A POUND OF FLESH

A POUND OF FLESH

SOPHIE JACKSON

Gallery Books

New York London Toronto Sydney New Delhi

Gallery Books
An Imprint of Simon & Schuster, Inc.
1230 Avenue of the Americas
New York, NY 10020

First Gallery Books trade paperback edition June 2015

Interior by Robert E. Ettlin

Manufactured in the United States of America

10 9 8 7 6 5 4 3 2 1

Library of Congress Cataloging-in-Publication Data

Jackson, Sophie
A pound of flesh / Sophie Jackson. —First Gallery Books trade paperback edition
pages cm
1. Prisoners—Education—Fiction. 2. Tutors and tutoring—Fiction. 3. Secrets—Fiction. I. Title.
PS3610.A35524P68 2015
813'.6—dc23

2014047106

ISBN 978-1-4767-9559-1
ISBN 978-1-4767-9562-1 (ebook)

For Mum. I am forever in your debt.

ACKNOWLEDGMENTS

This book would never have existed without many people's love, support, and encouragement.

Firstly, thank you to my family, especially my mum who, despite her eye-rolling at my ever-changing obsessions, became my own personal cheerleader during this whole process. From when it all went wrong and I thought this book was never going to happen to when it finally became right and I was neck deep in edits with the end seemingly so far away, she was always there calming me down, pulling me through, telling me that *of course* I could do it. You're my hero and always will be. I love you.

Sally, Rhian, Babs, Irene, Nicki, Caro, Sash, and Lisa, the original PAW Princesses. Who would have thought it? Your continued support throughout this entire journey, from your patience with my tri-monthly (sometimes longer) chapter posts, our read-along Skype sessions, our Manchester meet-up to the announcement that *PoF* was going to be published, will forever be invaluable to me. You are all wonderful women and friends, and I am truly blessed to have you in my life.

To my amazing friends and my incredible online family: Steph, my workout queen, Kim, my lobster, Afiyah, my Minion twin, Lauren, my Stucky lover, Tara Sue Me, for your invaluable advice and support, J M Darhower for your inspiring words, Liv, Laura, Rose—I could go on and on. I am insanely lucky to say that there are too many of you to mention. Your unrivaled excitement made the hard parts of this so much more bearable and the good parts so damned enjoyable. To every reader, reviewer, blogger, manip maker, banner maker, to every voter of every fandom award, to every hugger, texter, caller, and tweeter, you are all of you awesome and my love for you is immeasurable. You are the reason this is happening. Thank you for accepting my crazy fixations and for having so much belief in this and in me. Thank you for putting up with the good, the bad, and the ugly. I am proud and privileged to know each and every one of you. Lettuce spoon.

To my beautiful Pennsylvanian soul mate, Rachel. My original cherub. It seems like only yesterday that I sat down at your computer and wrote the prologue to *PoF*. Who knew, huh? We've come a long way, baby, and my love for you is still as strong as it was when you sent me that first online review. Your creative talents and your sunshine personality are so precious to me. You're a truly wonderful friend, your family is beautiful, and I can't wait to spend more laughter-filled summers with all of you.

To my superstar agent, Lorella Belli, the hardest working person in the literary world! What a journey it's been. Never once did you let me get downhearted when things looked bleak, never once did you lose hope when I was ready to throw in the towel. You are the most inspiring of people. I am in awe of your faith and fight, and I know without either this book would still be just a dream. Thank you so much for everything you have done and continue to do for *PoF* and me. I am beyond grateful. And to my U.S. co-agent, Louise Fury. Your love for the characters of this story will forever make me smile. You rock. Thank you for being the most awesome of sidekicks.

To my fabulously fabulous editor, Micki Nuding, who's put up with so much from me! You have the patience of a saint, woman. And to all the team at S & S and Gallery Books: Thank you for taking a chance on me and my story, and for making my dream a reality.

And, finally, to you for getting to the end of this long-ass thank-you note. Here, have an Oreo and a Coke. You damned well deserve it.

PROLOGUE

The pound of flesh which I demand of him
Is dearly bought; 'tis mine and I will have it.

—The Merchant of Venice, Act 4, Scene 1

The hurried sound of their feet on the sidewalk matched the frantic pace of her heart, while her father's grip on her hand was almost painful. Her short nine-year-old legs struggled to match his strides, causing her to stumble, all but jogging to keep up. There was a tightness in his jaw she'd never seen before, and his eyes, usually so bright and carefree, were as dark and angry as the sky above them. Foolishly, she felt the sudden urge to burst into tears.

A sound behind them made her look back. From out of the mouth of an alley slunk five hooded men who, despite keeping their heads down, kept up with her father's swift gait, stalking them like wild animals.

Her father may have uttered words of comfort, words to soothe the fear that crept across her neck, but they were eaten up by the sidewalk when something hard and fast came from behind them, sending her father sprawling, taking her down with him. Disoriented, with knees that burned from skidding across the concrete, she looked up and screamed as a baseball bat connected with her father's back twice, conjuring sickeningly dull thuds from his body.

She didn't see the direction from which the hand came that

struck her hard across the face, sending her tumbling over the curb and into the street, stars dancing in her vision and her father's furious bellow ringing in her ears. He staggered to his feet and launched himself at one of their attackers. She watched in horror as fists, feet, and bats rained down on him in retaliation.

Above the cacophony of shouted demands for his wallet, through the barricade of bodies surrounding him, her father yelled at her to run. He pleaded and begged as they battered him, but cold struck her, freezing her solid. How could he ask her to leave? She had to help him, save him! Tears ran down her face and an animalistic cry erupted from her throat.

He groaned in agony when another fist met the side of his head, and his knees hit the ground as she started toward him. She reached out to him, but her arm was unexpectedly pulled hard in the opposite direction. She whimpered in relief, expecting to see a police officer or her father's security detail—but it was someone not much taller than she was, in a dirty black hoodie.

She screamed loudly when he began to drag her away from where her father was being beaten, fighting and screaming at him to let her go when he hissed at her from under his hood. Did he not realize that her father needed her, that he would surely die without her help? But the stranger kept going, pulling her down the street into the doorway of an abandoned building, two blocks from where the terrifying sound of gunfire filled the air.

She screamed for her father, yanked her hand hard from her rescuer's grip, and began running back in the direction of the attack. She hadn't made it far when she was wrestled to the ground by strong hands that pinned her down. She continued to scream underneath him, fighting with everything she had, but soon her body became heavy and exhausted, and her cries and screams became wracked sobs that stuttered into the cold ground beneath her forehead.

The weight on top of her disappeared and two hands lifted her, pulling her back into the freezing doorway. She slumped against him and mewed in pain into his dirty hoodie. She needed to get back to her daddy. She needed to see that he was okay. He *had* to be okay. An arm around her shoulder and an icy hand against her cheek was her undoing, and she wilted further against her unknown rescuer.

She may have stayed that way for hours; she may have even fallen asleep. The next thing she knew, she was being carried by a man with a beard toward an ambulance. She opened her tear-swollen eyes and saw police and paramedics surrounded by a sea of red and blue flashing lights.

Their expressions, which would haunt her for the rest of her life, told her unequivocally that her father would not be tucking her into bed that night.

Or ever again.

1

Wesley James Carter, Arthur Kill Correctional Facility inmate and all-around punk, smirked at the disgruntled prison guard who'd been demanding his prison number for the past ten minutes. To say that Carter's insolent behavior and amused expression were agitating the overweight, balding man would be an understatement. Dude was nearly foaming at the mouth.

It was Friday, and five minutes after the guard had clocked out.

All the more reason for Carter to be a difficult bastard.

The guard ran an impatient hand over the back of his plump neck and his tired eyes narrowed. "Listen," he warned in a low, dangerous voice that no doubt worked like a knife to the throats of other inmates. "It's very simple. You give me your number. I put it on this form that I have to complete for your corrections counselor, and then I get to go home."

Carter raised a defiant eyebrow and glared at the pudgy shit.

Undeterred, the guard sat back in his swivel chair. "You don't give me your number and my wife gets pissed. She gets pissed and I have to explain to her that some cocky punk kept me waiting. Then she'll get more pissed and yell that our tax dollars are what keep losers like you in three meals a day and coveralls." He sat forward. "So, last time. Number."

Carter glanced nonchalantly at the guard's fist gripping the baton attached to his belt and exhaled a long, bored breath. Any other day, he'd be ready for the douche to take a shot; he'd take the beating with a smile plastered on his face. But today, he wasn't in the mood.

"081056," Carter answered coolly, unable to resist a small wink.

With a fierce scowl, the guard scribbled the number on the form, then wheeled his seat over to give the form to a young blonde admin assistant. The fat fuck was too lazy to get up and walk the six steps.

Carter waited while Blondie typed in the number that had been his adopted name for the past nineteen months. He knew what charges would appear on the monitor: car boosting, handling a dangerous weapon, drug possession, drunk and disorderly conduct to name just a few. Contrary to popular belief, he wasn't proud of the list of crimes and misdemeanors, which could fill up two full screens. Nevertheless, it did give him a sense of self, which was something he'd been searching for aimlessly most of his twenty-seven years. He was still searching for it and, until he found that *something* the list was all he had.

Whatever.

He rubbed a palm across his buzz cut. He was sick of thinking about it.

The sound of paper ripping from an ancient printer had him back on point.

"Well, Mr. Carter." The guard sighed. "It appears your stay with us stretches for another seventeen long months. Being caught with coke will do that."

"It wasn't mine," Carter uttered flatly.

The guard gave him an insincere look of pity before grinning. "Damn shame."

Carter didn't respond, knowing that his parole application was mere weeks away, and snatched the form with a quick hand.

Flanked by another stern-looking guard, Carter strode past the desk and down a long, narrow corridor toward a white door, which he opened with a loud slap of his palm. The room was claustrophobic and sterile, and reeked of confessions. Despite the many hours he'd spent in the godforsaken place, it still made his pulse quicken and his palms sweat.

With a straight back and stiff shoulders, he walked toward the cheap wooden table where a large ape of a man smiled as Carter approached.

"Wes," Jack Parker, his corrections counselor, greeted him. "It's good to see you. Please take a seat."

Carter pushed his hands into the pockets of his coveralls and dropped ungracefully into the chair. Jack was the only person who used his first name. Everyone else called him Carter. Jack had been insistent about it, explaining that it was a way the two of them could build a trusting relationship.

Carter had explained that was a crock of shit.

"Got a smoke?" Carter glanced dismissively at the guard standing at the door at the other end of the room.

"Sure." Jack tossed a pack of Camels and a book of matches onto the table.

Carter's long, pale fingers grappled with the wrapper. It'd been two days since his last cigarette. He was desperate. Two broken matches and a string of curses later, he finally inhaled the thick, lush smoke. He closed his eyes, held his breath, and, for a split second, all was right with the world.

"Better?" Jack asked with a shrewd smile.

Blowing the smoke across the table, Carter nodded.

Carter was impressed when Jack resisted the urge to wave the smoke away. They both knew doing so would only encourage Carter to do it more; he gripped on to any sign of weakness or irritation with the tenacity of a terrier.

It was a defense mechanism, apparently.

They'd discussed it in one of their first sessions. The mechanism was so well executed that Carter came across as strong, dominating, and, the majority of staff and inmates at Arthur Kill would agree, intimidating as hell.

Jack pulled a seven-inch-thick file from his briefcase and opened it, flicking through the numerous reports, court statements, and testimonials that, over the years, described Carter as being a "menace to society," a "strong-willed character," and an "intelligent individual who lacks the self-confidence to assert and channel it correctly."

Again, whatever.

Carter was tired of hearing how much potential he had. Yeah, he was intelligent, and fiercely loyal to the people he cared about, but for as long as he could remember, he just couldn't seem to find a path that fit. All his life he'd been drifting, never welcome or comfortable in a place for long, dealing with his fucked-up family and friends who couldn't stay away from fucking drama for more than five minutes.

At least in lockup, shit was simple. Real-life problems were like urban myths told by those who visited from time to time. Not that Carter had many regular visitors.

Jack turned to the final page of the file and wrote the date at the top of the blank piece of paper, then pressed the record button on the small digital voice recorder sitting between them.

"Session sixty-four, Wesley Carter, inmate number 081056," Jack began in a monotone. "How are you today?"

"Peachy keen," Carter replied, stubbing out his cigarette while lighting another.

"Good." Jack wrote a small note on the paper in front of him. "So, I attended a meeting yesterday regarding your enrollment in a couple of classes here at the facility." Carter rolled his eyes. Jack ignored it. "I know you have strong views on the subject, but it's important that you do things to challenge yourself while you're in here."

Carter dropped his head back and frowned at the ceiling. Challenge? The whole place was a damned challenge. It was a challenge to get through each day without blowing his freakin' gasket at some of the dumb fucks in the place.

"There are a few options," Jack continued. "English literature, philosophy, sociology. I explained to Mr. Ward and the education specialists that although you'd had problems with your previous tutors, you've changed from the seventeen-year-old high school dropout you used to be. Right?"

Carter cast him a skeptical glance.

Jack placed the tips of his fingers under his chin. "What would you like to study?"

"I don't care." Carter shrugged. "I just wish they'd leave me the fuck alone."

"It's all part of the conditions for the chance of early parole. You need to show progression in your rehabilitation. And if taking a couple of classes while you're here does that, then you have to play the game."

Carter knew that, and it infuriated him. Since the age of fifteen, he'd been passed from one lawyer, parole officer, and counselor to the next, with no thought about how or if he would ever do something more meaningful with his life. Though what meaningful meant, Carter had no fucking idea.

Nevertheless, after nineteen months at Kill, he was starting to think spending the rest of his days locked up wasn't the attractive prospect he'd initially perceived it to be.

As a wayward, arrogant, angry teenager, he'd enjoyed having a revered reputation. Now the excitement and thrill had waned. Court, detention centers, and prison were old news, and he was getting bored with the law institution as a whole. If he didn't change his shit, he'd be on the wrong side of thirty wondering what the fuck happened to his life.

Jack cleared his throat. "Have you had any visitors recently?"

"Paul came last week. Max is coming Monday."

"Wes." Jack sighed, pulling off his glasses. "You need to be careful. Max—he's not good for you."

Incensed, Carter slammed his palm on the table. "You think you have the right to say shit like that?"

Carter knew that Jack considered Max O'Hare a disease, infecting everyone around him with his drug issues, long criminal history, and his ability to land his friends in deep shit—Carter's being in Kill a case in point. But Carter had owed Max big-time. Being in prison was simply squaring a debt, and he'd do it again in a heartbeat.

"No," Jack soothed. "That's not what I think at all—"

"Well, good," Carter interrupted. "Because you have no idea what Max has been through, what he's still going through. None." He took a long pull on his smoke, staring at Jack over the burning embers.

"I know he's your best friend," Jack said after a moment of tense silence.

"Yeah," Carter agreed with a sharp nod. "He is."

And from what he'd heard from the guys who'd visited, Max needed him now more than ever.

• • •

Even when Kat Lane was asleep, the world around her was shadowed and oppressive, riddling her dreams with fear. Her small hands gripped the sheets, twisting in desperation. Her closed eyes clenched and her jaw tightened while her head pressed into the pillows beneath it. Her spine was rigid and her feet moved in her sleep as she found herself running, panicked and terrified, down a shadowed alley.

A sob rose from her throat, trapped in a never-ending slide show of the night that had happened almost sixteen years before. "Please," she whimpered into the darkness.

But no one would come to save her from the five faceless men who chased her. She shot up into a sitting position with a scream, sweating and breathless. Her eyes darted around her pitch-black room before, realizing where she was, she closed them and cupped her hands to her face. She exhaled through a rough throat and brushed the tears away, trying to calm herself with slow, deep breaths.

She'd woken this way every day for the past two weeks, and the grief that hit her every time she opened her eyes was all too familiar. She shook her head, exhausted.

Her doctor had told her not to stop taking her sleeping pills all at once, but to lower the dose gradually. Kat had dismissed her advice, determined to make it through one night without the aid of chemicals. It seemed her determination was wasted. She beat her fist on the mattress in frustration, then flicked on the bedside table lamp. But the light didn't ease the fear and utter helplessness her nightmares brought her.

With a defeated sigh, she got up and went toward her bathroom, flinching at the bright lights. She glanced at her reflection in the mirror and frowned. Christ, she looked a lot older than twenty-four. Her face appeared drawn, her green eyes dull and lifeless. She traced the dark shadows under them, then ran her hand through her hair. Instead of being its usual voluminous chestnut red, it hung lank and dry past her shoulders.

Her mother had told her that she'd lost weight, but Kat had dismissed her words. She always had to comment on something.

Kat was in no way skinny—having always been more curvaceous than skin and bone—but her size-ten jeans *had* become a little loose recently.

She opened the cabinet and pulled out a bottle of sleeping pills. She desperately wished for the night when she wouldn't have to rely on medicine to sleep. It wasn't like the pills helped all that much anyway; they simply numbed a pain that would never disappear. After taking two blue capsules, she padded back across the bare wood floor to bed.

Kat had realized a long time ago that there was no sleep deep enough to escape her nightmares. They were ingrained, part of who she was, and she'd never be rid of them. She knew no pill or therapy would ever erase the darkness and grief within her. Subsequently, she'd grown into a woman who was fiery and strong-minded. It was a safe way of keeping other people at arm's length, hiding her despair and fear behind a quick wit and sharp tongue.

She sank against her feather pillows. Would it ever get easier?

She didn't know. All she could focus on was the fact that sunrise would mean a new day, another day away from her past.

2

The following morning, Kat got into her car outside her apartment building in SoHo. The nightmares always left her cloudy and tense, and wondering why the hell she'd taken a job teaching in a prison.

Since she'd started tutoring a little over a month ago, it had not only brought on the nightmares but was also creating a deep division between her and her mother. Their relationship had always had its ups and downs, but when Kat had called to say she was going to work at Arthur Kill, the argument that followed was the most awful they'd ever had. Eva Lane was a complex and stubborn woman, and she would never understand Kat's need to do the job.

Kat understood her mother's and some of her friends' concerns. Although there were no murderers, their crimes were worrisome enough: vandalism, car theft, drug use and possession. But she knew without a doubt that this was what she wanted to do. For deep inside, a sworn promise to her father itched at her soul.

It had been there since her father had died. It was there the day she finished high school, and the day she graduated from college with an English literature degree. Teaching was what Kat had wanted to do since she was a kid, and she'd loved every second of it.

She'd been lucky enough to travel to London and China, teaching in private schools that made her fall in love with the job more and more. She made friends, experienced other cultures, and built enriching relationships that would never be broken. Nonetheless, she knew deep down that working in $50,000-a-year schools wasn't fulfilling the promise she'd made.

Gifted, hardworking children weren't whom she was meant to help.

"We have to give back, Katherine," her father had said the night he died.

She'd considered taking a job at an inner-city school, but that option didn't scratch the relentless itch, either.

Working in a prison was what quelled it.

She had to be nearer to her fears, nearer to men who thought little of breaking the law, of turning other people's lives upside down with no consideration of the consequences. She had to be closer to understand what could make a person capable of such behavior. She hated her fear; she hated the root of it, and she knew she had to face it head-on—even though she was terrified of it.

Her therapist had been very concerned about her decision, asking constantly if Kat was happy with her choice, if she thought it was right for her and why, even using her mother's worries to try and talk her down.

But it was Kat's choice to make—no one else's. And once the decision was made, there was no going back. Whatever the outcome, whatever her mother would say, she would live with it, because Kat knew what it would have meant to her father.

• • •

The building of Arthur Kill, Staten Island, looked as if it had fallen right out of an episode of *Prison Break*. Guards with huge, angry-looking dogs patrolled tall lookout towers surrounded by wreaths of vicious barbed wire fencing.

Kat pulled up to the gates of the parking lot and waited for the officer on duty. After silently taking her ID badge, he disappeared into the guardhouse and soon returned, directing her toward the morose-looking structure she worked in.

Once parked, Kat glanced to her left to see a large group of inmates playing basketball behind a huge metal fence. With their green coveralls tied at the waist, their sweat-covered chests gleamed in the hot June sunshine. The walk from her car to the building seemed miles long, especially when she heard wolf whistles and catcalls from the basketball court.

She hurried her step and grabbed the handle of the large door like a lifeline. Inside, pushing her bangs back with a flustered hand, she was welcomed by a low chuckle. She looked up to see Anthony Ward, the narcissistic prison warden.

Ward was in his late thirties, and while his face was round and youthful, his hair was combed and gelled to within an inch of its life. He assessed Kat with dark gray eyes and a quick smile that revealed a large dimple in his left cheek. "Miss Lane," he said, extending his hand.

Kat ignored it and tried to compose herself by running a palm down her knee-length charcoal skirt. "Mr. Ward."

Pulling back his hand with an embarrassed nod of his chin, he stood poker straight in an effort to look taller. Kat noticed he did this a lot, especially around the inmates. It didn't work. Poor guy was born stumpy.

"So," he began. "How are you? Settling in well?"

Kat smiled. "Yes. I think so." Her classes had been fairly event-free so far. And her students no longer used the F word like a comma when they spoke to her.

Ward adjusted his tie. "Good. Well, don't forget I'll be observing your session this morning. And anything you need, just come and see me."

"I will, thank you."

She walked past him, ignoring the way his eyes stayed on her chest a touch too long. His lecherous tendencies and his inability to view the inmates as anything other than scum rubbed Kat the wrong way. He didn't see how the inmates could possibly better themselves while incarcerated, unknowingly making Kat's job appear pointless. As a result, she avoided him as much as she could.

When Kat entered her classroom, she was grateful for the cooling breeze of the AC window unit. The rest of the facility was like a damned sauna. Twisting her hair off her neck, she turned when her teaching assistant, Rachel, entered looking flushed.

She blew a breath through her cherry-stained lips. "Christ, it's hot as Hades today," she complained, flapping her T-shirt in a futile attempt to cool down.

Rachel had been a lifesaver since Kat started. Qualified in assisting the inmates with learning difficulties, Rachel had helped Kat get to know her students quickly—especially Riley Moore, a colorfully large personality who suffered terribly from dyslexia. Not that it had stopped him from achieving a business degree from NYU.

Riley was one of her favorite students. Inside for dealing stolen car parts, his six-foot-three frame and broad shoulders would put Atlas to shame. He was funny and flirted with both women shamelessly. Unlike Ward, however, Riley was charming and uttered every word with his tongue firmly in his cheek. It was hard not to find his relentless yet harmless innuendos endearing, especially with his dancing hazel eyes and bearded cherubic face.

There were four other students in the class, all of whom worked hard and tried to keep themselves in check. Kat was more than a little proud at how quickly she'd brought them all to heel. Their progress had been fantastic.

At two minutes after nine, Riley's booming voice broke the quiet. Kat grinned when she turned to see him, flanked by a guard, followed by her other students.

"Miss L!" he bellowed, holding up his hand for a high five, which Kat met with a small slap. "Good weekend?"

"It was lovely, Riley. Thank you. And yours?"

"Ah, you know." He shrugged. "Causing shit here and there, making Ward's hair recede more and more by the day."

Kat repressed a snicker as Ward entered the classroom with her other students: Sam, Jason, Shaun, and Corey. Jason smiled meekly from under his floppy brown hair, while Corey and Shaun lifted their chins in greeting. Sam scurried to his desk and sat down without any gesture at all. At first this had bothered Kat, but now she accepted it as part of the routine they'd built up. A routine that, Rachel had explained, was paramount to the men in Kill. For many of them, a schedule was all they had to keep them sane.

Ignoring Ward at the back of her classroom, Kat began her lesson, reviewing their last session and asking the men to describe their favorite places by using metaphors and personification. They set about writing quietly.

"Okay," she called, bringing the class's attention back to her. "Who's brave enough to read theirs out lou—"

The classroom door flew open so hard, it smacked into the wall behind it. A harassed-looking guard, breathing raggedly, stared at Ward, who shot to his feet.

"I'm sorry to interrupt, sir," the guard gasped. "But we have a situation in room six."

"Who?" Ward barked, storming across the room.

"Carter, sir."

Ward's eyes narrowed and his mouth snapped into a sharp line. When the door slammed shut behind him and the guard, Kat looked around the room.

"Carter?" she asked.

Riley laughed loudly, immediately clearing the tension Ward forever left in his wake. "Carter. Dammit. That boy never fuckin' changes."

3

"You're not sleeping well, are you?" Ben, one of Kat's closest yet most irritatingly observant friends smiled sadly as a waiter placed a triple espresso in front of her.

Even without the numerous yawns she'd been stifling all through dinner, Kat knew she looked like crap. Even Estée Lauder couldn't hide the weariness around her eyes. Besides, he'd known her for six years and nothing got past him. "I tried," she replied, shaking a packet of Sweet'N Low.

"You're still having nightmares?" Beth asked from her seat at Kat's left. She and Kat had been friends since high school and, despite Beth only returning to New York a few months earlier after teaching in Texas for four years, they'd fallen back into their friendship easily.

It was nice to have her close again, completing their friendship trifecta, even if their constant worrying drove her near distraction. Kat knew they both meant well, but, along with her mother's continuous anxieties about Kat's job, it was becoming exhausting.

Ben shook his head. "You can always call me, you know?"

Like protective siblings, he and Beth frequently offered to stay the night when the nightmares hit, or offered the spare beds at their places, but she always declined.

"And wake you and Abby?" Kat asked with a lift of her shoulders. "Why would I call you?"

"Because we're your friends and we care about you," Beth said before spooning a large helping of crème brûlée into her mouth.

"Especially with this job," Ben added.

Kat glared. "Don't start."

Ben held his hands up. "Who's starting?"

Kat stirred her spoon around in her cup. "This job—"

"Is important to you—we know," Beth interrupted. She was a little sharper around the edges than she'd been in high school, but her chestnut eyes and crazy cropped ash-blonde hair reaffirmed she was still the same girl Kat had known for years. "But we still worry."

Ben rested a hand on Kat's. "You have a lot coming up in the next few months."

Kat dropped her gaze to the table.

"Your father's anniversary isn't far away. Just know that Abby and I are here, okay? We love you."

"And I love you, too." Beth grinned. "Even though Adam bought me a diamond, you're still my number one, you know." She wiggled the finger that held the gorgeous square-cut diamond engagement ring.

Kat tried to smile. "I know. Thank you both."

Ben replied, "And remember, I'm a lawyer. If anyone in that place gives you a hard time, I'm your man. You know I could dig up shit on the pope if you needed me to."

Beth and Kat laughed. It was probably true. Ben won most of his cases through sheer dogged determination, dirt digging, and favors. Like a hunting dog, he could sniff out scandal and blackmail at twenty paces.

"Hey, has your mom called?" Beth asked.

Kat exhaled hard. "Three times last night alone."

Beth's brow furrowed. "She called me, too. She's worried, that's all."

Kat hummed sardonically. "Look, I know you're Team Mom—"

"I'm not team anyone," Beth countered. "I simply see where she's coming from. It must be difficult for her."

Kat huffed. "Difficult for *her*? She's been on my case since I took this damned job. 'It's unsafe.' " She mimicked her mother's tone. " 'I'm putting myself at risk working with those animals,' blah, blah, blah." Her shoulders slumped. "Why can't she be supportive?"

"She means well," Ben said. "She'll come around."

"Sure," Kat replied, unconvinced.

• • •

Carter woke, having slept soundly; maybe he'd worn himself out plotting against Anthony Ward. He smiled. The motherfucker really had no idea who he was messing with.

He was to stay in his cell until four—two hours to go—which was when his twenty-four-hour punishment was over. For pushing a chair into a wall. What bullshit.

Maybe he'd pushed it a little harder than he should have, but his philosophy tutor had most definitely overreacted. And Ward? Well, he just knew all of Carter's buttons to press.

Jack soon arrived with a rescheduled visit for Max and a disappointed look on his face, which made Carter's insides clench. He appreciated Jack's gesture, given the man's thoughts on Max, and once again, he kicked himself for acting like a dick with his counselor. His mouth just ran away with him sometimes.

"So, I take it we don't like philosophy?" Jack had asked with a small grin. "Aristotle not doing it for ya?"

"Not exactly."

Jack nodded and rubbed the back of his neck. "Thanks for the shit storm from Anthony Ward, by the way. I owe you big-time for that."

"About that," Carter mumbled from his bed. "My bad."

It was the closest to an apology Jack would get.

"Yes, it is," Jack agreed. "Jeez, Wes, you're better than that."

Carter sighed despondently and pulled his knees up to his chest. "The guy was talking crap, Jack. He deserved it."

"Well, whatever your reasons, you have a lot of making up to do."

"Oh, yeah?" Carter snapped.

"Yeah," Jack returned, undaunted. "I've enrolled you in Literature. I know you like to read." He gestured to the shelves on the right wall of the cell, filled with battered, dog-eared texts. "And the tutor is a woman, so maybe there won't be as much hostility."

"Hostility?"

"You know what I mean," Jack said sharply. "You promised you'd try, so prove to me you are. I had to kiss that son of a bit—" He glanced toward the prison officer standing two feet away. "I had to speak nicely to Ward to give you another chance. Don't tell me I've wasted my time here."

Carter sat forward, running his hands over his buzzed hair. He was at a dead end. Ward had not only Jack's balls in a vise but his, too. He wanted nothing more than to beat the arrogant shit with his book of "rules," but he couldn't let Jack down again. He was stressed, frustrated.

"You'll do fine," Jack said quietly, moving a step closer. The guard behind him shifted, too.

"Yeah," Carter muttered. "We'll see, won't we?"

Even after his long sleep, fatigue began to creep silently over him. The walls had started to close ever so slightly, making his head heavy. Twenty-two hours locked in one room could do that to a man. Even him.

"Tomorrow morning," Jack said with an encouraging nod. "The tutor is Miss Lane. She's very good. Try to be . . . Just try, okay?"

"Okay." Carter held up three fingers. "Scout's honor."

Jack smiled. "And just to be safe, I've made sure all the chairs in that classroom have been bolted to the floor."

Carter laughed loudly. "Good thinking, J," he called before the guard shut the door of his cell, leaving him alone once again.

• • •

The final two hours of the punishment crept by at a snail's pace, and Carter almost knocked the guard off his feet when he finally opened the cell. He stretched his arms back, cracked his neck, and hurried toward the yard.

"Yo, Carter!"

Riley Moore's thundering voice traveled across the basketball court.

Carter smiled. "Moore," he replied, strolling toward the giant man.

"Where ya been?" Moore asked with a slap against Carter's shoulder. "I've missed your punk-ass face."

"Give me a smoke and I'll tell you all about it."

Riley pulled a cigarette from his pocket and flicked Carter a match. They made their way to a small seating area at the back of the court.

"Move!" Riley barked.

Carter snorted when the two newbies who'd been sitting in their spot scattered like leaves. He sat down, closing his eyes to the sun beating down on him, letting the smoke whisper from between his lips.

"So what gives? You been somewhere jerking off since yesterday?" Riley laughed and lit a cigarette.

"If only," Carter replied, watching the basketball game across the yard. "No, it was Ward."

"No shit," Riley murmured with a shake of his head.

"I had a slight disagreement with one of the tutors and he put me on twenty-four-hour punishment."

"It's on, man." Riley bumped Carter's fist. They'd known each other many years, both inside and outside Kill. If Carter needed him, he'd be there.

They both turned when they heard a loud bout of whistles and jeers from courtside.

Riley snorted. "Talking of tutors," he said, cocking an eyebrow.

Carter followed his stare through the fencing to see a redheaded woman with the sexiest curve to her ass he'd ever seen. Wrapped deliciously in a black knee-length skirt, she crossed the parking lot toward a sweet Lexus sport coupe. Her awesome legs disappeared into black heels that, even from Carter's viewpoint, were hard-on-inducing.

"Who the hell is that?" he asked, trying to see past the other inmates who were milling at the fence like kids at a damned zoo.

"That's Miss Lane," Riley answered, leaning back on his elbows. "My lit tutor. She's cool, actually."

Carter snorted. "Well, at least that's a plus." He snuffed out his cigarette on the bench.

"What?" Riley frowned, confused.

Carter waved his hand toward where the car had disappeared. "The tutor will be one good thing about doing lit."

Riley chuckled. "You're doing lit, too?"

"Yeah," Carter answered with a roll of his eyes. "Jack wants me to prove to the powers that be I can 'improve' myself inside. Some shit about how it could help toward an early parole. I'm not holding my breath."

"Sounds like a crock to me."

"Agreed," Carter replied, leaning back and lifting his face to the blazing sun.

4

Kat dropped her bag by the front door before walking over to play the answering machine, and immediately heard her mother's voice, urgent and clipped.

"I'm assuming you're still alive and well, even though I haven't heard a peep from you since Saturday. I hope you haven't forgotten that you're coming to the house this evening for dinner. If you aren't here by seven, I'll be sending Harrison out to make sure you're all right. Bye."

Kat sighed and pressed call back on her phone, leaving it on speaker. She walked over to her tropical fish tank and sprinkled food across the smooth water, smiling when they came to the surface and puckered and kissed at the flakes.

"Katherine?" Her mother's anxious voice filled the living room.

"Yes, Mom, it's me. I'm alive, I'm safe, and I'll be at the house at seven, so cancel the search party."

Kat could have done without having to have dinner with her mother after the day she'd had. She'd woken late that morning after, once again, being awake half the night having the same vivid dream repeatedly. She'd tried to go another night without her pills and had done nothing but regret it as soon as her head hit the pillow.

It was a new dream this time. There were no faceless men or wet sand, but her father was still there. He kept whispering something to her and, try as she might, she couldn't get near enough to hear him. That was when the hooded stranger came and pulled her back from him.

Just as he had done all those years before.

He was still a stranger to her—both in and out of her dreams—after apparently disappearing without a trace from the doorway of the building in which he had held her as she cried for her father. She truly believed the police and her mother thought she was insane when she tried to describe what had happened: that a hooded unknown had pulled her from seeing her father beaten to death on a cold, wet night in the Bronx.

All she knew was that he was definitely male and he couldn't have been much older than she was. But he was never found. Regardless, he was still there in her subconscious, desperately dragging her away from her father.

An hour and a half later, tired and frustrated, Kat was sitting at her mother's dining table, fighting to clear the horrendous tension that shrouded the room. It was a losing battle; it had been that way ever since Kat had applied for her job at Kill. Nevertheless, trying her hardest not to be discouraged by her mother's blatant apathy, Kat enthused to her mother and her mother's partner of ten years, Harrison, about how well her students were doing, how hard they were working, and how focused they'd become. Kat described what she felt when her student, Sam, had written prose so poetic it had damned near brought her to tears of pride. She spoke about the surge of adrenaline that only a teacher knows when their students show understanding of a subject, but her mother didn't even try to hide her scoff.

Her mother, as much as Kat loved her and tried to understand her point of view, was still extremely prejudiced about criminals and what should be done about them. As much as Kat had tried her best to quash her mother's fears, her pleading was ignored. The thought of Kat being near them, let alone teaching them, made Eva sick to her stomach.

The arguments that had taken place had been epic in their ferocity. Kat had tried to reason with her mother that, as hard as it was to understand, they weren't the same men who'd killed the man they both adored. After her therapy sessions, where she had discussed the same fears, it had surprised Kat how easy the words came off her tongue.

Nevertheless, despite Kat's efforts, the dinner was, as always, overwrought and awkward. Kat left early, making excuses about grading her students' work.

Once through her apartment door, she kicked off her shoes and wandered over to the answering machine, which was flashing, and pressed play. She grabbed a bottle of white wine from the fridge and poured it into one of her larger glasses. After dinner with her mother, Kat was definitely ready for a drink.

"Miss Lane, it's Anthony Ward. I wanted to give you a heads-up that a new inmate will be joining your class tomorrow. He's . . . difficult, but I'm sure you'll be just fine. I'll explain in the morning. Have a good evening."

Kat stared at the machine. A new inmate? Difficult?

"Cheers, Mr. Ward," she muttered, sipping her drink. She sat cross-legged on her sofa, glass of wine still firmly in hand, as a new message began.

"Hey, Lane!" Beth's voice was excited. "It's me! So. Reminder. It's nearly my birthday, which means wine and food, and did I mention wine? Huh. I'll text you the details. Call me."

Kat laughed into her glass.

With the uncomfortable dinner at her mother's house still fresh in her mind, Kat was certain that Beth's birthday party was just what she needed.

• • •

"Good morning, everyone." Kat smiled while her students took their seats.

"Morning, Miss L," Riley answered with a huge yawn. "And may I say how nice you look today?"

"You may," she answered with a playful warning look.

"You look nice," he responded, giving her a wide closed-lip smile.

"Thank you, Riley," she replied, unable to hide her own grin.

She handed out their previous day's work, entitled "My Favorite Places," and gave them a couple of minutes to read her comments.

"What does 'not entirely appropriate' mean?" Corey asked from his seat at the back of the class.

Kat approached him. "It means, Corey, I don't really want to read about every one of your conquests or the marks you gave them out of ten, including"—she whipped the paper from his desk to find the offending sentence—"her mouth was like a vacuum."

At this, Corey barked a huge laugh that echoed around the room, his afro hair bouncing as he did. Everyone else sat in unimpressed silence. "Oh, come on," Corey insisted, waving his sheet of work. "That shit's funny!"

"You're a prick," Jason muttered from his seat, dissolving Corey's smile instantly.

"Jason," Kat warned, unease prickling her skin.

Corey retorted with a string of colorful language before he kicked the back of Jason's chair. Hard. "Fucking asshole."

"Hey," Kat said, alarm rising inside her. "Not now, guys. Let's just keep calm and—"

"The hell?" Jason snapped back, ignoring her. He began to stand from his seat and turned to Corey, his height and wide shoulders dwarfing Kat. "You gonna say that to my face, you ugly fuck?"

"Hey," Kat repeated louder, maneuvering herself between them.

Corey stood, tall and lean, his ebony skin gleaming under the harsh lights of the classroom. "I'll kick your ass, shithead. Just name the day."

"Guys, please—"

"I'd like to see it, you jumped-up little bastard." Jason gave a come-closer gesture with his hand.

Panic began to engulf Kat's throat. She held an open palm toward each of the men as they threw threats and words, conjuring terrified sweat from her forehead. If either of them threw a punch, she would be right in the middle of it. She froze, dread solidifying her joints. Officer Morgan and Riley tried to get in between them, trying to protect her. She could hear Rachel calling for her to move back.

But she couldn't.

The fear pounded her head. She tried to remain calm, remembering the anxiety breathing exercises her therapist had given her, but her heart slammed against her ribs, taunting her. Kat clenched her eyes shut against the sixteen-year-old memories that pushed and clawed through the bars of the cage where she kept them locked in her mind. They were desperate to see her fail and crumble.

Breathing deeply, Kat grappled for the reins, trying frantically to gain control. She knew she couldn't allow her students to behave like that. It was her classroom, her time, her job, her promise.

She opened her eyes, clenched her fists, and filled her lungs. "HEY!"

Rendered speechless, everyone stared at Kat as her yell ricocheted around them. Riley, who was standing at her side, trying his best to shield her from whatever shit was about to fly, blinked in disbelief. The awed silence lasted all of thirty seconds before the door flew open, and Ward stormed in with a face like thunder.

"What the hell is going on here?" he roared.

The group surrounding Kat slowly began to disperse when two officers appeared in the doorway. Kat took another shaky breath and rubbed her drenched palms down her trousers. She cleared her throat and turned to her boss.

"Nothing to worry about, Mr. Ward. Just a differing of opinion. As you can see, they're all fine now. Aren't you, Corey?" She leveled a look at him that demanded obedience.

He nodded sharply, still glaring at the back of Jason's head.

"It didn't sound like nothing." Ward eyed the room, throwing a pointed stare at each inmate until he was seemingly satisfied that they were under control. "I'd like to bring in your new student." He turned his head toward the door. "Carter?"

. . .

Carter had been standing in the corridor with Officer West, grinning and listening to Ward try to assert what piss-ass authority he thought he had. He pushed from his place against the wall and wandered into the room, dragging his feet with every step.

The first thing he noticed was Riley across the room, acknowledging him with a nod and a smirk. He then glanced casually at the others in the class, trying to discern where he came in the pecking order. He was almost always at the top, but he made it a point to check first.

In this case, Riley dominated. Just.

He sneered when he took in the other faces. Jason could be cocky, but he knew his place and Sam was as quiet as a mouse. No problems there. Corey Reed, however, was a pain in the ass. Carter glared and smiled when he slumped down into his seat. An annoyed feminine cough pulled him from his visual tormenting of the little bastard.

He turned toward the origin of the noise, finding the delectable Miss Lane, arms crossed over her ample chest, eyeing him in a way that made his hackles rise. She, like every other person not in coveralls, thought she was better than he was. He didn't have to be a mind reader to know it. She may have hidden it well behind her sexy blouse and heels, but she was just like them. They were all the fucking same.

He shifted his weight casually onto his right foot and stared right back at her.

"Carter, this is Miss Lane. Miss Lane, this is Wes Carter," Ward explained.

"Just Carter," he spat, keeping his glare firmly on his new tutor. Ward knew better than to use his first name, for Christ's sake.

"Well, it's nice to meet you, Carter," Miss Lane offered.

He rolled his eyes. "Yeah, whatever."

"You can take a seat." She gestured to a desk and chair behind him.

Carter ignored her, surveying his surroundings.

"Take a seat, Carter," she ordered.

His stare snapped to her. Her mouth was pressed into a hard line, almost daring him to defy her. Game on. His eyes wandered lazily down her body. Hot. Curvy in all the right places, with an ass that would look spectacular with his hands all over it. He smirked at that particular image.

Carter was tall, at least six-two, and broad-chested. He towered a good nine inches over her and carried at least seventy pounds more than was on her feminine frame, yet the feisty redhead stood firm, not moving an inch, meeting him glower to glare. If her stick-up-the-ass, bitchy attitude hadn't riled him so much, he might have stopped to consider how turned on he was by it.

Damn.

"Here, Carter." It was Rachel's voice, which broke the strange electric mood enveloping the room. She motioned to the seat closest to him.

Carter, as loath as he was to break his gaze with his tutor, took a deep breath, and moved toward the seat. The air shuddered out of him when his blue irises dropped from Miss Lane's wide green ones, which flickered with fire.

"Well," Ward murmured, "any problems . . . you know where I am."

He gave a tight-lipped smile and, after they uncuffed Carter, left the room with the two officers.

• • •

Kat was unable to tear her eyes from the new addition to her class. He was fine to look at with his buzz cut; wide, strong shoulders; two days' worth of stubble; and long legs that stuck out from underneath the desk, but his attitude made him sharp around the edges. There was a dangerous aura around him that screamed *No entry.* She noted a lick of black ink poking out from the collar of his coveralls, curving up his neck.

How very badass.

She'd seen the way he'd taken in the other students in her class—conceited and arrogant—and she didn't like it. He was obviously an egotistical jerk who saw himself as above everyone in her class, including her, which irritated her beyond distraction. Despite his ability to shut everyone up with his dark scowl and brooding hostility, it was her classroom. Not his.

Kat's aggression was surprising and uncharacteristic, but the adrenaline still pumped through her body after the almost-fight, and the last thing she needed was a cocky jerk like Carter adding to it.

Kat took a second to compose herself and then started the activity, explaining it quickly and clearly, and within five minutes, they were on task. It appeared the altercation had been forgotten, or, knowing Jason, been left for another time.

She walked with purpose toward Carter's desk and placed an A4 book in front of him. He never moved to acknowledge her request for him to place his name on the front of it.

"Carter," she said again, annoyance creeping up her spine. "Could you please write your name on the front of this booklet?" She noticed the corners of his mouth twitch. "Is something funny?"

His eyes met hers, crystal blue, fiery, and furious, but he never said a word.

She pulled a pen from her pocket. "Is this what you need?"

She could have sworn his eyes softened, but it was a change so minute and fleeting, she shook the thought away. He raised his hand and took the pen from her, allowing the tip of his finger to catch the side of her knuckle. The contact was like bare skin to a naked flame. The burning jolt of heat shot from the tip of her finger deep into the pit of her stomach.

Bewildered, Kat watched Carter write his name across the top of the booklet, before throwing the pen down and sighing sarcastically. He sat back in his seat, looking like he owned the place. Kat had no doubt in her mind he thought exactly that.

"I know you're behind, having just joined us today, but I'm sure you'll catch up."

His face showed no emotion or thought, so she continued regardless, explaining the word association task the class had done twenty-four hours before in preparation for their creative writing assessment. "So, you can start with that," she said. "Write a word that means something to you and then all the words associated with that."

Still nothing.

She bit her tongue and placed her hands on her hips. "Once you do that, you can write about why that word is important to you."

He sneered.

"I'm sorry," she ground out. "Is there a problem?"

He glared at her, his face strong and terrifying. "Do you think I'm stupid?"

She blinked. "No. Why?"

He snorted. "It's a little bit basic, wouldn't you say, Miss Lane?"

Her jaw tightened. No matter how intelligent Carter assumed himself to be, his attitude made her want to rip the smug smile off his pretty face. And what a pretty face it was. The lashes that framed his baby blues were sickeningly long, lying on cheekbones that were sharp yet masculine. His mouth was plump in all the right places and puckered when he conjured up his smirk. His nose looked as if it had been broken a couple of times, with the small bump visible on its bridge.

"We're starting with these tasks before we dive into the literature," Kat explained through gritted teeth. "All roads to every answer start with the basics."

"Nice," he retorted, pulling his eyebrows together in a way Kat could only determine as condescending. "Read that little gem in a fortune cookie, did ya?"

Kat placed her palms onto the desk in front of him, invading his personal space, smelling smoke and warmth. "No, I didn't," she hissed. "So just do what I ask. Otherwise, there's the door. Don't let it hit you on your smart ass as you leave."

The entire room pulsed with blasting silence. Carter stared back at Kat for mere seconds before he sat up straight in his chair, leaning even closer. She was momentarily shaken when his hot breath whispered across her cheek.

"Watch your mouth," he seethed.

The guard shifted closer. Kat swallowed.

"No, Carter. This is my class, not yours. So do what I ask or leave. The choice is yours."

She spun on her heel and walked toward Riley, whose wide eyes and open mouth suggested he was as shocked as she was that she'd tested the patience of the most volatile person in the room. Kat couldn't explain it. She knew her conduct had been risky and maybe a little unprofessional, but she couldn't allow her students to behave that way. She had no idea where her bravery—or stupidity—had come from. Maybe it was a deep-rooted need to assert herself after her mother's unsupportive words from the night before; maybe it was the fear that still prickled her skin from the confrontation between Corey and Jason.

Something about Carter set her on edge. If she weren't so angry, she might have enjoyed the energy suddenly flooding her veins.

She managed to ignore Carter for the next fifty minutes, glancing at him occasionally to see him sitting in smug silence. She hadn't seen him even attempt to do what she'd asked.

Asshole.

The officers came to collect her students as she was finishing her closing plenary.

"Later, Miss L," Riley chimed, following Jason and Rachel out of the door.

Carter barged past everyone, including her, with no regard whatsoever.

"Yeah, see you later," she muttered.

As soon as the door shut, Kat sank back against her desk and exhaled. It was glaringly obvious that Carter was going to be a difficult son of a bitch.

Great. Just what she needed.

Pushing off the desk, she collected her students' booklets and pens. She looked reluctantly at the last booklet, placed on the desk where Carter had been. She stared at it, gnawing on her bottom lip in frustration.

What was it about Carter that had her so wired?

She approached the booklet as a soldier would an undetonated bomb and turned it around, opening up to the first page. Her eyes widened and her breath caught when she read the word that meant so much to the man who had conjured so much emotion from her.

DEBT.

5

For twelve hours, Carter had done nothing but fume and ruminate over the ways in which he could make his new tutor's life hell. He was still astounded that she'd spoken to him the way she had.

No one spoke to Carter like that.

No. One.

Fucking. Ever.

For hours after their meeting, he'd been unable to rid himself of the rage she'd sparked within him, the absolute fury at being spoken to in such a way and, unbelievably and more infuriating than all of that combined, the wild lust that had shaken his entire body.

It was almost as if an electric current had shot between them when she spat her words at him. Goddamn her heavy breaths and her venomous tone, which made parts of him twitch and pulse—parts that had been dormant for a long time, parts that made him want to do wild and wicked things to her all over his desk until she knew how he expected to be treated. He was seething at himself for thinking those things about a woman he'd met for all of fifty-five minutes.

Yeah, she was hot; any red-blooded male could see that, with her auburn Dana fucking Scully hair, full pink lips, voluptuous ass, and killer rack. Christ, her fire was sexy as hell. The desire and hunger which slammed into him had been so unexpected, it had caught him off guard, and in a place like Kill, that was some dangerous shit.

Miss Lane was a sanctimonious nobody who needed to learn

fast that he would not tolerate her speaking and acting so . . . unafraid of him.

He rubbed the bridge of his nose, remembering the look on her face when she hissed at him. There was not an inkling of fear or a spark of anything that would suggest he intimidated her. She'd burned with energy so fierce he could taste it in the air between them. He'd even done what she'd asked from him and written the one word he lived by every day.

Not that she'd understand, let alone have experience of it in her pretty, perfect little existence.

The other thing that had irritated him was the fact that the other guys in the class seemed to like her—even Riley, who'd laughed while Carter had fumed and spat out his incredulity during a cigarette before lunch. Carter couldn't deny he'd been unprepared for the protective tone in Riley's voice and the hint of warning in his eye.

"You expect me to respect some broad who was probably born with a silver spoon in her fucking mouth and hasn't had to want for anything?"

"It couldn't hurt," Riley had answered with a nonchalant shrug.

Carter had snorted and shaken his head. There was no way.

"So," Riley had said, breaking the silence. "She's hot, right?"

Carter couldn't stop the laugh that erupted. "Oh yeah."

Riley had slapped his back hard enough to make him flinch. "That's one for the spank bank, my good man," he'd offered with a wink.

• • •

The following morning, after several cups of coffee, Kat began setting up her classroom. After a relatively good night's sleep, she'd started seeing the situation a little more objectively. She'd surmised that Carter was in a highly tense and emotional environment, and her demanding him to do what she wanted was not going to make him any less uncooperative. It was going to be hard as hell, but she'd decided she was at least going to try. She glanced at his empty seat, imagining his slouch and his penetrating stare. Lord. This was going to be harder than she thought.

What she read in his file hadn't been a surprise. Carter was the poster boy for rebellious deviants. Sentenced to thirty-six months for cocaine possession in the second degree nineteen months previous, Carter, since the age of fifteen, had been in detention centers or incarceration of some description at least six months out of every twelve.

He'd dropped out of school at seventeen, where his GPA had been above average. He'd excelled in sports and English and listed Salinger, Steinbeck, and Selby Jr. as his favorite writers. It was clear that he was intelligent, a fact that he'd made apparent with his comments about her class and how "basic" he found the work. Kat bristled at the memory.

She knew she could have him removed from her classroom to make a point that she was in charge. But then he would have won. Giving up and running away, or ignoring the issue, would not do for Kat Lane. She would never be forced to run away from anything ever again. He would not defeat her, and it vexed her that he'd even tried.

Because of her eagerness to get the morning out of the way as fast as humanly possible, she was pacing the front of the room when the inmates entered, led by Jason, who threw a large smile in her direction. Riley bowed and followed him single file. She turned from laughing at Riley and her breath caught. Her heart started to stutter when Carter strode into the room, ignoring Kat and pushing Corey out of the way to get to his seat.

The irrational irritation and heat she'd apparently quelled with her hypothesizing and promise to try reared instantly when their eyes locked for a split second.

Clearing her throat, Kat made her way to her desk. "I'm glad we're all here. Today we're going to start our poetry study, which we will do for the next week before we start our Shakespeare play."

Kat rested her backside against her desk, her skin tingling. She'd seen Carter's reaction to the poem she'd distributed, and had managed to stay quiet by biting her lip so hard she nearly drew blood. She focused on getting her words out and not on the desire she had to pull a face, stick her tongue out, or perform some other equally inappropriate gesture.

Jesus—mature, much?

She took a deep breath. "I'd like to start by asking what you all know about poetry."

The room remained silent. Riley perused the ceiling as he always did, as though the answer was written there, while Jason and Corey looked at her like she'd grown three additional heads. Sam kept his eyes on the desk in front of him, happy to keep quiet after the fiasco of yesterday's session. He hated confrontations.

Jason slowly raised his hand, meeting Kat's eyes with trepidation. "They can rhyme?"

"They can, absolutely," she answered with a smile. "Just like the poem we'll be studying, but that's not always the case."

"They're always about pansy-ass shit like love," Riley complained from his seat.

"That is true in some cases, Riley, but not in this one," Kat replied with a shake of her head. "Would I do that to you?" Riley chuckled.

The undeniable sound of Carter mumbling something into the back of his hand had Kat's head swiveling in his direction. "I'm sorry, Carter, I didn't catch that."

He dropped his hands to the desk and shot her a daggered stare.

"We have a very simple rule in this classroom," Kat added when the silence continued. "You have something to say, you say it. Okay?" The smile she gave was sugary sweet.

"Or else what?"

Kat cocked her head to the side, studying him. He was undeniably attractive, hiding a rage that simmered beneath his skin.

"Or else you can leave. It's that simple." Kat moved closer, speaking quietly. "I've told you before. This is my classroom. My rules. You do as you're asked." Kat lifted the left corner of her mouth in her own derisive grin. "Not too basic for you, is it?"

"Basic," Corey muttered behind his hand.

Before Kat could say anything else, Carter slammed his hand down hard enough to split the wood of the desk and shoved his chair back with such force it clattered into the desk behind it. Furious silence blanketed the room.

"Something fucking funny?" he growled down at Corey before shooting a glare at Officer West, who'd moved from his position by the door. "Care to share?" Carter continued, taking a step toward his prey. "I don't appreciate being left out of a joke."

Kat was spellbound.

She moved slowly. "Carter, calm down."

Carter ignored her, bending at the waist to eyeball a wary-looking Corey. "Are you laughing at me?"

"Come on now, Carter," Officer West murmured while throwing a worried glance in Kat's direction.

"Carter, sit down," Kat urged, hiding the panic in her voice with firmness and authority. "There's no need for this. Cool it."

"Yeah, man," Corey continued. "Cool it."

In a quick move, Carter put his hands under the edge of Corey's desk and flung it hard against the wall with an almighty roar. The sound of the wood careening into the plastic-covered brick resonated around the room like a death knell.

Everyone was immediately on his or her feet, with Officer West grabbing his baton and lunging at Carter before he got closer to Corey, paralyzed in his seat. Kat's body seized up behind a psyched-up Riley, who protected her with his size as three more guards descended onto Carter.

Kat watched in alarm around Riley's mammoth biceps as Officer West threw Carter against the wall. The officers—called by the panic alarm hit by Rachel—were upon him in a second. Kat flinched when she heard Carter's grunts and curses as they pushed and pummeled him hard while cuffing him.

"That's my fucking wrist!" he yelled into the face of one of the officers before being slammed into the wall again face-first. The officer twisted his wrist farther with a sadistic smile on his face, making Carter shout out in obvious pain.

"Hey!" Kat cried, whipping under Riley's arm, past a laughing Corey. She stormed over to the rabble of angry men.

Carter, whose left cheek was pressed into the wall, eyed her furiously. She scowled at the guard who'd tried to snap the bone in his wrist.

"I saw that," she fumed, pointing to Carter's cuffs. "You don't need to hurt him. It's unnecessary."

"Oh, Miss Lane, it's very necessary," the officer countered with a hard voice. "You need to keep them in check, see." He pulled Carter into an upright position.

Kat immediately saw blood trailing from Carter's left nostril, down his lip. "He's bleeding!"

"He's fine," the guard barked. He thrust Carter forward but was halted by Kat's firm, unmoving hand on his chest.

"Wait!" She paused for a second before going to her purse and retrieving a pack of tissues. She pulled one out and walked back to Carter, whose face read a million and one different things.

He started to protest when her hand moved to his face. "You don't need to fuc—"

"Shut up and let me help you," she bit with a finality and insistence that shut Carter's mouth with a snap. He took a deep breath when the tissue in her hand swiped at the blood.

His eyes on Kat's face left a trail of warmth from her hairline down to her nose and mouth. Trying her hardest to ignore the fact that her heart was about to burst, Kat focused hard—watching the swiping motion of the tissue—but felt every movement he made. Every time he breathed and it whispered across her hand under his nose, she swallowed, and every time his mouth twitched, her lungs squeezed.

She wiped gently but determinedly until his face was a damn sight better than it had been after the officers had manhandled him so violently. He hadn't deserved their treatment. She stared intently around his face and noticed a mark starting to appear on his cheek.

The urge to touch the appearing bruise shook Kat to her core. She cleared her throat and dropped her gaze from his. She seemed to have no power over her hand or its intentions as it started to move toward the skin under his eye, where his bone jutted out in all its sculptured glory. She wanted to ease the redness of it through her fingertips and soothe the ache she just knew was burning under his skin, but she couldn't.

"All done," she muttered, wiping a spot of blood on her thumb.

Carter frowned. He opened his mouth, but no words came. Instead, he scoffed before the three guards marched him past her and out of the classroom.

Kat heaved a sigh and tossed the bloodied tissue into the trash can.

6

Kat rolled over and shut the alarm off before it even turned on. She was wide-awake and had been for over an hour.

She'd tossed and turned all night thinking and deliberating about what her next move would be with Carter. Their second lesson had been a complete disaster, and that was putting it mildly. She'd tried to be calm. God, how she'd tried. But it wasn't enough. She'd still managed to become enraged by him.

She had no idea what it was about him. He was, after all, just like the other men she taught. Well, that wasn't exactly true; he was a lot more combative and exceedingly more aggressive and—she winced at the thought—a lot more attractive, too. She'd tried not to see him in any other way than as her student, but it was hard to ignore the man who drove her crazy.

She rubbed her palms down her face. She knew better than to get involved in any way with any person she taught. The nonfraternization policy of the prison was clear and succinct, and Kat loved her job too much to put it in any kind of jeopardy. She was a professional and no one, not even Carter, could make her forget that.

But Carter was at his most stunning when he was furious. His rage seemed to make his skin glow and the frown lines, which Kat imagined were indentations caused by his hatred for everything around him, dissolved, leaving his face serene and flawless. He was, in those moments, the most breathtaking creature she had ever seen.

As scared as she was when he'd flung the desk at the wall during her class, she'd been unable to tear her eyes from him, watching with fascination as the beast inside him roared. He was animalistic and, for that brief time, utterly uncaged. It was that thought alone that made parts of Kat's body come alive in spectacular fashion; it was a side of Carter she desired and detested with equal fervor.

Regardless, no matter what her body thought of the matter, Kat knew the guard twisting his wrist was completely unacceptable. Carter hadn't deserved that.

And she would tell Anthony Ward that very thing when she got to work.

But, for whatever reason, Anthony Ward was not at work when she got there later that morning. A little disheartened and still a lot confused, Kat began preparing her classroom, trying her hardest not to think about whether Carter would turn up. She pulled at the hem of her blouse in frustration when she realized the part of her that wanted him in her classroom far outweighed the part that didn't, and cursed loudly.

"Wrong side of the bed this morning?"

Rachel's voice floated from the doorway, clearing Kat's head for all of five seconds before the battle within started again in earnest. She smiled and raised her eyebrows, unable to articulate correctly why she was cursing to an empty room.

"He's been removed," Rachel said plainly while placing her bag on her seat.

Kat turned. "What?"

"Carter." Rachel shrugged. "Ward told him his temper is out of control. He's a danger to himself and others."

"Shit. How did he take it?"

Rachel gave her a wry smile. "As Carter always does: with a few curses and a growl." She took a step toward Kat. "This is going to affect his parole."

Kat's eyebrows lifted in surprise. She didn't even know he'd been considered for it.

"When is his parole application up for review?" Kat asked.

"The end of the month."

Kat's newfound need to work with Carter instead of against him surprised her. She'd known him all of two days, spoken maybe a dozen words to him, mostly through gritted teeth, but still she knew, deep down, somewhere in her stomach, there was something about him, something more—something that set him apart from the other students in her class. Something that called to her in a way she could never explain.

His ambivalence was frustrating as all hell, and he had a smugness that could force any sane person to drink. In spite of all that, Kat had the overwhelming desire to put things right, to help.

That was her debt, after all.

Kat nodded in resolve.

"What?" Rachel asked. "What are you thinking?"

Kat smiled, her fortitude rising to the surface. "I'm thinking Mr. Carter is going to have to start dealing with being around me more often."

• • •

"Harder!"

Carter grunted.

"I said harder! I didn't feel a thing!"

Carter grunted again, louder this time as his fist slammed hard into the red protective shield that the prison's gym officer, Kent Ross, was holding in front of him.

"My three-year-old hits harder, and she's a girl! Again!"

Carter's eyes clenched and his knuckles turned the same shade of white as the bandages around them when, with a terrifying yell, he began pummeling the shield with everything he had. The hate, anger, desire, need, and want burst from him through his fists with such force that Ross staggered backward.

After thirty seconds, Carter's arms began to slow as the adrenaline burn began through his intricately inked shoulders, down his equally patterned biceps, and into his forearms, which screamed under the relentless pounding. He gasped and panted, and almost kissed Ross's ugly-ass face when he said they were done.

Carter loved the workout; it was the only part of his anger management he enjoyed. The in-house shrink had suggested Ross work with Carter after one of his notorious tantrums, in an effort to vent some of the tension.

Carter slumped against the blue mat he'd been standing on and lay on his back, his chest rising and falling heavily. He really needed to quit smoking. His knuckles smarted and his face throbbed from where the guard had smashed him into the wall during Miss Lane's class. He was drenched with sweat.

"You did good," Ross muttered, peering over Carter's limp body, holding out a bottle of water.

"You nearly killed me," Carter replied, taking it from him with a shaking hand.

He groaned when he sat up, his muscles protesting immediately, and downed half of the bottle in three giant gulps, dribbling some down his back in an attempt to ease the heat.

"You need to quit smoking," Ross grumbled, making Carter laugh. "You pushed hard, though," he continued. "More than usual. Something on your mind?"

Ross and Carter had built up a straightforward relationship over the twelve months they'd been working together. Carter respected Ross's no-bullshit attitude and liked the way he demanded more from him. Nevertheless, Carter wasn't entirely convinced that he could tell him what he wanted to know. He scoffed inwardly because Jesus if even he knew what he could say to describe the fucking carnival currently taking place inside his head.

Truthfully, he was amazed it was only a desk he'd thrown in Miss Lane's class. He'd never in his life been so completely filled with fury that the only way for it to manifest itself was to pick up the desk and hurl it as hard as he could. In retrospect, it was a dumb idea, but he'd had no control of himself.

The one thing that did bother him, and had since he walked from Ward's office after the "incident meeting," was the fact that he was subsequently banned from Miss Lane's lessons. Indefinitely. He wasn't allowed near her or her lessons and, for some reason that was not sitting well with him, it pissed him off.

The irony was not lost. He'd bitched and moaned about being enrolled in a class. Yet there he was, confused as all hell because a part of him wanted to be in her class, listening to her wax lyrical about poetry and shit he already knew. He wanted to sit in his seat at the front of her class and stare at her, trying to intimidate her.

Miss Lane was well and truly under his skin, and he wasn't sure whether to be disturbed or delighted by it. He hardly knew her, had hardly spoken to her, yet he couldn't get her face out of his head. It was just so damned . . . pretty.

Fuck. He was losing it.

He huffed and supped the dregs of his water out of the bottle before launching it toward the garbage can, where it landed with a crash. Ross sat down next to Carter with a thump.

"I heard about your . . . episode . . . in class," he offered diplomatically. Carter's face immediately went grave. Ross held up his hands in defense. "Hey, man, no judgment here."

Carter paused and dropped his eyes. Ross waited.

"It's just . . . ," Carter began. "Straight off, I don't give a shit about these lessons. I mean, I'm not stupid. I read and I know what I know, but . . . I have to do them for my parole."

Ross remained quiet.

"But this woman . . ." He stopped himself, wanting nothing more than to bite his own tongue off. "I don't know," Carter finished quietly, more to himself than to the man sitting to his right.

It was the most honest explanation he could give, because, the truth was, he *didn't* know. He didn't know why he wanted to be back in Miss Lane's class. He didn't know why she made him feel so off balance, and he didn't know why she'd cleaned him when he was bleeding.

The one thing he did know was that he'd liked it. He'd liked her doing it and he'd liked her being so close to him. It'd given him a chance to look at her properly. He'd been with many attractive women and seen even more, but there was something different about Miss Lane. She was natural, curvy, wore hardly any makeup, and he was damn sure her tits were what God had given her.

He was a tit man, and they were stellar.

He'd thought about touching them.

Nevertheless, the table incident had put an end to that.

Shit.

His parole officer was going to be pissed.

• • •

"Good morning, Miss Lane," Ward offered as Kat approached his desk. He gestured to the chair at the other side.

"Good morning."

"So," Ward said, patting his palms on the arms of his seat. "What can I do for you?"

Kat swallowed down her nerves. Straight to it. "I heard that the incident with Carter could affect his application for early parole."

"There's no 'could' about it," Ward answered brusquely. "He's not going anywhere for the next seventeen months. He'll serve his whole sentence and like it."

Something in his tone set Kat on edge.

"Yes," she countered, keeping her voice pleasant. "I understand he has a meeting with his parole officer scheduled soon."

Ward nodded.

"And I also understand it isn't just good behavior that can affect the decision of the parole board." Kat's eyebrow cocked when she saw the look of surprise washing over Ward's face.

He sat forward in his seat, resting his elbows on the desk. "Miss Lane, where are you going with this?"

"I've taken the liberty of setting up a meeting with Carter's corrections counselor, Jack Parker, this afternoon and would very much like to speak with his parole officer during her visit. I know either yourself or Jack can arrange that for me—"

Ward held a hand up to stop her. "I'm sorry, but I have to ask again. Where are you going with this, Miss Lane?"

Kat swallowed. "I want to tutor Carter."

For a moment, Ward was utterly perplexed. "You did," he countered, "and he's been removed because it's apparent to everyone that the two of you don't get along."

Kat ignored the sting in his words. "That may be so, but maybe I wasn't as patient as I should have been with him." Yeah, no shit, Sherlock. "I want to help him in any way I can." Her face warmed under Ward's scrutiny. "I also know he's banned from all other subjects, too, so his options are minimal. I think that if I can get Carter on a one-to-one, the chances of him losing his temper will significantly reduce."

Kat had considered this particular point in detail before she entered Ward's office. The fact that Carter intimidated her students was one of the reasons she had lost her shit with him. If it were just the two of them, it would surely make things better, right?

Ward sat back in his chair, seeming totally mystified. "Miss Lane," he muttered. "Just to clarify here, you want to tutor Carter . . . one-to-one . . . because you want to help him with his application for early parole?"

She smiled widely.

Ward stared at her incredulously. He shook his head. "I can't allow it."

"Hmm," she mused, chewing on the inside of her mouth in annoyance. "Can I ask why?"

He smirked derisively and straightened his shoulders. "I cannot authorize you to be put in a room with Carter alone—"

"There would be a guard," she interrupted.

Ward exhaled heavily. "Splitting hairs aside, Miss Lane, you've been hired by the facility to teach a group of inmates during an allotted time. On a timetable. Not to work as a one-to-one tutor." He lifted his hands to the heavens in mock sympathy. "It's not in your contract, and the facility can't afford to pay you extra for this."

Kat smiled at Ward, but it was in no way pleasant. She knew he'd take this angle and knew without doubt that it made no difference to her whether she was paid to do the job or not. As a rule, she never spoke about her family's wealth, as in the past it had made people uncomfortable, but with Anthony Ward, it wouldn't trouble her one iota. Being the daughter of a successful senator and the granddaughter of another ensured her bank account was always comfortable.

"Mr. Ward," she began with a wry tone and an unwavering stare that made him shift uneasily in his seat, "I'm not doing this for the money," she spat at him from behind a tight-lipped smile.

Ward sat back in his seat. "I have to admit I'm puzzled here, Miss Lane," he said after a tense moment of silence. "You seemed to detest each other on sight. What exactly would you be doing this for? What would you be getting out of it?"

"I am a teacher, so by definition my job is to teach. That's what I want to do. Carter obviously finds it difficult to be in a classroom environment with other students, so the only solution is to take him out of it." Her glare became fierce. "I believe I can help him, and his learning will be all I will get out of it. Besides," Kat continued, deciding to hit his pride, "if he gets granted his early parole, won't that make your life easier?"

She knew there was definitely no love lost between Ward and Carter.

The side of Ward's mouth twitched. "I still have to say no, Miss Lane. It raises too many questions, and the extra guard time—"

"Yes, talking of guards, has the guard who assaulted Carter been reprimanded in any way?"

"Assaulted?"

"Yes," Kat replied. "He twisted Carter's wrist. It was unnecessary and utterly antagonistic. I was shocked."

She sat wide-eyed with a hand on her chest. She wanted Ward to receive the message loud and clear. She knew the officer hadn't been reprimanded, despite his behavior having been caught on the security cameras in her classroom.

"I see," Ward murmured. "Well, of course we don't tolerate violence against any inmate. I will look into it."

"Good."

With her family's connections, Kat had big friends in very high political places. It would only take one phone call for them to be all over Ward's ass. He cleared his throat and pursed his lips.

"If I agree to this," he offered with disdain and a dismissive wave of his hand, "what makes you think Carter will even go for it? He's known to be a stubborn pain in the ass, as you well know."

Kat smiled at that. "I'm sure if you let me talk to him about it and make him see that I'm only trying to help, he may see past his pride and accept it. If not"—she shrugged—"I'll forget the idea."

"And this is done on your own time. No payment," Ward reinforced with a finger pointed at Kat.

"Absolutely," she agreed, wanting to rip his finger from its socket. "And I'll give you a schedule so you can arrange the guard. Preferably not the one who assaulted my student," she added.

"Fine."

"Great." Kat smiled with a clap of her palms onto her thighs. "I'm meeting with Jack at two. Can I have access to Carter? I'd like this cleared up before I leave for the weekend."

Ward huffed and folded his arms. "Have them radio me down and I'll see he gets to you."

"Thanks, Mr. Ward," she said with a saccharine smile before she left, closing the door very quietly behind her.

. . .

Later that afternoon, Jack Parker listened with rapt attention to the pretty redhead as she relayed her proposal to him in detail. He'd been exceedingly intrigued when he'd gotten a call requesting a meet with Miss Katherine Lane. His first thought was that she wanted to log a complaint against Wes and his behavior—and he wouldn't have blamed her—so he was shocked as hell when she told him she wanted to help with Wes's parole application.

Whether Wes would go for it was another matter altogether. His temper was always getting him into shit that Jack had to get him out of, and the incident with the desk was no exception. Wes's being banned from lessons was a huge blow to his parole application, so Jack was all for hugging Miss Lane to death when she offered to help.

"I have to say I'm amazed Ward went for this." Jack smiled, sipping from his coffee cup.

Kat laughed. "Well, let's just say I know how the game is played."

Jack's grin widened. It was about time Ward was put in his place. "Is that so?"

Kat smirked behind her cup and said no more.

The door to the bland, airless room opened and a resigned-looking Carter appeared, followed by two guards and a severely pissed-looking Ward.

"Hi, Wes," Jack offered, standing.

"Hey," he muttered before his eyes swept to the woman at his side. "Miss Lane," he offered without inflection.

She sighed. "Carter, would you please take a seat?"

• • •

Carter observed her defensive stance. She looked fucking good, he had to admit. He was sure she did it on purpose just to torment him. He slammed down in his seat and smiled at Jack while wiggling his fingers in a give-me-what-I-want gesture. Jack pulled out a box of cigarettes and some matches and threw them on the table. Carter pulled one out, placed it to his lips, lit it, and sucked in the smoke with a slow hiss.

He watched Miss Lane as he exhaled, her green stare unwavering.

"You've got ten minutes," Ward barked. He headed toward the door with wide strides and louder feet.

"We might not be done in ten minutes," Miss Lane retorted. "We'll radio you when we're finished."

Ward stopped dead in his tracks and put one hand on his hip while rubbing his forehead with the other. "Fine."

Jack and Carter exchanged impressed looks. Carter was happy as hell she stood up to Ward, if not a little jealous that Ward was getting a tongue-lashing and he wasn't. Absurdly, Carter wanted nothing more than for her to start mouthing off at him.

"So, is someone gonna put me out of my misery and tell me why I'm here?" he asked instead, glancing between Miss Lane and Jack.

Jack eyed him and his attitude disapprovingly before gesturing to Miss Lane to talk. Carter waited while she cleared her throat, intrigued by her nervousness. It was a new look for her, all fidgety hands and tense shoulders.

"Well, I think it's safe to say that you attending my classes hasn't really worked out that well."

He scoffed. "Yeah, no shit, lady."

"Wes," Jack warned with a curl of his lip. Carter rolled his eyes and signaled for Miss Lane to continue with a lift of his elbow.

"I understand your parole officer will be coming in soon to discuss your application."

He shrugged. "Yeah, so?"

She kept her gaze firm and steady, a fact that made Carter's fingers twitch. "And I also know that your participation in my lessons was to help with your application."

Carter huffed out the last of the smoke and extinguished the cigarette in the ashtray with three very deliberate and sharp drops of his hand. He continued to stare at the woman in front of him while he slumped back into his seat.

"In English," he said finally, hiding his smirk when he saw the familiar intensity burst in Miss Lane's eyes.

There she is.

"In English," she snarled, "I'm offering to tutor you on a one-to-one basis so you can apply for early parole despite your acting like a complete asshole, even when people are trying to help you."

Jack stared in amazement at the little spitfire. Carter let his eyes roam down the curves and skin of her face and neck in fascination as a red heat flashed across her. He licked his lips. Damn, she was hot when she was pissed.

Abruptly, Miss Lane stood from her seat, scraping it hard against the floor before it fell back with a loud clatter. She looked at it, not moving to pick it back up and, instead, grabbed at her bag, dropping it twice before she got a secure hold on it.

Jack stood with her while she struggled. "Miss Lane?"

"Forget it," she snapped. "I'm not wasting my time. It's obvious you're incapable of being anything other than ungrateful when someone offers to help." She pulled her bag onto her shoulder. "But I get it. I get that accepting my offer wouldn't help the totally-cool-badass persona you've got going on here, and I get that you're terrified someone might see you for the intelligent person you actually are. I'm sure Mr. Ward will be thrilled that you'll be seeing out the rest of your sentence, but who cares, right?" She spun on her heel.

Well, fuck.

Seeing the fire and challenge in her eyes and hearing the truth in her words, Carter suddenly realized the lifeline she was offering, a way of getting the parole he so desperately wanted, and his childish behavior was going to make her walk out of the room, leaving him with nothing. As infuriating as he found Miss Lane to be, he couldn't deny he was touched that she'd agreed to help him.

He cleared his throat. "Miss Lane?"

She stopped marching toward the door. Her shoulders rose as she turned to him with an impatient expression.

"I, um," he began, tapping his fingertips along the edge of the table, unused to showing gratitude, let alone feeling it. "Look I—I appreciate that," Carter stammered, his eyes flitting around the room.

Miss Lane glanced at Jack, who appeared equally speechless. "Don't worry about it. It was stupid of me to—"

"No," he interrupted. "It wasn't stupid. It was a good idea. I think . . ." Carter glanced at Jack for assistance.

"Wes," Jack coaxed. "Are you saying you want Miss Lane to tutor you?"

Carter dropped his eyes to the table, reaching for the cigarettes.

"Well, okay," Jack whispered. "Miss Lane?"

"So," she said, taking a slow step toward the table. "We're going to do this?"

"I said so, didn't I?" Carter growled through a fog of smoke that curled into the air around him. A bemused look crossed Miss Lane's face before she retook her seat.

Twenty minutes later and with her diary filled with the times and dates she and Carter were meeting, Miss Lane stood once again from the table and held her hand out to Jack.

He shook it enthusiastically. "Thank you, Katherine. We'll talk more, I'm sure."

"Absolutely," she replied with a smile. "And call me Kat." She glanced at Carter. "See you Monday."

But Carter remained mute, unmoving. Still as a statue, he kept his eyes fixed on the door as it closed behind her. His pulse thundered in his ears while the sound of her name reverberated through his skull with each ferocious beat of his heart.

Katherine. Katherine. Katherine.

Once they were alone, Jack turned to him with a huge-ass smile on his face. "Wes, this is great!" He clapped his hands together. "This is really great, right? Wes?" Jack repeated, sliding his hands into his pockets. "Wes, are you—?"

"What did you call her?" Carter croaked. His airway squeezed, making him gasp. He pushed a slow hand to his chest where a tightness, the likes of which he'd never encountered, pulled taut and unforgiving.

"What?" Jack asked in confusion.

Carter's eyes closed. He swallowed. "What did you call Miss Lane?"

Jack frowned. "I called her Katherine. Why?"

Katherine Lane. Katherine fucking Lane.

As the world around him tilted, making the room swim horrifically, Carter dropped his head like a lead weight to his knees. His breath hitched and tripped over itself as it fought to get to his lungs.

It couldn't be. There was no way.

No.

What were the odds?

The chance was minute.

He grabbed at his scalp in disbelief.

"It can't be her."

He pulled in as much air as he could, but it was useless. The walls were closing in while panic and disbelief gripped him mercilessly by the throat. He was choking.

Jack dropped to his knees in front of him. "Who, Wes?" he urged. "Wes, talk to me. Who are you talking about?" He grasped Carter's shoulder.

"It can't be," Carter mumbled.

"Who? Miss Lane?"

"No," Carter replied, vaguely aware of the alarm creeping into Jack's voice. "She's not Miss Lane, she's— Oh fuck."

"Who?" Jack asked, tightening his grip on Carter's shoulder.

Carter finally looked at his counselor through eyes that could barely see, his vision fogged with memories so thick he could almost touch them.

Thick, wavy hair. A blue dress. Gunshots. Screams.

He grabbed for Jack's arm and squeezed, clinging for his life, needing to be grounded, needing something to keep him from falling apart completely. He choked back a sob.

Long gone was the strong, arrogant twenty-seven-year-old man. Once again, he was a scared shitless eleven-year-old, desperate for someone to love him, frantically trying to save the life of a tiny, petrified girl.

He tried to answer Jack. Fuck, he tried. He wanted to tell him everything. He wanted to beg him to get him out of the room before he lost his shit altogether. He was losing his shit. Was this what dying felt like?

Like a broken dam, Carter's memory burst wide fucking open, each image like a firework exploding in his vision, whizzing around his brain, squealing in his ears. He dropped his head, squeezing his eyes shut and clutching the lapel of Jack's jacket, scrunching the wool in his palm, willing his whole body to calm, to relax and back the fuck up. Infuriatingly, the more he tried to slow his breathing, the more his body closed up.

He grunted in terror when his throat shrank more and more, and slumped his sweating forehead heavily against his counselor's shoulder, speaking the words he never thought he'd utter since that horrific night sixteen years before.

"Jack," he whispered. "She's my Peaches."

7

"I have to get to my daddy!"

"Keep moving! We have to get away from them. They'll kill you! Move!"

"Wes?"

"No! He needs me!"

"Wes. Can you open your eyes for me?"

"Stay still!"

"Wesley. You're all right."

Carter lunged up from the clinic bed into a sitting position, wide-eyed and gasping. He glanced around, almost frantic, and jumped when a hand touched his arm. He turned to see Jack standing next to the bed, his face creased with concern. He swallowed hard, trying like hell to coat his sandpaper throat. The fuzziness in his head was still front and center. Fuck, he felt like death.

"Where am I?" He blinked and looked around the room at the whitewashed walls and the surprised expressions of a doctor and two guards.

"You're in the facility clinic, Wesley," the doctor answered.

"It's Carter, and who the hell was talking to you, Doc?" he snapped. The doctor flinched and took a step backward.

"Wes," Jack said softly. "You had a panic attack."

He coughed a laugh, ignoring the heat of embarrassment that crept up the center of his body. "Says who?"

"Says me," the doctor interjected.

Carter stared at him for a beat. "I'm outta here." He swung his legs to the right so they were hanging off the bed. "Where are my shoes?"

"I'm afraid that's not possible," the doctor began.

"I wasn't asking!" Carter yelled.

His head pounded from deep inside his skull. His eardrums had pulled tight enough to split, and, oh, look at that, little black dots were hovering and dancing in his periphery. Fantastic. He scrunched his eyes shut for one split second to gain his bearings, listing forward.

Jack placed his hands on his shoulders to keep him upright. "You need to calm down," he murmured. "Just relax. You've been out for a while. You need to take it easy."

Carter grasped the bridge of his nose to try to ease the throbbing behind his eyes. He'd never felt anything like it. It was like a goddamn circus had taken up residence in between his ears, and dammit all to hell if he didn't feel completely drained. He couldn't even fight Jack when he pushed him back against the pillows on the bed. He exhaled and frowned at the crowd standing and staring at him, as though waiting for him to explode.

"Does your head hurt?" the doctor asked.

Carter glared hard at the man, too damned exhausted to come up with any witty shit.

"I'll go and get some painkillers," the doctor muttered and scurried out of the room.

Carter was surprised to see the two guards also leave, glancing nervously at Jack as they did.

"Well, hell, at least I can still clear a room," Carter muttered.

Jack pushed his hands into his pockets. "We need to talk."

"About what?"

Jack fixed Carter with a penetrating stare. "You know what."

Carter's head dropped back against the bed.

He was entirely too confused and still in a state of complete shock to talk about . . . well, fucking anything, least of all the huge revelation that had hit him in the head like a damn brick.

It was her. Peaches. The girl he'd dreamed about for sixteen years.

The girl he'd saved—

"Wes," Jack pushed. "It's confidential, if that's what you're worrying about."

"I'm not worried about anything, Jack. I just have nothing to say. Goddammit!" Carter fisted the bedsheets, wanting to tear them into small strips so they matched the tumultuous sensation vibrating through him.

The sound of a chair being pulled across the floor toward his bed reminded Carter that Jack was a stubborn and persistent son of a bitch who wasn't about to let him off lightly without some kind of explanation.

Jack leaned his elbows on the side of the bed. "Wes, we've known each other a lot of years. We've talked, we've argued, we've sat in silence—but I swear to God, boy, you've never scared me as much as you did yesterday."

Carter's eyes flew to Jack's tired ones to see only truth behind his words. His confession made Carter feel strange. He didn't give a shit about other people's thoughts or sensitivities usually, but knowing that Jack had been worried made Carter feel . . . something.

"Yeah, well," he murmured with a shrug while looking at the ceiling, "I'm fine."

"What's Peaches?"

A tremor of anxiety swept up Carter's spine, causing a wave of nausea to crash through him.

"No one important." The words were forced, whispered.

"So Peaches is a person?"

Carter pushed his fingertips to his temples and closed his eyes. "Jack, please," he groaned. "Leave it."

He hoped that the desperation lacing his voice was enough to stop Jack's persistence. Surprise crossed Jack's eyes and Carter knew he'd dodged the bullet for the time being. He just didn't have the energy or the inclination to try to explain something or someone he'd thought about every day since he was eleven years old.

He had to get his own head out of his ass before he could do that.

He had to get his own head out of his ass before Monday, when he had his English Literature session.

A one-to-one session with her.

With Miss Lane.

With Peaches.

• • •

Carter was sitting behind a wooden table when his Peaches entered with a wide smile at the guard. It dropped minutely when she registered Carter's purposefully listless appearance, though her confident gait never wavered.

"Good afternoon," she said, pulling books and papers from her mammoth bag.

Carter kept his eyes trained to the floor while his thumbs spun around each other on his lap. Fuck, he was sweating. She cleared her throat.

Carter lifted his head, praying his voice would work. "Good afternoon, Miss Lane."

Her green eyes flickered with surprise at his uncharacteristically amenable greeting. He gave a small smile, trying to appear blasé. On the inside, Carter wanted nothing more than to hightail it out of the room like a pussy. He was sure she could hear his heart pounding painfully in his chest.

She pulled up a chair. "We're going to do exactly what the class has been doing so you don't fall behind."

He kept his eyes on her, taking all of her in. He watched her movements and the expressions rippling over her face, trying to see the young girl he remembered like a crumpled photograph in the depths of his memory. Jesus. After sixteen years, she was sitting across from him, oblivious to their connection. Nevertheless, he knew she could feel his stare. He wondered if she felt the same way he did when she looked at him.

"This is the poem we'll be looking at." She placed a piece of paper in front of him.

He sat forward reading the title on the top of the page. " 'Tichborne's Elegy'?"

"Yes," Peaches said. "What of it?"

"Do those idiots in that class of yours even know who Chidiock Tichborne is?"

"They do now," she answered evenly while she pulled the lid off her pen. "And what do you know about him or his poetry?"

Carter heard the challenge in her voice. He focused on that and not the sensation of the heat coming from her knee near his, under the table.

"I know enough," he replied, crossing his arms.

"Please," she offered with an open palm, "regale me."

"Regale you?" he mocked. He rubbed his chin. "He was born in Southampton, England, in 1558," he started. "In 1586 he took part in the Babington Plot to murder Queen Elizabeth and replace her with the Catholic Mary, Queen of Scots. But they were shit out of luck. He was arrested and eventually hanged, drawn, and quartered."

Stifling a laugh at her shock, he said, "This poem is the one he wrote while he was awaiting his execution. Kind of inappropriate to be studying this in a prison, don't you think, Miss Lane?"

"You like history."

Carter shrugged. "It's okay. I prefer English literature." He allowed his loaded answer to settle between them.

She wet her lips. "So, tell me about the poem."

"He uses paradox and antithesis." He trailed his finger across the page in front of him. "Opposites and contradictions. He does it to highlight the tragedy of what he's going through, which, when you think about it, is pretty stupid."

"Why would you say that?"

Carter laughed. "He made his mistakes, so he has to pay the price. His debt."

"You sound like you know something about that."

Carter raised his eyebrows and glanced around the room with large, obvious eyes.

"I know you're paying for your mistakes. But he was so young, too young to die. Don't you sympathize with Tichborne in some way?"

"Sympathize? No," he answered firmly. "Envy? Yes."

"Why do you envy him?"

Carter kept his eyes on the table between them. "The fact he's about to die," he muttered. "He begins to see things much more clearly. He has focus, clarity. I envy him that."

"You want clarity?"

Carter smiled. "Wanting and needing are two very different things, Miss Lane," he answered. "I need clarity. I need focus."

Then he stared at her, because Jesus if there was anything else he could do or say at that moment. Carter knew that finding out who she was was the first step to him having any kind of focus in his life for years. And even though he spoke about Tichborne like he knew what the fuck he was talking about, it was only with his Peaches sitting in front of him that he truly understood his own need for it.

"Peaches," he whispered, taking in every inch of her face: the red hair that had engulfed him when he threw her to the ground and she'd fought against him to get back to her father, and the eyes that had cried heartbroken, terrified tears.

"What?" she asked quietly. "What did you say, Carter?"

And, just like that, the moment was gone.

As if he'd woken from a dream, Carter sat up straight, glaring at the guard before he slumped back in his seat.

"But, you know," he mumbled, grabbing the cigarette Jack had given him out of his pocket, his barrier snapping right back up. "What the hell do I know, right? You're the genius teacher."

A small voice in the back of his head screamed and shouted at him for being such a dick as her face changed from calm to furious. But it was okay, he told himself. He could cope with her anger. It was hot. Her anger turned him on. It was all the other shit that scared him to death.

"Yeah," she snapped in response. "I am, and I want you to do these activities." She slammed another piece of paper in front of him covered in questions and tasks. "I'm sure with all your worldly knowledge you won't have a problem, right?"

She flashed him a look that dared him to say something back, to refuse. He didn't.

Instead he picked up the pen she'd dropped on the table between them and began doing what she'd asked because, as she sat staring at him in all her rage and loveliness, Carter knew he'd have done anything she'd asked of him.

Anything at all.

8

Kat set the collected notebooks and pens in neat little piles on her desk, glancing at her students as they were escorted out of the room back to their cells.

"Good work today," Kat praised Riley as he approached with a timid smile. "Who knew Shakespeare would increase your enthusiasm for the written word?"

She was bursting with pride at the effort Riley had put into his writing. He was trying so hard and, although his dyslexia frustrated him, it was obvious that he was very smart.

Riley smirked, rocking back on his heels. "Yeah." He shrugged as his index finger touched Kat's copy of *The Merchant of Venice*. "I don't care for that poetry bullshit, but I kinda like this Bill dude."

Kat laughed and leaned against her desk, crossing her arms over her chest. "What can I do for you, Riley?"

He immediately seemed nervous and cracked his knuckles loudly. "You know it's my parole board meeting next week, right?"

Kat nodded.

"Moore!" the guard behind them shouted. "Time's up!"

"Excuse me!" Kat barked, standing up straight. "Mr. Moore wishes to discuss something important with me about his education, and doesn't need you"—she thrust an accusatory finger his way—"yelling at him while he does so."

The guard at once looked lost for words. Kat turned back to her student. "Sorry, Riley, carry on."

He clapped his hands together. "Um . . . yeah, so, it's my parole board meeting next week, and I was wondering . . . " He tapped his fists against one another. "I mean, I know you're helping Carter out." He shifted from foot to foot.

"What do you want me to do, Riley?" Kat asked gently, placing a palm over his knuckles in an effort to calm him. "You can ask me anything, and if I can help, I will."

Riley's shoulders appeared to slump in relief. "Jack said you'd say that, 'cause you're cool and shit."

Kat laughed. "Thank you."

"Would you give a . . . a character reference in front of the board? You know, help me get some extra points by telling them how awesome a fucker I really am?"

Kat had received a request for a written character reference that morning from a very agitated Anthony Ward. It seemed he still got all sorts of uppity when his inmates were granted their freedom. Asshole.

Kat squeezed Riley's forearm. "I'd be honored to."

"Really?"

"Yes, really," she replied before he clutched her to his mammoth chest, almost suffocating her .

"Fucking A, Miss L!" he cried, hugging her hard.

• • •

Kat hurried down the corridor toward the session room, late but excited. She was more than a little eager to get stuck in Carter's mind again. She'd been struck dumb by the knowledge Carter had shown in their first session. She'd known he was intelligent. She'd read it in his file, but Christ. He was something else. The man was intelligent and educated in an extraordinarily seductive way.

She smiled at the guard on the door and walked in, seeing Carter standing in the far corner of the room, fisting his hands together with a droopy, almost finished cigarette dangling from his lips. His face was hard and became even harder when he looked at her. He yanked the cigarette from his lips, causing ash to fall to the floor.

"Oh," he sneered. "And here was me, thinking you were too fucking busy to keep an appointment."

Kat slowly placed her bag on the table. She held her tongue, remembering Rachel's words about routine being vitally important to the inmates.

"I'm sorry," she said. He strode across the room from one side to the other, his long legs eating up the small space over and over. "I was talking to Riley after class and then I met Jack on the way here and—"

"What?" Carter yelled, making the guard by the door reach a hand to the baton on his waistband.

"What?" she echoed calmly.

"And what the fuck did he say to you, huh?" Carter bellowed, taking a giant step toward her.

Kat crossed her arms, standing firm against the untamed wrath on his face.

"We just talked about your parole officer coming next week," she replied. "He wants me to talk to her about our sessions. He thinks it'll help your application if I'm involved directly."

She watched the ire in his eyes dim and his strong, large chest began to slow. He swallowed hard and Kat stared at his Adam's apple bobbing at the front of his throat. She shook her head free of the inappropriate thoughts entering it. Not least, the one where her tongue traveled the length of the black neck tattoo that was teasing her mercilessly. She wondered how far down his body it went . . .

She refocused. "Carter, I apologize. I'm here now, so we can get to work." She dropped her arms to her sides, trying to appear nondefensive, and gestured to the chair by the table.

Carter ran a hand down his face and finally moved to his chair, where he sat slowly and extinguished his cigarette. "So, what exciting shit have you got for me today, Miss Lane? Because, I have to tell you, I'm on the edge of my seat in anticipation."

"We're staying with Tichborne for now," she replied, ignoring his sarcasm. "I wanted to go over the work you did for me yesterday."

"Great," Carter responded dryly, pulling another smoke from his pocket.

While Kat moved her chair to his side of the table, he clicked at the guard to bring him a match, which he did. Carter inhaled the smoke deeply before starting to exhale but stopped abruptly when he noticed she was so close. He stared at her as she sat down, crossed her legs, and began sorting through papers.

"What?" she asked.

With the cigarette still hanging from his mouth, he glanced down at the minute space between them and then at the space she'd left at the other side of the table.

"Oh, please," she scoffed. "What're you afraid of, that you'll catch teacher cooties?"

Carter pulled the smoke from his lips. "No, I'm not worried about that shit. I'm just surprised."

"Surprised?"

He scratched his forearm with his thumb. "At how well you hide your fear."

Her eyes narrowed. "I'm not scared of you."

"Oh, Miss Lane, don't tease me." He smiled sexily.

She stared at him for a beat before she sat back and crossed her arms. "And why should I be scared of you?"

Carter moved forward in his seat, releasing the smoke down his nose so it parted temptingly when it hit his top lip. "You should be scared, Peaches," he murmured. "I've done things that would make your pretty little head spin, and, you being this close"—he gestured with his chin between them—"well, let's just say"—his eyes met hers—"it just makes me want to be bad all over again."

Holy. Shit.

The air in Kat's lungs left her in an abrupt whoosh.

Carter smiled, seemingly pleased with himself, and sat back.

Arrogant bastard.

"I take it you liked my work, huh?" He began to look through the comments she'd made on his writings.

"It's— I, um . . . yeah, it— What?"

"I said you liked this shit." The edge of his mouth twitched with a conceited smirk. "So are we doing some work today or what?"

Still embarrassingly incapable of stringing a full sentence together, Kat pulled the papers closer while leaning forward, placing her arm only half an inch from his. She felt the buzz, the crackle, the hum. She managed to keep her arm in that position for about sixty seconds before she had to move it away.

For the next forty-five minutes, Kat watched Carter complete task after task, dutifully and perceptively. His discussion points were insightful and the sound of his voice as he became more and more enthusiastic about the poem made her insides twist in the most delicious ways. His brow creased adorably when he concentrated and his eyes grew impossibly darker when she said something that challenged him. Sparring with him about iambic pentameter, imagery, and metaphors was undeniably sexy.

An academic type of foreplay that left Kat craving more.

Before she knew it, the guards came to take Carter back to his cell. She packed up slowly, unable to refute the heavy sensation filling her stomach at the thought of not seeing him for two days.

As she reached the door, she heard Carter stand from his seat. "Miss Lane."

She turned. "Yes, Carter?"

The left side of his mouth lifted. "See you Monday."

• • •

With a birthday card and beautifully wrapped present in hand, Kat walked into Beth's favorite Italian restaurant in SoHo and laughed when she spotted her friend. A huge, flashing TWENTY-FIVE badge covered the left side of her pink knee-length dress, accompanied by an even pinker sash.

"Kat, you're here!" she cried excitedly as she approached.

"Of course, I wouldn't miss it!"

Beth stood stock-still, looking at her friend in a way that made Kat brush her hands nervously down her black silk top and black jeans. "What? Why are you looking at me like that?"

"Something's different about you." Beth gasped, then grinned. "You're all glowy and— Holy hell. What's his name?"

Kat's mouth popped open, then she gave a small snort. "God, you're crazy. Move your ass."

Beth obediently followed Kat's index finger, which was pointing toward the bar. "Just making an observation," she replied with her palms up.

Kat hummed skeptically. "Well, observe this instead." She smiled, handing Beth her present. "It's from me and Mom."

The red Hermès clutch purse was exactly what Beth had not-so-subtly asked for in the run-up to her birthday. She clasped it to her chest and cooed lovingly. If only everyone could be so easily pleased.

Kat glanced around the bar area as they waited for their drinks. "Adam's not here yet?"

Beth shook her head as she handed the bartender a twenty. "He had to work late. He'll be here soon."

"The life of a CFO, huh?" Kat smiled.

"He's working so hard with his brother," Beth said. "We're like ships passing in the night. When I'm not grading and planning for school, I'm planning the wedding, which we've decided will be next summer. FYI, you're going to be a bridesmaid."

"Oh God," Kat joked.

"Be nice," Beth scolded. "I will not be Bridezilla!" They laughed. "What about you, anyway? How's life behind bars?"

"It's like nothing I ever imagined." Kat described her amazing students and the sessions with Carter, while also recounting the hair-raising moments with Corey and Jason.

"You look happy, Kat," Beth stated sincerely as they took their drinks from the bar. "And it's a good look on you."

Kat's cheeks flushed. "It's a good feeling to finally be doing something that feels right."

"Your father would be proud."

"I think so. I'm helping, and it feels really good." Kat ran her index finger around the rim of her glass.

"Then why the face? What's wrong?"

Kat hesitated. "I just wish my mom would see how happy I am. I mean, Jesus, we can barely be in the same room for five minutes, we fight so much." And it hurt. "She's convinced something's going to happen to me, instead of trusting me and being proud. It's like nothing I do is good enough, and I'm doing all of this to spite her."

Beth squeezed Kat's shoulder. "She'll always worry, hon. That's what moms do. Even more so in your case."

"I know, but—"

"Maybe try to show a little more understanding."

Kat clenched her teeth. She didn't want to hear it. She loved Beth dearly, but her constant understanding of Kat's mother was starting to grind. "So," she said, changing the subject. "Apart from working tirelessly, how's Adam?"

"He's good. He invited his brother, Austin, tonight. He's the CEO at WCS. He got divorced last winter and Adam's determined to get him 'back out there.' He's really nice and very handsome."

It took Kat a moment to recognize the tone in Beth's voice. "Oh no, no, no," Kat exclaimed with a shake of her head. "I don't need a man right now."

"Pffft. If you say so." She gave a mock serious scowl. "Is reclaiming your chastity at twenty-four, like, a thing now?"

Kat pushed her friend playfully. "Shut up!"

Beth laughed while her eyes widened over Kat's shoulder. "He's here!" She all but skipped across the restaurant and kissed and hugged Adam. He was only a couple of inches taller than Beth, with neatly cut brown hair. He was dressed in a dark blue pair of jeans and a red button-down. He had green eyes and beautiful white teeth.

"Nice to see you, Kat," he said as she approached. "What can I get you to dri—"

"Sorry I'm late. Traffic was fucking terrible and the cabdriver was a complete ass!"

Kat turned toward the voice to see a head of chaotic black hair. It was that just-got-out-of-bed look, and he worked it well. The man was tall, towering over Kat and Beth, who was still at her side, and smiled at them both before turning his attention to Adam, who slapped him on the back before ordering a round of drinks.

"Kat, this is Austin Ford, Adam's brother," Beth said. "Austin, this is my friend Kat Lane."

"Hi," she said, holding out her hand. "Nice to meet you."

Austin stooped and took her hand, placing a soft kiss on the back of it. "Likewise." He smiled.

Yeah, he was very attractive. He had broad shoulders covered in a black polo shirt that was open at the neck, showing a black string that hung down underneath it. His arms were tanned and strong-looking, which matched his masculine, angular face. He resembled Adam but appeared rougher around the edges.

Kat studied him discreetly while sipping her martini. He had all the traits she usually went for and, if he was as nice as his manners, he'd be golden. Yet a feeling of unease in the pit of her stomach made her pause in her visual examination of Austin. It twisted uncomfortably, settling like a weight deep within her.

The sensation became stronger when Austin smirked.

It was an unnervingly familiar gesture, which made Kat's skin heat.

"So what do you do, Kat?" Austin asked, noticing her stare.

"I'm a teacher," she answered quickly. "English literature."

"Like Beth," he offered. "That's great. What school do you teach at?"

"I teach at a prison, actually. Arthur Kill."

Austin's eyebrows disappeared into his hairline. "Wow," he said, glancing surreptitiously at his brother, who coughed uncomfortably into his palm.

Kat frowned. Okaaaaay.

"Beth didn't mention it," Adam said quietly, staring at his fiancée.

Beth shrugged. "Why would I?"

"Kill, huh?" Austin mused, his eyes still on his brother. "What a small world. We know a guy who's spent time there. It must take some patience."

Kat nodded, the loaded looks between the two men making her very curious.

"Come on," Austin said, gesturing Kat toward their table. "Tell me all about it."

• • •

Monday morning couldn't come fast enough for Carter, and he made sure to take out all his nervous energy on the punching bag Ross held in front of him.

He'd been allowed into the prison library Sunday afternoon. After learning from a verbose Riley which play the class was studying, Carter immediately found a copy of *The Merchant of Venice* and some analytical studies on the text, which he proceeded to read from cover to cover through the night. He'd read the play before and knew the characters and storyline, but, once he was finished, he knew he was ready for anything his Peaches could throw at him.

He was sitting at the table of their usual room when she entered. Shit, she looked great. Her hair was down and a soft wave had appeared in the sections that framed her face. As much as Carter loved her hair, he loved seeing her face more, and he was at once annoyed that it was partially covered. He crossed his arms to stop the urge he had to push it behind her ears.

"Good afternoon, Miss Lane. How are you today?"

She paused, looking puzzled. "I'm well, and yourself?"

"Oh, I'm great." All the more for seeing you.

"So, today we start Shakespeare," she said, eyeing him carefully while she lifted all her resources from her bag and placed them in order on the table between them. Carter thought her perfectionist traits were at the very least adorable, and at the very most irritating as shit.

"Goodie," he replied, resting his forearms on the edge of the table.

Peaches reached back into her bag and pulled out a pack of Marlboros, which she threw at him.

"Shut up," she said playfully.

Carter grinned and pulled one out. He placed it between his lips. "Yes, ma'am."

Once the cigarette was lit, Peaches once again moved her chair around to Carter's side of the table. He was a little more prepared for it this time, but it didn't stop the pulse of desire that shot through his body when she crossed her legs. She had fucking awesome legs. They curved in all the right places, and they weren't skinny. There was enough there to grab on to. Suck on. Have wrapped around his—

"*The Merchant of Venice,*" Peaches said, placing the play in front of him. "Tell me what you know." She rested her cheek in her palm.

He shifted in his seat. "Set in Italy, it's classed as a comedy but many believe it was a tragedy due to the treatment of the main character Shylock." Carter picked up the book and thumbed through it.

"Who's Shylock?"

"Shylock is the loan shark who just happens to be a Jew in a predominantly Christian Shakespearean society. Unlucky for him."

Peaches laughed. "I guess so. I'm interested, though, why do you say it's a tragedy? What is tragic about Shylock?"

"He's classed as a villain because of his religion."

"He's classed as a villain because of his demands for payment of a loan," Peaches countered.

"Bullshit," Carter continued firmly with an index finger pressed into the center of the book. "The demands he makes are fair."

"Really? Demanding a pound of flesh to pay off a monetary debt is fair?"

Carter exhaled. She'd no idea how relevant her words were to him and the life he lived. "If you can't pay a debt, you shouldn't give your word." His gaze roamed over the piece of hair hiding her left cheek, and he imagined what it would feel like between his fingers.

"His call for a pound of flesh may sound macabre," he continued, "but the way he's reviled because of his religion is even more so. He's vilified because of his faith; his demand simply reinforces it. His demand is expected because of the prejudice of the narrow-minded bastards around him."

Peaches stared at him. "You know a lot about debt?"

"I do," he answered. "Do you?"

"I know what it's like to give your word to someone," Peaches said after a moment. Her eyes rested on the play, opened at Shylock's most infamous speech. "I know what it's like to pay that word off because you have no other choice but to see it through because you love that person so much it would be a tragedy if you didn't."

And that's when it happened.

Carter couldn't help himself. It was as if his body was working of its own accord, drawn to her, desperate for her touch. She just seemed so damned sad. His hand moved slowly toward her hair before he tucked it behind her ear. He could barely breathe as his fingertips touched the soft skin at the back of her ear, at the line of her jaw.

The guard by the door cleared his throat.

Peaches instantly sat back and brushed her hand down the skin he'd touched. Carter rubbed his fingertips down his thigh to ease the heat that resided there.

"I'm— Shit," he mumbled, grabbing for another cigarette. "I shouldn't have. Sorry." He lit his smoke and inhaled three times in quick succession. "You just . . . you looked upset, ya know, and— Fuck it. I shouldn't . . ."

All he'd wanted to do was make her feel better, smile, maybe.

"Carter," she said, placing a hand on his shoulder. His eyes shot to hers, cigarette dangling from his speechless mouth. "It's all right." She gave a small smile. "I appreciated it. Thank you."

Carter blinked. "Yeah," he offered. "Yeah. Whatever. Cool."

Peaches released his shoulder after giving it a reassuring squeeze and pulled the book closer. "Shall we continue?"

Carter groaned and rubbed his palms down his face. "Bring on that Shakespeare shit, Peaches."

"Peaches?" she asked with a dip of her chin. "You keep calling me that. Where does that come from?"

Panic sliced through Carter. "It's, um . . ." He fingered the cigarette pack. "I dunno. Why? Does it offend you?"

"No, I was just curious."

He pulled long and hard on his smoke. "I can just call you Miss Lane, if you prefer."

She was silent for a few seconds. "No," she replied finally. "Most people call me Kat, but I guess you can call me Peaches—on one condition."

"What's the condition?" he asked with a wry grin.

Peaches folded her arms, pushing her boobs up in ways that looked all kinds of awesome. "If I can call you Wes."

Carter stared at her. Well, hell. His name had never sounded so soft, so . . . nice. "I— That's a . . . I'm not sure. I mean, only Jack calls me that," he stammered, throwing his cigarette into the ashtray. "I'm not— I mean, Christ." Both hands found his scalp.

How could he explain his hatred of his Christian name? That was a long-ass, depressing story.

"Okay, I get it. Carter it'll be," she said, touching his right shoulder blade. "Actually, instead, maybe I'll name *you* after a fruit. How about Kiwi?"

The burst of laughter that exploded from him felt new and fantastic. Peaches laughed along with him. Dammit, she was gorgeous when she laughed. Her whole face lit up and her eyes crinkled, almost disappearing. Carter was mesmerized.

"Okay, enough of this." She chuckled. "Let's get to work."

The discussion points she produced elicited heated debates, which they both enjoyed more than they should have. They argued and undermined one another, but the atmosphere was playful and light and, Carter couldn't deny, sexy as hell.

"Shit," Peaches cursed, taking Carter by surprise. "It's late."

He glanced at the clock. They'd run over by twenty-five minutes. "Time flies when you're having fun, right?" The wink he sent her way caused her cheeks to pinken. "You, um, you got a date or something?" Carter asked as she rushed, throwing her shit into her bag.

"Oh no!" She gave a vigorous shake of her head. "I don't have a date. I—I'm single." She snapped her mouth shut and briefly closed her eyes.

Carter could barely hide his elation. Or his relief. She belonged to no one. No man had claimed her, made her his. His mind boggled. Christ, were they all fucking insane?

"Hey, Miss Lane," he called with a grin as she set off with her things across the room. "I enjoyed today."

"Me too," she answered, mirroring his smile. "Oh, and Carter . . ." She turned back to him while the guard opened the door. "The name's Peaches."

9

Carter was anxious. He was anxious and nervous and dammit, where the *hell* was Peaches?

He was sitting in a nicer room than normal, alongside Jack and his rat-faced attorney. Diane, his case manager, was due in fifteen minutes and Peaches *still* hadn't arrived. She was definitely in; Jack had told him so when he'd asked indifferently of her whereabouts. He hadn't been able to ignore the way Jack eyed him. That shit made him nervous.

The door opened and Carter's leg ceased its bouncing when Peaches entered. She was stunning in a pale blue top and black pencil skirt. Her hair was up in a loose twist and Carter immediately wanted to unfasten it and grab a handful, just so he could smell it, to see if it still smelled of the sweet peaches he remembered.

"I'm sorry I'm late," she told Jack while glancing at Carter.

He caught the look and smiled. Jack cleared his throat at his side and Carter's face dropped instantly. Shit. Jack was aware of there being "something" between the two of them, and had asked frequently about Peaches ever since his stupid ass had passed out. It was only a matter of time before Jack would figure it all out.

He'd have to be more careful. He knew he'd been a lot calmer around her. Where Peaches was concerned, his temper had been under control and, as positive a thing as that was, it could prove to be very dangerous. With that thought, he slouched in his seat, averting his eyes from her, and went to work picking at the cuticle on his right thumb.

As if on goddamn cue, Ward entered the room, followed by

Diane. She was a striking woman in her midthirties, with large dark eyes and brown hair that rested just under her shoulder blades in deep waves.

Ward began by making the introductions to Peaches, who blushed wonderfully when Diane praised her on the work she'd done. Diane walked over to Carter's table and, without a word, pulled out all the necessary papers. She took a seat opposite Carter and began writing at the top of the application form.

"How are you?" she asked him. "You look well."

"I'm just dandy," he answered in his usual blasé, cocky tone.

Diane ignored it. "The parole board is convening in six weeks. Your hearing will be then. But I have a few concerns regarding some instances that may have an impact on your application."

Carter bristled.

"I have evidence here," Diane stated while she held up another form, "that you've shown aggressive behavior toward other inmates, staff, including Miss Lane and Mr. Ward, and have threatened guards while in their charge."

"That's because one of them assaulted me," Carter fumed. "Damn near broke my wrist!"

"Wes," Jack warned with an imperceptible shake of his head.

"I'll be sure to look into that," Diane assured Carter, making a note in her diary. "But, regardless," she continued, lifting her head, "you have far more negatives than positives at this point. The question is, what are you doing to counteract these incidents?"

"As you know," Jack said after a moment of tense silence during which Carter pretended that his right shoe was the most fascinating item on the planet, "Wes has been working with Miss Lane on a three-day timetable, studying English literature."

"Yes, I do know this," Diane answered. "How have the sessions been, Miss Lane?"

Peaches smiled. "They've been excellent. Carter's worked well.

He's engaged and has many perceptive ideas about the topics we've discussed."

Diane made a quick note. "I understand that Carter and you had a couple of, shall we say, run-ins when you first started."

Peaches crossed her legs. "That's correct."

"But not anymore?"

"No. Carter and I have come to an understanding in terms of his conduct during the sessions. Carter's attitude has been positive and cooperative. It's clear that he wants to learn and do well."

"That's great, Carter," Diane said with a nod.

"But?" he and Jack said in unison.

"But the board members aren't stupid. They're aware that your attending these sessions could be a way of simply scoring points with them."

"With all due respect," Jack interrupted, "isn't that the point?"

"Yes, of course," Diane concurred. "But Carter needs to show that he's doing it because he wants to and views everything he learns as useful in the long term." She turned to Carter. "That's what parole is all about, Carter: the long term." She fixed him with a sharp stare. "I have to be honest. Despite your eligibility date, the board may see your past conduct as your way of not observing the rules of this institution."

Carter's gaze flickered to Peaches, disappointment radiating through him.

"How long-term are we talking?" Carter's lawyer asked as he scribbled on a yellow notepad. "How long will Carter's parole be?"

Diane sat back. "As per his eligibility, if the hearing examiner grants his parole, that would mean he's released fifteen months early."

"So twelve months," the lawyer finished for her.

"I would expect so. I would be surprised if they agreed to anything shorter. The first nine months would be monitored closely by myself, an assigned parole officer, and Jack, should he wish to continue with his meetings postparole."

"So, do we keep doing the tutoring sessions post-parole?" Peaches asked.

"That would definitely be something to consider," Diane replied. "It would show the board Carter is dedicated and serious about his rehabilitation, but you need to discuss that among yourselves and decide before the hearing. Is there anything you would like to ask or add, Carter?"

Carter cleared his throat. "If, um, if I continue with the sessions when I'm released, we do those for how long? I mean, do we do them forever?"

Diane shook her head. "At the end of your initial nine months of monitoring, you'll meet again with the board and the situation will be reviewed. If Miss Lane does agree, then she will have to keep rigorous notes detailing what you've studied and what the outcomes are, as well as meet with the board to explain them."

"That's not a problem," Peaches said firmly.

"I'm pleased to hear it." Diane turned back to Carter. "But you know there will be other terms to meet, including regular drug testing and curfews."

Yeah, parole was all fun and fucking games.

. . .

Carter looked like he was ready to start smoking his coveralls when Kat walked in.

"Please, for the love of all that is holy, tell me you have some—"

"Cigarettes." Kat smiled, holding up a pack of Marlboros. "Here ya go, Champ," she said, tossing them to him.

He pulled them open and grabbed at one.

She watched as Carter inhaled the smoke and closed his eyes. He did it twice more before he looked at her.

"Thanks," he murmured through a smoky haze.

She moved around to his side of the table, glancing at the guard, who now appeared unworried by her proximity to his inmate. She flattened out the text of *The Merchant of Venice* in front of Carter and sat back with her own.

"I wanted to have a look at this particular speech." She motioned to the page. "I was interested to hear your interpretation of it."

"This speech? How predictable."

Kat huffed. "Predictable or not, it's an important part of the play and I want to hear what you think of it. But maybe your answer will be just as predictable as my speech choice." She'd grown to enjoy riling him.

Carter cocked an eyebrow. "Okay, Peaches," he said, sitting back in his seat. "I'll bite. What do you want to know?"

"Amaze me."

He snorted and blew out the last of his cigarette. "The speech is spoken by Shylock."

"Wow," Kat retorted with wide eyes. "That's awesome! Shakespeare scholars the world over will be peeing themselves in excitement at your amazing insight!"

Carter chuckled. "Okay, Peaches," he replied. " 'I am a Jew . . .' "

Kat's mouth popped open. She listened to him quote the entire speech without looking once at the page in front of him. Instead, his eyes bored into hers, blue and bright. Hearing him speak Shakespeare's words was indescribably erotic. His eyes burned with a passion Shylock would no doubt have conveyed to the courts as he expressed his anger at the wrongdoing that had befallen him.

Trying hard to remain composed, Kat said, "Impressive. But you still haven't answered my question."

Carter raised his eyebrows. "It's mainly about revenge. He's understandably pissed about the way he's been treated because of his religion and he vows to match the 'villainy' with his own. Only his 'villainy' will be a lot worse. Shylock's a badass."

"So, does that excuse Solanio and Salerio's treatment of him? He's a badass; surely he deserves everything that comes to him?"

Carter scoffed. "They're only treating him that way because they're narrow-minded shits who see nothing but a label on Shylock. For them, 'Jew' means 'evil.' But the blatant anti-Semitism isn't the most important aspect of the play or speech."

"It's not?"

"No," Carter replied, firmly sitting forward. "Shylock says, 'If you prick us, do we not bleed? If you tickle us, do we not laugh? If you poison us, do we not die?' He's making the point that no matter his religion, or label or whatever, he is human just like the bastards who treated him like shit. People everywhere, every day, make judgments about others because of their color, religion, background, race, sexual orientation . . . criminal history."

He glanced up at her.

"The world is a shitty place, and Shylock's the only one in the entire play with the balls to make a point about it. The irony that the supposed unintelligent, evil, uneducated Jew has such courage is what makes the shit important. The fact that he's a Jew is simply a plot device." He exhaled and rubbed his chin with the palm of his hand. "Shakespeare could have made him an inmate at Arthur Kill if such a place existed then."

Kat was astounded. His fervor made her wonder what bigotry he'd encountered to make him sympathize with the character so much. Had he been treated a certain way because of his time in prison?

He slumped back, grazing the back of his hand against her knee, and her breath caught at the contact. "People think he's barbaric because he promises revenge, but who the fuck can blame him? If they've labeled him as such, why shouldn't he live up to it?"

"He could have surprised people," Kat answered, noticing a definite change in the tone of the discussion. "He could have behaved differently, calmly, and shown that he was a good person."

Carter shook his head. "It doesn't work that way. If the shoe fits—or the label." He pointed to himself. "Criminal. There's no amount of good that erases that shit. It's easier to live up to people's expectations than try to change them. It avoids disappointment for all involved."

Kat frowned. "Then why are you here, and why have I said that I'll help you get parole and put up with your grumpy ass for potentially another twelve months?"

Carter smiled briefly. "I don't know, Peaches. Why did you?"

Kat kept her eyes on him for a long time before dropping them to the play. "I have my reasons."

"Your own pound of flesh."

Her head snapped up at his words, but he was busy playing with the cigarette box. He took a deep breath. "And I'm here because . . . I had to be." Confused, Kat opened her mouth to speak, but he interrupted her. "Did you really mean it?"

"Did I mean what?"

"That you'll carry on with our sessions."

"Yes," she answered. "I want to help in any way I can."

Carter's mouth twitched. "Why?"

Kat smiled. "Because I'm a glutton for punishment."

Carter coughed a surprised laugh. "Fair enough. For a moment I thought it was because you just wanted to be near my hot ass without guards and cameras, but, you know. Whatever," he deadpanned.

Kat cupped her palms to her face. "I am so transparent." She laughed at Carter's snort of amusement. "Now shut up and do this work." She pushed a sheet in front of him, along with a pen.

"Yes, ma'am," Carter replied with a wink that sent parts of Kat's body into a small frenzy.

No guards or cameras, she mused as she watched him start writing. She let her eyes explore him from his sexy buzz cut to the sharpness of his stubbled jaw. Her blood warmed in excitement when her mind began to wander.

. . .

"Fucker!"

"Motherfucker!"

"Shithead!"

"Shithouse!"

"Bitch!"

Carter stopped moving and stood slowly from his stooped position, halting the basketball by grasping it in one large hand. He cocked a puzzled eyebrow at Riley who was panting with gritted teeth and red cheeks. Carter watched him for at least twenty seconds before realization passed over the big fuck's face.

"What the hell you waiting for?" Riley growled, standing a little straighter.

"Did you just call me a bitch?"

Riley stood to his full height and glared back at him. He sniffed and glanced around at the other two inmates who'd been playing the fast-paced, almost violent game of basketball for the past forty minutes. They both began to shift uneasily from one foot to the other. Riley leveled his stare back at Carter.

"Yeah," he answered, jutting his chin out in defiance. "I did. So what?"

Carter frowned and then smirked. "Just checking," he replied before launching the basketball over Riley's head to his partner, Greg, who caught it and threw it, like a goddamn pro, through the hoop, winning the game by two.

"COME ON!" Carter roared with clenched fists. He ran over to Greg and grabbed him roughly around the neck, rubbing his knuckles a little too vigorously over his head. "MY MAN!"

"You fuckin' cheat!" Riley yelled with a pointed finger. "You—You cheated!"

Carter laughed and shook his head after he released a relieved-looking Greg. "Losing without dignity or grace is not attractive, Moore," he commented as he sauntered toward him.

"Yeah?" Riley questioned with his tongue planted in the right side of his mouth. "Well, Carter, I may not have dignity or grace, but I sure as hell have a fist for your face and a foot for your cheating ass."

Carter stopped midstep, caught the glint in Riley's eye, and within seconds was running like a bat out of hell across the court as Riley lunged his two-hundred-pound-plus frame in Carter's direction.

"Come here, you pussy!" Riley cried, chasing Carter around the incredulous-looking inmates and guards.

Carter panted as he weaved and ducked from the ape's grasp, unable to keep the huge smile off his face. His overwhelming happiness and smug satisfaction were halted abruptly when he realized he had nowhere else to go and was facing a brick wall with a huge human gaining on him. He spun around to face his pursuer and plead surrender, and felt every bit of air leave him in a huge gust and a loud strangled groan, as Riley plowed hard into him. Riley grabbed him in a headlock before Carter could even blink or protest and was dragged back, groaning and digging his heels in, to the center of the yard, where even the guards were laughing and jeering at the punk ass cursing through an almost-crushed windpipe.

"Riley," Carter gasped, grabbing at the tree-trunk forearm around his neck.

"I'm sorry, what?" Riley asked loudly. "I don't speak 'cheating fucker.' You'll have to speak clearer."

Carter couldn't help but let out a choked bark of a laugh. "Riley!" He gripped his wrist with his long fingers. "Man, please! I'm— Dammit! Riley, I'm sorry!"

Riley smiled and winked at the large amused crowd that had

gathered and released the neck that had been resting comfortably in the crook of his arm.

"Bastard," Carter muttered. The gathering dispersed disappointedly when they realized that it really was all in good fun and that no one was going to have their ass handed to them.

Riley snorted. "Cheat."

"Touché," Carter conceded with a wry smile.

"Yo, Miss L!" Riley boomed, startling Carter.

He turned around to see Peaches walking from her car, half-hidden by a huge bag, toward the main entrance, waving discreetly toward Riley. Carter let the right side of his mouth rise in a small smile in her direction and frowned when she dropped her head and hurried on her way. Carter rubbed his stomach when a twinge of something uncomfortable curled deep and heavy. It'd been plaguing him for days.

Riley dropped his arms. "What was that about?" He stared, waiting for an explanation.

Carter rubbed his face before walking over to his regular seat and pulling out a cigarette. He lit his smoke, inhaled, held it, and exhaled with a shake of his head.

"She's been weird for a couple of weeks," he confessed, nodding toward the car lot.

"Miss Lane?" Riley clarified, to which Carter nodded and passed the smoke over to him.

Carter had tried to ignore Peaches' behavior, but it'd been getting progressively harder with each session they had together. It'd started a few sessions after the initial parole meeting with Diane. She'd come into the tutoring room, barely looking or speaking to him for the entire hour. He hadn't pushed the issue, sensing it was something that he maybe didn't want to know about. But after two weeks, Carter's patience was rapidly disappearing.

"Do you think it has something to do with your parole?" Riley passed the cigarette back.

Carter feigned indifference, even though he was petrified that was the reason behind her sudden distance from him. Maybe she was regretting having agreed to tutor him outside of the facility. Maybe she wanted to pull out but didn't know how to.

Carter was no stranger to being let down, but, fuck, could Peaches really be like that? He hated the feeling of powerlessness she brought to him. It wasn't even the thought of not being granted parole—even though that would suck major ass. It was more to do with the fact that he wouldn't have a legitimate reason to see his Peaches outside of Arthur Kill.

He blew the smoke down his nose in a huff of annoyance, knowing the circle he was going in inside his head would not change one fucking iota until he said something to her.

"Just ask her, Carter," Riley offered, looking out toward the fields at the back of the facility.

Carter snorted. "Yeah, sure, Riley."

Riley clicked his tongue. "Pussy."

"Whatever," Carter retorted, dragging the last of the smoke for all it was worth before blowing it into Riley's smug face. "Loser."

Riley's thunderous laughter and his palm slamming into Carter's back in jest ensured Carter's determination to confront her that very afternoon.

But fuck it all to hell if Peaches wasn't wearing the most delicious gray skirt and pastel pink silk top when she walked into the session room five hours later, making all the coherent thoughts and blood in his head run in one very specific direction. Goddammit. He exhaled and mumbled something profane as she dropped the resources and Carter's smokes on the table between them.

"Something wrong?" she asked with a quick look in his direction.

Carter chuckled into his hands and shook his head. "Nothing at all. Carry on." The woman would be the death of him.

Carter cupped his face in his hands and watched her almost bury herself inside the Mary Poppins bag she'd brought with her.

"Peaches," Carter muttered around the filter of the smoke resting on his bottom lip. His name for her had stuck well, and he used it liberally. Deep down he was stoked she let him get away with it without questioning how or why.

"Mmhm?" came the mumbled reply from the dark depths.

"What the fuck are you doing?"

Peaches froze before she rose slowly from the cavernous monstrosity and gave a small, embarrassed smile. "Just—um, looking for something."

Carter grinned. "What, Jimmy Hoffa's necktie?" He raised his eyebrows at the guard, who hid his laugh behind his right hand.

Peaches rolled her eyes at the two of them. "No, smart-ass."

She pulled out her chair next to him as she did during every session and laid out Carter's work. She paused before explaining the comments she'd given him and asking questions raised by his answers. They were still very much involved in *The Merchant of Venice*.

"You say here that the character of Portia is the most intelligent character in the play, but you don't explain why," she said, reading over Carter's work. He watched her tuck her hair behind her ear. "Could you explain?" She sat back, putting some distance between them while averting her stare.

"Why do you do that?" Carter blurted out.

"I'm sorry?"

"That," he repeated, pointing at the way she was sitting. "Why did you move away like that?" His eyes widened when after a few seconds she hadn't answered. "Forget it," he murmured, pulling his work closer.

"No," Peaches said firmly, placing her hand on the same piece of work. Carter's eyes met hers. "What did you mean, Carter?"

He mumbled again, grabbing the pack of smokes to fidget with. Peaches waited patiently. "Are you wigging out because of my parole?" he snapped.

His question appeared to shock the hell out of her, but he didn't give her time to respond.

"Because, frankly, I would much rather you be honest with me and tell me now. I mean, fuck, I don't wanna be standing in front of those smug losers all hopeful and shit, for you to turn around and say that you ain't gonna see this through because of . . . whatever."

• • •

Kat blinked. She opened her mouth to speak, but no words emerged. How could he think that she would wig out on him? Hadn't she proven her commitment to his case and parole with all the work she'd been doing?

Yes, she'd been behaving differently with him, but there was no way she could explain to him why. She'd rather die first.

The truth was, two weeks ago, Kat's nightmares had stopped. She would have been eternally grateful, if they hadn't been replaced by the most sensual dreams she'd ever had. They'd started tame enough, but over fourteen nights they'd become steamier and steamier. Usually, this wouldn't have been a problem—she'd had racy dreams before, of course; however, the man starring in her personal porn show was none other than one Mr. Wesley Carter.

Ever since she'd started having the dreams, she'd officially been in hell.

How could she have such mind-blowing dreams about a man she hardly knew? And what the hell was she going to do about the fact that she was potentially going to continue seeing him for at least another twelve months, outside of the guarded, well-monitored, keep-your-hands-to-yourself-and-we'll-all-get-along-fine environment of Arthur Kill?

Not that she would ever dream of putting herself or Carter in a position such as that. No way. She was still his tutor and he was her student. She was in a trusted position and she wouldn't jeopardize what she'd worked so hard to build. The nonfraternization policy would no doubt be enforced during his parole, too.

"Why do you think I wouldn't see this through?" she asked finally. "What gave you the impression that I didn't want to help you get parole?"

"I don't know. Shit, you just seem different. Like you're worried about something or nervous. I didn't know whether it was the thought of carrying on with our sessions that had you freaking out."

He hid the hurt in his voice well, but his eyes betrayed him when they dropped to the table. He'd noticed her distance. Suddenly, Kat didn't know whether to feel flattered or terrified that he had noticed at all. She swallowed down her panic and moved closer to him.

She fought down the overwhelming urge to touch his face. "I'm here for the long haul. I really want to help you get parole, and I want to keep our sessions going."

Carter let his eyes meet hers.

"I'm sorry if I've made you doubt that. I won't let you down. You can count on that one hundred percent."

Kat was surprised at the vehemence of her own words but knew in her heart she meant them. Pound of flesh or not, she was going to help Carter, and no one could change that.

It took a moment for Carter to speak. "Okay."

They sat for a few moments in silence, neither one of them finding it uncomfortable.

"Are you very nervous about your parole application?" Kat asked eventually after watching Carter put his cigarette out. He shook his head. "Shylock," she murmured. "As brave as ever."

"So says Portia," Carter countered with a smile.

"The most intelligent character in *The Merchant of Venice*," Kat said with a flirty undertone.

"Well, she did save Shylock," Carter responded.

The metaphor was not lost on Kat. She knew Carter saw himself as less because of his life choices, much like people saw Shylock as less because of his religion. The comparison was tenuous, but to Carter, Kat knew, it was very real.

"That she did." Kat's eyes landed on his work. "But if we're talking literary characters, I'm not sure that Portia is the right one for me to be compared to."

"Oh, no?" Carter asked. "Who were you thinking? The Queen of Hearts from *Alice's Adventures in Wonderland*? Hecate from *Macbeth*?" He snapped his fingers with inspiration. "The White Witch in *The Lion, the Witch and the Wardrobe*?"

Playing off his jibes, Kat grabbed her pen, and began to make a shopping list. "No," she deadpanned. "But thanks for reminding me what I need from the store: axe, cauldron, Turkish Delight."

"Okay," he said with a chuckle. "Seriously, who would you choose?"

"That's easy," she replied. "I would want to be Walter from *Walter the Lazy Mouse*."

Carter looked puzzled. "Not a velveteen rabbit or a spider named Charlotte?"

Kat shook her head. "No. The girls at school used to read those. But for me, it was always Walter." She turned toward him. "Do you know the story?"

"Tell me."

"Walter was a very lazy mouse," Kat began. "He's so lazy he won't get up for school or go out with his family or play with his friends, and soon they all forget about him. His family moves away one day while Walter is asleep."

Carter slumped in his chair, listening intently.

"He decides to look for his family," Kat continued. "He meets many creatures on his travels, including frogs that can't read or write. Walter tries to teach them, but, because he missed so much school through sleep, he can't remember how to."

For a quick, heartbreaking moment, she heard her father's voice as he read the story to her.

"Peaches," Carter whispered.

Sadness weighed heavily on Kat's shoulders. "My dad used to read it to me when I was a little girl. He used to do all the voices."

Carter folded his arms on the table. "He sounds—he sounds like a good guy."

A small smile tugged at Kat's mouth. "He was. He would say no matter what the obstacles, if I was determined like Walter, I could do anything I put my mind to."

"And did you?" Carter asked, taking her by surprise.

"Did I what?"

"Did you do whatever it was you put your mind to no matter what the obstacles?"

Kat smiled, embarrassed. "I'm here, aren't I?"

"Yes, you are."

• • •

Carter noticed her eyes go to the wall behind him and cursed quietly.

Time's up.

Carter watched, trying to feign indifference but silently mad as hell that she had to go, as she started to pack up her belongings.

"I might have a look for that book in the prison library, you know," he said casually. "Do you think Arthur Kill library would stock children's literature or is that just wrong on too many levels?"

Peaches failed to hide a smile.

"What the fuck am I talking about? Riley probably has it hidden under his pillow to read on cold, lonely nights. I'll ask him."

She giggled and Carter smiled at the sound.

"In all seriousness," she said, pulling her bag onto her shoulder, "if you do find a copy, would you let me know? I lost mine." The heartbreak on her face was clear.

"I will," Carter answered sincerely.

"Hey, Carter," she called as the guard unlocked the door for her. "Thanks for today."

He smiled as the door closed slowly behind her. "Anytime, Peaches," he whispered to the empty room. "Anytime."

10

Those who didn't know Eva Lane personally considered her aloof and arrogant. But no one, not even those who disliked her, could deny her strength.

When five thugs, high on whatever they'd taken that fateful night, had ruthlessly murdered her husband, Senator Daniel Lane, she'd remained stoic and calm in public. She received condolences from voters, strangers, and many of her husband's colleagues with a smile and a nod of thanks. Everyone had marveled at her composure.

But deep down, she'd been dying. Her heart had been ripped out, leaving a gaping hole that couldn't be filled with words of sympathy or touches from loved ones.

Daniel had been everything to her and when she was told he'd died, been beaten so violently that his brain had bled, causing a massive stroke, she'd considered taking her own life to be with him. An easy, selfish, and desperate way out. How could she possibly go on living when the only man she'd ever loved was gone?

For weeks after his death, Eva had taken to the bed they'd shared and cried. She'd screamed, shouted, thrown things, hit things, hit herself, but the pain remained. The hole was wide and cavernous, and nothing could staunch the grief every time her eyes opened and she realized her Danny was still dead.

Nothing except her daughter.

Her little Katherine, who'd witnessed the murder of her precious father, who was silent, pale, and desperate for her mother to give her words that would pull her from the grief consuming her so entirely. Eva knew she'd been selfish in her own sorrow, that her little girl needed her, and Eva needed Katherine, too. Yet Eva could barely look at her without seeing her husband. Every movement, mannerism, and look her daughter gave was so much like her husband that, for a long time, Eva could spend only small amounts of time in her company.

It broke Eva's shattered heart further and contributed to Katherine's belief that her mommy blamed her for the death of her hero-worshipped father. She should have stopped those bad men, she'd whimpered. If that stranger hadn't been there, she might have been able to. The anguished "what-if's" of a nine-year-old girl who wanted nothing more than to see her father walk through the door again.

During therapy, Eva slowly began to realize what she was doing to her child. She was devastated when she heard Katherine's thoughts about Eva's blame. She also understood how lucky she was that she still had her daughter at all—how close she'd been to losing her, too.

And she would be forever grateful for whatever divine intervention occurred for keeping her baby safe. She had a beautiful, living, breathing connection to her cherished husband—and she would always treasure and protect her daughter, for the rest of her life.

Unfortunately, as well as looking just like her father, Katherine had inherited his determination. She was stubborn to a fault and, once decided on something, she was never swayed. Eva knew that her attempts at keeping her daughter safe were bordering on smothering, but dammit, didn't Katherine see the risk she was taking?

It pained Eva to see her daughter dismiss her worries so easily. She'd tried relentlessly to steer her daughter away from the path she had chosen, to no avail. She sighed heavily now.

"Mom, you look like you're suffering from gas. What's up?"

Eva's eyes shot daggers across her Upper East Side apartment to where Katherine was fixing her hair, looking beautiful in her new birthday dress. "There's no need to be crude. I was just thinking." Eva cradled her wineglass. "How's Ben?"

Katherine shrugged. "He's good. Busy. He's coming tonight with Abby."

Eva sighed wistfully. "It's wonderful that he's settled down, married, and in a respectable job."

Katherine took a deep breath, her arms falling to her sides. "I know you're desperate for grandkids, Mom, but can we hold off just a little longer before I settle down?" She picked up her glass and gulped her wine. "And my job *is* respectable. I'm a teacher. A good one."

Ignoring the retort about the job, Eva laughed. "Oh, darling, as much as I would love grandchildren, I just want you to be happy, and with someone who'll look after you and love you. There's no rush, you're young." She paused. "But there's no one you're interested in?"

Katherine avoided her mother's gaze as she picked up her purse. "No. I'm happy as I am. In all aspects of my life."

Eva stared at her daughter, wishing she could explain her fears better. She sighed. "I hope so."

• • •

The Spanish restaurant in TriBeCa in which Kat had chosen to celebrate her twenty-fifth birthday was bustling. She, along with her friends and family, sat around a large circular table drinking wine and nibbling at the delicious breads laid out in its center. Her mother sat to her left, quiet but attentive, while Ben, Abby, Harrison, Beth, and Adam, God love them, with jokes and liberal pours of wine, tried to clear the tense atmosphere between mother and daughter.

"Carter got parole?" Ben exclaimed. "That's great, Kat!" He lifted his champagne glass.

Kat laughed and did the same, ignoring the look of disdain that flashed across her mother's face.

"So, when do your sessions start?" Beth asked.

"Sessions?" her mother interjected, her dark eyes flashing. "What sessions?"

"Kat meets with this . . . Carter three times a week," Beth answered, her stare on her entree. "No security or anything."

Eva blanched. "What?"

Great, Beth.

Kat breathed deeply, counting silently in an effort to keep her temper. "It's part of Carter's parole, Mom," she answered, frowning over at Beth. "Very few tutors get the opportunity to do it. It's important. You should be proud."

Her mother gawked, her eyes damned near falling out of her head. "I would be prouder if you taught children in a middle-class elementary school. I mean, really, Katherine." She put her glass down. "What makes these people, these prison officials, think that putting my daughter in danger will change these monsters one iota?"

"I'm not in any danger," Kat assured her again.

Her mother blinked. "Your father thought the same. He was all for campaigning and helping the less fortunate, and look at the thanks he got."

Kat's heart thudded in her chest. "Carter's not like them. He's trying to better himself.

"Don't dismiss my concerns, Katherine."

"She's allowed to worry, Kat. We all are," Beth added. Adam placed a hand on her shoulder. Kat opened her mouth to ask what the hell her friend was playing at.

"Of course I am," Eva said instead. "You're my daughter."

Her mother's words strengthened Kat's fire of determination. "Yeah," she snapped. "And it's your *daughter's* birthday dinner, so can you just let it go tonight?" Kat closed her eyes, beating down her anger. "I've contacted the library on Fifth and Forty-second to reserve the reading room. He's released on Tuesday. Our first session is a week from then."

"Well, that's great news," Harrison said before Eva could say any more. He smiled sympathetically across the table at Kat. She returned his gaze before looking at Beth, who was murmuring quietly to Adam.

What the hell was going on? Sure, Beth had always spoken up about Kat's mother, all but excusing her overbearing protectiveness, but this was something else.

Adam cleared his throat. "Austin's here," he said as his brother came toward the table with—much to Kat's embarrassment—a gorgeously wrapped present.

"Hi, guys." Austin shook Adam's hand and lowered his voice. "I just got off the phone with Casari. We got 'em."

Adam's features sharpened. "Austin, man, I told you; be careful that—"

"Later," Austin bit out. He hugged Beth and turned to Kat. "Happy birthday," he said, laying the gift in front of her. He leaned down and kissed her cheek.

"Austin, you really didn't have to—"

"Nonsense. It was just something that made me think of you when I saw it in San Francisco. Open it, please."

"I will. Austin, this is my mom, Eva Lane, and her partner, Harrison Day. Mom, this is Austin Ford."

Her mom's eyes widened when Austin kissed her hand. "A pleasure," he uttered before he shook Harrison's hand and took a seat at Kat's side.

"Quite. A young man with manners," her mom murmured with a pointed look at Kat. "How very rare these days."

Ben snorted from across the table, making Kat smile. With all eyes on her, she started ripping at the deep purple paper to find a large transparent box, which contained a beautiful snow globe. Instead of snowflakes falling around the miniature Golden Gate

Bridge, millions of small stars and bits of crystal spun and glittered as they caught the light.

"Austin, that's gorgeous." Beth gasped.

"It is," Kat agreed. "Thank you."

"You're welcome." He kissed her cheek again, allowing his lips to linger a little longer than before.

Austin was once again a pleasure to be around, and Kat decided that she liked it when his finger would graze her arm or his hand would lightly catch the skin of her back when he rested it on the back of her chair. She liked when their eyes met and she liked the sound of his laugh and the way he said her name.

But there was still . . . something off. She was attracted to the guy. But a few times she'd shifted uneasily in her seat because that undefinable discomfort settled deep within her. Kat tried to ignore it, but it never disappeared.

• • •

Standing on the sidewalk outside of the restaurant after dinner, Ben hugged Kat warmly. "Happy birthday. Jesus, your mom was in rare form tonight. She needs to lower the dose."

Kat chuckled into his shoulder. "She's a nightmare. She and Beth both."

"Yeah," Ben agreed. "What was that about?"

Kat shrugged. "Who knows? I can't even . . ."

"I think your mom's a little taken with your friend." Ben glanced at Austin, who chatted amiably with Eva. Ben's face turned serious. "You need any info on this guy, give me a call, okay? Dirty little secrets are my speciality. Plus it gives me an excuse to play on Google." He smirked when she pushed him away lightheartedly.

Kat turned to Abby. "Please take your husband home and smother him with a pillow."

Abby laughed, taking Ben's hand.

"Come over for dinner soon," Kat told them. "I'll make my special meatballs."

The hug Kat shared with her mother was awkward. "Happy birthday, Katherine. Call me. Tomorrow. As soon as you're home from working with those— Just call me."

Kat held her eye roll. "I will. I'll see you soon."

Kat hugged and kissed Adam and Beth. "Everything okay?" she asked them both.

"Yeah," Beth replied with a small smile. Adam nodded. "Just tired." Beth looked over at Austin. "Maybe Austin can take you home, huh?" She winked conspiratorially, gestured unsubtly toward Austin mere feet away, and muttered indelicately about "getting in there."

Austin laughed as Kat blushed and shook his head. The two of them stood on the sidewalk, neither knowing what to do next.

"Can I give you a lift?" he asked, pointing toward his car.

"Sure," she replied.

The Range Rover was spacious and smelled of leather and cologne.

"You have good taste in music," Kat noted as the CD changed from one song to another while they moved through the city traffic.

"Thanks," Austin replied. "I don't get to indulge it much, other than when I'm in the car." He looked at her for a moment.

"Did you enjoy your trip to San Francisco?"

Austin cocked an eyebrow. "It was work. No matter where you are in the world, if you have to work, it's never good."

"I guess. Though I bet it wouldn't be too bad if it was the Maldives or the Caribbean," she mused.

Austin chuckled. "It was good," he continued. "I finalized a big deal. I also thought of you. A lot."

Kat stared at her hands, wordless. They'd exchanged many texts since their first meeting. His were never pushy, always considerate. Hearing him say the words, though, was a little different.

"I'm sorry," he offered. "Too fast?"

She replied with a slow shake of her head.

"You look wonderful tonight, Kat." His dark eyes flitted down to her legs. "That color is great on you."

She ran her hands down her red wraparound dress, the compliment stirring indistinct emotions.

They spent the rest of the car journey this way, comfortably happy to share the silence once the music stopped. Austin put the car into park and turned off the engine when they reached Kat's building. She slowly unclipped her belt and reached for her purse and birthday gift bags from the footwell.

"Thank you," she said as she tucked her hair behind her ear. Her stomach felt heavy. She cleared her throat to try and push the odd sensation away.

"No problem," Austin replied. "I had a good time."

"Me too." She met his gaze and smiled gently.

Austin smiled back. "I know we've only met a couple of times, but I've enjoyed every minute." As always, his gaze was steady with a hint of CEO intimidation. "Would it be okay for us to have dinner sometime?"

She hesitated only briefly. "That . . . sounds good." Austin grinned, making his face softer.

Kat's breath caught in her throat. His eyes were determined and dark. The only sound in the car other than her heart thumping was the creaking of the leather seat as he slowly leaned closer. She didn't move. She wasn't sure that she could. The feeling of wanting to bolt but also wanting to stay exactly where she was sent a shiver up her back.

Austin stopped, his face only two inches away. "Kat," he murmured before he leaned closer and his lips found hers.

Kat stayed still as their mouths melded. It felt . . . nice.

After a moment of stillness, Austin cupped her left cheek and opened his mouth. Kat reciprocated by opening hers. She began to lose herself in the sensation of kissing Austin and surprised herself when she moaned softly as their tongues touched. Her hand found the back of his head, and she leaned closer. The feeling in her stomach twisted, but she fought to ignore it. She hadn't kissed anyone in so long.

Why should she deny herself this? Who was she denying herself for?

Austin hummed when Kat's tongue rubbed his, and he sucked its tip before she withdrew it from his mouth.

His hand dropped slowly from her cheek and slid down her bare arm as they moved together, synchronized, their heads moving slowly from one side to the other. His hand met her knee and he moaned deep in the back of his throat. His palm rubbed gently across her skin before moving slowly up the outside of her thigh. Kat tensed but moaned again when his fingertips danced under the hem of her skirt. He pulled his lips away for one split second and leaned his forehead against hers.

"Kat, we either need to stop right now or . . . Jesus."

Kat leaned back, seeing the lust and truth of his words on his face. She blinked, trying to clear her head. This wasn't her. Although Austin was handsome and undeniably charming, she wasn't about to lose herself in a night of crazy fucking.

"I think we should slow down," she said, finally moving back in her seat.

Austin exhaled and rubbed his hands down his face, apologizing into his palms.

"Don't be sorry," Kat said. "I'm not. It's just . . . maybe we should take things slowly?"

He smiled and lifted her hand to his mouth, planting a soft kiss on her knuckle. "Slowly works for me."

"Good." Kat pulled the handle on the car door. "Thanks for the lift. Good night, Austin."

"Good night, Kat."

She was still in a haze as she made her way across the lobby of her apartment building and, at first, didn't hear Fred on the welcome desk calling her name.

"Miss Lane!" Fred waved to catch her attention before she reached the elevators. "Miss Lane!"

"Yes, Fred?" she asked, approaching him.

"Good evening, Miss Lane." He grinned, revealing two adorable dimples that took the attention away from the large gap between his front teeth. "I have a package for you. It was delivered this afternoon."

From under the desk, he pulled out a square parcel wrapped neatly in brown paper. "I didn't catch the man's name, but he said it was important to get this to you."

Kat eyed the package curiously. "Thank you, Fred."

Once she entered her apartment, she dropped everything on the sofa, changed into sweatpants, and grabbed a glass of apple juice before parking herself on the other end of the couch cross-legged. Just as she reached for the mysterious brown package, her cell phone pinged with a text. Austin.

I really enjoyed tonight.

Kat sat back with a sigh, letting the tips of her fingers whisper over her mouth.

I did, too. Thank you for the gift. It was beautiful.

A beautiful gift for a beautiful woman.

Kat still hadn't thought of a reply when he texted again.

I look forward to our dinner. Happy birthday, Kat. Sweet dreams x

Good night.

She set the phone by her side. The odd sensation that had remained all night in her abdomen immediately bloomed and curled tightly. She placed her hand against it, trying to push it away.

How ridiculous.

Austin was great. He was a nice, safe guy, and there was no way she was going to let a silly inexplicable feeling stop her from having something that could be incredible. It had been too long since her last relationship—a three-month fling with a compulsive liar and cheater—and she deserved some happiness. Resolute, she reached for her apple juice and heard a light thud come from between her feet. She looked down to see the brown paper square Fred had given her.

"What are you?" She picked up the mysterious package and began tearing the paper open.

A gasp left her when she realized what it was. She stared through tear-filled eyes at the 1937 first edition of *Walter the Lazy Mouse* in her hands. "How?" She ran her fingers reverently over the front cover. "Oh God."

She opened it up and saw a brief message neatly written in black on the inside of the front cover:

> *Peaches,*
>
> *Here's to achieving anything you put your mind to, no matter what the obstacles.*
>
> *Happy birthday.*
>
> *—Carter*

11

Carter had barely slept. He was pumped and excited, much like a small child on Christmas morning.

At seven on the morning of his release, he was busy packing up his books and other belongings into a small box with great enthusiasm. The sheet of paper stating he had officially been granted parole was now his most treasured possession, and, at regular intervals, he would open it up and reread it, just to make sure that shit hadn't changed in any way.

It hadn't.

Carter's civilian clothes were what he'd worn when he entered the facility. He was smug as shit when he saw that his gray Ramones T-shirt was now tight across his arms and chest, thanks to Ross's vigorous workouts. He smiled and shook his head, pulling at the sleeves in an effort to give his biceps a little more room.

"I'll be damned," he muttered before he pulled on his dark-wash jeans and his black boots. Denim and cheap cotton had never felt so fucking good. Next were his rings. He placed the thick silver band on the thumb of his right hand, a silver-and-black Celtic cross on his middle finger, and a sweet Harley-Davidson insignia on his left index finger.

"You nearly ready?"

Carter turned with a smile to see Jack leaning against the open door of his cell.

"Pretty much," Carter replied, fastening his brown leather belt around the waist of his jeans. "When can I go?"

Jack glanced at his watch. "Doors open in ten. We're waiting on Ward."

"Fan-fucking-tastic," Carter muttered. He looked around his cell to see if he'd left anything behind, then picked up his box and pulled it close.

"So." Jack pushed his hands into his pockets. "I delivered your little gift."

Carter avoided his counselor's gaze. "Great," he replied casually. "There was enough cash?"

"More than enough, and I wrote exactly what you asked me to."

Carter's stomach somersaulted, thinking about Peaches receiving the book. He wondered if she liked it. He wondered if she thought it too much or too cheesy.

"I have to ask . . ." Jack continued, inspecting the toe of his right shoe.

"What?" Carter snapped.

Jack smiled knowingly before looking up. "I just wanted to know how the hell you managed to find a place that sold the book on such short notice," he finished with an innocent shrug.

Carter's shoulders collapsed in relief. "Peach—she, Kat, Miss Lane, had . . . um, well, shit, she mentioned it during one of our sessions, so I, I looked it up on the Internet in the library and put a hold on it. I was going to get it once I was out, but last week, when she mentioned it was her birthday . . ." He glanced up, shifting from one foot to the other, altogether uncomfortable as all fuck. "It's not a big deal, man. Stop looking at me like that."

"Hey," Jack said behind a small chuckle. "I didn't say a word. I thought it was a great gift: very thoughtful."

Carter watched him cautiously. "Really?"

"Really," Jack replied with a sharp nod. "I bet she loved it."

Carter's stomach twisted again. He hoped so. It was the least he could do for her; after all she'd done and had put up with from him.

"Inmate 081056," Ward called, sauntering into the doorway of Carter's cell. "I'm here to escort you off the premises." He pulled at the cuffs of the white shirt he was wearing under a dark navy blazer.

"Goodie," Carter murmured with a sardonic glare. Carter followed Ward, a guard, and Jack toward the back entrance of the facility, where he signed one more release form and received yet another copy of his parole conditions.

"How many of these does one person need?" he asked incredulously, pushing the piece of paper into the depths of his box.

"Well," Ward retorted while he clicked the top of his pen, "we all know how forgetful you can be when it comes to rules, Carter."

Carter picked up his box. "It was a rhetorical question, dickwad."

Ward's eyes shrunk in irritation. "What did—"

Jack stepped between the two men. "Come on now, Wes. Time to go." He pushed on Carter's shoulder, guiding him toward the exit.

Carter kept his stare on Ward before he allowed Jack to walk him out the door. The sun was hot for mid-September. Carter closed his eyes and lifted his face, breathing it in.

"That good?" Jack chuckled at his side.

"Yeah," Carter answered. He opened his eyes slowly and began rummaging in his box. It took him a few minutes of cursing and muttering before he found his Wayfarers and placed them onto his face. "Now I'm fucking ready," he said with a wide smile.

Jack laughed and rubbed his chin. He looked across the very far side of the lot to see a familiar large, black-haired figure leaning arrogantly against the front passenger door of a very hot muscle vehicle, smoking a cigarette.

"Is that Max?"

"Don't start," Carter warned with raised eyebrows. "He's here to pick me up because I sure as shit ain't walking home."

Jack scoffed. "Well, it's a definite conflict of interest to have him come and pick you up when—"

"Look!" Carter stopped Jack's lecture dead in its tracks. "This is my release day. I'm finally free of this place and I'm currently in a good mood. Please don't piss on my parade, J. I've had my fill." Carter's voice was firm but pleading.

"Fine," Jack surrendered. "Fine."

"Okay." Carter sighed. "So, I'll see you next Friday?"

"Yeah," Jack replied. "Your place at six. Don't forget."

Carter shook his head. "Like that's even possible with the six pieces of paper I have to remind me."

Jack raised his hand and patted Carter on his shoulder. "Take care."

"Sure," Carter replied. "I'll see ya." He began walking toward Max, who was grinning like an idiot; his mirrored aviators glinted in the sunlight.

"What's up?" he drawled around the plume of smoke that slipped from his mouth.

Carter smiled, despite the disheveled appearance of his friend. His AC/DC T-shirt was creased and his jeans looked as though they'd not seen a washing machine in a hella long time. "Not much; just released from prison, ya know."

"Same old, same old, huh?"

"You know it." Carter placed his box on the hood of the car and shook Max's hand before they hugged with a slap of the back. "It's good to see your ugly face," he said, taking the smoke Max was offering. He regarded his friend as he took a much-needed drag. His hair was longer and he looked like he'd not shaved in a while. "How ya doin'?"

Max's face pinched. "I'm okay."

Carter sighed. "You sure?"

"Yeah, dude." The smile Max offered was small. "Was that Parker?"

Carter nodded and leaned against the car.

"Carter!"

The two men looked up to see a flustered-looking redhead waving hesitantly and weaving through the parking lot toward them.

"Who the fuck is that?" Max pulled his shades down until they were resting at the tip of his nose. Carter immediately noticed the size of Max's pupils and the dark lines under his eyes that screamed lack of sleep. He was fucking high. Jesus. It wasn't even 8 a.m.

"No one," Carter answered with an exasperated shake of his head. "Hold this a minute."

He handed Max the cigarette and began jogging between the cars over to his Peaches. He didn't need Max ogling her while they spoke. If he was high, the asshole might say anything.

"Hey," he breathed, coming to a standstill in front of her.

"Hey," she replied. "I'm sorry." She glanced behind him. "I—I know you probably want to get going but, well, I—"

"It's no problem," Carter interrupted. "That's just my buddy Max. He's taking me home." He pulled his shades off and tucked them in the neck of his T-shirt. "What's up?"

Her gaze wandered over him in a way that made his heart race. "I got your present, the book, and I . . . I just wanted to say thank you. It was—" She bit her lip hard.

"Did you like it?" Carter asked nervously, slipping the tips of his fingers into the pockets of his jeans.

Her eyes widened. "Like it? I loved it. It was perfect and extremely thoughtful. Thank you."

Carter rocked back on his heels. "Well, you know." He scratched his head. "You said you'd lost yours and, well, now you have one."

"Yeah," she said quietly. "I've read it twice already. It's wonderful."

Carter smiled wider. She seemed so happy. "Good. You're welcome, Peaches."

"I also wanted to give you this." She reached into the pocket of her gray pants and pulled out a small card covered in numbers. "Our first session is scheduled for Tuesday at four at the library on

Forty-second. Here's my cell number and my . . . my home number in case, well, in case you can't make it or you're gonna be late or whatever." She waved her hand dismissively. "I just thought you should have some way of being able to contact me."

She handed Carter the card. Was she blushing?

"That's a damn good idea. Thanks." He pushed the card into the back pocket of his jeans.

"So," she continued. "I'll see you then?"

"Sure," he answered. Her flustering was unsettling but cute as hell.

"Good," she replied, taking a step back. "I'll let you get going. Take care."

He saluted with two lazy fingers at his temple. "You too." She smiled bashfully, turned, and walked back toward the facility.

Once she was through the door and out of sight, he blew out an uncomfortable breath. "Fuck."

Peaches was normally so in control. He relied on her discipline to keep him calm. Their sessions would sure as shit not work if they continued to behave this way with each other. Maybe the whole tutoring thing was going to be an utter bust. He put his shades back on and headed back to the car.

Max was chuckling. "Something you wanna share?" He waggled his eyebrows.

"No," Carter snapped back at the double entendre. Realizing how protective he sounded, he laughed, attempting to hide his annoyance. "She's just a lit tutor, that's all."

"Tutor, huh?" Max asked, glancing back at the door she'd disappeared through. "Well, fuck, she could tutor me anytime with that ass. That's some hot junk in the trunk."

Carter held his tongue and smiled tightly while keeping his eyes on the handle of the car door. "Really, I hadn't noticed."

Max snorted and pulled his car keys from his pocket. "That settles it, brother. We need to get your ass laid."

This, Carter had to laugh at and agree with wholeheartedly. He needed to relax and clear his mind of all this bullshit. He was a free man and he was ready to enjoy every minute of it.

• • •

Carter had never been a homebody.

From the age of nine he'd been shifted from one wretched place to another. If it wasn't from one boarding school to another equally pretentious one, he would, usually after coming to blows with his father, crash on friends' sofas or floors. He always got itchy feet from staying in one place for too long.

That's just the way his life was: unsettled.

So he was surprised when he was hit with an overwhelming sense of relief as he pushed the key into the lock of his loft apartment on the corner of Greenwich and Jay in the TriBeCa neighborhood of Manhattan. He pushed the door open and took a moment to allow the smells of the place to wash over him.

Max nudged his back. "You planning on going in there?"

"Yeah." Carter took a step into the apartment and closed the door behind Max, who had his box.

Carter threw his keys onto a small table and surveyed his home. High ceilings, wooden floors, and cream and brown furniture. His vintage guitar collection remained on the walls along with the black-and-white photographs from a local artist he'd collected over the years. Ornamental Harley and Triumph parts scattered the apartment, shining in the sun that swept in through the ten-foot-tall windows.

Max had arranged a cleaner to visit once a week while Carter was in prison, to make sure everything was just so.

"The place looks good, right?" Max asked.

Carter smiled. "Yeah, it does. Thanks."

"Hey, no problem." He moved around to the large double stainless steel fridge and opened it to display a large stock of alcohol. "Surprise," he said with a laugh. "Just for you, my friend." He opened two bottles of beer and handed one to an amused Carter.

"To your freedom," Max said solemnly as they clinked their bottlenecks and then took a gulp. Carter had never been happier that alcohol wasn't prohibited as part of his parole conditions, even at ten in the morning.

He belched loudly in appreciation and grinned. "I needed that."

Max handed him another. "So, Carter, free man extraordinaire, what's the plan for the rest of the day?"

Carter sipped his beer thoughtfully. "Well, I need a goddamn shower. And a haircut and a good sleep in my own bed."

Max rolled his eyes. "Jesus, Carter, is that the best you can come up with?"

"No." His face became serious. "I want to see my baby."

Max grinned.

"Is she okay?" Carter asked. "Have you taken care of her?"

"She's fucking gorgeous and, yes, I treated her as if she were my own."

"Take me to her."

He followed Max out of his apartment and galloped down the stairs of the building toward the private underground garage. Max flicked on the light switch and Carter gasped when he saw his pride and joy, looking so fucking spectacular, she took his breath away.

"Hello, beautiful," he whispered.

He reached out to let the tips of his fingers touch the pristine leather seat of the black Harley-Davidson Sportster. Kala. He swallowed hard when he grasped her handlebars. It'd been too long. Max whistled and, as Carter turned, threw the Harley's keys at him, which he caught against his chest. "She looks awesome, Max. Thank you."

"She's had an oil change and a polish. I did it myself, of course; I wouldn't let those greasy-pawed dogs at the body shop anywhere near her, as much as they whined."

Carter brushed his knuckles across the V-twin engine reverently. He hadn't realized just how much he'd missed riding. A luscious image of his Peaches straddling his bike with her knees tight against his ribs as they rode to the coast, holding on to him while he pushed the bike hard and fast, slid lusciously into his mind. He discreetly adjusted himself and stood from his crouched position at the side of Kala, once more letting his hands glide over her exquisite metal.

"I'll see your fine ass later," he promised before he walked back over to Max and back up the stairs of the building.

"Okay, man, I have things to see and people to do." Max smiled, leaning against Carter's apartment door.

Carter frowned. His friend had aged considerably over the past few months. There were lines on his face that hadn't been there before. "You stay out of shit, you hear me?"

Max scoffed. "Everything's cool, man." But the glaze in his eyes suggested otherwise.

Max ran a hand through his dark, unruly hair and smiled nonchalantly. "Things are handled. No point getting stressed, right? I've learned that I can't control shit." He sniffed.

"Max—"

Max clapped a hand to Carter's shoulder. "I'll be back later with food and women. About seven, okay?"

Carter sighed, holding his tongue. "Sounds good." He and Max clasped hands and stared at each other for a moment in silent understanding.

"It is good to have ya home, man," Max muttered.

"It feels good."

Max squeezed Carter's hand. "For what you did for me and— To get put away when you weren't even . . . I can't ever thank you enough—"

"Hey," Carter interrupted. "It's all good, brother. I owed you."

Max exhaled hard, anguish and heartbreak clear on his face. "Yeah. I'll see ya later."

Once Max left, Carter closed the door and fell against it with a loud sigh. He glanced around his apartment, wondering what the hell he was supposed to do. At Kill he'd had a routine, a schedule, people to tell him when and where he needed to be. Now he was free to do what he wanted, when he wanted. Within reason. It felt strange.

With a despondent exhale, he glanced at the clock on the wall and his mind instantly went to Peaches. She'd be in class right now with Riley and company.

Outrageously, jealousy bloomed in his stomach. "Get a grip, idiot," he muttered. He grabbed his beer from the counter and made his way to his bedroom.

He'd have Peaches all to himself come Tuesday evening, anyway. He smiled while he stripped off his clothes and made his way to the shower. He was more than ready to wash away all remnants of Kill from both his body and his mind.

12

Kat pulled her bag up onto her shoulder as she made her way into the library. She walked toward the grand welcome desk and smiled at Mrs. Latham, who'd worked at the library for decades. She was there the day the Daniel Lane Reading Room opened after his passing.

"Good afternoon, Kat," she said, pushing her glasses up her small nose. Her whole face, surrounded by curly gray hair, wrinkled when she smiled.

"Good afternoon, Mrs. Latham. You're looking well."

"Thank you. You're here to use the reading room?" She flicked through a schedule book on her desk.

"I am." Kat extended a printout. "I've booked it indefinitely for these days at these times."

"Ah, here we are, dear." She handed Kat the sign-in sheet, which was empty. Carter hadn't arrived yet.

Kat signed her name. "When my student gets here, can you tell him to come straight through once he's signed in?"

"Of course."

Kat wandered through the immaculate building toward the reading room constructed as part of her father's wishes in his will. Kat had always loved to read and her father had wanted to create somewhere that not only she but other people could go to lose themselves in the pages they read.

His plan was to do it before his fiftieth birthday, which he never saw.

Kat dropped her bags onto one of the large oak tables and sat down. She pulled out all her resources for Carter so they could get straight to work. She didn't want to dilly-dally. She got flustered enough in his presence.

The truth was, after seeing Carter so . . . civilian, as he left Kill, Kat had finally accepted that maaaaaybe she had a wee crush. The vision of his buzz cut and bright blue eyes, his body wrapped in a tight T-shirt and low-riding jeans, accosted Kat once again.

Why did it have to be the Ramones? She loved the Ramones. She loved them even more stretched across Carter's wide chest and large biceps. She'd been unable to tear her eyes from his tattoo, either. Cursive black and red flames of delicious ink dressed his skin to the elbow of one arm and to the wrist of the other; the intricate vines, patterns, and words she couldn't quite make out were stunning.

And very, very sexy.

Dammit. She'd been a train wreck. All she'd wanted to do was thank him for the amazingly thoughtful birthday present he'd given her and she'd ended up stammering like an idiot.

It was so stupid, and not simply because she was the teacher and he was her student (how cliché). Carter was from a different world. He was a different species to her, and not because of his criminal past, although that was definitely a factor. He was angry and big-headed, hostile, and cocky. He was everything she should run away from, screaming. But she couldn't deny he was equally smart, sensitive, and funny.

Christ, what a mess. Why couldn't he be a normal guy? Like Austin.

She glanced at her cell phone. Austin had texted her twice since the morning to wish her luck with Carter and to tell her that he was thinking of her. He was impossibly sweet, but still the uneasiness remained.

Kat started as if struck by a lightning bolt.

Was Carter the reason she was so damned uneasy with Austin? Was he the cause of the heaviness in her stomach, the discomfort, the whisper of wariness, and the reason her heart galloped?

Shit. She pushed her bangs from her face. Enough was enough. Kat knew she had to grow up and stop acting like a teenager. It was her first session with Carter outside of Kill and, by God, she was going to act like the professional she was.

Resolute, she crossed her legs and waited.

As the minutes passed, her foot began to tap the leg of the table. Fifteen minutes went by and she was still alone. And now pissed.

She checked her phone for any missed calls or texts from him. Nothing. She bit the inside of her mouth in fury. She should have known he'd let her down. He was a newly released criminal who had wild oats to sow. Why the hell would he waste time with her, even if it was part of the conditions of his parole? She was stupid to think that he'd meant it when he'd said he wanted to keep their sessions going.

Another fifteen minutes passed, and, with a string of quiet expletives, Kat began to pack her things. Screw him. If he didn't want to take it seriously, why should she care?

A hand on her shoulder made her scream.

"Shit! Don't!" Carter urged with his hand out to her in surrender. "Fuck. It's me."

She clutched a palm to her forehead, gasping for breath. "Christ. You scared me."

"No shit," he replied while his eyes danced up and down her body, making her stomach tighten. He grumbled something and ran a hand across his hair. A hand that, Kat noticed, was covered in oil.

In fact, most of him was covered in oil.

She studied him from head to toe. His hair was shorter; he'd obviously made a trip to the barber. His face was, as always, epically handsome, but now it had a smear of oil across its right cheek. His

T-shirt, which was a black Strokes affair, was tight and dirty, and his jeans, Kat could only assume, used to be blue denim.

"What the hell happened to you?" She tried to ignore the twist of lust that unfolded in her belly when she saw the bike helmet in his hand.

Carter smirked. "I had a fight with a V8 engine and lost. That's why my ass is late."

The cocky look on his face reminded Kat she was pissed. She stood up and flicked her hair over her shoulder. "Yes, you're late," she growled. "So the session is canceled." She whirled back around to continue throwing her resources back in her bag.

Carter's laugh was disbelieving. "Are you kidding me?"

"No," Kat snapped, keeping her back to him. "You're late, and I'm not here for shits and giggles while you mess around with your toys. You didn't even text or call to let me know!"

Carter grabbed her arm and spun her until she faced him. She gulped at the anger on his face.

"Hey," he barked, his nose only inches from hers. "Stop bitching and throwing shit for a minute, and calm the fuck down."

She caught his scent in her nose and on the tip of her tongue. It was deep, smoky, and metallic and made her lungs tingle.

"Let. Me. Go," she ordered through gritted teeth.

Carter stared at his hand on her arm and let go immediately. "Sorry," he muttered, though his eyes were still thunderous. "Look, don't leave, okay? Just let me explain."

She crossed her arms. "Fine. Explain."

Carter's eyes narrowed. "As stated in my parole," he started through tight lips, "my job is working at a body shop that my best friend owns." He gestured at the oil all over his clothes. "Max was having trouble with the engine on a Corvette. I offered to help just before I left and it went to shit. I would have called or texted you, but I was busy making sure that two-hundred-pound engine parts weren't falling onto the heads of my coworkers."

Kat considered what he'd said. He was so masculine and strong, standing in his dirty clothes with a day's worth of stubble. He oozed carnal sex. When he'd gripped her arm he hadn't hurt her, of course, but the sizzle of his hands on her was hard to ignore. It was still there, buzzing deep inside her in places only he could reach.

She dropped her arms and shrugged. "Fine. Whatever."

"I'm sorry. What?" Carter bent down so he was eye level with her.

"I said fine. Let's get on with it," she retorted sharply. Condescending ass. She gestured brusquely to the chair on the other side of the table.

Carter dropped into the chair and began rummaging through his bag as Kat watched surreptitiously. He pulled out a large pack of Oreo cookies and placed them on the table.

Kat gaped. She hadn't had an Oreo in years. She'd never been able to bring herself to, since they were a thing she and her dad had had. He'd always eat the center; she'd eat the cookie. Together they could demolish a whole pack in minutes. "You're not allowed to eat in here."

He glanced around the otherwise empty room. "Are you gonna tell on me?"

Kat sat down with a thump. "Just don't make a mess."

"Sure, Peaches." He took a cookie, pulled it apart, and licked the cream center.

Fascinated, Kat watched his tongue as it flicked up, down, and around. How could eating a cookie be so sensual, for God's sake? She cleared her throat and pushed his work toward him. He put the two cookie parts back together and rested them carefully on a napkin.

Carter perused the paper in front of him. He looked up to see her staring at the remains of his Oreo. "What? You want my cookie?"

"You . . . um, you only eat the inside?"

"Yeah," he answered. "I don't really care for the rest of it. You're free to have the side I haven't had my tongue all over."

Her cheeks flamed. "No. I'm good. Thank you."

"Well, the offer's there. And don't worry"—he dropped his voice—"I won't tell, either."

Kat held her smile. Barely. "Tell me what you know about this poem."

He glanced down. "Well, well. This is quite a change from 'Tichborne's Elegy.' You make me blush."

Kat waved her hand for him to continue.

" 'The Flea' by Donne takes a usually insignificant action—killing a flea—and turns it into a sexually deviant metaphor."

"Sexually deviant?" Kat questioned with a thick throat. His dark gaze and sexy smirk were not what she needed to stay focused and professional.

Carter dropped his chin. "Don't get coy with me, Peaches. You know as well as I do the poem is about Donne wanting to fuck his mistress."

The way his mouth curved around the word "fuck" made Kat's pulse race. "Care to elaborate?"

"When Donne talks of the blood that the flea has taken from both him and his mistress, he's talking about sex, their bodies coming together."

"Hmm," Kat mused, keeping her eyes on the table and away from the devastatingly long lashes that swept over Carter's cheekbones.

Carter shifted his chair closer to her. "Is that an *I agree with everything you just said, Carter* hmm, or a *You have no fucking clue what you're talking about* hmm?"

"No, no, you're absolutely right," Kat said, looking down at the table, cursing her choice of poem. What the hell had she been thinking?

Without word or hesitation, Carter pushed her hair behind her ear and lifted her face to his. The sensation of his callused fingers against her skin shot through her body like a bullet.

"Peaches," he murmured. "Where are you? You're miles away."

"I was just thinking . . . I know there's a critique on this poem here somewhere." She pulled her chin from his fingers and stood up. "I'll go and find it. Why don't you make some notes on your copy so we can discuss them when I get back?"

She hurried toward the shelves holding all the literature and critical works of each of them. She had to get away from him.

• • •

Carter watched her go and slouched down in his seat. He picked up another Oreo and began to lick.

Had he done too much with the hair-and-chin thing? Fuck if he knew. He didn't want her to think he was taking advantage of the no-guard, no-camera situation, although he'd thought about nothing but that since the minute he'd woken up. Dammit, recently she was all he thought about.

Three Oreos later, she still wasn't back. He checked the time on his cell and blew out an impatient breath.

"Fuck this," he grumbled, standing from his chair. He shoved his hands in his pockets and wandered in the direction she'd disappeared.

"Peaches?" he stage-whispered, searching each aisle.

He'd checked four of the motherfuckers before he finally found her standing on a tall ladder, reaching for a book on the highest shelf. He walked up to her, slowly and silently, his eyes level with the backs of her calves. He couldn't help but lick his lips at the sight of the soft creamy skin. She hadn't noticed him standing there, leaning against the shelves, tracing the curve of her leg with his gaze. His hand twitched of its own volition and, before he had any comprehension of what he was doing, he was reaching out to stroke the back of her knee.

"Carter!"

He jumped at her screech but then righted himself as she wobbled on the step and slipped back, grabbing at the books in an effort to stop her fall. He clutched at her waist, grazing the undersides of her magnificent boobs, making sure she didn't hit the floor. She landed against him, resulting in a resounding "Oomph" when his back collided with the opposite bookshelf.

"Seriously, Carter, that's twice today you've scared the hell out of me," she grumbled, pushing away from him.

"Yeah, don't mention it," he muttered, rubbing the bottom of his spine. "I just saved your life."

"*You're* the one who made me fall," she pointed out.

She'd taken a step back from him. What the hell was that about? He shifted near her, placing the flat of his palm against the spines of the books at the side of her face. He could smell her hair. Fuck. It did still smell of peaches.

"Is everything all right, Miss Lane?"

The two of them startled at Mrs. Latham's voice. Carter blinked, realizing how close they'd been standing to each other.

"Yes, I'm fine," Peaches replied to the old woman, who was eyeing Carter. He smirked.

"I heard a scream." She adjusted her glasses.

"Yeah," Carter interrupted. "That was me. I saw a spider. Fucking huge. I'm terrified of them. Kat saved me."

He flashed her his trademark smile to seal the deal, but the small librarian didn't look impressed.

"Well, as long as you're okay, Miss Lane."

"I'm fine, thank you, Mrs. Latham," Peaches assured her.

The old lady took one more disapproving look at Carter before disappearing back toward her desk. Peaches collapsed into giggles. He laughed, too, watching her nose crease up and emit a small snort.

"Spiders," she managed.

"What?" he asked, resting against the bookshelf next to her. "I hate them."

She shook her head. "You're one of a kind, Mr. Carter."

He beamed. "You know it."

They stared at each other for a small moment, seemingly lost in their own thoughts, before Peaches slapped the large book she'd grappled from the shelf into Carter's stomach.

"Jesus!"

"Here," she said with a smile. "Let's find out more about your deviant sexual metaphors."

Carter laughed and watched her fine ass walk away. "I thought you'd never ask," he muttered, following quickly after her.

13

"Fuck it!"

Carter looked up from the screwed-up carburetor in his hand to see Max kicking the tire rim of the V8 Pontiac GTO he'd been cursing at for the past hour.

Carter walked over to him, wiping his grease-covered hands on a rag he pulled from his pocket. "Whoa, whoa, man, chill out. We don't hit the ladies. What's up?"

Max threw his hands through his hair. "This piece of crap." He gestured toward the car.

Carter's eyes widened in mock horror. He placed his palms against the driver's door of the burnt-orange vehicle. "Don't listen, baby," he whispered to the car. "He doesn't mean it."

Max shook his head. "Whatever, man, I'm done."

Carter frowned and propped his forearm on the car roof. "You're done?" he asked in a baiting tone. "You give up so easy?"

"No," Max snapped back defensively. "I just can't—the fucking thing's still idling high and— For fuck's sake, Cam, turn that fucking shit down!"

Cam scurried to the stereo in the corner of the room and turned the Foo Fighters down to a dull roar.

Carter kept his stare on Max, knowing there was more to his bitching than the car's high idling.

Max turned away from Carter's meaningful look and opened a can of Coke he then proceeded to gulp. Once it was gone, he turned back to his friend, falling against the wall before sliding down. His eyes met Carter's briefly before explaining quietly, "My blood sugar's low, man."

Having been diagnosed with hypoglycemia when he was a kid, Max managed to keep his blood sugar on a fairly normal level, but he was a cranky son of a bitch when it dropped. Carter reached into his back pocket and retrieved his bag of mini Oreos, throwing them at his friend.

Max put one in his mouth and hummed in pleasure. He offered the bag to Carter, who took two for himself.

"So, what else is up?" Carter asked after a moment of Oreo-appreciative silence. Max averted his eyes from Carter, who dropped to the floor next to him. "Since when do we keep secrets, Max?"

"I don't have any secrets," Max answered with a shake of his head. He looked so weary. "You know all there is to know."

"Oh, really?" Carter countered. "So, if I know everything, when exactly were you going to tell me that you're doin' blow on the regular again?"

Max kept his eyes on the floor between his feet. "It's just recreational, man."

"I thought you were going to cut that shit out," Carter said in exasperation.

"I know. I tried; you know I did. But it takes the edge off." He rubbed his face with a somnolent hand. "I'm not . . . I'm not sleeping great. Truthfully, I haven't slept great since . . . since she . . . Look, it gives me a boost."

Carter's stomach clenched for his friend and his inability to speak about the woman who'd broken his heart. He looked so lost. He nudged Max's shoulder with his own. "I'm here if you wanna talk about Liz—"

Max's head snapped up, his eyes burning. "Don't."

Carter sighed. "Okay. But you need to be honest with me." Carter gave Max a pointed stare, which Max accepted with a slow nod.

Honesty had always been so important to the friendship they'd built over the years: honesty and trust.

"Dude, you look like shit. Your temper's raw. You're handling an expensive habit. Paul told me the books for the shop aren't good. If you kick this shit, you know I can help you with the money side of—"

Max shook his head. "No, Carter. I don't want your money. I've told you before."

"It's not my money," Carter bit back. "It's Ford money."

"Whatever," Max continued. "I'm not taking it. After you went to Kill for me and Liz . . ." He trailed off, the name clogging his throat with emotion. Then he coughed a bitter, cold laugh. "What a waste of fucking time that was."

"Have you heard from her?" Carter hedged softly. Max rarely spoke of the woman who, by walking out on him and disappearing without even a "fuck you," had shattered his heart six months after Carter was sent to Kill.

Max shook his head before he dropped it back against the wall. "Nothing. Not even a fucking text. Nothing since the day she left."

Carter placed a hand on Max's shoulder and squeezed, hating what Lizzie Jordan had done to his best friend. Because of her, the son of a bitch was brokenhearted and nursing a coke habit that was liable to land him in prison, or worse.

"The offer's there, okay?" Carter said softly. "I've got your back, man, you know that, but I'm on parole. I gotta watch my back, too."

His parole wasn't the only reason to keep his nose clean, though. Contrary to popular belief, he'd pulled away from all the drug shit a year before he was sent to Kill.

"It's all good," Max said, his mask of indifference sliding over the pain. "It's under control, I promise. Hey, I'm meeting a couple of guys next week for a sweet deal that'll clear everything. You want in?"

Carter's infuriated eye roll made Max laugh. "Asshole. Yeah, let me just call my parole officer and ask if that's okay." He thumped Max's arm. "You be fucking careful, you hear me?"

Carter's cell phone vibrated in his pocket. Standing and moving away from Max, he pulled it from his overalls and smiled.

Peaches.

Try not to be late again.

"That your tutor?" Max asked with a knowing smile. "Shit, son, when you gonna hit that?"

"Shut up," Carter grumbled.

Max laughed again, his game face back on. "What's with you and her, huh? Is it that way?"

Carter cleared his throat. "No," he breathed. "It's not that way." He licked his lips and looked at his best friend.

"Sure," Max teased. "If you haven't boned already you're desperate to, man. It's written all over you. Not that I blame you. Damn."

Carter held back the growl of possessiveness that threatened to creep up his throat. "It's complicated." He paused. "She's . . . she's Peaches."

Max's eyes popped wide. "Peaches? The girl in the Bronx, with the dad who— No shit?"

Carter raised his eyebrows. "Shit."

The night Carter had saved her, he'd told Max everything. It was only then, with his friend at his side, adrenaline still coursing through his veins and the sound of gunfire still resonating around his head, that he'd openly wept from the fear.

Max scrambled from his place on the floor. "Does she know? I mean, have you said anything to her?"

Carter clutched the bridge of his nose. "No. I haven't. I wouldn't even know where the fuck to start."

Max crossed his arms over his chest. "I hear ya." A small smile tugged at the edges of his mouth. "Damn, brother, after all these years. You found her."

Carter smiled small and rubbed the back of his neck. "Yeah."

Max smacked a playful hand to Carter's biceps. "Get on that. Girl done grown up good."

Carter snorted. No shit. Though Max's suggestion that he hit it and quit it would ordinarily have his panty-dissolving smolder firmly in place, with his Peaches it seemed too . . . crass. She deserved more than that.

He glanced at the clock. It was three fifteen. Less than one hour until he saw her. He texted back.

I wouldn't dare.

And he was only half kidding. He'd been more than a little surprised at her reaction to his tardiness at their first session. She'd looked ready to rip his head off, and he could see where she was coming from, but, damn, girl had a temper. Not that he was one to talk. But after the whole stern-talking-to, falling-off-ladder debacle, the session had gone pretty well.

It was strange how time passed so fast when he was with Peaches. It seemed so easy to be with her. He liked her sass and enthusiasm. It made him remember his own love of the written word, and he liked talking to her about the writer's word choices and the intricacies of it all.

In fact, he liked talking to her, period. Talking to her—and now touching her. He couldn't help but think about how soft her hair was when he'd pushed it behind her ear, or the silkiness of her skin at the back of her knee. Would her skin be that soft all over?

He cleared his throat and shook his head of the image of her wrapped around him as he pounded into her among the bookshelves.

Christ.

He wanted more. And not just in the let-me-see-what-you-look-like-naked sense.

What would it be like just to have an everyday conversation with her? The day she'd spoken about her father and the book he read to her was one of the best days he'd had inside Kill. He'd gotten a glimpse of the Kat Lane who existed outside of the prison walls, and now that he, too, was outside, he wanted very much to see more.

What might her reaction be if he asked her some more personal questions? Only questions about her likes and dislikes, not like her bra size or anything—though he'd wondered about that shit, too. They looked like they would fit in his hands perfectly. His body immediately reacted to that particular thought, which was more than a little embarrassing when he was surrounded by a bunch of guys.

His body still seemed to find it impossible to settle down when he was around her or when he thought about her. Regardless, as much as he would have loved to suggest they just get fucking down to it, he knew she wasn't that type of girl. He was fairly certain that if he ever heard of any man treating her that way, he would have no problem with fucking. Their. Shit. Up.

His possessiveness could be a problem.

"Carter?"

He came from his thoughts and looked at Cam, who was motioning toward the entrance of the body shop.

"There's a guy here to see you, man."

"Who?" Carter asked, putting his coffee down.

Cam shrugged. "No clue. He just said he needed to talk to you urgently."

"Don't they all."

He stopped midstride when he saw who was waiting for him on the sidewalk outside the shop, in a suit that must have cost at least two thousand dollars. Carter cursed and rubbed his palm down his face in aggravation.

"Austin Ford."

Austin nodded. "Carter."

There was a moment of overwrought stillness while the two men observed each other. Impatient as always, Carter was the first to break it.

"What are you doing here?" he asked with an incensed shake of his head.

"You haven't been returning any of our calls," Austin answered, his tone calm and arrogant.

"You dipshits can't bully me on the phone, so you decide to come down and do it in person?" he retorted.

"We're not bullying you, Carter. These papers need signing."

Carter pulled his smokes from his back pocket and lit one, taking a huge drag. He pointed at Austin with the cigarette still between his fingers. "Those papers were drawn up without my consent as a way of shifting me out of the picture. That, my friend, is fucking bullying: underhanded, conceited bullying."

"Carter." Austin rubbed the bridge of his nose. "You don't want anything to do with the company. You've said that time and time again, yet when we offer you a way out, you dig in your heels and say no."

"Bullshit," Carter snapped. "You're offering me a way out because the Fords are scared shitless that WCS shareholders will find out your company is owned by a criminal. Ironic, really, when you consider the men you've been making deals with. Casari ring any bells?"

Austin's eyes narrowed infinitesimally. "Carter. Rumors aside, we're family—"

Carter's eyes blazed. "Don't play the family card with me, Austin." He flicked his cigarette away, missing Austin's left arm by millimeters. "You weren't my fucking family when I was doing time in prison, so don't pretend you give a shit now!"

Austin held his hands up in submission. "Okay, okay. I get it."

"No," Carter continued, stepping toward him. "You *don't* get it. We may be related, but that doesn't mean I wouldn't think twice about laying your ass out, right here and now, just on general principle."

Austin refused to back down, even when Carter was nose to nose with him. "That wouldn't be too good for your parole, now, would it?"

"Fuck you, you sanctimonious shit," Carter hissed. "Don't stand there looking down your nose at me like you're cleaner than a nun's bedsheets. I could make one phone call about your dealings with Casari and the Feds would be all over your ass."

"And of course you have proof about Casari and me, right?"

The two men glared at each other, neither blinking nor stepping back.

"We okay here?"

Austin's eyes flickered toward Max, who was leaning against the wall with his arms crossed over his wide chest.

"Yeah," Carter answered, never taking his eyes from Austin's face. "My cousin was just leaving."

Austin exhaled in resignation. "Think about what I said, Carter. We'll be in touch." He headed back across the street to his car.

Carter watched the car pull away, then turned to Max with a face like thunder.

"What the fuck was he doing here?" Max asked with raised eyebrows.

Carter slumped against the wall next to him. "They're still tryin' to buy me out."

"What did you say?"

"I told him to go fuck himself," Carter replied with a shrug.

Max bumped his shoulder. "That's my boy."

Carter cracked a smile, allowing his body to calm down.

Fucking family? What the hell did Austin know about being family?

The Fords were all the same. All they cared about was getting their hands on his money and having more power. And as much as Carter despised every cent that entered his Swiss bank account every month, he wasn't about to slink off like some black sheep just because the Fords wanted him to.

Suddenly he bolted upright, wide-eyed and frantic. "Shit!" He patted his chest and jeans pockets as though searching for something. "What time is it?"

"It's three forty-five, man, why? Where's the fire?"

"Fuck!" Carter cried, running full speed back into the shop to grab his bag and keys. "I'm fucking late! I'm late!"

He pulled on his leather jacket and shades, and ran back out of the shop toward Kala. "My session!" he called back to Max, then pulled on his helmet and threw his leg over the bike. "I'm late and I said I wouldn't be! I told her I wouldn't be!"

"Oh, the tutor," Max replied as Carter steered the rumbling bike onto the road with his feet. "Hey, if you're not interested, tell her I'll show her a damned good time! I always had a thing for redheads."

He laughed when Carter flicked him the finger before revving the Harley and speeding off like a bat out of hell.

• • •

Kat drummed her nails on the library table in annoyance, wondering why the hell she'd thought Carter had meant it when he'd said that he would be on time.

Oh yes—because she was stupid.

She was stupid for thinking he'd be on time. She was stupid for looking forward to their time together and resenting him for cutting it short. And she was really stupid for having taken time to reapply a little lip gloss before she reached the library.

She pulled the copy of *Walter the Lazy Mouse* he'd given her out of her bag and reread the note he'd written. "No matter what the obstacles . . ."

Well, she thought dryly, the biggest obstacle right now was the fact that the guy would be late to his own funeral. She closed the book and glanced at the clock once again. Four ten. She'd waited thirty minutes the last session. She'd wait twenty this time. She picked up her phone, checking for any messages or missed calls from him. Nothing. The only text she had was from Austin, telling her to have a good day and asking if she had plans on Saturday.

She heaved a sigh, avoiding looking across at the shelves of books where Carter's large, strong, muscular arm had grabbed her and held her so deliciously—

"Dammit!" She dropped her forehead on the table. "It's just a stupid crush. Get a grip. Just because he's pretty doesn't mean you—"

"Who's pretty?"

Oh. Holy. Shit.

Kat sat up very, very slowly.

"My . . . shoes," she answered, extending her foot so Carter could see the gunmetal-gray Gucci pump. "Aren't they pretty?" She kept her eyes on her shoes, trying to calm her racing heart.

Carter cocked puzzled eyebrows above eyes that raked over the foot, ankle, and leg she was showing him. "Um, they're not really my style, but, yeah, great." He pulled off his jacket and flung it over the back of his seat, grimacing. "So, I know I'm late. And I know I said I wouldn't be."

"Yes," she answered sharply, eager for the change in topic. "Again. I know you have stuff you need to do, but so do I. And your being constantly late just isn't going to work. We've already lost fifteen minutes."

"Give me a break here, Peaches. It's only our second session. I'm still trying to find my groove and shit with everything. It won't be like this forever . . . I'm trying, okay?"

Kat noticed his face was softer, more vulnerable. She frowned. "What happened?"

Carter sat back, looking surprised. "What?"

"Why were you late? What happened?"

He inhaled deeply and rubbed his neck. "There was a . . . family issue I had to deal with and I lost track of time."

Family? That was the last thing she thought he was going to say. She knew nothing about his family. "Is everything all right?"

"Um . . . yeah, everything's fine." His eyes darted away. "Can we start now?"

Kat saw the tension creep back into his jaw. The truth was, she barely knew the man sitting before her, and it was cause for concern. She was lusting after him, yet all she knew for sure was that he'd done time, he had a good education, and he worked in a body shop with his best friend. The fact that he made smoking look sexy as all hell and looked fucking amazing in jeans and Ray-Bans was inconsequential.

Although . . .

Damn.

"I see you came straight from work again," she noted with a tip of her head toward his red White Stripes T-shirt smothered in oil.

"Yeah, I get covered in the stuff." He glanced at her from under his lashes, his gaze like a hot finger pressed to her skin. "Sorry for being late." He rubbed his hands down his face. "Christ, I need a cigarette."

Kat stood, scraping her chair across the linoleum floor. "If you need a smoke, let's go outside and have a smoke."

"But you don't smoke."

Kat put her hands on her hips and took two steps toward the door. "I like to watch," she sassed. "Come on."

• • •

Carter watched her for a moment, then followed. Outside of the library, in the warm sunshine, they went to the smoking area.

She gestured with her hand for him to spark up. He smiled

and did as she suggested, pulling on the thing for all it was worth. Leaning back against the wall, he caught a waft of her perfume, and closed his eyes briefly at the sweetness of it.

The top of her head only came to his shoulder; how had he not noticed that before? Maybe it was because her confidence, her no-bullshit attitude, made her seem taller. Her hair caught the sun, causing the red and gold to shine. His desire for her grew exponentially every time he saw her and, as he watched her gaze out at the traffic, the stirring she always caused began deep in his stomach.

"Why did you want to become a teacher?" he asked, needing a distraction from his rising libido.

Her head snapped toward him, her big green eyes wary.

"Sorry," he mumbled around his cigarette. "I didn't mean to pry. It's none of my business." He stared at his feet until she answered.

"My dad. Before he died, I made a promise to him." She lifted her face toward the sky. "He always taught me that it was important to give back, to not take anything for granted. I loved reading and writing, and becoming a teacher just seemed to . . . ignite something in me." She glanced at him. "Sounds corny as shit, right?"

He shook his head. "There's nothing wrong with passion, Peaches."

"Did you want to be anything, before prison?"

Carter crossed his legs at the ankles. "There was a time when I wanted to be a doctor." He'd never told anyone that.

"A doctor?"

"Yeah, a surgeon, actually. Don't look so surprised. I'm good with my hands." He wiggled his fingers.

"Is that why you work in the body shop?"

"Nah. Apart from doing it to help Max, I do that because I love engines. Taking it all apart, seeing how it works, and then putting it all back together." He closed his eyes. "The sound they make is pretty awesome, too."

The first time he'd blasted Kala to New Jersey one hot summer afternoon; her engine had been so loud his bones had vibrated.

Carter opened his eyes to see her gazing back at him, innocent and wanting. She was such a fucking paradox. The stirring in the depths of his stomach twisted sharply until it began to bloom into something more, something bigger.

It was more than yearning. It was craving. No, he was ravenous for more of her—in every way she'd allow him to have her.

He sucked in a breath against the crushing need to kiss her.

She blinked. "What?"

He cleared his throat, the need to place his mouth against hers rising like a tidal wave through his body. "Nothin'."

Well, this shit was new.

He didn't kiss women—ordinarily, they kissed him. Usually, they begged. He'd wanted to do unspeakable things to Peaches since he'd first seen her, but kiss her? That had never crossed his mind.

Until now.

"So, what do you like to do when you're not, you know, getting covered in oil?" Her smile was awkward. Her smile was fucking adorable.

He wanted to lick her bottom lip. Maybe suck on it. "I like to play guitar." His voice was rough. "Watch TV. Drink. Ride my bike. Nothing exciting."

"Yeah, I noticed your helmet."

"Yes. My baby."

Peaches laughed. "Boys and their toys."

"Damn straight."

She toed the floor. "My dad rode a bike when I was little. I love bikes."

Of course she fucking did. As if she could be any more damned perfect. Jesus. He stubbed out his smoke and flicked it to the side. "We should go back in."

Nodding, Peaches pushed from the wall. Carter followed behind closely, watching the luscious sway of her hips as they went inside. There, out of nowhere, a big, bearded asshole with a huge bag smacked hard into her, sending her flying. Carter grabbed her waist, pulling her upright against his chest before she hit the deck.

"Shit!" she gasped, grasping his forearm.

"Watch it," the asshole sneered without a second glance. "Blind bitch."

Carter took three huge strides and grabbed the asshole's wrist, making him spin around. The bastard winced as Carter squeezed the pressure points he knew would hurt like a bitch.

He tried to pull from Carter's grasp. "What the hell, man?"

"Carter," Peaches called, hurrying to his side.

He ignored her and twisted the asshole's arm farther.

"You're gonna break my wrist!"

Carter growled, "And I will, if you don't apologize to this lady."

The asshole opened his mouth, but no sound emerged.

"Apologize," Carter ordered.

"I'm sorry," he groaned, but Carter kept his grip.

"Carter, he apologized. Let him go," Peaches said.

Smirking at the fear in the asshole's eyes, he squeezed once more for good measure before he released him. The asshole stumbled back, clutching his wrist. He grabbed for the bag he'd dropped on the floor and hurried away, Carter's stare burning holes in his back.

Peaches spun around, pushing his biceps. "What the *hell* was that?"

Before he could answer, she stormed back toward the reading room, heels hard on the floor, arms jackknifing at her sides. By the time he reached her, she was banging shit around on the table.

"What the fuck did I do?" he asked, his voice low.

She didn't answer him as she flung herself onto her chair.

"Are you mad?" he asked incredulously.

"We have work to do," she snapped, throwing him a fiery glower.

Carter's annoyance peaked. He crossed his arms. "Hey, I asked you a question."

"Yes, I'm mad," she shot back in a low hiss.

"Why?"

"Why?"

"Yes. Why the fuck are you mad?" Her ingratitude made his skin crawl, while her rage made his dick harder than titanium.

She spoke through gritted teeth. "I'm mad because you nearly broke a man's wrist in the middle of the library, because you're an idiot who seems to have forgotten his ass is on parole and who can't keep his temper."

Before she could take another breath, he was looming over her, his hands gripping the armrests of the seat she was sitting in, trapping her against the leather at her back. She leaned back, her eyes narrowed, but he moved closer.

"About done?" he seethed, his eyes boring into hers. "Let me tell you something, Miss Lane. Your ungrateful ass would be smeared across the library floor if I hadn't caught you, and that shitkicker will now think twice about treating any woman that way again. So don't bitch to me about what I should and shouldn't do. You're my tutor, not my keeper. Get that shit straight right now."

His body heaved when Peaches' gaze flickered to his mouth.

Dammit, he wanted to kiss her, to taste her, lose himself in her, to nip and bite and steal every breath she had.

His breathing slowed. "Are you scared?"

She shook her head. So stubborn.

"You should be," he warned. "You have no idea what I'm capable of." Her pupils enlarged and goose bumps erupted up her neck. He watched them, fascinated.

"When you're done," she said quietly, "we have work to do."

Carter slowly released his grip on the chair. He glanced at the warm flush of her cheeks and took his seat, reaching for the poem.

"Read through it," she said with authority. "Highlight the lines, phrases, words that you like, and we'll discuss it once you're done."

• • •

An hour later, as Kat packed her bag, Carter's cell phone burst to life.

Grumbling, he answered it. "What's up, J?" His eyes rolled good-naturedly. "Yeah, I'm with Miss Lane now." He smiled. "Yeah, she's— I mean, it's good."

Kat continued to put her things away, skimming over the notes Carter had made on the poem. Even his damned handwriting was beautiful. It was clear and flowed from one cursive swirl to the next, genteel and calm. How ironic. She watched him surreptitiously, remembering the murderous look on his face as he'd almost broken a man for pushing into her.

It was blatantly clear that under the intelligence, quick wit, and striking face lurked something dark and treacherous. She couldn't allow herself to forget that for one moment. He unbalanced her. His brooding demeanor worried her. How could he go from being so charming, so funny, to behaving like an animal?

She was so confused. Hot, fiery longing for him rushed through her veins, and the more she tried to extinguish it, the hotter it burned. She glimpsed his mouth, lingering on the soft dip of his top lip. For one split second, when he'd pinned her to the chair, she'd truly thought that he was going to kiss her, and, by Christ, she'd have let him.

"Yeah, I'll call you," Carter said into his cell. "Later." He ended the call and pushed his cell into his pocket.

" 'Miss Lane,' huh?"

He shrugged. "Peaches is my name for you. No one else's."

"So I gather," she replied, ignoring the covetous tone of his voice even though it sent warm flutters through her chest.

"So, our session Friday." He grimaced and pulled his beanie over his ears. "I'm not going to be able to make it."

Disappointment teased at Kat's throat.

"I have my first meeting with Diane. Jack's coming," he explained. "I'm sorry."

"It's not your fault. It just means we have to book those two hours elsewhere." She retrieved her planner from her bag and flipped the pages to the date. Carter picked up his bike helmet and walked to her side.

Kat groaned in frustration. "I can't make tomorrow. I have a work meeting and the library shuts at six and I haven't requested a stay-open . . ." She trailed off, deflated.

"It's not a problem."

"Actually, it is," she countered. "We have to have six hours a week, per parole orders."

Carter stared at the floor. "Well, um . . . what are you doing Saturday?"

"Saturday?"

Carter shifted his weight from foot to foot. "Ye— Well, yeah."

"I haven't booked the room for Saturday."

Carter huffed. "Are you being obtuse on purpose? We could meet on Saturday if you have nothing planned. Go to the park or something and study there. I don't know."

"The park?"

"Holy shit, woman!" Kat smiled at the same time that Carter eyed her distrustfully. "Are you playing with me, Peaches?"

"I'm sorry," she said with a small giggle. "I'm just surprised. I thought the last thing you'd want to do would be to study on a Saturday."

"I'm a good student, what can I say?" Kat snorted. "So," Carter pushed, "are you busy Saturday?"

Kat looked at him with trepidation. His face appeared eager, apprehensive, and very young. She didn't need to check her diary. She knew she was free. Austin's text flashed through her mind.

"No, I'm not busy," she answered, wondering fleetingly if she would go on to regret the words that now slipped so easily from her mouth.

The resulting smile on Carter's face was beatific. "Well, good. Saturday it is. What time?"

"One?"

"One is great. Fifth Avenue and Fifty-ninth entrance?"

"Perfect."

• • •

Carter tucked his helmet under his arm and gestured for Peaches to lead the way.

The pair meandered through the nearly deserted library and out into the cool New York City evening. They descended the front steps and turned onto the sidewalk.

"Is this your bike?" she asked, approaching the exquisite piece of machinery.

"This is she," Carter said fervently. "Kala."

"Kala?"

"Fire. It means art, too, but it was the fire part I liked."

"She's beautiful."

"Thank you."

"I always liked the 2010 Harley Sportster Forty-Eight," she continued. "It was so much sleeker than the Nightster. Faster engine, too."

The sound of Carter's jaw popping open and his cock straining against his fly was heard as far away as Philadelphia.

Holy. Fuck.

He watched her small hand skim across the leather of Kala's seat, knowing it was the sexiest thing he'd ever seen. His mind was immediately accosted with obscene images of Peaches spread naked on Kala.

Peaches riding Kala.

Peaches' thighs tight around his waist.

He moaned softly, deep in his throat.

Usually, if a woman touched his bike, Carter would go ape shit, but somehow, seeing Peaches do it made him dry at the mouth and twitching at the crotch.

"You know your bikes," he stated.

"Not really," she replied with a shrug. She touched the handlebars. Carter licked his lips. "I would ride with my dad sometimes when we went to the beach on holiday twice a year. It was my favorite time with him."

"If you ever . . ." Carter pointed to the bike, tongue-tied. "We could. The beach isn't that far away."

He rubbed his hands together as if that would explain what the hell he was trying to say so inarticulately.

"Maybe one day," she muttered.

"I'll hold you to it."

Her cell phone began chirping from her pocket, shattering the moment.

"I'll see you Saturday," she said, walking backward away from him.

Carter rubbed his chest, where warm excitement wound around his lungs. "You bet."

• • •

The following Friday evening, Jack and Diane arrived at Carter's apartment to amuse him with their usual bullshit about rehabilitation and being in the right mind-set to make a "valuable contribution to society."

Jack, Carter conceded silently, wasn't as bad as he'd feared he would be. He simply begrudged them both for taking his Peaches' time away from him. They'd stayed at his apartment, drinking coffee and discussing his work at the body shop, his workouts with

Ross, and the anger therapy he was still to start. Jack, the sly shit, had waited nearly an hour before he'd brought up the library sessions. Carter had answered his questions, pleased that Diane had received Peaches' paperwork detailing the progress they'd made, while dodging Jack's suspicious stares.

"So"—Jack glanced at the bathroom door Diane had just gone through—"you and Miss Lane are okay?"

"Yeah," Carter replied with a nonchalant shrug. "We're fine. Good, actually." He smiled. "The sessions are . . . interesting and we get a lot done."

Jack inclined his head. "And you're behaving?"

"Of course I'm behaving. Why wouldn't I be?"

Jack put his coffee cup down. "I didn't mean that, Wes. Miss Lane's already stated in her papers that your attitude is much improved."

Carter was a little surprised by that considering what had happened with the fat asshole and his lack of manners.

Jack breathed deeply. "Wes, I meant . . ." He lowered his voice before continuing. "I meant are you managing the sessions with it being just the two of you?"

Carter tried to hold Jack's stare but found his eyes settling on his own sock-clad feet, fidgeting nervously on the floor.

Was he managing with it just being the two of them? Yes.

Was he about ready to blow a fuse with the tension between him and Peaches? Fuck yes.

He lifted his head and gave Jack a pointed look. "I'm not an idiot, J."

"I know you're not," Jack agreed. "But you have to understand the implications of, you know, if—if anything . . ." He trailed off. "The nonfraternization clause she signed—"

"I know." Carter dropped back in his seat.

He knew Jack had seen firsthand the chemistry between Carter and Peaches. Carter stared at Jack, silently accepting the line that lay between himself and his tutor. As blurred as it had become, he knew he couldn't cross it. He knew he shouldn't cross it.

The silent question that hung between them was whether he had the strength to remember that or, rules be damned, cross it anyway.

14

After stopping at the clinic to give mandatory blood and urine samples, Carter decided he was starving and, with half an hour before his park session with Peaches, the golden arches of McDonald's started beckoning him mercilessly.

With the brown bag in hand and Kala parked safely away, Carter took a seat outside of FAO Schwarz and began people-watching while he ate his Big Mac. He groaned in satisfaction when he took a bite of his burger, not realizing how much he'd missed that shit while he was inside.

Once he'd polished it off, along with the large fries and large Sprite, he sat back and tried to relax.

It was the first time he'd really slowed to any kind of stop since his release, and, as much as he liked being busy, he also appreciated the need to simply take a moment. Before Kill, he would quite often sit in Central Park or Battery Park with a full pack of Marlboros and a bottle of Jim Beam, sit back, and enjoy being still.

Under the warm New York sun, Carter watched the crowds on Fifth Avenue. He smiled when two twentysomething girls smirked flirtatiously and giggled as they passed him. They were so blatant that Carter—used to such reactions from most females—couldn't help but pull down his shades and smile back.

It worked like a damn charm, making the two girls stammer and stumble away from him. Carter snickered into the back of his hand and pushed his shades back in place. Too easy.

He sat back, his attention falling on a couple who were kissing not ten feet from him, oblivious to the world around them. The guy held his woman's face, lost in a kiss that was gentle and slow.

Carter frowned, confused. How could that be pleasurable? He'd never kissed that way—when he'd kissed at all—and he'd certainly never "made love." Although Max had spoken about making love with Lizzie, Carter wasn't even sure such a thing existed. Before that relationship had gone to shit, Carter had watched dubiously when his best friend had kissed and held his woman carefully, softly, as though she was the most precious thing in the world. It was clear that he'd cherished her. Not that that shit had made a difference when she'd decided to walk away.

Carter liked sex. No, he liked fucking, and when he did, there was nothing soft and tender about it. Maybe he was a prick for doing it that way, but he'd never had any complaints. Every woman who'd left his bed had done so satisfied, and many had come back wanting seconds.

No, Carter thought, pulling his stare from the man and woman, soft and tender wasn't his bag at all.

Looking across the busy street, he caught a glimpse of red hair. He craned his neck, looking past the people standing in front of him, his mouth lifting into a smile. It was his Peaches, wearing . . . goddamn her. She was wearing a loose-fitting white T-shirt that showed her neck and shoulders and black jeans. She was dressed, as always, with an edge of class. She oozed sexiness without even trying.

The strange feeling that had occurred in his stomach outside the library three nights before began to snake its way through his intestines. It was the oddest sensation—the hunger—and he didn't like it. It wasn't the sensation he didn't like as much as it was the unease and the overpowering sense of being out of control that accompanied it.

He knew, had he not had his wits about him, he would have

kissed Peaches on the steps of the library. After his conversation with Jack, their kiss would have been . . . it would have been . . .

Carter's mind went blank.

How would he feel if he kissed her?

Hard and horny? Most definitely.

Even more desperate to feel what it would be like to be inside of her? God yes.

Happy?

Carter rubbed his palms down his face. Shit. This thought process was far too deep for a Saturday afternoon. He needed to get his head out of his ass and focus on why he was there.

He glanced down at his watch and raised his eyebrows in surprise.

Son of a bitch.

She was late.

By nearly fifteen minutes.

Oh, baby, he thought with a smile and a playful shake of his head. He lifted from his seat, grabbed his jacket and helmet, and strolled toward her. He approached from behind, allowing his eyes to dance over her curves. She was ending a call on her phone when he stepped close enough to smell her hair. He bent down to her ear.

"What time do you call this, Peaches?"

She yelped, spinning around in a swirl of white tee and auburn hair. Her face was spectacular in its shock of wide eyes and open mouth.

"Carter," she gasped. "What is with you and scaring me all the damn time?"

Carter didn't reply, reveling in her feistiness. He simply cocked an eyebrow and crossed his arms, waiting for an explanation for her tardiness.

She dropped her cell into her bag, avoiding his gaze. "I got held up."

"Mmhm," Carter hummed. "And here I was thinking that I was the most important man in your life."

He was messing with her, but a part of him really wanted it to be the truth. His greediness for her was becoming ridiculous.

Peaches huffed and put her hand on her hip. "Delusions of grandeur," she snipped back. "Besides," she continued, "I wasn't with a man."

Carter's jaw unclenched in unprecedented and unexpected relief. "I suppose I can allow your lateness to slide this time," he deadpanned through a long breath that made pieces of her hair move. He shifted closer, lowering his voice in warning. "Just don't let it happen again."

She swallowed. "Or else what?"

Carter stared at her, stunned at her question, and hard as all hell that she was ogling the tattoos visible beneath the three-quarter-length sleeves of his Beatles T-shirt. "Oh, Peaches," he whispered. "Wouldn't you like to know?"

Something bright flashed within her eyes, but it was gone before Carter could identify it. She flicked her hair over her shoulder and shrugged.

"Not really," she replied with an unimpressed scrunch of her nose. "Come on. We have work to do."

A small laugh escaped Carter when she stormed past him into the park. He had to jog a little to catch up with her, but, once he did, he pushed his free hand into his jeans pocket and followed her lead.

"So," he said as they made their way through the gates and across the cobbled path, "where are we doing this?"

She glanced up at the blue sky and smiled. It was a beautiful day, unseasonably warm. "I thought we'd sit by the boating pond. I know a great spot."

"Great."

As was always the case on a warm Saturday, the park was teeming with people and Carter found himself weaving from one side to the other to avoid being pushed or shoved by kids or dogs.

• • •

Kat noticed how out of place among the normal run-of-the-mill New Yorkers and tourists Carter appeared—not for any other reason than the fact that he was so striking in all his tall, tattooed, buzz-cut glory. She couldn't help notice the admiring glances he got from the other women they walked past.

Kat had secretly been dreading meeting Carter outside of the library. She realized that technically, she wasn't doing anything wrong by being with him in the park, but deep inside, she knew she was on shaky ground. She hadn't told Beth, her mom, or Ben about the session, knowing she was bound to get some sort of lecture from one, if not all, of them.

Not that it seemed she'd have the opportunity to speak to Beth, who had been uncharacteristically quiet of late. Since Kat's birthday, there'd been a couple of text messages but nothing more. Ben, to whom she'd been speaking when Carter had startled her, was also seemingly mystified by Beth's weird behavior. Something was definitely up.

"You okay over there, Peaches?"

Carter's voice pulled her back to the park. She looked up to see the top of his nose over his shades bunched into a concerned frown.

"Yeah, I'm fine," she answered. "The spot's just over there."

She made her way over to the grass and pressed a hand down to check its dampness.

"Here," Carter muttered as he laid his jacket down. "You can sit on that."

"The grass is dry," Kat insisted.

He shrugged. "Just sit on the damn thing. It won't kill ya."

Kat dropped her stuff on the ground. "Thank you."

Carter dropped down onto the grass, his arm grazing hers. He lit a cigarette leaning back on his elbows, blowing the smoke down his nose. Kat watched him furtively as he looked out across the water, glancing at the children climbing all over the Alice in Wonderland statue situated to their right. He looked devastatingly beautiful.

"I, um . . . I brought you something." She reached into her bag.

He raised his eyebrows in expectation. She pulled out her hand to reveal a large pack of Oreos. He grinned and she threw them onto his lap.

"You shouldn't have." He chuckled.

She waved him off. "They're more for me," she muttered, seeing a questioning expression cross his face. "I know what a grumpy ass you can be without your Oreos, and I don't need your attitude." She smiled before delving back into her bag. "And no. I didn't bring milk."

Carter sat up, ripping the pack open. "I love these things."

"I noticed."

"You want?" he asked, holding the pack out to her while his tongue began doing indecent things to the white cream in the center of a cookie.

She watched, entranced. "Um, no, I'm good."

Was it even possible to be jealous of a cookie?

She turned from him, grabbing the session resources. She handed Carter his copy, and asked him to refresh her on what they learned about the sexually deviant Donne poem. He didn't disappoint. It seemed that her gift of calorific cookie beauty had unleashed his garrulous side. She loved listening to him. Hearing his voice, even when he cursed, was like wrapping up in velvet. Much like its owner, it was filled with contradictions. It was soft but firm, loud but quiet, commanding and submissive.

Behind her shades, she closed her eyes and listened. It was a lullaby, easing some place hidden inside of her.

"You like this poem," she stated when he became quiet.

Carter appeared indifferent. He lay back on the grass, next to where Kat was sitting cross-legged. "I like the metaphors he uses, even if I don't agree with them."

Kat waited for him to explain. He breathed deeply, which made his T-shirt rise from the waistband of his jeans, showing a black strip of underwear and a white slice of stomach. She tried not to notice. Really. She did.

"I just don't buy the whole *Sex is like heaven and I'm surrounded by cherubs while I'm getting off* thing," he said finally.

Kat shifted on the denim jacket at his words. She had to keep reminding herself that Carter spoke freely when it came to sex.

Carter propped himself up on his forearm. "Sex is just sex. It's two people wanting the same thing and doing what needs to be done," he muttered with a shrug. "It's raw, hard, and, I don't know, I mean, for me"—he pointed to himself—"When I'm in bed with a woman . . ."

His words came to a grinding halt. He looked away.

"Carter?"

"What?" he murmured, playing with the grass he was sitting on.

"You were saying?" Kat encouraged with a dip of her head, trying to catch his eye.

"It doesn't matter. I don't get it, so whatever." He pulled the grass out with his fist.

• • •

Carter couldn't believe his mouth had run away with him like that. Speaking to his Peaches about his being with other women was just . . . weird. He didn't feel embarrassed or ashamed but more uncomfortable with her knowing. Which, considering his reputation, was fucking absurd. She was bound to assume his sexual record was about as clean as his criminal one, yet he still couldn't find the words to talk to her about his past sexual exploits.

Regardless of whether she wanted to know or not, he wasn't about to tell her, just as he was sure as shit not going to ask her about the guys she'd been with. His fists tightened at the mere thought.

"You know," she said, pulling her hair off her shoulders and pushing it up into a messy bun, "I could kill for a popsicle."

Carter, who'd been watching her play with her hair, nodded. Talking about sex was doing nothing for his attempts at being a gentleman. His gaze meandered across her body. The curve of her neck as it met her shoulders just ached for his mouth along it. He had no doubt in his mind she would be delicious.

"What can I get you?" She pushed her shades up into her hair.

"I'll have a popsicle, too." He reached into his back pocket. "Here." He pulled out a ten-dollar bill. "Let me get it."

She looked at the money and raised an eyebrow. "Why do you have to pay?"

Carter smiled. "Because I want to. Now get off your feminist high horse and take the fucking money. I owe you for the Oreos anyway."

With a small smile, Peaches took the bill. "Fine. What flavor do you want?"

Carter reached for his shades and pulled them down his nose, leaning toward her. He stared right at her and whispered, "Peach."

Once purchased, and with her own raspberry ice, she sank back onto the grass next to Carter, who was lounging on his back. They were silent as they enjoyed the blue sky, the warm breeze, and the cold flavored ice.

"This is nice," she murmured after a moment.

Carter didn't reply but licked the remaining juice off the wooden stick in his hand.

She sighed. "I used to come and sit here with my mom and dad when we stayed in New York. We'd play hide and seek and he would always pretend he couldn't find me, even when I knew he could see me." Peaches closed her eyes. "He liked sitting here," she continued. "He liked it in the fall. The leaves would surround us and we'd just sit here."

"My dad and I would play here, too," he offered. Her eyes snapped open, clearly surprised at his divulging personal information.

Avoiding her gaze, Carter trailed his finger slowly along the strands of her chestnut-red hair lying on the grass. "We'd play by the pond before we would start on the statue." He gestured with a tip of his head in the direction of the bronze structure covered in small children. He kept his eyes on his finger. "And my mom would . . ." He exhaled. "My mom would come and take me. It was a passing-off point. Neutral ground for them."

After an age of silence, he heard her sigh. "Maybe we saw each other. It's a small world, after all." She looked straight at him. "Sometimes I feel like we've known each other longer than we have. Weird, right?"

He sat up again quickly, pulling out a cigarette. "Yeah," he managed. "Really weird."

Peaches followed his position and pulled the bag and her knees closer. "So, I have a question for you," she said, rummaging in her bag.

Carter blew out his smoke, staring despondently at the ground between his bent knees.

"Which one do you want?"

He frowned when he saw her holding two books in each hand. He coughed a laugh. "I don't have a fucking clue. Why?"

Peaches gave him a pointed look. "We have to study a text, and I wanted your input. Choose one."

"I haven't read any of them," he confessed. "I know the basics of this one, but other than that I'm at a loss."

"Well, I love this story," she said, pointing to the book to Carter's right, the one that he knew the basics of. "I haven't read it for a very long time, but it always stayed with me."

He picked it up and read the blurb, his cigarette dangling from his lips. "*A Farewell to Arms* by Ernest Hemingway."

"It's a really wonderful story," Peaches added. "But I have to warn you, apart from the descriptions of war, it's essentially a tragic love story."

Carter flicked through the pages. "Yeah, I know that," he grumbled. "I'm sure I'll live."

She pulled out a pad and pen and made some notes. "Do you want to take it home and read it? I can assign you maybe two chapters that we'll discuss next session?" She huffed. "What's that face for? We have to do this, Carter. I'm not asking you because I'm being a bitch."

"I know that." He tapped the book against his knee. "I just thought I was past being given homework."

She smiled. "We'll talk about the chapters next session and then we'll read some more together."

"Fine," he muttered with a wave of his hand. "Whatever."

"You say that a lot," she retorted with a smirk. "Maybe we need to work on your vocabulary as well."

Carter stared. "Are you fucking around with me?" he asked, narrowing his eyes playfully.

She giggled and he poked a finger into her ribs. She squeaked loudly, surprising them both.

"Peaches," Carter whispered devilishly. "Are you ticklish?" He glanced down her body, silently calculating how many places he could touch to make her squeak some more.

She adjusted her top, flustered, and picked up her resources to put back into her bag. "Not at all."

"Oh," he retorted dryly. "Well, that's good, because I would hate to do this"—he poked her again, causing her to shriek—"and make you squeal like a girl."

"I *am* a girl," she snapped, pushing her stuff into her bag.

Carter laughed and handed her the remaining papers. "You know what I mean." He poked again.

"Quit it!" Peaches said in a high-pitched voice, slapping his hand away. "You're so childish!"

"Tell me something I don't know," Carter replied. He stood up and brushed off the grass attached to his ass.

With his helmet in his hand and his jacket over his arm, Carter set off at a slow walk along the edge of the boating pond. It was late afternoon and the park was a bustle of people, running, walking, and playing. Peaches caught Carter looking down at her. She blushed and smiled. He pushed his hand into his pocket as the urge to do something shook his body once more. He thought back to the conversation he'd had with Jack and cursed himself. He was a damned fool if he thought he was going to be able to maintain the friendly, flirty relationship he'd built up with her.

He'd thought about kissing her, and now he wanted to . . . what? Hold her? Yeah, he wanted to hold her, and, fuck, he didn't hold women. That was too intimate, but dammit if she wouldn't fit perfectly under his arm.

"So," he croaked. "This wasn't so bad, right?"

"No," she replied. "It was very pleasant, Mr. Carter. You continue to amaze me with your literary intellect."

He glanced away. "It helps having a great teacher, you know."

"Th-thank you," she stammered. "But if you're trying to butter me up to get more Oreos, you're barking up the wrong tree."

• • •

Kat laughed uneasily, brushing off his praise by speeding up her steps. His hand gripping the crook of her elbow stopped her. She glanced up in question when he pulled his shades from his face. When she saw his eyes, she stopped breathing altogether. His eyes were the brightest blue she'd ever seen and they seemed to look deep into her, caressing the parts of her that were aching.

"Carter?" she whispered when he took a step toward her. Standing so close to him, Kat felt very small.

"Peaches." His gaze wandered around her face. "I didn't say it to— I meant it. I think you're . . ."

Kat's heart thumped wildly. His touch on her arm was so comforting she daren't ask him to remove it, and when his eyes stayed on her mouth, she felt it between her legs. She instinctively wet her lips with the tip of her tongue. No man had ever looked at Kat the way that Carter did.

"Carter," she said again, placing her hand on top of his. "Are you okay?"

He was still staring at her in a way that made her back arch and her nipples tighten. His mouth continuously opened and closed as though he wanted to say something but didn't know how. Eventually he dropped his head with a muttered curse and looked out toward the path.

His back snapped straight. "Shit," he hissed. He grabbed her forearm and pulled her back in the direction they'd come.

"Carter!" Kat protested as he dragged her around a corner and pushed her backward against a tree, dropping his helmet and jacket at her feet.

He leaned over her, his arms above her head, gripping the bark with his fingers, while the apples of his cheeks turned a ferocious red. Kat's anger turned quickly to concern when she watched him peering cautiously around the tree, mumbling and cursing.

"Carter, what's wrong?" His eyes darted from left to right while he tried to hide her with his body. He shook his head. "Carter, talk to me," she urged, placing a palm on his shoulder. "Who is it?"

"My cousin," Carter answered in a quiet voice that belied his huge frame.

Kat jumped when his palms slammed against the bark above her head. "Goddammit." He blew out his cheeks and leaned harder against the tree, trapping Kat with his arms.

"Calm down." She rubbed her palm a little from side to side before moving it down until she could feel the hard edge of his left pectoral against the side of her thumb. He was so strong.

"I wanna see him on my time, ya know? On my terms." Carter's eyes pleaded with her to understand.

"It's all right," Kat soothed with a soft voice, keeping the motion of her hand. "You don't have to do anything you don't want to."

Gradually, his body started to relax under her stroking palm. He continued to look at her in a way that made her skin prickle. As yearning washed over her, Kat was suddenly aware of how close they were standing. Their chests touched when each of them breathed, and his nose hovered by her hairline.

"You smell good," he whispered. "Do you know that?"

Kat swallowed. Her hand stilled on his chest.

"You do," he said, dropping his shoulders farther, bringing his face closer to hers. "You smell really fucking good."

"Thank you," she replied, shifting her back against the bark of the tree.

Her body was burning up, even with the breeze around them. He was so close. She knew she should push him away, but every time the thought entered her mind, she wanted to do the complete opposite. She wanted him closer.

"What are you thinking?" Carter's hands slid down the tree until they were resting above her shoulders.

The blue of his irises reminded Kat of the Caribbean Sea, and the pucker of his top lip ached to be licked. She noticed a small scar on his chin, and her fingertips itched to touch it.

"I'm— I'm thinking that we need to, we need to get— I need to go home," she stuttered and his nose grazed her left temple.

"Do you want to go home, Peaches?"

"I should," she replied. "I need to."

Carter moved his head back, his eyes hooded and sexy. "Can I tell you something?"

Kat could do nothing but nod. Carter's stare prowled down her face, coming to a dead stop at her mouth.

"I really, really, really want to kiss you right now."

"Cart—"

"I know I shouldn't, and I don't usually kiss, but, fuck, I want to." He trailed his thumb across her mouth. "I want to find out what your top lip tastes like." He licked his own. "And then compare it to the bottom." He exhaled. "I'm desperate to know if your tongue tastes of peaches."

Kat's eyes fluttered closed at his words. "We— I . . . please," she murmured. "Don't." The word fell from her but it made her stomach clench all the same. She was amazed she had the energy to utter the one syllable at all.

"Would it be so bad?" He moved, his breath washing over Kat's face like a lusty fog. "God, you're so pretty."

Everything in Kat's body was surging toward the man in front of her. Her core purred, her pupils dilated, and her heart beat wildly. She knew they were about to cross a line—a huge dangerous line that had her career written all over it.

"Carter," she whispered again, in one final attempt to stop what she knew in her heart was inevitable. "We can't do this."

"I know," he answered, cupping the side of her face. He tilted his head, his mouth a luscious whisper across the edge of hers. "Just one taste. Just one. That's all I want."

And then his lips pressed against hers.

Oh God.

She was kissing her student.

Her beautiful, lost, broken, angry student who'd tickled her and bought her a popsicle. Who'd told her he thought she was pretty and given her a precious gift for her birthday. A man who was so full of contradiction it made her head spin.

She knew it was stupid. She'd promised she wouldn't be stupid and there she was. There she was with . . . oh shit, his tongue in her mouth. His taste. His dark, rich taste with a hint of smoke. It was sublime. It was as though she'd been searching for it her entire life. He made her feel light and heavy, excited and terrified, all at the same time.

Despite her thighs clenching together with desire, her lust couldn't erase the panic rising up the back of her throat.

She placed her hand on his shoulder and pushed. "Please," she muttered against his lips.

"Peaches," he moaned, taking her hand and words in the wrong way. He kissed her harder, plunging his tongue farther into her mouth and pressing his hips firmer against her stomach.

Kat shook her head, making their lips slide against one another. "Please stop."

But the words didn't reach Carter's ears. She knew. He was too far gone.

"Please, I can't," Kat said again, pushing a little harder. "Stop, Carter."

Her words finally met his ears. "What?" he asked through his daze, his lips barely stopping.

"Stop." She pushed again and he moved back, but not far enough. "I said stop!"

She pushed with all her strength and, this time, he stumbled back.

• • •

Carter stared at her in utter confusion, taking in her perfectly plump red lips, before she covered them with her hand. Gathering his wits, he realized with a terrifying jolt that she was crying. Carter's heart dropped to the soles of his shoes.

"Peaches," he murmured. He took a step toward her but stopped when she held up her hand. "I— What the . . . ? Shit, did I hurt you?"

She shook her head. "No. You didn't hurt me."

"Then what?" He risked taking another step and breathed easier when she didn't stop him. The urge to be near her, now that he'd tasted her, was so fucking strong.

"We just . . . I can't believe—" She looked up. "Do you realize what could happen if people knew what we just did?"

Yeah, he did know, but right then he couldn't have given a shit. "Peaches," he said, holding out a hand, which she didn't take. "It's okay."

Her head snapped up. "Okay?" she exclaimed. "There is *nothing* okay about this, Carter. I'm your teacher!"

"Don't yell at me," he fumed, his temper rippling. "I know exactly what you are. I also know that you liked it just as much as I did."

"Regardless," she snapped, "it can't happen again. It *won't* happen again."

Searing pain sliced across Carter's chest, and he covered it with anger. "What-the-fuck-ever. Like I give a shit if it happens again."

Her eyes met his and he immediately saw the hurt. He swallowed down his pride. "Peaches, I— Shit— I . . ." He hesitated, feeling that, somehow, "sorry" wasn't nearly enough to fix the moment.

"I'm going home," she muttered.

Carter noticed how tired and small she looked. He was almost desperate with need to take care of her and make it better.

She started to turn from him, and he took another step toward her. "Peach—"

"Don't," she begged, closing her eyes. "Just . . . don't." Her shoulders fell. "Carter, I'm sorry that I—I didn't mean to lead you on. The kiss was— I need to go home." Her eyes opened slowly. "I'll see you on Tuesday." She kept her eyes on his for a beat before she turned away.

Carter stood silently and watched her walk away, certain that she was taking half of him with her.

15

Carter's entire apartment shook as he slammed the door shut behind him. He launched his keys and jacket against the wall, threw his helmet on the sofa, and collapsed against the breakfast bar of his loft. He'd been struggling to breathe properly since Peaches had walked away from him.

She'd walked away.

Christ, that had hurt.

When Carter had put his mouth to Peaches', he'd lost himself. She felt so good pressed against him and yet, he could do nothing but handle her as though she would fracture under his fingertips. He'd never kissed a woman that way before. He'd surprised himself at his own tenderness. The hunger for her that resided deep within him was desperate to take her wild and hard against the tree, but the moment they touched he knew there was no way he could do that to her. He beat the hunger back and held her as gently as he could.

Their lips had moved together so slowly and tentatively. But Carter had wanted more.

With her pulse thrumming under his fingertips, he'd kissed her with everything he had. But it wasn't enough. He wanted to feel more of her. He wanted her to touch him.

He'd fucked up. He shouldn't have kissed her. Peaches had even told him not to. But he'd done it regardless. He just didn't have the fight left in him anymore.

He knew, now that he had experienced the feel of Peaches on his lips, he had to have it again. And he knew that was an impossibility, just as she had told him. Nevertheless, Carter couldn't help but suspect her determined promise that it wouldn't or couldn't happen again was a carefully constructed front that hid her own desires for him. She'd kissed him back, for fuck's sake. She wanted it, too. Didn't she?

He rubbed his brow at the realization that the situation just wasn't on their side.

Carter wasn't stupid; he understood she had a lot more to lose than he did and that, should their kiss be found out, she could be in a whole heap of shit. But he didn't have to like it. His temper and selfish side started to escalate.

He thought back to what he'd said to her. *What-the-fuck-ever. Like I give a shit if it happens again.*

He was a lying son of a bitch.

The fact was her words had hurt. He'd been hurt before, by many people in his life, but Peaches seemed to know how to cut him to the quick. He wasn't so much of a dick that he couldn't admit it. She'd hurt him and he was pissed.

He glanced at the clock, a bitch of a headache starting in his temples. It was just before five, and he needed something to help him chill out and cut loose. He needed to stop thinking about Miss Lane, with her soft lips and peach-flavored tongue.

He pulled out his cell and found his contacts list. The line rang three times.

"Yo, Carter! How was your date—I mean, session?"

"Eat a dick, Max," Carter snarled, striding toward his bedroom.

"Whoa, such hostility! It didn't go well, I take it?"

Carter pulled his T-shirt over his head and dropped down onto the corner of his bed. "No. It didn't," he snapped. "Look, what have you got planned for tonight?"

"Not much. Why, you thinkin' of something?"

Carter ran a hand down his face. "I need to get shitfaced, and quick. Where can we go?"

Max laughed. "I know just the place, my man. Come to the body shop in an hour."

"I'll be there in thirty."

. . .

"Keep moving!" the stranger hissed from under his hood. "We have to get away from them. They'll kill you! Move!"

"I can't! My dad!"

The stranger didn't stop to listen. Gunfire filled the air. Kat screamed. She began running but was wrestled to the ground. He was heavy on top of her back and smelled of cigarettes.

The sidewalk was so cold.

"Stay here," he breathed into her hair as she wriggled beneath him. "You can't go back. He told you to run, for Christ's sake."

Kat shot up from her bed, gasping and hoarse from the scream that died slowly in her throat. Her face was wet, as were her clothes, from the sweat pouring from her.

She leaned against the headboard, taking in a huge lungful of air when she remembered she was in her bed. It had been a while since she'd had such a dream, yet the effects of it were just the same. With a groggy head, she lifted herself from her bed and made her way to the bathroom, knowing a bath would relax the muscles in her neck and back that were still tense.

After her long soak, and a good hour of tears, she pulled on a pair of sweats and a hoodie and put on the DVD of *School of Rock* for some light Jack Black entertainment. A knock at the door had her glancing at the clock, wondering who would turn up at her door past eight on a Saturday night.

Her heart thumped hard when she peered through the peephole. She unlocked the dead bolt and pulled the door open, leaning on it with her hip. She stayed silent for a moment, not knowing what to say.

"Can I come in?" Beth asked in a quiet but firm voice.

"Sure," Kat answered, standing back to allow her to enter.

Beth stepped in and stood awkwardly while Kat shut the door behind her.

"Can I get you a drink?" Kat tucked her air-dried hair behind her ears. Beth nodded.

Kat shuffled to the kitchen. Once Kat had poured Beth's drink and handed it to her, she walked, without a word, back toward the sofa and sat. Beth followed and sat at the far end of the couch, sipping her drink.

Kat placed the TV on pause as Jack Black started singing about straight As, then she turned to her friend. "How are you?"

Beth gave a small smile. "I'm okay." She placed her glass on a coaster on the coffee table. "How are you?"

Kat crossed her arms, feeling weirdly defensive. "I'm fine. Tired."

Beth clasped her hands in her lap. "Austin said you weren't well. That's why I came: to see if I could do anything for you."

Kat sighed, thinking about the text that she'd sent Austin, the lie she'd written to get out of going for drinks with him, unable to see him after the kiss with Carter. "I don't need anything." She saw an uncomfortable shift in her friend. "So where've you been? You haven't replied to any of my texts."

"I know," Beth conceded. "I'm sorry. There's been some family stuff Adam's been dealing with." Her eyes darted to a pile of Carter's work lying on Kat's coffee table.

"Is everything okay? You should have called." Kat blinked at the answering silence. "Have I upset you? You seem, I don't know . . . off. And that whole performance at my birthday dinner—I just . . . get the feeling something's wrong."

Beth moved closer to Kat on the sofa. She sighed and pressed her lips together. "No." She cleared her throat. "No, nothing's wrong, I— I just worry about you. You know, working at Kill and with Carter one-to-one outside of the prison. I wanted—I want—to make sure you're all right."

Kat stared at Beth for a beat, wondering what it was that she wasn't being told. Too tired to figure it out, she searched for the right words. "It's been a shitty day."

"You wanna talk about it?"

Kat barked out a laugh and shook her head while making a mumbled noise of words that made no sense. "Not really," she answered, her throat closing up again. "I'm just a stupid, stupid idiot."

Beth sat back. "Kat, what happened?" She paused before asking, "Did he hurt you?"

Kat's head snapped up. "What?" she asked incredulously. "Why would— Who?"

"Carter," Beth answered. "Did Carter hurt you? That's who you're talking about, right?"

The tears Kat had tried like hell to keep back dropped down her face. Her face scrunched up with despair and a sob broke from her throat.

"Oh God." Beth pulled Kat into her side. "I knew it. Shhh, it's okay. If he hurt you, we can send his ass back to Kill. Adam and Austin can—"

"No, Beth!" Kat sobbed. "I fucked up. Me." Beth stayed quiet. "He didn't hurt me. He would never hurt me."

Kat didn't know why, but she'd always known Carter would never do anything to cause her physical pain. She felt safe with him, even when he'd thrown a table across her classroom. There was something in his eyes, something in the way he moved around her, that made Kat feel secure and impervious to any danger.

She knew—deep in her soul—that he would protect her if she needed him to.

"Kat, what the hell happened?"

Kat sniffed. "He kissed me. And I kissed him back."

16

"Well, shave my ass and call me Priscilla! It's a motherfucking Kill reunion up in here!"

Riley's booming bass voice smacked Carter and Jack around the head like a baseball bat before his mammoth body launched from Carter's apartment doorway at the two of them and pulled them into a death squeeze.

"Oh, I'm so happy," Riley chimed sarcastically as Carter grumbled and pushed his oafish ass away.

"Dammit, dude," he said, stretching his back out of the concertina Riley had made of it. "Calm the hell down."

Riley smirked. "I see freedom hasn't chilled your uptight ass out any. I, on the other hand, have been free for forty-eight hours and everything is awesome!" He turned to Jack before Carter could respond. "How's it hanging, J?"

Jack chuckled and straightened his jacket. "I'm hanging fine, Riley. Good to see you. I'll see you on Thursday for our meeting." He slipped past him and waved. "We'll talk soon, Wesley."

Carter nodded and closed the door behind him while Riley sauntered into the apartment and looked around the place like a prospective buyer or some shit. Carter sighed.

"What can I do for you, Moore?"

Riley patted his enormous chest with his palms and smiled. "You got any beer? I'm about parched."

With two beers in hand, Riley dropped himself onto the couch while Carter fiddled with his cell phone, feeling disgruntled. It'd been two days since the kiss in Central Park, and he still hadn't heard from Peaches. Not that he'd expected to, but it didn't stop him from being fidgety as all hell. He had no idea what he was going to say to her when they met for their session.

"Am I keeping you from something?" Riley asked nonchalantly, sipping his beer.

Carter shook his head, threw his cell to the side, and lit a cigarette. "So how's it feel being out? Forty-eight hours? I'm surprised I've not seen your ass sooner."

Riley smiled. "You know me, Carter: places to see, people to do."

Carter laughed and raised his eyebrows in agreement.

"Not that you're not important to me or anything," Riley added with a wry wink. "But I had to get some shit organized."

Carter paused. "You getting involved with hot parts again?"

Riley frowned. "No. No, man. That was a mistake I will not be reliving. I just had a few deals to settle. Jack here for the usual?"

"Yeah," Carter replied. "Diane was here earlier. She'd have loved to have seen you." The two men snorted.

Riley and Diane hadn't always had the best relationship. To say that she didn't understand his foul-mouthed humor was an understatement.

"She wants me," Riley answered coolly as he sat back and kicked his feet up. "What can I say?"

"Of course she does." Carter chuckled but stopped abruptly when his cell beeped with an incoming text. Max. Dammit.

"That your new . . . female plaything?" Riley winked.

"No. It's not my new 'plaything,'" he barked before looking back at the cell screen.

"Okay, okay," Riley retorted before he lit his own smoke. "Chill yourself, asshole. It was only a question."

Carter exhaled and rubbed his forehead with his fingers. "I know . . . just . . . It's not like that."

"Things are going well with Miss Lane, I assume," Riley commented smoothly.

Carter extinguished his smoke and blew rings toward the ceiling. "Just swell" was his curt reply.

Riley hummed as though daydreaming. "Damn," he said in a low voice that he saved for seduction and all things nasty. "I do miss her tight ass in those pencil skirts." He licked his lips. "And those legs? I could have smooched on those bad boys for—"

"Shut the fuck up, Moore!" Carter bellowed. He snapped his arm up and pointed at Riley menacingly. "Watch your mouth about her."

Riley lasted all of three seconds with Carter's finger in his grill before his face creased into a smile the size of the Hoover Dam.

"Well, I'll be goddamned." He snickered with his hands up. "You and Miss L, huh? Nice."

Carter's arm dropped instantly and a groan of realization and frustration left him. He rubbed his palms down his face and mumbled into them.

"It's not like that, okay? I mean, I want it— I want her to . . . fuck." He snatched his beer from the table and fell back into his chair.

Riley chuckled and sat forward, resting his elbows on his knees. "Look, man, I'm not interested in the hows, whys, or what-the-fuck-ever. I'm just glad that I won the bet I had with myself."

Carter narrowed his eyes. "Bet?"

"Yeah, I bet myself how long it would take for you two to bone once you were out." He smacked his huge chest with both of his fists. "Guess I won, huh?"

Carter blinked in shock. "For Christ's sake, Moore. We haven't even— Shit, it's not about boning."

"Oh yeah, I know, but you get my drift." Riley smiled and put his smoke in the ashtray. "Hey, talking of fucking hot women, a few of us are going to hit a couple of bars tonight. You in?"

Carter shook his head. "Nah, man, I've got stuff to do."

Riley waggled his eyebrows. "Or someone . . ."

Despite himself, Carter couldn't help but laugh.

• • •

At the end of Kat's class at Kill the following Tuesday afternoon, she found herself walking toward Jack's office. Her feet and legs became sluggish, almost willing her not to keep going. But she had to. She needed answers and direction. And, truthfully, even with talking with Beth about her anguish from hurting Carter, there was no one else.

Gathering herself, she knocked lightly against the door.

"Come in."

Jack smiled when he saw Kat peer around the doorframe. "Miss Lane," he said, standing from his seat. "Good to see you. What can I do for you?"

Kat bit her lip and allowed her body to slide gradually into the room. She closed the door, grasping the handle as if her life depended on it.

Jack looked concerned. "Are you all right?"

Kat tried to smile back, to reassure him, but it fell flat. She cleared her throat and rubbed the back of her neck. "I need to ask you a hypothetical question," she muttered.

Jack frowned. "Hypothetical." Kat nodded. "Well," Jack continued, "I'll certainly do my best."

He gestured for Kat to take a seat before he sat back down and placed the papers he'd been reading back into a folder. Kat slinked over to a chair and sat down. This was hell. She fisted her hands in her lap and averted her eyes. She never behaved like this. She was usually so sure and steadfast.

"Miss Lane," Jack said, sitting forward. "Are you sure you're all right?"

"Yes," she rasped through a dry throat. "I was just— I was—"

"Did Carter do something wrong?"

Kat shook her head. No. Everything Carter had done had been oh so right.

"I saw him yesterday," Jack continued. "He seemed anxious about something. Wouldn't tell me what it was, of course—"

"Who do I speak to about quitting as his tutor?"

The words tumbled from her mouth with such speed, she was amazed they came out in the correct order. As the words settled around them, all she felt was pain. Not physically, but emotionally. She was angry at herself for asking the question she never thought she would. Her eyes became blurry, but she swallowed the tears. She'd done enough crying to last her a lifetime.

"Why would you want that?" Jack asked in a soft voice. "Are you sure he didn't do something?"

The smile that tugged at Kat's lips was weak but reassuring. "I'm sure," she murmured. "Who do I speak to and what are the procedures?"

"Kat," he said, "why do you want this?" He held his hand up when she started to jump in with an answer. "What I mean is if he hasn't done anything wrong, or violated the conditions of his parole, how are you going to justify quitting as his tutor?"

Kat closed her mouth, defeat skating down her neck.

"The fact is," Jack continued, "if you want to quit as his tutor—and you have every right to, if you so wish—you have to give just cause to the board."

"Really?" she asked in a voice that was quiet and beaten.

Jack rested his elbows on the desk. "It will cause questions, and I'm not sure you'd want to answer them."

Well. That was that.

"Kat, if I may?" Jack made to stand and gestured toward the chair at Kat's side.

"Sure," she replied, watching him come around his desk and sit down next to her.

"I don't want to upset you with what I want to say."

"It's okay, Jack. I'm willing to listen to just about anything right now."

Jack cleared his throat and fiddled with his tie clasp. "It's clear that you two are . . . fond of each other. But if you and Carter are involved in a relationship that is more than simply teacher/student, then I have to warn you. I have to tell you that, even with Carter on parole, you're still working for the prison, and, as such, you're contravening the teacher code of the facility, including the non-fraternization policy you agreed to and signed, as well as placing yourself at risk of prosecution."

Kat's face crumpled. That all sounded horrifically scary. "Jack, Carter and I aren't—"

"But," Jack interrupted with a hand on Kat's forearm, "if you aren't together until the probationary period of his parole is over, then there would be no problem."

Kat knew this already. She knew she'd have to wait until her contracted time with Carter was over before they could be together. If she wanted them to be together.

Was that what she wanted?

She wanted to see what was between them, of course; she couldn't deny that. But it was useless. The odds were stacked against them both.

"And to be totally clear," Jack said, "if you and Carter are together and nobody *knows* until the end of his probationary period, then there would be no problem."

Kat lifted her head. Was he being serious? She narrowed her eyes in an attempt to see through his bullshit but came up wanting. He was being totally serious.

"Are you saying that—"

"All I'm saying is that what people don't know can't hurt 'em."

Why was he willing to be discreet about her relationship with Carter? He had nothing to gain from it. "Why are you saying this?"

Jack squeezed her hand. "He needs you, Kat. Even if he hasn't truly realized it yet, he needs you."

She shook her head. "I can't do this."

Jack smiled. "Kat, you're the only person who *can*. You put him in his place, you don't take his bullshit, you've reached out to him in a way no one else ever has. Take your time, and try not to panic or worry. What more can you do?"

Kat thanked Jack for his time and understanding. She trusted him to keep what had been said between them. Despite the fears she had about her friends and family and their reactions toward her and Carter's relationship, it made her heart feel less heavy, knowing there were people who saw it as something positive.

She decided that she'd start to do the same.

17

Kat shifted in her seat while Carter read Hemingway in the library that afternoon. He was sitting with his ankle resting on his knee. Black jeans, boots, gray AC/DC T-shirt, tattoos, rings, and a black beanie covering his buzz cut.

Their greetings at the beginning of the session had been torturous at best, with Kat wanting nothing more than to hightail it home and lose herself in a couple of stiff drinks. Never had she felt more chaotic, more off balance. Her mind whirred unrelentingly with question after question, punctuated with words from her conversation with Jack and her talk with Beth, before it would go back to the kiss.

Oh God, the kiss.

Throughout their session, her gaze landed unapologetically on Carter's mouth. She cleared her throat when he glanced up at her, as if sensing her staring, and halted in his reading. Her cheeks warmed. She averted her eyes back to the page.

Carter frowned before he continued: "'I had treated seeing Catherine very lightly, I had gotten somewhat drunk and had nearly forgotten to come, but when I could not see her there I was feeling lonely and hollow.'"

"Okay, stop there." Kat laid her copy of the text facedown on the desk between them, alongside the Oreos and can of Coke Carter had brought. "In regard to the last few pages, what do you notice about the change in Henry's attitude toward Catherine?"

Carter fidgeted and his fingers became wedged under the edge of his beanie while he scratched his head. His eyes flickered to hers nervously.

"He's, um, he's confused by his feelings." He picked up his can of Coke and took a long sip.

"How do you know that?" She watched his Adam's apple dip and rise in his throat.

"Because he misses her, you know, when, um, when she's not there."

His eyes met Kat's for a split second, but that was enough time to send a burning-hot dagger of desire straight through her center.

"How do you know he's confused?"

Carter smiled with the right corner of his mouth. A knowing look shimmered across his high cheekbones. "A hunch." He looked at the text. He scratched at his jaw. "He's . . . 'hollow.' He's empty without her."

His blue gaze lifted from Hemingway's words. What Kat saw there made her heart almost stop.

Usually, when Carter's eyes were on her, Kat saw raw sex and desire. It always tinged his irises, making them a cloudless blue. That was still there, but more prevalent than that was a remorseful haze surrounding every inch of his pupils. It was so clear, Kat knew without his saying a word how he was feeling. He was sorry. And she felt the exact same way.

She had no idea how long they sat—looking at each other, lost in each other—and only returned to where she was when Carter touched her. His palm was warm and comfortable on the back of her hand, and the hot fizz of energy that was always present between them breathed a sigh of relief.

It seemed like forever since he'd touched her.

Carter edged forward. "Peaches," he said, allowing his thumb to smooth its way across her skin. He kept his eyes on the table where their hands joined. His hands felt so good. Fleetingly, her mind began to imagine how they would feel on other parts of her.

Her attraction to Carter was slowly turning into something more, something scary and irrevocable. She was tired of denying it, of course, but she still had to tread a careful path.

Carter's hand squeezed hers. "About Saturday—"

"It's fine."

"No," he retorted firmly. "It's not. It was— I mean, yeah, the kiss was . . ." He raised his eyebrows. "Look, whatever you think of me, I didn't kiss you to be a dick. Honestly."

"I know, I—"

"The thing is." He paused, his brows almost meeting in the middle. "The thing is, I might not have flowery fucking words or anything, but I'm . . . I'm serious about you."

Dizziness accosted Kat, making her grip on Carter's hand tighten.

"I know it's not the perfect situation." He pointed to himself. "I'm just a . . . and you're . . . but, fuck, I'm happy to have anything you're willing to give me at this point. Just sitting here with you would be enough."

The sincerity of his words made Kat want to fall into his arms and never leave them. Unable to articulate how hard her heart was beating, she simply uttered, "Okay."

Carter appeared satisfied with her answer. "Okay?"

She smiled.

"Are we good?" he asked quietly, watching her carefully.

Kat cleared her throat. "We're good."

Carter exhaled, seemingly torn. "I'm glad, but I need you to understand something, Peaches." He licked his lips. "I'm not sorry, and I'd do it again in a fucking heartbeat."

Oh God.

Realizing she was staring and barely breathing, Kat dragged her eyes from Carter and quickly pulled a folder full of papers from her bag. Change the subject. Change the subject . . .

"Do you want these now?" She placed them on the table.

Carter scowled. "And what are 'these'?" He slid the folder toward himself.

"Your resources for next week."

Carter blinked, confused.

"I'm going away," Kat clarified. "With my family, to Washington, DC." She let her fingertips dance along the edging of the table. "It's the anniversary of my father's . . . We do it every year. I'll be out of town from Sunday to Sunday."

Carter's face changed imperceptibly. He didn't look happy. After scratching the back of his neck, he slid his hands into his pockets. "Um, yeah, okay." The frown was tight above the bridge of his nose.

"Just do what you can," Kat encouraged. "I've assigned you some more reading and questions, and we need to talk about an assessment paper . . ."

She trailed off when Carter's dark, somber gaze met hers.

"Text me," she said without thinking. "Or call me if you need any help. Don't hesitate. I— Yeah, just, just call me."

"I will."

Kat tried to smile but it was harder work than she expected. Leaving to be with her family at this time of the year was one thing; leaving Carter for a whole week was another. She was suddenly very hollow indeed.

• • •

Carter was edgy: edgy and fucking miserable, to be quite honest, despite it being Saturday night.

He took a huge gulp from the fifth bottle of Corona placed in his hand by Max and rubbed a finger along his eyebrow. Seriously, seven days. How hard could it be? He only saw his Peaches three times a week anyway, so technically it was only six hours he'd be missing.

Big. Deal.

He sighed. Yeah, it *was* a big deal. They'd had their last session a day ago and already he could feel an uncomfortable sensation of wanting and emptiness curl within his stomach at the thought of not seeing her.

Dammit.

Paul, Max's head mechanic from the body shop, knocked Carter's elbow, which was resting on the bar.

"What's up?" he asked above the music. "You look like someone pissed on Kala."

Carter stood from his hunched position. "Nothin'. I'm good."

"Don't lie," Paul smirked. "You hate this club, don't you? It's all right to admit it to me. Max loves it, but I don't see the appeal."

Two statuesque blondes sauntered past, causing the two men to stare at their minimal clothing and flirtatious smiles.

Carter chuckled. He clinked his bottle against Paul's. "Where is Max?" he asked, narrowing his eyes toward the dance floor in the hopes of spotting his friend.

"Outside having a smoke," he replied with a wave of his hand. "With his new friend Laura. He's shitfaced already, high as a damned kite, yammering on about some deal he's doing tonight."

Carter rolled his eyes in frustration. From the snippets he'd heard from the other boys at the shop, since Lizzie had left, Max had lost himself in many women. As much as Max played that he was okay and lived for bedding the females he did, Carter knew he was simply trying to fuck the pain away. With the amount of coke Max was doing, it was clear that the one-night stands weren't working. Asshole was on a slippery slope.

"He needs to get out of that shit," Carter muttered.

"No doubt," Paul agreed. "But he's not going to listen to either of us, you know that. He's in too deep. When that bitch left, she took the best parts of him with her."

Carter knew that Max had hit the blow hard as soon as she'd left. It had been so difficult for Carter stuck in Kill, unable to be there for his friend. "Was it really bad?"

Paul sighed. "Yeah. Tried to act as if he wasn't dying on the inside after losing his woman so soon after losing the baby. Pretended he was all right while he shoved that shit up his nose." Paul sipped from his beer. "I'm just waiting for something to happen, for shit to hit the fan and—"

"I won't let anything happen," Carter snapped.

Paul smiled knowingly. "I know, man." He clapped Carter's shoulder. "I know. But you and I can't always be there for him. He's a grown man and a law unto himself. I worry."

Carter knew what Paul meant. Despite their friendship of nearly twenty years, Max would do what he wanted, no matter the consequences. His stubbornness was what the two men argued about most. His best friend was broken, that shit was clear as day, but Carter had no idea how to fix him, or even if he could.

Carter and Paul stood watching the dance floor writhe and bounce. "Sidebar: it's about time we found you a woman, Carter." Paul nodded toward a group of women grinding and dipping to the beat.

"Come on, man." Carter sighed. "I don't need a woman."

"Why?"

"Because women are hard work and fucking trouble. I have enough of that with Max."

Besides, he didn't want just any woman. He wanted one very specific woman.

Laughing in agreement, Paul set down another two drinks on the bar. Carter grabbed eagerly at the Jack and Coke and took half of that shit down in one. Yep. That was what he needed. He needed to stop thinking about his Peaches and nut up. He needed to stop obsessing, worrying, fantasizing—

Carter paused with the glass at his lips and blinked twice. Jesus. Was he hallucinating now? He almost broke his neck trying to see—over and around the writhing rhythmic bodies—the auburn-haired woman dancing about thirty feet away from him.

Holy. Mother. Of. God.

It was Peaches.

And fuck him running if she wasn't wearing the sexiest dress he'd ever seen. It was black and silk and dipped so low at the back he could almost see the dimples above her ass. Shit. And a bare back meant only one thing.

No bra.

His cock, immediately hard, started biting through the buttons on his fly to get at her, while his heart thumped like a damn hammer. Her body moved like water: graceful and flowing effortlessly. Her hair was up in a twist that was sexy and elegant and the heels she wore would have looked amazing . . . on Carter's shoulders.

He swallowed and smiled as she dipped and mimed the words to the song. Her hands moved against her hips, causing jealousy to burst through Carter's body. It should have been his hands, his fingers gripping her tightly. He managed to drag his eyes from her to see she was ostensibly dancing with a small blonde girl who was wrapped around some dude with a mohawk. She was cute, but Peaches was sex. No, scratch that. More like hot, raw, up-against-the-wall fucking, and Carter immediately wanted all over that shit.

And apparently so did the guy standing five feet to Peaches' left.

A growl built somewhere deep and dark within Carter's chest and his hands balled into fists when the asswipe walked toward her, fiddling with his hair as he did.

Before he could consider his actions, Carter was pushing away from the bar, leaving Paul shouting at his back. He shoved his way through the crowd toward Peaches and the prick who clearly didn't like his head on his goddamn shoulders. Carter had never been so protective about anything in his life, and the adrenaline that coursed through him was a thing of beauty.

Just as the jerkoff reached out for Peaches' waist, Carter grabbed his arm and twisted it. Hard. Prick stumbled as Carter pushed him backward. Carter leaned in closely to his ear to make sure he heard every word.

"You do not fucking touch. You do? I'll rip your arm from the socket. *Capisce?*"

Prick didn't even argue. Carter released him and mouthed: *Fuck off.* He didn't need to be told twice. Carter exhaled his growl as the douchebag slunk off into the depths of the crowd, before he turned toward Peaches. Luckily, she hadn't noticed the exchange, or him, which was perfect.

He moved behind her and lifted his hands.

The blonde Peaches was with noticed his move. Her face was a picture as she took Carter in from head to feet, intrigued and lascivious, but Carter couldn't have given a shit. All he cared about was touching the delicious creature in front of him.

Peaches, sensing someone behind her, made to spin around. Carter grabbed the tops of her arms, holding her in position—her back against his chest—and put his mouth to her ear at the same time the opening bars of Blackstreet and Dr. Dre's "No Diggity" began to blast around the club. He moved his nose closer. She smelled incredible.

"Do you know what you're doing to every man in this club, Peaches?"

Her body stiffened in his hands. He loosened his grip and let his palms slide down to the crooks of her elbows. He smiled when he saw gooseflesh pop up all over her and pulled her back against him.

"Do you know what you're doing to *me*?"

His hands moved farther down, over her soft forearms, to her wrists and then to her hands. Carter waited for her to tell him to stop, praying to everything that was holy that she wouldn't. Instead, she turned her head toward his so her nose grazed the right side of his jaw.

"What do I do to you, Carter?" she purred, twisting her fingers in between his and squeezing his hands against her stomach.

"You make me want to commit murder against every man who's looking at you and thinking about touching you."

She moaned and he saw the twists of a smile on her lips. Her plump, glossy lips.

"Are you jealous, Carter?" She moved her hips, oh so slowly, against him.

He pushed back and that time he heard a gasp when his cock pressed against her luscious ass.

"So jealous." Moving his nose farther into her hair, he lost himself to the awesome scent of sweet, juicy peaches. "Can you feel it?" He pushed against her again and moaned deep in his throat when she rotated her hips in reply.

He released her hands but kept his palms flat against her silk-covered stomach. He edged them outward until he came to her hips. As he'd imagined, they fit perfectly in his large hands. He clutched on to them, holding her against him, and dipped to the music. Carter couldn't hold back his groan when she started dancing, pressing herself into him, and leaning her head to his so they were nose to cheek.

Peaches' hands found his. She grasped them and began to move a little faster.

"What are you doing?"

"I'm dancing with you, Carter. Why? What does it feel like?"

"It feels fucking perfect." His hands moved up her sides so that his thumbs were brushing the undersides of her breasts.

What he would give to feel them. To feel her nipples tightening under his fingertips. To have his mouth on them. To taste the skin all over her body. He ground his hips into her again and placed a soft kiss on her shoulder. Her response was to lean her head back and curl her arms upward, behind his neck.

Carter groaned into her skin when her nails moved up to his scalp. Their bodies moved together from side to side. Peaches' ass was placed perfectly in his crotch while he moved his hands lazily up and down the sides of her body. When his palms reached the edge of her dress on her thighs, he was bold enough to let his fingertips dance across her soft skin. Her nails bit into his head. She moaned.

"I want you," he murmured into her ear, before placing another kiss in the hollow behind her ear. "God help me, I don't care if it's against the rules. I want you so fucking much."

She turned her head, looking him straight in the eye, and smiled like a vixen. "I want you, too."

Carter spun her around, grasped her hand, and pulled her toward a dark corner of the club. He pushed her against the wall, nose to nose, his hands at either side of her head. "Say it again," he demanded.

"What?" she asked, her eyes large and glazed with alcohol.

"Tell me that you want me," he ordered. "I need to hear that. You have no fucking idea."

"I want you."

Before she could say another word, Carter grabbed her face and crushed his mouth to hers, letting the delicious burn of her confession seep into his bones, into his soul. Her hands were immediately on his neck, tugging and pulling him closer while their tongues were pushing from his mouth to hers. She tasted incredible. Jesus, he'd almost forgotten how good she felt. He ground into her like a prick, but, shit, he couldn't help it. He needed friction against her. He wanted inside her.

The kiss was hot, hungry, and wet.

He pushed and she pushed back, blazing his body with desire fierce enough to leave him breathless. And her scent? Fuck. Her scent dazed Carter in such a way that he almost didn't hear his name being called.

Three times.

He pulled back, placing gentle kisses along her jawline. "What, baby?" he groaned against Peaches' lips.

"It wasn't me," she said, turning her head toward where the voice had originated.

Confused, Carter turned to see Paul standing there, looking all sorts of chaotic.

"What?" Carter snarled, shielding the woman in his arms.

"I'm sorry, man," Paul stuttered. "It's Max. He left. I couldn't stop him. He was muttering something about that deal and some guys followed him out and— I don't know, but they looked like they meant business."

Carter's heart dropped. His mouth went dry. "I'll— Shit. Give me a minute."

Paul nodded sharply and left.

Carter let go of Peaches' waist and slammed a palm against the wall. "Fuck!"

Peaches grabbed his face. "Hey. If he needs you, go." Her eyes were soft but demanded no bullshit.

He dropped his forehead to hers. "But I need you." He'd never said anything more honest.

She smiled against his cheek. "I know, but—"

Carter pressed his lips to hers. "No buts," he mumbled. "For the love of God, please no buts."

She laughed and rubbed her hand down the side of his face. The comfort he took from her touch was indescribable. "What I was going to say was it would be impossible to do anything tonight."

Carter was crushed.

"I leave in the morning, and you have a friend to look after. Tonight is not the night."

He knew she was right. He knew Max needed him. He knew taking Peaches home and fucking her seven ways from Sunday was not the way he should go. But couldn't they catch a break?

"Will you—will I hear from you next week?" he asked, not giving a fuck that he sounded needy.

"Sure." Her eyes roamed his face, as though memorizing him before their time apart. He liked it. "I think we need to have a long talk."

Her words made Carter cold. "Okay," he conceded and then groaned in frustration. "I gotta go. I'm sorry."

"Go," she said with a soft smile. "I'll see you soon."

Without a pause, his mouth met hers again, nipping and sucking desperately at her lips. He pushed from the wall.

"Be careful," he ordered with a pointed finger. "Text me when you get home tonight."

Peaches laughed and saluted him.

"I mean it," he said, no hint of playing in his voice.

Her smile dropped. "I will. I promise. Go and look after Max."

18

Carter heard Max before he saw him. The idiot was shouting something about leaving him the fuck alone. There was scuffling and a yelp. Carter strode into Max's sitting room, past a furious-looking Paul, to find Max draped across his couch, looking three sheets to the wind, with a busted nose and a right eye that was closing up nicely.

"Fuck's sake," Carter muttered.

"Carter!" Max called with a wide, blitzed, drunken smile. "Check this out!" He proceeded to lift his shirt to show several large bruises and a cut along his rib.

Carter's head snapped toward Paul and Cam, the latter of whom was sitting in a corner of the room with a joint in his hand and a whore on his lap. "Where the fuck were you when all this went down?"

Paul held his hands up and shook his head. "Don't bring it here, man," he warned. "The idiot left us, told us to stay where we were. I did my best!"

"No doubt," Carter conceded. "Were the cops involved?"

Paul shook his head. "The fuckers hauled ass before they made an entrance."

Carter walked over to Max, who had shut up and mellowed while he watched his friend Al spark a smoke and hand it to him. Max moaned when he inhaled and blew out the smoke but flinched and grimaced when he tried to move. The bastards had sure given him a beating.

"How many were there?" Carter asked Paul.

"I don't know," he replied. "There were two when I got there, but there could have been more."

Yeah, no shit. Max looked like he'd been set upon by the entire National Guard.

Laura, Max's latest toy, still in her club outfit, appeared from the kitchen with a bowl of water and a towel. She gave Carter a tight smile before she kneeled at Max's side and began trying to clean him up. "Trying" being the operative word, as Max swatted her away while mumbling expletives.

"Stop it, O'Hare," she snapped, "before I put you on your ass for real!"

Max grinned at her, cigarette dangling from his bloodied lips, and winked with his good eye. "You know you make me hard when ya talk that way."

Laura rolled her eyes and continued to dab at Max's mangled face.

"We need to get your dumb ass to the hospital," Carter said. Laura unfastened Max's shirt and the full extent of what had been done to him could be seen by all. Carter's teeth clenched when Max jumped as Laura ran the towel across his ribs.

"I'm fine," Max answered. "Besides, the hospital asks questions."

"Max," Carter argued. "If we just take—"

"I'm not going," Max said in a tone that demanded compliance. "The docs will call the fuzz. I don't need them on my case. Not that they'd find shit. The fuckers took my coke."

Carter ran a hand across his jaw and exhaled in frustration. "How much?"

"Enough." Max eyed him curiously. "I thought you were at the bar. Paul said something about you disappearing."

Carter avoided Max's stare and grabbed for the cigarettes in his back pocket. "Yeah," he muttered. "I went for a walk."

Max snorted and winced all at the same time. "A walk, huh? And what's her name?"

Ignoring his question, Carter opened his lighter. He shook his head, watching Max flail when Laura tried to put an ice pack on his face. "The fuck were you thinking?"

"Don't worry," Max soothed with a drunken wave of his hand. "I'll get that coke back. I swear to God, I will. You've got my back, right?"

Carter sighed and took a long pull from his smoke. "Sure, Max."

He lifted from his seat and pulled his cell from his jeans pocket when he felt it vibrate: a text. Peaches.

I'm home and fine.

Carter smiled. He allowed his index finger to linger along his bottom lip, remembering the feel of her mouth on his, and the sensation of having her in his arms. He knew there were parts of himself—unknown, unexplored, and dormant parts—that whispered certain words in an attempt to label what it was he was feeling for her. So far, he'd dismissed them swiftly and fervently and simply continued to lust after her body and mind. He didn't want a goddamn label, he just wanted his Peaches in as many ways as she would allow.

He glanced at his bruised friend, fighting the ball of unease and anxiety that swelled in his stomach at the thought of being arrested because of Max's stupidity. At this rate, Carter would be back in Kill before Christmas.

The text message from his girl shone bright and clear. He thought of the feel of her under his hands, the way her body moved against his, the promises they made.

No, Carter thought. He couldn't allow himself to be put back inside. He would not lose his Peaches.

• • •

The skies in DC were gray and stormy, the weather as gloomy as the faces of the two women walking through the vast graveyard. Kat walked slowly with her mother's arm tucked through her own while they ambled to the headstone that had changed very little in sixteen years. Her mother tightened her hold when the plot came into view.

Kat clasped her palm over her mother's. "You okay?"

Eva nodded. "Seeing it again after so long is always the hardest part." They walked across the path, closer to the grave. Kat always allowed her mother to speak first and, as Eva placed a deep red rose against the black marble, Kat turned away and left her to her private moment.

Wandering slowly down the path, Kat allowed her mind to travel back to New York.

Saturday had been a complete shock—her neighbor's bachelorette party taking an unexpected but very exciting turn. A rush of warmth dissolved in her stomach when she remembered the sensation of Carter dancing, grinding, and touching her.

Words spoken and texts sent since the night in the club only confirmed that Kat wanted Carter in ways she'd been fighting since the day they met. She wanted to be with him. He was stripping her bare of everything she'd ever known, and she had to admit she liked it. It was scary, exhilarating, and dangerous, but she was eager to do what she could to be with him in any way possible.

The lines initially drawn between the two of them were now smudges, merging into the ground at Kat's feet. Now more than ever, she was prepared to cross them, knowing deep within her heart that Carter would be waiting for her on the other side.

Streaks of soft tear lines were visible down Eva's cheeks when Kat arrived back at her side.

"Are you all right?"

A look of contentment surrounded Eva's eyes. "I am now," she replied, walking away. "Take your time, Katherine."

Kat looked at the gold lettering on the marble stating the date of his death. It seemed like only yesterday. She pulled her coat closer around herself and crouched down so she was eye level with his name.

"Hey, Daddy," she whispered. "I'm sorry it's been so long since my last visit. Life's pretty crazy." She smiled, mapping the *D* of his name with her index finger. "Work is good; my students are great." She laughed lightly, proudly. "They really listen to me now, and it feels like I'm making a difference. Daddy, I . . ." Lifting her face toward the angry sky, she closed her eyes. "I think about what you said to me that night all the time, about making a difference, about giving back. And I need you to know that I'm trying so hard to do right by you." She took a deep breath. "I wanted to tell you that I—I have feelings for . . . someone and I'm scared you'll think badly of me." Kat peered at her mother. "I know Mom will."

Like a flipbook in her mind, Kat recalled all the comments and harsh looks her mother had sent over the past few months, every time her job was mentioned. "She doesn't understand why I do what I do, and sometimes . . . sometimes, it makes me feel pulled. Trapped, as if I'm trying to do right by both of you, when I know I should be doing right for myself. That's what you taught me, and . . . he makes me feel right. He's made some mistakes, like we all have, but . . ." Kat's hand gripped the top of the marble.

"But you have to know that he's a good man. He's taken some wrong turns in life and he can drive me absolutely crazy, but there is good there. I just know it." Seeing her grandmother's grave at the side of her father's, she smiled.

"I know that wherever you are, you're happy and looking out for me. I feel it in my heart every day." Tears fell down her face. "I love you so much, Daddy, and I miss you. Please understand how I feel. I could fall so hard for him."

As the words left Kat's mouth—for one split second—the wind disappeared and the clouds parted above her, allowing a sliver of sun to shine through. The momentary warmth hit her back, making her body relax. And as she blinked at the sun she knew, deep in her soul, that her father had given her and Carter his blessing.

• • •

The plane ride from DC to Chicago had been comfortable and Kat smiled when Harrison met them at the airport terminal. Eva hugged him hard while he whispered lovingly into her hair. Kat had always been grateful for the infinite understanding that Harrison seemed to show in regard to her mother's grief for her late husband. He seemed to know what she needed and when and never sounded wounded when she made the annual trip to Daniel's graveside. Harrison and her father had been good friends for many years when he passed, and, although Kat's mother had fought it, the two of them together made complete sense. Watching the two of them get reacquainted after three days apart, with kisses and small smiles, caused a small tug of yearning to occur in Kat's chest. She wrapped her own arms around herself, trying to fool her body into thinking they belonged to a blue-eyed ex-con.

It didn't work.

Harrison had arrived in Chicago the day before and had hired a car that the three of them piled into. Eva's mother, whom Kat lovingly referred to as Nana Boo, always arranged a get-together at this time of year at her sprawling estate on the outskirts of Chicago. It was, she said, a way of celebrating the life of a man who had brought her daughter so much happiness, as well as a beautiful granddaughter.

As they drove through the city and out into the country, Kat pulled out her cell phone. It had been a few days since she'd heard from Carter. She couldn't deny that she was missing him. A text from Austin came through as soon as she turned her cell phone back on.

Hope you enjoy Chicago. Text me to let me know you're there safely. Sorry I couldn't make it.

She swallowed in resignation. Beth had thought it a nice idea to invite Austin to Chicago for the celebration. Kat hadn't been convinced, and had been relieved when Austin had had to cancel because of work. Texting excuses that got her out of drinks and dinner with him was one thing. Seeing him face-to-face? She'd have much preferred Carter there. She glanced at her mother and imagined the shitstorm his presence would cause. She exhaled heavily and began to type out a text.

Just wanted to make sure you weren't finding the work too hard.

She scoffed inwardly, knowing without doubt that Carter would be able to complete the work tied to a chair and blindfolded. Kat's cheeks immediately warmed as that image flashed behind her eyelids; only, in this fantasy, he was naked. Her cell vibrated against her thigh. Kat's heart responded by doing a weird flip-flop staccato beat.

I'm good. The work is fine. Boring doing it alone tho. Missing me, huh?

Kat smiled and shook her head at his arrogance. The fact that he was right was irrelevant.

Oh yes, Carter, missing you enormously (sarcasm) Just arrived in Chicago.

Thought you were in DC? You're missing me. I can tell.

Kat snorted, garnering a curious look from her mother. "Who are you texting?" she asked. "Is it Austin?"

Kat's smile disappeared. "Um, no. It's just a friend."

Eva nodded, still doubtful. "Well, I hope it's not those . . .

people from that prison, or that creature you spend time with in the library. I still can't believe they allowed you to be alone with him when he's so dangero—"

"Mom."

Her mother sighed. "They should know to leave you alone this week."

We were in DC for three days. Visiting my grandmother in Chicago. You may deny it, but I know you miss me hugely.

I miss you. There. Happy?

The ferocious speed of Kat's pulse would say most definitely. She smiled wide, biting down on her lower lip.

It's okay, Carter. I miss you, too.

I can still taste you on my tongue.

A moan slipped from Kat's throat. The soft, teasing throb in her core became a furious pounding. The man was relentless. Kat allowed her mind to meander to dark, naughty places where she and Carter could do things she'd only ever read about.

Kat was no shrinking violet. She'd had four lovers with whom she'd enjoyed some decent sex. Nonetheless, whenever she thought about sex or variations of the act with Carter, Kat couldn't help but think that he would blast her past sexual experiences out of the water. He was so commanding and passionate that Kat had no doubt he would be the exact same way in the bedroom.

She wanted him to command her, claim her, fuck her—

She placed a hand over her mouth, surprised by her shamelessly indecent thoughts.

Carter wanted her; he'd told her so. But was that all? Was it just about a hot, passionate fuck to him? Kat was desperate to find out.

Law of averages suggested that men like Carter weren't relationship material and were more than likely to run in the opposite direction at the sound of the word "monogamy."

Kat blinked at her reflection in the window of the Lexus.

Was she truly thinking about a relationship with Carter?

As in, like, long-term?

Yes. Yes, she was.

Can I call you tomorrow, Carter?

Anytime.

"We're here, Katherine." Eva's voice broke into Kat's daydream, and she looked up to see that, sure enough, they were parked on the stone drive of Nana Boo's estate.

The house was as beautiful and imposing as Kat remembered. A wide smile pulled her face when the huge oak front door opened, and Nana Boo appeared with her black-and-white dog, Reggie, pushing to get past her. Jumping from the car, Kat slapped her thighs and whistled. Reggie dashed toward her, barking happily and wagging his tail like a damn whip. He jumped up, tongue slobbering.

"Reggie!" Nana Boo chided. "Get down!"

The dog immediately obeyed with a sheepish glance toward his mistress. Kat laughed and hurried over to her grandmother, who threw her arms around her, squeezing tightly. She smelled of peppermint and lavender.

"Oh, my darling girl," Nana said softly. Kat clutched tighter at her grandmother's words.

Small, wrinkled hands cupped Kat's face. Her grandmother's sparkling green eyes emitted nothing but love and warmth, and Kat was instantly calmer, reassured. Nana Boo always had a way of making her feel better. It was a grandmother's gift.

Eva hugged her mother hard before they all made their way into the house.

Nana Boo had organized food and drinks to be served the following evening for the thirty or so people invited. Ben would be there, along with his wife, Abby, and his mother and father, colleagues of her father and numerous members of several charities Kat's father had contributed to or supported, as well as Beth and Adam.

Kat continued to suspect there was still something going on with her best friend and, despite Beth's words to the contrary, a part of her worried she herself had done something very wrong to upset her.

She lifted her bags onto the bed of her childhood room and tried to ignore the uneasy foreboding sensation lurching in her stomach.

19

The following afternoon, the house was filled. Serving staff offered entrees and champagne while Kat watched her mother float effortlessly from one person to the next, her smile fixed and her manner easy. Having grown up in a political family and been married to one of the youngest senators in the country, Eva could work a room with the best of them.

Ben, Abby, Beth, and Adam had arrived to a whirlwind of kisses and hugs from her and Nana Boo. As Kat watched them all exchange pleasantries, she was struck with how familiar Beth and her mother had seemingly become. She'd noticed it during her birthday dinner, but now, seeing the two women embrace and talk quietly, it appeared that, somewhere along the line, they'd become friends.

"How are you?" Kat asked, kissing Beth on the cheek.

"Good," Beth said as she glanced at her fiancé, who was looking decidedly uncomfortable. "And you? Any news?"

"Nothing exciting." Kat toed the floor, her face heating under the scrutiny of her friend.

"Something you wanna share?" Beth inquired with a tilt of her head.

"Not right now," Kat said firmly, but followed it with a small smile, trying like hell to take the defensiveness out of her tone. She wasn't sure it worked. She so wanted to share with Beth, with all of them. But something—something that made her turn cold—stopped her.

Nana Boo was the only person she trusted implicitly with her true feelings for Carter. The quiet and covert conversation with her grandmother the previous night when Eva and Harrison had gone to bed had been wholly different from the ones with her mother and Beth. It had been easy, open, and filled with laughter. Nana regaled Kat with the latest gossip from the bridge club and the handsome new guy, Roger, who was her new golfing partner.

"He's rough and ready," Nana had explained with a laugh. "Which I like."

Kat had curled up on the sofa with a chamomile tea and let herself get swept away by the soft tones and gentle words of her grandmother. She loved how Nana Boo knew what to say to make her smile, and the enthusiasm that the old lady exuded started to chase away the dark anxiety that had resided in Kat since the trip began. Kat heard herself laugh, and her smile was entirely genuine as Nana detailed her distaste for the new lady who had joined her salsa class.

"A floozy, darling, plain and simple" was her no-holds-barred description of the newly widowed Ms. Harper. "So," Nana Boo had said, smiling. "What's new with you? I've missed you."

Kat had sighed and plucked at a loose cotton thread at the bottom of her sweatpants. "I've missed you, too, Nana," she'd confessed. "I'm . . . I'm all right. Busy."

Nana had hummed and sighed gently. "Kat, I know when my only granddaughter is not herself."

Kat had laughed without humor and wrapped her free arm around herself. "It's complicated."

"What aspects of life aren't?" Nana had asked with a smile. "Darling, I love you very much, and I want to help if I can."

"Thank you."

"I know your mother worries, Kat. It's her prerogative."

"I know," Kat had answered with an exasperated sigh. "But she worries too much. I'm an adult, Nana. I can make my own decisions. I can look after myself."

"I don't doubt that, my darling. You were always so strong. So like your father."

"And stubborn like my mother?" Kat had asked wryly.

Nana Boo had laughed. "Without a doubt." She'd been silent for a beat. "I know your job causes your mother great concern, but I am so very proud of you. I hope you know that you can talk to me about anything. You have my absolute confidence, angel."

Kat had closed her eyes and leaned her head back against the sofa, knowing the truth of her words. "I . . . I'm . . ." Kat had clapped a warm palm to her forehead in an effort to ease the throbbing persisting at the backs of her eyes. "God, I wouldn't even know where to start."

"Start at the beginning," Nana Boo had encouraged.

So Kat had. Nana had been excited to learn about Arthur Kill and Kat's study sessions with Carter. She'd been surprised, to say the very least, when she heard about the man who was slowly stealing his way into Kat's heart, but, being an old romantic, Nana Boo had promised to be there for her every step of the way—going so far as to invite them both to Chicago for Thanksgiving.

"I want to meet the man who has brought that smile back to your face," Nana Boo had said tearfully.

Kat wasn't sure that she and Carter were anywhere near the meeting-the-family stage quite yet, but she'd offered to think about it. She couldn't begin to express how much her Nana's support and confidence meant to her. Words just didn't seem adequate.

"Just promise me that you'll try to talk to your mother, Kat," she had said. "You don't need to tell her everything, just try."

"I promise," Kat had conceded.

But when she'd brought up the subject of her job in conversation that morning, Kat had been met with huffs and tapping fingers. Eva interjected continuously with disagreeable and venomous comments. Her tone had been condescending and dismissive at best and Kat's patience had begun to dwindle even further. Something was about ready to give. Kat was sick of the whole it's-oh-so-dangerous spiel. Just once she'd like to be treated like an adult. She wanted understanding, not judgment.

As the celebrations continued, the bland, polite conversation began in earnest among Beth, Adam, and Eva, while Kat stayed at the side of the room, smiling politely at those who approached and spoke so respectfully of her father. As much as she wanted to be sociable, Kat couldn't find it in herself. The inexplicable distance between her and Beth, mixed with the exasperated glances from her mother, made her heart ache.

"—outside the prison with that cretin, Carter." Eva spat Carter's name as if it were a dirty word, pricking Kat's ears and dragging her from her safe spot by the wall into the conversation.

"Mom, he's not—" Kat began, but stopped when three sets of disapproving eyes landed on her.

The heaviness in her stomach began to spread and she wondered why, when surrounded by her family and friends, she felt so alone. Carter's voice was all she wanted to hear. She needed to talk to him and take comfort in his no-bullshit honesty, to be assured that the risks she was willing to take with him would be worth it.

"Never mind," she muttered before excusing herself and hurrying up the stairs to the bathroom, with Reggie close on her heels. Leaving the dog in the hallway, Kat closed the door and leaned her forehead against it.

Jesus, it was like being suffocated. She wanted her father. She wanted to see his face, hear his calm, patient voice, and smell his warm, deep cherry scent. He'd know what to say to make it right. He always did. Either that or he would squeeze her to his chest so hard she would forget what she was so upset about in the first place.

The tears threatened to spill, but it wasn't the time.

Going to the messages on her cell, she typed a quick one to Carter. Kat's thumbs flew over the screen.

Are you busy? Wanna talk?

The knock at the door of the bathroom coincided with Kat's thumb pressing the send button. Opening the door slowly, she wasn't surprised to see Beth standing on the other side.

"Hey."

"Hey," Beth replied. "You all right?"

No more bullshit. Cards on the table. "No."

Beth's eyes dropped to the floor. "I didn't think so."

Kat lifted her shoulders in question. "What's going on, Beth?" she asked. "I mean, I feel like I'm missing something. You were so supportive when I started at Kill. You sat with me while I spilled my guts to you about Carter, and now— I don't know."

"It's . . . difficult to explain."

"What's difficult? I thought you were on my side. Is this because of Austin?"

Beth's head shot up.

Kat closed her eyes in regret. "I'm sorry if I led him on, but we only kissed that once, and I was clear that we should take it slow, if at all. I'm so confused with everything. I didn't—"

Beth's face flashed with incredulity. "Are you—are you sleeping with Carter?"

Kat's temper flared. "Not that it's any of your business, but no, I'm not."

"This is getting out of hand, Kat. Do you even know him?" Beth continued, becoming vehement. "I mean, has he told you about all the times he's been in jail, told you the reasons why?"

"How the—"

"Your mom's right. You're putting yourself in danger, your work, your—"

"You don't know him. He's different."

"Oh, Katherine, please." Beth crossed her arms. "That's lust talking, nothing more."

"Don't speak to me like I'm a child, Beth," Kat snapped, moving closer. "I get enough of that from my mother. I don't need it from my friend."

"I'm speaking to you like a child because you're acting like one, and because I love you and want what's best for you, and because I've held my tongue for too long. He's. Your. Student, Kat, and a criminal. You're putting your whole career on the line for a stupid crush that's going nowhere."

"And what the hell would you know?" Kat's voice burst from her louder than she intended.

"I know a damn sight more than you," Beth replied tellingly.

"Then why don't you enlighten me, huh?"

"Everything okay here?" Adam's concerned voice came from the top of the stairs.

"No," Kat retorted.

Adam glanced nervously at his fiancée, who looked back with a tiny shake of her head.

Kat's hands rested firmly on her hips while her eyes flicked between them. "It seems I'm a little out of the loop here. Is someone gonna tell me what the hell's going on?"

Adam placed his hand in Beth's. His eyes were determined yet cautious as he took a deep breath and said, "He's my cousin."

Kat saw Beth's stare drop to the floor. "Who's your cousin?" she asked impatiently.

As Adam opened his mouth to answer, Kat's phone began singing in her hand. She grimaced and glanced at the screen.

Carter.

Adam reached out to tap her cell phone with his finger. "*He* is my cousin."

Kat slowly pressed decline as Adam's words buzzed in her head, her brain trying to make sense of them, to put them in an order that she could understand.

Carter was Adam's cousin.

They were related.

But that would mean . . .

"Oh, God." Kat swayed and grabbed on to the doorframe.

Austin.

Beth reached for her, but Kat pulled her arm out of her grasp.

Beth immediately appeared contrite. "I wanted to tell you, but—"

"You knew," Kat whispered. Her head throbbed with an emotion so heavy it almost brought her to her knees. "When I told you about kissing Carter. You knew."

Adam nearly choked. "You kissed him?"

"Yes," Beth answered resolutely. She placed a hand on Adam's chest but kept her eyes on Kat. "I did know. Adam told me. But, Kat, it wasn't my place."

"Bullshit!" Kat's palm slapped the door of the bathroom. All the pieces began to fall into place: the distance between her and Beth, the loaded looks between Adam and Austin when she told them where she worked and about Carter's parole. Their deceitfulness screamed through her.

"You could have told me at any time; you both could have," Kat seethed. "And Austin! But you all chose not to because, like every other person in my life, you treat me like a kid who doesn't know any better."

"I thought you'd get over it," Beth protested. "I thought you'd move on before you got in too deep. We all thought if you gave Austin a chance—"

"Wait. 'We'?"

"Adam told me Carter's done some serious shit. He's bad news and he's your student, Kat. Do you not understand the ramifications of that? You kissed your student!"

"Yeah, I did. Twice," Kat exploded. "And I fucking enjoyed it."

"Katherine!"

All three of them turned to see Eva standing with a look of disgust directed straight at Kat. "You—you kissed that . . . that man?" she asked, her voice dangerously quiet.

Breathless and trying to numb out the shame of what she was about to do, Kat pushed past Beth and Adam, and headed to her bedroom. The smothering was reaching epic proportions, and the hammering in her brain was sending her almost hysterical. We? They'd all known, all tried to keep her away from Carter. The new friendship between her mother and Beth, the persistence of Austin. It all made sense now. She suddenly felt sick.

"I need to get out of here," she muttered, bursting into the room and grabbing at her bag, throwing in her toiletries and clothes from the day before. Hoisting it over her shoulder, she turned and almost fell over her mother standing in the doorway.

"Where are you going?" Eva eyed the bag and the white-knuckle grip Kat had on it.

"I'm sorry, but I need . . . I need to get out of here, Mom," Kat answered, avoiding the gaze she knew would make her feel tiny and shitty all at the same time. "I'm sorry."

"Sorry?" Eva spluttered. "You're not going anywhere. You will stand there and explain to me just what the hell has been going on!"

But Kat knew she couldn't, wouldn't explain. She couldn't be around people, much less the people who refused to understand—people who lied to her and treated her as if she were stupid. There was too much to process, too many questions with no answers. She needed to be alone.

"I can't, Mom. I have to go . . . just for tonight." It was a lie. Kat knew it as soon as the words left her mouth. Her plan was to get into a car and not stop until the gas ran out.

"I won't allow it, Katherine. You will put that bag down, pull yourself together, and apologize to Beth. How dare you behave this way."

Kat barked a sardonic laugh. "Apologize? Me? I have nothing to apologize for!"

"Enough! From what I've heard tonight," Eva said in a low voice, "there are plenty of things you need to apologize for." Her eyes widened with disbelief. "My God, Katherine, what the hell were you thinking? He's dangerous."

Kat gripped her temples. "Oh my God!"

"He's just like those creatures that killed your father: evil, heartless. Is that who you want to be with? Do you understand how much you're hurting me? How much you'd hurt your father if he were here?"

Kat's breath caught hard. She stared hopelessly at her mother. Her eyes began to sting with furious tears. "I'm sorry I've let you down." She moved around her, holding in her sobs. "I need to get out of here."

Eva grabbed her arm. "You are not leaving. You are here for your father!"

That lit the fuse. "I know why I'm here, Mom," Kat shrieked. "I was there the night those creatures fucking killed him, remember?"

The shock of the slap to the left side of Kat's face stung much more than the slap itself. Her mother had never struck her before, but, deep down, underneath all the confused anger swallowing her soul, Kat knew she deserved it. She registered a gasp from her mother but didn't stay around to hear what she had to say. She yanked her arm from Eva's grasp, exploded out of the room, past Adam and Beth, and bolted down the stairs.

Ben was at the bottom, utterly perplexed. "What the hell's going on?" He followed her to the cloakroom.

"Can I have the keys to your car?" Kat stuttered, grabbing her coat. She could hear the voices of her mother and Beth getting louder as they came down the stairs after her.

Ben shook his head. "It's a rental. I can't." He rubbed her biceps. "Just stay and talk this out."

A small, pale hand appeared over her shoulder, holding a set of car keys. "Take mine, darling," Nana Boo said. Kat turned to her in surprise. "It'll be an excuse for you to come back."

"Nana," Kat whimpered, taking the keys. "I'm so, so sorry. I can't expla— Oh God. I just, I need to—"

"I know," her grandmother interrupted with a small smile of understanding, and cupped the side of Kat's face. She stroked her cheek with the flat of her thumb. "Go. I'll look after your mother."

Kat whispered, "Thank you," and, with her bag in hand, she ran outside to the Jaguar XJ, unlocking it as she approached.

Her bag was thrown in, the keys were in the ignition, and her foot was to the floor as she sped down the driveway away from her friends and family. Kat tried her hardest to ignore the intense relief that consumed her as the miles mounted between them, and wished like hell for guilt to take its place.

It never did.

. . .

Carter had had a shitty week. And, because he was a bastard, he'd made everyone else's week shitty, too.

He knew he'd been short-tempered with the guys at work, and his counseling sessions and home visits had been filled with uncooperative grunts and shrugs simply because he couldn't be bothered to deal with it all. The only good thing about the week had been Carter's session with Ross. He'd kicked seven shades of crap out of every piece of equipment that could handle it and, although it had made him feel better, he was still edgy as fuck.

He was starting to drive himself crazy. Hence why he'd decided to stay in on a Saturday night while Max and the boys went out. He really wasn't in the mood for any of Max's stupid shit. The asshole's face was still a complete mess, but he was determined to go out, get wasted, and fuck anything with a pulse instead of dealing with his grief. Again.

Carter lit another smoke, and began strumming the opening chords of Kings of Leon's "Fans" in an effort to relax. He peeked once again at his cell phone.

Nope. Still no fucking word.

The reason his panties were in such a goddamn awful bunch was simple. Peaches. The woman was gonna give him a heart attack, way before any pack of Marlboros or bottle of alcohol would. Dealing with her being away from him for a week was one thing. Having her ignore him, after they'd texted three days before, was another.

For the life of him, he couldn't figure the shit out.

The last he'd heard from her was a text asking if he could talk. He liked that she'd texted him, and he liked that she wanted to talk to him even more. Truthfully, he'd never had a relationship with a woman where conversations on the phone had happened. But he'd been more than enthusiastic to speak to Peaches.

He shoved the quiet cell phone across the leather. He wasn't going to call her again. It'd gone to voice mail the other four times he'd tried, and his seven texts had gone unanswered.

He rubbed the heel of his hand across his sternum to soothe the heartburn that'd been plaguing him for days, and continued to strum, humming along.

The knock at the door of his apartment was as unexpected as it was inconvenient. If Max thought he could come and drag Carter's miserable ass out into the city, he was in for a big surprise.

"Fuck off," he mumbled, and flicked his smoke into the full ashtray. But the knocking came again, and this time, it was relentless. Slamming his guitar down onto the chair, Carter stormed barefoot across the loft to the door. Pulling back the dead bolt while still muttering curses, he swung the door open, ready to punch whichever motherfucker was disturbing his pity party for one.

Catching the door before it hit the wall, the ferocious expression on his face dropped like a rock in water.

"P-Peaches?"

She was standing there, looking a little worse for wear, in skinny black jeans and a red hooded top. Bizarrely, she was wearing flip-flops. Her hair was pulled up into a messy ponytail and her eyes were bloodshot and rimmed in mascara as though she'd been crying for days, or—from the way she was swaying—drinking.

"What're you doing here?"

She rested against the doorframe and smiled, but it was forced and was gone far too quickly. Her eyes were flat, missing their shine.

"I came to see you," she replied with a playful tap of her fingertip against his nose. Carter frowned. "Can I come in?"

"Um, yeah, yeah, sure," he replied.

He watched her walk in like a timid animal, and closed the door behind her. Keeping his grip on the handle, he closed his eyes for a beat, trying to collect himself. He took a deep breath and turned around to find her staring back at him in a way that made his pulse race.

"Peaches," he began, "how did you know where—"

Carter's words were eaten up by Peaches' mouth as it smashed into his own. She came at him with such force that his back thumped hard into the door behind him. Her hands were suddenly everywhere: his hair, his face, his chest—oh shit—his ass.

She felt good. So good, pressed against him, eager for him, wanting him. He wondered if she was wet and moaned into her mouth when her tongue slammed into his. She groaned loudly in answer and pushed her hips into his, begging him. He wanted to take her: hard, right there, slamming against the door, but the whole thing just seemed . . . wrong?

She kissed him with a desperation that wasn't sexy. It was needy and panicked.

His hands, wrapped tightly around her waist, moved to her

face, where he pushed her back. She panted against his cheek with her eyes closed and her lips still in a full, gorgeous pout.

"Peaches," he gasped before swallowing. "Shit. Just . . . wait a second."

"No," she replied, burning her gaze into his. "I want you. I want you now"—she licked his throat—"inside me, fucking me, taking me."

"Fuuuuck," Carter moaned, rotating his hips against her, pushing his erection against her soft stomach.

"Yes!" She took his bottom lip between her teeth. "I can feel how hard you are, Carter. Tell me you want me. Tell me you want me and that you want it as much as I do."

"Want it?" Carter growled incredulously. He bent, grabbing the backs of her thighs, and yanked her off her feet so her legs wrapped around his waist, her heat pressing perfectly against his belly button, her flip-flops falling to the floor.

"Peaches, I don't want it." He pushed his face into her neck, smelling her peach-scented hair, and bit her skin, making her gasp. He sucked her earlobe. "Jesus Christ." He lifted his face and placed his nose at the side of hers. "I fucking *need* it."

Their lips met again, passionate and raw. My God, Carter had never experienced a need like it. It was all-consuming, heady. It swelled in his body, ready to erupt like a volcano: ready to erupt into her.

Her hands gripped the back of his neck as Carter staggered through his living room, bumping into the back of the couch. He leaned against it for one second while his hands shifted up and under her top, her soft skin against his palms.

Setting off with a grunt while Peaches moved her mouth to his jaw and began nibbling it in the sexiest, most sensual way, Carter moved toward his bedroom, wishing to all fuck that his bed would meet him halfway.

Carter was harder than he'd ever been in his entire life as his knees hit the side of his bed with a dull thump. Peaches lifted her mouth from his and pulled hard on his shoulders, toppling him, and making him fall forward onto the bed, on top of her. The feel of her legs wrapped around Carter's waist while he ground against her was incredible. He bent her neck back and started kissing, licking, and biting her from her chin to her collarbone and back again. He was suddenly frantic with the need to consume her: every part of her.

There were no words for her taste. No fantasy had come close. "Perfection" seemed insanely inadequate.

He groaned, pushing his hips into her again, hungry for any kind of friction, and watched in awe as her back arched in pleasure. He had to get inside her, had to feel her around him.

Carter lifted onto his forearms and searched her face for any signs of hesitation. If he saw any he'd be devastated, but he had to know that she was sure. He could smell the sweet scent of Amaretto on her breath, which meant she wasn't as sober as he would have liked, but the way in which she responded to his touch suggested she was as ready as he was.

Their eyes connected and a flash of something heart-wrenching crossed the green of her irises. He pulled back in concern. "Peaches," he murmured, but her fingers pressed hard against his lips.

"Don't," she whispered. "Don't think. Please. I need you to not think and just be with me." She pulled his face back to hers and smothered his mouth with long kisses that set his bones alight.

Carter tried to listen to his gut, he tried to listen to the sensible part of his brain, but her mouth and hands were far too distracting. Swallowing his conscience with one huge gulp, he gripped the zipper of her top and pulled it down in one fluid movement.

Jesus.

No bra.

"Shit." He licked his lips and just fucking stared. She was gorgeous; her dark stiff nipples ached to have his lips and tongue around them. "You're— My God, you're perfect."

Before she could reply, Carter's mouth fell against her right breast, where he hollowed out his cheeks and sucked as hard as he could. Sweet fruits. Her breasts were so perfectly heavy and full in his hands. With a guttural moan, Peaches' legs wrapped farther around him, and her nails scored the fabric of his T-shirt. She gasped and whimpered into his buzzed hair.

"I need to feel you," she groaned, pulling at the shirt's hem. "Please let me feel you against me."

Without a second's pause, Carter released her nipple, grabbed the neck of his T-shirt, and yanked it over his head. He crashed back down onto her, grunting at the feel of her bare skin against his.

While he continued to worship her, she released her arms from the confines of her hooded top and—as soon as she was free of it—he grabbed her hands and pushed them above her head, crushing them into the mattress of the bed.

Their tongues met again between their mouths in the open air, twisting and dancing amid soft moans and silent confessions of feelings too big and scary to say aloud. Peaches gripped Carter's fingers between hers and lifted her head from the bed, urgently seeking from him what Carter was more than willing to give. He wanted to give her everything, anything.

Fuck, he already had. He knew in his heart that she owned him.

"Say it," she gasped against his cheek when he began licking at her jaw. "Say you want me. I need—I need to hear it. I need to hear it."

Carter growled into her cleavage. "I want you." His teeth grazed her sternum. "I've always wanted you."

My whole life.

"Again," she croaked, her voice trembling. "Tell me this is right. Tell me we're right."

Carter, stunned at her words, glanced up.

What he saw knocked every ounce of breath out of him. Her eyes were clenched shut, her face in an almost grimace of pain, and a small shimmer could be seen at the inside corner of her right eye. She was crying.

"Peaches," he whispered, and lifted his body, terrified that he'd done something wrong, something she didn't want. "What's wrong? Did I— Was I too rough?"

Goddammit, he'd tried to be gentle.

She shook her head from side to side, her eyes remaining shut. "You'd never hurt me," she murmured. "Would you, Carter? I know you'd never hurt me or lie to me. Would you?"

"Never," he replied, his throat constricting in fear and confusion. "Please look at me."

She remained quiet, keeping her eyes closed, but the lone tear trickling down her cheek spoke volumes.

"Christ, Katherine," Carter begged in a voice even he didn't recognize. "Please talk; you're scaring the shit out of me."

At his words, her eyes snapped open. The fire behind them was so fierce, Carter was momentarily dumbstruck.

"What did you call me?"

Carter stared at her, baffled. He shrugged. "I called you Katherine," he answered in a calm voice. "Why?"

"You never call me that," she retorted venomously.

"I know, I just . . . It just came out."

"Get off me."

Carter balked. "What?"

"Get. Off. Me!" She wrenched her hands free of his and pushed against him so hard, he landed on his back, bouncing as the bed took his weight.

"What the fuck?"

But she didn't answer him. Instead, she grabbed for her hoodie, her hands shaking and her face twisted in anger. Carter watched her, helpless.

"Peaches!" she yelled, pulling on her top. "You always, always, always call me Peaches!"

"I know, but—"

"Only my mother calls me Katherine! My mother. Why tonight, huh? Why did you call me Katherine tonight?" She wasn't even looking at him while she struggled to fasten her zipper. She seemed close to losing her shit completely.

"I don't know," Carter yelled back. He rubbed his face in frustration. "Christ, would you just breathe for a second? What the *fuck* is going on?"

Her eyes flew to his, huge and fierce. "What's going on? I'll tell you what's going on. I came here for a good, hard fuck that I thought was a sure thing, and all I get is your damn mouth. That's what's going on, Carter!"

Even though her words stung, the fury inside him outweighed any part that hurt. He launched himself off the bed, beating her to the bedroom door, blocking that shit with every inch of himself.

"Get out of my way!" she demanded, moving to his right and trying to push under his arm. She was strong, but Carter wasn't giving in.

"Not until you tell me what's wrong with you," he growled, knowing if he shouted the walls would crumble.

"You are what's wrong with me." She pushed again.

He stood firm and, for the first time since they'd entered the bedroom, Carter saw a glimmer of light shine behind her eyes. He'd surprised her.

"Talk to me."

She moved to his left and pushed. "No!"

"Open your mouth and fucking speak!"

"No!"

He searched her face, seeing only tears, anger, and a profound sadness. "Why are you here?" he asked with a shake of his head. "Why? Why are you at my apartment, looking like death, after you've ignored my ass for two days?"

The force of her pushing dropped and her fingers began to grip into his skin. That shit hurt, but Carter was determined. "Why are you here, wanting me to fuck you, huh? Is this a game? Am I some sort of sick rehabilitation joke to you?"

She stood up straight and glared at him. "A joke," she repeated. "My God, Carter. Do you think I find anything about this situation funny?"

"How the fuck would I know?" Carter asked sharply. "You don't tell me anything." His palms slapped the doorframe in frustration. "I get ignored or I get half-truths and mixed messages."

She sucked in a shaking breath and stumbled back from him, yanking her sleeves down over her hands. Her face was desolate and pained, and Carter was sure, from the relentless ache inside him, he was suffering every single ounce of it.

"What the hell happened to you this week?" he demanded. All he could think was that someone had hurt her, and, if that were true, that same motherfucker would be read his last rights.

She began pacing, muttering garbled words. Carter, despising the unfamiliar behavior he saw, took a tentative step toward her, moving slowly away from the doorway.

He sure wished he hadn't. As soon as she saw he'd moved, she made a mad dash for freedom. Carter moved to stop her and, in her haste to move out of his way, she skidded on the wood flooring and careened heavily into Carter's arms, smashing the air from his body in a loud whoosh.

"Peaches, please," Carter begged as the pair of them landed in a jumbled heap on the floor. She was still fighting him, still demanding him to let her go, but he wouldn't give in.

"I can't," she sobbed. "You . . . you have to let me go." Her hands were still pushing at his bare chest, but her strength was waning as the sobs began to overtake her.

"I'm not letting you go. I don't give a shit what you do." He held both of her wrists so they'd stop flailing about and stared deep into eyes awash with tears.

"I can't. I can't be here. Everything. Everyone hates— I hurt, I . . . Carter."

Carter tucked her head under his chin and rubbed her hair in an effort to calm her. "Shhh. I'm here. I'm here. I won't let you go. I'll never let you go."

Her small shoulders shook and, when Carter loosened his grip on her wrists, she threw her arms around his neck and held him as tightly as he imagined she could. And that was fine. He wanted her to hold him. He wanted to soothe whatever pain she was going through and then find the culprit and make them pay dearly.

"I want my dad," she whimpered into his throat, his skin becoming wet from her tears.

Carter froze, his hand stilling against her. "What?"

"My dad. I miss him so, so much." Her voice was hoarse and weak, but the desperate grief lacing her words was like a foghorn.

"I know." Carter closed his eyes and placed a gentle kiss on her head. "I know, sweetheart."

"I'm sorry. I'm so sorry," she repeated, each word punctuated with a soft hiccough.

Carter continued to rub her hair, stealing soft kisses along the part. "What're you sorry for?"

"I . . . I couldn't help him. I couldn't stop them. What they did to him. I couldn't stop them." Her arms tightened around Carter's neck. "He told me to run. I shouldn't have run."

Carter's heart thundered. Did she remember? Did she know he'd pulled her away, saved her?

"Today," she whispered. "Sixteen years ago today, and I miss him so fucking much, Carter."

Outwardly, Carter was motionless. Inside his skull, his brain moved a million miles a second. Could it really have been sixteen years since they'd first met under such violent, horrific circumstances?

"It was today?"

Her fingers tightened at the nape of his neck, and her nose rubbed along his jaw.

Carter clenched his eyes shut. Holy shit. He pulled her closer, burying his face into the space between her neck and shoulder. She was perfect against him, so soft and delicate. Images and sounds of the night in question flashed behind his eyelids and blared loudly inside his head: her screams, her whimpers, the police gunfire, the color of her dress, and the paleness of her skin.

"I missed you so much," she whimpered. "I missed you so much this week, Carter. I couldn't stop thinking about you." She kissed the tip of his shoulder. "I had my whole family around me, and all I wanted was you."

Carter's eyes rolled back at the sound of her words and the feel of her lips on his skin. "Shhh, you're here now," he replied. "I'll look after you."

After a moment of silence, Carter pushed his free arm under her knees and pulled her securely to him. After a couple of attempts, on wobbling legs, he managed to stand, cradling her in his arms. He walked slowly toward the bed; his nose pressed against her wet cheek while he whispered words of comfort to her: "I'm here. It's okay. Hold on to me."

Never letting any single part of her go, he lay down on the bed and held her closely.

And, just as he had sixteen years before, in a cold doorway in the Bronx, he held on to his Peaches so fucking hard as she grieved for the father who'd been so cruelly taken from her.

20

Kat opened her eyes and was certain of two things simultaneously. First, she wasn't in her own bed. It was far too comfortable and large to be hers. Second, she wasn't alone. She was being spooned, quite generously, by a very large, very warm, masculine-shaped body.

Kat let her gaze travel down the bare, muscled forearm holding her firmly around the waist, allowing her eyes to wander slowly up past his elbow to the black, gray, and red of the tattoos that decorated the smooth skin: an eagle, flames, and vines that wound their way across strong muscle. Before she got farther, she clenched her eyes tightly as flashes of the night before accosted her.

She'd behaved like a lunatic: embarrassed herself and treated Carter like a damn punching bag. Was she insane? Jesus, what had she been thinking, getting a cab to his apartment when she was drunk?

Speaking of which, her mouth felt like she'd been breathing almond-flavored sandpaper all night, and her eyes were sticky from the tears she'd cried for the better part of three days. How could she have let Carter see her this way? He grunted quietly into her hair, making the area between Kat's legs heat instantly at the memory of him above her, rutting against her, sucking, licking, and whispering delectably deplorable words.

Christ. They'd almost had sex!

Granted, that had been her game plan from the minute her stupid, drunken ass had called Jack for Carter's address and hailed a cab, but that was beside the point. She hadn't been thinking clearly. She rubbed a hand down her face and shifted a little more, taking Carter's wrist in her hand as gently as she could while lifting it from her waist. His response was quick and immediate. He clamped his arm back around her, pulling her body hard against his. Kat could feel his crotch pressing nicely against her ass, and bit the inside of her lip to stop the moan of surprise from escaping.

Was he hard?

Carter muttered a curse into the nape of her neck. "Where ya goin'?" His breath was warm and his voice was gruff from sleep.

"Um, bathroom?"

Carter's grip on her didn't loosen instantly. Instead, he smelled her hair and mumbled something indecipherable before he lifted his arm and rolled back. Kat tried to ignore the bereft feeling that entered her spine when the cold air hit, and pushed the covers back with a sigh.

Her legs were a little unsteady when she stood up from the bed and wandered sleepily toward the en suite, not daring to look back at the man she'd left alone. She closed the door with a small click and dropped her forehead against it with a thump. What was she doing?

Well, the answer to that was fairly self-explanatory. She'd used Carter as a screaming board and potential booty call, in order to clear her head of the anger and the grief that had ripped her wide-open the day she'd left her grandmother's house. She'd driven for fifteen hours straight from Chicago to New York. And that was after she'd smashed her cell phone against the sidewalk when it had begun to ring incessantly.

Why the hell did her mother or Beth think she would want to speak to either of them again?

Kat stumbled back from the door, looking around at the beautiful marble floor and stunning shower stand, and shuffled over to the huge rectangular mirror hanging on the wall. Jesus Christ, she looked like death. She grabbed some toilet paper and ran it under the faucet before wiping vigorously at the skin under her eyes in an attempt to erase the mascara lying there in all its hideously smudged glory. Her face looked exactly how she felt: tired, angry, and alone.

She threw the paper into the toilet and leaned against the side of the sink. No, she thought. That wasn't right. She wasn't alone. The fact that she was standing in Carter's apartment proved she wasn't. He was the only one who seemed to understand her, who seemed to know what she needed or even wanted. He knew her in a way no one else did, and it was in a way that both thrilled and alarmed her.

She just wished she'd thought a little bit more about the consequences before turning up on Carter's damn doorstep and telling him she wanted him to fuck her.

But the truth was, the only thing she'd thought about as she'd driven through the night was getting to Carter. The only person she'd wanted to see was Carter. The only arms she wanted around her, the only chest she wanted to press her face into, the only mouth she wanted against hers, and the only scent she wanted to breathe in were Carter's.

She used the toilet, washed her hands, rinsed out her mouth, and moved back toward the door, cupping an ear to it, listening for Carter on the other side. It was silent. As quietly as she could, she turned the handle and opened it, peeking around the doorjamb.

Carter's voice was soft and deep. "Hey."

He was sitting on top of the covers, against the headboard of his bed, bare-chested and crumpled, with his jean-clad legs crossed casually at the ankles. His jeans sat comfortably under his belly button, showing a trail of coarse, dark hair that disappeared to, well, farther down.

Realizing she'd not noticed the artwork on his body while she was grinding all over him, her gaze wandered over his wide shoulders that were covered in the ink she'd seen on his arms. From his neck, the artwork moved past his collarbone to his strong stomach. He was a masterpiece. He was muscular, of course, but he didn't scream *body beautiful*; he screamed *strength and safety*. He had a smattering of hair in the center of his chest that sat like an exclamation point next to his masculinity.

Kat cleared her throat and walked back into the bedroom. She stopped about two feet from the edge of the bed, not really knowing what she should say or do. She twisted her hands together at her stomach. She eventually glanced up to see Carter's face was gentle, expecting nothing. She breathed a little easier and gave him a small smile.

"How ya doin'?"

"I'm okay."

He raised a knowing eyebrow. "You're a shitty liar." He shook his head and patted his palm on the bed space next to him. "Come here."

Kat's body flushed. "What?"

Carter simply continued patting the bed.

He looked extremely appealing and mischievous, but there was also a tenderness in his eyes that Kat could do nothing but trust. She took another tentative step, and watched Carter pull the covers back for her. She stopped again, wondering if it was a sensible move to get back into his bed.

"Carter, I—"

"Peaches," Carter interrupted with a dip of his chin. "It's six thirty on a fucking Sunday morning. Now, I don't know about you, but I could sure as hell sleep another few hours."

Kat laughed at his expression. She was so very tired. Her whole body was exhausted.

"All right," she murmured. She kneeled on the bed and shuffled ungracefully under the covers. Carter tucked them around her.

She froze for a moment, loving the softness of the mattress and pillows, before she turned her head back toward Carter. He was looking down at her, leaning over her on his forearm. The tenderness of his eyes had dissolved into something else that made Kat's mouth dry. He looked hungry.

"I thought you were sleeping, too?" she asked with a nod toward the bed.

His eyes seemed to snap back into focus and he frowned in response, clearly confused. "I will."

"So why are you not under the covers?"

Carter's cheeks tinged pink and he shifted away from her, the muscles in his chest tightening minutely.

"Yeah," he muttered. He glanced down at himself. "I didn't want you to feel uncomfortable. I'll just stay here. I'm fine."

After watching his face for a few seconds, Kat released a disbelieving laugh. Hadn't this man been between her legs with his mouth on her nipple not seven hours earlier? Hadn't she cried and sobbed into his neck as she told him she needed and missed him, while he promised to never let her go?

She snorted tiredly, nuzzling the pillow under her head. "Carter, shut up and get under the covers."

He stayed where he was for a while, but she could feel the bed jiggling as though he was shaking his foot or something. Was he nervous? Just as she was about to turn back around and tell him to move his ass, the covers lifted and his body moved smoothly underneath them. He was close enough to her that she could feel the heat radiating from his body and she instinctively moved back.

"Are you cold?" His voice, although concerned, sounded tight.

"A little." She pulled the covers tightly into the crook of her neck.

After a moment of silent and heavy stillness, Kat felt Carter's hand slide hesitantly along her waist. His little finger lightly grazed the skin of her hip before he pulled her body firmly against his so they were spooning, just as they'd been when she'd first woken up.

At first, Kat tensed, and silently willed her body to keep calm and stay quiet. It was embarrassing to simply think about how much his touch affected her. Her heart raced, her skin tingled, and the juncture between her thighs throbbed with an aching need. But, as she felt Carter's solidity press into her back and his muscular arm wind around her, Kat's body began to melt and relax.

"Is this okay?" Carter whispered, his breath caressing the skin of Kat's neck like silk.

"Yeah," she answered. "It's okay."

With a contented smile, Kat placed her palm over the back of his hand—against her stomach—and pushed her fingers, little by little, into the spaces between his.

It didn't surprise her that they fit perfectly.

• • •

It was a little before eleven when Carter opened his eyes again.

For a split second, he wondered where the fuck he was, until he realized Peaches' hair was covering his face like a peach-scented, auburn mask. He moved his head back. Contentment tugged at his stomach when he saw they hadn't moved from their original position, and their hands were still entwined against her body. Like a creeper, he watched her sleeping before she began to stir.

After an awkward cup of coffee, over which they shot each other fleeting glances and shy smiles, and after she'd agreed for him to take her home, Carter led a nervous-looking Peaches down to the garage in the basement of his building.

"You've ridden a motorcycle before, right?" he asked, trying like hell to hide the lusty excitement pumping through his body.

"Yeah," she replied as they approached Kala. "But riding with you? That's a little different."

Carter passed her a helmet. "And why's that?"

She gestured meekly with her hand toward Carter, making him look down at himself in confusion: black boots, dark blue jeans, dark blue vintage Zeppelin T-shirt, leather jacket.

She was watching him in a way that made his jeans feel tight. The fact that she was wearing one of his sweaters did nothing to help. He cocked an eyebrow and cleared his throat to get her attention. Her eyes snapped up and he chuckled behind his hand.

"So, Peaches," he growled, popping his collar. "You thinkin' I'm sexy right now?"

Her cheeks flashed pink. "Shut up," she muttered and pulled the helmet onto her head.

He snorted. "You're too easy."

He threw his leg over Kala's seat and put on his shades. He cocked his head back and grinned. "Ya comin'?"

With one lithe movement, her leg was over the seat, her thighs at either side of his. Carter shook his head of the explicit visual flashing behind his eyes and grumbled a few choice expletives, as he turned the key in the ignition. He could feel her pressed up against him and could only imagine what it would be like to turn around and have her in that very position.

"You ready?" he called over the grumbling engine.

"As I'll ever be," she called back.

Carter smiled when her arms and thighs gripped him as he revved the engine. With her heat pressed into him, the smell of rich gasoline, and the sound of Kala's engine roaring, he was pretty damn close to heaven.

Glancing up and down the windy street outside his apartment building, Carter tapped the clutch and they set off at speed, across the city, toward Peaches' apartment.

• • •

Carter was probably the most casually sexy man Kat had ever met. He oozed sensuality without even trying, whether he was wearing prison-issue coveralls or a blue Zeppelin T-shirt that made the color of his eyes pop. Seeing Carter on a motorbike took that casual sexiness, multiplied it by about a billion, and served it with a side helping of hot fucking and hour-long orgasms.

He was sensational sitting astride the damn thing, and Kat had to work hard at trying to keep herself together. Her craving for him had certainly spiked to new heights of ridiculousness, which was why she was all sorts of puzzled with herself when she invited him up to her apartment.

She unlocked her apartment door and gestured for Carter to enter in front of her. He smiled tightly and stepped in. She followed and watched him place his bike helmets on the side table. The silence was thunderous, and the tension between them, as they stood opposite one another, shifted from heated sex to anxiety and back again.

"Drink?" she offered.

"Sure. Orange juice?" His voice was rough and rich.

He followed her to the kitchen, where he stood, filling her apartment with his height and broad shoulders and waited while she poured him the juice. She felt his eyes on her, just as she'd watched him in his own kitchen that morning. It was bizarre how aware of him Kat was. Her whole body seemed to gravitate to his. But it'd always been that way; she'd just been too busy trying to keep up a professional demeanor with him to notice it before.

"Are you hungry?" she asked as he wandered around her sitting room, his eyes settling on her collection of watercolors.

He laughed. "I'm starving." He rubbed his belly.

She placed her glass down and walked over to the fridge. "Let's see what I've got."

There wasn't much, but there was enough to make bacon-and-tomato omelettes. Carter didn't look convinced when Kat offered him as much, but she assured him she was a master at any type of egg cuisine.

Kat placed all the ingredients on the countertop. "Hey, Carter, can you cook bacon?"

Carter rolled his eyes. He shook out of his jacket. "Of course. Why?"

"I need you to brown the bacon while I take a shower." She turned back to him and grinned. "Think you can handle that?"

"Please," Carter retorted, grabbing the pack of bacon. "Go and have your shower, and leave this shit to me." He grabbed her shoulders and moved her out of the way. "Be gone," he said firmly, pushing her out of the kitchen space. He waved her away and gave her a grin that made his face crooked.

Kat held back the pathetically girly sigh threatening to break, and turned toward her bedroom. Once there she pulled off the sweater Carter had given her. With a swift glance back at the door—making sure she'd closed it properly—she held the sweater to her face and breathed in his cologne. It was lush and heady. She pulled it from her nose, folded it, and laid it on her bed.

Showered and redressed in black jeans and a Blondie T-shirt, and with her damp hair in a knot at her neck, Kat sauntered back into the kitchen to find Carter leaning casually against the counter, reading *Walter the Lazy Mouse*. She watched him turn the page, seemingly engrossed.

"How's the bacon coming along?"

"Shhh," he replied. His eyes never left the page as he put his index finger to his lips. "Walter's asleep."

Kat grinned. She grabbed a bowl, a pan, and a knife for chopping the tomatoes.

Carter moved around her and placed the book back carefully next to the flowerpot where it had been since Kat had left it there two days before. When she'd arrived back from Chicago, she'd read it aloud to a captivated audience of a framed picture of her father and a bottle of Amaretto.

Good times.

Kat was surprised at how well Carter worked in the kitchen. He seemed domesticated, which was, at the very least, sexy as hell.

"It's rude to stare," he pointed out as she watched him whisk the eggs.

"Sorry."

She hadn't even realized she had been staring; it was just the muscles in his forearm and the way in which they flexed and tensed as he moved fascinated her. Coupled with his tattoos, he was quite the sight to behold. She rubbed the back of her neck with her sweating palm, cleared her throat, and resumed her tomato chopping.

"You're all flushed." Carter's voice came from behind her, directly into her left ear.

Kat's spine straightened instantly. He put the bowl down next to her chopping board and leaned against the counter, trapping her between his arms.

"Wanna tell me what you're thinking about?" he asked in a low rumble she felt in his chest pressing against her back.

She moved her head back, resting it on his shoulder. "No."

Carter laughed quietly and ran his nose up along her jaw to her earlobe. "From the color of your skin," he whispered, "I can bet it was something really fucking good."

"Mmhm."

He laughed quiet and sexy. "Peaches." His hands meandered their way to her waist.

"Yeah?"

"The bacon's burning."

Kat's eyes flew open and the smell of the burning meat registered instantly in her nostrils. She shoved past a chuckling Carter and yanked the frying pan from the heat. It was smoking and a little crisp, though it wasn't entirely unsalvageable. Kat glared at Carter, who was trying his hardest to look innocent, and failing miserably.

For the next ten minutes, while Kat cooked the omelettes, Carter asked her about Arthur Kill. He asked about her students and told her about Riley's visit to his place after he'd gotten parole. It was apparent that Riley and Carter's love of cars, and all things metal and fast, was what had brought them together.

This led to Kat asking him about his love of bikes and the origin of it. She loved how his face lit up when he spoke about Kala. Carter explained that Max's father had been a mechanic, and he'd practically lived in the shop from the age of nine, watching and listening as cars and bikes were brought in, disassembled, and rebuilt over and over. Carter had learned everything he knew about engines right there.

Despite his initial protestations, Carter devoured the omelette she placed in front of him, with a few grunts and words of appreciation. It was oddly normal, having Carter sitting at her dining table.

They'd both finished, with their empty plates between them, and were arguing playfully over who was better, the Beatles or the Stones, when Kat's apartment phone began ringing. The sound made Kat's heart stutter.

Carter turned around and gaped at the still ringing phone. Kat could see he was curious as to why she hadn't answered it, but, to his credit, he didn't say anything. Kat fisted her hands in her lap when the answering machine kicked in.

"Katherine, it's your mother. I know you're home; Nana told me. We need to talk. I— There are things to be said, dealt with, and the way you left . . . Beth is frantic and still very upset. I don't understand you. Call me."

The beep of the message ending thundered around the apartment and rattled Kat's very core. If her mother thought she was going to apologize to anyone, then she was sorely mistaken. Kat hadn't done anything wrong. None of them understood her heart. None of them.

Carter placed his forearms on the table. His face was concerned, with a tinge of anger around his blue eyes. "Are you okay?"

Kat nodded, not trusting her own voice.

"Wanna talk about it?"

She shook her head sharply but gave an apologetic smile. He sat back, his eyes still on her. She wrapped her arms around herself and exhaled through pursed lips in an effort to calm down. She was embarrassed that Carter had heard her mother, but was also comforted by the protectiveness he exuded. Deep in her heart, she was so glad he was there.

"Peaches?" At the sound of Carter's voice around her pet name, two large tears fell onto her arm. "Do you wanna get outta here? Go somewhere?"

She wiped at her face. "Where?"

He shrugged and smiled. "I don't know."

Kat smiled back.

"You want to?" he asked again. "Just you and me?"

She agreed without hesitation, knowing she wanted nothing more than to just be with him, away from all the fuckery going on around her.

"Good." He stood determinedly, pushing his chair back with his legs, and walked to Kat's side. He held his palm out for her and waited with patient eyes.

As soon as Kat's palm touched Carter's, she was better, calmer, freer. It was the strangest sensation, but she had the sudden urge to tell him so, to tell him she was home with him. To tell him it was the simplest gestures of his that had the largest effect on her heart.

Carter pulled her up and cupped her cheeks in his hands.

"Just you and me," he repeated in a soft whisper. His eyes roamed across her face while his fingers stroked a piece of her hair. "For one day. Let's just forget all of the bullshit, and be you and me."

Kat looked up into Carter's open face and saw everything she'd ever wanted or desired.

I want you.

I want to be with you.

I need you so much.

I think I love you.

Closing her eyes at the warmth of that realization, Kat pressed her cheeks into Carter's palms and smiled. "You and me."

21

Carter had no idea where he wanted to take Peaches, but she seemed fine with that, which was a huge relief. Carter had no idea what a romantic or intimate gesture was, he just wanted to put the smile back on her face. He would have to make it up as he went along and pray that whatever he thought was cool and perfect would be perfect for her, too.

Carter drove for miles, flying over the Brooklyn Bridge next to a hot Porsche that tried to overtake his ass. Carter pulled back his right hand and blasted Kala past the bastard. He smiled when Peaches laughed behind him.

They drove to East New York, through Cypress Hills, cruising by the park and along Broadway, all the way back to Manhattan. It was the first time Carter had truly stretched Kala's legs since he'd been out of lockup, and it was awesome. He lost himself in having Peaches behind him, around him, particularly as the wind whipped at them when they crossed the water, back to the island. They couldn't talk, but Carter knew that was probably what she wanted, although he'd laughed loudly when she'd squealed and giggled into his back as he'd revved Kala hard down Forty-seventh, shooting them through traffic like a bullet.

He could feel her hands through his jacket and—on two occasions—he placed a hand over them, stroking and squeezing. He wanted to reassure her, make sure she was okay, and, each time he had, she'd clutched his fingers back in response.

It was almost six in the evening when Carter pulled up on Fifth

Avenue, next to Central Park. It'd started to rain a little, but it didn't seem to matter. If it meant there would be fewer people around, then Carter was all for it. He sat for a moment with Peaches still clinging to him, listening to Kala's engine tick as it began to cool beneath him.

"You all right back there?" he asked, unclipping his bike helmet.

"Yeah," she murmured. "I'm so relaxed, I almost fell asleep."

He rubbed her hands, which were still grasping him, and turned his head toward her. "You want me to take you home?"

To his relief, she shook her head. "No. I'm not ready to go home yet."

"Good," he replied with a small smile. "Me neither."

Carter helped her off the seat, with his hand in hers. He made to pull away once she was standing, but she held on, slipping her fingers through his. His eyes widened in surprise.

She glanced up at him, her lip wedged between her teeth. "Is this okay?"

Carter smiled. It was more than okay.

Walking leisurely through Central Park, hand in hand with Peaches, was a strange experience. Carter felt ten feet tall, but, at the same time, he was tiny and vulnerable. The chaos surging through his body made him feel exhilarated and scared to death. It was intense.

"You still with me over there?" Peaches asked as they made their way toward the spot by the Alice in Wonderland statue that had become their own, even after just one visit.

"Yeah," he answered. "Why?"

"You just seem, I don't know, nervous?"

Carter laughed a strange, strangled type of sound. "Nah, I'm good."

She looked at him askance, but didn't push.

The rain eased. They took off their jackets and sat down on

them. Carter took a moment to glance over at the Alice in Wonderland statue. It was hauntingly beautiful.

"Here."

The air in Carter's chest exploded out of him when Peaches slammed a book hard against him. "What the—"

"I haven't heard you read for a week," she said with a hand on her hip. "So read."

Recognizing the copy of *A Farewell to Arms*, he laughed. "Yes, ma'am."

While he found the page they'd reached during their last session together, Peaches got herself comfortable by leaning against his side with her head on his shoulder, and her arm resting on his thigh. Emboldened, Carter put his arm around her waist and held her close. As Hemingway's words rolled off his tongue, she snuggled closer, relaxing and melting into him. She was warm against the chill of the air. He put his cheek against her hair while rubbing his palm along her arm.

"I love hearing you read," she whispered when he came to the end of the chapter. "Your voice is . . ."

Carter laid the book down on the damp grass. "What?"

"It's familiar to me, like I know it better than my own."

Carter's heart stuttered. Of course she knew his voice. It was all he had thought to use to keep her calm the night her father had died. "And that's a good thing?"

"Yeah. It's a good thing."

Her smile was wide and honest. Carter allowed his arms to encircle her waist and rested his chin on her shoulder, breathing her scent.

"Will you tell me more about the statue and your parents?"

Carter shifted and exhaled a grumbled, uncertain noise. "I, um, I don't—"

"It's okay if you don't want to," she said. "I was just curious."

Carter glanced at the statue again. He wanted to share with her.

The only way they could possibly move forward with whatever the hell was happening between them would be if they knew things about each other. Hell, his family would be a good place to start.

He kept his eyes on hers, anxiety creeping up his spine, but all he saw was encouragement and affection. There was no judgment, no condescension, no trickery.

"My dad met my mom when they were eighteen," he said through a long exhalation. "They were young, stupid, and from different sides of the tracks. My mom was from a very wealthy family. Her father—my grandfather, William Ford—owned one of the first communication companies in the country, WCS. James Carter, my father, on the other hand, had barely two cents to rub together and made what money he did have from playing music at clubs and painting."

Carter rolled his eyes at the romance of it all. "That's how he met my mother. She heard him playing piano one night and approached him." He clicked his fingers. "That was that."

Peaches played absentmindedly with the edge of his T-shirt; her silence encouraged him to tell her more, to tell her everything.

"To my mother's family, my dad was never good enough. He was trouble, a bum, worthless, but my mother rebelled, and they stayed together. They got a cheap, crappy apartment after my grandfather cut off my mother's money, and, within a year, she was pregnant with me." Carter clasped the bridge of his nose, easing the tension headache that teased behind his eyes. "She hid the pregnancy for a long time." Carter laughed without humor. He dropped his hand. "She hid me."

Peaches' hand found his chin and pulled his face up. "Hey. It's okay."

Exhausted with the tumult of emotion washing over him, Carter placed his forehead against hers. She leaned right back, strong and steady.

"My mother went back to her family," he continued. "My father had no money and she ran back to them like a coward. My grandfather told her to give me up, and she fucking considered it. It was only because my father turned up at the family house, shouting and demanding his rights, that they relented. My grandfather didn't want a scene or gossip for the family."

"Carter."

"Long story short, my grandmother—my mother's mom—was disgusted with her daughter's behavior. She fought for me and told her she had to face her responsibilities. A trust fund was drawn up for me, and full parental rights were given to my father." He scoffed. In a small voice, he added, "The bitch didn't even fight it. For me."

"Unbeknownst to my grandfather," he said with a self-satisfied smile, "my grandmother put her WCS shares in my name on the day I was born. She had lawyers draw up a secret, binding contract they've never been able to dissolve. My cousins are still trying to dissolve it and get me out of the company." Peaches tensed. "They only discovered it the day she died. That was sixteen years ago, and even then her shares were worth a little under . . . fifty million dollars."

He waited. Peaches blinked. "Fifty?" Carter nodded. "Million? Holy hell." She shook her head, bewildered. "Carter, why are you here? You have so much going for you. With that amount of money, you could go anywhere, do whatever the hell you wanted, and start over."

Carter shrugged. "I don't have access to the bulk of it. It's trussed up in shares and— I don't care. It means exactly dick anyway. I don't need their money."

The Fords—specifically his cousin Austin—had managed to freeze his assets when Carter was first incarcerated. Fucker. Apparently, even as an adult, Carter was still gossip that was frowned upon by his family.

"Do you ever see your mother?"

Carter shook his head. "She died of cancer when I was eight."

"Oh God, Carter, I'm so—"

"Don't apologize for her," he snapped. "She doesn't deserve it."

"You don't mean that."

"Don't I?" He took a deep breath. "All she did was deny me. She didn't want me. The only reason she took me once every two weeks was because my grandmother ordered her to in her will. Ordered her to. She just liked pissing her father off. She went through a rebellious phase and got knocked up."

"What about your father?"

Carter clenched his jaw. "He lives in Connecticut with his new wife. I don't speak to him. Can we— Can we talk about something else?" He shifted his head sharply to the side so his ear touched his shoulder, and groaned when it gave a loud click. "I need to move."

He stood, shaking his arms out. He had a lot of pent-up energy that needed releasing. He pulled out his pack of smokes and lit one, taking a huge pull. He turned to see Peaches sitting, watching him, gripping her shins while leaning her chin on her knees. He needed to divert the attention somehow. He'd never been comfortable under a microscope and, even though he knew that she wasn't asking him to be nosy, telling Peaches personal stuff was still difficult for him.

"So, are you gonna tell me what happened this past week while you were away?"

Tit for tat and all that.

Peaches twisted her hands together awkwardly and pursed her lips. Carter waited, vaguely aware it had started raining again.

"My mother is a difficult woman," she whispered.

Carter could only imagine how her mother reacted to her job. He wondered fleetingly how she'd react to her daughter's choice in men.

"She still sees me as a nine-year-old kid instead of a twenty-five-year-old woman. She thinks anybody with a criminal history is capable of evil just like the men who killed my father."

Carter flopped back against a tree, smoking silently.

Well. That answered that.

"She doesn't agree with my life choices. She thinks I can't make my own decisions, and the ones I do make are never the right ones, even my teaching."

"You're an amazing teacher, Peaches."

"Thank you." She dipped her head. "Well, it's what my dad wanted for me."

Carter couldn't look away from his girl, peaceful and stunning in the twilight. They'd shared so much together over the past few hours, but Carter knew there was still so much he needed to tell her. He just didn't have a clue how to broach any of it.

They needed to reconnect somehow, find what they had left in her kitchen when they'd cooked the omelettes. Determined, Carter threw his smoke away, pushed off from the tree, and walked to her. He held out his hand.

"What?" She cocked her head.

"Come here." He grinned.

Without hesitation, she placed her hand in his. Her touch tingled and buzzed and shot up Carter's arm like a lightning bolt. He pulled her to her feet and led her until they were standing next to the Alice statue. He pulled her close and held her left hand up in his right, with his other on her waist. Slowly, he began moving from side to side, watching confusion creep across her face.

"What are you doing?"

He lifted his arm and twirled her slowly underneath it. "I'm dancing with you."

He placed his hand tighter around her waist and leaned her so far back she squealed and clung to his shoulders. They both laughed when he brought her back up, and Carter did an internal happy dance when she pushed her cheek against him.

"Is that—is that Otis Redding you're humming?"

Embarrassment teased his neck. "Um . . . yeah, I think so—'These Arms of Mine,' I think. I don't know. Why?"

She giggled. "I wouldn't have pegged you as an Otis fan." She eyed his Zeppelin T-shirt.

"Shut up," he chided and pushed her face into his chest, smiling at her muffled laughter.

As he continued to hum, they moved together slowly, gracefully, from one foot to the other, in a complete circle, holding each other in the gentle rain.

"My dad loved Redding's music," she whispered. "He'd play '(Sittin' on the) Dock of the Bay' at full blast all the time. He drove me and my mom freaking crazy."

"He had good taste."

"He played it in the car on the way . . . the night that . . ."

Carter's arms tightened around her instinctively.

She cleared her throat. "It's weird the things you remember, huh?"

His stomach tensed. Was this the moment he asked? Was this the moment he told her who he was, what part he'd played? Was this the moment he put everything they had built together on the fucking cliff edge, and waited for the inevitable tumble?

If he truly wanted her to be his, he knew the answer was yes.

Closing his eyes, he let the words come.

"What do you remember of the night that he—ya know—when he passed away?"

She lifted her face to the evening sky. "I remember everything."

Carter's stomach hit his shoes. "You do?"

"Yeah, everything," she murmured, placing her cheek back against his chest. "I remember the car ride from DC. The hotel, visiting his rehabilitation shelter, the walk to the sandwich shop, the moment they hit him with the baseball bat."

His lips pressed against her hair. "I'm so sorry."

He hated that she'd been hurt. He hated that he hadn't been strong enough to stop the bastards from killing her father. And he hated that he knew, deep down in his soul, that Peaches would hate him for it, too.

"Don't be," she said. "No one could have saved him. Not even me, even though I tried like hell."

"You were nine." He knew she would have tried, if she'd been able. She would have fought with all of her might to stop them from hurting her father.

"I ran," she whispered. "I ran away when he needed me."

Carter's face collapsed.

"Don't do that to yourself." He waited. Breathed. "He told you . . . to run, Kat."

She froze in his arms. Carter shut his eyes and clasped his hands at her back, suddenly terrified she would bolt. He couldn't let her run again. He couldn't lose her.

"What?"

Carter held his breath. "He told you to run."

She moved her head back. Her eyes told him the pieces were falling together, slowly but surely, and all he could do was plead with his own for her to wait, listen, and try to understand.

"Carter." Her voice shook. "How do . . . how do you know that?"

He stared at her, praying he wouldn't have to say the words aloud, but knowing with every inch of himself that he had to. He had to tell her. "You told me last night."

She didn't look convinced.

She cocked her chin, studying Carter's face. The cogs of her mind turned behind her emerald-green eyes. They flashed with pain and shock at the same time she gasped loudly, shoving him, breaking his hold on her. She stumbled back.

Carter's heart shattered.

"I . . . I want to know what you remember." His arms dropped to his sides. They were useless without her in them.

"Why?" she pushed, with anger in her voice. "Why do you want to know? Why, Carter?"

He took a step closer and she instinctively took one back. Carter's teeth clenched.

"Because," he started, rubbing his hands across his beanie, terrified, "I was— Because . . . Peaches."

"Fuck's sake," she cried. "WHY?"

Her yell ricocheted around them as the rain clouds broke, and the heavens opened above them. But it didn't matter. Carter was numb. He stared at her and lifted his arms minutely before letting them fall, defeated. He dropped his chin, gathered himself and the fear pounding in his head.

"Because I was there."

The look on her face tore Carter wide-open, making his legs unsteady. Christ, she looked sick. She started shaking and gasping for air while mumbling words he couldn't decipher. She clamped her eyes shut while her mouth continued to move in incoherent ramblings.

"No. No. No," she repeated. "It wasn't— I can't."

The rain pummeled Carter. "It was me," he whispered. "It was me, Kat."

She was instantly mute, staring at him as though he were a stranger. She opened her mouth, but he didn't let her speak.

"I was in the area near your father's rehabilitation center. I'd been with Max, but we'd had a fight, and I—I'd left him at a friend's. I was having a smoke and heard a scream, so I went to see what was going on and . . . I saw them. I saw you. I saw them hit him with the bat."

"Stop," Kat rasped.

"I saw the guy hit you—"

"Stop, Carter."

"Your father told you to run and you didn't. Why didn't you run?"

"Fucking stop!"

"NO!"

He took three strides toward her and yanked her into his arms. She began to fight him. Her skin was slick from the rain, making it hard to get a good grip. She hit his chest and arms as she screamed at him to let her go. But he didn't. He couldn't.

"I grabbed you," he cried above her protests. "I grabbed you and ran with you. I've never been so scared, Kat. I had to drag you; you fought me so fucking hard. You fought me like you're doing now, like you did last night. But I couldn't let you go. I couldn't. They would have killed you, just like they killed him."

Kat sobbed in his arms, buckling at the knees.

"We landed on the floor, and, your hair, Kat. Goddammit. Peach-scented hair. My Peaches."

Her head snapped up and she screamed in his face. "GET OFF ME!"

At the fury in her voice Carter released her and stepped back, only to receive a white-hot slap across his face.

For a few seconds the only sound around them was the rain pounding the trees. He couldn't look at her and see the hate in her eyes. He was paralyzed, desolate, but he couldn't stop telling her. He had to tell her.

"I held you," he muttered, "for two fucking hours, in a freezing-cold doorway, talking to you."

"You," Kat accused. "You stopped me from . . ." She could barely speak through the wracking gulps of air. "I could have— I could have . . . He was my father!"

Carter turned back to her, his hurt, angry tears merging silently with the rain running down his face. "He told you to run. I couldn't watch them kill you."

"You had no right!"

"No right?" he argued back, his voice rising to match hers. "Your father wanted you safe, Kat. I . . . I saved you!"

"No, you didn't, Carter!" she shouted back. "No, you didn't, because I fucking died that night, too!"

Carter gaped at her. She may as well have punched him in the fucking stomach. How could she think that?

A dangerous calm shrouded her. She glanced about herself. "I . . . I need . . . I." She pushed past him toward her jacket and bag, her feet splashing in the huge puddles that had formed with the rain.

"Kat," Carter implored. "Don't . . . please!" He grabbed for her arm but she yanked it from his grasp and shoved him away.

"Don't!" she cried with a finger in his face. "You fucking liar! You're just like the rest of them! Just don't!"

He blinked at her. Stunned. "I never lied!" he yelled, fury rising through his body. "What are you talking about?"

"You never told me!" She pushed him again. "How long have you known and you never told me? That makes you a dirty. Fucking. Liar!"

Devastation curled Carter's shoulders.

Kat's palms found the sides of her forehead. "I . . . I can't be—be . . . no—anywhere near you. I have to . . ."

She turned from him, grabbed her bag, and set off at a dead run.

Carter exploded after her, calling for her to stop, yelling at her to think about what she was doing in the dark, in the middle of Central Park, but she ignored him. He could have caught her easily. He could have wrestled her to the floor just as he'd done sixteen years before, but what would have been the fucking point?

She hated him and didn't want to be near him.

She'd called him a liar.

Was he?

Carter stopped dead at that thought, and watched helplessly as she ran from him. Breathless, his whole body felt skinned. He clutched his chest in a futile attempt to stop the searing hurt that twisted there. Unable to breathe, he bent his head back and roared loudly into the sky, releasing the frustration and rage heaving through his bones. He kicked the base of a nearby tree several times, bellowing out words and sounds he'd never heard himself use before while praying to all hell that the hurt would stop.

Exhausted, Carter's hands dropped to his knees while his eyes followed the path she'd taken.

When he could no longer see her and his voice was hoarse, he staggered back to his jacket and bike helmets and stumbled back to Kala.

22

Carter wasn't sure how long he'd ridden his bike around the city. The only things he knew were that he was soaked to the bone, and there was a quarter-empty bottle of Jack in his hand.

He rolled Kala back into the garage and parked, kicking her stand down to take the weight. Carter flopped against her, ghosting his hand across the leather seat where Kat had sat behind him, around him, with him. His hand shook inexplicably, so he took a large gulp of Jack, hissing at the burn. The only comfort Carter took from the whiskey's heat was it reminded him that he was still capable of feeling something.

He snorted in derision and took another hit.

Dirty fucking liar. Dirty fucking liar.

With lead feet and a body that was disturbingly empty, Carter made his way back up the stairs, climbing the six floors to his apartment. He didn't care how long it took him or that it would have been easier to take the elevator. All he cared about was getting into bed with his Jack and praying he didn't wake up for days. He shoved the stair door open with his shoulder, stumbling a little, and stopped dead.

Sitting in a tight ball at his apartment door—soaking wet and shivering—was Kat.

Carter slumped against the wall. A relief that almost crippled him washed down his back like warm water. Despite mascara covering half her face and her hair dripping all over, she'd never been more fucking beautiful.

They stared at each other for an eternity, silent words passing between them: words too big for a hallway as small as the one they found themselves in. Eventually, and with a strength he hadn't known he possessed, Carter pushed from the wall and began approaching her—slow and cautious—as though moving toward a wild animal.

He was mere inches from her when she struggled to her feet and sagged, wet and heavy, against his door. She looked as tired as he felt.

With his eyes fixed on hers, and no words spoken, Carter pulled his keys from his pocket and leaned around her to unlock the door. He wasn't sure, but he thought he heard her take a deep breath of him. He didn't care, though. He wanted her to. He wanted any part she was still willing to give him.

If he was a dirty fucking liar, then he would be *her* dirty fucking liar.

Kat stepped hesitantly into the apartment. Carter set the bottle of Jack on the counter next to the coffee mugs that remained from that morning, when shit was still unicorns and fucking rainbows, and turned back to her, shaking out of his jacket. She was drenched and shaking with cold.

"Shit," he muttered. "You need a towel."

He made to step past her, toward the bathroom, but she stopped him in his tracks with her palms firmly on his waist, and her forehead pressed hard against his chest. Carter's breath shuddered out at the contact. He couldn't move. He didn't know what he was meant to do. Last time he'd tried to touch her, she'd screamed and run away. He couldn't cope with that shit again.

They stood motionless. Her shoulders shook with the sobs tumbling from her. He wanted to rub her back or touch her hair . . . but, dammit, he daren't.

"I'm sorry," she whispered. Her hands clutched his sides tightly, the water in his T-shirt running down her knuckles.

Carter's throat constricted.

Gradually, her hands slid up his chest to his neck. She lifted her head.

"I'm sorry." Her small fingers grasped at his skin and her breath burned hot across his collarbone. "I'm— Oh God, Carter. I'm so sorry."

Carter tried to clear his throat of the huge lump of emotion blocking it while she continued to whisper her apologies. With each one that left her, another piece of the punk-ass wall Carter had built around himself came tumbling down at her feet.

"I don't need a towel. I need you." Her body shook against him. "I need you so much."

Carter's head collapsed against hers. "Peaches." His arms wound around her. "You have me." He gripped the bottom of her shirt in his hands. "You always have."

She bit her lip. Her face crumpled and her hand smoothed carefully over the cheek she'd struck. "Like you have me."

Reaching up onto her toes, she placed her hot lips under his eye, murmuring again about how sorry she was. How she would beg for his forgiveness. How much he meant to her. Her lips were perfect as she kissed slowly and tenderly across his face, across his eye, his brow, and down his other cheek to the corner of his mouth.

Carter froze when her tongue brushed across his bottom lip. His hands automatically gripped her waist so that he remained upright on his wobbling knees. He wanted her so much. Jesus, would she ever know how much? How insane he was for her?

He bent down, desperate for her touch, and their lips met in the softest, slowest, most sensual kiss. He opened his mouth to her, his breath leaving him in gasps and shaking groans when her tongue met his again. He closed his lips around it, and sucked gently while his hands moved from their place on her waist, up and under her shirt.

His palms slid easily against her wet skin and the kiss instantly deepened with a loud groan from them both. Carter swallowed every breath she gave him, owning each one, and pulled her closer, wanting her to feel how hard he was and how much he craved to be inside of her.

Needed to be inside of her, consumed by her.

Her hands moved to the bottom of his shirt, where she tugged in question. He moved back so she could pull it over his head. Her mouth was immediately on his chest, licking and kissing, nibbling and driving him crazy.

Perfect. Her lips were fucking perfect.

"I'm sorry," she murmured into his skin.

Carter was suddenly desperate for more of her mouth, her taste, and crushed his lips hard against hers, forcing his tongue inside. She moaned loudly, holding him closer. He pulled at her shirt and ripped it over her head, mourning the few seconds her lips weren't pressing against his.

Her pale blue bra was next to go. Carter groaned when he saw the nipples he'd gotten to know so well the night before. They were erect and stunning, and reacted instantly when Carter's thumbs caressed them.

"Oh, God," Kat murmured.

He did it again. Her head lolled back, elegant and beautiful.

"You like that?" He kissed her again. She gripped his shoulders in reply. Her nails dug into him and he grunted in pleasure. His hands grabbed both of her heavy breasts, roughly kneading the soft skin while her nipples puckered in his palms.

"Yes," she answered in a breathless gasp. "Please. Please. I'm sorry. I'm so sorry."

Carter halted her words with his mouth. "Stop. You're here now." He pushed her hair from her face as it dripped down her nose. "Just you and me."

He cupped her face, rubbing at the wet skin under her eyes, and kissed her. Her hands held his forearms securely, letting him lead it. Carter tried to rein in his desire—fuck, he tried so damn hard—but all too soon, the fire between them began to strengthen, their passion for each other igniting into flames.

With a feral growl that sounded like her name, Carter bent down and picked her up, smiling against her mouth when her legs and arms wrapped firmly around him. He gripped her ass and groaned when her naked breasts slid against his chest, the rainwater acting as a natural lubricant.

Without any stumbling this time, Carter carried her through his apartment to his bed and kneeled, laying her down and spreading his weight protectively across her. He let his hands roam across her skin, up her sides, across her breasts, to her neck and stomach as they panted and moaned between crumpled lips.

Unable to resist any longer, Carter's mouth eventually followed the path of his hands, hungry and wanting more of her body. He growled when she arched, and he jerked his hips firmly against hers when she grabbed at his ass.

He bit the underside of her right breast and she yelped before moaning in pleasure.

"More," she whimpered into his hair. "Please, Carter. More."

"Anything." His hand dropped, quickly, to the button on her jeans and pushed it through.

He pulled at her zipper and hooked his fingers into the denim waistband. He waited, suddenly nervous, wanting to make sure she was okay, that this was what she truly wanted. He glanced up at her from under his lashes.

Tell me you want this. Tell me you want this as much as I do.

She gazed at him and caressed his cheek. "Don't stop."

She lifted her hips and he pulled her jeans down. He let his knuckles graze along her thighs and calves, and laughed when he got to her ankles and discovered she still had her boots on.

"Sorry." She giggled.

He began to untie them. "No problem," he replied, kissing

her ankle while he removed one boot and sock, and then the other.

Finally free of any obstacles, Carter yanked her jeans all the way off and kneeled on the edge of the bed, taking her in. She was breathtaking. Feminine. Sexy. Gorgeous. Her skin was pale and unblemished, and looked as soft as he knew it was under his fingertips.

He moaned low in his throat, unable to move, happy to just look at her.

"Carter," Kat whispered in concern. She lifted up onto her forearms and caught his eye with a dip of her chin. "If you don't want to do this, I understand after what I said, and did, I—"

Carter swallowed her words with a hungry mouth. "I want," he gasped into her mouth. "I really fucking want." His hand slid down her waist, to her hip, and played with the side of her panties, hesitating. "Can I? Can I touch you?"

"I want nothing more than your fingers on me."

"Christ." He tucked his hand under the cotton of her panties and ran his knuckles down her soft, naked lips. "Wet," he growled as his hand traveled up and down.

Kat hummed, collapsing back onto the bed, pulling Carter down with her. "For you."

As though her words were kerosene on a naked flame, Carter's fingertips pushed up between her lips in search of her clit. He hit it with his thumb first, and grunted. They both moaned at the contact. Carter's index finger moved down and slipped easily against the silky wetness lying there.

Closing his eyes, he nibbled her shoulder and breathed against her skin. The tip of his finger circled her entrance teasingly, garnering a sigh from her. The fluid movements of her hips, along with husky sounds rumbling from her throat, entranced him. He couldn't wait any longer. He slipped that shit right inside of her.

Warm. Wet. Transcendent.

She cried out when his finger began moving slowly in and out of her, right up to the knuckle.

He dropped his head and circled her nipple with the tip of his tongue. Kat grunted, gripping his shoulders.

She gasped while winding her hips around in a sharp, desperate figure eight. "More."

Carter pushed another finger into her and immediately upped the speed at which they were fucking her. Kat cried out and her hands pulled at his shoulders, hard. Carter closed his eyes and listened to the wet noises filling the room as he pumped his hand against her and feasted greedily on her delicious body. It was the sexiest symphony he'd ever heard.

His thumb found her clit once more, and another finger started to creep up inside. The last thing he wanted to do was to hurt her, but, fuck, he wanted so much of himself inside of her all at once he couldn't stop. He kept his eyes on her face as he pushed.

Gently. Carefully.

Kat's back arched, and a long guttural groan erupted from her when Carter began to pump his curled fingers.

God, she was magnificent as she bucked and thrashed.

More.

Carter's biceps tensed.

Harder. Faster.

He wanted her orgasm. He wanted to hear it.

Taste it. Smell it. Own it.

"Carter." Kat grabbed for him. "Oh, I'm—"

"That's it, baby," he panted and licked her throat, tasting the salty tang of her sweat. "Give it up. I want it." He nibbled her earlobe, tasting apricot and candy. "You feel so good around my fingers." He licked her jaw: honey. "Fuck, you taste so good." He sucked her nipple hard into his mouth: vanilla.

Desperate for her to climax, Carter began slamming his fingers into her, rubbing and curling and flicking her clit. She grabbed at him and Carter moaned with her when she came hard, pulsing, and twitching, and flailing under him.

"Jesus fucking Christ," he gasped when her body squeezed his fingers.

She crushed her lips to his, whimpering into his mouth.

"Goddamn," Carter murmured.

He allowed his hand to slide and tease as she panted and whispered into his neck. Her words were low and jumbled, but the shudder in her body told Carter all he needed to know: he'd made her come good. Kat glowed beatifically beneath him. He slowed his hand and kissed across her chest, up toward her jaw. Her pulse raced. She was resplendent.

"Are you okay?" He placed a gentle kiss on her open mouth. She laughed and put a hand to her throat. Her eyes closed but he could see them moving under her lids.

She blew a breath out between her lips and opened one eye to look at him above her. "Carter, your hands are genius."

This, Carter had to laugh at. He pulled his hand out of her panties and wiggled his fingers in front of her. The skin of his fingers glistened in the light and, Carter had to admit, it was the hottest thing he'd ever seen. Well, that was until Kat took them into her mouth and sucked on them like a vacuum. Carter's hips bucked of their own accord at the same time that he moaned obscenely loud.

"Oh, God." Her tongue swirled around each digit. He ground hard into the bed, desperate for release.

Kat pulled his fingers from her mouth with a loud popping sound, and moved to kiss him, gripping his face in her small hands. He could taste her on her tongue.

"What the hell are you doing to me?" Carter growled.

She pulled her mouth away and began kissing his face. "I want to make you feel good," she whispered. "I've wanted you for so long, Carter."

He held her close as her touches and kisses started changing from soft and wanting to desperate and frenzied, and her small whimpers slowly morphed into louder sobs.

"It was you," she muttered into his shoulder in between licks and bites. "Oh God, Carter, it was you."

"Shhh," he soothed. "Kat, it's okay. It's okay."

"You saved me." She wept into his skin. "I knew you were real. I knew. Everyone said I'd imagined it, that you weren't real." She trailed her pointer finger across his bottom lip. "But you are."

Carter's bones dissolved at her words. She understood. Wherever she'd been tonight, whatever she'd done after she'd run from him, she'd realized what he'd said was true. He had saved her.

Her legs wrapped around him, pinning him to her while she cried into his shoulder. "I'm so sorry I hit you." She smothered his cheek with kisses. "Forgive me, please?"

She continued to touch him while her words of thanks and realization tumbled from her mouth. Carter didn't stop her. He needed to hear her say all she had to. He needed to have this moment with her. She pushed his shoulders and rolled them both over, sitting astride his waist. Carter kept his eyes closed, with his hands on her ample hips, and let his other senses take over, focusing on every other part of her: the warmth from between her legs, the sound of her breathing, the power in her touch, and the smell of her perfume.

"You held me." Her palms explored his stomach. "I remember the way you smelled." She pushed her nose into the crook of his neck and took a huge breath. "It was you. You whispered in my ear, telling me I was safe. I know now. I know why your voice makes me feel so protected." She dropped her forehead to his and let her lips whisper across his mouth.

He *had* spoken to her—into her hair—until his voice gave out and the sirens came near. His eyes began to sting under his lids. He clenched them tight. Her hands swept over his skin, up his sides to his neck, and down again, memorizing him.

"Kat," Carter breathed, unraveling under every movement. "Keep touching me. Touch me everywhere." His hands gripped her sides and caressed the skin up to her ribs. "God, don't stop."

She shook her head, her hair falling all around him. "Never."

Their lips met again, softly, but with a passion that wrecked him.

"Your arms," she muttered against his neck. Her hands slid along his biceps. "I feel like I know them so well." He could feel her nails leaving imprints in his skin when she pulled them down to his forearms, and then to his hands, where she entwined their fingers together. "Strong and protective." She kissed the crook of each of his elbows. "I was meant to be in your arms, Carter," she said, the ardor back in her voice. "I missed them. I missed you." She whispered by his ear. "I've missed you my whole life."

Carter nuzzled her neck, licking the delicate column up to her jaw. "I missed you, too. My Peaches."

She smiled against his cheek. "Always."

Carter exhaled loudly, expectantly, when her hands moved gradually down his body, outlining the grooves of his muscled stomach and the hair below his belly button. When they finally reached the buttons of his fly, Kat's hand cupped him through the denim of his jeans and rubbed up his full length, hard and slow.

Carter's hips lifted eagerly to meet her incredible palm. It was insanely erotic, having her rub his dick the way she was, knowing he was naked underneath; her hand could be wrapped around him in mere seconds, stroking and making him beg.

Holy shit, he would beg. He'd beg her for anything.

Kat kept up the movement of her hand: up and down, gripping and rubbing, purring and sighing and feathering his chest with kisses.

Carter's abdomen began to tense. "You're gonna make me come if you . . . if you keep that shit up."

She smiled and grabbed him tighter. "And that's bad?"

He took hold of her face and pulled her mouth roughly to his, hot and hungry. "I'd much rather be inside you when that happens."

"God, yes." She moved her delectable ass so it was resting on his thighs.

With wide, excited eyes, Kat looked down at his button fly and began to pop each one open, slowly, cautiously. Fisting the bedsheets, he waited for her hands to touch, waited for the softness of her palm against him. It would feel so damn good. He rotated his hips impatiently.

It was then that Carter looked at her, and what he saw set every nerve ending in his body aflame. Kat was gaping at his cock, which was pushing readily through his open fly, and, Jesus, she looked hungry for it.

Like, animal hungry. Like she wanted to devour him.

He wanted her to devour him, to overwhelm him, intensely, desperately. But he had to be sure.

Carter sat up, taking Kat by surprise, and wrapped his arms around her. "We don't have to," he murmured, rubbing her nose with his in a gesture he hoped was reassuring. He pulled his face back and pushed her still damp hair away from her face. "I want you. I've always wanted you. But I want it to be right. I want it to be perfect."

Her face softened. "We're meant to be this way. Do you not feel that?"

"Kat," he said incredulously, kissing the tip of her shoulder, "I felt it from the moment you found me again."

She cupped his face. "So don't be afraid," she insisted. "Just be with me."

And they kissed.

And Carter lost himself to her.

Every. Single. Fucking. Part.

He lay down, bringing her with him with his hands in her hair, holding her as close as he could. She melted against him, curving into his body: a perfect fit above him. Slowly, and with his mouth still fixed to hers, Carter rolled over, covering her once again, wrapping himself around her from head to toe; their limbs aligned exactly.

Releasing her lips with a quick flick of his tongue, and with a tender kiss to her chin, Carter pushed up on his palms and moved so he was standing at the end of the bed. Keeping his eyes on hers, he removed his boots and socks. His hands were at the hips of his jeans when he saw her fingers were at the edge of her panties.

Without a word spoken, they pushed down their respective clothing and saw each other—naked—for the first time.

Carter's gaze roamed down her body as Kat's eyes did the same to him. She was perfect, every dip and curve of her. She was pink. Bare. And aching for his mouth all over her. Carter inhaled a shaky breath, seeing her equally captivated and enthralled by him.

Kat smiled, teasing. "You're very sexy."

Carter laughed, easing the nervous tension, before he kneeled on the bed between her legs, willing himself to keep his shit together. He was so hard he ached and pulsed with every breath.

Never had he been so insane for a woman.

He wanted all of her at once. Every part of her. He wanted to make her his. Mark her. Come in her. Come on her. He wanted to fuck her, to lick her, to feast on her. He wanted her panting, moaning, coming, and loud. He wanted her fast, hard, soft, and gentle. He wanted her above him, below him, in front of him, and at his side.

He ran both of his trembling hands across his scalp, terrified that they would hold her too tight if he let them. He dropped them to his sides, helpless, and held his breath.

"Kat, I—I want . . ."

In a move that made Carter's head light, Kat took his hand in hers and lifted it to her lips. She placed tiny kisses across his fingertips and knuckles, nuzzling his palm and breathing in his wrist before she held it against her cheek. Her eyes met his and every ounce of air held inside him left his body in a rush, leaving his heart stammering and stuttering, and his knees so weak that, had he been standing, he would have surely fallen.

He had fallen. He'd fallen so hard.

She tilted her head up, her beauty damn near blinding him. "You and me."

He nodded with a slack jaw and a pounding heart. "You and me," Carter answered; his thumb traced her cheek. He watched her lie back down and settled on his knees between her thighs.

Taking her ankle in his hand, Carter lifted it to his mouth and placed soft openmouthed kisses around it, moving down to her foot, where his tongue slid along her instep. Next were her calf and the dip behind her knee. She giggled when his tongue came out to taste her there, but grunted when his palms ghosted over her skin, leaving gooseflesh in their wake.

Taking his sweet-ass time, Carter crawled up her body, kissing every piece of skin he could see along the way. Her thighs were full and lush, and he spent extra time kissing and nibbling at those while pushing his nose into the crease of her groin. He smelled, but he didn't allow himself a taste. He wanted to save that delicacy and savor every moment later.

Kat moaned and grabbed at him and, by the time he reached her stomach and his tongue was in her belly button, she was heaving under him and dragging his face up toward her mouth.

"Carter." She groaned when he resisted her impatient hands. "Stop teasing."

He chuckled into her right breast and squeezed her left one. He moved over her and flicked at her lips with his tongue. Her hands grabbed his ass, nipping the skin with her nails.

"Fuck. That feels good," he muttered into her neck.

She did it again, lifted her legs up to her sides, and rested her heels on his lower back.

Carter hissed and dropped his head back as the tip of his cock brushed her wetness. Her heat was extraordinary. His hands cupped the sides of her face and he moved his lips across hers, languid and worshipful.

Dammit, he couldn't wait to be in her. He moved his hips minutely.

Yes, so deep, wet, tight, and—

Fuck.

He dropped his face onto her shoulder with a heavy thump and yelled loudly into her skin as his hips retreated. His cock rested heavy and hard on her thigh.

"Carter?" Kat asked nervously. Her hands rubbed down his back.

He smacked his hand down on the mattress by Kat's head, ready to throw himself under a bus, or a cab, or fucking both, and lifted his head while avoiding her gaze.

He silently fumed, glaring at the pillow above her head. "I—Shit, I don't have any condoms." And why would he? He'd been in prison for the best part of two years. Not much tail to be had there. "Kat?" he asked, in confusion. She looked nervous and she was definitely blushing. "What is it?"

"Well, I—" She cleared her throat and started to make small circles on his shoulder with her fingertip. "I am covered, I mean, you know. And I'm clean."

"Covered?" he repeated.

"Mmhm. And you have to go for your checkups, right?" she asked, to which he nodded like a mute idiot. "So, we know you're clean. And I trust you. That is, if you trust me?"

She was adorably uneasy as she finished her sentence and her eyes were suddenly everywhere but on Carter's face. He lifted her chin and kissed her.

"I *am* clean," he said, his eyes flickering between hers. "And I do trust you." He kissed both of her cheeks. "With my life," he added quietly. "But I'll only do this if you're sure."

She seemed to breathe a sigh of relief and pressed her heels right back into his ass, lifting her hips to his.

"I'm really, really sure."

Carter moaned and shifted back to his original position. The tip of his cock slid along her.

Kat whimpered into his mouth. "I want to feel every inch of you."

With a loud groan, Carter moved his arms underneath her, gripping her shoulders, anchoring himself, crushing her to him. He needed to be secured to something for fear he would lose his damn mind when he put himself inside her.

"You ready for me?" he asked, stroking her face.

"I've always been ready." She pressed her lips to his.

"Goddamn, you're beautiful," Carter breathed when their foreheads met.

He knew he should have said something more profound, but words escaped him. Keeping his eyes on hers, Carter waited. Kat's hand gripped him, guiding him toward her heat. Once she released him and smiled, Carter pushed forward slowly, and the tip of his cock slipped into her.

They both gasped at the sensation and Kat's hips jerked. Carter held her shoulders tightly and opened his mouth against hers, breathing and gasping, all hot breath and wet lips. Kat mewed and closed her eyes. Carter pushed a little more and grunted into her cheek.

Kat bowed under him when—unable to stop himself—he pushed harder, sliding farther, until his hips were flush with hers, and he was fully sheathed within her. Kat cried out loudly, and tightened her thighs around his waist and her arms around his neck.

"Carter," she moaned and kissed his throat when his head fell back in utter ecstasy.

His eyes rolled. "You feel—it feels . . ."

"Perfect."

Yes, it was, and Carter could do nothing but bask in having Kat all around him.

"Move in me."

Leaning his head close to hers, watching her face as it twisted and contorted wonderfully, Carter pulled his hips back bit by bit before pushing back in. A shaky moan rumbled through him at the concentration it took not to pump his hips hard. He pulled back again, her body gripping, and caressing, the entire length of him. It was magnificent.

Running his hand down from her shoulder to her hip, Carter continued with long, deliberate, patient strokes while his mouth began to devour the woman in his arms. Kat was equally hungry for Carter's mouth. She sucked on his lips as he moved in her.

Kat whimpered, pushing her breasts up, rubbing her nipples against his. Her face was spectacular as he thrust deeply. Her brow furrowed above dark, lustful eyes, and her lips pursed. Carter could see a small sprinkling of sweat on her cheeks that sparkled when the light from the doorway hit her.

Carter panted. He licked her neck up to her ear and pushed into her again. Kat bit her lip before she lifted her hips, making Carter moan. He'd never been that vocal during sex before, but goddamn, no sex had ever felt this good before.

Kat's head dropped back and her hands pulled urgently at his waist. "You feel so good inside me, Carter."

"Holy shit." Carter covered her mouth with his. "Don't," he mumbled with a shake of his head.

Her dirty little words would be all he would need to end him.

"Can you go faster?"

He replied with a sharp shove of his cock that made Kat's breath catch and her body rise. "But if I do, I won't be able to stop." He glanced down between their bodies to watch himself move in her. He twitched at the sight. "You feel too good."

He moved his right arm from her hip and grabbed hold of her thigh, pushing her leg up farther so her knee was near his shoulder. The angle must have been a good one, because the groan that left her was stunning.

"There?" Carter asked in between deep loud pants. "You want it right there?"

He pushed harder and his eyes nearly dropped from their damn sockets when he slipped in even deeper. His hips began to move faster.

Kat cried out. "Don't stop."

Carter was pretty damn certain wild fucking horses wouldn't have been able to stop his ass. "Does it feel good?" His mouth latched on to her neck, where he began sucking and licking.

"Yes. Yes."

He moaned and thrust twice, sure and hard, making Kat's back lift from the bed. She held him closely, her nails making deep grooves into the flesh of his back. He wanted her to mark him. He wanted her brand on him.

His hips began slapping the backs of her thighs, hard. "I want . . ." The feel of her around him, her sounds, and smells were too much. He was starting to lose himself and he didn't know whether to feel elated or scared to death.

"Anything." She bit his earlobe, sensing his panic. "Have anything."

"I need harder." He released her other shoulder and placed his palm on the mattress by her head. "I want you harder."

Kat ran her hand across his hair. "You want to fuck me, Carter?"

All he could do was curse loudly in reply. He wanted more.

He rotated his hips and slammed into her. Kat yelled and Carter felt his body start to heat from the inside out, as his thrusts became firm and sure. His eyes shut of their own accord.

His body was no longer his own. It belonged to her. He was

sucking air in through his teeth, every muscle in his body screaming for release. The sheets were just about ready to rip, he was gripping them so hard, and the headboard of the bed had begun to tap solidly against the wall.

"Please." Kat gripped his face and brought his ear to her soft lips. "I want you to fuck me."

Carter flew upright onto his knees, holding his weight as he pulled Kat's body flush against his, her breasts crushed between them, gripping her by the hip and shoulder, and began pounding into her, deep, powerful strokes that made Kat scream. She clawed at him while his mouth bit and smothered as much of her as he was able, while the cries of "fuck," "harder," and "Kat" filled the room until the walls could barely contain them.

Carter simply couldn't stop fucking the beautiful woman in his arms. He didn't want to stop. He wanted this forever. He wanted *her* forever. He wanted to have this moment on loop for the rest of his life. Her taste. Her smell. The small cries of pleasure she was breathing in his ear. The shouts for more and the sounds of their bodies slamming together.

He gasped when their mouths met again, teeth and tongues everywhere at once.

And then Carter felt it.

Deep in his stomach as his balls tightened again, and his thighs took on a life of their own.

He was coming.

He tried to tell her. But Kat merely held on to him and rode every thrust. Carter buried his face into her hair and grunted in sync with the delicious sound of slapping skin. But suddenly, Kat's body changed. She became rigid in his arms.

Her eyes widened in surprise. "Oh God. It's . . . it's right there."

Carter clenched his teeth, willing his orgasm to hold off. This was what he'd dreamed about: Kat, in his arms, coming all over him. And he'd be damned if he'd miss a second of it.

Her head fell back and her hips swiveled, seeking out any kind of friction. Carter's thumb was immediately on her, flicking, pinching, and rubbing the pleasure out of her. She was so slick. Carter gasped out her name.

"Please," he begged, biting down on her shoulder. "Please. What can I do?" Carter's thrusts started to become sloppy and out of rhythm. "Goddammit, Kat, tell me."

She lifted her head. Her eyes hooded, dark, and full of passion. "Kiss me."

So he did. With his nose crushed against her face, Carter smashed his mouth to hers, sliding his tongue in and out, fucking her in every way possible. She responded almost instantly. Her arms tightened around his neck, and her legs jerked at his sides as her thighs held his waist in a bone-crushing grip.

"Yes. Yes," Carter growled, trying like hell to keep his erratic pace.

Kat's head fell back and Carter watched her take a huge breath and cry out at the top of her lungs as her orgasm crashed into her. "WES!"

At the sound of his name ripping from her throat, Carter's spine snapped, and he exploded inside of her with such force that he fell over, landing on Kat's body. Waves of euphoric release crashed over him, leaving him breathless, groaning, and crying out for his Peaches while she mumbled unintelligible words into his sweat-covered neck and shoulder.

Nothing had ever felt that fucking good. Nothing would ever come close. No woman would ever come that close. With a strange feeling of contentment, as he rode the best orgasm of his life, Carter realized he'd been ruined. Kat had ruined him. And he couldn't have been fucking happier.

"God. God. I can't." Carter slowly returned to Earth, not entirely sure all his limbs were attached and in working order. He did realize, however, that his full weight was pressing Kat hard into his bed, and that was just unacceptable. He made to lift off her on shaking arms and knees, but she held him fast, crushing him to her.

"Not yet," she murmured. "Don't leave me yet. Just stay a while longer."

Carter was without the energy to argue. "Mmkay," he managed into the pillow at the side of her head, to which Kat laughed, a sweet, high sound.

Her hands and fingertips danced lazily across his back. He fought the urge to fall asleep. With a sigh and a small kiss to her neck, Carter slipped his softening body from hers. Despite still being on top of her, he was instantly bereft.

"Damn, woman. That was . . ." His mouth came to a grinding halt. He opened his eyes, needing inspiration.

"It was," she finished for him. She was lovely in her postcoital glow. Carter kissed her again.

"You know," he said, releasing her lips and gazing down at her. "Maybe Donne had it right." He let his index finger trail down her nose to her gorgeous beestung lips.

Kat tried to suppress her smile, clearly recollecting their session in Central Park. "Oh yeah? About what?"

He tucked her curling hair behind her ear and traced her lobe with his thumb. "About being with someone," he murmured. "About it being like heaven." Kat's eyes closed at his words. "Too much?" he hedged with caution in his voice.

She shook her head. "No," she replied. "It was exactly like that." She reopened her eyes.

Carter let his gaze wander from her forehead to her chin, taking in every line and soft edge. He realized that her smile had widened.

"It's rude to stare," she chided.

He chuckled at her using his words from earlier that day and rubbed the tip of her nose with his own. "I'm not sorry." He watched her carefully for a while, looking for any signs of regret.

"Are you okay?" he asked. "I mean, about what I told you? About who I am."

"I'm more than okay." She pulled his lips to hers and kissed him.

Carter's eyes closed and he exhaled in contentment. Their tongues touched briefly, tenderly, and Carter's lips were still moving when she pulled away. His eyes fluttered open to see her gazing adoringly at him. His heart halted for one beat.

Physically and emotionally exhausted, Carter shifted down Kat's body and rested his ear against her damp chest, smiling when he heard her heart thumping behind her ribs. Her fingers moved leisurely from his shoulders to his scalp. He was almost asleep when he heard her whisper his name.

"Carter?"

"Yeah?"

Her hands stilled. "Thank you."

He frowned. "What for?"

She didn't reply or move.

He lifted his head and rested his chin on her sternum. "Sweetheart, what are you thanking me for?"

A lone tear slipped down her temple. She swallowed hard before answering. "For saving my life."

23

Carter froze, his rough chin resting on her smooth, soft skin. His lips twitched with a response, but, for the life of him, he had no clue what to say. With a soft sigh, he moved back up her body and cupped her face in his hands, resting his weight on his forearms at either side of her head.

"Kat," he whispered with his nose inches from hers. He waited for her to look at him. "You're here." He let his thumb trace her pink cheek and watched the color deepen under his touch. "That's all that matters."

There was conflict in her eyes: fear, affection, hurt. Carter felt a sharp twist of unease. He knew she didn't regret what they'd done. The way she'd held him, ridden him, whispered delicious words into his ear assured him of that. But he was hopelessly aware of the dangers surrounding her because of their actions.

The fact that he cared for Kat would make no difference to how people, her mother specifically, regarded him. He was an ex-con and, as such, was an untrustworthy bottom-feeder. No pretty words or fancy declarations could change that shit. She would never see him as anything else. Her fear and narrow-mindedness would blind her to what he truly felt for her daughter.

Carter's heart squeezed. He had to pray that whatever the two of them had found together was enough to keep Kat with him for as long as possible. He wanted more with her, from her, and he was willing to step up to get it. She was worth all of the shit that would come his way, and he would be there to protect her as best he could.

Once Kat had been to the bathroom, giving them both a chance to clean up, she crawled back into bed, allowing him to wrap his arm around her shoulders, pulling her into his side. She held him snugly around the waist. His palm rubbed across her back in comforting circles while her fingertips danced around his nipple. As new as the sensation was of cuddling a woman in his bed, the familiarity of it with Kat was as warm as the blankets around them.

Carter pressed his lips to her scalp. "Where did you go tonight?"

He didn't want to upset her, but he was aching to find out what had led her to his doorstep after she'd screamed such hatred. What had triggered the realization that he had saved her rather than holding her back from helping her father?

"I wandered for a long time." Her fingers gripped Carter's side. "I didn't know what to do. I was just— I just hurt. Everywhere."

Carter held her closer.

"I eventually got home." She paused. "I think I got a cab." Her lips moved against his skin. "I called my mother."

Carter's hand halted its movement against her shoulder blade. "What?"

Kat scoffed. "I know. I must be fucking stupid to call her, huh?"

"Peach—"

"As soon as she heard it was me," she interrupted fiercely, "she started telling me how disappointed she was about what happened at my grandmother's. She said I was ungrateful for the people around me, the people that cared about me. That she only wanted what was best for me and I was too self-involved and caught up with you to see it."

He swallowed. "She knows about me?"

She lifted from his shoulder to look at him. She was so close Carter had to shift his head back into the pillow to see her better.

"She knows I care for you." Her index finger moved along his bottom lip. "She knows that we kissed."

A cold shiver darted down Carter's spine as the last seven days began to fall into place. "That's why you left your family and friends. That's why you came back from Chicago." He smiled wryly. "They know."

Kat shook her head. "They think they know what's going on, but they don't. They have no fucking idea." The anger was clear in her voice. "Carter, you have to understand, my own mother thinks my choices are wrong and that I'm still a kid who knows nothing. She doesn't know how much I love my job, how much I love what I do every day, how much I love—" Her eyes burned with fury. "You're the only person who treats me like I'm me, who makes me feel like what I'm doing is right and meaningful. There's no bullshit, no hiding with you."

Her lips twitched with the beginnings of a smile. "And I began to see how hard it must've been for you to tell me about who you are." Her palm slid down his jaw. "Carter, I know the only reason you didn't tell me was because you were scared. You're the only person on this planet who knows what I went through. And do you want to know something really ironic?" Her eyes blazed. "My family, my friends, the cops, my fucking therapist, they all said you weren't real, that you were a figment of my imagination, a result of post-traumatic stress." Kat nuzzled his cheek. "But you're the most real thing in my life."

Carter couldn't answer. He was speechless and crazy for her touch. "Kat" was all he could utter before their mouths met. Three little words whispered relentlessly through Carter's psyche, bubbling furiously, whipping away his breath. Swallowing them and the fear that forever accompanied them back down, Carter rolled Kat onto her back and settled at her side, lifting one of her legs over his hip. Although she moaned, the movement was not sexual in its intent. He wanted her again, but he wanted to reassure her more that he was real and that he would always be that way with her.

"Stay with me tonight." He pushed her hair back, needing to see her whole face. "Please, Kat, just . . . just for tonight." He searched for an answer in the depths of her eyes. "But don't stay because you're upset. Stay with me because you want to."

The pleading words came from nowhere. All Carter knew was he meant them, and he needed her to say yes.

The smile that appeared on her face could have lit up Broadway. "I'm not going anywhere."

• • •

The lobby of WCS Communications was just how Carter remembered it: pretentious, repugnant, and reeking of money. Even the damn furniture looked uncomfortable, as if the shit had been stolen from a torture chamber. Carter scoffed at the irony of that particular thought. The fact that he was in the building at all was torturous in itself. Fuck's sake, he was ready to crawl out of his skin.

With a deep breath, he walked toward the raven-haired woman at the reception desk, hating the loud sound of his booted steps on the shiny wood floor, and waited patiently for her to finish her call.

"I have a two o'clock with Austin," he grumbled when she did, rubbing his hand across his jaw.

"Mr. Ford."

Carter blinked. "Excuse me?"

"Mr. Ford," she repeated. "You have a two o'clock with Mr. Ford. Not Austin." She smiled contemptuously.

"Whatever," he snapped. "Just do your job and tell the prick that Carter's here, will you?" The sound of her mouth dropping open bounded around the large room. "Thanks, Buttercup."

He turned toward the heinous cream sofa situated ten feet from the desk and slammed down onto it. He adjusted himself to try to get comfortable, but the postage-stamp-sized cushions were about as cozy as having glass up his ass. The whole place appeared constructed just to make its occupants feel uneasy, and it was working. No wonder the receptionist was so fucking uptight.

"Wes."

The hair on Carter's neck stood on end and his lip lifted into an animalistic snarl at the sound of his cousin's voice. Fucker knew Carter hated his given name, but he still insisted on using it frequently whenever they were in each other's company.

"We're ready for you," Austin said, his poker face in full play.

Carter followed Austin into his office and immediately tried not to vomit at the elaborate artwork on the walls, the ostentatious desk, and the ridiculously incredible view over the rest of New York's Financial District.

Fucker was totally compensating for something.

There were three other men standing in the room: Adam, who nodded cordially at Carter when he entered, and two others he'd never met before.

"Take a seat," Austin said, gesturing to the high-backed leather seat situated by the humongous desk.

Carter sat down ungracefully, placing his ankle onto his knee. He blew out an impatient breath and tapped his fingertips against his thighs.

"So," he drawled, glancing around the room. "Who are you?" He pointed to the suits standing by the window.

"This is Steve Fields, WCS's lead attorney, and David Fall," Austin answered. "He's head of accounting and finance."

"'Sup, Dave?" Carter smiled when he got no response. "I'm Carter." He pointed to himself before whispering loudly, "Your boss."

Austin coughed. "Well, actually, Wes—"

"Save the 'Wes' shit, Austin," Carter barked, losing his patience. "Just explain to me why the hell I'm here so I can leave as soon as humanly possible. There's only so much pretense and dick-sucking I can handle."

Anger flared in Austin's eyes. "Fine," he replied. "You're here so we can discuss the immediate dilution of your shares in WCS Communications."

"Is that right?" Carter asked with a backward tilt of his head. Austin raised his eyebrows in reply and walked around his desk to take his leather-and-wood throne. "And just how do you think that shit's gonna fly, Austin?" Carter continued. "The shares are in my name. They were given to me by our grandmother. The contract that was drawn up is legally binding on a scale that even your pathetic excuse for a law team can't change it." He waved his hand indifferently toward the lawyers. "You can't dilute the shares because of the provisions on them. Granddaddy tried for years. It ain't gonna happen."

Austin looked at Steve and David. The two men sat down at Carter's right. Adam remained standing to his left. Carter was being cornered. They were using blatant intimidation tactics.

"That's why you're here." Austin smiled tightly. "So we can discuss the provisions in detail."

Carter smirked. "You mean you wanna discuss how much it's gonna cost you assholes to get rid of me, right? Can't have an ex-con owning a billion-dollar company, now, can we? What would the papers say?"

Carter shook his head and turned to look out of the window. "It must really bug the shit out of you that I have the biggest shareholding in the company you were primed to take over, huh?"

"Not as much as it must bug the shit out of you that we have control over your money every month." Carter's head snapped back to Austin, whose face was pinched and hard. He sat forward. "I'd bear that in mind before you start with your sanctimonious bullshit, Carter. I kept your ass out of prison once; I can sure as hell get it back in there."

Carter became very still. "You threatening me, Ford?"

"No," Austin replied, "just reminding you that you're not the only one with a set of cards to play."

Carter was silent for a considerable amount of time before he continued in a low, even voice. "The money I receive, I have every right to claim. It's mine. In fact, I should get more—"

"You would, if you didn't have a criminal record."

Carter hid the flinch of rage that pricked at his throat when Austin interrupted him. In truth, Carter couldn't have given two shits about the money. He never had. What he cared about was that he was the rightful owner of the shares of which Austin spoke. Adam, who placed a very formal-looking document in front of Carter, broke the game of stare-down between Carter and Austin.

"You haven't brought any legal representation," Adam said pointedly. "It would be better if—"

"I can read, Adam. Just explain what it says and cut to the chase," Carter barked, making his cousin flinch. "My lawyer can peruse that shit at his leisure."

Adam fiddled with his cuffs and exhaled. "Upon dilution of your current shares, the money you receive monthly would be tripled. For life," he said. "Instead of paying for an acquisition with shares, we're offering you new shares in the firm. Shares worth in the region of five million—"

Carter snorted in derision. "Five million? Are you shitting me?"

He looked incredulously from Adam to Austin and back again. Both men remained silent. Carter rubbed his face in disbelief, aching for a smoke. "We all know the shares I own are in excess of five *hundred* million," he scoffed. "I was expecting to be impressed with your offer, not insulted." Carter pushed the papers across Austin's desk and slammed back in his seat. "Try again."

Austin visibly bristled and took a deep breath that made his shoulders lift. "For someone who claims to not give a shit about the business, you sure seem to be protective and knowledgeable about it all."

"Austin," Carter fumed. "There is a huge fucking difference between not giving a shit and not appreciating being handled and played by an asshole who thinks he's God's gift because he wears an expensive suit. I went to prison, not fucking dunce school. Your offer is shit. You know it. I know it. So, like I said, try again."

The silence was deafening. "Fine," Austin murmured. "I'll get my law team and finance team to reevaluate, and we'll get back to you."

"Can't wait," Carter retorted. "May I be excused?" he asked with his hands on the arms of his chair.

Austin didn't answer but dipped his chin minutely, his stare fierce and angry.

"Thank fuck," Carter grumbled. "I have a literature session to get to."

As Carter stood, he noticed both his cousins react instantly to his words. Adam, who was still standing to Carter's left, shifted nervously, while Austin rubbed his palms together.

"Oh yes," Austin said as Carter began walking across the office. "How is Kat?"

Carter froze with his hand on the door and gripped the cold steel in his fist. The question hung around the room like a putrid smell. It was, to anyone who didn't know better, a simple, polite question. To Carter, the question reeked of a possessiveness that nobody but him had any right to feel. How the fuck did he know Kat?

Carter's heart pinched. He turned slowly, attempting to keep his expression neutral. Still, as soon as his eyes met Austin's, Carter knew he was on thin ice. Asshole knew. What exactly wasn't clear, but he knew something. Carter's eyes darted to Adam, who was now apparently fascinated with his shoes.

Carter took a breath. "Kat," he replied through a tight throat, "is just fine."

Like a snake ready to strike, Austin smiled. "Oh, good," he said with too much enthusiasm. "I was hoping she was."

"Were you?" Carter seethed. His right eye twitched and his nostrils flared.

"Absolutely," Austin replied, standing from his seat. He moved around his desk. "Oh, didn't you know? Adam's engaged to Beth, who's known Kat for years. We're friends, Kat and I. I knew she had family to see in DC and Chicago, so I haven't seen her since her birthday party."

Carter swallowed and bit his tongue so hard he could taste blood. "Birthday party?"

It was then that Carter noticed the absence of Austin's wedding ring.

"Oh, yeah," Austin answered. "We had dinner. Then I drove her home. We had a great time." He fucking grinned. "She loved my gift. She's a great girl. Beautiful, too, but I guess . . . you know that."

Carter shook with ferocious violence.

Austin and Kat had dinner? She'd been with him. In his car. Alone? Had she invited him up to her apartment? Did that mean they'd . . . ?

Bile rose in his throat at the same time an agonizing pain hacked through him.

Austin continued. "I'm planning to take her out again, you know, go on a date and get her mind off work and less important matters." Austin gestured toward Carter and grinned. "Like her students."

Through the furious red haze, Carter could see the son of a bitch was goading him, taunting him, like a kid with a stick through the bars of the lion's cage, waiting for the inevitable snap, wanting him to lash out and play right into Austin's greedy fucking hands.

Sure enough, the rope of sanity Carter was holding on to within himself was thinning rapidly, while the grip he had on it was tenuous at best. He wanted nothing more than to grab Austin by his neck, rip off his balls with his bare hands, and throw him out of his office window.

But then, where would that leave him? Where would that leave Kat? His ass would be sent back to prison quicker than he could say, *Fuck you, Ford.* Parole would be a thing of the past. He and Kat would be a thing of the past.

With Herculean effort, and with the image of his Peaches the night before, writhing and begging for him as he fucked her in his bed, Carter took a huge breath.

"Well, Austin," he said through clenched teeth, "I'll be sure to let Kat know you were asking about her."

Austin was instantly perplexed. Carter turned back toward the door.

"But I wouldn't hold your breath for that phone call," Carter added, glaring over his shoulder at his cousin.

"Oh, really?" Austin spat, no longer hiding the aggressive jealousy in his voice. "And why's that?"

"Well, as you pointed out, she's busy with her students. And with me"—he glanced down at his own crotch before looking back at Austin with a smug-ass grin on his face—"her hands are always full."

Without waiting for a response, Carter yanked the office door open, causing the hinges to squeal in protest. The inevitable slam behind him was all that Carter heard as he stormed through the lobby, past the raven-haired bitch at her desk, while lighting a cigarette and flipping a finger at the No Smoking sign above the WCS exit.

• • •

As the clock struck five after four, Kat found herself alone in the reading room of the library, playing on her newly purchased iPhone. She'd had a free couple of hours between leaving Arthur Kill and her session with Carter, and had managed to make it home to upload all that she needed onto it. She couldn't live without her music. Not for another day.

She'd been more than a little hesitant about putting the rescued SIM card from her old phone into it, and as the phone began to beep incessantly with missed calls, voice mail messages, e-mails, and texts, she suddenly realized why. She scrolled through them slowly. Beth's name, her mother's, Ben's, Adam's, Austin's, and Carter's all made appearances. After listening to the fifth voice mail from her mother, she deleted the remaining six, not wanting or needing to hear her abhorrence one more time.

The one name she did pause at was Carter's. He'd sent a number of texts on the days she'd been driving from Chicago back to New York, and each one seemed more frantic than the last. The texts from Beth, on the other hand, were short and succinct:

Call me.

We need to talk.

I'm so sorry.

Kat didn't allow herself to get mad. Beth wasn't worth it, and besides, anything she had to say was worth shit at this point.

Austin's messages, as always, were charming and concerned:

Hey, Kat, hope you're well. Give me a call.

Kat, Adam called. He and Beth are worried about you. I am, too. Regardless of what they've told me, I'm here if you need a friend. X

Thinking of you. Austin. x

"Fuck," Kat muttered, deleting every one before throwing her cell into her bag.

Despite his omitting his link to Carter, Austin was a polite, handsome, charismatic guy. She'd enjoyed his company and enjoyed the kiss they'd shared. It was . . . pleasant.

In retrospect, Kat realized that there was never the burning passion with him that she felt every time she was in Carter's presence. The small flickers of attraction she had for Austin were nothing compared to the all-out inferno that occurred each time Carter touched her, kissed her, fucked her.

Her insides clenched at the memory of his large, solid body between her thighs, his heavy breaths and moans of *more* in her ear, his unrelenting hold on her hips, and his exquisite face as he chased and rode every orgasm. God, he was glorious. He'd obliterated every past lover she'd had, leaving her feverish with her want and hungry for more. The aches of pleasure he'd left in the muscles she hadn't known existed were luscious.

Her skin blushed with the recollection of his stubbled kisses and the sensation of his silver rings, which had pinched her thighs as he'd slammed home, leaving vivid red marks that he'd licked in apology. Fuck.

She glanced at the empty doorway of the reading room. Where the hell was he? Kat knew Carter had "stuff" to do, and, as far as he knew, she was still without a cell phone, which explained the silence.

Nonetheless, Kat was hit abruptly with a worrying thought. Would Carter start to take liberties with their sessions now that they'd been intimate? Would he really think she wouldn't kick his ass all over Manhattan for being late just because he'd given her numerous orgasms?

Kat's leg twitched as her anger increased. He'd be in for one hell of a surprise if that was the case. Punchy and agitated, Kat rose from her seat and began to wander around the reading room, heading for her favorite section: poetry.

With the tip of her index finger placed against the spines of the books, Kat meandered down the aisle between two huge mahogany bookshelves. The smell of the leather, ink, and wood was rich and comforting, and reminded her of her father's library at the house they'd owned in Westchester. Her father would read Rossetti and Blake to her when she was very young, and always when she was upset or hurt. She stopped when she came to the romantic poets, specifically Wordsworth, immediately needing his imagery of an English countryside and swaying daffodils to ease her mind.

Suitably calmed and incredibly nostalgic after reading three of his poems, Kat replaced Wordsworth and pulled down a small black book with gold-leaf font filled with sonnets, poems, and declarations of love. Holding the book in one hand, she leafed through the yellowing pages with the other when suddenly every single hair on the back of her neck stood on end.

Someone was behind her.

Before she could think about who it was or what they were doing, a large hand clasped her shoulder and swung her around, backing her into the shelves of the bookcase. The book she'd been holding fell from her hands to the floor with a loud slap.

Dizzy from being spun at speed, it took Kat a moment to find her bearings and focus on the face before her, and when she did, she wished immediately that she hadn't.

The tip of Carter's nose was inches away, while his breath washed over her face in strong heated waves. His broad chest pressed firmly against her.

But that wasn't what made Kat's throat close in panic. It was the expression on his face. His eyes were so dark the blue was almost indistinct, and the edges of his perfect mouth curled up into a hateful snarl. He was ferocious. She opened her mouth to speak, but Carter's hand was at once covering it, holding her words tightly in a palm that smelled of smoke and mint.

"Don't," he rasped. He closed his eyes and shook his head. His nostrils flared and his hold on her tightened. "Just don't speak."

Kat's eyes widened, but she nodded in compliance, causing the metal of his rings to rub against her skin. She watched him, fascinated by his jaw as it clenched and twitched along with the small beads of sweat scattered along his hairline and buzzed sideburns. She knew what that sweat tasted like.

He blew air out from between his pursed lips before he finally began to speak. "I just came from a very . . . interesting meeting." He spoke every word quietly to his large boots.

With his right hand still covering Kat's lips and his left hand squeezing her hip, Carter gradually lifted his head and let his stare rest on hers. His eyes filled with every conceivable emotion. The overwhelming urge to hug him and take away the pain lacing his words struck Kat in the gut.

"Do you know who my meeting was with?"

Kat frowned, shaking her head. Carter's smile was grim. He moved forward, stopping only when his lips were by her cheek.

"My cousin," he whispered. He stood back so he could see her face. "Austin Ford."

A shiver ran through Kat's body when the fury in his eyes ignited with his words. She knew her face had paled with nausea. What the hell had Austin said? Carter's response was immediate. His jaw loosened at the same time that his hand dropped from her mouth. His left hand remained holding her, his fingers pushing deeper into her hip.

"It's true?" Carter murmured through lips that barely moved. A small V appeared between his eyebrows as his gaze flitted questioningly over her face.

Kat took a breath. As caught off guard as she was by his behavior, she had to remain calm for both of their sakes. "Is what true?"

The slam of Carter's fist connecting with the mahogany shelving at the side of Kat's head echoed around the room like a nuclear bomb.

"Don't play with me, Kat!" Carter thundered. "Don't you fucking dare!"

"I'm not," she replied evenly, blinking back his angry words.

"Just a yes or no," Carter continued darkly. "That's all I want."

Kat's heart sank. Dread crept up her spine. "I don't know, Carter. What are you asking me?"

"Austin. The fucking . . ." He released a long hiss of breath, steadying himself by leaning his body against her. "He said that—that you . . . Did you?"

"Did I what?" she whispered.

Carter's eyes flashed rapidly between light and dark. "Did you fuck him?"

Kat's mouth dropping open made an audible pop. "Sweetheart."

"NO!" he barked. "Don't do that. Not now. Just yes or no." He kicked at the bottom shelf before dropping his forehead and muttering into Kat's shoulder. "Did you fuck him?"

Kat stood, almost paralyzed, with Carter breathing into the skin of her neck.

"Did you, Kat?" he asked again in a voice close to defeat. "Please tell me."

Slowly, so as not to alarm him, Kat raised her hand from where it had been hanging lifelessly at her side and brought it to Carter's face. He flinched at her touch. Not to be deterred, she persevered and eventually her fingertips were dancing lightly across his cheek and jaw.

Carter eventually looked at her, his face furious.

"No," Kat murmured, moving her palm from his cheek, down his neck. "No, I didn't. I didn't." She rubbed her hand around in a small circle, praying it would ease him.

His relief was evident only in the way his grip on her lessened. His face still held a million and one emotions and questions. He licked his lips and shifted from one foot to the other. "You didn't?"

"Never, Carter."

His eyes moved down her body. It wasn't in the sexual way Kat had started to grow used to; instead, it was as though he was seeing her for the first time since he'd twisted her into the books.

"You didn't," he whispered finally, apparently seeing what he needed. He took an unsteady step back, releasing Kat, and stared at her in a way that made her want to laugh and cry all at the same time. He was worn and weary, having become the complete antithesis of the raging creature he had been. Kat stood up straight and made to take a step toward him.

Carter put his palm up to stop her. His eyes dropped to her feet. "Don't," he said with a frown. "I'm . . . I . . . Just stay there."

Even though it broke her heart, Kat stepped back. She stood, watching Carter slowly morph back into the man she knew. The tightness of his jaw dissolved, along with the tension across his shoulders, but the sadness in his eyes remained.

"I didn't know," he muttered. "I didn't know you knew him. That you—"

"He's not important—"

"You had dinner with him." Carter jutted out his chin, daring her to deny it.

Kat pressed her lips into a tight line. "There was a group of us. For my birthday. It wasn't like a date or anything—"

"He drove you home," Carter added. Kat dipped her chin in affirmation and Carter's face scrunched as though suffering a raging headache. "You were alone with him."

Kat bit her lip while her hands fisted at her waist. How stupid she had been to keep this from him. She'd cursed her family for not being truthful, and she'd done the exact same thing to the most important person in her life. She was no better than they were.

"I'm sorry," she said. "I'm sorry I didn't tell you, but I only found out that you were related at my grandmother's last week."

He looked toward the ceiling. "Did anything happen?"

Kat exhaled. The sound was the only confirmation she gave.

"You kissed him?"

Her eyes met his briefly as she whispered a tiny "Yes."

Carter's head snapped back. He hit it hard against the large books behind him. "Shit."

"Carter." Kat took a tentative step forward. "Please, talk to me."

"There's nothin' to talk about," he retorted, glaring over her head.

"There's plenty to talk about," Kat said firmly. "You're upset, and I want to make it right. You have to let me explain."

"Explain what?" Carter snapped. "Explain that while I was in prison, wanting you more than I've wanted anything in my life, you were allowing my cousin to stick his filthy tongue down your throat?"

"Hey!" Kat took another step while pointing a finger in his face. "That isn't fair. I didn't know he was your cousin, and I didn't know you wanted me! You treated me like a goddamn pariah every time I saw you. How the hell would I know?"

Carter avoided her stare and toed the floor petulantly.

Kat dropped her finger as his words sank into her heart . . . *wanting you more than I've wanted anything* . . . Had he wanted her that much even then? She moved closer and placed her hands timidly on his hips. "Carter." She moved her hands to his shoulders. "Look at me."

He ignored her. His hands had turned into fists so tight his knuckles were white. Kat's hands continued moving to his neck, which was flushed with his temper, up to his sharp jaw, covered in the rough stubble that had marked her so wonderfully.

"Carter, look at me." Kat pulled his face to hers. His eyes rested on her chin. "Please."

He shifted once more, slouching so that Kat was no longer on her tiptoes. His eyes moved up her face slowly. He stared at her, not speaking. He eventually moved his hands to her waist, squeezing her once before closing his eyes.

"I hate that he's touched you," he whispered.

"He hasn't."

A mystified expression crossed his face. Kat rubbed her hand down his temple.

"No one has ever touched me like you." She drew her nose across his chin, breathing in his rich scent. "No one has ever kissed me like you."

"Kat," Carter whimpered, placing his forehead against hers.

"I never wanted him."

"Peaches."

"Carter, listen to me," she urged, taking his hands. "I liked him; he was charming." Carter made to pull away, but Kat held firm. "And yes, we kissed. But do you know why we didn't do more? Why I couldn't do more? Why every time he asked me out, I avoided giving him an answer?"

Carter stared at the floor.

"Ask me why."

A soft groan rumbled in his throat. "Why?"

"Because every time I was with him, every single time he touched me, I thought of you."

Carter's eyes were desperate to believe her, but something in the way his mouth twitched and his eyebrow lifted told her he was doubtful.

"It's the truth," she added. "I promise you. I wanted you, too. For so long. I still want you so much. I . . ."

"What?"

"I'm so sorry that he upset you and made you hate me."

"I don't hate you," he admonished. "I couldn't. It's him I hate. I hate what he stands for—his greed, his pretentious arrogance, and the fact that since we were kids, he's wanted things of mine he has no fucking right to want."

The double meaning in his words wrapped around Kat's lungs. *Mine.*

Quietly, Carter told her what had happened at the meeting, detailing Austin's intentions to remove Carter from the company he legally owned.

"Austin and I never got along," he explained. "Adam and I are closer in age so, when we ever did see each other as kids, we'd play together. Austin was the firstborn of our generation, the one to take over the company from our grandfather. He was groomed for it and became cocky and arrogant. Even at the age of fifteen he was a smart-mouthed prick.

"I remember one particular day," he continued, "when my

mom had taken me from my dad for the weekend; we were at my grandparents' house, which was a fucking nightmare anyway because my grandfather couldn't stand the sight of me."

Carter shook his head.

"My grandmother was completely different. She was cool. She would bake cookies and buy me awesome presents for Christmas and birthdays. She was the reason why we spent so much time at their house. My mom would dump me there, and my grandmother and I would hang out." Carter scratched his head. "I think it was Thanksgiving. Austin started the minute he arrived. He was a smart motherfucker. He was never obvious with his little comments about how I wasn't wanted, how he'd heard from my aunt that I was a disappointment to the whole family. He was relentless. Adam just stood there, not saying a word. When it was just the two of us, he'd apologize for his brother, but never in front of him."

Carter smiled wryly. "Nothing fucking changes. The little comments about my father, and the fact that I was more or less a dirty little secret, went on for the whole weekend. And eventually I snapped. I punched him in the face. He hit the floor, but I couldn't stop. I punched, smacked, kicked at him, and the whole time, all I could think was that I wanted him to hurt just as much as I did. My grandfather pulled me off him, and he got a couple of slaps for his troubles. Until he slapped me back. He said I should have been given away, and that I would do nothing but bring shame on the family. Just like I had done since the day I was conceived."

"Oh, Carter," Kat whispered, placing her hand on his neck.

"My grandmother went bat-shit crazy." Carter laughed lightly. "I think I get my temper from her." Kat smiled. "She took me from him and we went to her beach house." He paused, lost in the memory. "She cried. I remember, she cried and apologized. I didn't know why she was apologizing. She hadn't done anything wrong." Carter looked down at his hands and shook his head. "I hated seeing her cry."

"How old were you?"

"Six." Carter cleared his throat. "Within two years, my mom was dead," he continued. "And I was being sent to boarding school via my mother's wishes in her will. My father, he just went along with it . . ." Carter trailed off, clearly uncomfortable.

"I was thrown out of most of the schools I went to. I hated every fucking minute. If I wasn't thrown out of school, I ran away. The older I got, the more I came to understand that if I made a big enough noise, caused enough shit, the more likely it was that the Fords would have to deal with me instead of shipping me off in the hopes that I'd never come back."

Kat's hand rubbed circles on Carter's shoulder. Her heart broke wide-open for the small boy within the man before her.

"I don't know how he was with you, Kat," Carter said, "but Austin Ford is dangerous. He's selfish and greedy." Hate lit his irises. "And it makes me fucking sick that he's been anywhere near you."

"I'm sorry." What more could she say?

Not caring where they were, Carter wound his arms around her waist. "I'm sorry, too. I'm sorry I scared you."

"You didn't."

"Yes, I did." Carter rubbed his palm over the small of her back. "And I'm sorry. I'm just . . ."

"I know." She knew how hurt she would be if the circumstances were reversed.

He pressed his lips together. "The idea of you being with anyone makes me wanna tear the city up," he confessed. "But him?" He shook his head slowly. "Thinking that you'd been with him fucking killed me." His heart thrummed under her palm.

"I'm with you," she whispered. "I promise. I don't want anyone else."

His eyes burned. "I don't want anyone else, either. It's so perfect when it's just us, away from all this shit."

Kat fought through the haze of delight his words brought, thinking carefully for a moment. "You know, I have a friend . . . Ben."

Carter's brow furrowed, menace skipping across his face. "Ben? A friend, huh? Should I be worried?"

Kat brushed away the deliberate anxiety wrapping his question with a roll of her eyes. "Hardly. He's a lawyer, among other things." She bit the inside of her mouth. "He could help you. With Austin."

"How could he help?"

Kat chuckled. "Ben could find dirt on just about anybody. That's his job." She shrugged. "I don't know. Maybe he could find something you could use against him."

Carter's lips twitched. "Fight fire with fire, you mean."

"It's worth a shot, right?"

Carter considered her offer. "I know Austin has been known to do business with some dodgy fucking characters. Adam has always been the one to clean up his shit."

Kat smiled. "That sounds like Ben's forte."

Carter regarded her carefully. "You'd do that for me?"

"I want you to have what's rightfully yours. You deserve that."

His exhale shook from him. "You're something else, you know that?" The pad of his thumb whispered across her bottom lip. "Thank you. I owe you." He paused. "Maybe I could do something for you." He nibbled his lip adorably, hesitant. "We could— I could take you . . . I mean, do you— What, um, I was wondering. I . . . Dammit." He rubbed his face. "I'm shit at this."

Kat made to move back, to give him some space, but his hand flew to her waist, stopping her.

Carter closed his eyes and spoke in one long breath. "Do you have plans for this weekend? Because if you don't I'd like to take you somewhere. If you don't want to I understand, but I'd really like you to come with me. I want to spend some time with you. I mean, I don't know . . ." He muttered a number of colorful curses before he shoved the tips of his fingers into his jean pockets.

Kat folded her hands together nervously. "Just us?"

Carter's eyes shot up, blazing blue and hopeful. "Yeah."

She cupped his cheek, smiling warmly. "I'd love to."

Carter blinked, not attempting to hide his surprise. "Really?"

Kat laughed. "I said so, didn't I?"

His chest rumbled with a low self-mocking laugh.

He glanced toward the empty reading room doorway and reached for her hand, clasping it gently between his large fingers. He tilted his head to the right. "I know it's against session rules, but I'm fucking dyin' to kiss you."

Kat instinctively licked her lips.

"Just a small one." His thumb snuck under the edge of her blouse, skimming her stomach, igniting the glowing embers in her blood. "Just a small taste."

Kat moaned deep in her throat, hearing the words he'd spoken the first time he'd ever kissed her. As soon as their lips met, her body relaxed. She forgot about the rules and risks. She forgot about Austin, her mother, and Beth.

All that mattered were his hands on her face, the strength of his body, and the way his tongue possessed every inch of her mouth.

She grasped his belt loops and pulled him closer, not giving a damn whether anyone saw.

24

Kat answered her cell phone on the third ring. "Ben, how are you?"

His smile could be heard in his answering words. "I'm great. How're you?"

"I'm okay."

"That's good. That's good. So, um, Beth called last night. She said you've still not spoken."

Kat sighed. "No."

Ben hummed. "Kat, I—"

"I know, Ben," Kat interrupted sharply. "I'll talk to her when I'm ready, okay?"

"Okay."

Kat pressed her lips together and took a deep breath, fighting off the sadness that pressed heavier every day she didn't answer Beth's or her mother's calls. "So did you get Carter's e-mail?" she asked, changing the subject quickly. "Were the details enough?"

Ben chuckled. "Oh yeah. That's what I was calling to let you know. Everything's ready to go with Ford tomorrow. What Carter sent was fantastic. Tell him thanks. How did he get hold of that stuff?"

"I have no idea. I didn't dare ask."

"Well, it made for very interesting reading. Seems our boy Austin has been playing with those he shouldn't. The Feds would have a field day with this shit, and if his shareholders got a whiff, having an ex-con on the board members list would be the least of his worries."

Kat didn't doubt it. Since she had asked Ben to help Carter with reclaiming his business, Ben had been working like a demon, calling in favors and hunting for any type of dirt he could find. Unsurprisingly, it hadn't taken long.

"You're meeting tomorrow?" Kat asked, getting into her car in Arthur Kill's parking lot.

"Yeah." Ben laughed. "Austin must be curious to have set up the meeting on a Saturday."

"You'll let me know how it goes?"

"Of course."

"Great." Kat leaned her head back against the seat. "Thank you, Ben. Truly. You don't know what this means to me."

"Of course I know what this means to you, Kat. Why do you think I agreed to do it?"

Kat smiled. "You're my favorite."

"I know. You just remember that when your millionaire boyfriend wants to loan out one of his supercars."

"He doesn't have any supercars, Ben," Kat replied with a laugh.

"Then he's a damn fool. You take care, yeah?"

"I will. Love to Abby."

Kat left Arthur Kill with a suitcase in the trunk and a flutter in her heart. After ending the call, she turned off her cell phone, ignoring the two voice mails from her mother. They hadn't spoken in over a week and, although Kat missed her, the relief that came from not having to hear the relentless daily diatribe outweighed it all. Guilt had threatened, but she'd pushed it down, deep into the gulf that continued to widen between the two women.

This weekend was about her and Carter. Everything else was irrelevant.

Excitement bloomed in her belly. He'd been incredibly coy about what he had planned and where they were staying, giving her brief directions and cryptic clues she'd spent the whole week trying to figure out.

Thankfully, the drive was easy enough. Kat wasn't the best with directions, but she knew she was headed toward the coast, specifically the Hamptons, which confused her to say the very least. West Hampton Dunes was an extremely affluent area, filled with people who were more Labradors, pipes, and slippers rather than metal, tattoos, and leather. Kat smiled. She was sure Carter stuck out like the proverbial sore thumb around these parts.

The closer she got to the address on her GPS, the bigger the houses appeared. Not that she should have been surprised after Carter's confession about his wealth. He could easily afford any house along the East Coast and still have change left over. Not that she gave a damn about any of that. He could have had five dollars left in the entire world and she'd still lov—

Her smile grew, undaunted by the direction her thoughts had taken. She turned up the volume on the car stereo and sang along.

The sky turned a stunning pink and orange above the rough gray sea, and the sand dunes rolled for miles. Even though it was cold, Kat wound down her window and, after putting on her shades, let the fresh ocean air blast into the car. It smelled wonderful. It smelled of freedom and fun. It smelled of her father. Christ, she missed the beach. It'd been too long.

Turning a long corner, Kat faced an endless stretch of sand upon which stood a beautiful two-story white house with a dark blue roof. The house was exquisite, made up of white paneling with a wraparound porch and balconies on the top levels. It reminded Kat of the large family homes she'd seen in the South as a child with Nana Boo.

Coming to a stop, Kat killed the engine and gradually opened the car door. The air swept around her, whipping her loose hair around her face and pounding her skin with sand. She gazed at the picture-perfect scene before her, wanting nothing more than to go running into the ocean.

• • •

There had been so many moments in his life where Carter had felt disappointment or frustration in some form or another that he had lost count. Depressingly, since the day of his birth, the two emotions had seemingly followed him everywhere he'd gone, running concurrently with everything he did, along with every choice he made.

From learning about his mother's desire to "get rid" of him, and her subsequent intolerance of him as a child, to the day his own father sent him away to a strange boarding school at the tender age of nine—even though the small dark-haired boy had begged and pleaded for his daddy not to—Carter had learned to become immune to the sting of things going to shit.

He was used to it, he shrugged it off, and, in many ways—as cynical as it was—Carter had started to expect the worst in all situations and people. At least that way he was never taken by surprise, and the arrogant, devil-may-care armor he covered himself in continued to protect him from any and all pain that came with being around fuckers and fuckups.

Carter was an angry son of a bitch and had accepted that particular fact years ago. He didn't like it and he hated the roots of it, but, shit, how else was he supposed to feel after everything he'd been through? He'd resigned himself to being that way his whole life.

Well, until Peaches came back into his life.

Kat.

The woman had been an enigma to him from the get-go. She'd driven him fucking crazy—still did—but, as time had gone on, along with his prison release and the changes in his and Kat's relationship, Carter had begun to realize that, as much as she could rile him and get on his last damn nerve, she also managed to calm him.

After the most intense fucking of his life, while he'd held a sleeping Kat in his arms, in his bed, Carter had experienced something that he was utterly unfamiliar with: peace.

It wasn't that his brain turned off completely while she was around, or that he had had some cheesy spiritual enlightenment while they'd come together. It was simply that Kat seemed to help lower his brain volume. The frustration, anger, and disappointment that twisted constantly within him were blunted by Kat's presence. He could breathe better, relax, feel more himself—and he'd basked unashamedly in his newfound slice of serenity.

Certainly, his Kat was a paradox. Her touch and words grounded him, while her kisses made him fly. At times she made him want to rip the city up in rage, but she could also make him smile like no one else. Her hugs and caresses dazed him as much as her furious verbal slaps, and Carter still wasn't decided about whether her fiery anger turned him on more than her sexual passion.

The juxtaposition was intense and, for Carter, absolutely perfect. Just like she was.

Her fire and strength, and her tenderness and sensitivity, were what made Kat so special. As ferocious as she could be, she could also be soft and quiet: molten fire and relaxing warmth. Carter loved that she kept him on his toes. He loved the spontaneity and the passion that smoldered continually between them, and he loved that she met him with every touch, kiss, and thrust with as much intensity as he felt.

She was everything he needed or wanted. But, as much as he should have been embracing his feelings for this spectacular woman, Carter found himself entirely terrified by them.

He was a pussy, he knew, but it was the unknown, the unfamiliarity, and the vulnerability that he had opened himself up to that left a sheen of sweat on his brow and a flutter in his heart. His armor had been delivered a huge blow when he'd pushed himself into Kat that night.

She hadn't eased it off him with a gentle caress. No. She had torn it open with wild hunger, frantic touches, and whispered words that floored him, putting his chest and his heart in a seriously precarious position.

Carter couldn't imagine being without Kat, now that he had her, and the thought of losing her filled him with a dread that was almost suffocating. Disappointment and frustration were nothing compared to the inevitable pain that Kat's absence would cause. For all his assaholic, aggressive, don't-give-a-fuck showboating, Carter had left himself wide-open. Kat had crawled into the many spaces within him that he'd thought were lost and barren, and had brought every one of them back to life.

After watching her through the large window at the front of the beach house, he emerged cautiously from the side door. He wandered along the porch toward her. She seemed mesmerized. Carter prayed it was because she was pleased. Shit, but he was nervous. He'd never done anything like this before, and he wanted the weekend to be perfect, a chance for them to reconnect. With a large breath, he jogged over. His chest warmed when she beamed.

He reached up to her aviator shades and pulled them gently from her face. "There's my girl," he whispered. "So, what do you think?" he asked with a chin tilt toward the house.

"It's wonderful," she answered. "It's been so long since I've been to the beach."

"I figured." He scratched his chin and cleared his throat. "I remembered you talking about the beach, about your dad, how you hadn't been for a really long time, and I thought you'd like it."

Kat launched herself at him, nearly knocking him off his feet. She wrapped her arms tightly around his neck and kissed his lips hungrily. Carter wound his arms around her and held her closely, breathing every inch of her in, his entire body burning.

He staggered sideways, stopping only when his hip hit her car. He grunted into her mouth while their tongues were reacquainted and turned in a half circle so he could press her soft body against the car.

Her hands were on his face, gripping and caressing. Carter rubbed up against her like a damn cat. He hadn't been inside of her since their one night together, and he was about ready to lose his fucking mind. When his hips rotated into hers, she gasped and wrapped her legs around the backs of his thighs, wanting him closer. Carter obliged by grabbing her ass. He'd missed having her so close to him, so responsive. He licked and nibbled until Kat was panting and whimpering his name.

"We have to stop," she breathed. Her body betrayed her words when she clutched his face, yanking his mouth back to hers.

"Why?" he asked with a quirk of his eyebrow. "There's no one for a few miles. If I wanted to fuck you right here"—he shifted his hips, making her gasp—"I could."

Her lips curved up against his cheek before she placed a soft kiss right in the center of it. "Thank you," she whispered.

Carter looked at her questioningly. She was sensational with her swollen lips and windblown hair.

"For inviting me here, I mean. For knowing I would love it."

"You love it?"

"It's so pretty."

Relief seized his racing heart. "You wanna see inside?"

With a quick kiss to her lips, Carter held on to her until her feet once again found the ground. Carter grabbed Kat's suitcase and led her along the porch and through the front door.

She took hesitant steps along the hallway, glancing at the beech wood stairs leading to the first floor. She was quiet as she removed her jacket, making her way into the living room, with Carter following silently. She walked around, standing by the window that looked out onto the ocean and the sand banks covered in long, yellowing grass.

Leaning against the doorjamb, Carter watched her. She was undeniably perfect, standing in his house. He'd thought the same when he'd first seen her in his apartment in the city, but somehow, this was different. His present was merging with his past, making him feel oddly at ease.

After heaving her suitcase upstairs to the bedroom, Carter returned to find Kat glancing at the eclectic artwork on the walls. He knew from seeing her own art collection that she appreciated watercolors, but his throat narrowed in panic when she stopped dead at a selection of black-and-white photographs littering the wall above the roaring fireplace.

"This is you," she murmured, pointing to a picture of a young boy in shorts building a huge sandcastle.

"Yeah," he answered, moving next to her. "I was seven."

Her fingertips glided over his image. "You're so happy. Who took it?"

"My grandmother," he replied. "This was her house. The house I told you about—she left it to me." He glanced around. "It was our place." He gave her a one-shouldered shrug. "We came here a lot. Just the two of us."

"It holds happy memories for you?"

"Yeah, the few that I have from my childhood belong here." He swallowed. "I wanted to share it with you."

She placed a soft kiss on his shoulder.

Carter kissed the top of her hair. "Come on," he whispered. "I'll get you a drink. Food for dinner is all ready for cooking. You like shellfish, right?"

When she nodded, Carter moved closer to her mouth. "Great, I'm starving." His words carried an undeniable undertone, but he was under no illusions. The next few days were not just about being naked with her. They were about truth, honesty, stepping up, and being an adult. Now that she had wrecked his punk-ass armor, Carter knew he had to show her everything that lay underneath. It was daunting and scary, but he would do it for her. He had to.

They kissed again tenderly but with a promised passion. "Why don't you go upstairs, get changed into something really warm so you don't get hypothermia or some shit, and I'll start on dinner."

Strangely, she neither argued nor questioned him. "Third door on the right," he said. "I put your suitcase at the end of the bed."

"Thank you," she said before she disappeared up the stairs.

• • •

"What else?"

Kat chewed her lip as she thought. "Anchovies and olives." She made an "ick" face. "And lemons. I hate any lemon food—lemon cakes, lemon dressing." She grimaced and shivered.

"You drink Sprite," Carter pointed out through a cloud of smoke.

"That's different," Kat countered with a tone that closed the conversation.

Carter rolled his eyes.

"What do you hate?" she asked.

"Tomatoes," he answered swiftly, "anchovies, pineapple, any fish except shellfish, and macaroni and cheese."

"Macaroni and cheese?" Kat laughed. "What is wrong with you?"

Carter frowned. "I hate the fucking stuff."

"Okay," Kat conceded. "Favorite food?"

"Peaches."

"Yeah, yeah."

"I'm serious," he offered. "Peaches and Oreos." He grinned. "Favorite movie?"

"I can't pick just one."

"Fine, two."

"*The Goonies* and *Forrest Gump*. You."

"*Beetlejuice* and *Pulp Fiction*," Carter replied as he put his smoke out. "Favorite album?"

"*Rubber Soul* and *Revolver* by the Beatles. It's always been one album for me." She gestured for him to answer.

"Same," he smirked. "That and *The White Album*, tied."

They'd been at the question game for over an hour. Kat watched from her seat on the back porch, wrapped in a large wool blanket, snuggled and warm, while Carter cooked their dinner on the grill and answered every question she threw at him. The smell of shellfish encircled her in the fresh wind, mixing with the scent of the sea and Carter's cigarette smoke.

As well as looking unbelievably sexy in a large, black knitted sweater and dark jeans, Kat couldn't believe how calm he seemed. He looked like he belonged, settled and free, as though the weight he carried around with him in the city had been swept away by the waves crashing against the shore not one hundred yards away.

"You look peaceful here."

Carter finished his beer. "That's pretty much how I feel. There's something about the coast. It makes me feel different."

"Better different?"

"Yeah." His eyes glimmered, soft and gentle. "I'm so glad you're here."

"Me too."

The food was incredible. Kat told him repeatedly about how good it was, and, in return, Carter made salacious comments about how he'd heard those kinds of words from her before. Kat had convinced herself that playful Carter would be difficult to adjust to; she was so used to brooding, serious, cursing, huffy Carter—and she loved him dearly—that cute and cuddly Carter sounded ridiculous. Kat realized that, in this case, she loved being wrong. His honesty and smile came easier the more they talked, pulling Kat deeper and deeper into the arms of emotions that no longer frightened her. She only worried whether they would frighten him.

After they washed up, during which Carter let his hands rub all over Kat's ass, he led her down the porch onto the beach. It was dark, but small twinkling lights placed on either side of the walkway, and Carter's flashlight, showed the way.

While Kat placed the beer and the bag he'd given her to carry to the side, and took a seat on the cool sand, Carter went about starting a fire in the pit filled with driftwood and logs with a can of lighter fluid, a match, and much enthusiasm. Kat doubled over laughing when she saw his ecstatic expression once he got the damn thing ablaze.

"Me. Man. Build fire for woman," he boomed, pounding his chest and gesturing proudly to the pit.

Kat called him an utter loser, which encouraged Carter to attack her ribs mercilessly with his long, nimble fingers. He growled into her neck while he tickled her, and laughed when she tried to tickle him back. It was loud—a true belly laugh that came from deep inside of him.

It was wonderful.

Carter shuffled so his back was against a conveniently placed rock and pulled Kat between his legs, keeping the blanket around them both. He pulled two beers and a pack of marshmallows, graham crackers, and chocolate from a bag. She stared wide-eyed at the bag in his hand.

"You brought marshmallows?" she exclaimed.

Carter deadpanned: "Um, we have an open flame going on here, Peaches. Of course I brought marshmallows. We have to eat s'mores on the beach." He scoffed. "It's the law."

They ate at least three each before Kat called mercy and collapsed against Carter. "I'm so full. You always make me eat too much. I'm gonna get really fat."

Carter clicked his tongue next to her ear. "What bullshit." His hands moved under her layers of clothes and gripped her sides. "You're fucking perfect. I love the way you feel. Besides, I'll help you work it off later."

"I'm sure," Kat shot back and giggled when she heard him groan. "First, tell me more about the house and your time with your grandma." He handed her another beer. She was on her fourth now, and she needed to slow down. If Carter's aim was to get her drunk and have his way with her, then he wasn't far from achieving it. "Tell me about your friends, girlfriends . . . tell me everything."

Carter laughed. They continued to watch the flames lick and dance in the moonlight. The wind had died down now and the sky had cleared, dropping the temperature so that their breath was visible. Kat couldn't feel the cold, though, wrapped in her blissful bubble.

"Okay." Carter rubbed his hands across her stomach. "Well, my main group of friends work with me at the shop."

"Max's shop? Tell me about Max. How long have you known each other?"

Carter smiled. "Nearly twenty years."

"Is he a good friend to you?"

"Yeah, he is. He laughed his ass off when I told him I was bringing you here." He looked troubled, almost sad.

With a friendship of two decades, it was obvious there was more to their story, but Kat decided not to push. Like peeling the layers of an onion, he revealed himself to her a little bit at a time. He couldn't be rushed. He would tell her when he was ready. She had to trust that.

"I've never had a girlfriend," he continued. "I was never with girls long enough to warrant a label like that. This may be hard to believe, but I was a complete asshole with girls when I was a kid." His self-ridicule was adorable.

"No way."

"Way." The playfulness ebbed from his face as he held her close. His words were low and serious in her ear. "I want you to know something." He took a deep breath. "I won't ever be that way with you. I promise. You deserve more than that. I'm far from perfect, but I swear I'll do my best."

Kat relaxed into his chest. "Do you know what a good person you are, Carter?"

Carter let his nose touch the tip of hers. "I'm not a good person, Kat—"

"Bullshit." She turned in his arms.

Before he could argue, Kat pressed on. "You saved my life." She traced his lips with the tips of her fingers. "Don't ever tell me you're not good."

• • •

Carter's grip tightened. She was so warm and soft. "You feel incredible." He kissed down her neck to her collarbone, licking at her delicate skin. "You taste so good. You smell so good." Kat gasped his name. "Tell me I can be inside of you tonight."

Wordlessly, she moved her hand and grabbed him through his jeans. He groaned and bit down on her earlobe. She rubbed him firmly, drawing gasps of want from his chest, damn near making him come in six perfect strokes. Abruptly, Kat moved until she was on her knees between Carter's legs, leaving him hard and achy with the small distance between them. Carter pouted at the same time she scrambled to her feet. She grabbed their trash and blanket and, with the sound of her laughter bounding across the sand dunes, ran ahead of him into the house.

She wanted him to chase her? Game. On.

Leaving the fire in the pit to die down itself, Carter grabbed what trash and beer was left and, as best as he could with a hard-on, sprinted after her, making it to the back door as the wind slammed it shut. Opening it with a grumble and dropping everything to the floor, he motored through the house, grinning at every piece of Kat's crumpled clothing he passed.

Her hat, her boots, her socks, her scarf, her sweater . . . her bra.

She squealed when his heavy feet thundered up the stairs at the back of her, but all Carter could see was a flash of chestnut-red hair as she flew to the bedroom.

Dammit, she was quick.

Kicking open the bedroom door and making Kat scream in excited panic, he managed to grab hold of her arm, pulling her bare back against his chest. She gasped for air, but the moans came thick and fast when Carter's mouth latched hungrily on to her shoulder. She reached up and pulled at his neck, grabbing for him and begging for any part of him to be in her.

"You're gonna pay for that, my Peaches."

Carter twirled her and knotted his fingers into her hair, smothering her mouth with his, and, in three large strides, he backed her into the bedroom wall. The air left them both when they came to a dead stop. Her hands were everywhere. She grappled with his button fly and wrapped her perfect, warm hand around his cock as soon as it was free. He released her mouth and let his head loll back. He cried out when her thumb ran over the wet tip, sucking in a long breath through his teeth.

"Not if I make you pay first," she purred, licking her lips and dropping slowly to her knees.

Carter swallowed as her tongue flicked against him. "Oh fuck."

That's my girl.

25

The wind was fresh and the sky was blue the following afternoon as Carter and Kat rode Kala through Westhampton. Once again, he'd kept her in the dark about where he was taking her, loving the way she grumbled about not knowing every detail. Apparently, Kat Lane didn't like surprises. She'd changed her outfit three times just to prove a point, slowly driving him mad. It was a good thing she was cute as hell, or he'd have had to spank the sass right out of her. He'd told her as much, causing her to laugh beautifully and kiss him so hard he was rendered mute.

They rode for nearly an hour before Carter began to see other bikes ahead of them, heading in the same direction.

Slowing down so he could turn onto a large stone road, Carter smiled when the thick scent of diesel hit his nose and the sound of heavy rock music echoed around them. Amid large marquees and smaller stalls lay row upon row of muscle cars as far as the eye could see and, next to those, were the Harleys, Triumphs, Yamahas, Ducatis, and any other erection-causing piece of two-wheeled metal Carter could think of.

He pulled to a stop next to a glorious yellow '69 Corvette and switched off the engine. He unfastened his helmet and pulled it off. Kat shifted at the back of him. He turned to look at her. She was adorable, with pink cheeks and sleepy eyes.

He caressed the apple of her cheek with his thumb. "You fall asleep on me again?"

She hummed and removed her helmet. "It's so relaxing, just holding you while we ride. It's great."

Her words melted into secret, silent parts of him.

Kat glanced around. "What is this place?"

Carter stood from the bike, pulling his leg over carefully, and stretched. "This is heaven." He held out his hand to help Kat up, and placed both of their helmets in the detachable holder on the back of Kala's seat. "A gear head's mecca."

"Those cars are beautiful," Kat murmured, gazing down the line of Mustangs and GTs.

Carter pushed his hands into his pockets and rocked on his heels. "Max and I used to come here when we were kids with his dad. I wanted to show you where my love for all this grew."

Kat took a small step toward him. "Then show me."

They walked and talked, and explored the cars and the crazy people around them. Carter pointed out his favorite cars and bikes, explaining their model, torque, and horsepower like a kid in a candy store, drooling over a rare Vincent Black Knight.

"What are the stalls and marquees for?" Kat asked as they meandered past a hot Ford Torino.

"The bigger ones belong to the car dealers and specialists: GT, Harley, and GMC. They sell parts cheaper than in the stores. They use it for promotion and to hire mechanics, things like that." He gave her a smug sideways glance. "Riley used to have his own marquee here, you know."

"Really?"

Carter answered with a squeeze of her hand. "He's a crazy motherfucker, but he's a shrewd businessman. He'd never gloat about it, either. He got me some amazing deals on parts and helped me with my other bikes and stuff."

He pulled her toward the rest of the stalls. He smiled when, after walking for ten minutes, she stopped at the opening of one specific tent Carter knew well. Kat remained quiet while they stood watching a young blonde girl have a tattoo inked across her right hip. It was a Big Dog Motorcycles stamp, and Carter had to admit it was sexy as hell.

"You thinking about getting one?" he asked as he wrapped his arms around her. She made a kind of coughing sound and shook her head under his chin. He laughed. "Shame. I think you'd look fucking amazing with some ink on this gorgeous body." He rubbed himself against her ass.

"Don't they hurt?" she asked, taking a couple of steps closer with Carter still attached to her like a damned limpet.

"Nah. Of course, it depends where on your body you get it, but really it's more of a discomfort than a pain."

"Where did yours hurt most?"

"Under my bicep." That one had smarted. The ones on his chest had been sore, too, but Kat didn't need to know that. No fucker with a needle was going anywhere near her tits.

He wrapped his arm around her shoulder, grinning when she slid her palm into the back pocket of his jeans and led her back into the crowd toward the food and beer tent. Petey, a guy Carter had known his whole metal-loving life, stood at the humongous grill, serving chicken legs, steaks, burgers, ribs, sausages, lamb chops, and chili that he ladled out of a giant pan. He was a huge mammoth of a man with tattoos and a bald head, which he always wrapped in a red bandanna.

He grinned wide, showing off three gold teeth. "Carter!"

Carter shook Petey's hand. "Mr. Yates."

"Long time no see, my friend! I heard you were in Kill."

"Unfortunately. Got parole a few weeks ago."

Petey smiled. "So, are you here with Max? I haven't seen his ass in forever." His face grew somber. "I heard about Lizzie. That shit was rough."

"Yeah, it was." Carter turned to see Kat looking more than a little awkward, and took her hand, pulling her to his side. "But no, I'm here with my . . ."

What the hell was he meant to say? My Peaches. My Kat. My woman. My tutor?

He cleared his throat. "My friend Kat Lane. Kat, this is Petey. He's a legend 'round these parts, been here since the dawn of time."

Kat smiled at Petey and held out her hand. "Nice to meet you."

"You too." Petey eyed Kat appreciatively. "Well, I can certainly see why you're his friend. You're a stunner, kid." He glanced at Carter. "I've never seen Carter here with a girl before. This fucker must like you a whooooole lot."

"Yeah, yeah." He responded with his middle finger, making both Petey and Kat laugh. "Shut up and feed us, asshole."

With food on their plates and a draft beer each, they sat on a picnic bench and talked, ate, and watched the world go by. Kat asked him questions about the time he'd spent with Max and Max's father and what trouble they'd gotten into. He told her stories about the first time they'd gotten shitfaced in the back of Max's dad's vintage first-generation Camaro, and how Max had spent the following morning hungover, cleaning the vomit he'd splattered on the wheel trims.

"You two sound like you got into a lot of trouble," Kat stated with a smile into her beer. "You care for him very much, don't you?"

"Max is a force to be reckoned with sometimes. But he means well. He's been through shit I wouldn't wish on anybody." He took a deep breath, willing himself to tell her the full story, praying that she wouldn't run away. "You know that it was coke I got caught with that sent me to Kill for three years, right?"

Kat nodded.

"It wasn't mine."

"What?"

"When we were sixteen, Max saved my life," he explained carefully. "Pushed me out of the way of a bullet during a car boost that went wrong."

"Jesus."

"I owed him." Carter stared out across the field. "Before I was sent down, Max had a woman, Lizzie. They'd been together for years. He worshipped the ground she walked on." He sipped his beer. "Long story short, Max managed to get into some messed-up shit. Drugs. The coke I was arrested for was a setup. It wasn't his; he had nothing to do with it. Neither of us did, but some asshole dealer with a grudge tipped off the cops. I took the heat and the thirty-six months."

Kat blinked. "Why?"

Carter exhaled heavily. "Lizzie was pregnant."

"Oh."

"With his history with the cops, if Max had been caught with that shit he'd have been sent down for years. I couldn't let that happen. Man should be with his woman while she's pregnant with his kid."

"So you served time for him." Kat's eyes shimmered. "Just like that?"

Carter worried his lip with his teeth. "Didn't have much going on at the time. Nothing important, anyway."

Not like now.

"That was . . . Wow, Carter. I don't know what to say."

"There's nothing to say." He shrugged. "It didn't make much difference. Not long after I arrived at Kill she left him."

"What about the baby?"

Sadness gripped Carter's heart. "He died."

"He?"

Carter bobbed his head solemnly. "Christopher. Max's son."

"Oh God."

"Engaged, pregnant, planning their lives together, and then . . ." Carter closed his eyes. "Just like that. Lizzie took it so hard. They both did." Carter rubbed a hand across his head. "So she left. After promising that she'd be with him forever, she left without a word, no note. Nothin'. Max never got over it, losing Christopher and then Lizzie. Now he tries to find the answer to it all in booze, blow, and women." Carter shook his head. "He's on a downward spiral, and I have no fucking idea how to help him. He won't admit that he needs help. Sad thing is I lost something the day Lizzie walked away, too."

"What?"

His eyes met hers. "My best friend."

Kat slid her hand across the bench and clasped Carter's pinkie. With no words said, her touching him was enough.

For the next hour, she sat with her chin in her palm, watching Carter intently, never judging, never interrupting or commenting on the things he told her. It was liberating, cleansing, almost like therapy, to be so open and honest with her. He stopped talking and smirked in embarrassment. He'd been boring her to death with his life story.

"Jesus, sorry. Just tell me to shut the hell up."

"Never." She sighed. "I love listening to you. I want you to tell me everything. Carter, you're . . . you're like no one I've ever met." She glanced at their hands, linked on the tabletop. "I have something to ask you."

"Hit me."

"You know I told my grandmother, Nana Boo, about you . . . and me."

"Yeah," Carter replied, feeling his heart give an appreciative thump. He liked that she'd done that. It made what they had together feel more real, like what they shared was valid and true.

"Well." She hesitated and looked away.

"What is it?"

Kat dropped her chin and spoke in one long breath. "She's invited you to Chicago, to her house, to spend Thanksgiving with her, with us . . . I mean, you and me, she's invited us both, and I'd really like to take you and have you meet her, but I understand if you don't want to. I get it; I do—"

Carter cut off her adorable blathering with a searing kiss. He pulled back and smiled when he saw that her eyes remained closed and her lips were still in a needy pout. "You're cute as hell when you ramble."

"Shush," she retorted, opening her eyes.

Carter laughed. "So you're asking me if I'd like to spend Thanksgiving with you in Chicago, with your grandmother."

Kat nodded. "I still have her car, which I need to take back, so we can drive there."

Carter exhaled, a finger of anxiety creeping up his spine. "What about your mom? Will she be there?"

Kat shook her head. "No. They always spend Thanksgiving with Harrison's family. She spends Christmas with Nana Boo."

Carter nodded in understanding but couldn't shake the wary feeling smack in the center of his chest. He had to hand it to Kat; she didn't appear worried at all. She looked beautiful and hopeful that he would say yes, but Carter wasn't entirely sure he could.

"You don't have to make a decision now," Kat said, seemingly sensing his unease. "Think about it."

"I will," he promised. "Thank you for inviting me."

"Of course."

Shadows of unspoken words clouded her usually bright eyes. Carter frowned. "Are you all right?"

"Yeah." Her voice was small. "I'm . . . I'm great. Really. I just want you to myself for a while. Can we go back to the house? Is that okay?"

Carter leaned across the bench and kissed her again. "I'm all yours." He took her hand. "Let's get out of here."

• • •

Austin Ford stared hard at his reflection in the gilded mirror of his office's private bathroom and grinned at what he saw. He had to confess; he was a handsome son of a bitch. His hair was thick and dark with small flecks of gray that suggested sophistication as opposed to age. His face was firm, with laugh lines around his eyes adding warmth, and his figure was trim and fit, hugged fantastically by the Armani suit adorning it.

Overall, life was pretty damned good.

Yes, he still had issues with a family member who would forever be the thorn in his side. But that shit would be handled, too. With the friends Austin had and the favors he was owed, Wes Carter would soon be behind bars again. It was just a question of when.

A burst of auburn wavy hair and large green eyes flashed in the back of Ford's mind.

Kat.

Austin had always considered himself a charming bastard, and to lose Kat's affections to his shit-for-brains cousin stung more than he was willing to admit. What the hell did Carter have that he didn't? Fuck if he knew. Besides, once her convict was back behind bars and she realized what a fuckup he really was, she'd appreciate having a strong shoulder to cry on, a knight to save the day. Austin's pulse quickened and his palms perspired, but he reined his thoughts in swiftly. Now was no time for being anywhere but on the fucking ball.

He adjusted the large silk knot at his neck and took a deep breath.

Showtime.

He strode out of his bathroom and nodded sharply at Adam, who was, as always, looking like little boy lost.

"Get your shit together," Austin snapped. He pressed the button for his secretary on the phone at the edge of his desk. "We need to own this."

"Yeah," came his brother's reply.

"You can send him in," Austin ordered.

Leaning against the desk, Austin looked squarely at his accounts manager and litigator, who both had straight business faces that would have made any normal grown man shit in his pants. Everything was perfect.

There was a sharp knock on the door before the handle turned and a tall blond man in a fabulous gray Gucci suit walked confidently into the office. Austin was a little taken aback by the obvious ease with which he entered, but he covered it with a commanding smile and an outstretched hand.

"Mr. Thomas," he crooned. "Welcome."

"Mr. Ford," Ben replied.

• • •

Ben took Ford's hand and shook it firmly, keeping eye contact the entire time. He wasn't a pussy by any stretch of the imagination; he'd been in offices like this many times, and dealt with assholes like Ford on a regular basis, but what he was about to do was nothing he'd ever been involved in and, if handled badly, could be a complete and utter catastrophe. People he cared about were counting on him to keep his cool.

He swallowed and placed himself in one of the ridiculously luxurious chairs next to a huge glass table.

"Water?" Ford asked as he, too, sat down.

Ben's mouth was dryer than the Sahara, but he wasn't about to give Ford the satisfaction of seeing how uncomfortable he was. "No," he replied casually. He opened his briefcase, keeping his eyes fixed on what he was doing. "I'm good. This won't take long."

He ignored the derisive snort that came from Ford. "Yes, I'm sure it won't. But, alas, you were a little vague on the details when we spoke and arranged this meeting. Would you be so kind as to explain just exactly why you are here?"

"I am here on behalf of my client. Mr. Wesley Carter." Ben's gaze nailed Ford to his chair. He placed a folder on the glass table and watched as the color of arrogance and control slowly seeped from Ford's face. "The reason I was vague about this meeting, Mr.

Ford," Ben began, while calmly steepling his hands on the table, "is because, as you can surmise, the situation is a delicate one."

Ford remained stock-still. "How so?"

Ben smirked at the attempt at nonchalance and opened Carter's file. "As you're aware, your largest shareholder is Mr. W. Carter of New York, as was directed by his"—Ben looked up with a sparkle in his eyes—"your grandmother's will."

Ford sat back in his seat and crossed his right leg over his left, ready to pounce. "I'm very well aware of that, Mr. Thomas. What's your point?"

"My point is that my client has on several occasions asked for his share within the company to be acknowledged with an appropriate salary and input on all company decisions, including those at board level." Ben waited. He was met with nothing but stern, unforgiving eyes and silence. "He hasn't been granted either."

"Mr. Thomas," Ford began in a careful tone. "Your client has been in and out of prison for the past twelve years on charges ranging from drug dealing to carjacking. As I'm sure you can appreciate, it isn't in the company's best interest to advertise such unsavory behavior."

Ben smiled stiffly. "Of course, but still, regardless of the other shareholders knowing—more of which I'll come to in a moment—do you not think it important to pay my client accordingly or at least offer a gesture of goodwill?"

Ford shifted in his seat. "And what exactly would a gesture of goodwill look like?"

"A sixty-percent increase on his current yearly income, input on all decisions at board level, and an assurance that his shares will not be diluted with or without the threat of blackmail."

The air around the two men became stifling. One of the suits standing at the back of the room twitched uneasily. There was the sound of a throat being cleared.

"I'd be careful which words you choose, Mr. Thomas," Ford warned. "Walls have ears, you know."

"Oh," Ben answered unwaveringly, "I know." He dropped a handful of black-and-white photographs on the desk.

Ford, with eyes like granite, stared hard at him. "What's this?"

"Insurance," Ben answered smoothly. "To make sure that these requests are met without comeback on my client."

"Comeback?" Austin repeated.

"Yes." Ben placed a finger on the top photograph, which showed Austin smiling over dinner and shaking hands with Raphael Casari, a convicted felon known by the FBI for money laundering and drug trafficking. "As I understand it, Mr. Casari is not the kind of character one would have involved in a business such as yours, unless there were more, shall we say, dishonest things at hand." Ben smiled.

"Pictures prove nothing," Ford said indifferently.

Ben smiled. "True. Although these might." He slapped another two folders down.

Ford's eyes flickered over them. "And these are?"

"Statements." Ben sat forward. "Monetary statements, which, for some reason, were harder to find than your others. Mr. Ford, does the word 'embezzlement' mean anything to you?"

With that heavyweight punch, Ben knew the ground under Austin Ford's two-thousand-dollar loafers became unsteady. He glanced once more at the photographs and folder and pressed a palm down the front of his tie. He stared hard at Ben. The menace spreading through his features, pinching and sharpening, was truly terrifying. He was no longer the big dog. He had his ass against the wall, and he didn't like it.

"What. Do. You. Want?" he asked through gritted teeth.

Ben met Ford's glower. "My client owns sixty percent of WCS Communications, with a value of six hundred million dollars." He cocked an eyebrow. "If he were to cash in those shares, it would be one hell of a blow for your investors, right?"

"What. Do. You. Want?" Ford repeated in a breath that reeked of anger.

"I want you to honor the goodwill proposal for Mr. Carter, effective immediately. I want written confirmation of said honoring in triplicate, signed by yourself and your CFO, faxed through to my office and to my client by the end of business today. I want funds transferred to an account of his choosing by the same time and his name put back on the public shareholder list."

It was Ben's turn to sit forward. He dropped his chin and glowered at Ford. "If that doesn't happen, Mr. Ford, I'm sure the police would be interested to know just what business it is you do with Casari." He held up a picture. "Considering he's wanted by the Feds for crimes dating back some thirty years."

Ben released the photograph so it sailed elegantly back down to the table, drifting from side to side in graceful silence. He picked up his briefcase and stood from his seat at the same time Ford sprang from his own chair, moving so close to him, Ben could feel Austin's breath on his chin.

"You're playing a very dangerous game here, Thomas," Ford growled. "You and Carter. And you'd better know one thing: I don't lose. I always win. I always fucking win."

"Well," Ben answered quietly, standing toe to toe with him. "It doesn't seem that way in this case, now, does it?" Ben edged closer. "And on a more personal note, stay the fuck away from Kat."

After a beat of tense silence, Ben turned from Austin Ford and walked toward the office door.

"This is not over, Thomas," Austin seethed. "You tell your client this isn't over!"

"I will," Ben remarked casually. "Oh, and by the way," he said cheerfully, pulling the door open. He turned back. "You can keep those photographs and statements, Austin. I have copies."

26

The clouds had rolled in dark and thunderous by the time Carter and Kat arrived back at the house. The pair of them ran and shouted, laughing curses when the heavens opened above them. A flash of lightning made Kat squeal when they finally made it inside, making Carter laugh. Kat flipped him off and started removing her soaked clothes while her hair dripped down her face.

Disappearing up the stairs to change, Carter followed her, once he'd lit the large fire in the living room, with worry in every step. She hadn't been herself since they'd left the convention. Carter wasn't the most knowledgeable man in terms of women's moods, but something was definitely up.

He thought back, trying to remember when she'd become so quiet, distant. Was it what he'd told her about Max and his past? Was she upset about the whole introducing-her-as-a-"friend" thing?

With his eyes fixed on the bathroom door where she was changing, he pulled off his jeans and T-shirt, and, after he'd rubbed his head dry with a towel, settled for his trusty gray sweats and a dark blue NYPD hoodie. Oh, the irony.

Kat reappeared moments later and dropped her wet clothes into a bag. "Ben texted. The meeting went well. That stuff you gave him about Austin's deals with Casari worked like a charm, he said."

"Of course it did. Even Austin isn't immune to a little blackmail."

Kat shook her head and put her hands on her hips. Her face flushed with blatant annoyance. She looked hot as hell. "I can't believe Beth tried to set me up with him. He's far more of a criminal than you are, and then she has the audacity to talk shit about you and—"

"Hey." Fuck that shit. Carter didn't want to waste one more minute thinking about Austin Ford. "Kat, it's done, okay?" He rubbed his hands up and down her arms.

"It makes me so mad."

"I know. It makes me mad, too. But he's not worth it."

Kat huffed but nodded.

"So listen," he continued. "I've lit the fire in the living room, and I have a grotesquely large selection of DVDs. How about we watch TV, get warm, and forget about that asshole, huh?"

Her smile was small. "That sounds good."

Frowning, he wound his arms around her waist. "Is anything else bothering you?"

She buried her nose in his neck, hiding her face. "No."

Carter wasn't convinced. Nevertheless, he halted the desire to push her further. He didn't like it, but what choice was there? He'd trusted her enough to open up; he had to be patient for her to do the same.

• • •

Back downstairs, Carter poured some red wine, while Kat stood by the glass doors watching the formidable clouds roll over the sea. The sky was pitch-black.

"I love listening to the rain when I'm nice and warm inside," she said quietly as thunder rumbled above them.

Carter handed her a glass. "Me too," he admitted, sipping his drink. "Gran and I would do that a lot here."

"Yeah? Dad and I did, too."

After grabbing a shitload of snacks from the kitchen, Kat took her seat on the sofa while Carter fought with the DVD player. Kat laughed when he held up the disc case to show her what they'd be watching. *Beetlejuice.*

"I can't believe you have that!" she exclaimed. He sat down and lifted her legs onto his lap. "Hey, Carter, 1988 called, they want their movie back."

"It's awesome," he deadpanned, and hit play on the remote. "Shut up."

Carter was quickly engrossed in the movie, but all Kat could do was watch him. She could see the child inside him with each snort of laughter. He seemed so relaxed, and never once removed his hand from her knee, circling it with the pad of his thumb while he drank, ate, and smoked with the other.

The connection was wonderful and allowed Kat to reflect on the day they'd shared. Discovering that he had gone to prison for his friend had left Kat reeling. He was loyal and selfless and so much more than she had ever imagined. His trust and honesty with her was the most beautiful thing, and her heart ached to tell him so. She let her eyes wander down Carter's strong profile, feeling heavy with overwhelming emotion.

"What are you thinking so hard about over there?" Carter asked, his gaze still stuck on the TV.

"Nothin'," she answered, grabbing a handful of Pringles.

"Liar." He adjusted himself in his seat, facing her. "I told you before, you're shitty at that. What's up?"

Kat shook her head, which only made Carter smile wider. "I have ways of making you talk, you know," he threatened with a wicked glint in his eyes.

He placed his wineglass on the side table and moved like a predator up onto his knees, pushing her legs apart and moving her hoodie up her stomach to her chest. With a smirk, he placed a tender kiss above her belly button. Kat ran her right hand across the velvet texture of his head. His hands came up her sides and caressed slowly, his rough fingers handling her as though she was breakable. Her eyes drifted shut.

"I have so much I want to say to you," Kat confessed with a long breath.

Carter hummed into her belly. "So much so that you'll tell me what the hell has been bugging you since we came back?"

Kat licked her lips watching him shift up her body, placing kisses where he moved.

"Kat," he groaned in frustration, moving up so he was lying between her legs with his forearms at either side of her head. His face pinched. "Did you not enjoy today?"

"Of course!" Kat cried. "It was fantastic. I had so much fun. I loved being with you. I—"

Carter played with the tips of her hair splayed out over the sofa cushions. "Is it what I said to Petey about you being my friend?" He grimaced.

Kat chuckled. "No. Why?"

"Because it sounded fucking ridiculous. I was caught off guard," he replied, and then muttered into her neck, "You have to know you're so much more than that to me."

Kat's heart pounded. She placed her hands on his face and pulled his mouth to hers. "Take off your top," she said firmly. "I want to feel you."

• • •

Carter whipped the thing off over his head immediately and watched in awe when she, too, removed her hoodie, leaving her bare. She oozed sexiness, and the color of her alabaster skin against the dim lighting made him want to lick her from head to toe.

"Sit up," she rasped.

He obeyed, slack-jawed, as Kat straddled his waist and assaulted his mouth. He moaned. The sensation of her nakedness against him was incredible. Her nipples shifted, etching his skin with invisible lines of ownership, just as her mouth declared possession with every flick of her tongue and suck of her lips. His hands delved into her hair, gripping her close.

"God, Carter," she breathed, sending sparks of lust over his skin. "I want to show you. I want—"

She stood suddenly, leaving Carter's hands holding nothing but air, and pushed her pants to the floor so they pooled around her feet. Carter whimpered, recognizing the look on her face, the dark hunger in her eyes. She bent to his ear and brushed his lobe with her tongue. His fingers moved between her legs.

"No teasing," she whispered, pushing him away. "I need you too much."

Thank Christ.

He pulled his cock from his sweats, locked his hands around her hips, making her straddle him, and pulled her down, slipping into her easily. They gasped in unison as the lights flickered with the heavy roll of the storm. Holding his breath, Carter moved slow and deep, dragging a moan from her throat while she clutched his shoulders and rocked over him. He cupped her cheek, grunting when their lips met. She tasted of wine and desire.

A loud clap of thunder shook the house.

Kat pushed down, taking him in with small thrusts and slow rotations of her pelvis, surrounding him while he slid his palms down the curves of her waist, around to the luscious swell of her ass.

She was a fucking vision. She moved over him, in control, greedy, dominating, and hard, leaving him breathless. He'd never seen her this way before. There was something in her eyes, a passion, that made his heart race and his hips jerk, and when their mouths slid together, it grew hotter and more powerful. The fervor with which she fucked him pulled every conceivable emotion to the surface. She was letting go in a way he'd never seen, wild and unashamed.

It was magnificent.

It was different.

The two of them together was different. It was as raw, hot, and mind-blowing as always, but the desperation between them was so thick, Carter could almost taste it. As though reading his thoughts, Kat rode him harder, scoring his flesh with her nails, arching her back, taking him deeper, making his entire body burst into flames.

"So fucking good," he told her, his voice hoarse. "Don't stop. Take it all."

He continued to ramble incoherently, begging her as he wrapped his arms around her back and drove up, hard. She was sensational with her head thrown back, crying out, her neck elongated. His orgasm built, heavy between his legs, stretching to his stomach, which tensed and relaxed in microspasms as they fucked.

"Can you feel it?" she gasped. She moved harder, making Carter's eyes roll. He pressed his lips to her damp shoulder, nodding, growling. "It's us. It's you and me."

He'd tried to hold his orgasm off, but her words and the way in which her body held him were making every attempt futile. Each one uttered tore him apart in brilliant ways. Carter licked her jaw, clutching her hair in his fists, pleasure vibrating through every vein, every organ.

She slammed down again, rough, eager.

Fuck. Carter lost himself to the sensations her body stirred up, reveling in her, in what she gave him.

The wetness, the heat, the pounding heart almost bursting from his chest.

The gasps, the moans, the filthy words, the orgasm teetering on the brink of oblivion.

And then she was calling out for him, gripping him, clenching around him.

His hips drove upward. "Come with me."

Her mouth chased his, hungry and wet, as her arms embraced his neck. She whimpered and gasped for air. "Now. Now. Oh."

When all his energy started to push down into his groin, Carter fell back, watching in breathless wonder as Kat continued to pull it from him. She lifted and fell, she demanded and begged, she swiveled and tightened, she thrust and grasped until, with a furious bellow, Carter shattered into her. Carter's neck corded as his orgasm blasted through him like a rocket and smothered his entire body in white heat, her name leaving his lips with an agonized moan.

Bright lights blinded him, while his body twitched and shuddered beneath her. He held tightly, praying she would secure him to the earth and keep his heart from stopping altogether. She squeezed around him, milking him. He threw back his head with a cry of almost painful pleasure. "Sweet Jesus!"

"Wes," she screamed out, coming apart, bucking, and writhing in his lap. "Wes. Oh God. *Oh God.* I love you!"

With a giant flash of lightning and a deafening clap of thunder, the room was plunged into darkness.

27

As they came to a gradual stop, still wrapped around each other, their heavy, labored breaths filled the living room, illuminated only by the still roaring log fire. Carter's eyes opened slowly as Kat's words rang around them.

Like a statue, Kat remained on his lap. Her knotted arms stayed around his neck with her face pressed against his. Carter's brain moved at a thousand miles a minute, and he was damn sure he could feel her heart pounding in time with his.

He moved his thumb minutely, touching the delightful dimples at the bottom of her back, and took a deep breath. "Peach—"

"Shhh," she interrupted in a quiet, anxious voice. He could feel her shaking her head next to his. "Just. Shhh. Don't say anything." He made to move his head so he could look at her, but she held him fast. "Don't move. Please."

Confused, he continued to hold her in the same position, cocooned in her warmth. He exhaled raggedly in aggravation when she kept silent and still. Why the hell was she so quiet? Did she regret saying those words to him? Maybe it was a simple impulsive thing inspired by the amazing sex they'd just had.

Maybe she didn't mean it.

Astonishingly, Carter's heart paused at that particular thought.

"Kat," he whispered. "Please."

"I'm sorry." Her voice shook.

Carter swallowed hard. He heard her sniff and tried to move his head to look at her, but she was too damned strong.

"Kat," he admonished. "Look at me."

"I can't."

"Why not?"

"Because I—I can't. I shouldn't have . . ."

At the sound of the words, he gripped her wrists from around his neck and pulled them away, keeping her body close to him with his hand on her cheek. His gaze wandered over her face in question. He saw she was crying, her face pained, and immediately a huge rock of discomfort lodged in his gut.

He smoothed her damp hair from her face. "What shouldn't you have done?"

If it was a slip of the tongue—so to speak—then he wanted to hear her say it. As masochistic as it sounded, if Kat had said those words and not meant them, he had to know. He wanted to believe her, truly, but so many things in his mind made him doubt her words. He hated that there was any doubt at all, but he couldn't help it. He'd been programmed that way: to be suspicious and untrusting. He closed his eyes for a moment, trying his damnedest to rid himself of the uncertainty coursing through him.

Kat stared down at where they were still connected. "I shouldn't have said that."

Carter slumped and watched her wipe at her tears. He let his hands drop to his sides in defeat. The warm postcoital sensation inside him turned cold.

"It's all right," he said in a rough voice. "It happens."

He had no idea if that was true, but he wanted to make her feel better.

"What happens?" Kat pressed her palm tenderly in the center of his chest, tracing the cursive black ink with her fingertips.

Keeping his eyes on the flickering flames in the hearth, he answered: "I'm sure people say stuff like that a lot. You know, when they get carried away in the moment." There was a second of complete silence where Kat tensed in his arms. Lightning lit the room sporadically.

Carter's eyes fluttered closed when her hand touched his chin, bringing his face around to hers.

"You think I got lost in the moment?"

He shrugged.

Kat shook her head slowly from side to side and cleared her throat. "I didn't get carried away, Wes."

His name never sounded as good as it did when she said it. He held her stare, searching for any hint of a lie, but all her beautiful eyes told him was the truth.

"You didn't?"

Her head continued to shake, as she mouthed silently, *No*.

His chest heaved, as he tried to regain thought and the ability to speak. "Wh—" His throat closed around the word. He swallowed, and tried again. "If you weren't caught up in the moment," he muttered, "why are you sorry?"

Kat drew invisible circles around Carter's belly button. She stayed quiet for an age, driving Carter beyond distraction.

"I'm sorry because I didn't want to say it that way. I didn't know if you'd want to hear it. I was afraid you'd not want to hear it." Gradually she brought her head up. "I didn't want to say it while we were together this way."

"Why?"

"Because it's cliché. Tacky."

"Kat." He grabbed her wrists and shifted her back, sliding out of her body. He pulled her hands, clasping them over his heart. He breathed, collecting himself. "Did you mean it?"

His voice sounded so foreign. He felt so fucking small. Weak. Breakable.

Kat's forehead dropped to his. She trembled against him.

"Yes," she whispered. "I meant it. With everything that I am, I meant it."

. . .

Saying those three words to him—as scary and unexpected as it was—had made Kat's whole body light. She loved him with every part of herself, inside and out, good and bad, past and present.

His fingers were suddenly at her face, tracing her lips. "I want to hear it." He shook his head in bewilderment. "I didn't know how much until just now. Don't ever be sorry about saying that."

"But—"

He cut her off again with a burning kiss that made her toes curl. It was filled with lust, gratitude, and a long moan that came from his throat. He wanted to hear her say that she loved him. He wanted her to love him. Kat's body folded into him in relief.

"Can I tell you something?" Carter asked quietly when their lips separated. "You're the first person, the first person in my whole fuckin' life, to ever say those words to me."

Kat blinked.

"But your family," she began, garnering an amused and sardonic expression from him. Okay. Of course not. "Your grandmother?" she hedged. "Friends?"

Carter's eyes dropped to her mouth. "I was always 'precious' to Gran, and she did love me, but she never said the words. And my friends?" He chuckled. "We're not exactly the huggy, affectionate types. Max is like my brother, but . . . no, we don't say that to each other."

Kat was astonished. How could the man before her never have heard anyone tell him that he was loved? What kind of parents would allow that? How could he have lived for so long with no one telling him how special he was?

Without words, she kissed him again.

"Don't be sorry, for God's sake," he urged. "Christ, hearing those words from you . . . It doesn't matter where or how you said it. What matters is that you said it at all."

She held him close. With her lips by his ear, she whispered once more, "I love you."

He squeezed her and placed a gentle kiss on her throat. "Thank you for being my first."

She buried her nose into his buzzed hair. "Thank you for being mine." Carter sat back, looking at her in question. "I've told people I love them before," she clarified. "You know, family. But I've never felt this way about anyone, Carter."

Carter's grin lit the room.

"Wow." He licked his lips and dropped his head against the back of the couch. He kept his eyes firmly on her. "Look at you."

He continued to stare at her, holding her captive. Occasionally his mouth would open to speak, before he would close it again.

"It's okay," she soothed, running her palms down his sides. "Stop overthinking it."

His body shook with laughter. He kissed her forehead. "You know me so well."

"I do." She sat up. She could see the battle: the fear in believing her and the hope that it was true. Her heart squeezed. "I didn't say it to hear it back. It's okay."

"But—"

"No, Carter, really, I don't need you to say it. And I don't want you to think that you have to." She stroked his face.

He stared up at her. "Why do you love me, Peaches?"

The absolute incomprehension in his expression crippled her. Kat trailed her thumb across his jaw as thunder crashed above the house.

"I love you because you're very special." She kissed his right cheek. "You're generous." His nose. "Caring." His top lip. "Passionate." His bottom lip. "And you are, without doubt, the most beautiful man I've ever seen."

He leaned his forehead to her chin. "Christ, I . . ." He lifted his head sharply, eyes wild. "I have to show you how—why I— There's more."

She held his face in an effort to calm him. "Show me whatever you want. I'm not going anywhere."

He lifted her from his lap. With her cell lighting the way in the darkness, she hurried with her clothes to the downstairs bathroom, cleaned herself up, and made it back to him in time for him to wrap a large blanket around her shoulders. He had a flashlight in his hand.

He held out his hand for her. "Come with me."

Kat placed her hand in his palm and let him lead her up the stairs and along the corridor. He came to a stop outside the third door down from their room and put his hand on the knob. He turned it and pushed the door open. It creaked loudly, as though it hadn't been used for a long time. Kat was hit with a rush of cold air and a musty, aged smell.

With only the flashlight and the intermittent glimpse of the moon through the storm clouds, it was hard to see much. The small room was decorated with dark wallpaper, interrupted only by posters of cars and baseball players. A corkboard hung by the closet, covered in drawings and ticket stubs. White dust sheets hid the furniture, and the small bed was unmade with the mattress bare and unused. Kat turned to face Carter, who was looking at her patiently.

"This was your room," she stated.

He moved the flashlight over the walls, pausing on a picture of a Triumph. They both remained quiet until Carter placed his arm around her shoulders and guided her to the bed, where she sat down. He ran his hand through her hair once before he moved over to the closet. He mumbled and cursed when he opened it and started to pull out boxes of different sizes. He rifled through them slowly until he pulled out a small book held together with a rubber band.

He stood and moved back toward the bed, sitting down next to her with a long breath. He placed the book on Kat's now crossed legs, staring at it as though it would jump up and attack him. Kat moved her hand to Carter's right knee and gave it a reassuring squeeze.

Carter scratched his chin with the side of his thumb. "This is kind of a— It's a diary," he stuttered. "It sounds stupid, I know, but after . . ." He paused. "I just think it'll explain things better."

"You want me to read it?"

He laughed humorlessly. "Yeah, I— Fuck, Kat, I don't know."

His nervousness was troubling. "Okay."

With tense fingers, she pulled the rubber band off the book while Carter opened the small bedroom window and sparked a cigarette. Kat placed the rubber band on the bed and opened the front cover.

What she saw made her blink in astonishment and suck in a quick breath of shock.

Her head snapped up to Carter who shrugged apologetically. Stuck untidily on the first yellowing page was an article reporting the death of one Senator Daniel Lane. There was a black-and-white picture of him and Kat's mother taken on the day of his election. He was so happy and so handsome. Eva looked beautiful, too. She smiled a smile that Kat hadn't seen in a long time. Kat's heart clenched with yearning for the mother who'd told her daughter she could be anything she wanted.

Kat's eyes skimmed the article, knowing what she would find, the details she would read. Words jumped out at her in the flash-light beam: "horrifying," "distraught," "brain hemorrhage," "police shot two suspects." She swallowed hard and let her fingertips slide over her daddy's face.

Gingerly, making sure she didn't damage the paper, Kat turned the page. There were more articles detailing the funeral, the foundation set up in her father's honor, and the events Eva had attended in Daniel's memory. In each grainy picture of her mother, Kat noticed how she aged. The beauty and radiance so noticeable in the first picture had all but disappeared.

Her eyes pricked with tears. As they moved over the article, she realized that every time her own name appeared, it was either underlined or circled. It was the same on all the articles, including the first.

Silently she continued through the book, glancing at the articles he'd collected. She stopped when she came to a page covered in spidery handwriting. The first date was a month after Kat's father had died.

> *I dreamed of* her *again. Every time I close my eyes, she's there. She haunts me and I don't know why. Ever since that night, she's been inside my brain. I wish I could scoop her out like Gran used to do with the chocolate ice cream out of the freezer, but then . . . I think maybe I would miss her.*

Two weeks later:

> *I smelled her today. I was with Max and we walked past a fruit stall. Peaches. Sweet peaches. Her hair smelled of peaches. I bought some. Max called me a freak. I think he's right.*

Two days later:

> *I am crazy. I know I am. I saw her. I know I did. But it's impossible.*

Christmas:

> *Dad and I argued. He called me ungrateful. I called him a prick. He found my smokes. I lay on my bed and closed my eyes and I saw her and smelled her hair again. Fucking crazy, right?*

It calmed me down. I think that if I helped her that night then maybe she wouldn't mind that I use her this way. Maybe she wouldn't care. Maybe she doesn't even remember me.

Kat continued to read. The passages were small, no more than five lines each, but gargantuan in their significance. The hand that covered her open, disbelieving mouth became wet with tears. At the same time, the bed moved with Carter's weight. He wrapped his arms around his knees. He was uncharacteristically still at her side.

New Year:

I hold the world but as the world, Gratiano,
A stage where every man must play a part,
And mine a sad one.

February:

In Belmont is a lady richly left,
And she is fair, fairer than that word,
Of wondrous virtues.

"Carter," Kat choked, reading the words from *The Merchant of Venice*.

"I'm sorry. Shit. I knew I shouldn't have— I just wanted you to understand."

"What did you want me to understand?"

She needed him to explain. Reading his deepest thoughts was almost too much.

He took the book from her hand, thumbing through it, smiling wryly at some of his words and closing his eyes at others.

"That night," he started quietly. "The night we met. That night was the longest, most terrifying night of my life." He smiled. "But I wouldn't change it, not for a fucking thing." He touched the diary almost reverently. "I started this when I was eleven years old. Sixteen years ago." His voice seemed far away to Kat's ears.

His eyes flickered to her hair. "Kat, your smell was— It was like it took over my brain. I couldn't think about anything else. It calmed me when I was ready to murder my father, and even when I was at Arthur Kill, I would go back to that night and think about you. Those were the nights I slept the soundest."

He put the book to his side and clasped her hands. "I don't want to freak you out with this shit, I really don't, but hearing you say those words and not being able to say them back . . ." He shook his head. "I hoped this would help you see." He gazed at her. "Do you understand, Kat? Do you understand what you are to me?"

Emotion stopped the answer from leaving her mouth.

"Today, when I introduced you to Petey," he continued with a crooked smile, "I didn't have a fucking clue what to say to him. I went through a dozen labels, including 'my girlfriend,' but that just . . . doesn't seem *big* enough." His face creased to show his distaste for the word. "And I couldn't say 'my Peaches' because that shit is mine alone."

Yes. She was *his* completely.

"Kat," he whispered, pulling her closer. Their foreheads touched and Carter closed his eyes.

"I don't know what will happen when we get back to the city. I have no clue. But I do know that I want no one else but you. I want to be with you for as long as you'll have me. I want more nights like this one, and I want to be able to walk down the street holding your hand knowing that, for once in my life, every other fucker envies me and what I have."

Kat clutched his hoodie in her hands.

Carter pulled her into his arms and whispered into her neck, "You're everything to me, Peaches. You always have been. *Always.* You're the best thing I've ever had in my life." He kissed her. "You're *my* everything."

28

Leaving the beach house was hard for Kat. So much had happened in the two days they'd stayed there. She'd clung to Carter at the side of her car, never wanting to be away from him again, but knowing that real life waited for both of them.

The drive back to the city was long and uneventful, except for the moment that Carter flew past Kat's car on Kala like a bat out of hell, weaving through traffic like a lunatic. She wasn't sure he even noticed her, but Lord if he didn't look like sex incarnate riding the damned thing.

After texting Carter to tell him she was home safely, she prepared herself for an unexciting evening of unpacking her suitcase. He'd promised to stop over later, which, even after a whole weekend together, still caused excited butterflies to swarm inside of her. Fred smiled as Kat approached the front desk, her suitcase clattering at her heels across the marble floor.

"Good evening, Miss Lane," he chimed. "How are you?"

"I'd be better if you'd call me Kat," she admonished with a playful flash of her eyes.

"Apologies. Kat."

"My friend Mr. Carter will be here later. Will you send him straight up?"

Fred picked up a pen and made a note. "Is he the tall gentleman with the . . . tattoos?"

Kat smirked. "Yes, that would be him, but he's really not as scary as he looks."

Fred raised his eyebrows. "I'll take your word for it."

Kat laughed. "Good evening, Fred."

"Good evening, Kat," Fred replied with a tip of his hat.

She turned back from the desk, heading to the elevators. As her hand lifted to press the elevator call button, a figure moved behind her, catching her attention. As realization struck, Kat spun around with a surge of anger.

"What the hell are you doing here?" she spat.

Beth's face showed no sign of surprise at Kat's reaction. "I came to talk to you."

Kat let out a bark of sarcastic laughter. "I have nothing to say to you."

She turned back to the elevator and pressed the already lit button, praying for it to hurry up.

"You look well," Beth murmured. "You look really well."

"Why do you care?" Kat remarked with no inflection to her voice. She turned, crossing her arms defensively. "Look, you'd better hurry back. I'm sure Adam and Austin are eager for you to get back to them to tell them all of my dirty secrets."

"They don't know I'm here," Beth replied, anxiety prevalent in her wide eyes. "I told Adam I was going to get some ice cream."

Kat's anger turned to confusion.

"I'm so sorry, Kat. Truly."

Kat remained apathetic. "And?" she asked with a lackadaisical shrug of her shoulders. She was intrigued as to what had caused Beth's sudden attack of conscience, although, if it was a trap, then God help her.

"And I wanted you to know that."

"Fine," Kat countered, pressing the elevator button again. "You've said you're sorry. Now your conscience is clear, and you can leave."

Ordinarily, Kat's brusque attitude would have made Kat feel

bad, but a quick apology wouldn't erase the secrets hanging in the air around them like a noxious gas.

"You're in love with him, aren't you?"

Kat froze, unblinking, praying her poker face was enough.

"I know you," Beth said quietly. "I can see it." She stepped closer. "Is he good to you? Does he treat you right?"

Kat bit the inside of her mouth. She stayed silent, fighting the urge to run far away. She knew trusting Beth was a mistake.

"You look happy," Beth continued in a voice Kat remembered fondly. "Love suits you. I know he must be a good man to make you glow the way you are." Her eyes flitted over Kat's face. "I know it's too little too late, but I can admit when I'm wrong." She sighed despondently. "Adam explained a few things. He told me about Carter and Austin. The way Austin was when they were all growing up."

"Yeah," Kat countered sharply. "Carter told me about it, too."

Remorse whispered across Beth, weighing down her shoulders, making her smaller. "I know Carter isn't bad, and I know that with him you're safe. I should've trusted your judgment, and I didn't. For that I apologize."

Paranoia flared up Kat's spine. "So now you can go and confirm it all to Austin, can't you?"

"That's not why I came," Beth muttered toward the floor before she started to rifle through her bag. She pulled out two brown folders. "I wanted to give you these."

Kat took them. "And what are they?"

"They're jobs."

Kat cocked an incredulous eyebrow.

"Teaching jobs with starting dates for the new year," Beth added. "One of them is at the school where I'm currently working. I think you'd be perfect, so . . ." She cleared her throat and glanced at the ceiling. "I know I went about it in entirely the wrong way, and I will always be sorry for that, but I want you to be happy, and I know Carter does that. But if you're with him, you have to be careful. If Austin finds out you two are in love he could use it—"

"What? You tried to set me up with this guy. Why would you do that when you know what he's like?"

"He isn't a bad guy, Kat," Beth replied firmly. "But that doesn't mean he doesn't make bad decisions. He has to answer to many important people, and they want Carter out, too. He's under a lot of pressure. I heard about Ben's visit to the office. Austin's going nuts trying to find a way to get Carter out. Adam said he's never seen his brother so angry, so dangerous, and . . ." She pulled her bag onto her shoulder, breathing deeply. "Just look at the folders. If you're Carter's tutor and you're together, you're both at risk. Think about Ward, the board, the nonfraternization policy you agreed to. There is so much at stake."

"You think I don't know . . ." Kat snapped her mouth shut. She'd already said too much.

Beth's smile was small but knowing. "Think about it. I'm here if you want to talk. We could go for coffee, or . . ." Beth moved her hand toward Kat, but let it drop before she reached her. "I'm sorry and I miss you."

She hesitated before she closed her coat around herself. With one more repentant stare, she turned, walked across the lobby, and left.

• • •

Carter kissed Kat's hair and nuzzled her temple. They were fully clothed, under the covers of her bed, where Carter had placed her after she'd almost strangled him when he arrived at the apartment a half hour earlier. She'd flung herself at him and he'd shushed and soothed her, while she explained what had happened with Beth.

"I'm so scared, Carter. I'm scared she's doing this so she has proof that we're together. I'm afraid she'll go to Austin and he'll use that against you. I never thought that sending Ben would—

I'm terrified he'll threaten you and take you away from me. And I can't—I can't lose you, I . . ."

Carter kissed her, swallowing her concerns. The tremors of fear ran up her spine under his touch. He hated it. He'd fucking kill Austin if he dared to take his Peaches from him. Let the fucker try.

"He can't do anything. I won't let him." His voice grew dark, menacing. "If he wants the company he can fucking have it. The money means nothing. All I want is you."

She nodded hopelessly, turning Carter's anger into panic. He was losing her.

"We can't let them win," he said, seizing her chin. "After this weekend, you have to promise me you won't let them win." She shook her head, but it didn't appease him. He held her jaw. "Say the words, baby. I need to hear them."

"I won't let them win. I promise you."

He groaned in a mixture of frustration and desire.

His tongue lay flaccid and unusable at the bottom of his mouth. He gritted his teeth. How could he not tell her how he felt? His body was bursting at the seams with emotions for her, and he simply could not express any of them. He kissed her neck and knotted his fingers in her hair, silently fuming and cursing himself.

"If I take one of those jobs, I won't be your tutor anymore," Kat mumbled sadly against his rough cheek.

He'd think about having a new tutor and the antagonism he would feel toward them later. Now was not the time. "But I'll still have you, right?"

She slid her palm down the side of his face. "You'll have all of me."

He gripped the back of her knee and pulled it higher above his hip. She pushed her hands under his T-shirt, her nails grazing his back, while her tongue pushed into his mouth. He could taste her fear and pushed back just as hard to soothe her.

"Fuck them, Kat," he growled. "Come back to me. Be here

with *me*. Right now," he demanded. "Don't think about them. Just think about us."

There was so much to discuss. So much to think about. There was so much at risk that could tear them apart. Carter clenched his eyes shut, pushing his dread as far away as he could. As long as they were together, he thought, everything would be all right.

"Make me forget. *Please*," she begged. "Make me forget all of them."

Carter rolled her onto her back, hovering above her. "Anything."

29

Days passed, gradually folding into weeks as Kat and Carter continued to fold into each other. Cautious and careful, they continued to meet at the library three days a week, working as they were expected, while at night they worshipped each other's bodies in an effort to keep at bay the things that threatened to tear them apart. For those sweet, blissful hours when their limbs entangled and their names became frenzied gasps of pleasure, everything floated away, leaving them to imagine what being together without worry or recrimination would be like.

Carter watched his Peaches carefully from one day to the next, hopelessly aware that the strain of their situation had begun chipping away at her resolve. Outwardly, she appeared the same, beautiful and put together, but he'd begun to notice, when they were alone, she held on to him a little tighter, touched him more frequently, more fervently, as though terrified that what they'd built together would collapse around them at any second.

Carter wasn't naïve. He knew the obstacles. He worried just as much as she did. His cousin was an asshole of the highest order, no doubt plotting a retaliation that would be sure and swift. Max was still falling into blow with no regard for those who cared for him, and Kat's mother called incessantly, despite Kat's insistence that she didn't want to speak to her.

Shit outside of their bubble was not copacetic. Nevertheless, Carter knew he had to be strong for them both. He'd do anything to help see that smile of Kat's he adored so much, which was why he insisted she look through Beth's folder of good intentions for a new job when, after two weeks, it still sat untouched on her coffee table. And why he agreed to accompany her when she returned her grandmother's car to Chicago in time for Thanksgiving.

To agree to the latter, and doing family-type shit, highlighted just how insane he fucking was. But, truthfully, the thought of Kat being away from him for any amount of time was excruciating. He'd just have to nut up and shut the fuck up.

Kat's small hand shot out across the car's center console and covered Carter's leg, which jumped up and down in earnest. Unable to throw himself from Nana Boo's Jag and hightail it back to his apartment, Carter settled for decimating the side of his thumbnail, which he shoved inelegantly between his teeth, gnawing on it like a motherfucker.

"Sweetheart, relax." Kat glanced at him and then back to the road. "Everything is going to be fine."

Carter scoffed.

Fine? *Fine?* Was she insane?

Her confidence in both him and the situation was endearing as hell, but his brain had been on fast-forward since they'd left the apartment. Oh God, the fumbling, nervous verbal vomit that would no doubt happen when he met Kat's favorite family member was enough to turn his stomach inside out. His nerves were just about shot to shi—

"I love you."

Carter's eyes closed briefly before they slid over to the breathtaking creature next to him. His hand dropped loudly from his mouth to his lap.

"And Nana Boo will, too." She smiled, her eyes sparkling. "I just know it."

How the hell did she do that? She knew exactly what to say to help calm him down, and, although the need to leap out of the car was still heavy in his stomach, her words made it all the more bearable.

He kissed her temple. "Thanks." Even though the sentiment seemed grossly inappropriate for how she made him feel, it was all he had. Carter sat back, keeping her hand tightly on his thigh, fingers entwined, securing himself to her. With a deep breath, he stared out of the car window, watching the world whizz by. They had a long drive ahead of them: nine hours, a stop overnight in a motel, and then another six to Chicago.

He looked at the clock.

Only another eight and a half hours to go.

Terrific. Plenty of time to get riled up.

His cell phone chimed from his jeans pocket. He read the display: Max calling . . .

"Hey, man."

"Where the hell are you?" Max's words were sharp, high, and slurred.

The idiot was filling his nose at nine in the damn morning. The shit was getting out of hand.

Carter sighed. "I'm headed to Chicago, Max. Where are you?" The faint sound of a female voice sounded in the background. "Who's with you?"

Ignoring his question, Max retorted, "What the fuck are you going there for?" His tone made Carter bristle.

"Thanksgiving," he replied firmly. "Kat invited me. I told you about it, remember? You said you'd be chillin' at Paul's."

Max laughed, though it sounded humorless. "Oh yeah. You and Kat. The happy fucking couple."

Here we go again. There was a crash on the line, something hitting the floor, and high-pitched giggling that could only be chemical-induced. "Max. Are you okay? What's up?"

"It doesn't matter," he spat. "You clearly have better things to do, brother. You always do."

Carter's temper spiked. "That's not true. Don't be a dick, Max."

But the line went dead. Carter stared at the cell screen, incredulous and angry. He and Max had spoken little about his and Kat's relationship, not least of all because Max's bitterness and anger over Lizzie clouded his ability to see how happy Carter was. The more Carter felt for Kat, the madder Max appeared to become. Carter's joy was apparently of little importance to Max, who was too involved in his own despair. The amount of coke he was doing daily simply exacerbated the situation.

And Carter was powerless to stop it.

Every time he offered to help—be it money or support—he was met with resistance. Max's pride was almost as difficult to penetrate as his stubbornness. Carter and Paul had discussed an intervention—the only place for Max now was rehab—but both men knew that would only end badly.

"Everything okay?" Kat's expression was anxious.

"No." Carter sent a quick text to Cam and Paul, telling them to go to the shop and make sure Max hadn't choked on his own vomit or some shit. In irritation, he began fiddling with the radio, playing station commando for a good five minutes, appreciative of the fact that Kat didn't push further.

"Don't forget you have to call Diane when we cross the state line," Kat said instead.

"Yeah, I know," he replied, settling back in the leather seat of the Jag XJ and letting the sounds of Green Day's "Good Riddance (Time of Your Life)" relax into his bones. Carter hummed along and played the invisible chords of the song against the blue vein in Kat's wrist. He brought Kat's hand to his lips and kissed her knuckle.

She hummed. "Tell me what it is you're worried about."

He replied with a peevish shrug, like that shit would discourage her from asking questions. Truth was, there was no escaping Kat and anything she asked him. His ass remained trapped in a cream leather bucket seat traveling across the country at seventy miles an hour.

Awesome.

"Tell me."

Carter clasped the bridge of his nose. "I'm worried about a lot of things. I can't think of just one."

"Okay," she soothed. "But you should know there really is no need to—"

His patience snapped, his words bursting from him in a sharp rush. "For Christ's sake, I'm a criminal, Peaches. Of course there's reason to worry."

He didn't mean to bite, but he was beyond edgy. His spine was wired and his stomach was in knots, twisting frequently between fear and panic. Yeah, he was a fucking mess.

Kat remained silent.

He was instantly contrite. "Look, shit, I'm sorry, baby—"

"No, it's all right," Kat interrupted. "This is a big deal for you. I'm sorry I've not addressed that properly, I really am." Her sincerity made his chest tight. "Just say the word and I'll turn the car around. If this is too much for you, I don't want you to feel this uncomfortable."

What the hell had he done to deserve her?

"I don't want you to turn the car around." He breathed deeply, turning in his seat to see her better. "Not that I don't appreciate the gesture, but I want to be with you this weekend." Carter ran his free hand across his head. "I just want your grandmother to see I'm not just a . . ." He swirled his fingers toward his chest, thinking of a list of not-too-nice adjectives. "You know, and that I care about you."

Kat slowed the car as they approached a junction. "She will. My grandmother is the very best person I know. She doesn't judge."

She laid her palm against Carter's neck, running her thumb along his jaw. "We can just be us. You and me."

"Promise?"

"I promise."

• • •

They were only twenty minutes from the house when Carter's gut began to do backflips. His back was also all kinds of fucking sweaty, which was ridiculous considering it was colder than a witch's tit outside the car. It'd even snowed a little.

"You feel okay?"

Carter rested his head back, watching Kat drive. "I'll be fine," he murmured, pressing his cheek against the headrest. "I'm just gonna watch you until we get there."

She smiled with her eyes still on the road. "Like when you have a flu shot, huh?"

Carter frowned. "What?"

Kat glanced in the rearview, changing lanes. "When I was a little girl, my dad took me for my shots, and he'd always say that if I didn't look, it wouldn't hurt as bad. It wasn't as scary if you couldn't see it comin'." She smiled again, her eyes wistful. "I'd hide in his neck and pray for it to be over."

"Did it work?"

"Every time."

The sides of his mouth lifted. She'd spoken a lot about her father since they'd left New York. Carter couldn't deny he would like to have met Daniel Lane, regardless of how the man would have reacted to Carter dating his daughter.

"Do you think . . . ?" Carter wrapped his thumb around the side of Kat's little finger hopefully. "Do you think that he would have liked me?"

Kat pulled to a stop, as the lights changed to red, and turned to face him. "I think you and my father are more alike than even I realize. I think he would have thought you were awesome."

God, he wished that were true enough to erase the dark fear lurking just beneath his skin. "You do?"

"Yeah," she answered with no hint of doubt in her voice. "I do. Kiss me?"

Carter moved so their lips met. Keeping his eyes open, he watched Kat's roll back into her head. He let the tip of his tongue trace her bottom lip and sighed when she pulled back and continued to drive.

"I don't remember having my shots," he confessed quietly.

Kat glanced at him. "You don't?"

He shook his head, trying to recollect.

Kat scrunched her shoulders, making her voice bright and indifferent, but Carter knew she was feeling sorry for him. The sympathy prickled his skin like a nettle sting, making his molars grind.

"Maybe that's a good thing," Kat offered. "Having shots is awful."

It seemed like such a ridiculous thing to want to remember. He exhaled hard at the memories he did have. Hurt. Tears. Isolation. Hate. Fuck it, he thought, when the anger began to rise. There was no changing his past; he had to look forward, and having Kat at his side was one giant leap in the right direction. He squeezed her leg, his fingers whispering over the denim seam running up the inside of her thigh.

"Carter?" She swallowed.

He smiled. "Yeah?"

"We're here."

Carter snapped his head around to see a huge redbrick house appearing at the end of a long stone driveway, surrounded by gardens. Carter's heart gave a resounding kick behind his ribs. He was suddenly desperate for a cigarette. Frantically patting himself down, he found the pack of smokes in his jeans pocket and swallowed in relief. Thank God.

Unexpectedly, a terrible thought crossed his mind: Shit, what if Kat's grandmother hated smokers?

"Carter?"

Kat's voice sounded miles away and when he turned to look at her, Carter had the oddest sensation that he was floating underwater, unable to breathe.

Kat unclipped her seat belt. "Are you all right? You look a little pale."

Carter rubbed the center of his chest, willing his airways to open up. It didn't help. A wave of cold sweat crashed over him, shooting down his back like icy claws. He couldn't breathe. Christ. His lungs were seizing.

What was he doing? Why had he agreed to this fuckery? He didn't do this. He didn't meet families. It was laughable, really, thinking Kat's grandmother would accept him. She'd never accept him because he wasn't good enough. He'd never be good enough.

Stupid, stupid idiot.

"Hey," Kat said, pulling his hands from his face to her lap.

"Kat, I—I'm not . . ." He gasped. "I can't."

"You're fine, Carter. I'm here and you're fine." Kat put her hands on his neck and rubbed his pulse points with the pads of her thumbs. "Tell me," she murmured, kissing the fingertips of his right hand. "Tell me you know what you mean to me."

His lungs shuddered. "I know. I know. But I—"

Her forehead met his, holding it up, holding him up. "No. No buts. That's all you have to think about."

See? her tone whispered. *Easy.*

With three deep breaths, Carter's pulse slowed. Focusing on her fingers drawing circles on his skin, he managed to sit up a little straighter. He had to get a grip. He couldn't allow his fear to be the first thing Kat's grandmother would see. No way.

He moved forward, capturing Kat's lips. "I'm sorry."

"Don't be sorry. Are you okay now?"

He dropped his gaze to the floor of the car. "Just don't leave me, okay?"

"I won't," Kat said fervently, dismissing his neediness as quickly as he offered it. "Come on."

Before Carter could stop her, she was getting out of the car and bouncing excitedly around the hood.

"Here goes fuckin' nothing." Carter opened the car door and got out.

He shut the car door and pushed his hands into his pockets against the cold air and the sudden, colder memories of his own mother's house, the foreboding that settled in his bones every time he was dropped off at the front door and the look on her face when she opened it, regretful and inconvenienced. Christ, he'd just been a kid, scared shitless and alone. He swallowed and fought the memories back. They were soon forgotten when the front door opened and a huge black-and-white dog came bounding out, tongue flopping and tail wagging.

• • •

"Reggie!" Kat squealed and crouched down to him. He whined and barked in happiness.

She rubbed the mutt's belly until his back legs were scratching and kicking up like a lunatic. "I missed you, too," she cooed.

"Kat!"

She looked up to see Nana Boo, dressed in a huge parka and mittens, hurrying from the door, looking as wonderful as she always did. Trevor, her help, followed with a warm smile.

"Nana," Kat breathed, instantly at peace. She stood and allowed her grandmother to envelop her in one of her hugs.

"Angel." Nana Boo smiled into Kat's hair. "It's so wonderful to see you."

"You too."

Kat kissed her cheek before she pulled back. She glanced toward Carter shifting on his feet and rounding his shoulders in defense. She immediately grabbed his hand and pulled him with her. His grip on her hand was painful, but she would have taken all he had to ensure he was protected and comfortable.

"Nana," Kat said with a dip of her chin, "this is Carter. He's my . . . Wes."

Carter's head almost toppled off his neck he looked at her so quickly. His eyes were wide with surprise, but the smile threatening the corners of his perfect mouth told Kat her words were the right ones.

"It's a pleasure to meet you, Carter," Nana Boo offered with an outstretched hand and an ecstatic smile that creased her face in a thousand different ways.

Carter cleared his throat. "Nice to finally meet you, too," he said as their hands met.

Nana Boo's eager arms encircled Carter around his waist. She pressed her cheek against him and squeezed.

"Um, hi," Carter mumbled, while staring at Kat over the top of the aged woman's woolen hat. Kat smiled.

"I've been so excited to meet the man who's captured my Kat's heart," Nana Boo whispered.

She stepped back and wiped a finger under her shimmering eyes. "Oh my." She chuckled, observing the tears on her skin. "Silly old woman."

"Not at all," Carter said with a half smile.

Nana Boo cupped his cheek and tapped it tenderly. "And, darling, you're just as gorgeous as she described." She laughed at the speechless expression on Carter's handsome face, and snaked her arm through the crook of his elbow. "Let's get you inside. It's too damn cold out here. Kat, give Trevor the keys. He'll collect the bags."

Carter pulled Kat with him, gripping her hand as if his life depended on it. She rubbed her palm up and down his forearm in placation. God, he'd been truly terrified when they'd been in the car. The distress was almost visible around him, evil and unrelenting. She knew where it came from; he carried it around with him like a lead weight.

Kat bit the inside of her mouth. The hate she harbored for his family made her teeth snap. They'd treated him so appallingly, never loving, caring, or nurturing him as he grew, and he now considered himself unworthy, with no comprehension of just how incredible a man he had become. It was painfully tragic.

"Was the drive good? The car was all right?" Nana Boo asked. She shut the front door behind them and pulled off her hat.

"Yeah." Kat took a step closer to Carter's side, knowing his need for contact. "He didn't complain about my driving once." She smiled when she saw him roll his eyes, his finger twirling a piece of her hair on her shoulder. "You may have even turned him into a Jaguar fan."

Nana Boo's eyes lit up. "You like cars?"

Carter scratched his neck. "Yeah, I, um, I dabble."

"Carter likes motorcycles, too," Kat interjected, ignoring the pointed look he shot her.

Nana Boo gasped. "A real-life Steve McQueen! Oh, be still, my beating heart."

Kat giggled into Carter's shoulder and closed her eyes when she heard him burst with laughter.

"I wouldn't say that," he murmured. "But I like them."

"Well, I'll show you the Triumph I have in my garage later." Nana Boo winked. "You kids need a warm drink."

Carter stared after the little woman as she scurried past them to the kitchen.

"She has a Triumph?" His blue eyes twinkled.

Kat laughed. "And an antique Aston. Come on, Steve," she teased. "She makes a killer hot chocolate."

Seated around Nana Boo's huge wooden table, Kat allowed the warmth of her grandmother's house, love, and acceptance seep into her, filling up the gaps of shame and uncertainty that had opened over the past few months. Carter, with his free hand always touching her, sat and listened while, before, during, and after their dinner of enchiladas and Oreo cheesecake, Nana Boo told him story after story of Kat and her childhood escapades. Stories detailing Kat falling off horses, climbing trees, and smashing baseballs through windows kept Carter enraptured.

Seeing him so relaxed, hearing him laugh, and having him slowly realize there was nothing to be afraid of was more than Kat could have dreamed. All she wanted from their weekend with Nana Boo was for him to see he fit into her life. She wanted him to see there were people who didn't care about his past and the mistakes he'd made. It was important for Carter to understand not everybody would hold them against him. They didn't define him.

She listened when Nana Boo asked him questions about his hobbies, smiling when Carter became shy and modest about his musicality and his love of all things fast and metal. He explained about Kala, and his desire to buy another motorcycle, which led to Nana Boo telling stories about Kat and her father riding up and down the beach for hours, simply to have the sound of the engine in their ears and the wind on their faces.

"She's not changed," Carter mused, smiling at Kat, making her cheeks flush.

Nana Boo was amazing, laughing and joking and never asking questions that made Carter uncomfortable. She listened with absolute attentiveness. Gradually, Carter's shoulders lost their hard edge and his smile began to appear a little more easily. Even his grip on Kat's hand loosened.

Although he had yet to resolve one particular issue, and she knew it was driving him beyond distraction.

Kat smiled knowingly when she saw him squirm for the thousandth time. "You can have a cigarette, you know."

Carter glanced apologetically at Nana Boo. "I'm fine."

"Trevor smokes out on the back porch, dear," Nana Boo said dismissively while placing a bowl of Doritos and a sour cream dip onto the table. "Please feel free. You're on your vacation."

Carter eyes searched Kat's for permission. "It's fine," she assured him, finding his timidity endearing as hell.

"Okay," he conceded. He tapped his long fingers against the edge of the table, hesitating. "I need to call Max, too. I'll—I won't be long."

He stood up from his seat and strode toward the back door. Reggie, with claws scratching eagerly across the wooden floor, got up from his place under Nana Boo's seat and followed him. Carter looked at the dog by his side, cocking an eyebrow in question. Reggie sat down and thumped his tail excitedly.

"He'll follow you," Nana Boo explained. "He likes you."

"Okay," Carter mumbled, keeping his suspicious eyes on the dog before he opened the door and they both stepped out into the cold Chicago night. Kat stared at the door once it closed.

"He's wonderful." Nana Boo sipped her red wine. "He adores you, darling."

"I adore *him*," Kat confessed. She allowed her finger to trace the stem of her wineglass. "He was so nervous, Nana. He wanted to make a good impression so badly. I just wish he knew he didn't have to worry. He doesn't see himself clearly at all."

"He will in time, Kat. If he hears it enough, he'll see it." Nana Boo smiled to herself. "He reminds me so much of . . ." She shook her head.

Kat rested her chin in her palm. "Who?"

"Your father," Nana Boo replied. "He's just like Danny was when your mother first brought him into the house, all jittery and aching for a cigarette."

"Dad smoked?" Kat coughed into her wineglass.

"He quit when your mother became pregnant with you."

Kat looked at the table, smiling. "I never knew that."

"There's a lot I could tell you about your father."

"Please," Kat encouraged.

"Your grandfather never approved of your mother's choice of husband." Nana Boo smiled reminiscently. "No one was ever good enough for his Eva."

Kat exhaled a gust of sardonic breath. "Yeah, it must be a family thing."

This made Nana Boo chuckle. "Yes, your mother is very much like her father."

Kat thought for a moment, considering all the ways in which her mother had made her feel so entirely disgraceful for choosing Carter, for choosing Arthur Kill.

"She's protective because she loves you, Angel," Nana Boo murmured, seemingly reading Kat's thoughts. "She's terrified of losing you."

"She already has."

"You don't mean that, Kat," Nana Boo chided, making Kat feel instantly remorseful. She swirled the wine in her glass. "So, you have an interview for a new job," Nana Boo stated, seamlessly changing the subject.

"For a juvenile detention facility in Brooklyn," Kat confirmed. "It's to start in the new year."

The job had been one of the first that she'd come across in Beth's folder and, although Kat hated to admit it, the job sounded perfect. They'd accepted her application immediately. Despite the parts of her that were sad about leaving Kill, Kat was excited.

"And this is what you want?" Nana Boo asked.

"I want Carter."

Nana Boo's eyes sparkled with the romance of it all. "As long as you're happy. That's all that I care about. Your mother'll come around." There was so much conviction in Nana Boo's voice, Kat almost believed it.

Despite her hurtful words, and the animosity still between them, Kat would have given anything for her mother to be sitting at the table, having a glass of wine, being understanding and happy. Weeks had passed and still the two of them were at loggerheads. For Kat anger had given way to sadness and acceptance. Things between them would never be the same.

She dipped a Dorito into the sour cream with a weary hand, needing a distraction. "So, tell me more about why Grandpa didn't like Dad."

Nana Boo chuckled. "Danny had a few skeletons in his closet, just like your Carter." She eyed Kat carefully. "He'd done things before he met your mom that he wasn't exactly proud of, and your grandfather always had a bee in his bonnet about it. I have some things upstairs you can look at. I think it would be easier to explain that way."

"It's nothing bad, is it?"

"No. It's nothing bad." Nana Boo hesitated. "Unlike your mother, who thinks it unnecessary, I believe it's time you learned more about what they went through to be together." She placed her hand on top of Kat's. "I assure you it's nothing scary, and it'll make sense when you see what I have." She glanced toward the back door. "Just know that Carter and your father are very alike in many ways."

Before Kat could ask any more, the back door reopened and Carter hurried back in with lumps of snow covering his dark hair, followed by a very cold-looking Reggie.

"Jesus Christ, it's fucking freezing out there," Carter grumbled. He rubbed at his scalp, splattering water onto the floor. "I can't feel my damned fingers!" He stopped abruptly, clearly realizing what he'd said and in whose company. "Shit." He blinked. "Dammit, I mean, sorry."

Nana Boo snorted loudly and cupped her hands to her mouth

to stifle her giggles. "It's quite all right," she managed through her fingers. "I've heard a lot worse. I was married to Kat's grandfather for nearly forty years."

Kat's shoulders shook from holding in her own giggles. Carter exhaled and shuffled back to his seat, where he took an enormous gulp from his bottle of beer.

"Don't you worry any." Nana Boo snickered, patting his knee. "You just be yourself. You're perfect as you are."

• • •

"Are you sure it's okay?" Carter watched Kat roll her small weekend suitcase into their room, the room they were sharing under her grandmother's roof, with her grandmother down the hall.

"You know," Kat singsonged from her spot across the room, "for a convicted felon, you sure have prudish ideas about our relationship."

He rolled his eyes. She skipped into the en suite, pulling her sweater off. Prudish? Sure, that's why he had a semi on just from seeing her naked back.

"I'm not being a prude," he griped. "I— It's Nana Boo's house." He dropped his ass down onto the edge of the huge bed, ripping off his boots and socks.

He was rubbing the tiredness from his face when Kat reemerged from the bathroom, leaning against the doorjamb with a peculiar expression on her face.

"You called her Nana Boo," Kat whispered, fingering the hem of the Harley T-shirt she'd changed into. His T-shirt. The edge of it skimmed her creamy thighs, while the V-neck dipped between her breasts.

"Yeah," Carter replied. His eyes devoured her.

Kat walked toward him. She nudged his knees apart with her own, and placed her hands on his shoulders while he placed his on her hips.

She bent down and rubbed her nose against the side of his. "I love that you call her that."

Carter hummed when their lips met, gentle and warm.

"Are you feeling better?" She placed a knee on either side of his thighs on the bed.

Carter smiled against her throat. "I do feel better." He sat back a little, focusing on the way Kat's hair curled at the tips. "I feel good." He tilted his chin toward the door. "She's amazing." He shook his head in wonder. "She's just so— I mean, the woman made me an Oreo cheesecake! How cool is that?" He kissed her jaw.

Carter trailed his hands down her sides and tickled the back of her thighs. "For the first time, in a long time," he murmured, "I don't feel like I'm missing anything." He placed his lips at the side of her mouth. "I feel like I belong."

"You do belong," Kat soothed. "You belong with me."

Her words made Carter's body soft and malleable. He held Kat nearer and kissed her. He jumped back, however, as though caught doing something unforgivable when there was a light knock on the door. Kat crawled off him after kissing the tip of his nose, and walked to open it.

"I'm sorry to disturb you, dear," Nana Boo said from the other side. "But I wanted to give you this before you went to sleep. It's the details about your father."

Carter craned his neck to see around Kat, but could only make out a large, brown, crumpled envelope clasped in Kat's hand.

"Thanks, Nana," Kat said before kissing her grandmother's cheek.

"Good night, Angel," she hummed. "Good night, Carter," she called, with a smile lacing her words.

"G'night," he called back. She reminded him so much of his own grandmother it was, at times, a little overwhelming. Even her smell made him feel nostalgic, all sweet and floral, with large green eyes he saw every time he looked at his Peaches.

He whipped his sweater over his head and pushed his jeans down. Kat closed the door and tapped the envelope against her knuckles.

"What's up?" He pushed the covers of the bed back and slipped in between them.

"Nothing." She lifted the envelope. "It's just some stuff about my dad. Nana Boo wanted me to look at it."

"What stuff?"

"I don't know." She held it in both hands.

Carter sat forward and lowered his voice. "You, um, you want to look at it together?"

A look of intense love and gratitude lightened her face.

Carter pushed the duvet aside, patting the mattress. "Get over here."

Kat skipped over to the bed and got in next to him. He wrapped his arm around her shoulder, kissed her hair, and watched her open the envelope. He rubbed the top of her arm, watching her pull out a shitload of newspaper clippings and lay them carefully across her lap. She fanned them out, stopping at a few that detailed her father's death, his funeral, and the subsequent memorials and remembrance events that had taken place.

Carter squeezed Kat to his side when he saw a picture of her, taken the night of the murder. She was wide-eyed, clearly terrified, wrapped in a police-issue blanket that drowned her tiny frame.

"You were so damned small," he whispered, trailing his finger over her black-and-white face. He tucked a stray piece of hair behind her ear. "But so strong."

They spent a few minutes looking over the clippings before Kat suddenly gasped and cursed.

"What?" he asked with a smile. Her dirty mouth was all sorts of hot. He liked that he was rubbing off on her.

"Look at this." She handed him the paper, ignoring his lascivious glances.

The picture on the article was of Kat's mother and father, dressed to impress and looking like every other political couple Carter had ever seen. However, the headline caught Carter's attention: Senator Lane Served Time for Misdemeanors.

Holy shit.

His eyes flicked up to Kat's before he stared back at the clipping and began to read. The misdemeanors ranged from graffiti, being drunk and disorderly, dope possession, and, most impressively, car boosting. The penalties he'd been given were tame, due to the senator's age when the offenses were committed, and it was clear from the tone of the article that the senator's past had only been brought up in an attempt to blacken his name, but still, Carter didn't know whether to be exceptionally smug or stunned.

Either way, he was definitely intrigued.

"I can't believe Mom didn't fucking tell me," Kat fumed at his side. "After everything." Kat dropped back against the pillows. Her voice climbed in pitch. "After everything she said about my job, about you."

Carter picked up all the clippings and carefully placed them on the side table.

"How can she be such a hypocrite?" she asked through her teeth. "How could she say such awful things about my choices, when she made exactly the same ones?"

"They're not exactly the same," Carter countered.

Kat cocked an eyebrow.

Carter shifted. "Look, I'm not defending the fact she didn't tell you. That shit's not fair, but your dad boosted a couple of cars and sprayed a few walls with paint." He shrugged. "Compared to me, he's as clean as they come."

Kat's eyes darkened. "That's not the point, Carter. She omitted that information and made me feel like crap because I wanted to be with you and I wanted to do a job that would help me overcome my fears and make me stronger. She's done nothing but belittle me, you, and the decisions I've made, and all the while, she knew my father had a criminal record."

Carter cupped her face in an attempt to soothe her.

"It's not a competition based on who did the worst thing or did the longest time," she continued, disgusted. "In the eyes of the prejudiced assholes walking around with their judgmental noses in the air, you and my father are the same." She shook her head. "My mother knew that. That's why she didn't say anything." She moved closer, curling her body around his.

He ran his index finger down the center of her nose, following the outline of her top lip he knew tasted like raspberries. "Are you mad at your dad?"

"No," she whispered, trailing a finger around his nipple. "How could I be? He made some bad choices when he was a kid. So what? He's still one of the best men I've ever known." She hesitated. "Like you."

Carter couldn't pull his eyes away from her. Her words ruined him. There was no denying it. Christ, she was so damned beautiful, draped across him, with her fervor and fire heating the room around them both.

Unexpectedly, his chest stirred, as though a rope wound tightly around his insides, tugging them hard. He moved, trying to ease the pressure rising within him, up from his stomach, to his throat. Everything inside immediately was too big, as if some unknown force was making his organs swell and push together, overwhelming him. It whipped his breath away and set every nerve ending in his spine alight. His skin erupted in gooseflesh and his toes curled in supplication to whatever the fuck it was.

"What's wrong?" Kat asked, noticing his alarm.

Carter rubbed his eyes with the heels of his hands. "Just indigestion, I think."

Kat placed a soft kiss below his belly button. "Better?"

Carter grabbed the tops of her arms, pulling her closer, up his body. "No. You're too far away." He kissed her, needing her above him, below him, covering him, engulfing him.

He kissed her hard, breathing in the rush of life that came from her lips, the heat, and the color she'd brought into his miserably gray life. She kissed him back, concern evident in the gentle brushes of her lips. She pulled away, her gaze dancing, searchingly, over his face.

Carter swallowed. "I'm fine."

He tried to keep his voice calm, tried to show in his face that all was peachy fucking keen, but inside, a goddamn festival was taking place, and, for the love of God, Carter had no idea how to stop it, or if he even wanted to.

30

Kat awoke to the sound of banging that sounded like it was coming from Nana Boo's front door. Carter moved with a loud sigh, his arm wrapped protectively around her waist. He hadn't let her go all night. They'd done nothing but cuddle and spoon, even though his hard body had told her he'd wanted a lot more. There was something different. He was different. Something had appeared in his eyes. Something irrevocable and too big to deal with at—

With her face half covered by the pillow, Kat glanced at the clock to see it was a little after ten in the morning. How had that happened? Christ, she didn't even remember falling asleep.

"Who the fuck is making that noise?" Carter grumbled into the nape of her neck, pressing his delicious morning wood against Kat's ass. "They need to shut the fuck up and let me get back to sleep." He yawned. "I was having awesome dreams."

Kat snorted and rolled over to look at him, smiling at his adorable sleepy eyes and brushing her palm over his crotch. "I can feel how good they were."

Carter sighed and lifted his hips from the bed, chasing her hand. "Don't pretend that you don't love it."

Kat frowned when the banging stopped abruptly and raised voices, spouting inaudible words, echoed up to the room.

A concerned frown slashed between Carter's brows. He lifted himself up onto his forearms. "What the hell's going on?"

Kat shook her head, hating the heavy dread snaking up her back. "I have no idea."

Carter was swiftly on point, protective and cautious. "I'll go and check it out."

"No," Kat said, touching his shoulder as he pushed back the sheets. "I'll go."

"Peaches," he murmured with an annoyed glint in his eye.

"It's fine, I'll—"

"KATHERINE!"

The bubble around herself and Carter burst apocalyptically as the voice pummeled at the bedroom door. Kat's skin prickled in cold terror, while tears sprang to her eyes, forced to the ducts by fear and absolute fury.

"Mom."

"What?" Carter coughed, shooting to his feet at the side of the bed, eyes wide. "Your—your mom?"

Kat nodded slowly, robotically, gripping the blankets in her fist.

"Katherine, come out here! I know you're in there with him!"

Kat closed her eyes, unable to look at Carter for fear that she would fly out of the room and slap her mother senseless.

"Eva, calm down." Nana Boo's voice crept under the wood.

"No, I will not calm down. How could you have him in your house? How could you allow this to go on under your roof?"

"Because it is *my* roof, Eva, and I am your mother. I don't answer to you."

There was a beat of silence; the acidic tone of Nana Boo's words fizzled into the air.

"I should go," Carter muttered, making his way around the end of the bed.

Kat's heart dropped to her stomach. "NO!" she called out, scrabbling from the bed toward him, catching her foot in the sheet. "No, you don't have to go anywhere. Please. Don't go."

He avoided her eyes, looking past her, alarm making the muscle in his jaw jump. "I can't be here."

"Yes, you can," Kat urged, grabbing at his biceps. "You have as much right to be here as I do."

"Kat—"

"If you go, then I'm coming with you."

Before Carter could answer, the door of the bedroom swung open, smacking the back wall of the room with the momentum with which it was forced. Kat turned to see her mother glaring at the two of them: Kat in Carter's T-shirt, and he, bare but for his ink and a pair of black boxer briefs.

"Get out," Kat growled.

"I'm not going anywhere." Eva's eyes trailed down Kat's state of undress.

"Eva," Nana Boo chastised. "That's enough."

"Get some clothes on and come downstairs," Eva insisted through thin lips, ignoring Nana Boo. She shot daggers at Carter, causing Kat to move protectively in front of him. "Alone."

"I'm not doing a thing—"

"Now, young lady," Eva interrupted. She whirled like a dervish and marched out of the room, thumping down the stairway.

"What does she want, Nana?" Kat asked, desperate to feel Carter's arms around her. He didn't move.

His stillness and silence were terrifying.

"I don't know," Nana Boo replied with a despondent shake of her head. "I'm so sorry to both of you. She called asking if I'd spoken to you. I told her you were here together. I had no idea she planned on coming . . . I'm so sorry."

"Don't apologize," Kat urged. "It's her, not you."

Glancing over her shoulder at Carter, Kat's stomach rolled violently when she saw his face: angry, barricaded, and closed off from everyone around him.

Even her.

"I'll give you a moment." Nana Boo sloped out of the room, closing the door behind her.

Kat sniffed and moved toward her suitcase, ignoring the waves of dangerous calm rolling off Carter. When she started talking, the words came out quickly, bumping into one another.

"We'll go. We'll get out of here. I don't want to be here with her. Nana can lend us the car again and I'll grab my bag; you can grab yours—"

"No," Carter interrupted.

She stopped, stock-still in the center of the room.

"Go downstairs and see what she has to say." His voice was intense and direct, but his eyes flitted around the place, searching for a way out.

"But we can leave together," she insisted.

Carter bent to grab his sweater. "No, you need to speak to her, Kat."

Hurt gripped Kat's heart. She folded her arms, holding herself together. "Why? Why do you want me to talk to her?"

"Because it's time you did."

She watched him sit and pull on his socks. "You . . . can't leave," she whispered. Her voice broke. "I need you here."

"Kat."

"Please, Carter. Don't listen to her. Everything she says—it's not true. It's not. Please."

Her breathing started to accelerate, as the thought of him walking out of the door grew more vivid in her mind. Unable to move from her spot for fear that she would shatter, she gasped, "Please. I'll talk to her if you promise you'll stay."

They remained silent for an age, staring at each other, neither of them seemingly wanting to speak. The atmosphere around them was charged but uncomfortably different from how it normally was.

"Peaches, I can't—"

"You can."

"I'm no good for yo—"

"Don't you fucking dare say that!" Sadness gave way to anger. "You *are* good enough! Christ, you have to know that!"

Carter didn't answer and continued to look down at the floor. Kat's heart fractured painfully. Jesus, they were back at square one.

Kat took a tentative step toward him. "Promise me you'll stay. Promise me you won't leave."

He scrunched his eyes shut and bit his bottom lip, but she didn't care. She needed to hear the words. At that moment, it was the most important thing. Nothing else mattered.

"Carter."

"Okay," he answered in a lifeless voice. "I promise."

"Promise that you won't leave. Say it."

He lifted his head and looked at her, but something deep in Kat's heart told her he was seeing straight through her, and it hurt. It hurt so much.

"I promise I won't leave."

He was so crushed, so broken, and Kat hated that she was helpless in putting him back together. "Okay," she whispered. "Okay."

Silently, she moved around the room, pulling on a pair of jeans and sneakers. She tied his T-shirt at her right hip and pulled her hair up into a loose ponytail.

"I'll be right back." She stood at the doorway with the crumpled brown envelope in her fist. "And then we're out of here."

"Kat, I—" She waited for him to continue but, instead, he cracked the knuckles of his right hand and shook his head. "It doesn't matter."

With a lead weight in her stomach and a splintering heart, Kat opened the bedroom door. "I'll be right back."

• • •

She walked with purpose and dignity into the sitting room, unable to make out any of the words of the obviously heated conversation taking place between Harrison and her mother by a large bay window. The snow had fallen hard overnight, covering the gardens in a winter blanket.

Nana Boo was absent, which pleased Kat. Nana Boo didn't deserve to see or hear what was about to happen. The fact that her mother had come into Nana Boo's the way she had, and on Thanksgiving, made Kat's teeth grind. Seriously, who was the parent here?

Kat stopped with a straight back, arms folded, when Eva caught her eye. "I thought you were at Harrison's parents'? What are you doing here?"

Eva stared back. "Do not speak to me that way, Katherine."

"And don't tell me what to do," she retorted. "How dare you come into my room, into Nana's house that way?"

An edge of remorse stole across Eva's mouth. "Nana is fine. It's you I'm worried about, furious with, actually."

"Why?"

"Why? Because my daughter doesn't speak to me, answer my calls. My daughter, who not only works in a damned prison but is running around town with—with that—"

"Be careful," Kat warned when Eva waved toward the doorway.

Eva blanched and a flash of hurt lit her eyes. "I am here to put a stop to this."

Kat scoffed. "Do you know how ridiculous you're being?"

"What is ridiculous is you're putting your entire career, your reputation, and maybe even your life on the line for some delinquent waste of space—"

Kat flew toward her mother, stopping only inches away from her. "You do not speak about him that way!"

Kat's proximity and the ferocity emanating from her every pore made Eva pause.

"Calm down," Harrison said at her side. He raised his hand toward Kat's shoulder but dropped it. "Just both of you, please, calm down."

Eva swallowed. "You may not believe it, but I'm doing this

because I love you, Katherine. The prison is no good for you. He's no good for you."

"You don't even know him," Kat spat. "You never even gave him a chance."

Eva was incredulous. "And how was I supposed to do that when you carried on behind my back? I had to find out from Beth, from Nana!"

"And it's such a big mystery why I didn't tell you!"

"Because you knew it was wrong!" Eva countered. "For God's sake, you could get into so much trouble."

"You think I don't know that?"

Eva's face grimaced in puzzlement. "Then why are you—?"

"You have done nothing but make me feel like a disappointment ever since I started working at Arthur Kill. Nothing I've done since I took that job has been good enough for you; even the man I love is a disappointment in your eyes."

Eva scoffed. "Oh, please, you don't love him."

"With everything that I am," Kat said imploringly. "You have no idea what I've been through these past few months, Mom. How hard it was to face my biggest fears at Kill, to confront what has kept me awake for the past sixteen years."

Eva's face pinched.

"But Carter's been there for me, with me, helping me and caring for me when no one else would." Kat turned her face toward the ceiling, furious that her mother would even dare to cry. "When I left here that night, it was Carter who took care of me, and never once has he said or done anything to me that warrants such narrow-mindedness from you."

"He's a criminal."

"Like Dad?"

Eva took an unsteady step backward. Her face held an expression of complete shock, but her glistening eyes told Kat it was checkmate. Kat pushed the crumpled envelope against her mother's chest.

"I wonder," Kat mused. "Did Grandpa's hatred make you want

to walk away from the man you loved, or did it push you further into his arms?"

Eva stared at the envelope in her hands.

"You should have told me, Mom. It wasn't Nana's job to tell me about Dad's past," Kat said angrily. "Instead of judging me, instead of judging Carter; you should have been honest with me first." She willed her tears back. "How could you lie? How could you make me feel so alone?"

"I never wanted that," Eva answered. "I just . . . I want you protected, Katherine. You're all I—I didn't tell you because I want what's best for you."

"Carter is what's best for me. He may have made bad choices, but he's a good man and I love him."

Eva closed her eyes. "It doesn't matter. I can't lose my daughter, too. I won't. You're risking too much!"

"Carter isn't dangerous!" Kat exploded. "Jesus, Mom. He protects me. He's protected me since I was nine years old!"

Eva's face changed to one of perplexity. "What do you mean?"

"You wouldn't believe me even if I told you. You don't trust a thing I do or say."

"That's not true," Eva argued. "I just—"

"What, Mom?" Kat huffed in exasperation. "Worry? Get scared? Guess what? So do I."

Eva moved closer. "Listen to me, Katherine. Come home with me. Let's talk. I can't keep fighting with you like this. I want us to go back to how we were before all this." She wrung her hands together. "Don't you see? This is all because of that damned job, because of him."

Kat bit her tongue, halting the vitriol that threatened to spill. "I need to be with Carter." She turned on her heel and made for the door.

"Katherine, wait!"

Kat stopped, took a breath, and turned slowly.

"Talk to me," her mother urged, pain lacing her features. "I . . . I want to make this better. I want to make us better." Frustration and hurt were clear in the sharpness of her shoulders. "I hate that we're like this. I want . . . I want my daughter back. Please. I love you."

Kat fought back the urge to go to her mother and find comfort in her arms. God, she was tired. They'd never fought this way before, never been so far removed from each other. Even after Kat's father had died and Eva had fallen into herself, there were still moments of affection and hope. A part of Kat's heart wanted there to be a resolution to the bullshit separating them now, but she knew that wasn't going to happen. Too much had been said. There was no bridge big enough to cross the divide gaping between them.

"Until you accept that Carter is going to be in my life, I can't do that, Mom."

Without waiting for Eva to respond, Kat hurried back up the stairway, needing to get back to Carter, to have him tell her everything would be all right. She needed him around her, needed his scent in her nose and his skin under her hands. She needed his lips on her mouth and his voice in her ear.

The hallway to reach him suddenly seemed a mile long. She rubbed at a dead ache settling above her heart and pushed the bedroom door open, pausing in the doorway, holding her breath.

Empty.

She called his name.

"Katherine, please," her mother continued from the hallway, having followed her up the stairs.

But Kat didn't respond. Hastily, she stormed into the en suite.

Empty.

With her heart slamming into her ribs, she dashed back into the bedroom, calling his name.

His bag was gone.

She pushed past her mother, who was still muttering words such as "amends" and "love," and threw herself down the steps, running in a full sprint to the back door.

Cigarette. He's having a cigarette. He promised.

"Carter?" The back door flew open, showing only a thick layer of snow across the vast gardens.

Empty.

"Kat?"

Kat spun around, almost collapsing in on herself when she saw her grandmother's soft, concerned face. "Nana, where is he?"

She shook her head in bewilderment. "I don't know, sweetheart. I thought he was in your room."

"No. He isn't there." Kat gasped. "He promised me, Nana."

Kat grappled for her cell phone from her pocket and burst out of the kitchen toward the front door.

"Please pick up," she whimpered before the voice mail kicked in.

Her panic reached epic proportions when she threw open the front door to find only more cold stillness. Her breath erupted from her mouth in large gray plumes against the frigid air, while her gaze desperately sought Carter's tall, broad form against the white.

Yet, looking through eyes releasing frightened, angry tears, all Kat could see was a single set of large footprints leading down the driveway, away from the house.

Away from her.

. . .

The screen of Kat's cell phone lit the entire room as she pressed redial once again.

Voice mail.

She blinked heavy lids over weary, wet eyes.

She'd heard nothing from Carter for twelve hours. Not a text message and no phone call. Silence.

Her head throbbed, her heart was shattered, and her body was exhausted with worry. Every part of her body ached. The hollowness was paradoxically overwhelming.

Still, after many tears cried and hundreds of steps paced, she knew she didn't blame Carter for any of it. How could she? She couldn't blame him for finding a way out, an escape route. It had taken six hours, repeated hysterical calls, and numerous texts to him for her to recognize that. But she had.

Carter may have come across as impenetrable, unemotional, and indifferent, but Kat knew he was anything but. He was hopelessly open and fragile.

If anything, Kat was at fault for placing him in a situation in which he was clearly uncomfortable. She should have listened to her instincts and read the anxiety in Carter's eyes. She'd wanted to show him he was enough, prove to herself that she could help him, that she was strong enough to support him.

She had been so selfish.

Yes, he had promised, Nana Boo said when Kat had laid her head in her lap. Yes, she had trusted him to mean it, but the truth was he hadn't. He'd said it because she'd made him. He knew she'd needed it, and he'd given it to her. She wouldn't have spoken to her mother if he hadn't, and, in many ways, Kat was glad she had.

Not that it achieved much.

Rome wasn't built in a day, after all. Their conversations after Carter had left were uncomfortably stilted and curt, but they were conversations nonetheless. Kat had seen it, clear as day, on her mother's face: she knew it was her presence that had forced Carter to leave. And, whether she admitted it or not, a part of her had to feel responsible.

Kat rolled onto her back, clasping her phone tightly to her stomach. Glancing out of the window, she saw the snow was still coming down. She couldn't help but agonize about where Carter was and whether or not he was safe. She'd called the airport, but their flight booking hadn't been altered. She'd no idea whether he had taken another flight home, but something within Kat told her he hadn't. She'd decided after packing her bag she would leave Nana Boo's and catch her scheduled flight the following afternoon.

Nana Boo, of course, had urged her to stay, telling her that Thanksgiving should be with her family, but truthfully, being in the house with her mother, after everything that'd happened, simply didn't sit right with Kat. She'd texted Carter telling him where she would be, should he return to her, and left.

Family or not, she needed peace, quiet, time to think.

Just like Carter had.

Jesus, what he must have felt, hearing Kat's mother say the things she had. Eva's words had bulldozed every single piece of confidence and self-assurance Kat and Nana Boo had helped construct around Carter the previous day and night. She closed her eyes. God, she just wanted to tell him she loved him.

No matter if he never wanted anything to do with her again, Kat needed him to hear it.

She allowed herself a moment to release a few more tears. They were tears for Carter and the pain he was no doubt in. Tears of the anger she felt toward her mother for doing that to the man she loved; tears for Nana Boo and the awful situation she'd unwillingly become a part of, and tears for her father.

Jesus, how she missed him.

She was so sorry he wasn't there.

She was so sorry for everything. So sorry and so tired.

Before she could think any more about the shitty mess she'd found herself in, blissful, quiet sleep overcame her.

• • •

There was a noise.

Nestled on the edge of Kat's consciousness, in a place between dark and light, and reality and dreams, there was definitely a noise.

In her sleep-induced haze, Kat flung her arm out to press the alarm on the digital clock in an effort to stop the—

knock knock knock

Blinking back the sleep gluing her eyes together, Kat sat up, disoriented, slowly becoming aware of her surroundings.

Nana Boo's favorite suite. The Drake Hotel, Chicago.

With her now-dead cell phone still clasped in her hand and her clothes warm and damp from sleep sweat, she shuffled to the edge of the bed. She flicked on the bedside lamp, drowning the room in elegant light. She listened again, frowning in frustration, wishing her brain would shake itself awake so she could focus properly.

There was nothing.

Silence.

Of course there was only silence. Why had she expected anything else?

Maybe it had been a drea—

knock knock knock

Kat lifted from the edge of the bed and made her way across the bedroom and into the large sitting room of the suite, flicking lights on as she went. Who the hell? She couldn't remember ordering room service. Cursing herself for not noting the time, Kat dragged her feet toward the door, rubbing her face while simultaneously fixing the nest-like hair residing on her head.

knock knock knock

"Hang on a second," Kat called sleepily. "I'm coming."

Ignoring the peephole and muttering about the numerous locks on the door, Kat was still talking toward her feet when she finally got the thing open.

"Sorry," she apologized, suppressing a yawn. "I was asleep. What's the prob—"

Kat's words died in her throat when her eyes met the tall, unexpected figure standing before her. He wasn't even standing, in fact; he was sagging against the doorjamb with water dripping from his chin and down the sides of his tired face.

His beautiful, perfect face.

"Carter," Kat squeaked, dazed, unsteady on her feet, and still believing she was dreaming. "Where the— What are . . ."

Her eyes traveled down his body in disbelief. His clothes were saturated, clinging to his strong form, and the knuckles of his hands were white from the cold. His lips were tinged a dark blue and, as she stared at him with now-wide-awake eyes, she realized he was shivering.

"Jesus, you're freezing," she exclaimed, coming to her senses. "Come in and—"

"No," he rasped, shaking his head and licking the water that subsequently fell to his lips. "I can't."

Kat's heart stuttered. "Why?"

He kept his eyes to the floor. He shook from head to toe and made a pained noise that came from deep within him.

"Carter, you're going to get sick," Kat coaxed. "Please."

"No!" he said loudly, too loudly for a sleeping hotel. "I need . . ." His chin dropped. "I have to say something first."

Kat's knees started to buckle. This was it: what she'd dreaded the most. He was leaving for good. Her heart skipped several beats and her insides clenched in preparation for the devastating impact of his words.

She cleared her throat and exhaled. "Can I tell you something before you do?"

She took his silence as acceptance, even though his eyes remained glued to the sumptuous royal-blue carpet below their feet. Closing her eyes and praying she was able, she began to think of all the things she wanted to say to him.

"I'm so sorry, Carter," she started. "I'm so sorry for everything. I shouldn't have brought you here. It was selfish of me. My mother was— Everything she said was bullshit, Carter, I promise you. She's the only one who believes it. I hate her for what she said. I hate her for making you doubt everything I've ever said to you. And I don't blame you. I don't blame you for walking away because I would have done the same, and I'm sorry I couldn't protect you from the things you were so scared of. God, I'm just so sorry."

Kat dropped her forehead against the door, terrified it was going to be the last time she ever spoke to him. But she'd said all she could.

"I'm sorry, too," he uttered, making Kat lift her head. He was still looking at his feet.

"You have nothing to—"

"Let me fucking finish," he snapped, squeezing his eyes shut. "I need to say this without you interrupting or arguing with me, okay?"

"Okay," Kat agreed quickly.

"I have plenty to be sorry for," he ground out through his teeth, pressing his clenched fist against the wall. "I'm—it's—you're, you're . . . you're everything to me, and I'm sorry I was such an idiot to have believed I was ever good enough for you."

Kat pressed her lips together and cupped a hand to her mouth to stop the words of protest.

"I'm sorry I'm weak. I can't—I—you wreck me, Kat. Things you say to me. The way you . . . love me. They do things to me, your words; they make me feel things no one else has ever made me feel. I'm sorry I've done shitty things, and I was a fuckup—*am* a fuckup. I can't ever take my mistakes back. I hate that fact, but I can't. They're what they are and I'm who I am because of them."

His body collapsed farther against the door frame. Kat stayed rooted to the spot, desperate to touch him, comfort him.

"I'm sorry I left," he whispered. "I shouldn't have, I know I promised, but it was . . . so fucking hard." He pressed his forehead against the wall. "I was terrified that— Christ, I knew I should have just stayed in the room and not listened, but I wanted to know what she— I grabbed my bag and left," he admitted. "Snuck out of the house like the fucking coward I am. I didn't know what else to do. The walls were closing in."

"Carter."

"I felt sick when I heard her say those things," he continued. "Sick because I knew she was right. And I know you don't agree, but she's your mother, Kat, and she cares about you. She doesn't want you with someone like me, and I get that, I really do. Shit, it kills me, but . . . I get it." He shrugged one shoulder. "I figured it was better for everyone if I left." His long lashes pressed against his cheekbones. "I shouldn't fucking be here."

He stood, motionless, silent.

All Kat heard was the pounding of her heart. Her skin was clammy and the knot of helpless terror in her gut tightened incessantly. "Then . . . why are you here?"

The corner of Carter's mouth twitched. "Walking out of that door, Kat, was the hardest thing I've ever done." He pressed a hand over his heart. "When I left there was this pain, like a, I don't know . . . It was— It took my breath away. And the farther I walked away from you, the more painful it became. I . . . I thought I was dying."

She knew exactly what he meant. There'd been nothing but pain for her since the moment she'd realized he'd gone.

"I walked and walked," Carter continued. "I was so mad with myself. I knew I had to keep going, and I tried. You have to believe me. I tried so damned hard. But, my heart. Jesus, it was— It was fucking breaking."

He stood up as straight as his exhausted body would allow, and looked at Kat for the first time.

Their eyes met. His were aged, defeated.

"I hate that I've caused so much trouble," he said miserably. "You've had to defend yourself against people who should be happy for you. I have issues, I'm an angry fucker, and I have a terrible temper. I still have shit I need to tell you about myself, and I have no idea where to start because I'm scared shitless you'll run from me, and I know that makes me a selfish bastard for expecting you not to when I know that's the best thing for you to do."

"I—"

"Wait," he interrupted, breathless, taking a wobbling step toward her. He was so close, Kat had to lift her head to look at him, her eyes level with the sharp edge of his rough jaw.

"Please, Peaches. I want"—he exhaled in frustration—"I want to do the right thing. I know I should walk away. I know I should have put my ass on a plane and gone home instead of standing outside of this hotel for four hours in the snow. I know you deserve better. I know all of that, Kat. But the truth is . . . the truth is . . ."

Kat closed her eyes, swaying toward him. She shivered when his ice-cold hand cupped her neck and moved to her cheek.

"The truth is," he whispered, his lips by her ear, "I'm so damned scared to walk away. I can't. I'm hopeless without you."

Kat clutched his forearm, rested her head on his biceps, and released a soft, pained sound of relief.

His nose glided up her temple. "I'm yours. You have to know that. Christ. Tell me you know."

"I know," she whimpered. "I know."

Carter's body fell into Kat's, pushing her back, stumbling into the hotel room. She managed to shut the door with the edge of her foot as he buried his face into her neck and began to shiver uncontrollably, mumbling garbled words into her skin. His arms wrapped around her waist, gripping her tighter than he ever had before.

"Kat," he croaked. "I— Kat. Don't make me go. Please."

"Never," she promised ardently.

His body shook violently.

"Let's get you warm. Please, let me help you. You're so cold."

He stepped back reluctantly so she could unzip his jacket, which she pushed off his shoulders. He stood silently, looking downward, water dripping from his chin onto the floor, as she began to undress him. Wordlessly, and with his top half bare, and gooseflesh puckering every inch of his skin, Kat took his shaking hand and led him to the bathroom. Leaving him by the door, she switched on the five large showerheads, turning them to warm. She removed his boots and socks, unfastened his jeans, and helped him out of his underwear before she took off her own clothes.

As naked as they were together, there was no sexual charge, no fizzling atmosphere, no desperate hands or manic kisses.

With her palm in his, Kat guided him into the shower, moving so the water hit his body first. As they stood under the stream, she turned the temperature up gradually, not wanting to shock his body with the heat.

She pulled him into her arms. "Let me make you warm."

He wound his arms around her, dropping his face to her shoulder. He shook his head against her neck. "I couldn't leave. I know I should have, but I couldn't."

"I know. It's okay."

"I'm so scared. Fuck. I'm so scared." His voice broke. He pulled her closer, his large frame dwarfing hers, making her spine bend backward.

"Don't be scared," she insisted, rubbing his back. "I'm here."

Carter tried to move closer. "I can't lose—I—God. It hurts to even think about it." His voice became hoarse. "Help me," he begged. "Help me. I can't . . ."

"Carter," Kat urged. "Calm down. Please."

While holding them both upright and maneuvering as best as she could, she managed to guide them both down to the shower floor, a mass of heavy limbs that never unraveled or lost contact.

She'd never seen him this way before. Every barrier she'd ever come up against, every last piece of his armor that remained—the cockiness, the indifference, the anger, and the hate—was disintegrating before her, leaving his body with every drop of water that hit him, running off his trembling skin, and disappearing down the drain.

She cradled him, pulling him closer, winding her arms around his inked shoulders and her legs around his waist, while he pressed his coarse cheek against her chest. His shoulders quaked and heaved with gasps and hiccoughs.

She heard him moan at the same time his body shook.

Oh God.

He was crying.

She ran her hands up his back and neck, trying to calm him while struggling to keep herself together. "You're all right, sweetheart."

"I need—I need to . . ."

She kissed his neck. "Tell me what you need."

"Jesus, it's . . . it's, it's here." He grappled for her hand and pulled it to his thundering heart. "I've never felt anything like it." He licked his lips. "It hurts."

"Your heart hurts?"

His face collapsed.

Kat watched the hot water fall down his face.

"It's yours. All of it." He blinked his sodden lashes. "I know now.

"Kat, I . . ." Carter lifted his head and, with his nose at the side of hers, his arms wrapped around her, and with the steam of the water cocooning them both, he opened his mouth, gazed into her eyes, and breathed, "I . . . I . . . love you."

31

With her eyes flickering over Carter's terrified yet expectant face, Kat found herself without words. Over and over she opened her mouth to say something, something momentous or meaningful, but found that his confession had left her entirely dumbstruck.

He loves me.

"Carter," she breathed, closing her eyes. "I love you, too."

His hand moved to her neck, skimming her wet skin tenderly with the tips of his fingers, tracing the pulse point in her neck she knew was going crazy.

His stare remained fixed on her collarbone. "My Peaches." He pressed a soft, wet kiss to her throat. "You're mine," he said with his lips at her jaw.

She nodded, rubbing her cheek against his. The feel of his skin on hers made parts of her body clench and twist in subjugation.

"Every part," she whispered passionately.

"Jesus," he murmured by her earlobe. "It's so— I don't even have words."

She knew exactly what he meant. Theirs was a love beyond words, beyond reason, beyond even the two of them. It was indescribable, inexplicable, but unbreakable and unyielding. Their connection, their bond, was sixteen years in the making. Even though they hadn't known each other and had gone about their lives from one monotonous day to the next, they'd still been a part of each other, a silent, integral part that would always be, for as long as they both lived.

They were both powerless to stop it or deny it.

A surge of awesome strength swept through Kat's body, pumping adrenaline through veins already hot from Carter's declaration. It was an uplifting sensation, one she'd not experienced for a very long time. For the briefest of moments, with Carter in her arms and determination filling her from head to toe, she was truly unstoppable.

. . .

Kat kicked the quilt from off her feet. She was sweltering and, as nice as having Carter's body pressed against her was, she had to move to cool down.

Glancing at the clock, Kat wiggled out of the bed—where she and Carter had been asleep for the last five hours—pulling her T-shirt off and turning the thermostat down from hot-ass sauna to just warm enough. She hurried to the bathroom, where she splashed some cold water on her face and pulled off her sweats, changing them to a small pair of sleeping shorts.

Kat's skin immediately began to cool down. With a glass of water in hand, she wandered back into the bedroom to find Carter, still on his back, wearing only his boxer briefs. She smiled when she saw he'd kicked the quilt off, too. His hard stomach lifted and dropped hypnotically as he breathed.

He cracked an eye open and rubbed a palm down the center of his glistening chest, as she lay back down at his side. He looked deliciously rumpled.

She trailed her fingertips through the hair on his stomach. "Hey."

He turned his dopey, pillow-creased face toward her, smiling lazily. "Hey."

"How's your heart?"

He reached for her hand and placed it on the left side of his chest. "You tell me," he said, piercing her with an intense stare.

Kat bit her lip. "It's pounding."

"It always is when you're near me."

She took his wrist and did the same, placing his large hand over the top of her left breast. Unhurriedly, Carter lifted onto his elbow, watching his hand and her face with childlike wonder.

"It's flying." His gaze moved from his hand, leisurely up the curve of her neck, stopping hungrily at her lips before it rested resolutely on her eyes. His silence made the hair on the back of Kat's neck lift and tingle, while the air around them began to thicken and buzz.

"Do I do that to you?" he asked, tracing the gooseflesh along her arm.

"Every time you look at me."

The tips of his fingers danced lightly along the lace edge of Kat's bra. Her chest heaved at the sensation and her eyes fluttered closed of their own volition. With featherlight touches, Carter moved his hand over to her right breast, tracing every curve, caressing lightly, while purposefully missing the places Kat was desperate for him to touch.

Shifting his body closer, Carter began to draw languid figure eights up toward her collarbone, mapping its shape and pressing against the pulse points in the valley of her throat. It was such a simple thing, for him to touch her that way, but Kat was unable to hold back the soft whimper slowly building with every brush of his gentle hand. His index finger dropped from her throat and meandered knowingly, erotically, down between her breasts, over the fabric of her bra, to the soft skin of her stomach.

Kat held her breath when he reached her belly button. He circled it twice before his finger dipped into it teasingly. Unable to hold her head up any longer, Kat lay back against the pillows, giving herself over to her senses, while Carter continued his wonderful exploration of her more-than-willing body.

"Your skin is so soft here." His hand skimmed the waistband of her shorts. "So soft."

Kat gasped when his lips pressed onto the same spot, and purred when Carter's tongue licked along the trail his finger had just taken.

"Carter," she moaned.

"What is it, baby?" He moved gradually so his body was leaning over hers.

Kat's hands moved from his hair, finding his broad shoulders that flexed powerfully under her palms. His chest pressed against her.

"I miss your lips."

His thumb skimmed her jaw, as his stare burned across her mouth.

"Please." The word escaped Kat's lips as a wanton whisper.

Desperate need bubbled below the surface of her skin. The inevitable explosion of passion, always so present when she was with him, was only one touch away.

"Tell me what you want," he said gruffly. "Keep looking at me like that and I swear to God I'll give you anything."

"Kiss me," she begged. "Just kiss me."

• • •

Kat's mouth, pink, wet, and soft, entranced Carter. They'd kissed a million times, in a million different ways, but her request seemed so fucking huge that, for a split second, he could do nothing but stare. A divine image of her mouth around his dick immediately flashed before him, simultaneously drying his throat and weighing his body down to hers in seconds.

Skin to skin, flush and warm.

Carter tried to calm himself but struggled. Fact was, his body didn't feel like his own. It was as though something had taken it over, like it was being controlled by something.

Something bigger. Something incomprehensible.

He closed his eyes and exhaled a soothing breath.

Who was he kidding? Kat had taken him over. Kat had control over him.

She'd had a hold on him since he was eleven years old. And if he hadn't realized it before, he sure as shit knew now that he'd loved her every second, minute, and hour of those sixteen long years. He'd lost himself to her on a lonely, dark street one heartbreaking night in the Bronx, and now he finally understood that he'd never, ever truly found himself again.

Sixteen years. Five thousand eight hundred and forty-four days.

Jesus, how had he survived without her for so long?

He loved her, desperately, and, truthfully, it terrified him. He'd missed her without even knowing her and fantasized about her whenever he'd begun to lose himself to the bullshit surrounding him as he grew up. If he weren't so hypnotized by her, Carter would have laughed at his own blindness and the ridiculous denial he'd immersed himself in since Kat had come back into his life.

As subtle as it was, her body writhed underneath him. Her legs shifted against the mattress and her hips lifted, rocking toward him, seeking out any type of friction. She was exquisite. He opened his mouth, gasping into her. His entire body shook when he pressed his lips to hers, and he grunted when she pulled him down, deepening the kiss quickly.

Their tongues met, reunited, touching, tasting, and rubbing together, inside her mouth, then inside his. Carter gripped her waist with one hand and her face with the other as their passion began to snap and sizzle. Sweet Jesus, the heavy ache pounding between his legs was torturous. He ground his hips against her stomach, showing her what she did to him. Not that she would ever understand. She had no comprehension at all.

He'd been such a damned fool to think he could ever get away without speaking those three words to her. The three words he'd never uttered to another human being in his entire fucked-up life. They'd taken his ass by surprise, but the relief that came with them was more freeing than any parole board's release letter could ever be.

He moved his mouth from her lips to her jaw and down her neck. She bent backward, curving under him so that he could access any place he wanted on her gorgeous body. He began with her chest, yanking the straps of her bra down the tops of her arms so he could pull at the cups, releasing her to his eager hands and demanding mouth. With his eyes closed, Carter began to lick, suck, and tease, tugging her between his lips. He moaned when she scratched his back, pulling him closer while whispering her need for him.

Carter let his lips caress her hip, the soft flesh of her belly, all the way to her panty line peeking temptingly from beneath her shorts. He wanted her on his tongue. He wanted to feel her in his mouth and make her come so hard she'd see stars. He wanted to devour her, bury his entire face in that shit and never come out for days. He wanted her gasping and soaked. He wanted—

"I missed you," Kat breathed.

Astounded by the pained expression on her face, Carter rested his chin against her hip.

"I missed you while you were gone."

Carter's heart fractured. "I missed *you*." He brushed away the stray hair lying on her cheek. He shook his head. "God." He kissed her. "I was a fucking fool to walk away from you."

Walking away from her was as close to being burned alive as Carter imagined he would ever get. The pain had crippled him, rendering him immobile.

When the boys had visited him in Kill and tried to explain

how Max had fallen apart when Lizzie left, Carter had struggled to understand. Now he knew exactly what pain his friend had been through—was still going through.

Carter never wanted to feel that pain again. He doubted very much that he would even survive it a second time.

"I know why you did it," Kat whispered. "And if you walking away helped you realize that you love me," she continued in a hushed tone, "then I'm happy you did."

Christ, she was right. He'd walked away and cracked into a thousand pieces, bare, with nothing to hide behind. Realistically, Carter couldn't refute admitting his true feelings had been inevitable. And now that his finely executed punk-ass demeanor had been thoroughly fucked, Carter at last accepted just how exhausting it had been.

"Carter." Kat reached for his hand and placed his palm flat against her heart. "Show me," she whispered. "Show me how much you love me."

As his eyes scoured her face in question, Carter's brain flashed back through all the times they'd come together, thinking about the ways in which he'd touched her, kissed her, moved inside of her. *Show me.*

At the beach house.

On the sofa.

The very first time they were together, soaked from the rain, desperate, on his bed until dawn.

He'd loved her so much even then.

Without even knowing it, he'd shown her what she meant to him by using his body instead of his shitty, inadequate words. When the sensation of having his body inside of hers had been so overwhelming and he'd been unable to find his rhythm through the thick clouds of need, he'd simply breathed her in, kissed her languidly, or touched her in places he knew made her moan his name.

Those had been his favorite moments. Connected together but not moving. No frenzy. Just being. Those were the moments Carter was most at peace.

He brushed her hair back and kissed her. He was gentle, his mouth pressing into hers only a little, while his tongue whispered across her lips, tender and loving.

You're so beautiful, his kiss said. *You make me breathless.*

The moan from Kat's throat told him she heard it, felt it. He placed his hand on the back of her neck, lifting her to his mouth. She never resisted. She was incredible in her generosity. Pulling off his boxer briefs, he moved over her, shifting down her chin, kissing her throat, and licking her chest. He nibbled and grazed his teeth across her stomach. His hands slid up her thighs, opening them.

I've wanted you forever.

Her hands fisted the bed when he laid small kisses from one hip to the other. Kat bent her knees and rested the balls of her feet on his shoulders. He caressed the crease where her thighs met her body and spread her legs farther, as they beckoned Carter forward, her bare skin aching for his mouth. He kissed the top of her cleft, seeing the sparkle of the wetness lying there. Gently, pushing her lips back with his mouth, he let his tongue seek out her swollen heat and began winding it in slow circles that made her eyes roll and her spine arch.

Holy fuck. She was the most delicious thing he'd ever tasted. His fingers moved, slipping easily along her sodden skin, teasing and asking for more with every dip, twist, and stroke. Little by little, Carter pushed two long fingers inside her and moaned into her skin when she cried out and swiveled her hips against his face. She was so warm. He pulled them out and pushed them back in while he sucked and licked her.

"More."

I'd give you the fucking world.

He hummed and pushed his face closer, shaking his head from

side to side, purring against her flesh when her nails scratched deeply across his scalp. His tongue moved faster and his fingers slid deeper, as sounds started to erupt from her, breathless and begging.

"Oh my God. You're going to make me come."

Yeah, he fuckin' lived for it. She pulled at his shoulders, tugging and pushing while her hips ground against him, drenching his chin. She whimpered and called out, nonsensical words pouring from her mouth until her orgasm snapped and shook through her body. Carter gripped her thighs when they slammed shut around his head and she tried to move away from his voracious mouth. He devoured everything she gave him until she was begging him to stop.

I'll never stop loving you this way.

Eventually, Carter lifted his head and gazed up at her and the glow washing across her gossamer skin. Her chest heaved heavy, spent breaths. He prowled up her body, lathering her skin with kisses, needing the warmth to keep him grounded. He knew he had to be gentle, tender. The fog of lust had started to descend, hot, frenzied, and hard, but he breathed through it. Right then, chest to chest, her hands gripping his shoulders and her thighs around his waist were enough to calm him.

He moaned into her mouth when she kissed him, tasting herself on his lips. He rested his hands on the bed next to her ribs with his cock trapped between their bodies, wet, wanting, and thick. Every time she moved, she rubbed its entire length, driving him insane, making his hips shift and rotate. He grunted when she bit his neck.

I'm yours to mark.

She lifted her legs and placed her heels on his ass. They both grabbed for him, their desperation slipping through. Carter let go first and watched as Kat guided him, rubbing the tip of his cock along her wet flesh. He sighed, furrowing his brow, enraptured. Coming together that way made Carter's bones weak. She was soaked and so soft. Carter pushed his hips a little closer, a little harder.

Carter pulled her face to his, nibbling on her plump bottom lip. Kat's hand pushed so that—for one incredible moment—he slipped inside. The euphoria that always came with their unions blazed up his back and sent his hips into a frenzy.

"My sweet girl," he whispered across her throat and slowly began to push into her tight warmth. "That's it." A little farther. "Oh fuck."

He lifted his head and pushed, little by little, until he was completely enveloped by her. He was home. A small sob escaped her, but Carter caught it between his lips. The urge to thrust deep and hard clawed at the base of his spine, and his knees moved upward, pushing her thighs wider apart so he could get farther inside. Their fingers entwined by the sides of her head as Carter pulled back, releasing a long groan of breath. He chanced a look down to where they joined and panted at the sight of her all over his cock, glistening and beautiful.

He gasped, sliding back in. "Do you know I'd do anything for you?" he asked. "Do you know I think about you constantly? Sometimes I think I'm crazy. You make me crazy. I'm insane when I'm not with you. Jesus, Kat, I ache."

She grabbed at his neck.

"I need you so badly," he continued, breathlessly. "I need us. I need to feel us like this, because I swear to God, my heart, it beats only for you."

She squeezed his hands and kissed his neck. Their foreheads fused together and he lost himself in her heavy lidded eyes. He continued to move, slow but firm, tilting his pelvis so he reached the spot inside of her that made her breath catch. A small tightening began deep in the depths of his stomach. He gave a sharp thrust and gripped her hip harder than he probably should have. He grunted when she licked his jaw, nibbling on his Adam's apple in reply.

She held him close, arms around shoulders, holding tight. Never had Carter been so close to her. She was all around him, and he was at her mercy, defeated but entirely victorious. But, above all, above his need to come and his slow descent into euphoric bliss, Carter felt totally and unequivocally loved. The sensation wrapped around him in the same way Kat was, warm and safe, and it crushed him in ways that were entirely fantastic and impossible to describe.

It was the weirdest, most incredible thing.

It was so much more than making love.

It was erotic, passionate, naked, soul bearing—which ordinarily would have terrified Carter.

But not now. Not with his woman in his arms. With Kat, he could take over the fucking world.

Never had Carter been so exposed but so safe.

Never had he given himself to someone so freely and expected nothing in return.

His body lifted higher and higher. "I can't get close enough," he confessed with a frustrated growl. He pushed harder and harder, gritting his teeth and making sounds entirely alien to him, quickly being pulled under. He held on tighter. "I'm coming. Kat."

Carter's neck snapped back and he shouted and cursed. His cock pulsed with blinding force, as his orgasm ricocheted through him—leaving flashes of white behind his eyes and thundering in his ears—pulsing, hot, and relentlessly hard, into her body. He snarled into her shoulder while his entire body throbbed, writhed, and twitched.

He breathed easier. He felt free. He felt good. Could he dare to believe he was good enough?

Carter clenched his eyes shut, fighting back the salt water threatening to fall, overwhelmed once again by the woman in his arms, overwhelmed by what he'd shared with her, what they'd shared together. He kissed her collarbone and breathed through it. Carter's body shivered. He buried his face under her jaw and removed his sated cock from her warmth, cocooning himself within her arms and legs, the only sound being Kat's heart echoing in his ear.

His heart beat back in reply.

I love you, it thrummed. *I'm yours, but please, for the love of God, don't break me.*

"Thank you," he whispered. "Thank you for forgiving me. For loving me. I don't deserve any of it, Peaches." He held her close. "Thank you."

Kat murmured sleepily by his forehead, "I guess that makes us even."

Carter closed his eyes. He knew that wasn't true. As hard as his time away from Kat had been, Carter had had a lot of time to consider his options, and the one option that was simply impossible to comprehend was the one that saw them separated permanently.

He would not, could not walk away. He'd tried and it had crushed him.

Which left only one option.

He lifted his head and brushed her hair from her sleeping face. "Peaches."

"Mmm."

He drew an invisible circle under her lashes and across the flush of her cheek, considering his next words. There was no use in denying it anymore. He was responsible for the animosity between Kat and her mother. Of course, Eva hadn't given him a chance and would no doubt laugh in his face should he try to explain his feelings for her daughter; nonetheless, Kat had already lost one parent, and he didn't want her to lose another.

"We have to do something—something important—before we fly back to New York tomorrow. I have to do something."

She snuggled into him. "Yeah?"

Carter cleared his throat. "I need to talk to your mom."

• • •

Austin Ford paced like a caged lion in his office, gritting his teeth so hard Adam was convinced they would shatter. Hell, it would match the four-thousand-dollar vase that lay in a million pieces at their feet. Following Ben Thomas's impromptu visit, the much-anticipated fax had come through from the WCS board. Its message was clear: *Pack up your shit, boys. Your presence at WCS is no longer required.*

Adam, for one, hadn't been surprised, and, in many ways, it had come as a huge relief. For too long he had followed his brother through the valleys of aggressive mergers and bullying acquisitions. He'd stood back and watched in humiliated and embarrassed silence as Austin bartered and harassed people and businesses for his own gains.

Yes, he was one hell of an executive and he had made himself and those around him exceedingly rich. But over the years, he'd grown cocky. His manner was less genteel and more arrogant, and the wry smile of disappointment had now become a sneer of disgust that anyone would dare to refuse or stand up to him.

Nevertheless, Wes Carter had done just that.

Despite it being Thanksgiving week, Austin had put every lawyer and favor he had at his disposal on the fax the minute it slid through the machine. He wanted to find a loophole, a lose end, a clause, a fuck-you. He needed to find one. Adam knew that Austin would rather die than let Carter take over WCS, but that was exactly what was happening. There was no way around it, and one of Austin's cronies had delivered the news.

The vase had been the first casualty.

Adam watched his brother continue his furious journey around the office.

"You're telling me," Austin growled, "that there is no way to stop this?" His index finger smacked against the desk, pressing down hard into the fax.

Rick, his consultant, shifted on his feet and cleared his throat. "Yes, sir."

Austin's eyes grew impossibly wider. Adam had never seen his brother look so unkempt. His hair was ruffled and a light sheen of sweat covered his cheeks and forehead.

"I don't fucking believe this!" he bellowed. "How is this even possible?"

"Well, sir—"

"Don't answer me when I ask rhetorical questions, Rick!" Austin snapped angrily. "I can fucking read!"

Austin exhaled heavily and rubbed a palm over his mouth. "I thought we did everything in our power to cover this up." He gestured toward the black-and-white photographs Ben Thomas had left. "I was told that things were in place to keep my company safe."

Adam's anger surged. And not for the first time. Austin had always considered WCS his. In all the time he'd been in charge, Austin had never once acknowledged Adam's help or the work he did to keep him clean of all the shit he got into. Of course, there were the obligatory raises and single-malt gestures that would show up on his desk every once in a while, but neither made up for the amount of times that Adam had paid or bartered with people in order to keep his brother's indiscretion's off the board's radar, his dealings with Casari included. Adam had told him Casari was bad news, he knew he was watched by the Feds, but his brother hadn't listened.

Enough was enough.

The crunch, for Adam, was when it became a pissing contest over Kat, with Carter on one side and Austin on the other. It was pathetic, and Adam had wanted no part of it. He genuinely couldn't understand why Austin wouldn't just let Carter have his share of the pie. It would simplify things, keep Carter quiet. But Austin had had other ideas.

The photographs with Casari were all Austin's doing, and Adam had reached his limit.

Shit, everyone made mistakes, for Christ's sake, and it wasn't fair to keep Carter reliving his over and over. Kat was, as Beth had conceded, very much in love with Carter. The guy had a real chance at turning his life around and being happy.

Adam couldn't stop that from happening. And neither could Austin.

"Austin," Adam muttered. The other five men in the room shuffled and fidgeted.

"No, Adam," Austin barked back. "We need to figure this out, work out the next step."

Adam blinked in confusion and caught Rick's equally bewildered eye. Sighing, Adam took a cautious step toward his brother and clasped his hands at his front.

"There is no next step," he said quietly. "This is concrete. This is happening."

Austin's eyes narrowed. "What the hell is this?" he asked in disbelief. "Have you all lost your balls?" He eyed each man menacingly, finally coming back to Adam. "This isn't over. Not by a long shot."

Adam rolled his eyes and pushed his hands into his pockets. "It is over. It's been over for a long time. It's time to move on."

The look of absolute fury on Austin's face surprised even Adam. He tightened his fists at his side and dropped his chin. "Everyone out!"

Adam watched the staff scuttle out, closing the door firmly behind them. The room was oppressively silent for the thirty seconds it took Austin to reign himself in. He was furious, Adam knew, but honestly, he couldn't have cared less.

"What the fuck is wrong with you?" Austin murmured through tight lips.

"There's nothing wrong with me."

"Then what the hell are you doing standing there shrugging? Do you not understand what this means?" He held up the fax and shook it.

"I know exactly what it means," he answered calmly. He took

another step toward his brother. "It means that you and I each get a settlement that will ensure we never have to worry about money again, and Carter gets what's rightfully his."

Austin blanched. "I beg your pardon?"

Adam shook his head. "Oh, come on, Austin. Let it go. This is how it's meant to be! He's the rightful owner; it was written in black and white all those years ago. He deserves to have it back and not coveted by you!"

Austin lunged at Adam, but Adam was faster. It wasn't always so, but age brought a strength that he didn't have when they were kids. He pushed Austin away until his back was against the wall.

"Back the fuck off, Austin," Adam growled with a pointed finger in his face. "I am not six, and this company is not your goddamn G.I. Joe. Face the fact that, this time, your dirty little bastards couldn't get you out of this and move on with your dignity and name intact." He pulled back and adjusted his jacket. "Jesus, man, get a grip. You're losing it."

Austin swallowed. His face was beet red, his eyes wild.

Adam shook his head. "What happened, Austin?" he asked sadly. "I fucking defended you. I turned Beth against her best friend for you! I'll never forgive myself for that. Christ, man. I mean, this isn't you."

"This *is* me," he countered. "This is me keeping this company alive before some coke-headed fuckup drags it back to the gutter he came from."

Adam glared in disgust. "Like you're so fucking perfect." He chuckled without humor. "How can you be so self-righteous when you do the things you do?"

Austin's back straightened and a glimmer of caution appeared in his eye.

"Yeah," Adam whispered, glancing down at the photographs. "I'm sure the board would be interested to know who else you do business with. I don't need photographs to prove the shit I know."

Austin gave a wry smile. "You son of a bitch."

"Maybe," Adam countered darkly. "But I'm telling you: let this go, Austin. Walk away with your head held high. Forget Carter, forget Kat; take your stocks, buy a house, or go on a long vacation to butt-fuck nowhere, but walk away, or so help me."

Adam turned slowly from his brother, adjusting his tie as he did.

"Well, hell, Ads," Austin said. "That sounds like a threat."

Stopping, Adam looked back over his shoulder. "No threat," he answered before he walked toward the office door. With his fingers on the handle he continued, "It's a promise."

• • •

The tension in the car as Kat drove it back to Nana Boo's was thick, much like the snow that lay like a blanket all over the city. Carter stopped tapping his foot against the car floor and cracked his knuckles, in hopes that the tension that had set his spine poker straight would somehow ease. He was utterly exhausted. It hadn't been helped by the fact that he was running on seven hours of sleep over the past forty-eight hours. He closed his eyes.

"Are you okay?"

Carter kept his eyes closed, quirking an eyebrow in sardonic response. Like an asshole, he had no words of comfort for her even though he knew that Kat needed them from him badly. She silently craved assurance and support. He simply didn't know how to give it to her. He settled for placing his hand on her leg.

Contact was good.

He could tell from the tremor in her voice she was as nervous as he was about the upcoming conversation with Eva, and rightly so. Even though he had gone over and over in his head what he wanted to say, Carter knew he was walking straight into the lion's den, vulnerable and scared shitless.

He just had to make sure he didn't let Kat's mother control the discussion—if that was the appropriate word for it. Hell, it would be a heated one at the very least. He had to keep his head and allow her to have her say. That shit was vitally important. Carter was under no illusions; he understood why Eva behaved the way she did.

It was all about convincing Eva he loved Kat with his whole heart, that he would do anything for her, be anything for her. She was safe with him. He would protect her and cherish her until his last breath.

Hopefully, it would be enough. Jesus Christ, he hoped it would be enough.

If he could make Kat's mother see he wasn't all about the length of his criminal record, and that mistakes don't define a man, then he would be on the home stretch. Goddammit, he was a wreck. He wondered fleetingly if he would have time to have a smoke before battle commenced.

"We're here," Kat murmured, turning off the car engine.

Apparently not.

Carter swallowed and opened his eyes. "Peaches."

"Carter."

They spoke at the same time, nervous and quiet. Carter turned to her with a wry smile.

"Go on," he offered.

"No," she insisted with a shake of her head. "Please, what were you going to say?"

What was he going to say? He had no idea whether her name had escaped him simply because the sound of it and the knowledge she was close by comforted him more than he could express. Carter picked up her hand and brought it to his mouth, placing a courtly kiss in her palm.

He sighed. "Whatever she says, whatever she calls me or accuses me of. Whatever happens, I want you to promise me that you won't say anything."

Kat's eyes widened. "What?"

"You heard me."

If he was going to do this, he had to do it alone. What kind of mother wanted to see the man who loved her daughter as a weak, incapable prick? The last thing he wanted was for Kat to defend him. He was determined to fight this one on his own.

"I can't promise that, Carter."

"Please. I need you to do this for me."

Fire sparked in her eyes. "If she says—"

"I'm not going anywhere," Carter said firmly, interrupting her. "Look at me. I'm not going anywhere." He brushed the back of his fingers down the side of her face. "I swear to you. Do you trust me?"

She nodded. "But I'm terrified."

"I know," Carter whispered. He kissed her fingertips.

"I'll try and keep my mouth shut," she said with conviction. "But if she starts, so will I."

It was as much as he could hope for.

Standing on Nana Boo's porch waiting for someone to open the damned door, Carter clutched Kat's hand like a drowning man. He knew he was drawing all of his strength from her, but that was fine. When her small fingers tightened around his, he knew she was doing the same thing.

The sound of a dead bolt sliding home made his neck tingle and his throat dry.

Go big or go home, right?

Trevor opened the door with a wide, gracious smile as Reggie wagged his tail heartily at his side. "Miss Katherine. Mr. Carter. How nice to see you again. Please come in."

Kat smiled, but Carter could do little more than grimace. He literally had to pull his feet from the floor so he could walk forward. It was just his luck: the confidence and determination that had filled his body the day before had all but disappeared now that he needed it. With a jolt he suddenly felt very, very foolish.

Kat pulled both of his hands to hers. He pursed his lips and blew a breath of relief, so grateful for her, standing with him, on his side, ready to back him up in any way she could.

"Happy Thanksgiving!" Nana Boo smiled warmly at Carter and kissed his cheek. "It's so good to see you."

"Happy Thanksgiving." He stood back and fixed her with an apologetic stare. "I'm sorry about yesterday." Kat's hand pressed into the small of his back. "I'm an idiot and the last thing I wanted to do was to upset Kat. I mean, I know she'd have been upset," he mumbled. "I just— I wanted— I'm sorry I left, okay, and . . . yeah."

Nana Boo's face lit with an admiring smile, despite Carter wanting nothing more than the floor to swallow his ass whole. She placed her palm on his arm and rubbed it, coaxing his eyes back to hers. The warmth of her gaze and the tenderness in her touch filled Carter with nostalgic hope and love. For one split second, he was seven years old again.

"Thank you for the apology. But there really is no need. As long as you and Kat are fine, then I'm happy."

"We *are* fine," Kat said, moving closer to Carter's side.

He could have easily lost himself in Kat's gorgeous eyes, and he would have done so quite happily had it not been for the unexpected sound of a clearing throat that reverberated around the cavernous lobby like a vicious snarl. Kat's stare snapped instantly to her right, but Carter kept his front and center, tracing the delicate curve of his Peaches' face. He didn't need to look; he knew who it was and what to expect when he did.

The silence was about as comfortable as a quilt of glass, and everyone under it became unnaturally still. Even Nana Boo, normally so vibrant and full of life, remained motionless.

"What the hell is this?" Eva asked contemptuously.

Carter blinked slowly, lifting his head to face the woman he was there to see. She was standing in the living room doorway, looking spectacularly pretty and ageless in a pair of black jeans and a gray sweater. A tall man with dark hair and a Yankees hoodie stood behind her. He placed his hand on Eva's shoulder and gave it a small squeeze. Eva scowled at Carter, folding her arms across her chest. Her face was angry, defensive, but surrounding all of that were the markings of hope.

If she was hopeful, he'd cling on to that fucker like a vise. He could use it to his advantage. He could turn that hope into understanding. That's all he could ask for. He didn't need her blessing or her acceptance. He just needed her to understand.

"What the hell are you doing here?" Eva asked sharply.

Carter gripped Kat's arm, halting her retort in its tracks. Her furious eyes searched his face.

"It's okay," he said.

"I invited them here," Nana Boo answered, lifting her chin toward Eva, daring her daughter to question her actions.

Carter removed his hand from Kat's and stepped forward. Eva watched him carefully as he approached. The man behind her, whom Carter knew to be Harrison, stepped to her side, a subtle move that told Carter to watch his step. Eva's face betrayed no emotion when Carter reached her, stopping just two feet away. But, when he held his hand out between them for her to take, a flash of disbelief shot across her features.

"Hello," Carter croaked. He cleared his throat in annoyance, but kept his eyes on Eva's. "I'm Wes Carter."

The walls of the room seemed to bend and strain under the tension that emanated from everyone around Carter, including Eva, who still hadn't taken his hand. He kept it there, though, determined to show he was no pussy, even though his insides were ready to bust out of his ass and run for the hills.

"It's nice to finally meet you," he added when the silence became stifling.

Eva's stare was intense and downright bewildered. Carter wasn't sure whether she thought him to be completely insane or genuinely stupid. At that point, he'd have personally gone for the latter. She glanced toward her daughter.

"Did Katherine put you up to this?"

"No!" Kat shot back from behind Carter before he could take a breath. "I didn't. And I can't believe you're just standing there and ignoring his attempts at civility like a—"

"Kat," Carter said firmly, interrupting what he knew was going to be something toxic and unhelpful. He fixed her with a level stare and shook his head minutely. The anger never left the rigidity in her body, but, to her credit, she shut up.

Carter turned to Eva, whose eyes were flickering between the pair of them, and gradually dropped his hand. "Kat didn't put me up to this," he said. "I was the one who wanted to come here today."

Eva remained silent, cautious, and expectant.

"I wanted to come here and talk to you."

"About what?"

Kat shifted at his side. Still watching Eva, Carter reached out his hand, finding Kat's, and wrapped his index finger lovingly around her pinkie.

"I wanted a chance to explain."

"Explain?" Eva scoffed. "Explain what, exactly? Are you here to explain why you're endangering my daughter's future? To explain why the hell I should trust you with her when you're a convicted criminal? To explain what prospects someone like you could possibly have with a woman like Katherine? What exactly are you here to explain, Wes Carter?"

Her voice rose in volume with each word. Carter didn't miss the quiver behind it, though, and allowed that to ease his temper rising with each slice of her tongue. Kat's hand shook. She was aching to blow up at her mother, resisting only because he'd asked her to and he loved her all the more for it.

"I can explain all of that, if that's what you want," he offered in a tone more clipped than he'd intended. And, without knowing why, he took another step toward her. He saw Eva's eyes widen infinitesimally, though her chin rose defiantly.

"But I came here to explain that, despite what you think of me, or whatever conclusions you have come to about me and my intentions, I'm in love with your daughter. And no matter what you say or do, I'm not goin' anywhere."

Carter could have sworn he saw shock tease at the edges of Eva's mouth. "Is that so?"

"Yes," he answered with a sharp dip of his head, determination once again flowing freely through his body.

Kat moved closer, and he indulged in the warmth and security her gesture brought. Eva saw it, too, which conjured up another intense frown. She stared at her daughter, but Kat's eyes were on Carter, branding him as hers.

"I love you, too," she said, loud enough that everyone heard.

32

"What time is your flight, darling?" Nana Boo asked, shattering the quiet enveloping the sitting room.

"We need to be at the airport in a few hours," Kat answered from her seat at Carter's side. She drew invisible circles on the back of his hand encased in hers on her lap.

Eva, seated in the large, plush chair opposite, glared as though Carter had asked her to give up her only virgin daughter for a public human sacrifice. He simply looked back, strong and patient, waiting for her to combust with everything he knew she wanted to say.

Fleetingly, Carter wondered what she saw as she glowered at him.

Did she see the love he had for her daughter? Did she see what conflict he'd gone through to be at her side? Did she see how he would lay down his life to keep her safe? Or did she see his list of crimes? Did she see him as a poster boy for the major fuckups of society? Did she regard him in the same way she regarded the animals who'd stolen her beloved husband?

Yeah, he thought pessimistically. That's exactly how she saw him.

"I know you have a lot to say," he muttered. "I know you have strong opinions of me." He raised his eyebrows. "I'd rather you tell me so that maybe I can change them."

"That won't happen," Eva hissed back.

"You don't know that."

"Don't you dare tell me what I do and do not know. I know exactly who and what you are."

Carter held Kat's twitching hand fast. "Could you explain to me?" He sat forward. "Everyone deserves a chance to plead their case."

"You'd be fairly practiced at that," Eva remarked smarmily.

"Eva."

Everyone's head snapped toward Nana Boo, who was gaping at her daughter in a way that made Carter sink farther into his seat. Eva glanced at her mother before her eyes dropped deferentially.

"Yes," Carter said. "I've done time."

"More than once," Eva countered. She shook her head, bewildered. "Do you truly believe that I want my daughter with a man who considers spending time in prison an extended summer vacation?"

"I don't see it that way." Carter was resolute. "I'm not proud of my past."

"Maybe so," Eva snapped. "But the past did happen."

"Like Dad's past?" Kat interjected sharply.

Eva stared at her daughter for a beat, tears filling her eyes. "Don't you dare compare him to your father," she growled. "Your father . . . your father . . ." She bit her lip, and wrapped her arms around herself. "He may have done things he wasn't proud of," she continued before her eyes landed back on Carter, "but he did something to make up for it. He became someone who people admired, respected, loved—"

"Carter's done things I admire and respect," Kat seethed. "You have no idea what he's overcome, what he's fought against his entire life. You have no idea about the night that Dad died, about how Cart—"

"Kat," Carter interrupted.

He didn't want Eva to know about his role on the night the senator died. Not yet, anyway. This wasn't about winning points. A muffled sob came from across the room. Carter turned from Kat to see Eva's devastated face and Harrison stroking her hair.

"You think I have no idea about the night your father died?" she repeated breathlessly. "How can you . . . Katherine, that night . . ." She shook her head, at a loss for words. "The night your father passed was the worst night of my life," Eva said. Tears fell down her face. "I have no *idea*?" she repeated, giving a harsh snort of laughter. "I have never felt fear like I did when I received that phone call: debilitating fear that grips your very core, Katherine."

Kat dropped her chin to her chest and closed her eyes. "Mom, I'm sorry. I didn't mean—"

"And it wasn't just because I'd lost my husband," she choked, "as much as I adored him, loved him. No." She stared at Kat with shimmering eyes and the devastating memories lining her face. "The time when I was most scared, Katherine, was when I thought I'd lost you."

Kat squeezed Carter's hand, chewing the inside of her mouth.

"I knew your father would never let anyone hurt you, Katherine," Eva continued. "He would have destroyed anyone who tried. But when the doctor at the hospital looked at me . . . with those sympathetic eyes, I was sure you were . . ." She clutched her teacup. "I was sure those monsters had taken you from me, too."

"They didn't," Kat murmured, wiping at her left eye. "I'm here."

"Yes, you are," Eva countered. "With him."

"It's different. Carter isn't a murderer!" Kat snapped.

"No, he's a drug dealer. I'm so relieved," Eva replied, disdain dripping from every word. Before Kat could respond, she continued, "Do you think your father would be happy that you took a job in a prison, working with the type of men he died saving you from? Do you think he'd be sitting here giving you two his blessing? If you do, you're wrong."

Before Carter could stop her, Kat shot up from her seat, eyes blazing, the tears and gentle words forgotten. "He gave me his blessing, Mom! He gave me his blessing the day we visited his grave."

Despite Harrison's hand and urging not to, Eva stood. "Don't be ridiculous, Katherine. Your father wouldn't stand for it. I am not going to stand for it! You are so much better than this."

"You don't have any say in my life, Mom. I'm twenty-five years old!"

"You are my daughter, and I want you safe!"

"I. AM. SAFE!"

"How can you say that?" Eva shoved an accusatory finger toward Carter. "He's a convict, put inside for possessing cocaine, stealing cars, carrying dangerous weapons. He is not safe, and he is not who I want you with!"

"Enough!"

The room rattled with the deep, booming voice of Harrison. Carter gaped at him, speechless that he'd shouted as loud as he had, even though he'd been damn near doing the exact same thing himself. Harrison moved from his spot, behind Eva's chair, looking pissed. "That is enough from both of you."

Eva sighed. "Harrison, I don't think—"

"No, Eva," he interrupted. "Enough is enough." He rubbed his forehead with the tips of his fingers. "I'm so tired of seeing the two of you argue and fight. It breaks my heart." He looked at Kat. "I've never seen you like this. Either of you, and I can't keep my mouth shut any longer."

"I agree," Nana Boo muttered from her seat in the corner of the room. "Eva, I love you, but you need to back off."

"Back off?" Eva repeated. "Your granddaughter is 'in love' with a man whose wardrobe is filled with nothing but prison-issue coveralls."

Carter almost snorted at that one.

"That may be so," Nana Boo retorted angrily. "But what you seem to be oblivious to, is that the more you shout and dig in your heels, the more you will push them together. And if you're not careful, you really will lose her."

Eva blinked. Kat turned to Carter with an apologetic grimace. He took her hand and kissed her knuckles.

"Kat, come with Harrison and me," Nana Boo instructed in a tone that denied argument. "Eva and Carter, you two stay here." Her eyes softened when she caught Carter's eye. "I'm sure it will be easier for you to talk without an audience."

Eva blanched. "I am not staying in here with him."

"Why?" Nana Boo shot back. "You afraid he'll try to sell you an eight ball?"

Eva was rendered wide-eyed and mute while Carter smirked.

"Stay here," Nana Boo ordered. "Talk."

She ushered Kat and Harrison out of the room, never taking her eyes from Eva. Carter couldn't deny he was surprised Kat hadn't argued, but remained quiet. He fixed his eyes on Eva while she paced up and down the room like a caged animal. He glanced at the large mahogany drinks cabinet across the far side of the room and the decanter of what he prayed to Jesus was whiskey.

Bingo.

"Well, I don't know about you," he said with an exhausted groan. He stood and made his way over to it. "But I need a drink."

Eva watched him pour two fingers into a crystal glass. He gestured toward her with it.

"No, thank you," she bit back, dropping back into her seat. "It's a little early for me."

Carter sipped the bourbon and closed his eyes. Dutch courage never tasted so damned good. Eva avoided his stare, looking anywhere but him, staying annoyingly but not surprisingly silent. Fifteen minutes passed in the same manner until Carter couldn't take it anymore.

"Kat's a lot like you, ya know."

Eva cocked an unimpressed eyebrow.

"She is," he continued. "Caring, determined, passionate. Stubborn as all hell."

"If this is your way of getting into my good books," Eva said firmly, "believe me: it isn't working."

"Oh, I know that," Carter agreed. "Like Kat, you don't back down when it comes to things you believe in."

"Katherine doesn't know *what* she believes in."

"Bullshit. Kat is the most strong-minded person I know. You don't give her enough credit. What she believes in, she does without equivocation."

"Impressive language," Eva scoffed.

"Thanks. I had a good teacher."

Eva sat back and crossed her legs. "Yes, you did. As I understand it, you had an upstanding education, which you threw away without thought so you could run around dealing drugs and boosting cars."

"It wasn't quite like that," Carter remarked, sipping his drink.

"Semantics. The point is you've been in prison more times than most people in this country go on vacation, including your most recent stint for cocaine possession."

The corners of Carter's mouth pulled down impressed. "You've done your homework."

"I love my daughter. Of course I've done my homework." She eyed him. "I also know that you're the main shareholder in one of the biggest companies in the continental US, worth millions, and yet you continue to live this insignificant life of crime."

Carter cleared his throat, too unnerved to fill in the blanks. "Well, at least Kat won't go hungry, right?"

"Are you trying to be funny?"

Obviously not.

He wound his index finger around the lip of his glass and closed his eyes. "Look, would you understand what I meant if I said that my last time in lockup, the cocaine, was my pound of flesh?"

Eva frowned. "What?"

"A pound of flesh," he repeated, lifting his eyes to hers. "Do you know what that means?"

Bewildered, Eva answered, "A debt that must be paid?" She paused. "You dealt cocaine to pay off a debt?"

"No," he replied. "I was caught with the cocaine to pay off a debt."

Eva rubbed her forehead in annoyance. "I'm completely confused."

Carter exhaled and fingered the top of the cigarette box in his jeans pocket, needing the nicotine in his blood. He sighed and leaned his elbows on his knees, detailing the story of Max and Lizzie, from the moment Max pushed him out of the way of a bullet, to the day Lizzie left.

Eva waved her hand dismissively. "And you're telling me this because . . ."

Christ, she was a tough one to crack. "Because sometimes things aren't always what they appear to be."

"And sometimes they are exactly as they appear to be. One act of stupidity does not change a damn thing."

"Granted," Carter conceded. "I know I'm an asshole, I'll be the first one to admit it."

"Do you have any idea how worried I've been?" she asked. "Have you any idea about the amount of sleep I lost when she began working in that . . . prison?"

"I can imagine."

"No, you can't!" Eva snapped. "You have no idea. Being a mother is not easy, especially when your daughter insists on making everything so damned difficult."

"Kat didn't take the job at Kill to make your life difficult," Carter refuted. "She took the job to overcome her fears, to overcome what terrified her and kept her awake at night."

"And what do you know about that?" Eva spat.

"Enough." Carter pursed his lips in an effort to reel himself in. "Look, I know about her father. I know what happened. Her teaching criminals—"

"Animals."

"—is her pound of flesh."

"To whom?"

"To her dad."

Eva's face softened and her voice dropped in volume. "What do you mean?"

"The night he passed, she promised him she would give something back. She promised him she would become a teacher and help people, the way he'd done as a politician." Carter glanced toward the door his Peaches had gone through. "She just wanted to keep her promise. To pay her debt."

Eva sat back in her seat and stared out the window. The snow had started falling again. "I didn't know that."

"Like I said," Carter murmured. "Things aren't always as they appear." He took a deep breath. "I'm in love with your daughter, ma'am. I'm doing this because I want to do everything right. I'm doing this because she wants to be with me, and I want to be with her."

Eva's back straightened. "You barely know each other! You think because she's told you a few secrets, that you know her?"

"I know her better than you think."

"Oh, please! You've known her, what, four, five months?"

A heartbeat passed. "Try sixteen years."

Eva's eyes flickered, fierce yet puzzled.

Carter stared right back, waiting for the penny to drop.

Yeah, it was a big ask, but, hell, at this point what did he have to lose? He hadn't wanted his role in saving Kat to be the deciding factor as to whether or not Eva would accept him with her daughter, but the damn woman had driven him to it with her incapacity to see him without a list of misdemeanors and felonies tacked to his fucking forehead.

Jesus, he'd even brought up the fact that he went to prison for Max. He wouldn't have mentioned it, if not for having his ass against a wall with no way out. Desperate for Eva to see past his mistakes, he had nothing else to lay on the table.

"How have you known her for sixteen years?" Eva asked slowly. "There's no possible way. No way."

Despite her words of conviction, her eyes told Carter the pieces were falling into place. Her stubbornness was the only thing stopping her from seeing what was right in front of her.

"We met . . . in the Bronx," Carter said quietly. "She was nine. I was eleven."

Horror washed across Eva's features, but it changed swiftly to emotions that were as indiscernible as they were fleeting. She was warring with herself now, battling with what she believed—he was a hardened, dangerous criminal—and the actual truth—he'd saved her daughter's life.

"The news," Eva stammered. "It was all over the news. *Everyone* knows where they were that night. *Everyone* knows what happened."

Carter carried on, ignoring her accusation that he was a liar. "I heard a scream."

Eva closed her eyes.

"I was across the street and I saw everything: the punks with the bat, Kat, your husband. Christ—it happened so damned fast. He . . . Your husband was on the ground. They hit him with the bat, kicked him. He tried to fight back, but there were too many of them for one man."

Eva made a strangled sound and clapped a palm to her mouth.

"Kat was on the ground about two feet away," Carter continued, lost in the memory. "One of the assholes had hit her."

"Stop."

"She was wearing a blue dress. It was dirty from the sidewalk, ripped at the sleeve. Your husband screamed at her to run. He begged her over and over, but she didn't listen. And I knew that if those fuckers got hold of her, they'd kill her."

Eva looked up at him finally, tears spilling down her face.

Carter put his hand on his stomach. "Something in here, deep in here, told me to help her. I just couldn't watch them hurt her. It was so damned wrong."

"You—you," Eva hiccoughed, unable to form a full sentence.

"I ran to her," Carter said. "Grabbed her arm and ran. But I had to drag her most of the way; she was small, but she fought, ya know? She was so strong."

Eva wrapped her arms around herself, listening to him describe how he'd tackled Kat to the cold, wet ground.

"There was gunfire and she screamed, and all I could do was hold her and make sure that she didn't run back. I figured I was doing what her old man wanted. I was doing something good." He ran his hands across his hair. "Saving Kat's the only good thing I've ever done in my entire life."

Then they stared at each other for the length of two heartbeats, and he hoped they finally understood each other. They'd found their common ground. They both existed for the same reason, and, with that realization, he found it easier to breathe.

"Where did you take her?" Eva croaked.

"A doorway a couple of blocks down. Once she stopped fighting me, she cried until she fell asleep."

"Then you left her?"

"No," he replied. "I held her. Stroked her hair, talked to her until help came."

"But . . . you disappeared."

Carter gave a wry smile. "I already had a name with the police because of shit Max and I had done, and I knew if they caught me I'd have to answer questions. So . . ."

"You ran."

"Yeah."

"Where did you go?"

"Back to my friend's place. Max calmed me down, helped me through the shock of what happened."

Eva cast her eyes toward the doorway. "She knows?"

"Of course. I had to tell her."

"How did she take it?"

Carter smiled. "In her own way. But I'm here, right?"

"Yes, you are."

Carter exhaled and rubbed his face with a weary hand. "Look. I know we're never going to be the best of friends. I know you'll never see me as good enough for her, because I know that myself. And I didn't tell you this to win points. I told you because I wanted you to see I would never ever hurt her. She's everything to me. I want to give her everything she wants or needs. And I want you and Kat to go back to the way you were before I got involved. I hate that I caused this."

Eva's face glimmered with hope of the same thing. "It wasn't just you. We're all to blame in some part."

"I need you to know that I'm not here to do anything but love and take care of your daughter."

A timid smile played across Eva's mouth. "You know," she said wistfully, "you sound like Kat's father when you talk like that. He had to convince my dad he was good enough for me."

"And did he?"

"I think so."

"Have I convinced you?"

Eva stood and walked across the room to the large window. The silence and anticipation caused Carter's heart to race like a fucking V12 engine.

"My daughter is too much like me for her own good," she began. "You were right about that, and I can see how much she loves you." Her cheeks washed with an embarrassed pink. "I didn't want to see it, but it's clear as day. Still, having said that, I can't overlook the fact that Kat's putting a lot at risk by being with you."

Carter opened his mouth to protest, but Eva held up her palm, halting his words.

"I need *you* to know that Kat is the most precious thing in my life. She always has been. If anything happened to her, I don't know how I'd survive."

He knew exactly what she meant. If Kat ever ceased to be, so would he.

"But you saved her, didn't you?"

Carter swallowed. "Yes, ma'am."

"You saved her when her father couldn't. And if you hadn't been there, then I'd have lost them both."

"Yeah."

"So where does that leave us?"

Carter shrugged. "I don't know. But it's a start, right?"

Eva's face gave nothing away.

Carter peered toward the doorway again before slowly getting to his feet. He pushed his hands into his pockets and gestured with his head in Kat's direction.

"I'm—I'll go and see if she's okay."

Eva didn't reply, but kept her eyes on him as he walked across the room.

"Wes."

Carter stopped and clenched his eyes shut for a brief moment, then turned back to her, a rock in his gut and a desert in his throat. "Yeah?"

"Thank you," she whispered. "From the bottom of my heart, Wes, thank you for saving Katherine's life."

33

Once Wes left the sitting room, Eva was lost in thought, staring out of her mother's front window, watching the snow falling to the ground, crisp, clean, and beautiful.

She blinked slowly, picturing the face of the man who had been her everything. She loved Harrison with all of her heart, save for the one piece that would forever belong to Daniel Lane.

Eva wiped away tears and glanced over her shoulder when she heard the faint sound of laughter and the closing of a door. She had to give Wes his due. He'd stood his ground, never wavering. He'd spoken articulately—save for a few curses—and showed unquestionable love and protective loyalty for Katherine. Eva wasn't lying when she told Wes she hadn't wanted to see the love between them. It's what scared her most.

Her daughter was head over heels in love with Wes Carter. It was a love that many never found and no one could ever extinguish. It was a love that was far-reaching, powerful, and all-consuming. Eva could see it in Kat's eyes when she looked at him and when she glared at Eva in his defense. It was the same look Eva had given her father innumerable times when she'd first introduced Danny to the family.

Eva wanted nothing more than for Katherine to be loved in passionate, breathtaking ways. She wanted her consumed by love, desperate with it, unafraid to be made fragile by it, and filled with its strength. She wanted her to soar and spin and lose herself in a man who would love her just as much. She wanted it all for Katherine, and Katherine had it. But Wesley Carter couldn't be further from the man Eva had imagined.

After hearing his confession, her anxiety about the relationship had dropped considerably. The man had saved her baby, for God's sake. When he'd been only eleven years old. She was grateful beyond description, but the momma bear within her refused to back down.

She wandered into the kitchen to find her mother and partner seated at the table. Two bottles of wine sat opened, as well as a bottle of Jameson. Her mother's face was softer now.

"Hey," Eva said softly. "Where is—?"

"She's outside with Wes while he has a much-needed cigarette and a drink." Her mother sighed. "Come. Sit down."

Eva approached Harrison with a heavy stomach. It was love. It was guilt. It was embarrassment. It was apology. She sat down slowly and stared at his profile. Dark stubble flecked his jaw, and his dark brown eyes were troubled as they stared down at the glass of malt whiskey in his hands. They had so many things that needed to be said, but Katherine was her priority. She needed to make things right.

Eva glanced hesitantly at the back door.

"Tell her how you feel," Harrison said, his eyes still fixed on the table.

"I don't know how," she confessed.

"Yes, you do."

"We're so far apart."

"You'll find each other again. Be honest." He pulled off his hoodie and handed it to her. "It's cold out there."

Eva took it from him with a grateful smile. "I'm sorry, Harrison. And I love you. Very much."

"I know," he answered, looking at her for the first time.

She leaned forward and placed a tender kiss at the corner of his mouth. He turned in to it with a sigh. "Go," he urged softly.

Reggie's nails tapped happily against the floor as he followed Eva to the door. She dragged on Harrison's hoodie—loving the smell and how it drowned her small frame—and slowly pulled the door open. Her eyes immediately found two closely huddled bodies sitting on the porch step.

Wes had his arm around her daughter while his lips murmured soft, inaudible words against her temple. The air smelled of smoke and cold. The door clicked shut behind her, causing Wes to turn.

Eva dipped her chin in acknowledgment before Wes did the same. Katherine looked over her shoulder, her expression indecipherable.

Wes kissed Katherine's cheek and smiled. "I'll give you two a moment," he said before he stood, moving around Eva to the door.

"Thank you, Wes," she said.

The door shut behind him, and Eva swallowed before she tentatively stepped toward her daughter. "May I sit?"

"If you want."

Gathering her courage, Eva took the spot at Katherine's side. For a few minutes, the two women sat in silence. How could she verbalize the love she had for her daughter? No mother ever could. It was vast, immeasurable, and impossible to label with inadequate words.

"Katherine," Eva started quietly, petrified of saying the wrong thing. "I'm thankful you're both here."

Katherine remained quiet. Eva couldn't read the profile of her face except for the small twitch of her lip. Danny would get the same thing when he was nervous. To think she made her own daughter feel that way ripped her heart in two.

"I wanted to apologize to you." A heavy breath escaped her, and she closed her eyes. "I love you very much, sweetheart, and I want us to go back to the way things were. I hate fighting with you."

"We're never going to be the way we were, Mom. Too much has happened."

Eva fought down the alarm rising at the back of her throat. "I . . . I understand if you don't want to try."

Blazing green eyes met hers. "It's not that I don't want to try, Mom. It's the fact you can't bear to be in the same room as the man I love. Carter and I come as a package now. If you can't deal with that, then there's no hope for us to ever go back to how we used to be."

Eva fisted her hands together, willing her misgivings and distrust down into her stomach. "I understand."

"No," Katherine countered. "You don't." She closed her eyes and took a deep breath. "Just because he told you about saving me doesn't mean you understand what Carter and I are to one another."

"Then explain it to me," Eva urged. She wanted to understand. Needed to.

Katherine answered without hesitation. "I love him more than I could ever explain." Her voice never wavered in its fervency. "He understands me, he keeps me safe, and he loves me, too."

"I know he does." Love like that was undeniable.

"He's honest, sensitive, and one of the bravest men I've ever known. And I want to be with him for the rest of my life."

Although Eva's heart gave a panicked thump, Katherine's words really didn't surprise her. Of course she wanted to be with him forever. He was her other half, just as Danny had been Eva's. How could she deny her daughter the one thing she'd wanted for her since the day she was born?

"How does that make you feel, Mom? How does it make you feel that someday that man in there, whom you regard so hatefully, will be my husband, the father of your grandchildren?"

Eva pushed her hands under her arms and stared out at the

gardens, picturing her grandchildren running about the trees and flowers. She saw Katherine in a simple white gown with wildflowers in her hair, walking with Harrison down a path of white magnolias toward Wes, who would no doubt look devastatingly handsome in a black suit and white shirt unbuttoned at the neck.

It seemed so simple, so natural. And, in that moment, Eva knew it was inevitable. "It makes me feel terrified." The confession slipped from her lips in a whisper.

"Why?" Katherine demanded. "Why does the thought of my being happy scare you so damned much?"

Eva stared at her daughter, beautiful, strong, and determined. "It terrifies me because you're not my little girl anymore." She moved closer and moved Katherine's hair from her shoulder so that it spilled gloriously down her back.

"I've made some very bad choices during my life, not least the ones regarding how to handle your career and man choice, and for that I'm truly sorry. But please believe that when you have children of your own, you'll know exactly what that means. I would walk into hell and take on Satan with my bare hands if anyone threatened to hurt you. A mother protects her children no matter the consequences, whether they're five or twenty-five."

She cupped Katherine's face. "After your father died, knowing that my only connection to him was you scared the life out of me. I wanted to keep you even more protected, away from anything or anyone who could take you from me." Her eyes filled with tears when Katherine's face nestled into her palm.

"It's not an excuse for my behavior. And I never meant to hurt you, or smother you. You're so much stronger than I am, and I don't give you enough credit for that. I'm sorry. I know it'll take time for you to trust me again. I just hope you can. It's hard for me to let go for so many reasons, but I want you to be safe and happy, Katherine. That's all your father and I ever wanted."

"I know, Mom," she croaked. "I am. I'm happy with Carter."

Eva kissed her daughter's forehead softly. "I know, sweetheart. I know." Leaving all of her hope in Katherine's hands, Eva stood up. "I'll send Carter back out so you're not alone."

"Mom?"

She turned slowly, her hand on the door. "Yes, love?"

"I'm sorry—and I love you, too."

34

Two weeks later, Austin Ford was summoned to the offices of WCS. The board wanted a word.

After Ben Thomas's visit, he'd spent days and nights contacting every asshole with an outstanding debt to him. But it seemed nothing could dig his ass out of the cavernous pit Carter and his lawyer had found for him.

Austin approached the boardroom now with poise, ignoring the wary look from Helen, his office secretary, when he stopped at her desk.

"The board should be arriving at—"

"They're already in," she said, avoiding his eyes.

Austin cocked an eyebrow. "They are?"

"Yes, sir."

Well, that was . . . odd.

He took a breath, pushed the large mahogany door open, and immediately wished that he hadn't.

Fuck. Me. Sideways.

He stared incredulously at his cousin, who was standing at the head of the board table in a four-thousand-dollar tailored Dior suit. Standing straight and smiling as if he knew the meaning to life itself, he looked infinitely different than the bedraggled ex-con Austin had seen only months before. Austin instantly wanted to wipe the smirk off his face with a swift right hook.

"Morning." Carter gestured to the empty seat to his left. "Won't you take a seat?"

"I'd rather stand," Austin replied, eyeing the fifteen people around the table, including Adam. "Isn't this fucking cozy?" Austin dipped his chin in an effort to keep his temper. "I guess this is what they mean when they use the phrase 'hostile takeover.' "

"Perhaps," Carter replied. "But this isn't hostile, nor is it a takeover; I'm simply reclaiming what was already mine. The board members have unanimously agreed that the contracts signed by our grandparents clearly show that I am rightful CEO and majority shareholder of WCS Communications."

"Have they?" Austin growled.

"Yes, they have," Adam answered. He stood and took a step toward Austin. "And they would have done so sooner, had you not hidden it from them. We need you to sign over your rights. I've done mine. Legally, we have to do it in front of the board."

Austin narrowed his eyes at Adam. Where was the fucking loyalty? "I know," he hissed through gritted teeth.

"Don't worry," Carter interrupted. "I've made sure that you still have shares, and the payout you will receive is more than enough to keep you and yours secure for two lifetimes."

"It's not about the money."

"Exactly," Carter snapped. His voice lowered to a harsh whisper. "It never *was* about the money, Austin. It was about the fucking principle, a word that continues to elude you on a daily basis."

Austin regarded his cousin and brother, the cold fingers of defeat gripping his chest. "Where's the contract?"

"Here, Mr. Ford," said one of WCS's lawyers.

The sly, backhanded nature of the whole scenario started to surround Austin like a suffocating fog. Storming past Carter and Adam, he grabbed a pen off the table and signed his name. All his hard work, all his dreams, signed away in one brief moment. The taste of vomit became strong in the back of his throat.

"There is also a gag order for you to sign," the lawyer said. "It states that, should you besmirch Mr. Carter's or the company's name, the entire deal will be null and void and you will be entitled to nothing. Legal action will also be swift and indiscriminate."

"Yeah, I get it," Austin retorted. Throwing the pen down hard, he glared at the board members. "Good luck," he sneered with a thumb in Carter's direction. "You're gonna need it with this prick running the show."

He turned to Carter and smiled tightly. "Well done, Carter. Looks like you landed on your feet."

Carter shook his head. "No, I just got what I deserve. As did you."

"Whatever," Austin snapped, pushing past his cousin. He needed to get out, find a bottle of JD and a woman, and lose himself in both for a week.

"Oh," Carter said suddenly, stopping Austin in his tracks, "Kat says hi."

The sound of Austin's jaw snapping shut echoed around the room. He could practically hear Carter's smug fucking smile. With his temper unraveling, he shoved through the doors and left WCS for the last time.

• • •

"Just suck."

"I can't!"

"Of course you can. Suck!"

Kat coughed on the noodles Carter was dropping into her mouth and began to giggle. Carter laughed with her. The noodles slid down her chin and fell to her bare breasts. Quick as a flash, Carter dove onto her and began to lick and slurp the noodles into his mouth. He may have licked her nipples, too, because eating Chinese food naked was all about the perquisites.

His adventurous mouth moved to her chin, and then to her lips, where he kissed her, covering her in sweet-and-sour sauce.

She squealed, feebly trying to push him away. "You're an ass." She giggled.

"I know," he admitted with a waggle of his eyebrows.

He sat back against the pillows at her side, grabbed the box of Kung Pao chicken and his chopsticks from the side table, and returned to stuffing his face. Girl had helped him work up an appetite in the last hour, and he needed to refuel. Kat, still naked and smelling of their lovemaking, nibbled on garlic shrimp while watching some predictable Christmas movie on the flat screen.

Carter let the domestic simplicity of their situation soak in. The calmness of their relationship and the easy silence they enjoyed surrounded him like a cocoon. He'd never been more comfortable with anyone in his entire life, happier or more loved. All the shit that'd come and gone seemed insignificant, and, as God was his witness, he'd go through it all again if it meant being with her.

He swallowed his mouthful of food and licked his lips. "So, you're staying over tonight, right?"

He usually didn't ask—letting Kat decide when she stayed with him—but, weirdly, tonight he needed to hear her say she wasn't leaving.

He *never* wanted her to leave.

The thought made him sit up a little straighter. Startled, his mind tried to wrap itself around what that would mean.

What, forever?

Like, move in?

He kinda liked the idea—a lot. It definitely had its appeal. He glanced at her naked legs stretched down his bed. But it was more than that. He'd want her to move in because he loved her.

His brain kicked into overdrive. Shit, they'd been together only a short time. Yet they'd been through so much. Maybe it was a bad move to lay that on her. He didn't want her to feel pressured, and maybe she wouldn't want to live with him yet. He was anal about cleanliness and he was a grumpy motherfucker in the morning, not that she didn't already know that—

". . . because I'm meeting Beth for coffee, if that's okay with you?"

He slowly blinked back into the room to see Kat looking at him expectantly.

"I'm sorry, what?" he asked, dazed.

Kat laughed and cupped his cheek. "Are you okay? Where were you?"

"Nowhere." He put his food down and fisted his hands in his lap.

Kat noticed and her face turned serious. "You wanna talk about it?"

Did he want to talk about it? He gazed at her. "Um . . . I was just thinking."

Kat squirmed at his side. He noticed, in her nervousness, she'd pulled the sheets up to cover her nakedness. Carter clenched his jaw and little by little pulled it back down. She'd never been shy about her body. He wasn't about to let her start. He bent to her bare chest and kissed her lovingly between her breasts.

"It's nothing bad," he promised her, then laughed with uncertainty. "Well, I sure as shit hope not."

Kat's hands clasped his. "Whatever it is," she soothed, "you can tell me."

He rubbed his hands across his hair. Well, shit, this was a first. After a moment, he said, "So, I was thinking that, maybe—you know, if you want to. Because I do," he waffled. "I don't want you to feel obligated. But I think it'd be— What I mean is, I wondered if you'd—"

His cell phone vibrated on the side table, and he cursed. Max. Shit.

"Hold that thought," he fumed before he picked up his phone. "Dude, what's up?"

"Carter, I need a favor."

Carter's eyes darted to Kat. "Little busy now, man. Can it wait?"

"No, it can't," Max snapped. "Fuck's sake, man, you can't blow me off for your woman again!"

Carter's hackles went up. Something smelled off. "What is it? What's going on?"

"I'll explain when you get here," Max answered. "I need you at the shop in twenty, okay?"

Carter rubbed his forehead. This wasn't good. "Sure," he replied and hung up. He stood to retrieve his boxer briefs and jeans from the floor.

Kat's mouth pressed into a hard line. "You're going out?"

"Yeah." He began to fasten his belt. "I shouldn't be long, though. Max needs me for something."

Apprehension crossed Kat's face. "Something," she repeated quietly. "Something . . . illegal?"

"No," he said, going over to her. "I'll be right back."

She wrapped her hand around his wrist. "Please . . . He's not— What're you . . . You know what? It doesn't matter." Kat tried to smile. "You'll be careful, though, right?"

Since Carter had finally admitted to Kat about his doing time at Kill for his best friend, and Max's ever-worsening drug addiction, she was always anxious when Max's name was mentioned or when he called. She would never admit it, but he knew she worried that Max would land his ass back in jail. Truthfully, he worried about the same thing.

Occasionally, Kat would drop subtle hints about Carter working at a different body shop, or stopping working altogether now that his name was firmly back on the WCS shareholders list, so that he was away from any threat to his parole. At first, her concern had riled him and caused many a heated debate. Now? He understood where her fear came from. She was petrified of losing him, just as he was of losing her. She loved him and wanted to protect him and keep him safe.

Carter tucked a piece of hair behind her ear. "I would never jeopardize what we have, baby." He kissed her. "I'll text you when I'm there, okay?" He kissed her again, his mouth lingering on hers.

"Okay."

• • •

Carter left Kala standing by the shop door, texted Kat, and then lit a smoke. He surveyed his surroundings instinctively, watching for anyone who appeared suspect. Once he was sure there was no one near, he disappeared inside the shop.

With every step, his palms got sweatier, and his conscience spoke louder. *Bad idea*, it said. Yeah. No shit.

He found Max in his office, looking disheveled and sleep-deprived. His clothes were creased, his face unshaven, and his dark eyes were encircled by even darker lines. He, too, was smoking. The cigarette dangled from his lips while he cut a line of coke on the desk with a credit card that was no doubt maxed out. Despairing, Carter pushed his hands into his jacket pockets while Max snorted the line through a rolled-up twenty. He sat back, coughed, and rubbed his nostrils before standing and holding his fist for Carter to bump.

"Thanks for coming, man," he sniped when their knuckles finally touched. "I wondered whether I could pull you away from banging your precious tutor."

Same shit, different day.

"I've told you before," Carter replied sharply. "We're not 'banging.'"

Max gave a derisive laugh. "Ah yes. You *love* each other. That shit's a thing for you now."

Carter ignored his goading and the bitterness in his words. "What the hell am I doing here?"

"I got a tip from a guy I know," Max explained. "The fuckers who jumped me at the club: they're doing a deal tonight."

Carter lifted his shoulders. "So?"

Max's eyes flashed furiously. "The deal should have gone to *me.* Thirty thousand cash. That shit will clear my debts. I've called Paul; he's going to meet us there."

"Meet us where?"

"At the deal." Max's face turned malicious. "We're gonna show them not to fuck with me."

Carter's blood ran cold. "And how are 'we' gonna do that?"

Max gave a chilling smile. "I won't be pushed to the side. I used to run this fucking bitch. I either want in on their deals, or they need to learn some respect."

Carter blanched. "The hell are you thinking? Fuck, Max. This is the stupidest idea I've ever heard! And what if they say no to your proposal, huh? What are you gonna do, *make* them?"

Max scoffed. "Don't get all fucking virtuous on me, Carter. I'm barely keeping the shop afloat. I owe too much! I can't do anything else, man."

"I've told you," Carter replied in exasperation. "Let me help you. I'll give you the money."

Max shook his head. "No."

"There's gotta be a better way than this," Carter pleaded. "Who's this tip from, anyway? How do you know this guy isn't gonna snitch? We could turn up at the meet and be faced with fifteen motherfuckers baying for blood. Look at what happened last time you fucked with these assholes."

"The dude's cool. He won't rat," Max placated him. "It's fine. Trust me."

Carter opened his mouth to argue, but realized there was little point. His trust in his friend was at an all-time low, and Max was as stubborn as he was. Add in the coke, and the bastard was impossible to dissuade. There was no reasoning, no coercing. He'd made his decision, and damn the consequences.

His cell vibrated, and he knew who it was before he even looked at the screen.

Wake me when you get back. Be safe. x

With fear gripping his heart like a vise in his chest, he pushed his cell back into his jeans. "So what am I here for?" he asked quietly.

"You're the only person I trust to watch my back."

Carter snorted. "Lucky me. This is a mess, dude. Are you sure there's no other way?"

Ignoring Carter's question, Max moved around him and approached the wall safe hidden behind a picture of a Shelby GT. Once opened, Max reached in and pulled out two Glocks. He held out the first to Carter.

Carter's hesitation had Max's brow furrowing.

"I'm on parole," Carter said slowly. "If I'm caught— What the fuck do you think I can do with that?"

"You don't have to use the fucking thing," Max snapped. "Take it."

With a deep breath, Carter took the gun, thankful that he was wearing gloves. Ordinarily, it would have felt good. Guns always made him feel strong and undefeatable. Now the metal felt alien and dangerous in his hand.

He swallowed.

Now, he realized, he had Kat to help him feel strong. She made him feel greater than any gun, any drug, any boost, any deal. She gave him more strength than he'd ever thought possible. With her, he was truly invulnerable.

Holding the Glock in his palm and with the image in his mind of Kat warm in his bed, waiting for him to return safely, he suddenly understood the crossroads that lay ahead of him.

One road took him home, to his Peaches, his everything. The other took him back to where he'd been for so many miserable years. It was a dark place filled with bad memories, hopelessness, and fear. With Max on coke and holding a gun in his hand, that road took him straight back to Kill, back to being a worthless criminal with no prospects, no respect, and no future, all promises broken, all faith shattered.

It wasn't a place he ever wanted to go back to. He'd worked too damned hard to get to where he was now, and he couldn't give it all up. He couldn't give up his Peaches. She was all that mattered.

Max dropped a large bag heavily onto the desk and started to retrieve all manner of weapons from its depths.

"I can't," Carter said quietly, snapping Max's head up from the large knife in his hand.

"What?"

Carter shook his head and placed the gun next to the bag. "I can't do this."

Max's face was baffled. "What are you talking about?"

Carter gestured to the gun. "This isn't me anymore, man."

Max's eyes flashed in disbelief. "The fuck? I need you here."

"You don't, Max," Carter implored. "Look, I can give you the money. You don't need to do this shit. You don't need guns and coke. I've told you—"

"I'm not a fucking charity case! I don't want your money!" Max bellowed. "Why don't you understand?"

Incredulous, Carter ground his teeth. "Okay. Why don't you explain it to me? Let's get this shit out there."

"Yeah. *Let's* get this shit out there, Carter." With stiff shoulders, Max made his way around the desk. His steps were heavy, angry, but Carter stood firm. "You think because you have a woman who believes the bullshit you feed her about being a good guy, that you're above all this." He motioned around the small room with wide arms. "You're not. You're still the Wesley Carter you've always been. You'll never change. You can't."

Though Carter knew it was mostly the coke talking, the urge to smack his best friend in the mouth still thundered through him.

Max smirked at Carter's silence. "You think you're so fucking perfect with your grandmother's piggy bank. Not all of us have a fucking trust fund like you, Carter. Some of us have to pay our way."

Anger carved through Carter's chest. "Are you serious with this shit? You know what that money means, what I've been through over it. It means exactly dick. It always did! Jesus! Do you even know what you're talking about, or has the coke finally killed off what brain cells you had?"

"Respect is more important than money, Carter." Max held up the Glock, pupils black and menacing. "This is more powerful than owning sixty percent. This is more important than some Upper East Side bitch who sucks your cock—"

Carter's index finger snapped up to Max's face. "Don't you fucking dare," he spat. "You don't know a thing about her."

Max sneered, "You said you had my back. But you don't have shit."

"You selfish son of a bitch," Carter murmured, shaking his head slowly. He breathed, his temper starting to loosen. "I don't even know who you are anymore." He swallowed. "Do you remember the night you saved my life?"

"Of course I do. How could I not? I took a bullet for you."

"I'm glad you do." Carter's chest grew tight. "Because we're even now, Max. I've paid my debt. I did the time for you. I owe you nothing."

"Carter—"

"No," Carter snapped. "I'm done. I have everything I want in my life." He turned to go.

Max's eyes widened in disbelief, stopping him. "You're leaving to go back to what? To a woman?"

"I'm in love with her, Max. Don't you get it? She's enough for me. She made me realize I'm better than this."

"I don't believe this! She'll leave you, man," he spat. "Once she's done with you, she'll be gone like they all are. They take from you what they want, and then they're gone without a fucking word or care! Can't you see? That bitch is slumming it for a while, just like your mother did—"

Carter's fist connected hard with Max's face. His nose exploded with an almighty crack. He stumbled back, arms flailing, while Carter stood over him, filled with a rage so furious he could barely breathe.

Finding his bearings, with a face covered in blood, Max grabbed wildly for the Glock Carter had set on the desk and pointed it at Carter's head. His eyes were wild.

"Are you gonna shoot me, Max?" Carter asked, pinning his friend with a white-hot stare that dared him.

"Touch me again and see," Max growled, cocking the gun. "You owe me a bullet." He spat blood onto the floor.

Grief twisted in Carter's stomach. It was fucking tragic that it'd come to this. His best friend was lost in the depths of a drug that was slowly driving him crazy, insane with his heartbreak but too stubborn to ask for help. They'd traveled the same road for so many years, brothers in arms, but now they were headed in completely different directions.

Slowly, Carter turned toward the door of the office, the sensation of the loaded gun blistering through his leather jacket.

"You're leaving?" Max asked without inflection. "Just like that? You're . . . You can't. I need you here! Carter! CARTER!"

Carter reached for the handle. "I love you, brother, but I have to think of Kat now." He shook his head. "You're better than this shit." He pulled the door open. "When will you realize that?"

"Carter, I—"

When Max stayed silent, Carter turned back. His mouth dropped open when he saw a tear fall down Max's face. The Glock in his hand shook.

He gasped for breath. "You can't leave. Everyone leaves me. Not you. I'm— It's . . . Don't. Fuck, man."

The blood from Max's broken nose dripped onto his T-shirt, and Carter was immediately remorseful. "I need help. It hurts." They'd fought before, but never to the point where blood was spilled.

"I'm sorry I punched you, but—"

"No." Max took a deep, shuddering breath. "My fucking *heart* hurts." He closed his eyes. "I'm . . . It kills me that she's not here."

Carter took a tentative step toward the crumbling man, afraid to say anything.

"Every day I wake up, and she's not there," Max continued. "And I feel like I'm dying all over again." The gun in his hand dropped to the floor. "My baby, my son"—he gasped—"he would be . . . almost two. If he was . . . and she . . . and my mom's gone, dad's gone, and you're with your girl. And what do I have?" He looked around himself, helpless. "I have hangovers and nightmares that . . . terrify me, and I can't sleep. The coke . . . keeps me awake. It makes me forget for a while, and I can finally breathe." He gripped his hair and sobbed. "And then I remember again, and I'm suffocating without her." He groaned. "Christ, I miss her *so* fucking much."

Carter's chest cracked wide-open. "I know."

He'd die without his Peaches. She possessed his heart. If she walked away from him or gave it back, it would surely destroy him.

"Oh God," Max whimpered into his forearm. "What happened to me? I thought I'd forget, but I can't find myself. I'm so fucking lost. I mean . . . *look* at me. Make it stop, Carter. *Please* make it stop."

Carter reached out and pulled him into a tight embrace as Max sobbed into his jacket. "Don't leave me like she did. Help me," Max begged. "You're all I have left. Please. For Christ's sake, help me."

"I will," Carter promised. "I swear I will, brother."

EPILOGUE

A year later . . .

Shivering from the cold, Kat pushed the beach house door shut with her butt and trudged to the kitchen, where she heaved two sizeable grocery bags onto the counter. She pulled off her hat and gloves, unzipped her jacket, and made her way into the sitting room to find Carter slouched on the sofa, watching TV, chewing the ever-loving shit out of a toothpick.

Kat smiled, watching him. He'd given up smoking on his birthday in March, and now, nine months in, he hadn't caved. She was incredibly proud of him.

Noticing her once the commercials came on, Carter looked up and smiled. "Hey, beautiful. How was your day?"

"Long, but great," she replied. "The boys are really something. They're really starting to listen to me. Look." She held up a small silver key chain in the shape of a cat. "They gave me this for Christmas."

She'd struggled to keep her emotions in check when her class of twelve students at the Brooklyn Young Offenders Institute had handed her the beautifully wrapped gift. "I'll miss them this week."

Carter placed his chin on the back of the sofa, looking insanely adorable. "You'll have me."

Kat leaned over and kissed him. "Aren't I lucky?"

"Beth called," Carter whispered against her lips. "She wanted to know if we're still going to the benefit on New Year's. I told her yes. That okay?"

"Definitely. How was your day? Did Max call?"

Carter's face turned sad. "Yeah, he did." He sighed. "It breaks my fucking heart, his being in that place at Christmas, but I know it's where he needs to be."

Less than twelve months after his heartbreaking confession to Carter, Max was admitted into rehab, finally conceding that he needed professional help. His solo battle against his coke addiction had been valiant but short-lived. He was clean for only seventy-three days before he caved after seeing a woman he thought was Lizzie on a busy street in Brooklyn.

Carter and the boys from the shop tried their best to steer their friend onto the right path, keeping him busy, but Max's emotional scars ran too deep. Once Max had admitted defeat, after Carter had found him unconscious on his bathroom floor, Carter had footed the rehab center bill, also clearing the shop of the debts Max's addiction had created.

Kat cupped Carter's cheek as she kissed him. "Be strong. He needs you."

Carter exhaled. "I know."

"Hey, guess what?" Kat smiled. "I stopped at the store on the way home."

Carter's eyes brightened. "Did you get me something nice?"

She grinned. "Oreos, milk, and twelve cans of Coke."

He dropped his head back onto the sofa and sighed. "God, I love you."

Kat laughed and went back to the kitchen to put the groceries away. The lush domesticity that swept through her was as familiar as it was welcome. Living with Carter had been trying at first, but after almost a year, they'd finally found a new level of comfort that Kat cherished. Sure, his obsessive cleanliness and OCD habits still drove her crazy, but it was most definitely worth it.

They split their time between the beach house and the TriBeCa apartment, which they used primarily during the week and whenever Carter was needed at WCS. The beach house, however, would always be most special to them: a precious getaway they both treasured.

Once she was done unpacking, Kat poured two large glasses of milk and tucked the pack of Oreos under her arm. She handed one glass to Carter and sat down next to him, putting the cookies between them. Carter took all of two seconds to rip the pack open and begin devouring the contents.

"So, look, I was thinking while you were at work," he mumbled before swallowing the cream from his cookie. "I was thinking that we should exchange gifts today. You know, to celebrate your vacation time."

Kat looked at him askance. "But it's not Christmas for another four days. Can't you wait?" She'd caught him at least half a dozen times shaking and touching the parcels under the tree they'd decorated together two weeks before. "Besides, Nana Boo, Mom, and Harrison will be here then. I'd like to have some gifts to open with them."

Carter shot a longing gaze at the beautiful Christmas tree. "But . . ."

Kat laughed. "Oh my God, you're such a child."

He grinned, blue eyes sparkling. "Does that mean we can?"

"Okay. Fine," Kat caved. "But you only get to open one."

"Yes, Boss." He sprang up and hurried over to the gifts.

• • •

Carter kneeled next to the tree, pretending to search through the copious number of packages underneath it. He shook, poked, and prodded, and, once he was satisfied he'd made enough of a show, he picked up a small silver package and beckoned Kat over. When she was seated at his side, looking decidedly exasperated, he passed it to her.

"This is from me," he said softly, kissing her. "Merry Christmas, Peaches."

"Merry Christmas." She smiled, excitement creeping in, and began ripping the paper open.

"Oh, Carter," Kat gasped when she saw the miniature Alice in Wonderland statue, an exact replica of the one in Central Park. "It's perfect."

"Really?"

"Really," she answered, leaning over to kiss him.

"I wanted to get you this because Alice has seen us through so much."

Kat hummed. "I guess she has."

"And," Carter continued, "I thought she should be here for this part, too."

Kat looked quizzical.

Carter's heart almost burst from between his ribs as he pulled his hand from his pocket and held out a small blue Tiffany box.

Kat's eyes widened and snapped to his. "Carter, I—"

"Take it."

She did and, slower than Carter could bear, she opened it and gasped. The three-carat diamond-and-platinum ring sparkled perfectly under the Christmas lights.

Breathing deeply, Carter took her shaking hand, letting his thumb trace the cursive *C* she'd had inked on the inside of her wrist as a birthday gift for him. It was the sexiest fucking thing he'd ever seen.

He picked up the Alice statue. "I want you to look at this and remember how far we've come. Alice was there when we had our first nondate and I stole the best kiss of my life. She was there when we danced in the rain and I hummed Otis Redding in your ear. That was the same night I told you who I was, and you let me make love to you all night."

He put the statue down. "I was so broken when you found me again. But you put me back together and made me realize that the mistakes I've made don't define who I am. You believed in me when no one else would." He kissed her palm. "I know I'm a pain in the ass. I'm far from perfect. We both are. Your cooking leaves a lot to be desired and you leave your dirty laundry on the bathroom floor every morning and it drives me insane!" He chuckled when she pushed him playfully.

"But I love living with you, Kat. I love waking up with you every morning and seeing you smile, and falling asleep with you in my arms, knowing that I've never felt safer. I love our lazy days. I love laughing with you and fighting with you, because I know it means we get to make up. I love riding Kala with you. I want to put up a Christmas tree with you every year for the rest of my life."

His throat became thick and he squeezed her hands. "I've loved you every day since I was eleven years old. Will you marry me?"

Kat laughed through her tears. "Of course I'll marry you."

Carter laughed with her and pulled her into his arms, kissing her deeply.

Her lips and body merged with his so perfectly, so beautifully, as they always had. Pulling back, Carter took the ring from the box and slipped it on her finger. Staring at it, he knew it was always meant to be there. Staring at it, he knew he was finally home.

He cupped her face and kissed her again.

He owed the woman in his arms everything. He'd become the man he wanted to be for her, the man he liked being. And as their clothes started coming off when the passion between them burst into flames, Carter vowed to himself that he would continue to repay her every single day of his life.

It was his most deeply desired obligation.

His precious debt.

His beloved pound of flesh.

Max O'Hare is ready to move on with his life after successfully completing rehab and learning to explore his deepest fears and dreams through art. It's through art that Max meets Grace Brooks, the seemingly perfect girl. But why won't she tell anyone anything about her past? Will they slowly allow each other in or are they both too afraid to get hurt again?

Keep reading for a sneak peek of

AN OUNCE OF HOPE

by Sophie Jackson

Coming Fall 2015 from Gallery Books!

Max's sponsor arrived at the coffee shop with his customary smile and a yellow T-shirt decorated with—

"What the fuck is that?" Max asked with a puzzled shake of his head as they ordered their sandwiches.

Tate glanced down at himself and cocked an eyebrow. "It's a Minion dressed as Wolverine," he answered, clearly disgusted with Max's lack of comic book expertise. "What the hell else would it be?"

Max snorted. "I apologize. I'm obviously having an off day with DC—"

"Marvel! Jesus."

"Whatever."

Tate shook his head. "I don't even know why I keep coming back to see you."

"Because you love me," Max retorted as they took their lunches to their usual table.

Tate shrugged. "Someone has to, I guess." They sat in companionable silence, watching the world go by, while they ate. "So how have things been?"

Max nodded. "Okay. Got my six-month medallion." He took a mammoth bite of his chicken on rye.

When he was in rehab, he'd never imagined he'd get to this point—but the gold medal in his pocket proved he had. When he'd been awarded it at his last group session, it'd been the first time he'd truly felt a shiver of pride.

Tate grinned. "My man. Nice." They fist-bumped. "Any more 'off' days?"

Max shook his head. He and Tate stayed in frequent contact, exchanging texts at least once a day, with phone calls just as regular. Tate had been a true support for him, and the fact that he traveled three hours every week to see Max was testament to how seriously he took his role as Max's sponsor.

As always, they shot the shit about therapy, caught up on friends—with Riley at the helm, Max's body shop was booming; Carter was stressed with Kat's wedding planning—and drank coffee.

Suddenly, his coffee mug frozen in mid-air, Tate's attention moved to something on the street. Max followed his line of sight and smirked.

It was Grace.

Dressed in running gear, she was walking toward the coffee shop, looking at her watch, no doubt checking her run time. Her hair was pulled back, her ponytail bouncing, her running pants breathtakingly tight. Max's cock gave a nod of appreciation. He was annoyed he'd had to cancel his run with her this morning to meet Tate.

"Good Lord," Tate muttered as he watched her enter the shop and head to the counter.

"Like what you see?" Max asked. A curious and unfamiliar warmth crept across his skin.

"Um, yeah . . . Shit, do they all look like her around here?"

Max looked over at Grace, catching her eye. She beamed and waved. He smiled and dipped his chin back at her. "No," he answered. "She's one of a kind."

As Max expected, she soon sauntered across the shop toward them with latte and muffin in hand. "Hey," she greeted him, her green eyes dancing.

"Hey yourself. Good run?"

"Yeah. Weirdly boring without you." Her gaze moved to Tate. "Hello, you must be Tate, Max's sponsor. I've heard a lot about you."

Tate held out his hand. "All good things, I hope." He smiled widely.

Max rolled his eyes.

Grace laughed. "Oh, yeah, all good things."

Tate's head turned toward Max, who sighed. "This is Grace," Max introduced. "She's my running partner."

"Running partner, huh?" The expression on Tate's face said he thought Max was full of shit. Well, he could think whatever the hell he liked.

"Yes," Grace said. "You interrupted an important run today." Her playful smile was lovely, and Max watched Tate fall headfirst to its captivating power.

"Well, we can't have that, can we?" Tate played along. "Maybe I can buy you a coffee to make it up to you."

Max cleared his throat and crossed his arms, not knowing where to look while his sponsor hit on his . . . friend.

"Thank you, but I have some already," Grace answered, lifting her cup.

Max wasn't about to step in, unless she looked uncomfortable. Besides, Tate was harmless. An asshole, but harmless all the same.

"Hey, Max," she said, "could you meet me at the cottage by the stream later? I'm working, but I can be there at three thirty." She seemed nervous.

"Should I be worried?"

"Oh, no. I just need your help with something."

"I'll be there."

She smiled again. "Great. It was nice meeting you, Tate."

"The pleasure was all mine, Grace." Tate's eyes never left her until she disappeared down the street.

Max waited with bated breath.

"Okay," Tate ordered, his index finger pressed into the table. "Fucking spill. Who is she, and why the hell haven't you talked about her before? And don't give me that running-partner bullshit. She's hot for you, and if you aren't hitting that, I'm revoking your man card right now."

Max laughed despite himself. "She's not hot for me. It's not like that."

Tate gaped; mouth and palms open, looking a lot like his brother Riley. "She's *so* hot for you. How can you— Whatever. Why are you not all over her like a damned rash?"

Max ran a hand through his hair. "We're friends."

"With benefits?"

Max stared at his coffee mug. "Sort of."

Tate sat back. "We need more coffee and one of those fucking great muffins—and then *you*'re gonna tell me *everything*."

It was going to be a long-ass morning.

GOULD

Czas na pożegnanie

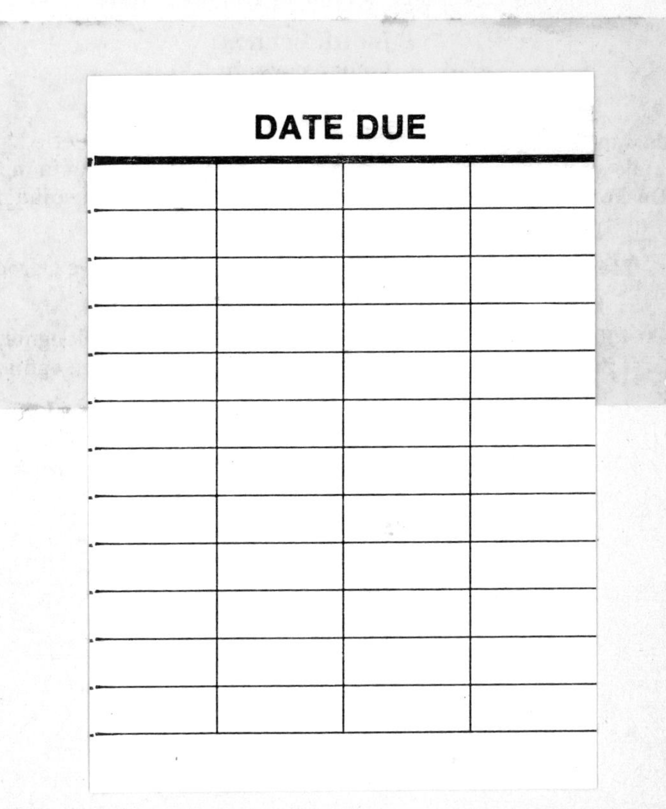

W serii Biblioteczka pod Różą ukazały się m.in.:

Maeve Binchy
Droga do Tary

Sandra Brown
Pojedynek serc, Pozory mylą

Jude Deveraux, Judith McNaught
Dary losu

Dorothea Benton Frank
Pojednanie, Wyspa Palm, Powrót do marzeń

Judith Gould
Grecka willa, Najlepsze przyjdzie jutro, Po kres czasu

Victoria Holt
Tajemnica Zuzanny, Indyjski wachlarz, Tajemnica starej farmy,
Tajemnicza kobieta, Wyznania królowej, Guwernantka

Judith Lennox
Trudne powroty

Judith McNaught
Coś wspaniałego, Zanim się pojawiłaś, Raj, Szepty w świetle księżyca,
Jak w raju, Na zawsze, Królestwo marzeń, Whitney, moja miłość,
Doskonałość, Fajerwerki, Mój własny anioł stróż, Podwójną miarą

Deirdre Purcell
Meandry uczuć, Rozmowy z Ambrożym, Marmurowe Ogrody

Karen Robards
Księżyc myśliwego, Księżycowe widmo, Pocałunek ognia,
Zaufać nieznajomemu, Po tej stronie nieba, Morze ognia,
Oszustka, Przebojowa dziewczyna

Nora Roberts
Klucz światła, Klucz wiedzy, Klucz odwagi, Skarby przeszłości

Mary Westmacott (Agatha Christie)
Brzemię, Niedokończony portret, Samotna

Barbara Wood
Oznaki życia, Zielone miasto w słońcu

Judith

GOULD

Czas na pożegnanie

Przełożyła Agnieszka Barbara Ciepłowska

Prószyński i S-ka

Tytuł oryginału
TIME TO SAY GOOD-BYE

Projekt okładki
Agnieszka Spyrka

Ilustracja na okładce
Corbis

Redaktor prowadzący serię
Ewa Witan

Redakcja
Ewa Witan

Redakcja techniczna
Elżbieta Urbańska

Korekta
Grażyna Nawrocka

Skład i łamanie
Aneta Osipiak

ISBN 83-7469-261-8

Biblioteczka pod Różą

Wydawca
Prószyński i S-ka SA
02-651 Warszawa, ul. Garażowa 7

Druk i oprawa
OPOLGRAF Spółka Akcyjna
45-085 Opole, ul. Niedziałkowskiego 8–12

Z wyrazami serdeczności dedykuję tę książkę
Trojgu muszkieterom z rodu Gallaherów:
Joyce Rucker
Suzie Bissell
oraz
Robertowi W. Gallaherowi

Rzecz piękna jest radością wieczną:
Jej uroda wzrasta, a będąc konieczną
Nie odejdzie w nicość, lecz dla nas odszuka
Przystań, gdzie sen słodki oczy nam zamyka
Zbawienny w ucichłym wytchnieniu.

John Keats, „Endymion"

Podziękowania

Pragnę wyrazić wdzięczność Terry'emu Rootowi, właścicielowi „Orchid Zone" w Watsonville w stanie Kalifornia, za to, iż znalazł czas, by mnie osobiście oprowadzić po tym nieprawdopodobnie urokliwym miejscu, a także podzielił się ze mną swoją imponującą wiedzą na temat orchidei. Jeśli pojawiły się w tej książce jakiekolwiek błędy dotyczące tego tematu, powstały wyłącznie z mojej winy.

Podziękowania z pewnością należą się także Nancy Austin i Billowi Cawleyowi – za ich bezgraniczną uprzejmość, która umożliwiła mi między innymi zapoznanie się z cudami hrabstwa Santa Cruz w Kalifornii.

Koniec jest początkiem

Wczesna jesień 2000 roku

Pogoda była dość niezwykła jak na tę porę roku.

Może przez szacunek dla wyjątkowych okoliczności.

Słońce ugrzęzło za ponurymi chmurami, w dół przedarło się tylko kilka bladych promyków. Jak okiem sięgnąć, ziemię spowijała mgła. W sinawym obłoku ginęły nawet potężne sekwoje.

Nieduża urna wykładana muszlami została wykonana na zamówienie.

Oto, co zostaje z człowieka, pomyślał. Tylko garść prochów.

Odwrócił się do towarzyszącej mu kobiety. Choć bardzo się starał panować nad bólem i rozpaczą, nie zdołał ukryć swoich uczuć. Ale przynajmniej wyprostował ramiona i uniósł głowę, gdy oboje razem podeszli do samochodu. Otworzył drzwi, a kiedy jego towarzyszka wsiadła, obszedł wóz dookoła i wsunął się za kierownicę. Urnę pieczołowicie ustawił tuż obok siebie, na tym samym siedzeniu. Przekręcił kluczyk w stacyjce, wrzucił wsteczny bieg i wyjechał na drogę prowadzącą wzdłuż brzegu oceanu. Skierował się na południe, w stronę fragmentu wybrzeża zwanego Big Sur.

Podróż mijała w milczeniu, ciszę tylko niekiedy przerywały zduszony szloch albo drżące westchnienia kobiety. Mężczyzna prowadził zatopiony w myślach, zdruzgotany stratą, skupiony na tym, co miał zrobić.

Mgła wtórowała mu w smutku, spowiła okolicę grubym płaszczem, ukrywając bujne piękno stromego brzegu. Tylko od czasu do czasu odsłaniała na chwilę jakiś wąski kanion, kamienisty stok czy wody oceanu, przez które widać było tarasowe dno. Zwieńczyła bladymi kręgami sosny i cyprysy, przysiadła na czubkach dębów oraz majestatycznych sekwoi, zmroziła perłową szarością niepowtarzalny blask morskich fal.

Kierowca zwolnił, szukając zjazdu z głównej drogi. Wiedział, że skręt nie jest dobrze oznaczony, a jeszcze na dodatek dziś skrył się we mgle. Nagle mężczyzna dostrzegł znak, tabliczkę z napisem „Sycamore Canyon Road". Gwałtownie wcisnął hamulec i ostro skręcił w prawo. Pasażerka, wyrwana ze smutnej zadumy, przestraszyła się nie na żarty, ale nie odezwała się ani słowem.

Gdy opuścił szybę, do wnętrza samochodu wdarł się ryk fal bezlitośnie atakujących skały.

Tutaj łatwo można sobie wyobrazić najgorszą tragedię, pomyślał. Choć to takie piękne miejsce. A może właśnie dlatego...?

Wóz toczył się w ślimaczym tempie, bo kierowca nagle stracił chęć, by wykonać to, po co tu przybył. W końcu zatrzymał auto i wyłączył silnik. Jakiś czas siedział bez ruchu, niewidzącym wzrokiem śledząc tumany mgły. Wreszcie odwrócił się do pasażerki.

– Niedługo wrócę – powiedział.

Nie czekając na odpowiedź, wysiadł, sięgnął do środka po urnę i ruszył samotnie ku plaży.

Stawiał długie kroki, więc szybko znalazł się na skraju urwiska. Tam przystanął i rozejrzał się w poszukiwaniu charakterystycznych punktów krajobrazu. Pośród lepkich, wilgotnych macek sinobiałego obłoku odnalazł znajomą ścieżkę wiodącą przez skały do oceanu w kolorze indygo.

Widok jak z bajki, pomyślał. Fale łamiące się na skałach, podmorskie groty, kamienne łuki... Tajemniczy zakątek promieniujący pięknem tak intensywnym, że aż bolesnym. Miejsce jej ostatniego spoczynku.

Odetchnął głęboko słonym morskim powietrzem. Ścieżka była wąska i stroma, tu i ówdzie nawet niebezpieczna. Zacisnął usta, przytulił urnę do piersi i ruszył w dół, ostrożnie stawiając stopy na mokrych kamieniach. Elegancki garnitur, włożony z okazji nabożeństwa żałobnego, podkreślał sprężystość muskularnego, silnego ciała, ale myśli mężczyzna miał odrętwiałe. Ta sama bezwładność, która kierowała jego wszystkimi czynnościami w ciągu ostatnich dni, teraz poprowadziła go nadmorską dróżką w stronę wody, ku spełnieniu trudnego obowiązku.

Stanął na plaży i rozejrzał się dookoła. Nikogo. Byli tylko we dwoje.

Przy pierwszych krokach stopy zapadły mu się w piasek. Przystanął i uniósł spojrzenie na daleki horyzont. Linia, gdzie ocean zlewał się z niebem, także zniknęła za mgłą. Przybyły spojrzał przez ramię na potężne skały, z których właśnie zszedł, jakby się wahał, czy nie zawrócić, czy nie zmienić decyzji, ale zaraz na nowo podjął wyzwanie. Od wybranego przez nią miejsca dzieliło go zaledwie kilkanaście kroków. Znali dobrze oboje ten skrawek wybrzeża.

Wiatr załopotał połami marynarki, porwał w górę krawat, rzucił mężczyźnie w oczy garść słonej piany i zmierzwił mu włosy. Na nic jego wysiłki, bo stojący nawet ich nie zauważył. Myślał tylko o jednym, wyłącznie o swoim zadaniu.

Dotarł wreszcie na miejsce. Rozejrzał się i pokiwał głową.

To właśnie tutaj, pomyślał.

Powoli wszedł do lodowatej wody. Ujął urnę w obie dłonie, obrzucił ją spojrzeniem pełnym żalu.

Jak pożegnać kogoś, kto był tak pełen życia? Istotę stale żądną nowych wrażeń, kobietę, której ziemska droga jawiła się jako radosna ścieżka, niekiedy kręta, pełna przygód, czasem tajemnicza, a zawsze intrygująca... Istotę, która stale podejmowała nowe wyzwania. Która dla niego była gotowa na wszystko. Z którą połączyła go namiętność. I prawdziwa miłość.

Po tej osobie została tylko garstka prochów.

W oczach mężczyzny pojawiły się łzy. Gdy otworzył urnę, nie mógł ich już powstrzymać – stoczyły się po policzkach, wpadły do oceanu.

Podniósł urnę w górę, wysoko, do samego nieba, pozwolił, by wiatr porwał popioły... jej prochy... i rozrzucił je na cztery strony świata.

– Żegnaj, najmilsza – wyszeptał. – Żegnaj.

Nagle przez chmury przedarło się słońce, złoty blask spłynął na ziemię, skąpał wodę w ciepłej poświacie. A jemu się wydało, że widzi, jak dusza ukochanej wzlatuje prosto do nieba, jak po świetlistej smudze wędruje z tego bajecznego ziemskiego zakątka w górę, do wieczności. Oślepiony nagłą jasnością spuścił wzrok i przycisnął urnę do piersi. W końcu ujął ją jedną dłonią, zamachnął się potężnie i rzucił w morską toń. Szybko zniknęła w głębinie. Wkrótce nie zostanie po niej nic, tak samo jak po ludzkich prochach.

Wyszedł na plażę i ogarnął spojrzeniem skalisty klif. W jej towarzystwie każdy spacer zmieniał się w pasjonującą wyprawę... Ruszył wąską ścieżką wśród stromych skał.

Jak teraz bez niej żyć?

Na szczycie przystanął, musiał uspokoić oddech. Zdjął marynarkę i przerzucił ją przez ramię. Ostatni raz spojrzał na morze. Mgła ustąpiła pod ciepłymi promieniami, świat był teraz jasny, barwny, radosny. Cienka linia znaczyła odległy horyzont, a bliżej brzegu wesoło baraszkowały wydry morskie. Nikt im tutaj nie przeszkadzał, czuły się swobodnie.

Jak ona je uwielbiała! Często je obserwowali.

Dziś ich widok nie sprawiał mu przyjemności, bo nie mógł się z nią dzielić radością.

Jak teraz bez niej żyć?, powtórzył w myślach.

Był pogrążony w smutku. I nawet ocean, zwykle niosący ukojenie, a nawet leczący rany, nie miał dla niego pociechy. Fale podnosiły się i opadały, gładząc piaszczystą plażę.

Mężczyzna ciężkim krokiem ruszył do samochodu. W ciszy.

Zupełnie sam.

Księga pierwsza

JOANNA I JOSH

Wiosna i lato 2000 roku

Rozdział pierwszy

Joanna Cameron Lawrence wcisnęła hamulec. Leciwy, ale wypieszczony mercedes kabriolet wolniutko wspinał się krętą wąską drogą prowadzącą przez pasmo górskie Santa Cruz. Jechała tędy wcześniej, lecz już dość dawno. Nie sposób jednak było zapomnieć, że droga należała do wyjątkowo niebezpiecznych, podobnie jak ta, która prowadziła do jej domu w Aptos, całkiem niedaleko.

Choć na jezdni wyznaczono po jednym pasie ruchu w każdą stronę – przynajmniej teoretycznie – w wielu miejscach obfite zimowe deszcze wypłukały ziemię i z szosy pozostał wąski pas asfaltu, tylko na jeden samochód. Przed takimi groźnymi przewężeniami ustawiano znaki ostrzegawcze, najwyraźniej w nadziei, że nie dojdzie do kolizji, choć ruch odbywał się po jednym paśmie.

Joanna wciągnęła głęboko w płuca chłodne górskie powietrze, przesycone wonią eukaliptusów. Po lewej stronie wyrastała skalista ściana, do której kurczowo przylgnęły domy, po prawej otwierał się kanion, a właściwie nieomalże przepaść. Strome ściany opadały miejscami nawet ponad sto metrów, nim sięgnęły dna, gdzie płynął strumień, potężny lub słabnący, zależnie od pory roku. Cyprysy, ogromne sekwoje, eukaliptusy i sosny tworzyły gęsto tkany baldachim, który z rzadka tylko przepuszczał promienie słoneczne.

Po przeciwnej stronie wąwozu, na zboczu sąsiedniej góry, od czasu do czasu także pojawiały się budynki, głównie domki letnie, zawieszone na skałach niczym gniazda i podobnie jak gniazda zbudowane w przyzwoitej odległości jeden od drugiego. Prowadziły do nich kruche mostki przerzucone nad parowem. Właściciele musieli parkować po tej stronie kanionu, gdzie prowadziła droga, i dostawali się do swoich siedzib na piechotę.

Najwyraźniej byli to ludzie nieustraszeni, godni podziwu. Mieli odwagę być inni oraz borykać się z wszelkimi niedogodnościami związanymi z mieszkaniem w tak niesamowitych warunkach.

Joanna zerknęła na jedną z mijanych skrzynek pocztowych. Numer wskazywał, że cel jest już blisko. Kobieta, którą miała odwiedzić, powiedziała, że tuż obok jej mostka znajduje się dogodne miejsce parkingowe...

Po prawej stronie ukazał się staruteńki kremowy dżip wagoneer upstrzony plamkami rdzy, zaparkowany w bocznej asfaltowej alejce. Tego właśnie auta miała wypatrywać Joanna. W ślimaczym tempie pokonała ostry zakręt i zaparkowała tuż za dżipem. Zaciągnęła hamulec i wyłączyła silnik.

Przejrzała się w lusterku wstecznym. No tak, to było do przewidzenia. Z przepastnej płóciennej torby wykończonej skórą wyjęła szczotkę i kilkoma energicznymi ruchami przeczesała włosy. Takie właśnie są skutki jeżdżenia kabrioletem. Spojrzała w lusterko raz jeszcze. Tym razem fryzura dała się zaakceptować. Joanna chwyciła torbę, wrzuciła do niej kluczyki i wysiadła ze swojej srebrnej strzały.

Postanowiła nie podnosić dachu. Na deszcz się nie zanosiło, samochód stał w miłym cieniu, więc nie musiała się obawiać, że blacha się nagrzeje, no i powinien tu być zupełnie bezpieczny.

Obeszła dżipa i stanęła przed drewnianym mostkiem. Dłuższą chwilę przyglądała mu się nieufnie. Ciągnął się i ciągnął, co najmniej dwadzieścia metrów. A Joanna Lawrence obawiała się tylko jednego. Wysokości.

Słodki Jezu, jęknęła w duchu. Kochana, naprzód marsz!, próbowała dodać sobie animuszu. Przejdziesz i tyle. Po wiszącym moście nad potwornie głębokim parowem. Po zbutwiałym drewnie...

Wzięła głęboki wdech i ostrożnie postawiła na desce nogę. Jednocześnie z całej siły ścisnęła poręcz. Postawiła na mostku drugą nogę i odważyła się odetchnąć. Mostek zachwiał się lekko pod jej ciężarem. Coś wyraźnie skrzypnęło.

Boże jedyny, miej mnie w swojej opiece!

Ktoś jej kiedyś mówił, że w takiej sytuacji należy spoglądać prosto przed siebie – za nic w świecie nie patrzeć w dół! Iść powoli, lecz pewnie, w jednakowym tempie.

Łatwiej radzić, niż zrobić!

Raz jeszcze odetchnęła głęboko, utkwiła spojrzenie w ślicznej chatce po drugiej stronie wąwozu i ruszyła – krok za krokiem, najpierw powoli, potem coraz szybciej. Przez całą drogę wstrzymywała oddech i mocno trzymała się poręczy.

Wreszcie przeszła! Mało się nie rozpłakała ze szczęścia. Taka krótka przeprawa, a wydawało się, że trwała wieczność! Joanna zerknęła przez ramię na pokonany kanion. Wyglądał teraz całkiem niewinnie.

Irracjonalny strach działał jej na nerwy, jak zresztą każda słabość, ale nie umiała go przezwyciężyć. Tak czy inaczej, tym razem wygrała. Wyprostowała się dumnie, obrzucając wyzywającym spojrzeniem Bogu ducha winny domek letniskowy.

Podobnie jak mostek, on także został zbudowany z desek w kolorze piernika, które miejscami wyblakły i upodobniły się barwą do kory otaczających go sosen. Okiennice miał ciemnozielone, a w podokiennych skrzynkach wesoło czerwieniło się geranium. Dach kryty cedrowym gontem z czasem posrebrzał, a komin i podmurówka z kamienia były obrośnięte soczystym mchem. Gzymsy i ganek ozdobiono ażurową kratką, po ścianach pięła się winorośl. Wzdłuż ścieżki prowadzącej do wejścia rosły krzewy.

Pięknie tu, pomyślała Joanna. I jak romantycznie!

Podeszła do drzwi. Ponieważ nie było dzwonka, uniosła lśniącą mosiężną kołatkę w kształcie ananasa i stuknęła nią dwukrotnie.

Otworzyły się niemal natychmiast.

W progu stanęła wysoka szczupła kobieta, mniej więcej w tym samym wieku co Joanna, czyli tuż po trzydziestce. Miała jasne włosy do ramion oraz błyszczące oczy o żywym spojrzeniu, w przedziwnym kolorze przywodzącym na myśl szylkret: niby ciemnobrązowe, ale prześwietlone blaskiem złota i ciepłem bursztynu. Do tego wysoko sklepione kości policzkowe, pięknie zarysowane łuki brwi, prosty nos oraz pełne, zmysłowe usta i cera bez skazy.

– Pani Lawrence, prawda? – zapytała z przyjaznym uśmiechem. Jednym spojrzeniem ogarnęła strój przybyłej: lnianą bluzkę barwy ecru, letnie jasne spodnie, espadryle. Swobodny, a jednocześnie elegancki.

– Proszę mi mówić po imieniu. – Joanna zrewanżowała się uśmiechem.

– Ja mam na imię April. April Woodward, jak oczywiście wiesz. Zapraszam.

Otworzyła drzwi szerzej i odsunęła się, przepuszczając gościa. W niewielkim przedpokoju zwracał uwagę imponujący, wykuty z żelaza stojak, w którym zgromadzono laski różnej długości oraz parasolki. Tu i ówdzie sterczała rączka w kształcie łba jakiegoś zwierzęcia. Na niewielkim sosnowym stoliku z dwiema szufladami leżał porcelanowy talerz na klucze. Podłogę przykrywał spłowiały i wytarty, niegdyś wielobarwny chodnik.

– Napijesz się czegoś, Joanno? – spytała gospodyni. – Mam zieloną herbatę. A może wolisz wodę mineralną?

– Uwielbiam zieloną herbatę – ucieszyła się Joanna.

– Z cukrem? Ze słodzikiem? Z miodem?

– Najchętniej z odrobiną miodu.

– Rozgość się, proszę. – April gestem wskazała salonik. – Zaraz wrócę.

Joanna powiodła wzrokiem za gospodynią ubraną w spodnie khaki i koszulę w drobne prążki. Mokasyny niosły ją miękko i cicho.

Wybrała sobie ogromną, wygodną kanapę, ustawioną przed kominkiem, który zdominował całą ścianę. W znacznym stopniu właśnie dzięki niemu wnętrze nabierało przytulnego charakteru. Zapadła się w miękkie poduchy i ciekawie rozejrzała dookoła. Pokrycie było chyba z prawdziwego lnu? Ściany wyłożono sosnową boazerią, z takiego samego chyba drewna zrobiono też półki, z których wprost wypływały książki różnej wielkości, sądząc po wyglądzie, często czytane.

Ujmujący salonik, pomyślała. Bezpretensjonalny i miły. Zapewne April jest podobna... W ogóle jaki to romantyczny domek, a jednocześnie nieprzesłodzony i nieprzeładowany. I pieniądze nie biją w oczy...

Wróciła gospodyni z niewielką tacą w dłoniach. Postawiła na stoliku dzbanek z herbatą oraz baryłkowaty słoiczek miodu.

– Nie chcę ci sprawiać kłopotu – odezwała się Joanna.

– Nie sprawiasz – zapewniła April. Nalała jasny gorący płyn do filiżanek, dodała odrobinę miodu i podała gościowi aromatyczny napój.

– Dziękuję.

– Nie ma za co. – April upiła łyk herbaty. – Z tego, co zrozumiałam – zaczęła rozmowę – chciałabyś zbudować coś w rodzaju groty.

– Tak – odrzekła Joanna. – Przywiozłam zdjęcia... Jedne z czasopism, inne skopiowane z różnych książek. Na pewno się zorientujesz, o co mniej więcej mi chodzi. – Odstawiła herbatę, sięgnęła do torby i z jej przepaścistych głębin wydobyła sporą żółtą kopertę. – Może wyda ci się, że trochę sfiksowałam... – podjęła, wyjmując zdjęcia – ale pokażę ci, co zamierzam osiągnąć.

April z uwagą obejrzała wszystkie fotografie.

– Fantastyczne – westchnęła, odłożywszy ostatnią. W jej szylkretowych oczach błyskały złote iskry. – Rzeczywiście tak ma być? – Stuknęła dłonią w odbitki.

– Jak najbardziej – potwierdziła Joanna pogodnie. Zadowolona była, że zdjęcia się April spodobały. – Widziałam fontannę i mury według twojego projektu w ogrodzie Ingrid i Ronalda Wilsonów. Niesamowite. Po prostu... nieziemskie.

– Serdeczne dzięki.

– No i coś mi mówi, że potrafiłabyś zrobić to, czego chcę.

– Dziwne... – zamyśliła się April. – W dzisiejszych czasach mało kto decyduje się na coś podobnego.

– A ja, owszem. – Joanna zaśmiała się w głos. – Śnię o tym po nocach. I wszystko mi jedno, czy ktoś uzna to za wariactwo czy też nie. Chciałabym zrobić tę grotę z dawnej stajni. To kamienny budynek, myślę, że będzie się nadawał. Nie jest bardzo duży, ale za to z miejsca, gdzie go zbudowano, roztacza się przepiękny widok.

– Grota... – mruczała April. – Jaskinia... pieczara...

Joanna z aprobatą kiwała głową.

– Tak, tak, tak. Właśnie. Chociaż wolałabym, żeby trochę przypominała pawilon ogrodowy, żeby nie wyglądała na dziką, zaniedbaną jaskinię. Najchętniej używam słowa „grota", chyba dlatego, że chciałabym ją całą wyłożyć muszlami i otoczakami. Ściany, sufit, podłogę... Tak jak na tych zdjęciach.

– Świetna myśl! – przyklasnęła jej April.

– Ale nie chcę ściągać wzorów z tych fotografii – zastrzegła się Joanna. – Wolę, żebyśmy stworzyły coś oryginalnego. – Znowu głośno się roześmiała. – Dobre sobie! Jeszcze się na nic nie zgodziłaś, a ja już uznałam, że mam twój talent do dyspozycji.

April tylko się uśmiechnęła.

– Mąż i ja hodujemy orchidee – podjęła Joanna – dlatego chciałabym mieć na ścianach wzór kwiatowy. Trochę jakby orchidee wyrastały z muszli i kamieni, nie wiem, czy dobrze to ujmuję?

April upiła łyk herbaty i zdecydowanym ruchem odstawiła filiżankę.

– Pokażę ci swoje portfolio – oznajmiła. – Zyskasz pojęcie o moich pracach.

– Z przyjemnością.

– Zaraz wrócę.

Gdy April wyszła z saloniku, Joanna dostrzegła na ścianie akwarele, na które wcześniej nie zwróciła uwagi. Wstała, by przyjrzeć im się z bliska. Były to scenki z natury, krajobrazy przedstawiające plażę, wydmy i morze. Na paru innych widniały tutejsze góry.

April wróciła z dużym, oprawionym w skórę albumem.

– O, widzę, że odkryłaś moje hobby – uśmiechnęła się do Joanny oglądającej akwarelki. – A w każdym razie jedno z nich.

– Są śliczne – odrzekła Joanna. – Mają mnóstwo wdzięku.

– Dziękuję. – April obrzuciła obrazki krytycznym spojrzeniem, niepozbawionym wręcz matczynej czułości. – Teraz pracuję nad roślinami. Maluję miejscową florę. Jeśli będziesz chciała, mogę ci później pokazać kilka obrazków.

– Chętnie obejrzę – przystała Joanna z ochotą. – Uwielbiam szkice kwiatów. Nawet mam przy sobie kilka... Zostawiłam w samochodzie. Prosto od ciebie jadę oddać je do oprawienia.

– Niektóre prace rzeczywiście warto oprawić... – April położyła album na stole. – Chodź, pokażę ci, co robiłam z otoczaków i muszli.

Usiadły obie na kanapie, gospodyni otworzyła portfolio i kartka za kartką pokazywała Joannie zdjęcia oraz szkice.

– Fantastyczna! – wykrzyknęła Joanna, wskazując ścieżkę ogrodową z gładkich kamyków poukładanych starannie w zawiły wzór.

– Mnie też się podoba – przyznała April. – Jak widzisz, muszli używałam niewiele i to w większości na zewnątrz... Tarasy, ściany, ścieżki, fontanny... Ale spora część moich prac jest dokładnie w tym stylu, o jaki ci chodzi. Najpierw ogólny zarys, potem wypełnienie go konkretnymi wzorami. Czasami z płytek ceramicznych, innym razem z kamienia. Surowiec zależy wyłącznie od wymagań klienta. – Podniosła wzrok na Joannę. – Dlatego mam pewność, że z otoczaków i muszli także potrafię stworzyć coś godnego uwagi. Zrobiłam kiedyś pokój mniej więcej w takim stylu, o jakim mówisz, ale nie mam zdjęć.

– Dlaczego?

– Mój zleceniodawca, prawdziwy krezus z Los Angeles, nie życzył sobie fotografowania gotowego dzieła. Nie chciał, żeby pomysły gdzieś „przeciekły", jak to ujął. Zdaje się, że miał na tym tle lekką obsesję.

– Człowiek nigdy nie wie, na kogo trafi – zauważyła Joanna filozoficznie.

– To prawda – zgodziła się April.

Joanna znów pochyliła się nad portfolio.

– Tu styl neoklasyczny, tam barok, gdzieniegdzie nawet rokoko...

– Klient płaci, klient wymaga – odparła April z uśmiechem. – Ale zawsze daję z siebie, ile tylko mogę. Staram się podsuwać możliwie najlepsze rozwiązania.

– Bardzo mi się podobają twoje prace – oświadczyła Joanna. – Mogłabym się nimi zachwycać od rana do wieczora, ale pewnie i tak nie powiedziałabym ci nic nowego. – Zamilkła, i upiła łyk herbaty. – Czy zajmiesz się moją grotą? – spytała poważnie.

– Z przyjemnością. – April pokiwała głową. – Ale zanim zacznę na serio myśleć o projekcie, chciałabym obejrzeć budynek.

– Fantastycznie! – ucieszyła się Joanna. – Jestem pewna, że stworzysz ósmy cud świata! – Przeczesała włosy palcami, zapatrzyła się gdzieś w dal, ale szybko otrząsnęła się z zamyślenia i spojrzała na April przytomniejszym wzrokiem. – Od lat zbieram otoczaki i muszle, mam ich mnóstwo... nie do uwierzenia. – Zaśmiała się, odrzucając głowę do tyłu, i w jej fiołkowych oczach zatańczyło światło. – Jak zobaczysz, ile ich jest, pewnie uznasz, że zwariowałam. Całe góry! Mimo to zaopatrzyłam się też w katalogi wysyłkowe, więc jeśli czegoś zabraknie, będzie można zamówić.

– Oczywiście wszystko okaże się na miejscu, ale bardzo możliwe, że katalogi się przydadzą. Pewnie trzeba będzie więcej materiału, niż się spodziewasz. Przede wszystkim jednak muszę obejrzeć budynek.

– Zajrzyj, kiedy zechcesz – zaproponowała natychmiast Joanna. – Choćby jutro. Chciałabym ruszyć z pracami jak najszybciej. Oczywiście – zmitygowała się – jeśli jutro masz czas.

– Chodźmy do studia. – April podniosła się z kanapy. – Zerknę do kalendarza, a przy okazji rzucisz okiem na moje szkice roślin.

– Świetnie. – Joanna także wstała i poszła za gospodynią krótkim korytarzykiem.

Znalazły się w wysokim pomieszczeniu, które najwyraźniej zostało później dobudowane do właściwej bryły domu. Mogło pełnić funkcję oranżerii czy przeszklonej werandy albo czegoś na kształt ogrodu zimowego, połączonego z bawialnią czy pokojem wypoczynkowym. Miało trzy ściany ze szkła, ogromne drzwi balkonowe prowadziły wprost do ogrodu, a sufit także był niemal całkowicie przeszklony. Wyraźnie położono tu nacisk na zapewnienie jak największej ilości naturalnego światła. Pośrodku stał ogromny stół roboczy, zastawiony słoikami z najróżniejszymi narzędziami pracy artysty: pędzlami, ołówkami, piórkami, rysikami, węglem i podobnymi przyrządami. Arkusze papieru wszelkich rozmiarów leżały chyba wszędzie, gdzie tylko nie zajmowały miejsca imponujące sterty książek. W wysokich stojakach tkwiło mnóstwo zwiniętych w rolki projektów, a z każdego kącika wychylał się jakiś kwiatek w wazoniku. Na wielkich sztalugach tkwiła przypięta klipsem akwarelka, jeszcze nieskończona, a już ciesząca oko. Zarys subtelnego kwiatu.

– Jak tu miło! – zachwyciła się Joanna.

– Ten pokój jest sercem mojego domu – oznajmiła April. Zajrzała do oprawionego w skórę terminarza. Kilka chwil z uwagą studiowała notatki, wreszcie podniosła wzrok. – Jutro jestem wolna. Mogę przyjechać o dowolnej porze.

– Wobec tego, koło południa – zaproponowała Joanna. – Obejrzymy budynek i zjemy razem lunch.

– Lunch... – April wyraźnie się zawahała. Zaraz się jednak uśmiechnęła. – Właściwie... bardzo chętnie – uznała. – Czemu nie?

– W takim razie przyjedź między dwunastą trzydzieści a pierwszą, dobrze?

– Przyjadę.

– To oczywiście twoje dzieło? – upewniła się Joanna, wskazując obrazek na sztalugach.

– Tak, tak. Jak widać, jeszcze nie skończyłam... To chyba werbena... Zapisałam gdzieś pełną nazwę...

– Pięknie oddałaś szczegóły. – Joanna przyjrzała się obrazkowi z bliska. – O, a na listku siedzi robaczek! Świetne!

– Dzięki. – April się zarumieniła. – Zobacz, tu mam skończone prace. – Otworzyła na stole duży album.

Joanna uważnie przyglądała się szkicom.

– Niesamowite – stwierdziła. – Najbardziej ujmuje mnie wyobraźnia. Potrafisz nie tylko wiernie odwzorować kwiat, ale jeszcze dodać jakiś drobiazg, który przyciąga wzrok, pobudza wyobraźnię. Tu biedronka, tam kropla rosy...

– Namalowanie samego kwiatu jest najłatwiejszym etapem tworzenia – zgodziła się April. – Znacznie trudniej wzbudzić zainteresowanie patrzącego, przyciągnąć jego uwagę. Stąd te drobne dodatki.

– Bardzo dobrze się składa, że lubisz malować kwiaty – uśmiechnęła się Joanna – bo naprawdę zależy mi, żebyś uwzględniła w grocie także orchidee.

– Doskonała myśl – przyznała April.

– Miałam taką nadzieję – wyznała Joanna z mniejszą pewnością siebie. – Nie wszystkie moje pomysły się sprawdzają, ale też Ingrid Wilson zapewniła mnie, że jeśli nawet się na coś nie zgodzisz, to przynajmniej mnie zrozumiesz.

– Nie przewiduję żadnych kłopotów – oznajmiła April z promienną miną.

– Ja także nie. Widzę przecież ten dom, całe twoje otoczenie... Mamy bardzo podobny gust. A nieczęsto spotykam pokrewne dusze.

– Dziwią cię nasze podobne upodobania? – zaśmiała się April.

– Trochę tak – przyznała Joanna otwarcie. – Ingrid wspomniała, że byłaś żoną Rogera Woodwarda, więc jadąc na spotkanie z osobą, którą wybrał sławny aktor, spodziewałam się poznać kogoś... sama nie wiem, jak to powiedzieć...

– Bardziej wyrafinowanego? – April zbyła kwestię lekkim wzruszeniem ramion. – Kogoś w hollywoodzkim stylu?

Joanna poczerwieniała lekko, ale uczciwie skinęła głową.

– Rzeczywiście. Okropna jestem, prawda?

– Nie, nie. Ludzie często mają wobec mnie podobne oczekiwania. Właściwie zawsze, jeśli tylko się dowiedzą, że byłam żoną Rogera. – Rzuciła Joannie poważne spojrzenie. – Nasze małżeństwo skończyło się przed wiekami. W poprzedniej epoce. Od dawna żyję własnym życiem i jestem całkowicie zadowolona ze swojego losu.

– To cudnie – rozpromieniła się Joanna. – Chyba mało kto mógłby coś takiego powiedzieć. – Zamilkła na chwilę. – Czas już na mnie. Cieszę się, że cię poznałam i mogłam obejrzeć twój dom.

– Bardzo mi miło. – April uśmiechnęła się lekko.

Razem wróciły do salonu. Joanna zarzuciła torbę na ramię.

– Zostawić ci zdjęcia czy zabrać?

– Jeśli możesz, zostaw. Chętnie je poprzeglądam.

– Dobrze. – Joanna podeszła do drzwi wyjściowych i w progu jeszcze się odwróciła. – Do jutra.

– Do zobaczenia.

– Dzięki za wszystko.

– Nie ma za co, naprawdę. – April zamknęła za gościem drzwi. Jakiś czas przyglądała się przez okno Joannie, która ostrożnie stawiała pierwsze kroki na wąskich deskach, kurczowo trzymając się poręczy.

Przemiła z niej kobieta, pomyślała. Chociaż trochę dziwaczna. A pomysły ma zaskakujące. Innymi słowy: przemiła dziwaczka.

Pokręciła głową w zamyśleniu.

Nawet nie podejrzewała, do jakiego stopnia nowa znajoma odmieni jej życie.

* * *

Joanna dotarła wreszcie do mercedesa, przechyliła się nad fotelem kierowcy i położyła torbę na miejscu dla pasażera. Otworzyła drzwi i z ulgą wsunęła się za kierownicę. Odrzuciła głowę do tyłu, kilka razy odetchnęła głęboko, żeby chociaż trochę uspokoić rozszalałe serce. Puls walił jej w uszach.

Powrót drewnianym mostkiem okazał się nie mniej przerażający niż pierwsze doświadczenie, na dodatek tym razem do potężnej dawki adrenaliny doszła jeszcze euforia.

Po kilku minutach zbyt szybki oddech zaczął się wyrównywać, a serce stopniowo wróciło do normalnego rytmu. Na próbę położyła ręce na kierownicy. Już nie drżały, ale za to były jak naelektryzowane. Trudno. Trzeba jechać. Zapięła pasy, wyjęła z torby okulary przeciwsłoneczne i wsunęła je na nos.

Uruchomiła silnik; potężny motor zamruczał jak wielki zadowolony kocur. Ostrożnie zawróciła na wąskiej odnodze i, rozejrzawszy się uważnie w prawo i w lewo, wyjechała na górską drogę.

Po prawej stronie wyrosła pionowa ściana góry, po lewej otworzyła się przepaść kanionu, jak gigantyczna rana w ziemi. Joanna, im dalej była od mostka, tym czuła się pewniej i nabierała szybkości. Jeździła takimi drogami całe życie i nigdy nie spowodowała wypadku. Wiatr bawił się jej włosami, to odsuwał je do tyłu, a potem znowu gładził ją nimi po twarzy. Chłodna, wonna bryza niosła ukojenie, pozwalała w całej pełni rozkwitnąć radości.

Świat Joanny nabrał ostatnio nowego wyrazu. Właściwie całe jej życie zmieniło się nie do poznania.

Roześmiała się wiatrowi w twarz i klepnęła dłonią w kierownicę.

– Człowiek nigdy nie wie, co los chowa dla niego w zanadrzu! – Patrzyła na drogę, ale właściwie jej nie widziała, ponieważ przed oczami miała smukłą postać April Woodward, jaśniejącą w promieniach słońca, zachwycającą, pełną czaru kobietę o hipnotycznych oczach barwy szylkretu, rzucających złote błyski.

Znalazłam ją, powiedziała sobie. Nareszcie ją znalazłam.

W tym momencie zdała sobie sprawę, iż sama nie wiedząc kiedy, dotarła do podnóża góry i lada moment miała się włączyć w ruch na drodze szybkiego ruchu, którą szybko dotarłaby do kolejnej górskiej serpentyny – wiodącej do jej własnego gniazda. Ale nie wybierała się jeszcze do domu. Zamierzała skręcić do miasteczka Capitola, by wstąpić do niewielkiego warsztatu, gdzie już wcześniej oddała akwarele do oprawienia. Najwyższy czas zrobić porządek z rycinami, które zabrała ze sobą w tym właśnie celu.

Ruszyła na północ, skręciła w zjazd do Capitoli i majestatycznie wjechała do nadmorskiego miasteczka, zabudowanego ciasno skupionymi wiktoriańskimi domkami o spokojnych pastelowych fasadach. Na wąskiej głównej ulicy odszukała warsztat ramiarza i zaparkowała przed wejściem. Zza siedzenia kierowcy wyciągnęła ciężką teczkę z rycinami.

Choć jej wejście do środka obwieścił dzwonek wiszący nad drzwiami, nikt się nie pojawił. Zaczęła wobec tego sama rozglądać się po zakładzie, usiłując dokonać wyboru spomiędzy setek wystawionych próbek ram. Jedne były wyeksponowane bezpośrednio na ścianach, inne przyklejone do solidnych tablic umocowanych na ciężkich obrotowych stojakach, kolejne umieszczono na planszach porozstawianych w każdym wolnym kącie. Schyliła się, by obejrzeć interesujący wzór jednej spośród wiązki listew opartych o ścianę. Nagle odniosła wrażenie, że jest obserwowana. Podniosła się i rozejrzała dokoła.

Rzeczywiście, w drzwiach wiodących na zaplecze stał Woody – młody człowiek opalony na ciemny brąz – i założywszy na piersiach muskularne ręce, bezczelnie lustrował ją wzrokiem. Joanna aż poczerwieniała z oburzenia.

Najzwyczajniej w świecie rozbierał ją spojrzeniem!

Zdarzyło się to już raz czy dwa wcześniej, ale nigdy nie robił tego aż tak otwarcie. Mogłaby się czuć wyróżniona, wyraźne pożądanie mężczyzny powinno jej schlebiać... Nic z tych rzeczy. Czuła się po prostu źle. Cóż, w każdym razie nie można było ramiarzowi odmówić biegłości w swojej sztuce.

– O, dzień dobry. Nie widziałam, kiedy pan wszedł.

– Ano, wszedłem – powiedział Woody, nie zmieniając pozycji.

– Przywiozłam sześć rycin – podjęła, wskazując pokaźną aktówkę. – Chciałabym, żeby pan je identycznie oprawił.

Woody przypomniał sobie, że pracuje w tym warsztacie.

– Pani pokaże. – Podszedł do wielkiego, jasno oświetlonego stołu. – Pani położy tutaj.

Rozłożyła na blacie ryciny i podniosła wzrok na ramiarza.

– Niebrzydkie. – Pokiwał głową, a gęste czarne loki powtórzyły jego ruch. Stanął obok Joanny i także pochylił się nad stołem. – Całkiem niezłe.

– Widzi pan, hodujemy orchidee, to nasz zawód i zarazem największe hobby, więc ryciny tym bardziej nam się podobają. Pochodzą z tysiąc osiemset piętnastego roku. Chciałabym je powiesić u męża...

Niespodziewanie poczuła na karku oddech mężczyzny. Jednocześnie zdała sobie sprawę, że niezbyt mocno, ale na pewno nie przypadkiem przesunął dłonią po jej pośladkach!

Obrzuciła go lodowatym spojrzeniem.

– Proszę tego więcej nie robić.

– A bo co? – Rozłożył dłonie gestem zranionej niewinności. – O co chodzi? Przecież nic się nie stało.

Joanna śpiesznie zebrała ryciny i wrzuciła je do aktówki.

– Zlecę tę pracę komu innemu – stwierdziła, otwierając drzwi.

– I dobrze – prychnął ramiarz, a kiedy drzwi już prawie się zamknęły, dorzucił: – Cnotka niewydymka!

Joanna szybko podeszła do samochodu, wrzuciła teczkę za siedzenie kierowcy i wsiadła.

Co za drań!

Już nie zachwycało jej wiktoriańskie piękno cichego miasteczka. Jak burza pognała do wyjazdu na drogę szybkiego ruchu.

Coś podobnego! Do tej pory nigdy się nie zachowywał tak skandalicznie!

Gnając do domu, do Aptos, stopniowo zapominała o przykrym incydencie, ponieważ wróciła myślami do April Woodward.

Ta kobieta okazała się dokładnie taka, jak powinna. Wysoka, smukła, ale nie zanadto krucha. Elegancka, lecz bez ostentacji. Z pewnością nie goniła za modą, nie wysilała się, żeby pokazać klasę. Po prostu ją miała – i już. Doskonale podcięte jasne włosy, bardziej piaskowe niż blond. Niesamowite oczy, wręcz hipnotyzujące. Rysy twarzy może nie klasycznie piękne, ale ujmujące, pełne czaru. A postawa, zachowanie, podejście do pracy! Trudno o kogoś lepszego. Natura twórcza, choć jednocześnie stojąca mocno na ziemi – a to szalenie ważna cecha u osoby, jakiej szukała Joanna.

Mimo wszystko, pomyślała, nie sposób przewidzieć, co może się stać, czy ta kobieta rzeczywiście jest najodpowiedniejsza do moich celów.

Coś jednak jej podpowiadało, że się nie rozczaruje.

Rozdział drugi

Joshua Lawrence pracował w niewielkim, oddzielonym pomieszczeniu w cieplarni, zwanym z przymrużeniem oka jaskinią rozpusty. Przysiadł na wysokim metalowym stołku, pochylony nad wielkim drewnianym stołem, aż rozjaśnione słońcem włosy opadły mu na niebieskie oczy. Zapomniał o bożym świecie, bez reszty skupiony na ważnym zadaniu.

Najpierw starannie poślinił koniec wykałaczki, obracając ją między wargami. Następnie uważnie obejrzał drewienko pod światło, trzymając je w dłoni osłoniętej cienką gumową rękawiczką.

– A teraz do dzieła – powiedział głośno.

W takich chwilach często mówił sam do siebie. Uśmiechnął się, całkowicie usatysfakcjonowany, i z zadowoleniem pokiwał głową.

Na stole przed nim stały dwie piękne orchidee, niezwykle rzadkie okazy: „Screaming Eagle" oraz druga, także z rodzaju *Paphiopedilum.* Obie zdobyły już ważne wyróżnienia. Szybkimi, delikatnymi ruchami Josh przeniósł nieco pyłku kwiatowego z jednej rośliny na drugą.

Czysty seks, pomyślał z niejakim rozbawieniem. Nie ma na świecie nic lepszego.

Cóż, w zasadzie miał rację w obu kwestiach. Właśnie zapładniał jeden z kwiatów pyłkiem drugiego.

Był to proces żmudny, wymagający ogromnej cierpliwości oraz wprawnej ręki. Ale też jedyny pozwalający krzyżować *Paphiopedilum.* Hybryd nie da się przecież uzyskać przez podział – szybką metodę skuteczną w wypadku wielu gatunków orchidei. Na szczęście ten staromodny sposób okazał się skuteczny i warto było długo czekać na ostateczny wynik, tak w każdym razie uważali Joshua Lawrence oraz jego elitarna klientela. Nowy kwiat otrzymywało się najwcześniej po sześciu, a bywało, że nawet i po dwudziestu latach.

Joshua Lawrence stworzył kilka najbardziej ekstrawaganckich orchidei na świecie. Miały one wyjątkowo piękne, błyszczące warżki, uderzającej urody okółek wewnętrzny, a także wprost nieprawdopodobną kolorystykę. Nic więc dziwnego, że jego okazy były cenione wśród kolekcjonerów na całym świecie. Choć miłośnicy tych egzotycznych roślin mieli do wyboru wiele hybryd, te od Josha cieszyły się wyjątkowym uznaniem i to zasłużenie, ponieważ wszystkie, bez wyjątku, charakteryzowały się ogromnymi kwiatami o cudnie ubarwionych listkach okwiatu, zdrowych pędach i dumnych prętosłupach. Miewały frędzelkowate działki, żyłki, cętki, prążki – a wszystko to w doskonałych kombinacjach kolorystycznych od dziewiczej bieli po smolistą czerń.

Kolejny raz poślinił wykałaczkę. Musiał zyskać pewność, że przeniósł dostatecznie dużo pyłku. Zerknął na zegarek, choć i tak doskonale wiedział, która godzina. Zbliżała się pora obiadu, a domowy interkom milczał jak zaklęty.

Dziwne. Joanna powinna się odezwać już dawno. Przecież jest punktualna, niezawodna. A już poza wszystkim, zwyczajnie lubiła patrzeć, jak zapylał kwiaty.

Zwykle gdy pracował w cieplarni na tyłach domu, jedli obiad we dwoje. Było to miejsce specjalne, oddalone od wielkich szklanych pawilonów, gdzie prowadzono masową uprawę storczyków. Właśnie tutaj, w tym rajskim zakątku sąsiadującym z domem, rosły najrzadsze, a co za tym idzie, najdroższe orchidee. Chroniły je wymyślne zamki, skomplikowany system alarmowy oraz gęsta sieć kamer wideo i czujników laserowych, działających dwadzieścia cztery godziny na dobę. Niezorientowanemu obserwatorowi takie środki ostrożności mogłyby się wydać przesadzone, jednak miały swój głęboki sens, ponieważ rośliny te warte były fortunę. Cenę pojedynczych egzemplarzy szacowano nawet na dwadzieścia pięć tysięcy dolarów, a każda sadzonka mateczna była w zasadzie bezcenna.

Joshua włączył przycisk interkomu. Raz, drugi, trzeci...

Cisza.

Co jest, do licha ciężkiego?

Skupił się znowu na orchideach i z wielką uwagą przeniósł pyłek ze „Screaming Eagle" na drugi okaz *Paphiopedilum*. Po kilku minutach, całkowicie usatysfakcjonowany, zakończył pracę nad tymi dwoma egzemplarzami. Wyprostował się i przeciągnął, wyciągając na boki mocne, opalone na głęboki brąz ramiona, aż zatrzeszczało mu w stawach.

Sięgnął do interkomu i znowu włączył przycisk.

Nadal cisza.

Cholera. Nawet Connie nie odbiera?

Odstawił zapyloną orchideę i przysunął do siebie doniczkę z następną. Miał powtarzać proces zapylania roślin z kilkoma egzemplarzami *Paphiopedilum*. Z niewielkiego pojemnika wyjął czystą wykałaczkę, wetknął ją w usta.

Gdzie ta Joanna?

Ostatnio w ogóle zachowywała się dziwnie. Stale była jakaś taka nieobecna i zamyślona... Czyżby coś ukrywała? Znikała gdzieś na całe godziny, nic nikomu nie mówiąc... Potrafiła się nawet rozzłościć na Connie...

Tak. Rzeczywiście coś musiało być bardzo nie w porządku, ponieważ Joanna Lawrence nigdy nie zachowałaby się niegrzecznie w stosunku do Connie Cespedes, niezależnie od humoru, fatalnego dnia czy przykrego pośpiechu. Dziewczyna była nieomal członkiem rodziny, a Joanna ją uwielbiała, między innymi za sprawą przekonania, iż właśnie ludziom takim jak Connie ten kraj zawdzięczał swoją wielkość.

Josh przyjrzał się w ostrym świetle wykałaczce i rozpoczął na nowo proces zapylania, usiłując się skupić na orchideach. Niestety, stale rozpraszały go niespokojne myśli o żonie.

Co się z nią dzieje?

Może powodem dziwnego zachowania Joanny była jej starsza siostra Christina? Niedawno wpadła z niezapowiedzianą wizytą, krótką, lecz w najwyższym stopniu irytującą... Nie, raczej nie. Choć odwiedziny szwagierki nieodmiennie okazywały się bardzo wyczerpujące psychicznie, po jej wyjeździe oboje szybko odzyskiwali równowagę. Poza tym, kłopoty z Joanną zaczęły się dużo wcześniej.

Czy przyczyną mogły być troski finansowe? Powodziło im się całkiem nieźle, choć w interesach, jak to w interesach, bywały okresy lepsze i gorsze. Ostatnio musieli się zmagać z braćmi Rossi, ich głównymi konkurentami, którzy dokładali wszelkich starań, by wykupić firmę. Bracia, pozbawieni skrupułów, gotowi byli zaprzedać duszę diabłu, byle przejąć ziemię i szklarnie Lawrence'ów.

Znowu wyrwało mu się ciężkie westchnienie.

A może to jakiś drobiazg? Na przykład... może powinna się zająć jakimś nowym projektem? Nigdy jej nie wystarczał dom i pomaganie Joshowi w prowadzeniu interesu. Zawsze szukała innych wyzwań. O, choćby ten przepiękny album o orchideach, który został ciepło przyjęty zarówno przez odbiorców, jak i krytykę. Skończyła go jednak już kilka miesięcy temu... Aha, czyli możliwe, że po prostu brak jej nowego pasjonującego zajęcia.

Wolno pokręcił głową.

Nie, nie. To nie to. Niemożliwe. Takie rozwiązanie byłoby zbyt proste. Na dodatek – trzeba także o tym pamiętać – ostatnio... od jakichś dwóch, może trzech miesięcy, wydawała się niespecjalnie zainteresowana seksem... Owszem, nie burczała na Josha, jak na Connie, ale też go nie pragnęła. W każdym razie nie tak jak dawniej.

Wyjął z ust wykałaczkę, uważnie obejrzał ją w mocnym świetle i ponownie zajął się orchideami.

A może się jej znudziłem? Czyżbyśmy przechodzili osławiony kryzys po siedmiu latach związku? Eeee, nie... to się przytrafia chyba tylko mężczyznom? Zresztą, byli małżeństwem od dziesięciu lat. Hmmm... Kryzys po dziesięciu latach?

Nie umiał określić przyczyny swojego niepokoju, ale był niezbicie przekonany, iż dzieje się coś bardzo złego. Odsunął zapyloną orchideę i wziął następną.

A może wszystko przez to, że jesteśmy bezdzietni? Kto wie?

Oboje chcieli mieć dzieci, ale zbyt długo zwlekali z realizacją planów. Gdy jakiś czas temu Joanna odstawiła tabletkę antykoncepcyjną – ich starania spełzły na niczym. Oczywiście zgłosili się do lekarza, przeszli wszelkie badania – i uzyskali orzeczenie, iż są całkowicie zdrowi. Cóż z tego, skoro nic się nie zmieniło. A teraz Joanna najwyraźniej nawet nie miała ochoty próbować!

Nagle pojawiła się myśl zdradziecka jak jadowity wąż.

Joanna znalazła sobie kogoś innego.

Josh ukrył twarz w dłoniach, zabezpieczonych lateksowymi rękawiczkami. Tyle lat wspólnego szczęścia. Pokochał ją od pierwszego wejrzenia, nie umiał żyć bez tej pięknej kobiety, beztroskiej i zabawnej, choć jednocześnie praktycznej i twardo stąpającej po ziemi. Ona także pokochała go od razu. Tak w każdym razie zawsze mówiła. A mijające lata scementowały ich miłość. Stali się nierozłącznymi kochankami, partnerami, prawdziwymi przyjaciółmi.

Co się więc teraz dzieje?

Ciszę spowijającą cieplarnię przerwał dzwonek telefonu. Joshua chwycił słuchawkę.

– Halo?

– Mówi Carl – odezwał się w słuchawce głos z hiszpańskim akcentem.

Joshua zaniepokoił się nie na żarty. Skoro dzwonił Carl, musiało się zdarzyć coś wyjątkowo ważnego i najprawdopodobniej złego.

– O co chodzi?

– Powinieneś tu przyjechać. Jak najszybciej.

– Ale o co chodzi?

– Coś niedobrze z nawilżaczami – wyjaśnił Peruwiańczyk. – Nie wiem, albo komputer, albo co?

– Cholera! – zaklął zdenerwowany Joshua.

Rzucił słuchawkę, w pośpiechu ściągnął rękawiczki i pognał do samochodu.

Rozdział trzeci

Christina Cameron von Leydon leżała na chłodnych gładkich prześcieradłach. Jedwabna narzuta ledwo osłaniała jej pełne piersi i ześlizgiwała się pomiędzy jędrnymi opalonymi udami. Podłogę w obszernej sypialni, wyłożoną marmurem, przykrywał aubusson, utkany ręcznie wełniany dywan w kolorze kości słoniowej przełamanej różem.

Drzwi łazienki zostały lekko uchylone.

Uśmiechnęła się z zadowoleniem. Za tymi drzwiami był on. Nie mogła się doczekać, kiedy wróci do sypialni.

W jednej dłoni trzymała dunhilla, w drugiej wódkę z tonikiem. Pociągnęła łyk i odstawiła szklaneczkę na nocny stolik. Zaciągnęła się papierosem. Wolną dłonią poprawiła włosy. Balejaż kosztował fortunę.

– Co najmniej tuzin różnych odcieni blondu i srebra! – oznajmiłaby z dumą, gdyby ją ktoś o to zapytał.

Normalnie miała włosy nieskazitelnie ułożone, teraz jednak po fryzurze zostało tylko smętne wspomnienie. Podobnie makijaż, który w miarę upływu lat nakładała coraz staranniej, w tej chwili stanowczo wymagał dłuższej chwili uwagi.

Nieważne. Naprawdę. Tego dnia nie liczyły się podobne drobiazgi. Ponieważ za owe mankamenty, za te rozczochrane włosy i niedoskonały makijaż odpowiedzialny był on. On – ze swoim niezaspokojonym apetytem na jej ciało.

Westchnęła z rozkoszą.

Wszystkie te seanse jogi, ci osobiści trenerzy, dwa liftingi twarzy, powiększenie piersi, a potem ich zmniejszenie, niezliczone kilometry na domowej bieżni i stacjonarnym rowerze, nie wspominając już o ciągłej diecie – wszystko to bezdyskusyjnie się opłacało. Christina miała trzydzieści sześć lat, a ciało nadal młode i zniewalające.

Nawet dla takiego mężczyzny, jak Peter Rossi, pomyślała.

Nareszcie wyszedł z łazienki. Widok jego ciała, muskularnego, prężnego, pięknie opalonego, także nie sprawiał przykrości. Peter Rossi, wysoki i szczodrze wyposażony przez naturę, miał czarne włosy, ciemnobrązowe błyszczące oczy i był próżny, ponieważ doskonale znał swoje zalety.

Dumnym krokiem podszedł do łóżka, napawając się wyraźnym zachwytem kochanki.

Christina pośpiesznie zgasiła papierosa. Usiadła, zsunęła nogi, objęła Petera w biodrach i wpiła palce w jego twarde pośladki.

– Eeech, laluniu – westchnął. – Niezła jesteś.

Zakrył jej piersi wielkimi dłońmi, ścisnął w palcach brodawki. Po chwili przesunął ręce na pośladki Christiny, wreszcie wsunął je między uda.

Christina poddała mu się całkowicie, pozwalając na wszystko. Zgadzała się, by jego dłonie błądziły, gdzie zechcą, by docierały do najtajniejszych zakamarków jej ciała. Oboje oddychali głośno. W pewnym momencie Peter odsunął się od Christiny, położył ją na łóżku. Przez tę chwilę już zaczęła tęsknić za jego dotykiem, już pragnęła go w sposób trudny do wyrażenia. Popatrzył na nią z góry, uśmiechnięty i zadowolony z siebie, potem ukląkł między jej nogami. Pochylił się, wsunął dłonie pod pośladki Christiny, przeciągnął językiem najpierw po jednym udzie, później po drugim, wreszcie uniósł jej biodra w górę. Christina jęczała i wiła się pod nim, dręczona pożądaniem, drżała i dygotała, wczepiła się palcami w jego czarne gęste włosy.

Peter usiadł prosto. Christina jęknęła, niezadowolona, że została pozbawiona ulubionej przyjemności, ale rozczarowanie nie trwało długo. Zobaczyła nad sobą muskularny tors, przez chwilę widziała też imponujących rozmiarów członek, ale już moment później Peter wszedł w nią wyjątkowo głęboko i zaczął poruszać się rytmicznie, jak szaleniec opętany tylko jedną myślą.

Christina, rozpalona jego żądzą, odpowiadała mu z całej siły, napierała na niego całym ciałem, aż w szaleńczym pędzie wspólnie osiągnęli szczyt. Peter krzyknął chrapliwie, ona natomiast pojękiwała, zalewana kolejnymi falami rozkoszy.

Wreszcie Peter opadł na nią i oboje walczyli o oddech, krańcowo wyczerpani, zroszeni potem, niezdolni do najmniejszego wysiłku.

– O, Boże... – wychrypiała Christina. – Peter, to było... niesamowite!

Przycisnął ją do siebie, trzymając za pośladki, i przetoczył się na bok. Pokrył jej twarz pocałunkami. Ciągle jeszcze miał nierówny oddech.

– Jezu! Christino! – wykrztusił w końcu. – Nie wiedziałem... Nie spodziewałem się, że może być lepiej niż poprzednio.

Roześmiała się lekko, mile połechtana jego słowami, zadowolona i spełniona.

– Ja też nie – przyznała.

Pocałował ją namiętnie w usta, powoli się z niej wycofując. Podparł się ramieniem, drugim objął Christinę i zajrzał jej w oczy.

– Prawdziwa diablica z ciebie – stwierdził.

– To świetnie, bo sam jesteś diabłem wcielonym.

Sięgnął nad nią i z nocnego stolika wziął papierosa. Zapalił go i podał Christinie.

– Dzięki.

Drugiego przypalił dla siebie. Głęboko zaciągnął się dymem i wydmuchnął siwą strugę w stronę sufitu.

– Ten twój były ma nie po kolei w głowie – uznał. – Po cholerę szukał innej?

– Ty mi to powiedz. – Christina wzruszyła ramionami. – Ja nie mam bladego pojęcia. – Wypuściła obłoczek dymu. – Wiem natomiast, że był takim samym łobuzem jak poprzedni, więc życzę mu szczęścia w życiu z tą podłą dziwką, bo zapłacił za nie fortunę.

Peter zaśmiał się krótko.

– Puściłaś go w skarpetkach?

– Jasne! Tak samo jak dwóch poprzednich.

– No i bardzo dobrze!

– Nie masz pojęcia, jak się cieszę, że się poznaliśmy – powiedziała. – Już myślałam, że ten weekend u Joanny pobije wszelkie rekordy nudy.

– Ja też nie narzekam – odrzekł Peter. Zgasił papierosa i zakrył pierś Christiny wielką dłonią. – Będzie z nas dobrana para.

– Na pewno, ale pamiętaj, musimy dotrzymać tajemnicy. – Przesunęła ustami po muskularnej klatce piersiowej mężczyzny.

– Co prawda, to prawda – zgodził się Peter. – Tym lepsza zabawa.

Dłoń Christiny powędrowała w dół. Jej partner natychmiast zareagował na dotyk.

– Hej, hej, hej! – Przykrył dłoń Christiny swoją. – Lepiej nie zaczynaj. Przecież wiesz: nie dość że mam spotkanie w Santa Barbara, to jeszcze kupę telefonów do odwalenia.

– Tak, tak, wiem – mruknęła nadąsana Christina.

– Nie martw się, laluniu. Wrócę wieczorem. Jeśli jeszcze będziesz mnie chciała. – W szerokim uśmiechu pokazał wszystkie zęby.

Żartobliwie szturchnęła go w pierś.

– Żebyś tylko się nie spóźnił!

* * *

Christina przede wszystkim wzięła gorącą, pachnącą kąpiel. Następnie starannie nałożyła makijaż, na koniec owinęła się długim jedwabnym szlafrokiem. Napełniła ponownie szklaneczkę wódką z tonikiem i stojąc na środku wspaniałego salonu w pięknym domu w stylu neoklasycznym, wolno popijała drinka. Przez szerokie balkonowe drzwi, ozdobione połyskującymi, suto marszczonymi firankami z jedwabiu, rozpościerał się wspaniały widok na odległy Pacyfik. Bliżej pieściła oko soczysta zieleń doskonale utrzymanych trawników, nieskazitelna biel ogrodowych rzeźb i przejrzysty błękit ogromnego basenu, gdzie nad brzegiem wspierał się na kolumienkach wdzięczny domek. O tak, widok był piękny, wart ceny, jaką musiała zapłacić za rezydencję na szczycie wzgórza w ekskluzywnym Montecito. Napawał spokojem, leczył rany po najnowszym rozwodzie.

Cóż za godny pozazdroszczenia zbieg okoliczności, pomyślała. Jak wspaniale się stało, że Peter przyjechał do Santa Barbara w interesach. Dzięki temu pomógł jej się otrząsnąć z niemiłych przejść. I to jak!

Akurat dzisiaj przyszło z sądu oficjalne orzeczenie o rozwodzie. Od dzisiaj była znowu kobietą wolną. Mąż numer trzy przeszedł do historii. Oskubała skurczysyna do czysta! I bardzo dobrze.

Odetchnęła głęboko i podeszła do miękkiego szezlongu krytego jedwabiem w kolorze ecru. Zrzuciła z niego poduszkę i wygodnie się ułożyła. Pociągnęła długi łyk ze szklanki, po czym odstawiła ją na stolik Giacomettiego, wyczarowany z mosiądzu i szkła. Wtedy dojrzała na blacie orchideę, urzekającą swą egzotyczną urodą. Od Joanny, rzecz jasna. Dla poprawienia nastroju.

Cóż, tym razem nie potrzebowała pociechy. Z całą pewnością. Tym razem jej się poszczęściło. Gdyby sprawy przybrały taki sam obrót jak przy poprzednich dwóch rozwodach, rzeczywiście narzekałaby na samotność i nudę, nieodłącznie związane z przykrym rozstaniem, musiałaby walczyć z poczuciem porażki, które ogarniało ją, gdy sobie uświadamiała, że małżeństwo się rozpada. Tym razem jednak, dzięki Bogu, sytuacja wyglądała zupełnie inaczej, gdyż w najwłaściwszym momencie pojawił się Peter Rossi.

Na samą myśl o tym przystojniaku krew zawrzała jej w żyłach. Miał przynajmniej dwa metry wzrostu, idealne ciało byłego zawodnika futbolu – jędrne, umięśnione, o doskonałych proporcjach – czarne włosy oraz ciemnobrązowe oczy. Młodzieniec tuż przed czterdziestką. Wiedziała, że nie pochodził z dobrej rodziny, ale wiedziała też, że twardo i bezpardonowo prowadził swoje interesy, miał wielkie ambicje, władzę, a jego fortuna stale rosła. Nie miał natomiast żadnych skrupułów. Tak, tak. O tym także wiedziała. Z całą pewnością nie był tak zwanym dobrym człowiekiem. Dla Christiny jednak pieniądze, władza i brak skrupułów stanowiły potężny afrodyzjak. Nie potrafiła się oprzeć takiemu mężczyźnie.

A do tego wszystkiego, pomyślała z krzywym uśmiechem, Peter Rossi był głównym przeciwnikiem jej siostry i szwagra. Bali się go jak diabeł święconej wody. I słusznie. Ponieważ bracia Rossi, startując praktycznie od zera, zbudowali potężne imperium, a teraz ostrzyli sobie zęby na firmę Joanny i Josha.

Christina uśmiechnęła się w rozmarzeniu. Peter Rossi powinien być dla niej owocem zakazanym, więc doprawdy trudno o coś smaczniejszego dla złaknionej kobiety.

Podnosząc szklaneczkę, raz jeszcze przyjrzała się roślinie na stoliku. *Paphiopedilum lowii.* Orchidea, rzecz jasna. Jakże by inaczej. Prezent typowy dla Joanny.

Leniwym ruchem zerwała kwiat o efektownych różowych płatkach poznaczonych tu i ówdzie zieloną siatką żyłek, a gdzie indziej nakrapiany fioletowymi plamkami.

Ładny gest ze strony Joanny, pomyślała.

Choć przecież Joanna doskonale wiedziała, że Christina nie przepada za orchideami. Kojarzyły jej się z dzieciństwem i wczesną młodością, z cuchnącym nawozem, a także dwiema jednakowo silnymi obsesjami ojca: na temat orchidei oraz ziemi.

Aż się wzdrygnęła.

Ależ my jesteśmy różne! Joanna właściwie zawsze zgadzała się z ojcem, uwielbiała te nieszczęsne kwiaty. Podobało jej się życie w dziurze zabitej dechami odległej o lata świetlne od rzeczywistości

Christiny. Kochała dom ojca, uwielbiała zajmować się rodzinnym interesem.

Joanna. Siostra, która zawsze miała wszystko, czego dusza zapragnie. Wszystko, o czym mogłaby marzyć kobieta. Uderzająco piękna, mądra, bogata. O tak. Nie tak bogata jak ja, ale zawsze miała pieniędzy w bród. I ten piękny dom... choć nie został zbudowany w tak atrakcyjnym miejscu... A przede wszystkim - Josh. Właśnie. Miała Joshuę Lawrence'a, wysokiego, dobrze zbudowanego przystojniaka o włosach rozjaśnionych słońcem i nieprawdopodobnie błękitnych oczach. Mężczyznę idealnego. Prawdziwego mężczyznę, a nie cherlawą namiastkę samca pozującego na macho.

Christina wyciągnęła się na szezlongu. Wzrok miała wciąż skierowany na kwiat, ale tak naprawdę już go nie widziała.

Zawsze skrycie zazdrościła siostrze udanego związku.

Cóż, wreszcie nie mam powodu do zawiści, pomyślała. Ani trochę. Ponieważ Joshua Lawrence w porównaniu z Peterem Rossim zasługuje co najwyżej na miano towaru z drugiej ręki. Owszem, ma klasę, ale klasa to jeszcze nie wszystko. A z pewnością nic nie kręci tak, jak kasa i władza. Albo szatański spryt.

Bezmyślnie skubała orchideę, rozmyślając o Joannie i Joshu, o ich farmie, o rodzinnym biznesie, który kiedyś stanowił własność ojca.

Coś mi się zdaje, że po śmierci tatuśka dałam się wystawić do wiatru, uznała. Dostałam tylko pieniądze, cała reszta przypadła Joannie. Wtedy wydawało się, że to niezły układ, ale teraz... Hm... Zasługuję na więcej. Z pewnością należy mi się część ziemi i udział w zyskach.

Spojrzała na orchideę przytomniejszym wzrokiem. Kolorowe płatki utworzyły na blacie stolika żałosną stertkę, kilka spadło na podłogę. Nawet nie wiedziała, kiedy oskubała łodygę.

Tak, zdecydowała stanowczo. Najwyższy czas odkroić sobie kawałek tortu, którym tak hojnie obdarowano siostrzyczkę. Z pomocą odpowiedniego mężczyzny... kto wie, co się może zdarzyć.

Rozdział czwarty

Szklarnia przypominała amazońską dżunglę: było tu ciepło, wietrznie i wilgotno, ale nawet ciężki i cierpki zapach nawozu nie robił już na Joshu żadnego wrażenia. Czegoś wszakże brakowało. Tego jednego istotnego elementu, ważnego składnika, którego brak mógł spowodować zmarnowanie roślin wartych setki tysięcy dolarów.

Para!, uświadomił sobie Joshua ponuro. Zniknęła cała mgła!

Włączane przez skomplikowany program komputerowy nawilżacze miały za zadanie w najodpowiedniejszych momentach spryskiwać rośliny tropikalnym deszczem, a jednocześnie wytwarzały wilgoć niezbędną im do życia. Teraz – nie działały. Zepsuły się albo może zostały celowo uszkodzone. Co gorsza, nie wiadomo kiedy. Na pewno w czasie weekendu, między piątkowym popołudniem a poniedziałkowym rankiem. W najgorszej wersji brak owej wyjątkowej tropikalnej atmosfery mógł już zniszczyć drogocenne rośliny.

Joshua obszedł całą szklarnię, uważnie obejrzał kwiaty, sprawdzając, ile ucierpiały.

– Akurat w ten weekend wyjątkowo tu nie zajrzałem, bo zajmowaliśmy się Christiną! Szlag! – Skończył inspekcję i popatrzył na ogrodnika. – Jakoś przetrwały. Wiesz, Carl, chyba tym razem mieliśmy trochę szczęścia.

– Najwyraźniej – mruknął Carl Cespedes.

Główny ogrodnik, odpowiedzialny za stan szklarni, był niezwykle wysokim, potężnie zbudowanym Peruwiańczykiem. Pochodził z kalifornijskiego miasta Indio. Szedł teraz za Joshem krok w krok. Na jego twarzy, zwykle przypominającej maskę, malowała się niekłamana troska. Opiekował się szklarniami jak własnymi, a weekendowy wypadek zaskoczył go w tym samym stopniu co Josha.

Sprawdzili system nawilżający pod kątem usterek mechanicznych i nie znaleźli nic. Wobec czego włączyli ponownie komputerowy program zraszania, a wówczas skomplikowane urządzenie natychmiast podjęło pracę, nie wykazując żadnych usterek. Ewidentnie wina leżała po stronie komputera. Albo z bliżej nieokreślonych powodów sam przestał działać, albo ktoś celowo go zresetował, w nadziei że orchidee uschną.

– Bóg łaskaw, że żaluzje działają – westchnął Josh. – W przeciwnym razie szkody byłyby niewyobrażalne.

Carl znowu mruknął potakująco. Obrzucił badawczym spojrzeniem żaluzje zamontowane na dachu szklarni. Miały one za zadanie imitować cień rzucany przez płynące po niebie chmury. Gdyby i osłony przestały się przesuwać, orchidee byłyby zbyt mocno nasłonecznione lub niedoświetlone.

– Wystarczyłaby jedna taka solidna wpadka, żebyśmy przestali istnieć na rynku – zauważył Josh. – A bracia Rossi tylko na to czekają. Wcale bym się nie zdziwił, gdyby mieli swój udział w tej awarii.

– Nadal chcą przejąć wasz interes?

– Jak najbardziej. I nic ich nie zniechęci. – Josh ruszył z powrotem do drzwi. – Po prostu zawzięli się na nas. – Joshua zamarł w pół kroku. – Zaraz, a może to rzeczywiście ich sprawka? – Gwałtownie odwrócił się do Carla. – Ale jakim cudem dobraliby się do komputera? Chwileczkę, czy Miguel coś słyszał albo widział?

– Nie. – Carl pokręcił głową. – Jak tylko się zorientowałem, że nawilżacze nie działają, zadzwoniłem do niego i spytałem. Nic nie widział, nic nie słyszał.

– Cholera jasna! – zaklął Josh. – Nic z tego nie rozumiem. Trzeba ściągnąć ekipę, która instalowała urządzenia, no i w końcu pewnie będziemy musieli wezwać policję.

– Po co gliny? – zdziwił się Carl.

– Co prawda nie znaleźliśmy śladów włamania, ale mogliśmy coś przeoczyć. Policyjni fachowcy mają swoje sposoby.

– No tak – zgodził się Carl, choć nie wierzył w taką możliwość. Jego zdaniem policjanci nie byli zdolni znaleźć niczego, czego on sam nie odkrył. Niezależnie od tego, jak bardzo by się starali.

– Aha, i zadzwoń do Miguela – polecił Joshua. – Chciałbym go wypytać.

– Już go ściągnąłem – odrzekł Carl. – Czeka w biurze.

– Czytasz w moich myślach – ucieszył się Josh. – Dzięki! – Przyśpieszył kroku. – Gdyby ktoś coś ode mnie chciał – rzucił przez ramię – to wiesz, gdzie mnie szukać.

Carl, jak to Carl, skinął głową w milczeniu.

Joshua ruszył biegiem w stronę okazałego wiktoriańskiego budynku. Dziewiętnastowieczny dom był biały, suto zdobiony wszelkimi elementami charakterystycznymi dla minionej epoki, przez co natychmiast przywodził na myśl tort weselny. Między szklarniami naszpikowanymi najnowszą technologią wydawał się wręcz nie na miejscu.

Zbudowali go przodkowie ojca Joanny, Cameronowie, którzy żyli z uprawy setek hektarów brązowej ziemi. Najpierw mieli brukselkę i truskawki, później karczochy. Wielu okolicznych farmerów na tym poprzestało, natomiast Mitchell Cameron, ojciec Joanny, poszedł inną drogą. Zakochał się w orchideach, wręcz padł ofiarą orchideomanii, zjawiska dość szeroko rozpowszechnionego w wiktoriańskiej Anglii. Choć był niepoprawnym romantykiem i marzycielem, wykazał się niezwykłym zmysłem praktycznym: już jako nastolatek kupował rośliny mateczne, wkrótce też postawił niewielką szklarnię i rozpoczął krzyżowanie gatunków, tworzenie nowych odmian. Gdy odziedziczył po ojcu farmę, zrezygnował z dotychczasowych upraw i całkowicie poświęcił się orchideom. Po kilku latach pieniądze zaczęły do niego płynąć szerokim strumieniem.

Wtedy poprosił o rękę prześliczną Julię Lenoir. Znali się od dziecka, gdyż dziewczyna mieszkała na sąsiedniej farmie. Julia chętnie przyjęła oświadczyny i wkrótce młodzi małżonkowie rozpoczęli budowę nowego, wymarzonego domu, zaprojektowanego z rozmachem w stylu McKim, Mead and White. Postawili go wyżej, na stokach pasma Santa Cruz, skąd roztaczał się niezrównany widok, gdzie wiała chłodna bryza, wolna od ciężkiej woni kompostu, nawozów sztucznych, środków owadobójczych i samych kwiatów.

Teraz mieszkali w nim Joanna i Josh, a w starym wiktoriańskim domu, idąc za przykładem Mitchella Camerona, pozostawili składy, magazyny i biuro.

Joshua dwoma susami pokonał drewniane schody prowadzące na ganek, pchnął połówkę dwuskrzydłowych drzwi i wpadł do przestronnego holu. Tam za biurkiem siedziała Luna, żona Carla. Ramieniem przyciskała do ucha słuchawkę i z zacięciem stukała w klawiaturę komputera. Josh zawsze się zastanawiał, jakim cudem wciska właściwe klawisze, mając tak długie paznokcie. Zwykle malowała je na ciemny fiolet. Była w połowie Wenezuelką, w połowie Żydówką, ale urodziła się w Stanach, więc miała amerykańskie obywatelstwo. Carl ożenił się z tą sekutnicą wyłącznie po to, by do-stać zieloną kartę. Od dnia, kiedy się poznali, darli ze sobą koty, a jednocześnie jedno nie potrafiło żyć bez drugiego.

– Cześć, szefie – rzuciła z uśmiechem, podnosząc wzrok znad monitora. Między pełnymi wargami, pociągniętymi szminką w tym samym odcieniu, co lakier do paznokci, błysnęły olśniewająco białe zęby.

– Cześć, Luno. Przestań wreszcie tytułować mnie szefem – powiedział Josh. – Będziesz tak uprzejma?

– Jasne, szefie. – Luna uśmiechnęła się jeszcze szerzej. – Miguel czeka w biurze – dodała.

– Serdeczne dzięki. – Joshua westchnął i ruszył ku podwójnym szklanym drzwiom, prowadzącym do niegdysiejszego salonu.

Miguel siedział w fotelu, całkowicie pochłonięty zabawą z Lucy, biało-szarą kotką, pełnoprawną mieszkanką wiktoriańskiego domu.

Joshua usiadł za biurkiem i obrzucił stróża uważnym spojrzeniem. Miguel był niskim, żylastym Meksykaninem po trzydziestce, chyba nieco ociężałym umysłowo, ponieważ każda reakcja wymagała od niego niebagatelnego wysiłku. Syn imigrantów, pracowników fizycznych, dostał zajęcie u Josha, ponieważ nigdzie indziej nie mógł nic znaleźć. Łagodny jak baranek i ufny jak dziecko, był bezgranicznie oddany swemu chlebodawcy.

Podniósł wzrok na szefa.

– Lucy to mnie lubi. – Uśmiechnął się uszczęśliwiony. – Nawet się ze mną bawi.

– Od razu przypadłeś jej do gustu. – Joshua odchrząknął. – Słuchaj, muszę ci zadać kilka pytań na temat zeszłej nocy.

Miguel wyraźnie się przestraszył; twarz mu pobladła, oczy się zamgliły, niewiele brakowało, a byłby się rozpłakał.

– Nie denerwuj się, nic strasznego się nie stało – odezwał się Josh uspokajającym tonem. – Chciałbym tylko się dowiedzieć, czy może zwróciłeś uwagę na coś szczególnego.

Miguel gwałtownie potrząsnął głową.

– Ja nie widziałem nic a nic. W ogóle nic.

Josh dłuższą chwilę przyglądał mu się z uwagą. Co właściwie skłoniło go do zatrudnienia Miguela w charakterze nocnego stróża?

– Jesteś zupełnie pewien? – spytał. – Nie widziałeś nic dziwnego, niezwykłego, niepokojącego?

Meksykanin potrząsnął głową jeszcze gwałtowniej.

– Nic, nic. W ogóle nic.

– A może coś słyszałeś? – drążył Josh. – Coś szczególnego? Innego niż zwykle?

– Nie, nie, nie! Wcale! – Miguel zamknął oczy i nadal kręcił głową, na jego twarzy pojawił się wyraz napięcia.

Wyraźnie cierpiał, mimo to Joshua musiał zadać mu kolejne pytania. Chociaż... co to da?

Dobrze, wobec tego niech będzie tylko to jedno, absolutnie konieczne.

– Miguelu, jak sądzisz... czy istnieje możliwość... że się na chwilę zdrzemnąłeś? Noce są długie, jesteś tutaj całkiem sam, więc...

Miguel wybuchnął głośnym płaczem, aż Lucy uciekła mu z kolan.

– Nie, nie! – krzyknął. – Nigdy! Ja nigdy nie zasypiam w pracy! Nigdy!

Po jego szarych policzkach płynęły potoki łez, a Josh miał ogromną ochotę zdzielić się po głowie. Podszedł do Miguela i uspokajająco poklepał go po ramieniu.

– Nie denerwuj się. Ja tylko pytałem. – Sięgnął do pudełka z chusteczkami. – Masz, uspokój się. Nie będę cię więcej wypytywał. Słowo honoru.

Miguel wydmuchał nos w chusteczkę, a potem grzbietem brudnej dłoni otarł policzki. Podniósł na pracodawcę spojrzenie przepełnione żalem.

– Lucy ode mnie uciekła...

– Zaraz wróci – zapewnił go Joshua. Nagle wpadła mu do głowy doskonała myśl. – Słuchaj, Miguelu, a może kupiłbym ci psa? Wytresowanego. Miałbyś towarzysza w nocy. Co ty na to?

Meksykanin zesztywniał z przerażenia. Osłupiałym wzrokiem spojrzał na Josha, jak gdyby zobaczył diabła.

– Ja... ja... nie! Ja się boję psów! – Zatrząsł się cały. – Strasznie się boję!

O Jezu! To tyle, jeśli chodzi o świetne pomysły.

– Dobrze, nie ma sprawy – zapewnił Meksykanina pośpiesznie. – Przyjmijmy, że w ogóle nic na ten temat nie mówiłem. Nie chciałem ci sprawić przykrości. O, zobacz, Lucy wróciła!

Całe szczęście! W samą porę.

Podniósł kotkę i posadził ją Miguelowi na kolanach.

– Widzisz, łasi się do ciebie.

Na ustach stróża od razu pojawił się uśmiech, jasny jak słońce po burzy. Pogładził ulubienicę, pomrukując z zadowoleniem.

Josh wrócił za biurko.

Zaiste, żaden dobry uczynek nie uchodzi bezkarnie, pomyślał z goryczą. Ale psa trzeba będzie kupić. Dobra, dosyć tego.

Sięgnął po słuchawkę, lecz zaraz ją odłożył.
– Miguel?
Meksykanin podniósł na niego oczy.
– Myślę, że Lucy przyda się trochę świeżego powietrza. Przy okazji poproś, niech któryś z chłopaków podrzuci cię do domu. Powinieneś się przespać przed nocną zmianą.
– Jasne. – Miguel wyszedł, starannie zamykając za sobą drzwi.
Wtedy Joshua wybrał numer cieplarni.
– Niech ktoś odwiezie Miguela do domu – polecił, gdy Carl podniósł słuchawkę. – Jak najszybciej, dobrze? Nie chcę, żeby się tu kręcił, w razie gdyby przyjechały gliny. Jak zaczną go wypytywać, umrze ze strachu.
– Oczywiście. – Carl przerwał połączenie.
Dopiero wtedy Josh zadzwonił do firmy, która zainstalowała komputerowo sterowane nawilżacze. Mieli pierwszeństwo przed policją. Leniwie stukając ołówkiem w blat, czekał, aż ktoś odbierze.
Oby mi powiedzieli, że system zawiódł, modlił się w myślach.
Niestety, zdawał sobie sprawę, iż z ogromną dozą prawdopodobieństwa taka wersja wydarzeń okaże się tylko jego pobożnym życzeniem.

* * *

Przedstawiciele firmy konserwującej komputerowy system nawilżania przyjechali, sprawdzili, co mieli do sprawdzenia, i zniknęli. Nie znaleźli żadnych wad w aparaturze, wobec czego doszli do słusznego wniosku, iż jedyną możliwą przyczyną awarii był błąd człowieka.
– Innymi słowy – powiedział Josh – mam przez to rozumieć, że ktoś zmienił ustawienie programu.
– Tak jest. – Dwaj technicy unisono pokiwali głowami.
Wkrótce po ich odjeździe przybyła policja. Ekipa dokonała szczegółowych oględzin całego terenu ze szczególnym uwzględnieniem szklarni. Stróże prawa nie znaleźli nic.
– Czy jest pan pewien, że nikt więcej nie zna kodu do pilotów otwierających bramę? – spytali Joshuę.
– Z całą pewnością – odparł. – Tylko Carl, moja żona i ja. Nikt więcej.
Odprowadził ich do samochodu.
– Na pana miejscu – odezwał się jeden z policjantów – przyjrzałbym się uważnie pracownikom. Ta awaria robi wrażenie celowego działania.

Josh pokiwał głową i grzecznie podziękował za radę, ale w głębi duszy nie potrafił uwierzyć, by któraś z pracujących u niego osób miała cokolwiek wspólnego z przeprogramowaniem systemu komputerowego.

Przyczyna musi leżeć gdzieś indziej, pomyślał z pełnym przekonaniem. Przecież jesteśmy sobie bliscy jak rodzina.

Gdy wszyscy obcy nareszcie odjechali, usiadł z Carlem w dawnym salonie.

– Najwyraźniej będziemy musieli sprawić sobie psa – powiedział. – Liczę na twoją pomoc w przełamaniu oporów Miguela. Jeśli nam się nie uda, pomyślę chyba o zainstalowaniu kamer wideo. Albo zatrudnimy nowego stróża, a dla Miguela znajdzie się jakieś inne zajęcie.

– Zrobię, co się da – obiecał Carl. – Ale wiesz, jaki jest Miguel.

– Tak, wiem – przyznał Josh. – Rano pogadamy.

– Dobra. – Carl obrócił się z fotelem, wstał i wyszedł z biura.

Joshua właśnie miał zamiar wybrać numer Joanny, lecz akurat w tej chwili rozległ się dzwonek telefonu.

– Halo?

– Czy mówię z panem Lawrence'em? – spytał męski głos.

– Tak, to ja. – Josh wytężył słuch, bo rozmówca najwyraźniej dzwonił z telefonu komórkowego i dźwięk tonął w szumie zakłóceń.

– Tu Peter Rossi.

– Witam pana. Czy może pan mówić głośniej? Bardzo słabo słyszę.

– Jadę, stąd kłopoty – odezwał się Rossi głośniej.

– W czym mogę panu pomóc?

– Zadzwoniłem spytać, czy przypadkiem nie zmienił pan zdania na temat sprzedaży firmy. W dzisiejszych czasach prowadzenie takiego biznesu najeżone jest wieloma niebezpieczeństwami. Odpowiednia dbałość o szklarnie to nie lada wyzwanie, tak ogromna odpowiedzialność niekiedy okazuje się ponad siły. Na pewno pan ze mną się zgodzi.

Josh poczerwieniał z wściekłości, ale udało mu się odpowiedzieć spokojnie.

– Nie mogę się z panem zgodzić. Nigdy się nie uchylałem od odpowiedzialności. – Rzucił słuchawkę na widełki.

– Cholera jasna! – wyrwało mu się. – Cholera żeż jasna!

Rozdział piąty

April nalała sobie kieliszek wina. Było to stosunkowo niedrogie, ale wyborne chardonnay Alexander Valley, którego zalety odkryła całkiem niedawno. Zamieszała podgrzewany sos i uśmiechnęła się zadowolona.

Woody'emu będzie smakowało, uznała.

Zrumieniła na maśle przeciśnięty przez praskę ząbek czosnku, położyła na patelni filet z dorsza, dodała domowej roboty gęsty koncentrat pomidorowy, posypała kaparami, dołożyła zielone oliwki z odrobiną zalewy, na koniec doprawiła pieprzem, solą i wrzuciła dwa listki laurowe.

Roger, jej były mąż, zawsze powtarzał, że w głębi serca April jest wielbicielką prostego wiejskiego życia, a nic tak nie odzwierciedlało jej upodobań, jak ulubione potrawy. Zawsze wolała dania możliwie najprostsze w przygotowaniu i jak najmniej wyrafinowane, najchętniej ze świeżych, sezonowych składników. Jeśli przygotowywała coś wykwintniejszego, to wyłącznie dla Rogera, który uwielbiał przesadę we wszystkim. Jego motto brzmiało: im bardziej skomplikowane, tym lepsze. Nigdy nie dość mu było przypraw, ozdóbek i wymyślnych dodatków.

Odstawiła kieliszek na stary kuchenny sosnowy stół o zniszczonym blacie i jeszcze raz wymieszała sałatkę.

Gotowe, uznała. Pociągnęła łyk wina i wróciła do kuchenki, by spróbować sosu. Doskonały. Wyłączyła palnik. Podgrzeje sos jeszcze przez minutę, kiedy już oboje z Woodym będą gotowi do zjedzenia kolacji. Spojrzała na zegarek. Gdzie on się podziewa? Zwykle przychodził wcześniej. I zawsze zostawał do późna.

Usiadła i zaczęła przerzucać kartki czasopisma poświęconego urządzaniu ogrodów, ale myślała o Woodym.

Zawsze wywoływał na jej twarzy uśmiech. W pewnym sensie przypominał Piotrusia Pana, miał w sobie coś z pluszowego misia i uwielbiał surfing. Był od niej starszy o rok, skończył już trzydzieści trzy lata, a zachowywał się jak szesnastolatek. Przyjaźnił się z Rogerem, gdy obaj dorastali, a teraz oprawiał obrazy w Capitoli. Miał kręcone włosy do ramion, muskularne, zawsze opalone ciało, a jego olśniewająco biały uśmiech ją rozbrajał. Gdy tylko pojął, że April nie jest nim zainteresowana w ten szczególny sposób, albo może nie jest gotowa do kolejnego związku, natychmiast zrezygnował z wszelkich sztuczek i na dodatek zrobił to z ogromnym wdziękiem. Może dlatego, że był przyjacielem Rogera? A może z szacunku dla niej? Nie miała co do tego pewności, ale była mu wdzięczna, że nie próbował żadnych numerów w stylu uwodzicielskiego Casanovy albo odtrąconego absztyfikanta.

Stopniowo stał się prawdziwym kumplem, a ich znajomość pozbawiona była komplikujących życie podtekstów seksualnych. April podejrzewała, że Woody jednak wciąż miał nadzieję na coś więcej, ale też nie poganiał jej, nie namawiał i nie naciskał.

Wypiła kolejny łyk wina i zamknęła magazyn. Znowu spojrzała na zegarek.

Dlaczego się spóźnia?

Zupełnie jakby ściągnęła go myślami: akurat w tej chwili usłyszała skrzypnięcie drzwi salonu.

– April? Heeej, gdzie jesteś? – dał się słyszeć głęboki baryton.

– W kuchni!

Woody stawiał długie zręczne kroki. Ręce wsunął w kieszenie wytartych lewisów, częściowo zakrytych przez wypuszczoną luźno koszulę w krzykliwe hawajskie wzory.

– Ale pachnie! – Pociągnął nosem. W oczach rozbłysły mu psotne iskry. Pocałował April w czoło.

– Nalej sobie wina. – Chciała wstać po kieliszek.

– Siedź, sam wezmę. – Wyjął go z szafki, nalał sobie chardonnay i usiadł naprzeciwko gospodyni. – Twoje zdrowie! – powiedział, unosząc szkło.

– I twoje. – Stuknęli się lekko kieliszkami. – Jak ci minął dzień?

– Miałem co robić. – Zabębnił palcami po stole. – Mnóstwo starych zamówień, sporo nowych... Odwaliłem trochę roboty papierkowej, no wiesz. Dzień jak co dzień. – Jego dłonie znieruchomiały. – A co u ciebie?

– U mnie wręcz przeciwnie – odrzekła April z dumą.
– Tak? A co się działo?
– Rozmawiałam o dużym zleceniu z pewną kobietą, która chce, żebym dla niej zaprojektowała... coś w rodzaju groty.
– Ciekawe! – Uniósł brwi.
– Chce zaadaptować kamienny budynek dawnej stajni – uściśliła April. – Zaplanowała wnętrze z muszli i kamieni, ozdobione freskami.
– No, nieźle! Widzę, że szykuje ci się większa robota.
– Rzeczywiście.
– Podejmiesz się?
– Jeszcze nie wiem. Jadę tam jutro, obejrzeć budynek i sprecyzować, jak by to miało wyglądać... – Urwała, by napić się wina. – Jeśli okaże się, że właściwie ją zrozumiałam, a taką mam nadzieję, bo podoba mi się ten pomysł, będzie to najwspanialsze zlecenie od wieków. I największe.
– Wobec tego trzymam kciuki.
– Trzymaj, bo jest za co – zgodziła się skwapliwie. – Freski, orchidee i...
– Orchidee? – Zaalarmowany Woody podniósł pytający wzrok na April.
– Moja zleceniodawczyni i jej mąż hodują orchidee.
Woody zesztywniał.
– Jak ona się nazywa?
– Joanna Lawrence. Jest...
– Wiem, jaka jest – odparł ponuro.
– Naprawdę?
– Jak najbardziej. Robiłem coś dla niej. – Pociągnął solidny łyk wina i zdecydowanym ruchem odstawił kieliszek. – Jest taka sama jak te wszystkie bogate baby. Rozpuszczona do granic możliwości, arogancka egoistka.
– Wydała mi się całkiem miła – zaprotestowała April. – Nazwałabym ją nawet kobietą z klasą.
Woody jednym haustem opróżnił kieliszek, a potem napełnił go ponownie.
– O, to prawda – zgodził się ironicznie. – Fakt, robi wrażenie kobiety z klasą. Ale w rzeczywistości jest tylko jedną z wielu nadzianych snobek. Uwierz mi, wiem swoje, wychowałem się w tych stronach i znam takich ludzi od podszewki. Szanowna pani Joanna Lawrence pochodzi z bardzo starej rodziny, jej ojciec był strasznym ważniakiem, starsza siostra lata z przyjęcia na przyjęcie i tak dalej.

Rozumiesz, jak zacznie balować w San Francisco, to kończy w Los Angeles. A wtedy robi w tył zwrot i zaczyna kolejną rundę po imprezkach dla forsiastych nierobów.

April słuchała tej tyrady z niebotycznym zdumieniem.

– Strasznie jesteś rozgoryczony – odezwała się w końcu. – W ogóle cię nie poznaję!

– Fakt, trochę mnie poniosło. – Odetchnął głęboko. – Tak czy inaczej, muszę cię ostrzec. Bądź ostrożna, nie daj się oszukać. Na pewno będzie chciała cię wykorzystać na wszelkie możliwe sposoby. Ludzie pokroju Joanny Lawrence myślą tylko o sobie.

April uważnie przyjrzała się przyjacielowi znad kieliszka. Widywała już Woody'ego w podobnym stanie. Zdarzało mu się szukać dziury w całym, miał talent do dramatyzowania. Tym razem jednak wyczuwała w jego zachowaniu jakąś istotną odmianę.

– Będę uważać – obiecała. – Dziękuję ci za ostrzeżenie. Bogiem a prawdą, zwykle nie wiem, z kim mam do czynienia, i jakim człowiekiem jest mój klient. Niektórzy naprawdę potrafią zaleźć za skórę... I rzeczywiście, w zasadzie im bogatsi, tym gorsi i bardziej skąpi. – Pokiwała głową w zamyśleniu. – No dobrze. A teraz, niech mi pan powie, panie Pearlman, czy jest pan głodny?

– Jak wilk! – zawołał. Białe zęby, kontrastujące z opalenizną, błysnęły w szerokim uśmiechu.

– Wobec tego, nakrywaj do stołu – zarządziła April. – A ja już podaję kolację.

– Nie ma sprawy. – Wstał i sięgnął do kuchennych szafek po naczynia.

Jakiś czas później, gdy na talerzach nie zostało już nic, April oraz Woody, wygodnie rozciągnięci na sofach w saloniku, leniwie popijali kawę. W wielkim kominku wesoło trzaskał ogień, więc niestraszny był im chłód wiosennego wieczoru. Ciepły blask spowijał ich twarze, meble, ściany.

– Zgadnij, kogo spotkałem w weekend – odezwał się Woody.

– Nie wiem, nie będę zgadywać, mów.

– Davida Jarmana! – zaśmiał się Woody.

– O rany! Nie psuj mi humoru!

– Nie żartuj! Myślałem, że chętnie o nim posłuchasz. – W oczach mężczyzny zapłonęły psotne iskierki. – Przyszedł z taką laleczką... mówię ci, Barbie prosto z pudełka. Tleniony blond, duuuże niebieskie oczy, nogi do sufitu, skórzana mini do pępka... – Nie wytrzymał i roześmiał się głośno.

April mu zawtórowała.

– Chyba wreszcie znalazł kobietę doskonałą.

– Ożeni się z reklamą chirurgii plastycznej!

– I bardzo dobrze. Dostanie, na co zasłużył. Z drugiej strony, kto wie, ta dziewczyna może być całkiem miła i niegłupia.

– Ależ oczywiście – zgodził się Woody kpiąco. – Z całą pewnością.

– A ja miałam nadzieję, że David czeka na mnie... – April westchnęła z udawanym smutkiem. – Niestety, ci milionerzy z Doliny Krzemowej zawsze tak się śpieszą, prawda? Nie mają czasu porządnie się rozejrzeć dookoła, tacy są zajęci robieniem kasy... Rany! – Klepnęła się otwartą dłonią w czoło. – I pomyśleć, że ja z nim chodziłam...! Z tym... z tym wulkanem testosteronu! I to ty – oskarżycielsko wycelowała w Woody'ego palcem – ty nas sobie przedstawiłeś!

– Rzeczywiście – przyznał się bez wykrętów – ale nie wiedziałem, że będzie się do ciebie przystawiał.

– Gadaj zdrów!

– Poważnie. – Woody usiadł. – Przysięgam ci, tego nie przewidziałem. Przecież wiadomo wszem wobec, że kiedy taki rekin finansowy pojawia się w weekend na plaży, chodzi mu tylko i wyłącznie o jedno. Bez żadnych niedomówień.

– Tym bardziej dziwi mnie, że nas ze sobą poznałeś.

– A skąd miałem wiedzieć, że akurat ty wpadniesz mu w oko? – bronił się niezdarnie. – Naprawdę, gdybym wiedział, tobym cię nie wystawił, słowo.

– Dobrze już, dobrze. Mniejsza o większość. Ale wyciągnij odpowiednie wnioski na przyszłość. Do tej pory na myśl o tym facecie dostaję gęsiej skórki. – Wstrząsnęła się z obrzydzeniem. – Swoją drogą – podjęła tonem filozoficznych rozważań – ten człowiek dowiódł, iż nie trzeba być zarozumiałym hollywoodzkim aktorem o potężnie rozdętym ego, żeby być zarozumiałym i mieć potężnie rozdęte ego. Magik od bajtów i kilobajtów, zbijający gruby szmal w Dolinie Krzemowej, może być tak samo zarozumiałym facetem i mieć równie potężnie rozdęte ego. – Roześmiała się głośno. – Jeden kit.

– Nie wszyscy mężczyźni są jednakowi – stwierdził Woody.

– Wiem, wiem. Ty taki nie jesteś. W każdym razie, tak mi się wydaje. Cóż, pewnie po prostu nie spotkałam jeszcze tego właściwego... – Podniosła wzrok na przyjaciela. – Ale mam już trzydzieści dwa lata. I coraz mniejsze szanse.

Woody wstał, obszedł stolik między sofami i usiadł obok April. Skromnie cmoknął ją w czoło.

– Zawsze masz mnie – rzekł poważnie.

– Wiem, dzięki. – Ścisnęła jego silną dłoń. – Jesteś kochany.

Mimo wszystko opanowały ją niewesołe myśli.

Jakie właściwie mam szanse?, zaczęła się zastanawiać. Od czasów gimnazjum bez przerwy chodziłam na randki. W końcu znalazłam sobie męża... Teraz spotykam mężczyzn, z którymi niejedna kobieta chętnie by się umówiła, a nawet z ochotą wyszłaby za jednego z nich za mąż. Dlaczego żaden mi nie pasuje, żaden nie wydaje się odpowiedni? Czy wina leży po mojej stronie? Czy do końca życia będę sama?

Poczuła się jakoś dziwnie. Trzydzieści dwa lata – i samotna. Bez rodziny. Zostali jej tylko dalecy krewni. Bez realnych perspektyw w kwestii zamążpójścia, oczywiście, jeśli wykluczyć z tych rozważań Woody'ego. Z drugiej strony, przecież kochała niezależność, wobec czego należało się liczyć z konsekwencjami takiego stanu.

Gdzieś w głębi serca czy może duszy jakiś głos szeptał cichutko, iż niedługo jej życie się odmieni. Czy na lepsze, czy też na gorsze – nie wiedziała. Miała jednak przeczucie, że wpływ na wydarzenia nie będzie jej dany.

Rozdział szósty

Joshua wjechał na szczyt wzgórza i zatrzymał swoją żółtą toyotę na żwirowanym podjeździe przed domem. Mercedesa Joanny nie widział ani tutaj, ani w szeroko otwartym garażu, natomiast w kącie dziedzińca na swoim stałym miejscu tkwił staruteńki plymouth voyager należący do Connie. Wyłączył silnik i wyskoczył z wozu.

Connie na pewno będzie wiedziała, gdzie szukać Joanny, pomyślał.

Gdy wchodził po kamiennych schodach, poczuł oszałamiającą woń chińskiej glicynii. Akurat zaczęła kwitnąć, na pergoli biegnącej wzdłuż ściany budynku otwierały się całe pęki niebieskofioletowych groniastych kwiatostanów.

Już miał przekroczyć próg, gdy przypadkiem opuścił wzrok na buty.

– O, szlag! – wyrwało mu się.

Jak zawsze przyniósł na nich imponującą porcję błota ze szklarni, nie sposób było ich oczyścić na wycieraczce. Skręcił w lewo, zdecydowanym krokiem minął długą pergolę, dotarł do furtki, za którą wąska ścieżka prowadziła przez ogród ku bocznemu wejściu z przedsionkiem. Otwierając przeszklone drzwi, zawołał Connie. Odpowiedziała mu cisza.

Usiadł na sosnowej ławie tuż za drzwiami, rozwiązał sznurowadła, zdjął buty i skarpetki. Na bosaka ruszył korytarzem do kuchni.

– Connie! – zawołał ponownie.

I znów nie doczekał się odpowiedzi. Tutaj także nie było żywej duszy, ale przez okno dojrzał osobę, której szukał na tarasie. Przy uchu trzymała telefon komórkowy. Jakże by inaczej? Connie, podobnie jak jej szwagierka, Luna, uwielbiała ploteczki przez telefon. Z kim rozmawiała i o czym – Josh nie miał pojęcia, gdyż jego znajomość hiszpańskiego okazywała się stanowczo niewystarczająca wobec gradu słów sypiących się z szybkością pocisków wystrzeliwanych z karabinu maszynowego.

Nie chciał przeszkadzać, więc cofnął się od okna. Spojrzał na niewielką czarną tabliczkę przy lodówce, ale i tam nie dostrzegł żadnej wiadomości od Joanny. Kompletnie nic. Sięgnął do chłodziarki i wyjął butelkę białego wina. Dobrze jest przepłukać gardło, zwłaszcza po długim dniu w upalnej szklarni. Nalał sobie kieliszek i całkiem zapomniawszy o Connie, podszedł do okna.

Tym razem dostrzegła go kątem oka i natychmiast przerwała rozmowę.

– Connie, mówiłem ci tysiąc razy, że nie musisz wyłączać telefonu na mój widok – odezwał się Joshua.

– Wiem, pamiętam – odparła z lekkim obcym akcentem. – I tak już skończyłam. – Uśmiechnęła się. – Takie tam, babskie plotki. – Ściągnęła z włosów gumkę przytrzymującą koński ogon i przeczesała pasma palcami. – Jak interesy?

– W porządku – rzucił Josh odruchowo, po czym dodał: – Chociaż nie do końca.

– A co się stało? – Twarz młodej kobiety wyrażała niekłamaną troskę.

Joshua przyjrzał jej się z namysłem.

– Napijesz się ze mną wina? – spytał z niewesołym uśmiechem.

– Zawsze znajdę dla ciebie parę chwil – zapewniła go. – I chętnie się napiję. – Wyjęła z lodówki butelkę i napełniła dla siebie kieliszek.

– Wyjdziemy na taras?

– Chodźmy.

Poszła pierwsza. Drobna, zgrabna, cała w czerni. Ubrana w prosty top z dzianiny i dżinsy, wetknięte w kowbojskie buty. Nikt by się w niej nie domyślił gosposi. A co więcej, posiadła zdumiewającą jak na swoje lata życiową mądrość.

Usiedli pod wielkim parasolem, przy ogrodowym stole z drewna tekowego, który najlepsze lata miał dawno za sobą. Kamienny taras był nadspodziewanie przestronny, prowadziły nań wyjścia z prawie wszystkich pomieszczeń na parterze, gdyż dom miał kształt podkowy. Przed nimi połyskiwał w słońcu basen, jego turkusową powierzchnię leciutko marszczył słaby powiew wiatru. W dali okryte mgiełką wiosennej zieleni pasmo górskie Santa Cruz urzekało surową urodą, najeżone spiczastymi wierzchołkami i pocięte kanionami.

– Mów, Josh, co cię martwi?

– Czy nie wydaje ci się, że Joanna zachowuje się ostatnio jakoś... dziwnie? – Westchnął ciężko.

Gosposia odwróciła wzrok.

– Hm... – Zabębniła pomalowanymi na różowo paznokciami w tekowy blat. – Bo ja wiem...?

– Jesteś inteligentna i spostrzegawcza... – Joshua wiedział, że jeśli Connie zacznie mówić, powie wszystko, co myśli. Mało tego, uwielbiała spiskować, co wcale nie oznaczało, że zniżyłaby się do złośliwości lub oszustwa.

– Wydaje mi się, że siostra wywiera na nią niezbyt dobry wpływ... – Rzuciła mu porozumiewawcze spojrzenie. – Wredna baba!

Joshua wbrew sobie roześmiał się głośno.

– Trudno to lepiej ująć – przyznał. Zaraz jednak spoważniał. – Ale nie w tym rzecz. Mam wrażenie, że chodzi o coś poważniejszego. Zaczynam się nie na żarty o nią obawiać. Dlatego chciałbym wiedzieć, co o tym sądzisz i co widzisz. Nikt nie zna Joanny lepiej, wiem, że nie macie przed sobą tajemnic.

Connie wypiła łyk wina i z uwagą odstawiła kieliszek.

– Cóż, chyba muszę ci przyznać rację. – Zapatrzyła się w dal. – Ciągle gdzieś ją nosi, a nawet jeśli zostaje w domu, wyraźnie myślami jest gdzieś indziej. To rzeczywiście dziwne.

Joshua bez słowa pokiwał głową.

Dobrze, pomyślał. Połknęła przynętę.

– Jest mało przytomna – podjęła Connie. – Jakby żyła we własnym świecie. I przestała mi mówić, dokąd się wybiera. – Popatrzyła na Joshuę znacząco.

– Mnie też nic nie mówi – przyznał. – Domyślasz się czegoś?

– Nie – odrzekła Connie. – Joanna w nic mnie nie wtajemnicza. Zaczęłam się już zastanawiać, czy przypadkiem nie ukrywa jakiejś większej sprawy.

– Uważasz, że ma jakieś poważne zmartwienie?

– Trudno powiedzieć. Ale rzeczywiście, bywały ostatnio takie chwile, że zachowywała się po prostu wstrętnie, to fakt. Potrafiła się koszmarnie czepiać o całkiem nieistotne drobiazgi.

Josh wiedział, że jego żona traktuje Connie jak siostrę, więc potraktował jej spostrzeżenia całkiem serio.

– Też to zauważyłem. I to też mnie martwi, bo takie zachowanie jest u niej całkiem niezwykłe.

– To fakt. – Connie znów zabębniła w stół różowymi paznokciami. – *Misterioso* – rzekła ponuro.

– Jak sądzisz... – Joshua nie zdążył dokończyć pytania, bo przerwał mu dźwięczny głos żony.

– Witajcie, kochani! – zawołała Joanna z entuzjazmem. Postawiła na podłodze kilka papierowych toreb z zakupami i przeszła na taras.

– Witaj, moja piękna. – Josh podniósł się i ucałował ją w policzek. – Napijesz się z nami?

– Chętnie.

Poszedł do kuchni po kieliszek, a Joanna serdecznie cmoknęła Connie i usiadła.

– Przerwałam wam babskie ploty? – Oczy jej błyszczały.

– Nie, coś ty – zaprzeczyła Connie. – Podziwialiśmy krajobraz.

– A od kiedy to masz czas na podziwianie krajobrazu?

– Od teraz! – odparła gosposia i obie wybuchnęły śmiechem.

Connie doskonale zdawała sobie sprawę, że Joanna odgadła, o kim rozmawiali, ale też miała błogą świadomość, iż przyjaciółka nie będzie z niej wyciągała informacji i pozwoli rozkoszować się tą drobną konspiracją.

Wrócił Joshua z kieliszkiem dla Joanny, postawił go na stole i usiadł.

– Dziękuję. – Joanna od razu podniosła wino do ust. – Mmm...! Wyborne. Jak ci minął dzień? – spytała męża.

Joshua był w rozterce. Nie chciał psuć żonie humoru, ale przecież nie mógł przed nią zatajać przykrych wieści.

– Byłem dzisiaj pracowity jak pszczółka – zaczął lekkim tonem. – Z największą starannością zapyliłem kilka naprawdę wyjątkowych okazów. Niestety, musiałem przerwać to fascynujące zajęcie, bo Carl zadzwonił z pilną sprawą. Wezwał mnie do szklarni na dole, okazało się, że zawiódł komputerowy system nawilżaczy. Liczymy się z dwiema możliwościami: błędem w programie albo celowym uszkodzeniem.

– Co takiego?! – wykrzyknęła Joanna. – Boże! Są jakieś straty?

Jezu Chryste, pomyślała zrezygnowana. Jeszcze tylko tego mi potrzeba.

– Tym razem mieliśmy szczęście, nic strasznego się nie stało, choć mogłoby się to skończyć katastrofą. Trudno nawet powiedzieć, jak długo nawilżacze nie działały. Mogły się zepsuć choćby i w piątek po południu. Pamiętasz? Cały weekend zajmowaliśmy się Christiną, żadne z nas nie zajrzało do kwiatów. – Przeniósł spojrzenie na Connie. – Kilkoro pracowników kręciło się po szklarniach, ale tylko Carl zauważył, że nawilżacze nie funkcjonują. Jesteśmy mu winni ogromną wdzięczność.

Gosposia tylko kiwnęła głową.

– Josh – odezwała się cicho Joanna – twoim zdaniem naprawdę istnieje możliwość, że ktoś celowo uszkodził system?

– Nie można tego wykluczyć – przyznał. – Z drugiej strony, należy brać pod uwagę fakt, że policja nie znalazła żadnych śladów włamania. Nic podejrzanego. Tylko że zdaniem fachowców z firmy, która instalowała urządzenia, nie zawiódł program komputerowy.

– Przepraszam was. – Connie wstała. – Muszę lecieć.

– Może jeszcze odrobinę wina? – zaproponowała Joanna.

– Nie, nie, dzięki. Naprawdę na mnie już czas. – Connie serdecznie ucałowała ją w policzek. – Do jutra.

– Trzymaj się – Joshua mrugnął porozumiewawczo. – Do zobaczenia.

Gosposia pomachała im samymi palcami, obróciła się na pięcie i już jej nie było.

Joanna popatrzyła na Josha w zamyśleniu.

– Powiedziałeś policjantom o braciach Rossi? O tym, że chcą przejąć naszą firmę?

– Nie. Bałem się, że mogliby nas posądzić o paranoję. Przecież Rossi nie zdecydowaliby się na takie ryzyko! A przy tym, policja nie znalazła żadnych śladów włamania...

– Tak... chyba masz rację. Coś mi jednak mówi, że ci dwaj mogli maczać w tym palce.

– Na pewno trzeba ich brać pod uwagę – zgodził się Joshua. – Wyobraź sobie, Peter Rossi zadzwonił do mnie do biura! Spytał, czy przypadkiem nie zmieniłem zdania na temat sprzedaży farmy.

– Coś podobnego! Co za bezczelność! Ten człowiek nie ma żadnych skrupułów!

– Na to wygląda. Krąży o nim pewna opowieść, która nie stawia go w najlepszym świetle... Pamiętasz, jak wykupili starego Giglio? A zaraz potem budynki na jego farmie spłonęły? Podobno były one niepotrzebne braciom Rossi, ale szkoda im było pieniędzy na rozbiórkę, więc wynajęli jakiegoś zbira, żeby je podpalił. Nie dość, że mieli mniej roboty, to jeszcze zgarnęli ubezpieczenie.

– Josh, moim zdaniem ci ludzie są niebezpieczni – oznajmiła Joanna z mocą. – I zdolni do wszystkiego.

– Mimo wszystko chyba sobie z nimi poradzę – odparł z uśmiechem. – Dosyć już o mnie, powiedz teraz, jak tobie minął dzień. – Nie wiedział, czy otrzyma szczerą odpowiedź. Oczywiście, robiła zakupy, to było widać, ale z pewnością nie siedziała w sklepach do tej pory.

Joanna aż się cała rozjaśniła.
– Och, Josh, wyobraź sobie, poznałam dzisiaj niesamowitą kobietę.
Ucieszył się z jej entuzjazmu.
– Kto to taki?
– Pamiętasz fontannę i mur otaczający ogród u Ingrid i Ronalda Wilsonów?
– Oczywiście. Faktycznie, piękne, a ty wprost oczu nie mogłaś oderwać od tych cacuszek.
– Zadzwoniłam do Ingrid i wyciągnęłam z niej, kto im zaprojektował te cuda – oznajmiła Joanna z dumą.
– Rozumiem, że ta osoba mieszka gdzieś w pobliżu?
– I owszem. Nazywa się April Woodward. Ma dom całkiem niedaleko. Od razu się z nią umówiłam i dzisiaj do niej pojechałam. – Przekrzywiła głowę i popatrzyła na męża zmrużonymi oczami, z figlarnym uśmiechem na ustach.
– Ty coś knujesz – uznał Joshua.
– Jutro przyjedzie do nas obejrzeć stajnię – oznajmiła Joanna. – Mam cudowne wrażenie, że jest równie zafascynowana moimi planami jak ja sama.
– Doskonale! – uradował się Josh. – Tylko... aż mi się nie chce wierzyć, że masz siłę na tak ogromne przedsięwzięcie. Rzeczywiście, fontanna i mur u Wilsonów bardzo mi się podobały, ale też wyobrażam sobie, ile pracy wymagało zbudowanie obu tych cudów.
– Czuję, że muszę to zrobić – odrzekła stanowczo. – Tyle lat zbierałam te wszystkie piękne muszle i kolorowe kamienie, zawsze marzyłam, by wykorzystać je do stworzenia czegoś w rodzaju groty.
– Och, kochanie, jesteś niesamowita! – Joshua ujął dłoń żony. Dawno już nie widział Joanny w tak dobrym nastroju. Wreszcie zyskał przekonanie, że znowu jest taka jak zawsze. – Muszę ci wyznać, że to twoje hobby zawsze było jedyną cechą budzącą we mnie niepokój. Moim zdaniem nawet graniczyło z obsesją.
– Rzeczywiście – roześmiała się Joanna – to silniejsze ode mnie. Wyobraź sobie, zawiozłam April zdjęcia, które zbierałam specjalnie na taką okazję... te przepiękne wnętrza, wykładane muszlami i kolorowymi płytkami... I wiesz co? – Spojrzała na męża oczami pełnymi entuzjazmu.
– No mów już, mów.
– Nie wzięła mnie za wariatkę! – oznajmiła Joanna z triumfem.
Oboje się roześmieli.
– Widzisz, Josh – podjęła po chwili – wydaje mi się, że April naprawdę rozumie, czego bym chciała.

– Zdumiewające! – wykrzyknął Joshua kpiąco. – Może też jest szalona?

– Ty wstręciuchu! – Joanna czule ścisnęła dłoń męża. – Bądźże czasem poważny. Posłuchaj: April zrobiła już coś podobnego do mojej wymarzonej groty, dla jakiegoś zleceniodawcy z Los Angeles. Więc takie zamówienie nie będzie dla niej całkowitą nowością, choć tamto było dużo mniejsze. No i tak. – Zamyśliła się na kilka chwil. – Jutro się przekonamy...

– Oby wszystko poszło, po twojej myśli... Czy jesteś zupełnie pewna, że masz ochotę na realizację takiego dużego projektu? Nie neguję twoich planów, ale...

– Joshua, ta grota jest dla mnie bardzo ważna. Muszę ją zbudować. Jest... jak spadek. To coś takiego jak ten album o orchideach, rozumiesz? – Obdarzyła męża tęsknym, zadumanym spojrzeniem. – To ma być cząstka mnie. Mój ślad na ziemi. Coś, co po mnie zostanie... kiedy mnie już nie będzie.

Joshua odetchnął z ulgą. Właśnie zyskał pewność, że nie ma powodów, aby się martwić zachowaniem żony.

– Jesteś bardzo podobna do ojca.

– Dlaczego? – spytała z uśmiechem, bo doskonale znała odpowiedź. Chciała ją jednak usłyszeć.

– Jesteś marzycielką o twórczym umyśle – rzekł Joshua. – Słuchasz podszeptów ducha, nieposplitych kreatywnych impulsów, które domagają się wyrażenia w niespotykanej formie. No i pragniesz zostawić po sobie wyraźny ślad.

Joanna spuściła wzrok i zarumieniła się lekko. Od wina i od słów męża.

– Chyba każdy chce stworzyć coś znaczącego. – Podniosła oczy na Joshuę. – Chcemy być potrzebni, zostawić po sobie coś pamiętnego, dzięki czemu nie przeminiemy z wiatrem, dzięki czemu choć odrobinę upiększymy świat.

– Wiesz co?

– Co?

– Kocham cię – powiedział Joshua cicho. – Kocham cię całym sercem.

Na ustach Joanny pojawił się drżący uśmiech. W oczach zalśniły łzy.

– Ja ciebie też kocham. Kocham cię nad życie.

Rozdział siódmy

April z godną pozazdroszczenia swobodą prowadziła ukochanego pordzewiałego dżipa niebezpiecznie wąską i krętą górską drogą. Zwalniała jedynie wówczas, gdy na skrzyżowaniach szukała charakterystycznych punktów krajobrazu, opisanych przez Joannę. Trasa przypominała tę, która wiodła do jej domu – była jednocześnie śmiertelnie niebezpieczna i zabójczo piękna, nakryta rozsłonecznionym dachem jodeł, cyprysów, sekwoi, eukaliptusów oraz dębów i pożłobiona przez wodę, która spływając ze stromych stoków, podmywała podłoże. Miejscami zmieniała się w jednopasmówkę.

Za ostatnim zakrętem uwzględnionym w notatkach od Joanny April wjechała na kolejny szczyt. Spodziewała się wszystkiego, ale na taki widok nie była przygotowana. Dżip ledwo się toczył, a ona zachwycała się przepychem naturalnego piękna. Pagórki i doliny przybrały się już w wiosenną zieleń, upstrzoną jaskrawymi plamkami dziko rosnących kwiatów. Bogactwo kolorów i kształtów zapierało dech w piersiach.

W pewnym oddaleniu widać już było żwirowany podjazd do domu Joanny. Prowadziła do niego droga ujęta w dwa rzędy starych jabłoni. Wjazdu na teren posiadłości strzegła para kamiennych słupów, zwieńczonych miedzianymi latarniami, które na zielono przyprószyła patyna. Ciężka brama z czarnego żelaza stała otworem, rozwarta w serdecznym zaproszeniu. Z takiego samego żelaza wykuto ogrodzenie otaczające sad i ogrody wokół domu.

Wjechała między kamiennymi słupami na obszerny dziedziniec. Po lewej stronie wznosił się duży dom kryty szarymi gontami, ze śnieżnobiałymi akantami i okiennicami. Wzdłuż ściany ciągnęła się pergola ciężka od niebieskofioletowej glicynii. Na prawo stała druga, obrośnięta różami, przywodzącymi na myśl dawne czasy. Tysiące bladoróżowych kwiatów spowijało ją słodkim obłokiem. Widać było, że mieszkają tu ludzie dobrze sytuowani nie od dzisiaj, dostatek zdążył się utrwalić, wspierany wszechobecną dbałością i miłością do tego miejsca.

Wysiadła z dżipa, wyciągnęła swoją dużą torbę i po kamiennych stopniach podeszła do frontowych drzwi. Pomalowano je ciemnozieloną farbą, była to zieleń z odcieniem granatu.

April zadzwoniła.

Na progu stanęła prześliczna młoda kobieta o kruczoczarnych lśniących włosach i błyszczących ciemnych oczach.

– Cześć – powitała gościa bezceremonialnie. – April, prawda?

– Zgadza się – odpowiedziała April z uśmiechem.

– Ja jestem Connie. – Odsunęła się na bok. – Chodź, Joanna czeka.

April ruszyła za gosposią, rozglądając się na boki. Piękno krajobrazu było niczym w porównaniu z zachwycającym wnętrzem domu. W przestronnym holu królował okrągły stół z czasów regencji, nad nim wisiał roziskrzony kryształowy żyrandol. W głębi szerokie schody prowadziły na piętro. Connie szła żwawym krokiem, więc April ledwo rzuciła okiem na mijane pokoje, ale nie sposób było nie zauważyć dobrze utrzymanego drewna, wypolerowanego srebra i brązu oraz harmonijnie dobranych obić i dywanów.

Dotarły do wysokich balkonowych drzwi na tyłach domu, za którymi rozciągał się rajski widok na kamienny taras i góry jaśniejące wiosenną świeżością. April odwiedziła wiele domów w tej okolicy, niektóre z nich należały do bardzo zamożnych ludzi, ale nigdy dotąd nie spotkała się z tak przecudownie spokojnym luksusem. Miała ochotę przesuwać między palcami lejące się tkaniny, gładzić ciepłe drewno, chłonąć otaczające ją piękno. Tymczasem jednak Connie stała przy drzwiach balkonowych z lekko zniecierpliwionym uśmiechem.

– Tędy – powiedziała, otwierając jedno skrzydło.

– Dziękuję.

Joanna siedziała przy dużym stole z tekowego drzewa, pod ogrodowym parasolem. Na blacie i kamiennej podłodze piętrzyły się książki i kolorowe magazyny. Na widok gościa wstała, zdejmując okulary przeciwsłoneczne.

– Cześć. Cieszę się, że przyjechałaś.

– Witaj – uśmiechnęła się April. – Nie do wiary, jak tu pięknie! Nie miałam pojęcia, że tutaj są takie rajskie zakątki! Mieszkam w okolicy już długo, a nigdy mnie nie podkusiło, żeby pojechać tą drogą. – Ogarnęła szerokim gestem basen, mostek, szczyty gór. – Naprawdę, jak w raju!

– Trudno się sprzeczać z tak trafną opinią. – Joanna wyciągnęła rękę na powitanie. April ujęła jej dłoń dość delikatnie i nie tyle nią potrząsnęła, ile lekko ścisnęła. – Chodź, usiądź i powiedz, czego się napijesz. Jest herbata, woda mineralna, jakieś soki... Nie wiem, na co masz ochotę?

April usiadła.

– A ty co pijesz? – spytała.

– Zieloną herbatę. Mrożoną.

– To jest to – odrzekła April zdecydowanie. – Tego właśnie mi trzeba.

– Mogłabyś przynieść dzbanek? – poprosiła Joanna Connie.

– Jasne. – Gosposia zniknęła w kuchni.

Teraz Joanna także usiadła. Uważnie przyjrzała się kobiecie po drugiej stronie stołu. Tak, rzeczywiście była piękna. I miała mnóstwo wdzięku.

– Wypijmy spokojnie, a potem cię oprowadzę, dobrze?

April z ciekawością rozglądała się dookoła, chłonąc oczami każdy krzew, kwiat i drzewo. Odetchnęła głęboko, zachwycona świeżymi woniami, które niosła lekka bryza.

– Niesamowite miejsce – oznajmiła z podziwem. – Pełne świeżości, ale takie... emanujące zmysłowością... A jednocześnie nasycone spokojem.

– Chyba trafiłaś w sedno – uznała Joanna po chwili zastanowienia. – Tak, tutaj panuje zmysłowy spokój.

– Długo tu mieszkasz? – spytała April.

Joanna pokiwała głową.

– Właściwie od zawsze. Nigdy nie miałam innego domu. Zbudował go mój ojciec, tutaj się wychowałam. Po ślubie krótki czas mieszkaliśmy z Joshem przy plaży, niedaleko Pajaro Dunes, w domku, który dostaliśmy od taty w prezencie ślubnym. Trudno go nazwać prawdziwym domem, to raczej pawilonik letniskowy, ale widoki były tam niesamowite. Po śmierci taty wróciłam do rodzinnego domu.

– Cudownie tutaj – westchnęła April. – I jakoś tak... jak nie w Kalifornii. To znaczy... I dom, i cała posiadłość sprawiają wrażenie, jakby tu istniały od zawsze. Rozumiesz, o co mi chodzi? Wy naprawdę zapuściliście tu korzenie.

– Rzeczywiście, większość kalifornijskich domów wygląda inaczej – zgodziła się Joanna z uśmiechem. – Pudełka z winylu postawione najdalej przed tygodniem...

Do stołu podeszła Connie z tacą, na której pysznił się pękaty dzbanek.

– Jest prawdziwy cukier, słodzik i miód – powiedziała, nalewając April mrożonej herbaty. – Co dodać?

– Sama to zrobię, bardzo ci dziękuję.

– Nie ma sprawy. – Odwróciła się do Joanny. – To ja już pójdę kończyć lunch, tak?

– Dobrze. Możesz podawać za jakieś pół godziny.

– W porządku. – Connie odmaszerowała do kuchni.

– Śliczna ta wasza gosposia – zauważyła April. – I pełna energii.

– Connie jest na wagę złota. Drugiej takiej można by ze świecą szukać. Mój tata przygarnął ją i jej brata, Carla. W zasadzie to prawie ich adoptował. Wtedy jeszcze nazywali się Consuela i Carlos, ich matka przyjechała z obojgiem z Peru. Mieszkali w obskurnej przyczepie w jednym z tych strasznych obozów dla imigrantów... No i w efekcie Connie pracuje u nas w domu, a Carl w szklarniach.

– Dlaczego zmienili imiona?

– Chcieli się jak najbardziej zasymilować. Nadal robią, co w ich mocy.

– Ach, czyli są tu nielegalnie.

– Carl ma już obywatelstwo – odparła Joanna. – Ożenił się z Luną Garber, pół Wenezuelką, pół Żydówką, ale urodzoną już w Ameryce. Ona też pracuje w firmie, prowadzi biuro. Tymczasem Connie... cóż, tutaj sprawa jest nieco bardziej skomplikowana.

– Opowiedz – poprosiła April zaintrygowana.

– Connie znalazła sobie odpowiedniego kandydata na męża. Oczywiście chodziło o białe małżeństwo. Pożyczyliśmy jej pięć tysięcy...

– Dla pana młodego?! – zdumiała się April.

Joanna pokiwała głową.

– Najwyraźniej taka jest zwyczajowa stawka za tego rodzaju przysługę. Pobrali się, ale niestety, nie przeszli testów urzędu imigracyjnego.

– Jak to? Nie wiedziałam, że coś takiego w ogóle istnieje!

– Pewnie któraś urzędniczka miała akurat zły dzień. Tak czy inaczej, w administracji szybko się zorientowali, że to oszustwo, bo młodzi niewiele o sobie wiedzieli, nie mówiąc o tym, że nie żyli ze sobą jak mąż z żoną. I w ten sposób Connie nie dostała zielonej karty.

– Biedna! Co z nią teraz będzie?

– Na razie wynajęliśmy dobrego prawnika specjalizującego się w takich sprawach. Ma niemałe osiągnięcia w podobnych przypadkach, więc jesteśmy dobrej myśli. Tyle tylko, że mąż Connie zniknął, rzecz jasna razem z gotówką. – Joanna roześmiała się lekko. – Zawsze musi być jakieś „ale".

– Na to wygląda. – April zamilkła. – Ta dziewczyna wiele wam zawdzięcza – odezwała się po chwili.

– Cóż... Zaczęła u nas pracować, mając zaledwie osiemnaście lat. Stała się nieomal członkiem rodziny. Jest mi równie bliska jak moja siostra. A do tego wspaniała. Mądra, rozsądna, ambitna.

– I śliczna – zauważyła April. – Aż dziwne, że do tej pory nie znalazła sobie prawdziwego męża.

– Rzeczywiście, można się temu dziwić – przytaknęła Joanna. – Connie od czasu do czasu umawia się na randki, ale jak dotąd nikt nie podbił jej serca. Najwyraźniej szuka tego właściwego mężczyzny i jeszcze na niego nie trafiła. A ma dość konkretne oczekiwania. Liczy się dla niej, jak wygląda adorator, jak zarabia na życie... Connie chce możliwie najdalej uciec od dzieciństwa w biedzie. No i po prostu jeszcze się nigdy nie zakochała.

– A to szalenie istotne – zaśmiała się April.

– Właśnie – przytaknęła Joanna. – W każdym razie, ja się podpisuję pod tym twierdzeniem obydwiema rękami. – Spostrzegła, że April skończyła pić herbatę. – Jesteś gotowa na wycieczkę do stajni?

– Jak najbardziej. Nie mogę się doczekać.

– Wobec tego chodźmy.

Poprowadziła gościa kamiennym tarasem do drewnianego mostka wiodącego nad basen.

– Pięknie zagospodarowany teren – zachwycała się April. – Po prostu idealnie.

– Prace zapoczątkował tata – wyjaśniła Joanna – ale Josh i ja też zrobiliśmy niemało.

Minęły basen, a potem szły między krzewami i drzewami, aż wreszcie April ujrzała dawną stajnię. Budynek wznosił się na łagodnym stoku, na skraju sadu. Stare jabłonie użyczały mu cienia. Widok na okoliczne szczyty był tu jeszcze piękniejszy niż z tarasu.

– Joanno! – wykrzyknęła zachwycona April. – Jak tu cudnie!

– To prawda. Między innymi dlatego właśnie chciałabym mieć tutaj miejsce do odpoczynku, medytacji albo odpowiednie na miłe spotkanie. Takie, gdzie można sobie spokojnie poczytać, pobyć z samym sobą lub z kimś bliskim, z dala od wszystkiego, co się dzieje w domu. Pracując nad albumem, przekonałam się, że choć dom jest duży, czasem niełatwo w nim znaleźć spokojny kąt. Wówczas przyszła mi do głowy myśl, by stworzyć takie szczególne miejsce, niedaleko, ale w pewnej odległości od domu. Miejsce odpoczynku lub pracy czy refleksji... Azyl.

Stanęły przed bramą stajni. April przyjrzała się Joannie z uwagą, chcąc odczytać z jej twarzy myśli i uczucia, lecz nie zdołała. Wolno ruszyła wzdłuż ściany. Gospodyni szła za nią krok w krok. Razem obeszły budynek dookoła. Na koniec weszły do środka. April długo rozglądała się po wnętrzu. Wreszcie oparła ręce na biodrach, stanęła w rozkroku i popatrzyła na Joannę.

– Wszystko jasne – oznajmiła z mocą.

– Tak? – Joannie zadrżał głos. Czy stajnia zyskała aprobatę April? Jest odpowiednia?

Twarz projektantki rozjaśniła się uśmiechem.

– Budynek jest doskonały. Idealny dla twojego przedsięwzięcia.

Bogu dzięki! Joanna odetchnęła z ulgą. Jej plany zaczęły nabierać kształtów!

– To świetnie – powiedziała głośno. – Cieszę się, że ci się podoba. Trochę się obawiałam twojej opinii, bo mogłabyś uznać, że jakakolwiek przebudowa byłaby szaleństwem, a co dopiero taka, jaką sobie wymarzyłam...

– Nie, nie. – April pokręciła głową. – W twoim pomyśle nie ma nic szalonego. Mówię szczerze. Budynek doskonale się nadaje na grotę. – Odwróciła się ku jednej ze ścian, gdzie niegdyś znajdowały się wrota boksów. – Sama popatrz. Tutaj aż się proszą balkonowe drzwi na całą wysokość. Inaczej być nie może. Zyskasz piękny widok na góry. A na pozostałych ścianach – obróciła się na pięcie, wskazując ręką – żadnych drzwi ani okien. Jak w jaskini. – Zatrzymała wzrok na Joannie. – Tutaj, w środku człowiek będzie otoczony freskami oraz wzorami z kamieni i muszli.

Joannie rozbłysły oczy.

– A więc spodobał ci się mój pomysł!

– O, tak – przyznała April. – Można tu stworzyć przecudne gniazdko, cichą przystań, miejsce o magicznym uroku...

Właśnie to chciałam usłyszeć, pomyślała Joanna.

– Musimy jeszcze ustalić terminy, harmonogram prac i tak dalej... Ale w zasadzie... tak. Chętnie się podejmę tej pracy.

– Cudownie! Już nie mogę się doczekać, kiedy zaczniesz. – Joanna odruchowo ścisnęła April za ramiona i serdecznie ucałowała ją w policzek. Zaraz jednak odsunęła się od niej i zaśmiała nerwowo. W normalnych okolicznościach nie pozwoliłaby sobie na podobne zachowanie w stosunku do osoby, którą ledwo znała. – Przepraszam. Wiem, że nie powinnam, ale... tak się cieszę!

– Nic nie szkodzi... – April poczerwieniała lekko. – Ja też bardzo się cieszę... A poza tym, mam wrażenie, jakbyśmy się znały od lat.

– Ja też – przyznała Joanna. – Chyba jesteśmy do siebie podobne. Obie praktyczne, ale z odrobiną fantazji, lubimy się śmiać, musimy być niezależne...

– Tak. Z pewnością wiele nas łączy. Gust mamy podobny...

Joanna ujęła April pod ramię.

– Chciałabym ci pokazać coś jeszcze.

– Co takiego?

– Chodź.

W kącie stajni połyskiwały ogromne foliowe płachty. Joanna pociągnęła jedną, a wtedy April zobaczyła przynajmniej setkę równo poustawianych metalowych i plastikowych pojemników. Piętrzyły się aż pod sufit.

– Zobacz. – Joanna otworzyła pierwszy z brzegu.

April zajrzała do środka i oczy zaokrągliły jej się ze zdumienia. W pojemniku znajdowały się starannie poukładane barwne muszle.

– Piękne! – westchnęła z podziwem. – Jakby dopiero co wyjęte z oceanu.

– Mnie też się podobają. Mam ich tutaj całe tysiące. Są posegregowane według rodzajów.

– Niesamowite!

– Mam nadzieję, że się przydadzą, może uda się je włączyć do twojego projektu.

– Na pewno! Przede wszystkim!

– Chodźmy na lunch. – Joanna zamknęła pojemnik. – Chyba że chcesz jeszcze coś obejrzeć?

– Na razie wystarczy. Muszę się oswoić z tym, co już zobaczyłam.

Joanna poprowadziła ją między jabłoniami, w górę po łagodnym stoku i obok basenu – z powrotem na kamienny taras.

– Connie doskonale gotuje – mówiła, idąc. – Przyrządza różne specjały peruwiańskie, odmienia je na swój sposób, czegoś tam doda, czegoś ujmie i efekty są nieprawdopodobne. Niestety, większość tych dań jest dość kaloryczna. A trudno im się oprzeć.

– To, co dobre, często bywa niewskazane – zaśmiała się April.

Stół już był nakryty do posiłku. Na śnieżnobiałym obrusie pyszniła się elegancka chińska zastawa, błyszczały wypolerowane srebra i lśniące kryształy w towarzystwie wykrochmalonych lnianych serwetek. Na środku stał wazon z delikatnymi, bladoliliowymi orchideami.

– Niepotrzebnie robisz sobie tyle kłopotu – zaprotestowała April.

– To żaden kłopot – odparła Joanna zdecydowanie. – Piękno powinno być nieodłącznym elementem życia.

April miała pewność, że nowa znajoma mówi z całkowitym przekonaniem. Ta kobieta nie szczędziła wysiłków, by świat wokół niej miał jak najwięcej uroku.

– Pierwszy raz widzę orchidee w takim odcieniu.

– Nazywają się *Cattleya skinneri*. Nie są szczególnie rzadkie ani trudne w prowadzeniu, a rzeczywiście mają przepiękny kolor. – Wskazała dłonią krzesło. – Siadaj, zapraszam.

Gdy tylko obie usiadły, jak za skinieniem czarodziejskiej różdżki pojawiła się Connie z ciężką tacą.

* * *

Po lunchu zostało niewiele, a był on przyrządzony z taką maestrią, iż nawet resztki jedzenia wyglądały apetycznie. Dno miseczek zabarwiła na różowo kremowa gęsta zupa z krewetek, doprawiona świeżą kolendrą, w równej mierze dla wzbogacenia smaku, jak i dla zapachu. Przepyszna *calsa* zostawiła na talerzach białe, złote i zielone smugi po purée ziemniaczanym, piersi kurczęcej i awokado, natomiast talerzyki deserowe wyglądały, jakby w ogóle nie były używane, tak dokładnie, co do okruszynki, została z nich zebrana doskonała tarta z owocami.

– Pyszności! – westchnęła April, składając serwetkę.

– Connie jest niedoścignioną kucharką – przyznała Joanna. – Wyobraź sobie, że nawet z Europy dzwonią nasi goście, prosząc o przepis na tę zupę z krewetek.

– Ktoś go dostał?

– Jedna osoba – zaśmiała się Joanna. – Pewna starsza dama z Francji, szalenie bogata wielbicielka orchidei. Przy tym kobieta z klasą, naprawdę ktoś, no i jedna z naszych lepszych klientek. Ubłagałam Connie, żeby jej zdradziła przepis.

– Złamała się jednak.

– Nie do końca. Jakiś sekret mimo wszystko zataiła.

Roześmiały się obie.

Nagle April się zorientowała, że gładzi kwiat opuszkami palców.

– Och, przepraszam! Sama nie wiem, jak to się stało.

– Nic nie szkodzi, naprawdę. Tak jak mówiłam, to nie są jakieś wyjątkowe okazy. Skoro ci się tak podobają, weź je, proszę.

– Nie umiem...

– Nie przesadzajmy. Nie są szczególnie wymagające. Dam ci potem kartkę ze wskazówkami, jak o nie dbać. Chcesz zobaczyć cieplarnię?

– Bardzo chętnie. Skoro mam zaprojektować grotę z orchideami, powinnam się z nimi bliżej zapoznać.

– Chodź, przedstawię was sobie.

Minęły mostek, potem domek nad basenem, a stamtąd krótka ścieżka prowadziła prosto do niewielkiej cieplarni.

– Nikt by jej tu nie zauważył! – zdziwiła się April. – W każdym razie z domu w ogóle jej nie widać.

– Takie było założenie – wyjaśniła Joanna. – Tutaj trzymamy bardzo rzadkie okazy. Wyjątkowe i cenne. No i Josh ma tu swoją jaskinię rozpusty.

– Nie całkiem rozumiem... – April miała ochotę się roześmiać.

– Nie przesłyszałaś się – odrzekła Joanna wesoło. – Powiedziałam, że Josh ma tu swoją jaskinię rozpusty. Nazwaliśmy tak miejsce, gdzie rozmnaża i krzyżuje orchidee. Robi to własnoręcznie. W niektórych przypadkach zapylenie jest wyjątkowo trudne. Joshua pracuje nad niebywale skomplikowanymi hybrydami. Stanowią one jeden z filarów tego interesu. W każdym razie, w naszym wypadku. Tworzenie nowych okazów, innych niż te dobrze znane, to naprawdę niebagatelne wyzwanie. Każdy hodowca stara się uzyskać krzyżówkę, która zainteresuje bogatych odbiorców, która ich zaintryguje, a co za tym idzie, dobrze się sprzeda. Proces tworzenia hybryd jest długi i żmudny, a w dodatku trudno mieć pewność, jaki będzie końcowy efekt. – Z kieszeni luźnych kremowych spodni wyjęła niewielkie urządzenie elektroniczne. Wstukała kod i wycelowała pilotem w wejście do cieplarni. Gdy rozległo się kliknięcie, pchnęła drzwi. – Musieliśmy tutaj założyć dość szczelny system zabezpieczeń, bo kwiaty mają sporą wartość.

April powędrowała za Joanną przez cieplarnię, a z każdym krokiem miała coraz większe oczy.

– Jak nie z tego świata... – wyszeptała w pewnej chwili.

Zaczynało jej się kręcić w głowie od bogactwa odcieni i ciężkich woni. Zewsząd uderzały ją wszelkie tonacje czerwieni, różu, zieleni i bieli, kwiaty fioletowe, żółte i nieomal czarne. Widziała wszystkie kolory tęczy, momentami odnosiła nawet wrażenie, że dostrzega jakąś barwę, której natura jeszcze nie stworzyła. Łodygi, liście, kwiaty, korzenie – każda część tych wspaniałych roślin zasługiwała na szczególną uwagę; i tych maleńkich, których trzeba było szukać wzrokiem, po te ogromne, przywodzące na myśl drzewa.

– Warto tu zajrzeć, żeby obejrzeć najrzadsze okazy, ale cieplarnia jest niewielka – powiedziała Joanna. – Zaczekaj, aż zobaczysz duże szklarnie! – Dostrzegła zapylony okaz *Paphiopedilum lovii.* – Jak ci się podoba ta?

April przyjrzała się roślinie uważnie.

– Niesamowita – oceniła. – Ta zieleń, róż i fiolet... Przepiękna.

– Josh usiłuje ją połączyć z jakąś inną... nie mam pewności z którą. A może nawet z kilkoma innymi? Żeby uzyskać jeszcze lepsze efekty.

– Czy dobrze słyszałem? – rozległ się za nimi głęboki męski głos. – Ktoś coś o mnie wspominał?

– Nie wiedziałam, że tu jesteś! – Joanna wyraźnie się ucieszyła na widok męża.

Przytulił ją mocno i pocałował w usta.

April patrzyła kątem oka, trochę zaskoczona tymi nieskrywanymi czułościami przy obcej w końcu osobie.

Jacy oni naturalni, jacy swobodni, pomyślała.

– Josh – odezwała się Joanna – poznaj moją przyjaciółkę, April Woodward. April, to mój mąż, Joshua.

Uścisnął jej dłoń; April odwzajemniła uścisk, patrząc Joshowi prosto w oczy.

Niesamowite, pomyślała. Skąd taki kolor...? Fantastyczny... Ten błękit... A uśmiech! Białe zęby, opalona twarz... I te włosy...

Nagle zdała sobie sprawę, że zbyt długo przygląda się obcemu mężczyźnie, że przytrzymuje mu dłoń. Szybko uwolniła rękę i spuściła wzrok.

– Miło mi cię poznać – powiedziała, znowu patrząc na niego. – Joanna właśnie chwaliła twoje osiągnięcia.

– E tam, to zaledwie czubek góry lodowej! – odparł z dumą. – Lepiej powiedz mi, April, co sądzisz o tym jej pomyśle. Miałaś czas się nad tym zastanowić?

– Bardzo mi się podoba – odpowiedziała April. – Przypuszczam, że zdołamy osiągnąć niebagatelny efekt.

– Już byłyśmy w stajni – dodała Joanna. – April zaaprobowała budynek i otoczenie.

– Bardzo się cieszę – odrzekł Joshua. – Obawiam się, że zazwyczaj ludzie nie pojmują nietuzinkowych zamierzeń mojej żony. – Ujął Joannę za rękę. – A szalone pomysły to jedna z cech, które w niej uwielbiam.

– Ooo, kochany! – wykrzyknęła Joanna z udawanym oburzeniem. – Niektóre z moich pomysłów sam uznałeś za wariactwo.

Joshua roześmiał się głośno.

– Cóż, nie mogę zaprzeczyć.

– Kochanie, może oprowadzisz April po cieplarni, a ja zajmę się paroma drobnymi sprawami w domu? April, dobrze?

– Tak, oczywiście.

– Nie boisz się, że cię zanudzę na śmierć? – spytał Joshua.

– Nie, skądże! Przecież te kwiaty są fantastyczne!

– No to do zobaczenia – rzuciła Joanna. Odwróciła się na pięcie – i już jej nie było.

– Co ci Joanna zdążyła pokazać? – spytał Joshua.

O rany, te oczy! Miały jakąś magiczną moc. Nie mogła przestać się w nie wpatrywać. A włosy... Miękkie, jedwabiste, wyzłocone słońcem...!

– Co widziałam...? – zastanowiła się, dochodząc do siebie. – Joanna pokazywała mi kwiat, który usiłowałeś zapłod... zapylić. – Wskazała *Paphiopedilum lovii.*

– I co, naprawdę cię to interesuje?

– Jak najbardziej.

Joshua widział, że April mówi poważnie, i jej zaciekawienie oraz uwaga sprawiły mu przyjemność. Efekt końcowy – dumny egzotyczny kwiat – jest przedmiotem zainteresowania wielu ludzi, ale mało kto się zastanawia, ile pracy, czasu, ile wysiłku i starań trzeba włożyć w stworzenie niepowtarzalnej rośliny.

Josh pokazał jej działanie komputerowo sterowanego systemu nawilżania oraz żaluzji. Potem włożył lateksowe rękawiczki i zademonstrował, jak za pomocą wykałaczki zapyla orchidee.

April patrzyła zafascynowana, gdy Joshua zwilżał drewienko, a następnie przenosił pyłek z jednego kwiatu na drugi.

– Nie razi cię taki widok? – spytał, podnosząc wzrok. – Niektórym wydaje się niehigieniczny, w innych nawet budzi obrzydzenie.

– Ależ skąd! – żachnęła się. – Przecież to jest... miłość.

– Masz rację!

Jakiś czas później ruszyli razem przez cieplarnię. Joshua pokazywał gościowi różne gatunki orchidei, opowiadał o ich charakterystycznych cechach, pochodzeniu, sposobach uprawy i tysiącu innych szczegółach, aż April poczuła, że kręci jej się w głowie. W pewnej chwili zwrócił uwagę na jej nieprzytomny wzrok.

– Zdaje się, że trochę przesadziłem – zmitygował się. – Za dużo nowości dla laika.

– Rzeczywiście... – przyznała szczerze. – Ale temat jest fascynujący i słucham z prawdziwą przyjemnością. Bije od ciebie prawdziwa pasja.

– Przejąłem miłość do orchidei od Mitcha Camerona, ojca Joanny. Był nieuleczalnie chory na orchideomanię, no i najwyraźniej mnie zaraził! Któregoś lata, jeszcze w czasach college'u, zacząłem pomagać w szklarniach... i już mi to nie przeszło.

– Więc to tak się zaczyna? Ot, po prostu?

– Właśnie tak. Po prostu. – Joshua błysnął zębami w uśmiechu.

Och, ten uśmiech...!

– W jednym czasie pokochałem orchidee, Mitcha Camerona i jego córkę.

– Co za zbieg okoliczności! – zaśmiała się April. – Widać, że uwielbiasz swoją pracę.

– O, tak. Z tego, co mówiła Joanna, z tobą jest podobnie.

– Racja... Choć mało kto interesuje się tym, co robię, a jeśli już, to najczęściej konkurencja.

– Mimo wszystko, uwielbiasz swoje zajęcie.

Podniósł oczy i po raz pierwszy spojrzał na nią uważniej. Do tej pory nie zwrócił uwagi na tę piękną twarz o regularnych rysach, na smukłą sylwetkę, oczy o trudnym do nazwania kolorze i złociste włosy. Aż trudno mu było uwierzyć, iż tak długo nie dostrzegł tuż obok siebie tej nieprawdopodobnie pięknej kobiety.

– To prawda – przyznała April. – Uwielbiam swoją pracę bezkrytycznie i wkładam w nią całe serce. Obojętne, czy układam muszle, czy ceramiczne płytki albo kamienie, czy tylko maluję akwarele, poświęcam się temu bez reszty. I kocham ten stan. Czuję się, jakbym była... idealnie zrównoważona. Wiem, że to mało konkretne określenie, ale chyba najlepiej oddaje istotę moich odczuć... – Na jej twarz wypłynął uśmiech pełen melancholii. – Świat wydaje mi się kompletnie zwariowany... – Westchnęła niewesoło i leciutko wzruszyła ramionami.

– W tym szalonym świecie – podjął Joshua – twoja praca niesie ludziom piękno i spokój. Sama decydujesz, gdzie ulokować muszlę, a gdzie kamień, jakie barwy stworzą akwarelę. To dziedziny, w których panujesz nad rzeczywistością.

– Ładnie to ująłeś.

Dziwne, pomyślał Joshua. April patrzy na świat tak samo jak Joanna. I ja. Podobnie jak ona jest marzycielką. I tak samo twardo stąpa po ziemi, choć ma żywą wyobraźnię. Nic dziwnego, że szybko się zaprzyjaźniły.

– Czas wracać – westchnął. – Czeka na mnie papierkowa robota, a jeszcze trzeba zajrzeć do szklarni.

– Dziękuję, że pokazałeś mi orchidee. Naprawdę jestem pod wrażeniem.

– Mam nadzieję, że nie poczułaś się przytłoczona nadmiarem informacji.

– Jakoś przeżyję – zaśmiała się April.

Wyszli z cieplarni i wolnym krokiem ruszyli w stronę domu. Po kilku chwilach ujrzeli Joannę siedzącą na tarasie. Uśmiechała się do nich z daleka.

Pięknie razem wyglądają, pomyślała. Świetnie do siebie pasują, wręcz idealnie! I najwyraźniej doskonale się rozumieją.

Pomachała im wesoło, a oboje odpowiedzieli tym samym gestem. Śmiali się głośno i wyraźnie dobrze się razem czuli.

Cudownie!

Gdy weszli na taras, Joshua pochylił się i ucałował żonę w policzek.

– Muszę przerzucić trochę papierów, więc będę w gabinecie. Potem zajrzę do szklarni.

– Jeszcze dzisiaj?

– Tak, zostało tam parę rzeczy do zrobienia.

– Dobrze, kochanie. Wobec tego pewnie zobaczymy się dopiero wieczorem.

Joshua odwrócił się do April.

– Miło było cię poznać. Mam nadzieję, że dobrze wam pójdzie ustalanie szczegółów.

– Ja też się cieszę, że cię poznałam – odpowiedziała April szczerze. – A z projektem poradzimy sobie na pewno.

Gdy Joshua wszedł do domu, Joanna gestem zaprosiła gościa do stołu.

– Czy możesz zostać jeszcze chwilę?

– Twój mąż jest wyjątkowo sympatyczny. – April usiadła.

– Rzeczywiście, to złoty człowiek. W zasadzie także w sensie dosłownym.

Obie się roześmiały.

– Prawdziwa z ciebie szczęściara.

Joanna kiwnęła głową.

– O tak, prawdziwa ze mnie szczęściara. – Jej wzrok powędrował gdzieś w dal, na ustach pojawił się zadumany uśmiech. – Jestem najszczęśliwszą kobietą na ziemi.

April odniosła wrażenie, że w głosie nowej przyjaciółki zabrzmiała nuta melancholii, a może nawet smutku.

Cóż mogło martwić tę cudowną kobietę? Nic, to pewnie tylko wyobraźnia.

– Przygotowałam dla ciebie kilka drobiazgów. I zanim odjedziesz, chciałabym, żebyśmy omówiły konkretne warunki. Jeśli nie masz nic przeciwko temu.

– Nie, skądże! Mów, słucham.

– Nie mam żadnego pojęcia o tym, jak zazwyczaj pracujesz, ale chciałabym najpierw zobaczyć ogólny szkic twojej propozycji i kosztorys. Będę musiała wybrać orchidee do groty, więc chciałabym wiedzieć, które twoim zdaniem okażą się najodpowiedniejsze.

– Na kiedy chciałabyś mieć te informacje?

– Za tydzień?

– Tydzień? – zdumiała się April. – Strasznie szybko!

– Zależy mi na czasie – oświadczyła Joanna.

Z pewnością mówiła całkowicie poważnie.

– Dobrze. Odłożę wszelkie inne prace, wtedy powinnam zdążyć w tydzień...

– Świetnie. Wobec tego jesteśmy umówione na przyszły tydzień. A jeśli chodzi o termin ukończenia prac... – Umilkła i zamyśliła się na chwilę.

April odniosła wrażenie, że Joanna zażąda wykonania tego ogromnego dzieła na wczoraj.

– Chciałabym, żeby prace zakończyły się – podjęła gospodyni – najdalej za pół roku. Byłoby mi bardziej na rękę, gdyby nie trwały dłużej niż cztery miesiące, jednak pół roku to ostateczna granica.

– Oj! – wykrzywiła się April. – Tydzień na szkice to jedno, ale pół roku na wszystko? Joanno, to ogromne wyzwanie!

– Jestem gotowa iść o zakład, że uwielbiasz wyzwania.

– Ech, przegrałabyś. Taki termin wymagałby ode mnie przełożenia wszystkich innych zobowiązań. – Dłuższą chwilę milczała, przygryzając wargę. W końcu podjęła decyzję. – Zgadzam się. Skończę tę pracę w ciągu pół roku. Cztery miesiące to termin praktycznie niemożliwy, nie mogę czegoś takiego obiecać, ale będę pracowała najszybciej jak można.

– To właśnie chciałam usłyszeć – uśmiechnęła się Joanna. – April, twoje dzieło będzie tego warte. Uwierz mi, nie pożałujesz.

– Tego jestem pewna – odparła z dzielną miną, choć właśnie się zastanawiała, czy aby właśnie nie zaczęła żałować, że się podjęła tego zadania.

– Zapakowałam ci te kwiaty ze stołu i instrukcję, jak o nie dbać.

– Och, bardzo ci dziękuję. Są rzeczywiście wyjątkowo piękne.

– Naszykowałam ci także swój album orchidei, żebyś mogła im się przyjrzeć, a za tydzień razem zdecydujemy, które wybrać do fresków. Co ty na to?

– Świetna myśl – przyznała April. – Dziękuję ci za wszystko. Obsypujesz mnie prezentami...

– Nic za darmo – zaśmiała się Joanna. – Robię to w swoim interesie, więc nie czuj się zobowiązana.

– Zbieram się – oznajmiła April. – Muszę zdążyć z pewnym projektem na przyszły tydzień.

– Czy chcesz teraz zaliczkę?

– Nie, umówmy się na przyszły tydzień.

Razem ruszyły do domu, gdzie przy frontowych drzwiach czekały przygotowane dla gościa pakunki. Na pożegnanie ucałowały się, jakby były zaprzyjaźnione od wieków, i April wyszła.

Joanna obserwowała ją, gdy wyjeżdżała z dziedzińca, a kiedy samochód zniknął jej z oczu, oparła się o drzwi i głęboko odetchnęła.

Znalazłam ją. Tak, Joshua, nie zaprzeczysz. Znalazłam tę właściwą kobietę.

* * *

April wolno posuwała się niebezpieczną górską drogą. W głowie wirowały jej tysiące myśli, a wszystkie związane były z uroczą i stanowczo nietuzinkową Joanną Lawrence.

Co za kobieta! Nieprzeciętna! Inteligentna i piękna... A w jakim domu mieszka...! Cudnym, doskonałym! Jak z bajki. Posiadłość na szczycie wzgórza... nobliwa i elegancka, a przecież jednocześnie pełna ciepła, miła, gościnna. I ta dbałość o szczegóły... począwszy od pergoli uginających się pod ciężarem winorośli, po nakrycie stołu.

Przyhamowała za znakiem ostrzegającym przed podmytą nawierzchnią szosy.

Trzeba się skoncentrować na prowadzeniu.

Nie było to jednak łatwe i wkrótce znowu błądziła myślami po doczesnym raju Joanny Lawrence.

Nie sposób zapomnieć o ważnym uzupełnieniu tego czarownego życia: o Joshu. Nieziemsko przystojny, o słonecznych włosach i mocno zarysowanej szczęce. Pięknie opalony, z klasycznym rzymskim nosem... Nieprawdopodobnie delikatny, cierpliwy, z mnóstwem uroku... A przy tym, podobnie jak żona, kochający życie. Co więcej, najwyraźniej nie zdawał sobie sprawy z własnej urody, a już na pewno się nią nie chełpił. Męski w każdym calu, swobodny w obyciu, pełen naturalnego wdzięku.

Joanna i Joshua Lawrence. Co za para! Można im jedynie zazdrościć – wzajemnej gorącej miłości oraz wspaniałego wspólnego życia.

Wyjechała na autostradę. Była coraz bliżej swojego skromnego, lecz przytulnego domku.

A jednak... April wróciła myślami do nowych znajomych, coś zgrzytało w tym baśniowym świecie dwojga cudownych ludzi. Chociaż nie, poprawiła się, ten rozdźwięk krył się w samej Joannie. Tak... W Joannie wyczuła... nie tyle fałsz, ile jakąś nieszczerość... O co może chodzić? I skąd w ogóle takie wrażenie? Dlaczego szuka dziury w całym? Skąd rezerwa, która kazała jej mieć się na baczności i wypatrywać drugiego dna? Może trudno po prostu uwierzyć w istnienie tak idealnego małżeństwa?

Zwolniła przy zjeździe z autostrady.

Może to przesada. Zbytnia ostrożność. Czasami nawet intuicja zawodzi.

Mimo wszystko... nie mogła się pozbyć wrażenia, iż na idealnym wizerunku prezentowanym światu przez państwa Lawrence'ów widnieje poważna rysa. Nie potrafiła jej zdefiniować, ale coś ją ostrzegało, że powinna zachować ostrożność.

Rozdział ósmy

Słońce rozbłysło ostatnim, najpiękniejszym odcieniem pomarańczy i skryło się za górami. Tylko niektóre drzewa i ścieżki zatrzymały jeszcze cętki światła. Powoli nadciągał wieczorny chłód. Reflektory w basenie nadały wodzie odcień nieco bardziej turkusowy niż światło dnia. Wielkie świece o zapachu kapryfolium porozstawiano w kryształowych świecznikach na stołach, na ogrodowym murze, a nawet na brzegu basenu.

Joanna uwielbiała pływać o tej porze. Właśnie skończyła codzienny trening. Położyła się na materacu i zapatrzyła w niebo. Lubiła pływać także wczesnym rankiem, ale gdyby musiała wybierać, zdecydowałaby się na porę wieczorną, by widzieć i podziwiać rozgwieżdżone niebo.

Z ukrytych głośników sączyła się japońska muzyka grana na instrumencie zwanym koto. Joanna ją uwielbiała i cudownie przy niej wypoczywała, lecz niestety, mało kto ją rozumiał: większość przyjaciół trzymała się od tego rodzaju tonów możliwie najdalej. Tylko Josh potrafił dotrzymać żonie towarzystwa przy tego rodzaju muzyce... też nie zawsze.

Tego akurat wieczoru miała basen tylko dla siebie. Zanurzona w bajecznym świetle, błogiej woni, słuchając egzotycznej melodii, przeniosła się w świat czarów. Jej ciało, umysł, wszystkie zmysły poddały się rozkosznemu relaksowi, zyskała poczucie całkowitego rozluźnienia i wewnętrznej równowagi.

Nareszcie spokój, pomyślała. Przynajmniej na chwilę.

Właśnie spokoju kazał jej szukać lekarz. Uśmiechnęła się smutno. Ostatnio coraz częściej potrzebowała owych chwil odosobnienia, by odzyskać siły. Niekiedy wydawało jej się, że gdyby nie te magiczne wieczory, przekroczyłaby próg szaleństwa.

Dziś zdołała odsunąć od siebie negatywne emocje, cieszyła się chwilą, nie martwiąc się o dzień wczorajszy ani o przyszłość, o następny tydzień albo miesiąc. Dziś nie myślała o kłopotach w szklarni, o Joshu i wszystkich obowiązkach, jakie na siebie przyjął... i jakie jeszcze na niego spadną.

Nie. Tego wieczoru była w optymistycznym nastroju. Myślała o tym, jak wiele dobra zaznała w życiu, i dziękowała swojej szczęśliwej gwieździe, opatrzności czy może losowi, iż dane jej było zakosztować życia w luksusie, roziskrzonego radością i pełnego miłości.

Zsunęła się z materaca i popłynęła do schodów na płytszym końcu basenu. Wyszła z wody, wypiła łyk koktajlu z białym winem i podniosła z leżaka miękkie prześcieradło kąpielowe.

Nagle silne ramiona uchwyciły ją w talii, a na szyi poczuła czyjś gorący oddech. Serce podeszło jej do gardła, ale natychmiast uświadomiła sobie, że to Joshua. Poznałaby jego zapach na końcu świata.

– Pięknie wyglądasz – wyszeptał, całując ją w kark.

– Cudownie pachniesz... Ale mało przez ciebie nie umarłam ze strachu.

– Na szczęście jednak przeżyłaś. – Leciutko skubnął zębami jej ucho.

– Tym razem mi się udało. Więc wyjątkowo ci przebaczę. – Odwróciła się i cmoknęła go w czubek nosa. – Zobacz, całkiem cię zamoczę. – Pocałowała go w brodę.

– Nieważne! Możesz mnie moczyć, kiedy tylko zechcesz.

– Jestem okropnie głodna. Ty też?

– Owszem, zjadłbym coś. A dokładnie rzecz biorąc, umieram z głodu.

– Świetnie. Wobec tego pomożesz mi przygotować małą ucztę.

– Co to będzie?

– Steki, pachnące i soczyste, pieczone ziemniaki z rozmarynem... wystarczy je zagrzać w kuchence mikrofalowej. No i oczywiście sałatka.

– Już mi ślinka cieknie. Hm... Niech no zgadnę, na czym będzie polegała moja rola...

– Tak, kochanie, dobrze się domyśliłeś. W czasie kiedy ja będę robiła sałatkę, ty zajmiesz się grillem.

– Z wielką chęcią.

– Wobec tego, ustalone. – Joanna przytuliła się do męża. – Zdejmę bikini i zaraz wracam.

– Może przygotuję w tym czasie drinki? Napijesz się killer martini?

– Z rozkoszą. – Już szła przez taras do domu.

Joshua ruszył w jej ślady, ale dotarł tylko do kuchni. Z zamrażarki wyjął butelkę zmrożonej stolicznej, z barku wermut i z wprawą zmieszał składniki w dzbanku. To znaczy, do sporej porcji wódki dolał kropelkę martini. Właśnie naszykował kieliszki, gdy pojawiła się Joanna. Włosy miała jeszcze wilgotne, ubrana była w króciutką tunikę z białego marszczonego muślinu odsłaniającą kuszący widok.

– Gotowe? – spytała.

Joshua jak dyrygent złożył ukłon, błyskając w powietrzu szklanym mieszadłem.

– Voilà! – zaanonsował z szerokim uśmiechem. Napełnił stożkowaty kieliszek nieomal po brzegi i podał go żonie.

– A gdzie oliwka?

– Nie będziemy psuć czystego, wzniosłego smaku alkoholu – odparł, podnosząc swój kieliszek.

– Skoro ci na tym zależy... – zaśmiała się Joanna.

Zadźwięczało szkło w toaście i oboje spróbowali trunku.

– Och, ale to mocne! – wyrwało się Joannie.

– Pij, kochanie, będziesz łatwiejsza.

– Jeszcze łyk i będę bezwolna. – Joanna wyjęła z lodówki talerz z dwoma stekami. – Proszę bardzo, to dla ciebie – oznajmiła. – Ja włożę ziemniaki do kuchenki i zajmę się sałatką.

– Krwiste, jak zwykle?

– Przypieczone na zewnątrz, różowoczerwone w środku – doprecyzowała.

– Do usług. – Joshua ustawił na tacy talerz ze stekami, dzbanek z alkoholem oraz własną szklankę i zniknął na tarasie.

Kilka minut zajęło Joannie zrobienie sałatki z różnorakiej zieleniny z dojrzałymi pomidorami, doprawionej czosnkiem, oliwą z oliwek i balsamicznym octem. Gdy kuchenka mikrofalowa cichym gongiem dała znać, że skończyła pracę, wyjęła z niej pachnące rozmarynem ziemniaki, ustawiła je na tacy razem z sałatką oraz kieliszkiem i wyniosła wszystko na taras. Usiadła przy nakrytym wcześniej stole.

– Zaraz będą gotowe? – spytała. Obrzuciła steki łakomym spojrzeniem.

– Za sekundę. – Joshua także usiadł przy stole i popijając martini, przyglądał się żonie. – Zmęczona jesteś? – spytał. – Może za bardzo się przejmujesz tym nowym projektem?

– Nie, nie – zaprzeczyła Joanna zdecydowanie. – Czuję się świetnie i jestem przekonana, że ta grota będzie wspaniała. – Umilkła. – Co myślisz o April? – spytała po chwili.

– Cóż... – Josh wyraźnie szukał odpowiednich słów. – Jest... jak najbardziej...

– Wykrztuś wreszcie! – zaśmiała się Joanna.

Wzruszył ramionami, nieco skrępowany.

– Wydaje się osobą odpowiednią do tego zadania... ma mnóstwo entuzjazmu i wydaje mi się... ech, sam nie wiem.

– No powiedz, powiedz.

– Co mam ci powiedzieć? – Joshua wycofał się rakiem.

– Spodobała ci się, co? Jest śliczna i przemiła, prawda? – Obserwowała męża z uwagą.

Joshua lekko poczerwieniał.

A w niej zakłębiły się sprzeczne uczucia.

Polubił ją, pomyślała. Zainteresował się nią i przypadła mu do gustu. W przeciwnym razie nawet by się nie zająknął.

Z jednej strony bardzo ją to odkrycie ucieszyło, lecz jednocześnie z drugiej... czyżby poczuła... zazdrość?

O, Boże!

Nie chciała widzieć u siebie tak podłego uczucia.

– Chyba lepiej zrezygnuję z tych wielkich planów. – Skrzywiła się lekko. – Coś mi się widzi, że wpadła ci w oko.

Joshua ujął żonę za rękę, przyciągnął do siebie i przytulił. Pocałował ją czule w usta, a potem zajrzał jej głęboko w oczy.

– Tylko przy tobie jestem szczęśliwy – szepnął.

Joanna lekko pokiwała głową, ale wzrok miała nieobecny. Joshua wziął ją na ręce i pocałował mocniej, goręcej.

– Kocham cię tak bardzo, że nie sposób tego wyrazić – powiedział ochryple. Jego wargi pieściły twarz żony, jej czoło, policzki, oczy i nos, a potem uszy i szyję. Pocałunki stawały się coraz bardziej namiętne, gorące, pożądliwe. Zsunął dłonie na jej krągłe pośladki i przycisnął Joannę do siebie.

Natychmiast spotkał się z żarliwą odpowiedzią. Joanna przylgnęła do niego, wsunęła mu ręce pod ramiona i pogładziła szerokie, muskularne plecy. Raptem zdała sobie sprawę, że na jej brzuch napiera nabrzmiały kształt. Odsunęła się od męża, zajrzała mu w oczy.

– Wyłącz grill – zarządziła z psotnym uśmiechem.

Joshua posłusznie sięgnął ręką za siebie i natychmiast znów zamknął Joannę w objęciach.

Rzeczywiście, pomyślał, steki mogą poczekać.

Jeszcze raz pocałował żonę w usta, po czym wypuścił ją z objęć i wziął za rękę.

– Chodźmy do sypialni.

– Idziemy – zgodziła się natychmiast.

Ramię w ramię poszli na piętro i od razu na progu w pośpiechu zrzucili z siebie ubrania. Joshua zapalił świece i dłuższą chwilę sycił wzrok widokiem żony. Zuchwale sterczące piersi z różowymi brodawkami, talia cienka jak u osy, długie smukłe nogi połączone rozkosznym trójkątem – a całość skąpana w miękkim złotym blasku chybotliwych płomyków.

Joanna także miała na co patrzeć. Stał przed nią mężczyzna szczupły, silny, proporcjonalnie zbudowany, niezaprzeczalnie przystojny i pięknie opalony. Gdy wsunął się w jej ramiona, objęła go mocno za szyję i wpiła się w jego usta.

Błądził rękami po jej ciele, całując ją namiętnie i z żarem. Wreszcie wziął Joannę na ręce i położył na łóżku. Rozchylił jej uda, ukląkł między nimi. Delikatnie gładził jej nogi, biodra, brzuch, aż w którejś chwili pochylił się i ujął wargami jedną z różowych brodawek. O drugiej także nie zapomniał; żeby nie była zazdrosna, pieścił ją dłonią.

– Josh – jęknęła Joanna ochryple – już, proszę cię, teraz. Nie wytrzymam dłużej.

Rozsunął jej nogi szeroko na boki i ukrył twarz między jędrnymi udami. Gdy sądziła, że nie zdoła już się powstrzymać, Joshua odsunął się, a potem płynnym ruchem wszedł w nią aż do końca. Gorącymi wargami pochłaniał jej usta.

Joanna objęła go mocno. Zaczęli poruszać się w jednym rytmie, coraz szybciej i gwałtowniej. Bardzo szybko porwały ją fale cudownych skurczów, pochłonęła ekstaza orgazmu doskonałego, który potrafił jej ofiarować tylko ten jeden mężczyzna.

– Josh! – krzyknęła z zaciśniętymi szczękami. – Oooch!

Wtedy on także znalazł się na szczycie. Zadrżał, a całe jego ciało napięło się i zesztywniało, wstrząsane rozkoszą.

Opadł wreszcie, przygniatając ją swoim ciężarem i pokrywając jej twarz pocałunkami.

– Kochanie – wydyszał – bosko!

– Tak... – szepnęła, z trudem łapiąc oddech. – O, tak.

Przetoczyli się na bok. Ich serca powoli odnajdywały spokojniejszy rytm.

– Joanno, jak ja cię kocham... – Joshua pogłaskał żonę po twarzy, zapatrzony w jej ogromne źrenice. – Nikt na tym świecie nie kocha nikogo tak mocno.

– Ja ciebie też kocham. – W jej głosie zabrzmiała nutka smutku, a w oczach pojawił się cień melancholii, lecz Joshua tego nie zauważył, gdyż silniejszy podmuch wiatru wpadł akurat przez otwarty balkon, uniósł kotary, wepchnął je do pokoju jak łopoczące chorągwie i przytłumił płomienie świec. Niewiele brakowało, a byłby je zagasił.

Joanna wzdrygnęła się odruchowo, lecz zaraz pokryła lęk śmiechem.

– Chyba powinniśmy się przenieść z jedzeniem do środka – powiedziała. – Może padać.

Joshua przytulił ją czule raz jeszcze.

– Jak zwykle masz rację. Chyba że wiatr zdążył wymieść stół do czysta i już nie ma się do czego śpieszyć.

* * *

Siedzieli w jadalni. Joanna odłożyła nóż i widelec, otarła usta serwetką.

Joshua podniósł na nią wzrok.

– Poddajesz się? – spytał z uśmiechem. – Wiem, że stek mógłby być lepszy, wiem, że nie jest zbyt krwisty, ale mimo wszystko nadaje się do jedzenia.

– Jest całkiem smaczny – odparła. – Po prostu już się najadłam.

W oczach Josha błysnął niepokój.

To do niej niepodobne. Joanna uwielbiała jeść, choć przestrzegała rozsądnej diety i liczyła kalorie. Z drugiej strony, chyba nie ma powodu do niepokoju? Trzeba było uczciwie przyznać, że sałata zdążyła przywiędnąć, steki, sądząc po smaku, równie dobrze mogły zostać ugotowane, a i ziemniakom dwukrotny kontakt z kuchenką mikrofalową nie wyszedł na dobre.

– Mogło być lepiej – stwierdził z kwaśną miną.

– Daj spokój, coś za coś. – Joanna uśmiechnęła się znad kieliszka.

– Racja. – Pogładził żonę po policzku. – Jesteś smaczniejsza niż najwykwintniejsza kolacja.

– Rzekłeś! – zaśmiała się. – Ja też nie narzekam!

Przyglądała się jedzącemu mężowi i myślała o cudownym zakończeniu tego dnia. Najpierw pływanie, cudowny relaks, dodający sił. Potem seks – idealny, doskonały. Tymczasem jednak czar wieczoru z wolna się rozpływał i zaczynała czuć jakiś niepokój.

Miała wrażenie, jakby uciekała przed groźną ciemnością, jak gdyby kradła chwile szczęścia z Joshem! Dlaczego?!

Doskonale znała odpowiedź na to pytanie, choć jeszcze nie potrafiła jej ubrać w słowa, zupełnie jakby milczenie odsuwało od niej ponurą rzeczywistość.

Nie, nie dopuści do głosu przerażającej prawdy. Jeszcze nie dziś. Jeszcze nie teraz.

Rozdział dziewiąty

Słońce ogrzało już poranną mgłę i dzień stawał się coraz cieplejszy. Josh zszedł do jadalni, przeciągając się, aż mu stawy zatrzeszczały. Odrzucił z czoła bujną grzywę włosów.

– Witam piękne panie!

Świeży, pachnący, ogolony, trącił żonę nosem w policzek i pokrył jej twarz deszczem pocałunków.

Jak chłopiec, pomyślała Joanna z rozrzewnieniem. Rozpromieniony i szczęśliwy, dumny z siebie nastolatek, który minionej nocy odkrył jeden z najwspanialszych sekretów życia.

Connie, zajęta wyłuskiwaniem krewetek, zajrzała przez łukowate przejście.

– Co to za radosny ptaszek zawitał nam tu z rana?

– Mam za sobą wspaniałą noc. – Joshua puścił do niej oko. – Spałem jak zabity.

Connie roześmiała się głośno i pogroziła mu palcem.

– Już ja swoje wiem. Bądź grzecznym chłopcem.

– Jestem grzeczny – odparł z pewną siebie miną. – Zawsze. Bez wyjątku.

Usiadł przy stole i zaczął przeglądać gazetę.

Gdy odezwał się telefon, Connie odebrała w kuchni.

– Josh, do ciebie – zawołała. – Dzwoni Carl.

Joshua podniósł słuchawkę w jadalni.

– Cześć, to ja. – Jakiś czas słuchał, odpowiadając monosylabami, wreszcie się rozłączył.

– Coś się stało? – zapytała Joanna.

– Nic szczególnego – odpowiedział i na powrót zajął się przeglądaniem gazety.

Joanna udawała zainteresowanie ostatnim numerem „Vogue", leniwie przerzucając kartki czasopisma. Wolno popijała kawę. Mimo cudownego zbliżenia wieczorem, przez całą noc prawie nie zmrużyła oka. Niespokojnie przewracała się z boku na bok, a kiedy w końcu zdołała usnąć, dręczyły ją koszmary tak potworne i realistyczne, że z ulgą przywitała ciężkie przebudzenie.

Joshua z apetytem pochłaniał babeczki truskawkowe z bitą śmietaną.

– Jadłaś już? – spytał, popijając czarną kawę.

– Tak – odpowiedziała, podnosząc wzrok znad magazynu. – Wstałam dzisiaj o pierwszym brzasku.

– Co zrobisz z tak pięknie rozpoczętym dniem?

– Mam tysiąc spraw do załatwienia – odparła. – Jak zwykle.

– Wrócisz na lunch?

– Jeśli będziesz jadł w domu, przyjadę.

– Świetnie. Jesteśmy umówieni. – W błyskawicznym tempie skończył śniadanie, wstał i pochylił się nad żoną. Ucałował ją w policzek. – Muszę lecieć. Będę mniej więcej o wpół do pierwszej.

Wypadł z domu nieomal w podskokach, a po chwili rozległ się warkot staruteńkiego land cruisera. Gdy ucichł, Joanna odłożyła magazyn i poszła do sypialni. Szybko włożyła lekkie szerokie spodnie khaki, ażurowy pulower i wygodne sandałki na płaskim obcasie od Gucciego. Chwyciła jeszcze słomkowy kapelusz oraz torebkę i zeszła do kuchni.

– Connie, wychodzę.

– Obowiązki wzywają? – uśmiechnęła się gosposia, nadal zajęta krewetkami.

– Tak.

Dziewczyna podniosła na nią zdumione spojrzenie, ale nie odezwała się słowem. Normalnie Joanna wyjaśniłaby dokładnie, dokąd się wybiera i w jakiej sprawie, a także zapowiedziałaby, o której wróci. Dziś jednak stało się inaczej. Dlatego też Connie, podobnie jak Joshua, zaczęła się obawiać, że dzieje się coś niedobrego.

Joanna szybkim krokiem przeszła do holu i z misy imari, stojącej na irlandzkim stoliku, wzięła kluczyki od samochodu. Z torby wyciągnęła okulary przeciwsłoneczne, wsunęła je na nos, wreszcie włożyła kapelusz i przejrzała się w ogromnym lustrze o złotych ramach.

– Ujdzie w tłoku – oceniła.

Wyszła z domu, otworzyła drzwi garażu i wsiadła do ukochanego mercedesa. Wiekowy kabriolet był prezentem od ojca. Zaciągnęła pod brodą pasek od kapelusza, uruchomiła silnik i skierowała wóz na podjazd.

Gdy minęła bramę i ruszyła krętą górską drogą, odetchnęła z ulgą.

Dzięki Bogu! Z dala od Connie, Josha, telefonów...

Od wszelkiej odpowiedzialności, od podejmowania decyzji.

Czekały na nią rozliczne obowiązki, a ona dziś po prostu nie umiała stawić im czoła. Zakupy musiały poczekać. Tak samo jak projekt groty, spotkania towarzystwa miłośników orchidei oraz wszelkie akcje charytatywne. A także przyjacielskie plotki, kłopoty koleżanek, ich codzienne zwycięstwa i porażki.

Chcę być sama. Muszę się spokojnie zastanowić.

Dotarła do wjazdu na autostradę i pod wpływem impulsu skręciła na południe. Dokąd właściwie zdążała? Tego nie wiedziała, ale musiała jechać. Pęd ją uspokajał. Poranny ruch był niewielki, wreszcie zaczęła oddychać swobodniej. Po jakimś czasie zdjęła nogę z gazu, zwolniła odrobinę. Lepiej nie łamać prawa, na tej drodze zwykle roiło się od patroli.

Stopniowo dotarły do niej ciepłe promienie słońca oraz podmuchy wiatru próbującego unieść jej kapelusz i zaczęła dostrzegać krajobraz. Po prawej stronie od czasu do czasu pojawiał się w dali Pacyfik roziskrzony złotym blaskiem.

Jechała przed siebie, nie myśląc, jaką drogą prowadzi ją los, gdzie jest i dokąd zmierza. Nie zauważyła, kiedy zjechała z autostrady, nie zdawała sobie sprawy, że znalazła się w okolicach Watsonville, że pnie się krętymi uliczkami miasteczka, wracając w góry.

Wreszcie szosa przemieniła się w drogę pełną ostrych zakrętów, miejscami podmytą i najeżoną znakami ostrzegawczymi – prawie taką samą jak ta, która prowadziła do domu April.

Zwolniła – i nagle zdała sobie sprawę, gdzie jest.

Boże jedyny! Trafiła tu jak po sznurku!

Rzeczywiście, wiodła ją jakaś niewytłumaczalna siła, potężniejsza od niej samej, od jej woli. W tym czarownym miejscu opuszczały ją nawet straszliwe bóle głowy, które zaczęły się przed pół roku.

Och, mam nadzieję, że nikogo nie spotkam!, pomyślała.

Skręciła w lewo i wolno pięła się krętą szosą prowadzącą na niewielki parking. Nie było tam innego samochodu. Objęła spojrzeniem wysoki parkan, obrośnięty pnącymi różami. Gałęzie uginały się pod ciężarem kwiatów. Wolno podeszła do wiekowego rosłego krzewu „Dainty Bess", obsypanego delikatnymi różyczkami w kolorze bladego różu. Głęboko wciągnęła w nozdrza słodką woń.

Weszła do ogrodu przez drewnianą furtkę i starannie zamknęła ją za sobą na haczyk, by nie narazić pięknych roślin na niepożądaną wizytę zwierząt. Rozejrzała się uważnie dookoła.

Nikogo.

Odetchnęła z ulgą. Powietrze było ciężkie od aromatu tysięcy różanych kwiatów. Wolnym krokiem ruszyła przez ogród pocięty ścieżkami, spoglądając od czasu do czasu na tabliczki z nazwami gatunków, odświeżając je sobie w pamięci. Niejeden miał rodowód sięgający początku dziewiętnastego wieku, a zapach roztaczały tysiąckroć piękniejszy niż tak popularne ostatnio herbaciane hybrydy.

Joanna przyklękła i delikatnie ujęła w dłoń ogromny kwiat „Comte de Chambord", pochodzący z lat sześćdziesiątych dziewiętnastego wieku. Zanurzyła nos w wonnych płatkach. Rzeczywiście, arystokratyczna ozdoba. Prawdziwy arystokrata wśród innych kwiatów.

Nazwy kolejnych gatunków wywołały uśmiech na jej ustach: „Duchess d'Brantes", czyli księżna, następnie „Marchioness of Lorne", a więc markiza, dalej „Lady Hillingdon", również kwiat wysokiego rodu, „Bishop Darlington" – tu dla odmiany dostojnik duchowny, „Honorine de Brabant" – prześliczna róża w paski, rozłożysta „Gruss an Coberg", pełna „Gruss an Aachen", a do kompletu jeszcze „Jacques Cartier" i „Louise Odier".

Krzewy zasadzono w przypadkowych, zdawałoby się, miejscach, rabaty otoczono starymi deskami, a ścieżki wijące się po ogrodzie były pokryte asfaltem albo wysypane piaskiem lub żwirem. Ogrodzenie także składało się z bardzo różnych elementów – od zardzewiałego drutu po wyschnięte drewno. Ale uroda kwiatów i cudne rajskie wonie sprawiały, że pozorny bałagan i zaniedbanie traciły jakiekolwiek znaczenie.

Ktoś, kto urządził tę czarowną kryjówkę pośród sekwoi, włożył w swoją pracę wiele serca.

Minęła niewielki placyk, gdzie wystawiono na sprzedaż sadzonki w doniczkach. Na rozchwierutanej ladzie obok roślin stało pudełko pełniące rolę kasy. Transakcje tutaj przeprowadzane oparte były na zasadzie całkowitego zaufania: kupujący wsuwali czeki lub gotówkę przez otwór w kartonie. Miło było widzieć namacalny dowód ludzkiej uczciwości.

Joanna przysiadła na drewnianej ławeczce, pobielonej przez czas. Cień dawała jej pergola porośniętą czcigodną różową „Cecile Brunner", która wspięła się na szczyt podpory i spływała z niej obfitymi kaskadami. Joanna odetchnęła głęboko, rozkoszując się cudowną mieszanką zniewalających woni, ciepłym dotykiem słonecznych promieni na stopach i chłodnym cieniem nad głową. Zamknęła oczy, ukołysana spokojem i ciszą tego miejsca, a wówczas myśli, oderwane od codziennych spraw i domowych obowiązków, zaczęły powracać do problemu, z którym musiała się uporać.

Najwyższy czas powiedzieć im o wszystkim... Sama już dłużej nie da sobie rady, bo oszaleje. Długi czas dźwigała ciężkie brzemię w pojedynkę, lecz każde bohaterstwo ma swoje granice.

Widać nie jestem taka dzielna, jak mi się zdawało. Muszę z kimś porozmawiać, wyrzucić z siebie przerażenie i ten straszny ból... Koszmarne uczucie bezradności wobec nieuniknionego.

Postanowiła najpierw zwrócić się do Joshuy. Najbliższego przyjaciela. Najukochańszego męża.

Powiem mu wszystko. Jemu pierwszemu. Powinnam się z nim podzielić tym zmartwieniem, choć w ten sposób przysporzę mu cierpień. Tak. Właśnie tak trzeba postąpić.

Ogromny ciężar, przygniatający jej serce, zelżał nieco. Rozbłysła iskierka nadziei, że z Joshem łatwiej jej będzie znosić ten posępny czas. Bo coraz trudniej przychodziło jej ukrywanie przed mężem fatalnej prawdy.

Tak, powiem Joshowi, obiecała sobie. Zasługuje na zaufanie, powinien wiedzieć, co się dzieje.

Czas jakiś błądziła po ogrodowych ścieżkach, nim wreszcie zdecydowała, iż najwyższy czas wrócić do obowiązków. Jeszcze tylko podziękowała w myślach opatrzności za istnienie tego czarownego zakątka, za pociechę, którą tu zawsze znajdowała, i za to, że wskazywał jej najwłaściwszą drogę.

* * *

Joshua siedział sam przy stole na tarasie. Kończył drugą kanapkę z tuńczykiem, przygotowaną przez Connie. W zasadzie uwielbiał zapach kolendry, którą ryba została obficie przyprawiona, ale ostatnio odnosił wrażenie, że gosposia dodaje kolendry do wszystkiego.

Albo po prostu jestem w kiepskim humorze, zmitygował się w myślach.

Spojrzał na resztki doskonałej sałatki z karczochów. Chyba też z kolendrą.

Upił solidny łyk mrożonej herbaty, odstawił szklankę i starannie otarł usta sztywną lnianą serwetką. Po raz kolejny zatrzymał wzrok na pustym krześle po drugiej stronie stołu.

Cudownie. Wspaniale. Tylko, niestety, bez Joanny. I właśnie dlatego był w takim podłym nastroju. Znowu zniknęła.

W południe zawsze jadali razem, jeśli tylko było to możliwe. Na palcach jednej ręki mógł policzyć, ile razy im się to nie udało.

Może wymagał od niej zbyt wiele? W końcu, ile małżeństw wytrwało w takiej zażyłości jak oni? Ile tego pragnęło?

Uświadomił sobie, że większość ich znajomych nie życzyłaby sobie takiej bliskości w domu i w pracy. Dotąd jednak im dwojgu odpowiadał taki stan rzeczy. Od samego początku, od zawsze tworzyli zgrany duet i nie wyobrażali sobie innego życia. Pewnie dlatego, że po dziesięciu latach małżeństwa kochali się równie mocno jak na początku znajomości.

Czy aby na pewno? A może Joanna...?

– Josh! – Mroczne domysły przerwał mu wesoły głos żony. Szła przez taras, rozjaśniona słonecznym blaskiem, uśmiechnięta, piękna. Uściskała go serdecznie. – Przepraszam za spóźnienie. – Przyśpieszony oddech zdradzał, że biegła.

– Gdzie się podziewałaś?

Z westchnieniem ulgi siadła przy stole i zsunęła torbę z ramienia.

Jak za sprawą czarów pojawiła się Connie z kanapkami i sałatką. Postawiwszy naczynia, zaczęła nalewać herbatę.

– Dziękuję. – Joanna uśmiechnęła się do niej. Przeniosła spojrzenie na Josha. – Załatwiałam różne sprawy – odparła wymijająco.

W zasadzie nie miał zamiaru przeprowadzać przesłuchania, ale nie zdołał się powstrzymać.

– Jakie?

– No wiesz – położyła serwetkę na kolanach – zwykła codzienna krzątanina... Nie ma o czym mówić. Zawiozłam ubrania do pralni, zrobiłam drobne zakupy... Naprawdę nic szczególnego.

Connie zmrużyła oczy. Już ona wiedziała swoje. Joanna wyszła z domu z pustymi rękami, a wróciła także bez niczego. Nie wyniosła prania i nie przywiozła sprawunków. Tak czy inaczej, gosposia nie odezwała się słowem.

Joshua przyglądał się żonie zaintrygowany. Rozmyślając podczas pracy w cieplarni, zdecydował, że najwyższy czas przeprowadzić z Joanną poważną rozmowę. Teraz, czując wyraźnie, iż nie dowiedział się prawdy, tym bardziej uznał słuszność swojego postanowienia. Musiał poznać przyczyny dziwnego zachowania żony. Chciał wiedzieć, dlaczego od jakiegoś czasu wydawała się dziwnie obca.

Z drugiej strony, wspomnienie minionej nocy odsuwało na bok wszelkie wątpliwości co do jej uczuć. Zeszłej nocy była taka jak dawniej: cudowna, kochająca, troskliwa, czuła – i namiętna, a seks dał im obojgu tyle szczęścia i radości. Po tej upojnej nocy Joshua wstał radosny jak skowronek i zaczął już nawet myśleć, że chyba mu się wydawało i w rzeczywistości nie dzieje się nic złego.

A jednak... może powinien wspomnieć, że zauważył jej... rezerwę? Zwyczajnie spytać, czy nie stało się coś złego, o czym powinien wiedzieć... nie robiąc z tego wielkiej sprawy?

Nie zdążył, gdyż uprzedził go dzwonek telefonu. Odebrała Connie, która składała na tacę puste naczynia.

– Halo? – Przez kilka chwil słuchała bez słowa, następnie podała komórkę Joshowi. – To Carl.

– Dziękuję. – Wziął od dziewczyny telefon. – O co chodzi?

Joanna przyglądała się mężowi, jedząc kanapkę. Wiadomość najwyraźniej zrobiła na nim duże wrażenie.

– Co powiedział? – spytała, gdy tylko Joshua zakończył rozmowę.

Uśmiechnął się szeroko jak kot z „Alicji w krainie czarów" – i na tym poprzestał.

– No powiedz! – Teraz była już mocno zaintrygowana.

– Wiesz, kto się zapowiedział z wizytą w szklarniach?

– Kto?

– Zgadnij.

– Josh, przestań! Mówże wreszcie!

– Pan Hara – oznajmił Joshua.

– Wspaniale! – ucieszyła się Joanna. – Świetnie! – Zerwała się z krzesła, ujęła twarz męża w obie dłonie i wycisnęła mu na czole głośny pocałunek.

– Dzwonił z samochodu. Jedzie z San Jose i będzie u nas niedługo, więc chyba już czas na mnie.

Joanna ucałowała go raz jeszcze.

– Iść z tobą?

– Nie musisz.

– Miałam zamiar poszperać w albumach i poszukać zdjęć dla April, ale jeśli się przydam...

– Na dole dam sobie radę sam, tylko gdybyś mi teraz pomogła spakować kilka roślin z cieplarni, będę ci wdzięczny po grób.

– Do roboty.

Trzymając się za ręce, poszli do cieplarni, wystawili z niej kwiaty wybrane przez Joshuę i na cztery razy zanieśli je do land cruisera. Wreszcie Joanna przesłała mężowi pocałunek, Josh pomachał jej znad opuszczonej szyby i pojechał do szklarni.

Zdawał sobie sprawę, że powinien na kolanach dziękować losowi. Pan Hara był jednym z najbogatszych ludzi na świecie, a jednocześnie najbardziej liczących się kolekcjonerów orchidei. Już sam fakt, że czyjś kwiat został wybrany do jego zbiorów, należało traktować jako ogromne wyróżnienie i niekwestionowany zaszczyt. Japończyk potrafił lekką ręką zapłacić piętnaście albo i dwadzieścia tysięcy dolarów za jeden kwitnący okaz, więc można się było spodziewać, że dziś zostawi przynajmniej sto tysięcy.

Mimo takich świetlanych perspektyw Joshua miał nieco zwarzony humor, ponieważ nie mógł się pozbyć przykrego wrażenia, iż coś ważnego zostało niedopowiedziane, a w powietrzu unosiła się jakaś niepewność związana z domem, z rodziną.

Muszę jednak porozmawiać z Joanną, zdecydował. Koniecznie.

Rozdział dziesiąty

Wiosna stała się nagle gorącym latem, więc April otworzyła w swoim starym dżipie wszystkie okna. Wiatr niósł wszechobecny zapach brukselki, który nie każdemu się podobał, ale ona akurat nie miała nic przeciwko temu. Po obu stronach drogi ciągnęły się pola, płaskie i równe jak stół. Z prawej zdawały się kończyć dopiero u podnóża gór, z lewej sięgały wydm na granicy z oceanem. Zawsze się zastanawiała, jak to możliwe, że takie atrakcyjne grunty, potencjalnie świetne tereny pod zabudowę, są wykorzystywane do uprawy warzyw.

Jechała dość szybko i uważnie przyglądała się mijanym znakom, by nie przeoczyć tabliczki wskazującej skręt do szklarni Lawrence'ów. Wiele razy jeździła tędy do Monterey i dalej, a nigdy nie zwróciła na nią uwagi.

Gdy poprzedniego dnia zadzwoniła Joanna z prośbą o spotkanie, April uznała, iż ma jej przedstawić wstępne szkice. W zasadzie zgodnie z umową powinna je skończyć na jutro, ale ponieważ wiedziała, że klienci często się niecierpliwią i oczekują jakichś efektów przed uzgodnionym terminem, była gotowa wcześniej. Tymczasem została mile zaskoczona. Joanna zaprosiła ją do siebie, słowem nie wspominając o szkicach.

Tak czy inaczej, z przyjemnością wyrwała się z domu. Ostatnie dni spędziła przy desce, rysowała, ścierała, poprawiała i ulepszała, pracowała właściwie bez ustanku, bez chwili przerwy, bo nawet jeśli nie siedziała z ołówkiem w ręku, to i tak myślała o tym projekcie. Woody, który próbował ją skusić uroczystą kolacją, również przegrał z grotą, bo April tak bardzo się starała dotrzymać terminu. Jeśli nie szkicowała, to przeglądała książki od Joanny, szukając pomysłów, natchnienia, inspiracji dla wyobraźni. A gdy pojawiała się wena, April znów gorączkowo przelewała obrazy na papier, pełna energii, gorączkowo rzucając na kartki liczne pomysły, których wystarczyłoby na kilka takich projektów.

Wreszcie uznała, iż pierwsze szkice są mniej więcej gotowe. Mimo wszystko zamierzała im poświęcić jeszcze trochę czasu ostatniego wieczoru przed oddaniem.

Po lewej stronie dostrzegła znak wskazujący drogę do szklarni Lawrence'ów. Nie widziała jeszcze szklarni orchidei z prawdziwego zdarzenia, jedynie tę niewielką cieplarnię z najcenniejszymi okazami, po której oprowadzał ją Joshua. Teraz April nie mogła się doczekać kolejnej egzotycznej wycieczki, jako że Joanna chciała jej pokazać możliwie najwięcej gatunków tych kwiatów.

Przejechała boczną drogą może pół kilometra, gdy z prawej strony zobaczyła szklarnie. Zatrzymała się na żwirowym parkingu, wzięła torbę, wysiadła i uważnie popatrzyła dookoła.

Osłaniając oczy dłonią, przyjrzała się dużemu domowi w stylu wiktoriańskim, z charakterystyczną dla tego okresu bogatą ornamentyką, otoczonemu przez oszklone pawilony – twory wyjęte z zupełnie innej rzeczywistości. Wszystkie były nieskazitelne, nawet cokolwiek przesadnie zadbane, a mimo to nadal stanowczo nie na miejscu.

Nie dostrzegła na parkingu mercedesa Joanny, poszła więc do bramy prowadzącej na podwórze, a potem chodnikiem do drzwi domu. Ogrodzony teren wokół budynku nie należał do rozległych, rosło tam zaledwie kilka drzew i krzewów, pięknie utrzymanych, ale nieproporcjonalnie małych w porównaniu z okazałą budowlą. Weszła na ganek, pchnęła skrzydło podwójnych drzwi i znalazła się w chłodnym biurze.

W holu urządzono recepcję. Było to pomieszczenie o dziwacznym kształcie, nieomal okrągłe. Na środku znajdowało się biurko, za którym siedziała uderzająco piękna kobieta o kruczoczarnych włosach, ogromnych smolistych oczach i zbyt mocnym makijażu. Rozmawiała przez telefon – z jej ust spływał wartki potok hiszpańskich słów. Podniosła wzrok, a zobaczywszy April, uśmiechnęła się i gestem zaprosiła ją, by usiadła na krześle. Dłonie miała wąskie, o smukłych palcach zakończonych długimi paznokciami pomalowanymi krwistoczerwonym lakierem. Ani na sekundę nie przerwała rozmowy. Oczy jej błyszczały, żywo gestykulowała wolną ręką.

April usiadła posłusznie na wskazanym krześle i szczerze zafascynowana obserwowała śniadą piękność. Zwróciła uwagę na jaskrawowiśniową szminkę, obwiedzioną konturówką w nieco ciemniejszym odcieniu czerwieni, fioletowe cienie na powiekach, rzęsy ciężkie od tuszu i rozświetlający róż. Z umalowanymi ustami pięknie kontrastowały olśniewająco białe zęby.

Nagle kobieta zachichotała, rzuciła krótkie „ciao" i odłożyła słuchawkę na widełki.

– Przepraszam – odezwała się z lekkim obcym akcentem. – To był miejscowy klient. Lokalny. *Loco*.

– Nic nie szkodzi – uśmiechnęła się April. – Jestem umówiona z Joanną Lawrence.

Młoda kobieta uniosła brwi, wyraźnie zdumiona.

– Z Joanną? Aha. Proszę zaczekać chwileczkę. – Wcisnęła guzik na aparacie, podniosła słuchawkę. – Kogo mam zapowiedzieć?

– April Woodward.

– April – powtórzyła recepcjonistka, jakby się uczyła wymowy. – W biurze jest pani April Woodward – rzuciła w słuchawkę. – Umówiona z Joanną, tyle że Joanny tutaj nie ma. – Chwilę słuchała, po czym się rozłączyła. – Zaraz przyjdzie do pani Joshua, pan Lawrence.

– Dziękuję.

Po niedługim czasie otworzyły się balkonowe drzwi z lewej strony holu i wszedł Josh, błyskając na powitanie szerokim uśmiechem. Ubrany był w sięgające do kolan spodnie khaki oraz tego samego koloru koszulę i wyglądał jak ogrodnik.

Nieziemsko przystojny, pomyślała April.

– Witaj! – Wyciągnął do niej rękę. – Miło cię widzieć.

April podała mu dłoń.

– Mam nadzieję, że nie przeszkadzam – powiedziała nieco zakłopotana. – Joanna miała mnie oprowadzić po szklarniach.

– Nie przeszkadzasz ani trochę – zapewnił ją Joshua. – Joanna pewnie się spóźni. Widzę, że Lunę już znasz.

– Niezupełnie. – Podeszła do biurka i podała rękę sekretarce. – Miło mi panią poznać.

– Mnie także. – Luna zachichotała po swojemu. – Właśnie rozmawiałam przez telefon... – wyjaśniła Joshowi.

– Jak zwykle – uśmiechnął się wyrozumiale. – Jak zwykle. Wejdźmy do mnie – zaprosił gościa.

April od razu spostrzegła, iż jego gabinet został urządzony w dawnym salonie. Na wprost wejścia, przed wykuszowym oknem, stało ogromne biurko. Za nim zobaczyła obrotowy fotel, przed nim dwa skórzane leniwce.

– Siadaj, proszę. – Joshua zamknął drzwi. – Zadzwonię do Joanny. – Przysiadł na brzegu biurka i wystukał numer.

April uświadomiła sobie, że wlepia w niego wzrok, więc szybko spuściła powieki.

Co ją naszło? Dlaczego nie może oderwać spojrzenia od tego mężczyzny? Od jego niemożliwie niebieskich oczu, złotych włosów, śnieżnobiałych zębów, opalonej skóry... O Boże!

– Cześć, Connie – odezwał się Joshua. – Czy Joanna jest może gdzieś w pobliżu? Już w drodze na dół? – Słuchał przez chwilę. – Rozumiem, dziękuję – powiedział wreszcie. – Trzymaj się. – Odłożył słuchawkę i odwrócił się do April. – Jest w drodze. Nie nosi telefonu komórkowego, więc nie potrafię powiedzieć, jak prędko do nas przyjedzie. – Przepraszającym gestem rozłożył ręce. – Mam nadzieję, że Luna nie kazała ci czekać?

– Nie, nie – zapewniła go April. – Zresztą nigdzie się nie śpieszę. – Nie wiadomo czemu poczuła się lekko skrępowana.

To niemądre, pomyślała. Ten człowiek jest mężem Joanny. Owszem, czarujący, miły, wręcz doskonały, ale to cudzy mąż. Poza obszarem zainteresowań.

Mimo wszystko z trudem skupiała się na rozmowie. Była niespokojna i czuła się odrobinę zawiedziona.

– Luna – podjęła niepewnie – jest wspaniałą sekretarką.

– Szatan, nie kobieta! – roześmiał się Joshua. – Ale też potrafi poprowadzić dziesięć rozmów telefonicznych jednocześnie i wycisnąć z klienta ostatni grosz. Mało tego, wobec tych, którzy zapominają o płaceniu rachunków, jest gorsza niż komornik.

– Wzór wszelkich biurowych cnót – podsumowała April.

– Rzeczywiście, jest świetna – przyznał Joshua. – Zresztą, nie odbiega od reszty rodziny. Jej mąż, Carl, pracuje u nas jako kierownik szklarni. Poznasz go dzisiaj. A jego siostrą jest Connie.

– Innymi słowy, prowadzicie interes dwurodzinny.

– Można to tak ująć. – Josh wstał. – Chodź, Joanna znajdzie nas w szklarniach. Nie ma sensu czekać na nią bezczynnie.

– Chętnie. Jest mi trochę nieswojo, że zabieram ci czas.

– A ja z przyjemnością wyniosę się z biura. Wolę pracować przy kwiatach.

April wstała i oboje ruszyli w stronę drzwi.

– Luno, będziemy w szklarniach – zwrócił się do sekretarki. – Poproś Joannę, żeby tam do nas przyszła.

Luna, oczywiście ze słuchawką przy uchu, pokiwała głową.

Wyszli na niewielkie podwórze, minęli bramę i skręcili w ścieżkę prowadzącą do bramy.

– Niesamowity dom – odezwała się April.

– Zbudowała go rodzina Joanny na początku dziewiętnastego wieku. Jak większość tutejszych mieszkańców byli farmerami. Potem jej ojciec rozpoczął uprawę orchidei, a pomysł okazał się trafiony. Wtedy zbudował dom, w którym teraz mieszkamy, a w tym urządził biuro. My podtrzymaliśmy tę tradycję.

Doszli do wysokiego ogrodzenia z drucianej siatki, otaczającego szklarnie. Gdy brama się otworzyła, ruszyli w stronę największego budynku.

– Dobry Boże! – wykrzyknęła April. – W życiu nie widziałam takiej wielkiej cieplarni!

– Jest ich tu siedem. Razem zajmują powierzchnię prawie trzydziestu tysięcy metrów kwadratowych.

– Trzydzieści tysięcy!

– Przeważającą część sadzonek sprzedajemy odbiorcom hurtowym. Dostarczamy hodowcom w całym kraju licznych odmian kwiatów, niedrogich i niezbyt wymagających. Zaopatrujemy także sklepy prowadzące sprzedaż wysyłkową. Natomiast naszą specjalnością są rzadkie i cenne gatunki. Tym się wyróżniamy spośród innych hodowców. – Otworzył drzwi szklarni.

April weszła i od razu stanęła jak wryta, oszołomiona ogromem przestrzeni wypełnionej niezliczonymi kwiatami o urodzie zapierającej dech w piersiach. Podobnie jak w małej cieplarni koło domu, tak i tutaj powietrze ciężkie było od wilgoci i zapachu kompostu.

– Chyba macie tu wszystkie orchidee, jakie rosną na ziemi? – westchnęła oczarowana.

– Rzeczywiście, niewiele nam brakuje. Jak dotąd mamy dwadzieścia tysięcy odmian klasycznych i ponad sto tysięcy zarejestrowanych hybryd.

– Niesamowite!

Ruszyli ścieżką, zerkając na tabliczki.

– Tutaj rosną te, które pozwalają nam zarobić na chleb. Innymi słowy, *Phalaenopsis*. Ta, na przykład, jest kupowana wyjątkowo chętnie, ponieważ kosztuje stosunkowo niewiele, a jednocześnie jest łatwa w utrzymaniu. Mamy takich spory wybór. Z tych samych powodów uprawiamy *Paphiopedilum* i *Cattleya*. W obu wypadkach ścieramy się z dość ostrą konkurencją tajwańską. Tym bardziej więc kładziemy nacisk na uprawę wyjątkowo rzadkich gatunków.

Na nich właśnie zarabiamy prawdziwe pieniądze. Zyskaliśmy także godną pozazdroszczenia reputację hodowcy oferującego najbogatszy wybór kwiatów.

– Jakim sposobem Tajwan może stanowić dla was konkurencję?

– Nasze prawo zezwala na wwożenie roślin bez ziemi. Wobec czego Tajwańczycy przywożą ledwo ukorzenione siewki, po czym doniczkują je w Stanach. W ten sposób zalali rynek niektórymi bardziej wytrzymałymi gatunkami. A teraz zaczynają wykupywać ziemię i stawiać szklarnie – od Vancouver po San Diego. Produkują ogromne ilości kwiatów, nie zwracając najmniejszej uwagi na ich jakość.

– Nieprawdopodobne!

– A jednak. My, na szczęście, słyniemy z rzadkich okazów i doskonałej jakości roślin. Dzięki temu przetrwaliśmy, gdy wielu innych hodowców musiało zamknąć interes.

Zwiedzali szklarnię za szklarnią, zatrzymując się tu i ówdzie, by poświęcić chwilę uwagi którejś wyjątkowej piękności albo wymienić kilka zdań na temat warunków uprawy. Joshua cierpliwie objaśnił gościowi działanie komputerowo sterowanego systemu zraszaczy, który strzegł odpowiedniego nawilżenia roślin. Odpowiedział też na wiele pytań o automatyczne żaluzje, które otwierały się i zamykały, dozując światło i cień, podobnie jak przepływające po niebie chmury. W poszczególnych szklarniach panowała różna temperatura i wilgotność, a także inne nasłonecznienie, zależnie od tego, jakie były tam orchidee. Wszystko po to, by zapewnić kwiatom warunki możliwie najbardziej zbliżone do naturalnych.

– Hodujemy rośliny pochodzące z najróżniejszych zakątków świata, wymagające krańcowo różnych warunków zewnętrznych. Mamy orchidee ze świątyń Machu Picchu, z Himalajów, a także z najbardziej tropikalnych rejonów Brazylii. Toteż musieliśmy w jednym miejscu odtworzyć różnorodne warunki atmosferyczne. – Joshua widział wyraźnie, że April słucha go z ogromnym zainteresowaniem i ciekawią ją nawet szczegóły techniczne. Wdzięczny był jej za ciągle nowe pytania. Spotkał w swoim życiu wielu miłośników orchidei, lecz mało kto był rzeczywiście zainteresowany czymkolwiek poza egzotyczną urodą kwiatów oraz informacją o ich pochodzeniu.

– A niech to! – wykrzyknęła April nagle. – Tak się zasłuchałam, że w ogóle nie robię notatek!

– Po co ci notatki?

– Chciałabym wybrać orchidee do groty. Zamierzałam od razu zdecydować, które będą najlepiej wyglądały pośród muszli i kamieni.

– Rozumiem z tego, że przyjmujesz propozycję Joanny.

– O tak! Z przyjemnością! Teraz już nie potrafiłabym odmówić.

– Więc to tak! – rozległ się za ich plecami znajomy głos. – Żona zawsze dowiaduje się ostatnia! – Joanna wzięła się pod boki i zmarszczyła brwi, mierząc dwójkę winowajców groźnym spojrzeniem.

April nie bardzo wiedziała, jak powinna zareagować na te słowa, ale zanim zdążyła się spłoszyć, Joanna wybuchnęła śmiechem. Potem podeszła i serdecznie ucałowała ją w oba policzki.

– Pojęcia nie masz, jak się cieszę! – zawołała. – Bałam się, że w końcu jednak mi odmówisz.

Joshua z radością przyglądał się obu kobietom. Cieszył go widok Joanny wreszcie rozpromienionej, pełnej zapału, pochłoniętej nowym projektem. Było też jasne, że znalazła doskonałą wykonawczynię swoich zamierzeń.

O tak, pomyślał. April jest naprawdę... wyjątkowa.

– Niewiele brakowało, żebym zrezygnowała – przyznała April. – Ze względu na termin. Muszę przesunąć realizację wszystkich innych zleceń. Ale po kilku dniach szkicowania zaczęłam widzieć tę grotę... – Zabrakło jej słów, więc tylko rozłożyła ręce. – Najwyraźniej połknęłam bakcyla.

– Chcesz powiedzieć, że zapadłaś na orchideomanię? – spytał Joshua.

– Szczerze mówiąc... – zastanowiła się – sprawa jest chyba nieco bardziej skomplikowana. Najwyraźniej nie mogę żyć bez projektu tej groty – a także bez orchidei. Jedno z drugim się splata... Nie sposób oprzeć się tak kuszącej propozycji.

– Tak właśnie podejrzewałam – oznajmiła Joanna. – Byłam przekonana, że znalazłam właściwą osobę do tego zadania.

– Witaj wśród swoich – uśmiechnął się Josh.

– Bardzo mi przyjemnie – odrzekła April z lekkim wahaniem. Nie była całkiem pewna, jak ma rozumieć to określenie.

– Znalazłaś jakieś kandydatki do groty? – spytała ją Joanna.

– Właśnie powiedziałam Joshowi, że zwiedzając szklarnie, zapomniałam o bożym świecie, o robieniu notatek też – przyznała April. – Ale muszę przyznać, że stanowczo jest w czym wybierać.

– Dziewczęta – wtrącił Joshua – zostawię was z tym trudnym zadaniem, bo wzywa mnie praca.

– Idź, idź. – Joanna ucałowała męża serdecznie. – Jak skończymy wycieczkę po szklarniach, będziemy w domu.

Josh przytulił żonę i oddał jej pocałunek.

– No to na razie. – Uśmiechnął się do April.

– Bardzo dziękuję za oprowadzanie. Jestem ci naprawdę wdzięczna.

Joshua raz jeszcze błysnął w uśmiechu śnieżnobiałymi zębami i zniknął.

– Powiedz mi – zapytała Joanna – widziałaś już wszystko?

– Chyba tak – April w zamyśleniu rozejrzała się dookoła – ale nie mam pewności.

– W takim razie przejdźmy się jeszcze raz szybszym krokiem – zaproponowała gospodyni – przy okazji pokażę ci, które kwiaty moim zdaniem pasowałyby do groty. Jeśli i ty pokażesz mi te, które tobie wpadły w oko, sporządzimy listę i porównamy spostrzeżenia.

* * *

Oranżerię urządzono w stylu neoklasycznym. Podłoga z gładkiego francuskiego wapienia stanowiła przepiękne tło dla ozdobnych roślin: palm, najróżniejszych paproci oraz, rzecz jasna, orchidei. Na środku stał ogromny stół zdobiony kamieniarsko-jubilerską metodą zwaną *pietra dura*, polegającą na tworzeniu niewielkich obrazków z precyzyjnie wycinanych kolorowych kamieni półszlachetnych. Centralną część blatu zajmował wizerunek gołębi na drzewie. Z sufitu zwisał kryształowy żyrandol z szesnastoma ramionami. Joanna i April zdecydowały, iż tutaj właśnie będzie się im najlepiej pracowało. Rozłożyły na stole wstępne szkice.

Gospodyni długi czas przyglądała się uważnie rysunkom, przekładając je i zamieniając miejscami, aż wreszcie podniosła spojrzenie na April, która oczekiwała werdyktu z niespokojnym biciem serca.

– Świetnie. Właśnie o czymś takim marzyłam.

Projektantka odetchnęła z ulgą.

– Cieszę się, że ci się podobają moje propozycje. Włożyłam w te szkice całe serce.

– Mhm... Trzeba oczywiście zmienić kilka drobiazgów...

O, nie... – westchnęła w duchu April z rezygnacją. Teraz się zacznie. Klienci zawsze wywracają wszystko do góry nogami. „Kilka drobiazgów" oznaczało zwykle gruntowne zmiany od podstaw.

Joanna dostrzegła jej zmieszanie.

– Nie ma się czym przejmować! – Jej głos od razu złagodniał. – Naprawdę chodzi mi o drobiazgi.

– Nie przejmuję się... – April wyraźnie robiła dobrą minę do złej gry. – Powiedz, proszę, co ci się nie podoba.

– Wszystko mi się podoba. Chcę ci jedynie podsunąć kilka sugestii! Rozchmurz się, proszę.

April musiała się uśmiechnąć.

– Teraz lepiej – uznała Joanna. Przełożyła kilka kartek, aż znalazła tę, której szukała. Był to szkic ściany, ozdobionej wnękami i innymi elementami architektonicznymi z muszli oraz kamieni. – Spójrz tutaj.

April pochyliła się nad rysunkiem. Tak ciężko pracowała nad tym projektem, że trudno jej było uwierzyć, iż coś należałoby zmienić.

– Oto doskonała wizja ściany we wnętrzu neoklasycznym – oświadczyła Joanna. – Piękna. Chciałabym zmienić tylko jeden element. Proponuję rozmyć granice.

April podniosła na nią pytające spojrzenie.

– Nie rozumiem.

– Wyobraź sobie, że ta ściana jest doskonale rozplanowanym ogrodem. Każdy kamyk, każda muszelka znajduje się dokładnie na swoim miejscu.

April skinęła głową.

– A teraz – ciągnęła Joanna – zobacz oczami wyobraźni, jak ten ogród się rozrasta. Jak rozkwitają kolejne rośliny. Tu czy tam wystaje gałązka, listek, kwiat. Pozwól tutaj na to samo. Niech od czasu do czasu któraś muszelka wymknie się spod sznurka, niech jakiś kamyk wyłamie się z szyku.

– Oczywiście! – rozjaśniła się April.

– Wiedziałam, że się zrozumiemy.

– Trochę baroku przełamującego czyste linie klasyki.

– Tak! Właśnie tak. Tu i ówdzie coś niespodziewanego, zaskakującego, z innego wymiaru.

– Kamień przełamany muszlą... Joanno! Jesteś genialna!

– Bez przesady! Po prostu długo się nad tym zastanawiałam. Frontony zaplanowałam z koralowca...

– Jak to!? – April była wzburzona.

– No tak... – Joanna straciła pewność siebie. – Dlaczego by nie?

– Joanno, koralowiec jest gatunkiem zagrożonym. I właśnie dlatego nie wolno go wykorzystać w grocie. – Widać było wyraźnie, że mówi całkowicie poważnie.

– To prawda. Z drugiej strony mam go całe kilogramy, zbierałam przez lata. Po co go marnować?

– Istnieje ważny powód, żeby go nie wykorzystywać. Znajdą się ludzie, którzy będą chcieli powielić twój pomysł. Zaczną kupować koralowce bez względu na źródło pochodzenia, a popyt oczywiście kształtuje podaż. I zaczyna się gospodarka rabunkowa.

– Nie przesadzaj.

– Nie przesadzam. Możesz wykorzystać wiele innych materiałów. Nie wolno narażać koralowców na zniszczenie.

Joanna westchnęła ciężko.

Odważna jest, pomyślała. Broni swojego zdania jak lwica. I przestrzega zasad.

– Wygrałaś – oznajmiła w końcu z uśmiechem. – Muszę przyznać, że teraz trochę mi wstyd. Wiedziałam, że to gatunek zagrożony, ale chciałam go wykorzystać. Uznaję jednak twój punkt widzenia.

– Masz tyle innych możliwości do wyboru, że na pewno nie będzie ci brakowało koralowca.

– Przekonałaś mnie – oświadczyła Joanna. – Aha, a przy okazji jeszcze jedno. – Podeszła do okna, gdzie pod parapetem wbudowano długą półkę na książki. Przełożyła kilka tomów i wyjęła sporą stertę katalogów. – Przejrzyj. – Położyła je na stole.

– Co to jest?

– Sama zobacz. – Wzięła pierwszy z brzegu katalog i wręczyła gościowi.

April zaczęła przerzucać kartki, a jej oczy robiły się coraz większe i okrąglejsze ze zdumienia.

– Niesamowite! – wykrztusiła wreszcie. – Skąd masz takie cudeńka?

– Swego czasu kupiłam trochę muszli w Monterey. No, może trochę więcej niż trochę – uśmiechnęła się Joanna. – Sprzedawczyni zapakowała je w karton od hurtownika, na którym była nalepka z jego danymi. Zadzwoniłam do dostawcy, do Oregonu... przedstawiłam się jako osoba wykorzystująca muszle do pracy i zamówiłam katalog.

Roześmiały się obie.

– Nie umiem kłamać, a tu naopowiadałam, że jestem artystką... że muszle są niezbędnym elementem moich dzieł... Było mi głupio, czułam się podle... Ale hurtownik połknął haczyk, nawet razem ze spławikiem, żyłką i całą wędką. Toteż uznałam tę metodę za skuteczną i od tamtej pory udawałam plastyczkę i prosiłam w sklepach o namiary na hurtowników.

– Pomysłowo! Dzięki temu z pewnością nie zabraknie nam materiału. Ja też korzystałam ostatnio z usług hurtowników, więc na pewno muszli będziemy miały pod dostatkiem.

– Chciałabym najpierw, o ile to się okaże możliwe, wykorzystać te, które sama zbierałam. Mają dla mnie wartość emocjonalną.

– Oczywiście. To nie podlega dyskusji. Powinnyśmy omówić jeszcze jedną sprawę... a właściwie dwie: kwestię wyboru kwiatów i koszty. W zasadzie miałam zamiar poruszyć oba tematy dopiero jutro, ale skoro już tu jestem i mam kosztorys, rzuć na niego okiem, dobrze?

– A może najpierw zajmiemy się orchideami?

– Nie ma sprawy. Kilka z tych, które widziałam dzisiaj, chciałabym narysować i sfotografować.

– Nie widzę przeszkód.

– Tyle tylko – podjęła April – że nie chciałabym ich wozić do domu, aby nie brać na siebie odpowiedzialności za cenne rośliny.

– To zrozumiałe. – Joanna w zamyśleniu postukała w usta palcem. – Czy mogłabyś pracować tutaj? – spytała. – Zapraszam cię serdecznie. Możesz zająć tę oranżerię. Będziesz miała doskonałe światło... Co ty na to?

– Nie będę wam przeszkadzała?

– Skądże! A już poza wszystkim, przecież i tak będziesz spędzała sporo czasu w naszym domu, prawda?

– W takim razie zgoda, chętnie się urządzę w oranżerii do czasu zakończenia prac konstrukcyjnych w stajni. Później będę mogła się tam przenieść.

– Wobec tego, ustalone.

– Pozostała jeszcze kwestia kosztów – przypomniała April. Sięgnęła do torby zostawionej na krześle i wyjęła kartonową teczkę. W środku znajdował się starannie sporządzony szczegółowy kosztorys. – Proszę. – Podała go Joannie. – Starałam się zredukować koszty do minimum. Chciałabym, żebyś się zastanowiła, czy wszystkie pozycje są jasne.

Joanna skupiła się na lekturze, April zaś, nie chcąc jej przeszkadzać, podeszła do okna. Zachwycała się przepięknym widokiem na basen, zieleń i góry.

– Widzę, że uwzględniłaś już prace hydrauliczne i stolarskie... – odezwała się gospodyni po dłuższym czasie. – W zasadzie sporządziłaś pełen kosztorys.

April tylko pokiwała głową.

– Moim zdaniem jest jak najbardziej do przyjęcia. Poproszę jeszcze Josha, aby rzucił na to okiem, ale nie podejrzewam, żeby miał jakieś zastrzeżenia.

– To świetnie. – Czekała na słowa zleceniodawczyni z biciem serca, bo rachunek opiewał na rzeczywiście niebagatelną sumę. Z drugiej strony, miała świadomość, iż praca zajmie jej prawie pół roku i będzie wymagała ogromnego wysiłku.

– Bardzo się cieszę, że się rozumiemy – powiedziała Joanna zadowolona. Wzięła do ręki niewielką kartkę. – Wypisałam sobie najważniejsze sprawy do załatwienia... Dam ci kod do głównej bramy... Zwykle jest otwarta, ale nie zawsze. Aha, oczywiście kod do cieplarni, żebyś miała dostęp do kwiatów...

– Cudownie!

– Jeśli będziesz chciała coś do picia czy do jedzenia, zwróć się do Connie. Niezależnie od pory. Zawsze mamy wszystkiego za dużo, więc pomożesz nam trochę ograniczyć marnotrawstwo.

– Z przyjemnością. Chociaż starym zwyczajem będę pewnie przyjeżdżała z własnym prowiantem.

– Rób tak, jak ci najwygodniej.

– Chciałabym teraz jeszcze zajrzeć do stajni. Muszę zrobić dokładniejsze pomiary. I poprawiłabym szkice.

– Oczywiście.

– Trochę to potrwa...

– Może wobec tego zostaniesz na kolację?

– Nie chcę sprawiać kłopotu...

– Nie przyjmuję sprzeciwu – oznajmiła Joanna. – Zapraszam cię na kolację z szampanem, aby uczcić rozpoczęcie wspaniałego projektu.

– W takim razie nie zgłaszam sprzeciwu.

– Całkiem słusznie. Jemy zwykle między wpół do ósmej a ósmą. Jeśli się nie zjawisz do tego czasu, przyjdę po ciebie.

– Dobrze. – April zebrała swoje rzeczy. – Do zobaczenia. – Wyszła przez ogromne drzwi balkonowe.

Joanna odprowadzała ją wzrokiem, aż straciła gościa z oczu.

Cudownie, pomyślała. Wszystko idzie jak po maśle.

* * *

Dopiero gdy w budynku stajni zapanował półmrok, April uświadomiła sobie, że zrobiło się późno. Tak była zajęta pracą, iż nie dostrzegła upływu czasu. Zebrała do teczki kartki z pomiarami i ostatni raz rzuciła okiem na szkice. Były to rysunki znacznie bardziej szczegółowe niż te, które pokazała Joannie – i uwzględniały sugestie zleceniodawczyni.

Niesamowite, pomyślała. Na jej ustach błąkał się lekki uśmiech. Jeszcze nikt mnie tak szybko i łatwo nie przekonał do swojego punktu widzenia.

Tego dnia zyskała nowe, ogromnie ważne doświadczenie: okazało się, iż potrafi zachować ustalone reguły i zasady, ale też nagiąć je do tego stopnia, by spełnić oczekiwania zleceniodawcy, a jednocześnie ulepszyć projekt.

Zarzuciła torbę na ramię i ruszyła między starymi jabłoniami w stronę domu Lawrence'ów. Wieczór był piękny, powietrze rześkie, a ją przepełniało cudowne uczucie spełnienia, satysfakcja z dobrze wykonanego zadania.

Z daleka dobiegł ją głośny śmiech. Gdy zobaczyła basen, aż przystanęła, by podziwiać niespotykany widok. Wszędzie rozstawione były latarnie ze świeczkami: nad brzegiem wody, na stołach i na murze, na trawie i na schodach, nawet na mostku. Joanna siedziała na tarasie, Joshua, zanurzony po pas, akurat prysnął na nią wodą.

– Co to za wrzucanie męża do basenu! – zawołał z udawanym oburzeniem.

– Przestań! – krzyknęła Joanna. – Widzisz, coś narobił? Będę musiała się przebrać. – Wstała, aby strzepnąć mokrą bluzkę i spodnie.

– Dobrze ci tak! – Wyszedł na brzeg, zamknął żonę w uścisku mokrych ramion i obsypał jej twarz pocałunkami.

Joanna pisnęła.

– No, teraz to już koniec – jęknęła. – Jestem zupełnie przemoczona. – Ale jednocześnie wcale nie próbowała się uwolnić z jego objęć.

April poczuła się trochę nieswojo, jak intruz podpatrujący idylliczną scenkę małżeńską, lecz nie mogła oderwać oczu od tych dwojga. Tak właśnie wyobrażała sobie szczęście.

Jaki on jest cudowny! Wysoki, przystojny i silny, ale delikatny, czuły, a na dodatek skory do zabawy i z poczuciem humoru...

Gdzieś w głębi serca ukłuła ją dawno zapomniana tęsknota za beztroską radością we dwoje. Obudziło się w niej pragnienie takiego życia ze wspaniałym mężczyzną, wypalone i pogrzebane w czasie nieszczęśliwego małżeństwa.

– A, jesteś nareszcie! – zawołał do niej Joshua.

Zawstydziła się, jakby ją przyłapał na gorącym uczynku, choć przecież nie robiła nic złego. Bezwiednie przybrała ton i postawę, jak gdyby dopiero co zjawiła się nad basenem.

– Cześć!

Jednak na nic się zdała gra pozorów.

– Śledziłaś nas!

– Nie, wcale nie! – zaprzeczyła odruchowo. – Ale widziałam, jak się całowaliście! – dodała przekornie.

Roześmieli się wszyscy troje.

– Chodź, napijemy się szampana – powiedziała Joanna. – Czekaliśmy na ciebie z otwarciem butelki.

– Bardzo to miłe z waszej strony. Ale niech Josh obieca, że mnie nie ochlapie.

– Masz to jak w banku – oznajmił z szerokim uśmiechem. Owinął się jedwabnym szlafrokiem i zaczął otwierać butelkę, która już czekała w wypełnionym lodem wiaderku na stole.

– Muszę się przebrać w coś suchego – uznała Joanna. – Zaraz wrócę.

– Tylko nie marudź! – zawołał za nią Joshua. – Bo wypijemy wszystko bez ciebie. – Spojrzał na April. – Usiądź – poprosił. – Czuj się jak w domu.

– Z przyjemnością. – Usiadła i popatrzyła dokoła z zachwytem. – Pięknie tutaj w blasku świec.

– Rzeczywiście – przyznał Joshua. – Nie wiem, czy Joanna już ci wspominała, ale z basenu też możesz korzystać, kiedy zechcesz. Zależy nam, żebyś się tu czuła zupełnie swobodnie.

– Jesteście kochani.

– Daj spokój. Przecież nam nie ubędzie. – Korek z głośnym pyknięciem wyskoczył z butelki, w powietrze uniosła się cienka smużka mgiełki.

– Voilà! – Joshua nalał szampana do trzech smukłych kryształów ustawionych na srebrnej tacy. Wcisnął butelkę z powrotem w lód, następnie podał gościowi kieliszek.

– Nie powinniśmy zaczekać z toastem na Joannę? – spytała April.

– Masz rację – przyznał. – Jestem niewychowanym prostakiem. – Roześmiali się oboje. – Wypiję tylko troszeczkę, nie zorientuje się, że miałem więcej. – Podniósł kieliszek do ust. – Zaraz, zaraz... Ale przed tobą się nie ukryję. Hm... Wobec tego lepiej zaczekam.

April w odpowiedzi tylko się uśmiechnęła.

– Muszę ci powiedzieć – podjął Joshua – że Joanna zdążyła mi już pokazać twój kosztorys. Moim zdaniem jest bez zarzutu. Widać tu rękę profesjonalistki.

– Dziękuję. Twoja żona ma dalekosiężne plany, więc nawet oszacowanie kosztów nie było łatwym zadaniem. Określenie płatności za zmiany konstrukcyjne wymagało sporo pracy, a do tego jeszcze wycena mojego wkładu...

– Zdaję sobie sprawę, że stanęłaś przed wielkim wyzwaniem – stwierdził Joshua. – Ale też, przyznam szczerze, bardzo się z tego cieszę, bo ten projekt wyraźnie uszczęśliwia Joannę. Jest bardzo podobna do swojego ojca, musi stale tworzyć coś nowego. Domek na plaży urządziła właściwie własnymi rękami. I to jak! Potem wydała album o orchideach, prawdziwy bestseller. Wiecznie coś zmienia i poprawia, a to zakłada ogród, a to zmienia wystrój któregoś pokoju, a przynajmniej kolorystykę wnętrza... stale coś nowego.

– Moim zdaniem można się z tego tylko cieszyć. Wolałbyś, żeby spędzała czas głównie na zakupach?

– Dziękuję Bogu, że mi oszczędził takiej przyjemności!

– Wróciłam! – rozległ się głos Joanny. Lekkim krokiem podeszła do stołu i usiadła. – O, jak miło! Zaczekaliście na mnie! – Podała April cienki szal. – Masz, zaraz będzie chłodno. A kolacja najwcześniej za pół godziny.

– Dziękuję. – April narzuciła szal na ramiona. Był wykonany z pashminy, delikatniejszej niż kaszmir, i cudownie miękki, a na dodatek w ciepłym odcieniu jasnego brązu, wyjątkowo korzystnym przy jej karnacji.

Joanna przebrała się w beżową bluzkę z jedwabiu i spodnie od kompletu. Na ramiona zarzuciła biały kaszmirowy sweterek. Wyglądała uroczo, ale zarazem wydawało się, że wcale się o to nie starała. Jakby piękno stanowiło nieodłączny, oczywisty element jej otoczenia i jej samej.

April jednak wiedziała swoje. Ponieważ jej praca polegała na dyskretnym eksponowaniu piękna w taki sposób, by wydawało się całkowicie naturalne, doskonale zdawała sobie sprawę, ile wysiłku kosztuje osiągnięcie takiego rezultatu.

– Wobec tego teraz – odezwał się Joshua, podnosząc kieliszek – nadszedł czas, aby wznieść toast. Za grotę! Za szalony projekt mojej żony, którego ukończenia wszyscy wyglądamy z równą niecierpliwością.

Mam nadzieję, że go doczekam, pomyślała Joanna.

Ale zaśmiała się tak samo wesoło, jak pozostała dwójka, równie srebrzyście zadźwięczał jej kryształ ze szlachetnym trunkiem.

April dawno już nie piła tak wyśmienitego szampana. Drobne bąbelki rozkosznie łaskotały ją w podniebienie. Swoją drogą, od dłuższego czasu nie miała żadnej szczególnej okazji do świętowania.

– Chciałbym wznieść jeszcze jeden toast – odezwał się Joshua.

– Jaki? – spytała Joanna.

– Za April. – Przeniósł na gościa spojrzenie błyszczących błękitnych oczu. – Za jedyną kobietę, która słuchając mojej żony, pojęła nie tylko jej słowa, lecz także myśli.

– Tak jest! Słusznie! – wsparła go Joanna entuzjastycznie.

Z drżeniem w sercu obserwowała, jak patrzył na tę wyjątkową kobietę. Rodziła się między nimi sympatia, a może nawet zażyłość.

April natomiast przełknęła kolejny łyk szampana i znów poddała się fali melancholii. Tak dobrze jej było z tymi dwojgiem, mogłaby zostać z nimi na zawsze. Obawiała się jedynie, że wzbierające w jej sercu uczucie nie zostało równo podzielone. A lwia jego część przypadła panu domu.

Rozdział jedenasty

Nadeszło lato w całej pełni, a prace w stajni posuwały się naprzód w zadowalającym tempie. Szybko wmontowano rząd balkonowych drzwi, ale nie zyskały one całkowitej aprobaty żadnej z inicjatorek powstawania groty, póki Joanna nie dokupiła potwornie drogich okuć i klamek – rzecz jasna z motywem muszli.

April przyjęła założenie, iż w chwili rozpoczęcia robót Joanna, jak każdy normalny zleceniodawca, zniknie z horyzontu i tylko od czasu do czasu będzie sprawdzała postępy prac. Pomyliła się jednak; ta klientka stale trzymała rękę na pulsie. Taka sytuacja mogła się okazać trudna dla obu stron, ale w tym wypadku praktyka szybko wykazała, że obecność Joanny przynosiła więcej pożytku niż kłopotów. Podsuwała cenne rady, pomagała w podejmowaniu ważnych decyzji, brała na siebie wiele obowiązków, słowem – często okazywała się niezastąpiona.

Na przykład niewielką fontannę, która miała stanąć pośrodku groty, uznała za nieodpowiednią, zbyt dużo było na niej barokowych ozdób.

– Sądziłam, że dorówna obrazom powstającym w twojej wyobraźni – zdziwiła się April.

– Sama bryła fontanny ma być tylko podstawą dla stworzonych przez ciebie dekoracji – odparła Joanna. – Dlatego musi być jak najskromniejsza. Ty ją obłożysz muszlami i kamieniami. Tak samo jak ściany. Wyznaczysz na niej linie wzorów, a następnie zatrzesz granice.

April przez chwilę mierzyła ją osłupiałym wzrokiem, aż wreszcie wybuchnęła śmiechem. Tak, tej lekcji z pewnością nie zapomni.

Gdy wreszcie dostarczono właściwą fontannę, Joanna doglądała prac hydraulicznych, pilnując, by wyloty rur znalazły się na odpowiedniej wysokości, a każdy zwrócony był w odpowiednią stronę.

Ale korzystała też z doświadczenia April. Szybko odkryła najoczywistsze źródło jej sukcesów – doskonały kontakt z wykonawcami, owocujący ich prawdziwym, szczerym wysiłkiem. Jeśli jakiś fragment stiuków wyglądał już „prawie idealnie" i był „właściwie poziomo", a fachowcy przestawali się nim interesować, April potrafiła ich skłonić do poprawek, do poświęcenia najdrobniejszemu wycinkowi dekoracji takiej uwagi, że w końcu rzeczywiście był idealnie poziomo i dokładnie tak jak trzeba – choć wymagało to odrobinę więcej czasu i pracy.

W nawale prac dni uciekały lotem błyskawicy. Gdy nadszedł czas, by April zajęła się układaniem kamieni i muszli, obie były zdumione, iż nastąpiło to tak szybko. Zaprzyjaźniły się przez minione tygodnie, stały się sobie bliższe, zmienił się ton ich rozmów. Któregoś piątkowego ranka, na początku czerwca, kiedy pozwoliły sobie na chwilę odpoczynku, Joanna zaczęła opowiadać o siostrze.

– Christina jest ode mnie cztery lata starsza, kuta na cztery nogi i szczerze mówiąc, niekiedy zachowuje się podle. Ale umie też być troskliwa, pełna życzliwości. Przeżyłyśmy razem wiele cudownych chwil. Uczyła mnie, jak się ubierać, malować, z nią pierwszą rozmawiałam o sprawach damsko-męskich, plotkowałyśmy o chłopakach... Nie wiem, co bym bez niej zrobiła, na dobrą sprawę zastępowała mi matkę.

– Nadal jesteście takie zaprzyjaźnione?

– Cóż... Swego czasu wiele nas łączyło... Teraz... Odwiedzamy się przy różnych okazjach... Ja zawsze dwa razy w roku zaglądam do Montecito, natomiast Christina... z nią nigdy nie wiadomo. Może pokazać się u nas raz w roku albo przyjeżdżać co weekend. Jest nieprzewidywalna. – Westchnęła głośno. – Ot, choćby ostatnim razem... ze trzy miesiące temu wpadła do nas jak bomba całkiem niespodziewanie. Jesteśmy takie różne...

– Pod jakim względem?

– Pod wieloma. Christina jest szalenie ambitna. Od dziecka pragnęła brylować w towarzystwie. Kocha pieniądze i szaleje na punkcie mężczyzn. Może powinnam powiedzieć, że jest zwariowana na punkcie mężczyzn z pieniędzmi i władzą... Tak, to chyba bliższe prawdy. A tacy ludzie najczęściej mają także wysoką pozycję towarzyską.

– Twoja siostra nie stanowi jakiegoś szczególnego wyjątku w kobiecym gronie.

– A jednak się wyróżnia. Wyobraź sobie, skończyła trzydzieści sześć lat i była już trzy razy mężatką. Wszyscy trzej mężowie mieli pieniądze, władzę i doskonałą pozycję towarzyską. Moja siostra obraca się wśród snobów z Montecito i Palm Beach, bogaczy, zainteresowanych tylko perfekcyjną opalenizną. No, może jeszcze w pewnym stopniu końmi. Niektórzy grywają w polo, większość dysponuje gigantycznymi funduszami powierniczymi i nigdy w życiu nie skalała się żadną pracą.

– Ty nie umiałabyś tak żyć.

– Rzeczywiście – przyznała Joanna. – I wiesz, co najdziwniejsze, wielu spośród nich to naprawdę nieszczęśliwi ludzie. Oczywiście nie wszyscy, ale Christina wyraźnie ma talent do otaczania się próżniakami, znudzonymi, niespełnionymi i rozczarowanymi życiem.

– Bez żadnych celów i pragnień.

– Właśnie. Dostają obsesji na punkcie własnych kłopotów, jakby z powodu niedoskonałej fryzury czy kreacji miał się zawalić świat. Najważniejsza pod słońcem jest kolejna operacja plastyczna. Albo oryginalna biżuteria. Lub najnowszy kochanek. Oto sprawy bezsprzecznie najistotniejsze na świecie! – Joanna pokręciła głową. – Powinni czasem popatrzeć dalej niż na czubek własnego nosa. Taki jest mój najlepszy sposób na chandrę. Zrobić coś dla drugiego człowieka. – Spojrzała na Joannę. – Czy to nie brzmi jak banał?

– Owszem, ale ja powiedziałabym to samo. Zawsze to powtarzam.

– Christina powinna się zająć działalnością charytatywną. Robić coś, co by komuś innemu przyniosło pożytek.

– Powiedziałaś, że dawniej byłyście mocno zżyte. A jak teraz układa się między wami? Skoro jesteście tak różne?

– Jakoś dajemy sobie radę. – Joanna zamilkła. – Chyba zaakceptowałyśmy to, że mamy odmienne podejście do różnych spraw – podjęła – i mimo tych rozdźwięków pozostałyśmy przyjaciółkami. Przed śmiercią tata zapytał nas, jak chciałybyśmy podzielić majątek. Miałyśmy zdecydować, która woli wziąć ziemię i orchidee, a która pieniądze. Christina bez namysłu wybrała pieniądze, a ja byłam zadowolona z jej decyzji, bo wolałam ziemię i rodzinny interes. – Urwała i zapatrzyła się w dal. – Chyba dokonałyśmy właściwego wyboru, chociaż nie był to równy podział. Moja część okazała się, przynajmniej z początku, dużo mniej warta niż gotówka i gruby portfel akcji, które przypadły w udziale Christinie.

– Zdumiewające, że mimo to nie ma między wami niesnasek.

– To prawda. Może właśnie dlatego, że jesteśmy tak różne. Ja nie dbałam o tamte pieniądze, Christiny nie obchodziły szklarnie i ziemia. – Zamilkła. – Przynajmniej wtedy – dodała.

– Jak to? Chcesz powiedzieć, że teraz jest inaczej?

– Właściwie... nie bardzo wiem, co o tym myśleć. Ostatnio Christina często wypytuje o firmę, chociaż zwykle w ogóle jej nie zauważała. Więc trochę to dziwne... – Wzruszyła ramionami. – Może po prostu się nudzi między jednym mężem a drugim i poczuła sentyment do rodzinnego biznesu. – Pokręciła głową. – Naprawdę nie wiem. Tak czy inaczej – uśmiechnęła się – choć byłyśmy i jesteśmy całkiem różne, choć życie poprowadziło nas odmiennymi ścieżkami, nigdy nie zapomnę, że zastępowała mi mamę, i zawsze będę jej za to wdzięczna.

– A co się stało z twoją mamą? – Jeszcze kilka tygodni temu April nie miałaby śmiałości zadać takiego pytania, teraz jednak nawet się nie zawahała.

– Utonęła – odpowiedziała Joanna. – Niedługo po moim urodzeniu.

– O Boże!

– Swego czasu mieliśmy żaglówkę i kiedyś mama z tatą wybrali się popływać po zatoce Monterey, niedaleko naszego domku plażowego. Nagle zerwał się sztorm, a na zatokę opadła gęsta mgła. Od razu podniosły się też wielkie fale. Rodzice natychmiast skierowali łódkę do brzegu. Oboje byli na rauszu, mama nie włożyła kamizelki ratunkowej, więc kiedy wypadła za burtę, właściwie nie miała szans. Tata szukał jej długi czas, oczywiście wezwał pomoc, ale wszystkie wysiłki spełzły na niczym. Następnego dnia morze wyrzuciło jej ciało nieomal przed domkiem plażowym. – Joanna podniosła na April smutne spojrzenie.

– To straszne. Podejrzewałam, że spotkało ją coś złego. Często wspominacie z Joshem o twoim ojcu, a wcale nie mówicie o matce.

– Dla mnie jej śmierć nie stanowiła tragedii – przyznała się Joanna. – Byłam wtedy niemowlęciem. W ogóle nie pamiętam matki. Christina ledwo ją sobie przypomina i też nie ma całkowitej pewności, czy pamięta rzeczywistą postać, czy też fotografie i historie, jakie jej opowiadano.

– Twój ojciec już się nie ożenił?

– Nie. O ile mi wiadomo, nawet nie spojrzał na inną kobietę. A łódź spalił. I do końca życia nie tknął alkoholu.

– Winił siebie za śmierć żony?

– Najprawdopodobniej. I ze wszystkich sił starał się nam wynagrodzić brak matki. Poświęcił się całkowicie, kochał nas całym sercem. Czasami nawet myślę, że musiał zaczekać, aż obie się usamodzielnimy i wyjdziemy za mąż, żeby zachorować na raka. Dopiero kiedy zyskał absolutną pewność, że znalazłyśmy swoje miejsce w życiu, pozwolił sobie umrzeć.

– Dziwne są koleje losu... Taki ojciec to prawdziwy skarb.

– O tak. Miałam najlepszego tatę na świecie. Bezsprzecznie. Był wspaniałym człowiekiem, godnym podziwu pod każdym względem. Nie mogę się pozbyć odczucia, że los jest niesprawiedliwy... okrutny, skoro życie takiego wartościowego człowieka zakończyła straszna śmierć, powolna i bolesna... – Przeniosła na April poważne spojrzenie. – Kiedy umierał, straciłam wiarę w boskie miłosierdzie. I chyba jej nie odzyskałam. Ciągle bez skutku usiłuję się doszukać jakiegokolwiek sensu w niesprawiedliwości... w okrucieństwie, jakie czasem niesie ze sobą życie. – Uśmiechnęła się melancholijnie. – Wybacz, nie chciałam wpadać w taki poważny ton. A wracając do naszej rodziny, muszę przyznać obiektywnie, że obie z Christiną wyrastałyśmy otoczone miłością i rozpuszczane do granic możliwości.

– Szczerze mówiąc, jakoś nie widzę, żebyś była rozpuszczona – odparła April. – Doskonale zdajesz sobie sprawę z własnej sytuacji i doceniasz to, co masz.

– Jesteś bardzo miła. Ech, wracajmy do pracy, bo czas ucieka.

– Skoro już mowa o pracy, to chciałam ci powiedzieć, że od jutra będzie przychodził mój pomocnik, Woody.

– To ten przyjaciel, o którym wspominałaś? Ten ramiarz?

– Tak. Już nieraz pomagał mi przy większych zleceniach. Doskonale radzi sobie z szybkoschnącym cementem. Skoro mamy skończyć budowę groty w jak najkrótszym czasie, Woody bardzo się przyda. Nie dopuszczę go do żadnych prac dekoracyjnych, ale niech położy grunt pod wzory.

– A co z jego warsztatem? – spytała Joanna.

– Znalazł sobie zastępstwo. Będzie też pracował u siebie popołudniami, nic mu się nie stanie, jak czasem posurfuje trochę krócej.

Joanna nie chciała zdradzać April, że zna Woody'ego Pearlmana. Przynajmniej nie teraz. Trudno było jej wyrzucić z pamięci przykry incydent w pracowni ramiarza, ale też nie sposób zaprzeczyć, że poprzednie dwa zlecenia wykonał wzorowo. Może za trzecim razem po prostu miał kiepski dzień.

– Ten Woody chyba bardzo cię lubi, skoro jest gotów wszystko rzucić, żeby ci pomagać – zauważyła. – Może nawet kocha się w tobie?

– Nie, nie. To znaczy... to nie jest miłość... Do licha! Właściwie, nie wiem.

– A ty co do niego czujesz?

April najpierw się uśmiechnęła, a potem roześmiała w głos.

– Z całą pewnością go nie kocham. W każdym razie, tak mi się wydaje. Przyjaźnimy się od dłuższego czasu, a znamy się kopę lat, ale tak czy inaczej jesteśmy jak brat z siostrą, a nie kochankowie. Tak mi się przynajmniej wydaje. Nigdy na jego widok nie miękły mi kolana, nie łomotało serce ani nic z tych rzeczy. Z Woodym można iść do kina. Albo załatwić konkretną sprawę. Jest świetnym kumplem.

Joanna słuchała tej opinii z rosnącą ulgą, ale nie zdradziła się ze swoimi rewelacjami.

Woody Pearlman nie jest wart April, pomyślała.

Miałaby, delikatnie mówiąc, pewne zastrzeżenia w stosunku do każdego mężczyzny, z którym chciałaby się widywać April, ale też trzeba przyznać, że Woody, ów niefortunny Casanova, przede wszystkim budził jej niechęć.

Temu facetowi chodzi wyłącznie o jedno!

Z drugiej strony, czym wytłumaczyć przyjaźń tych dwojga? Chyba należało przyjąć, że on traktował ich znajomość inaczej niż April. A kiedy dostanie, czego chce, rzuci ją bez skrupułów i zacznie się rozglądać za następną zdobyczą. Ponieważ ona nie będzie już stanowiła wyzwania.

– Przebiorę się i wyjdę Woody'emu na spotkanie – odezwała się April.

– Dobrze. W takim razie, do zobaczenia przy obiedzie.

– Joanno, czy ja aby na pewno nie nadużywam twojej gościnności?

– Daj spokój! A już poza wszystkim innym, dziś mamy szczególną okazję, bo przecież zakończyły się roboty przygotowawcze i zaczynamy prawdziwą pracę.

– Masz talent do wyszukiwania specjalnych okazji – zaśmiała się April.

– Dobrego nigdy za wiele.

– Wobec tego, do zobaczenia przy obiedzie. – April poszła zmienić ubranie w domku przy basenie. Z niejakim poczuciem winy uświadomiła sobie, że zastanawia się, czy Joshua także będzie z nimi jadł.

* * *

Woody wetknął ręce w kieszenie i z nieskrywaną ciekawością dłuższy czas przyglądał się dawnej stajni. Wreszcie potrząsnął głową, aż czarne loki rozsypały mu się na ramiona, i zagwizdał z podziwu.

– Muszę przyznać, że to będzie ekstra.

– A ja muszę od razu zaznaczyć, że to pomysł Joanny, nie mój.

– Zgoda, ale to ty odwaliłaś całą robotę nad projektem. A teraz przyczepiasz te muszelki. – Jego czarne oczy rozbłysły. – Najwyższy czas, żebyś zaczęła dostrzegać własną wartość.

– Lejesz miód na moje serce. A wracając do rzeczy: widziałeś już, co trzeba zrobić. Znajdziesz czas, żeby mi pomóc?

– Jasne. Dla ciebie zawsze. A mogłabyś uściślić, o co dokładnie chodzi?

– Chciałabym, żebyś zajął się wypełnieniem większych fragmentów przeznaczonych pod jeden rodzaj kamieni czy muszli. Tam, gdzie nie będzie konkretnych wzorów. Spójrz. – Poprowadziła go do roboczego stołu zarzuconego planami. – Choćby na tej ścianie. Widzisz te miejsca między stiukami? Można je pociągnąć szybkoschnącym cementem, bo tam chcę ułożyć identyczne muszle i kamienie bez wzorów.

– Aha. Nudna, łatwa robota, z którą sobie poradzi pierwszy lepszy kretyn.

– Właśnie. Ciężką i trudną pracę zatrzymałam dla siebie.

– Ty tu rządzisz – stwierdził Woody ze śmiechem.

April spojrzała na zegarek.

– Przepraszam cię, ale muszę już uciekać, nie chcę, żeby na mnie czekali z jedzeniem. Trafisz sam z powrotem?

– Pewnie! Ale jeszcze przejrzę szkice, jeśli nie masz nic przeciwko. Zorientuję się, ile jest tej przewidzianej specjalnie dla mnie nudnej roboty.

– Nie ma sprawy. – Zdziwiło ją takie zaangażowanie przyjaciela. Woody pracował szybko i dobrze, ale nigdy nie interesował się szczególnie tego rodzaju robotą, traktując swoją pomoc tylko jako obowiązek do odbębnienia.

– I w ten oto sposób, gdy w poniedziałek przystąpimy do żmudnej pracy, będę już znał na pamięć obszar swoich działań artystycznych.

– Och, Woody! – April nie mogła powstrzymać się od śmiechu. – Jesteś niemożliwy. – Cmoknęła go w policzek. – Czas na mnie. Do zobaczenia wieczorkiem.

– Trzymaj się. Miłej zabawy.

April poszła w stronę basenu.

Woody odprowadzał ją wzrokiem, śledząc bacznym spojrzeniem, póki nie stracił jej z oczu.

* * *

– Nie wstawaj. – Joanna zatrzymała April gestem. – Dam sobie radę, naprawdę nie potrzebuję pomocy.

– Dobrze, nie będę się z tobą kłóciła.

– I słusznie – wtrącił Joshua. – Ona zawsze wie, co robi.

Joanna wyniosła do kuchni tacę załadowaną brudnymi naczyniami. Właśnie skończyli główne danie. Nadeszła kolej na kawę oraz deser.

– Connie ma dzisiaj wolne? – spytała April.

– Tak. Jest pod tym względem niemożliwa. Zawsze bierze wolne dni znienacka i w ostatniej chwili. Z drugiej strony, nam to specjalnie nie przeszkadza. Joanna uwielbia się rządzić w kuchni pod jej nieobecność. Może w pewnym stopniu dlatego, że nieczęsto jej się zdarza taka gratka.

– Ma to swój sens – przyznała April ze śmiechem. – Ja także lubię coś upichcić od czasu do czasu, zwłaszcza dla przyjaciół.

– Ze mną jest tak samo – powiedział Joshua. – Raz na jakiś czas chętnie przygotuję coś specjalnego dla nas dwojga albo jakieś wystrzałowe danie w ramach wkładu w imprezę. Gdybym jednak miał to robić codziennie, raczej nie byłbym zachwycony.

– Jako podlotek bardzo poważnie podchodziłam do wszelkich działań w kuchni, nawet do zrobienia kanapki. Zawsze starałam się uzyskać szczególny rezultat. Na przykład chleb z masłem orzechowym ozdabiałam sosem czekoladowym...

– Skąd ja to znam! – zaśmiał się Joshua. – Do wszystkiego dodawałem keczup. Do kanapek z sardynkami, do zupy z puszki...

– Bleee! Teraz mnie skręca na samą myśl o takich delicjach. Ale trzeba przyznać, że kiedy młody człowiek czuje się samotny, stara się ubarwić sobie życie na wszelkie możliwe sposoby.

– O tak. Powiedziałbym nawet, że do tego nie trzeba być bardzo młodym ani specjalnie samotnym.

– Może i racja.

– Ty chyba nie narzekasz na swój los? Joanna wspomniała, że masz dom jak z bajki, rozumiem też, że zarabiasz na życie tak, jak lubisz. Wyglądasz na szczęśliwą.

– Tak, rzeczywiście. Czuję się szczęśliwa. Nie zawsze bramy raju stoją przede mną otworem, ale jest dużo lepiej, niż drzewiej bywało. A taki zleceniodawca jak Joanna to prawdziwy dar niebios. Przy okazji: gdzie ona się podziała?

– Jak ją znam, dopieszcza deser – wyjaśnił Joshua. – Co może trochę potrwać. Nie muszę ci mówić, że dążenie do perfekcji to główna cecha charakteru mojej żony. Wiesz to już na pewno równie dobrze jak ja.

* * *

Joanna obserwowała ich przez okno. Deser był już gotowy, kawa zaparzona. Nie potrafiła jednak oderwać wzroku od sceny na tarasie. Na policzkach miała mokre smużki po łzach smutku, radości oraz ulgi. Widok tych dwojga, rosnącej między nimi zażyłości, rodził w niej całkiem nowe refleksje. Rozdarta między poczuciem godności i przerażającą świadomością straty musiała iść dalej zdradliwą ścieżką, na którą wstąpiła z pełnym rozmysłem. Stała na niepewnym gruncie, bo w świecie emocji nigdy nic nie wiadomo. Bliskość tych dwojga mogła się okazać fatalnym błędem. Czy rzeczywiście podjęła właściwą decyzję?

Kimże ona jest, żeby tak igrać z ludzkimi uczuciami?

Ale też zaraz uświadomiła sobie przyczyny, dla których musiała rozpocząć tę grę – i doprowadzić ją do zamierzonego końca.

Z drugiej strony, co mam do stracenia?, spytała siebie. Absolutnie nic.

A co oni mogą zyskać?

Znała odpowiedź także i na to pytanie.

Oni mogą zyskać wszystko.

* * *

Woody zgasił światła w grocie i ruszył między jabłoniami w stronę basenu. Wiatr przynosił mu odległy szmer rozmowy, tutaj podobny do szeptu, akcentowany dźwięcznym stukaniem lodu o szkło.

Na skraju sadu zatrzymał się w cieniu. Z daleka obserwował sielankową scenę. Joshua Lawrence. Przystojny, jasnowłosy, bogaty. Trzymał April za rękę. A ona pożerała go wzrokiem. Oczywiście. Jakże by inaczej.

Piękny obrazek, nie ma co. Skrzywił się, obrócił na pięcie i obszedł taras szerokim łukiem.

Jak ona tak może! Kto jej pozwolił! A on? Podrywacz się znalazł! Żonaty! Z tamtą dzianą niedotykalską! A ta się ślini na jego widok! Dlaczego mnie nie chce dać tego, co powinna? A jemu pewnie dałaby ze śpiewem na ustach!

Na podwórzu wyjął z kieszeni kluczyki od vana. W tej samej chwili jego wzrok padł na toyotę Josha.

Staruszka, pomyślał. Ale świetnie utrzymana.

Chwycił kluczyk mocniej i przycisnął go do karoserii. Z potwornym zgrzytem wyrysował na żółtym lakierze długą, krzywą rysę.

Ma za swoje, kutafon jeden.

Wsiadł do swojego auta, uruchomił silnik i wycofał vana z takim impetem, że żwir spod kół strzelił wysoko do góry. Zadowolony był ze swojego wyczynu. Zastanawiał się też, w jaki sposób mógłby naprawdę wyrównać rachunki z tymi dwojgiem.

Rozdział dwunasty

Christina wbiegła po betonowych stopniach na chodnik. Szpileczki od Gucciego, warte fortunę, stukały głośno. Skrzywiła się paskudnie i pożałowała, że nie może się stać niewidzialna. Chciała się spotkać z Peterem Rossim gdzieś indziej, ale on nalegał. Koniecznie musiał ją ściągnąć w ten posępny zaułek, do sklepiku na końcu deptaka w Santa Cruz. Śpieszył się ponoć, miał jakieś niecierpiące zwłoki sprawy do załatwienia właśnie tam, a ponieważ późnym letnim popołudniem w takim miejscu nie ma ludzi, istniało bardzo niewielkie ryzyko, że ktoś znajomy ich zobaczy.

No jasne, pomyślała Christina. Ponieważ nikt znajomy za nic w świecie nie pokazałby się w tak żałosnym miejscu!

Peter mówił, że w okolicy jest mnóstwo przytulnych zakątków, gdzie będą mogli miło spędzić razem parę godzin. Nie potrafiła odgadnąć, czy przypadkiem nie przeprowadzał właśnie testu, który miał pokazać, czy Christina byłaby skłonna zadawać się z facetem z dołów społecznych.

No, jak dla niej to mógł pochodzić nawet z Marsa.

Skądś popłynęła smutna pieśń grana na flecie, ale niemal od razu zagłuszył ją ryk osiemdziesięcioletniej kolejki górskiej zwanej Giant Dipper. Towarzyszyły mu krzyki i śmiechy pasażerów. W powietrzu unosił się pomieszany zapach hot dogów, prażonej kukurydzy, waty cukrowej oraz piwa, olejku do opalania i potu. Dla Christiny – smród trudny do wytrzymania.

Boże! Co ja tu robię?!

Czuła tylko pogardę dla ludzi, których pociągają przejażdżki kolejką górską, fast foody i niezliczone kioski z upominkami, gdzie sprzedawano tandetne koszulki, muszle, sztuczną biżuterię oraz inne bezwartościowe gadżety. Z odrazą przesunęła wzrokiem po grupce spoconych, brudnych motocyklistów, ubranych w skóry, oraz ich równie zaniedbanych przyjaciółkach. Akurat w tej chwili podjechali do nich strażnicy miejscy w schludnych mundurach khaki. Stróże prawa na rowerach nie robili może wrażenia szczególnie srogich, ale pozory mylą. Christina uśmiechnęła się z satysfakcją.

Starała się trzymać jak najbliżej dobrze oświetlonych sklepów po prawej stronie ulicy. Ciągle nie widziała tego, w którym się umówili... Wreszcie znalazła: Ogród Posejdona. Kolejna nędzna buda z tandetą. Zwolniła i zajrzała do środka przez podwójne szklane drzwi. Może wypatrzy Petera? Niestety, widok zasłaniała para utleniona na blond. Oboje demonstrowali muskulaturę kulturystów, ona była ubrana w pomarańczowe bikini, które pozostawiało niewiele pola wyobraźni, on miał na sobie ledwo widoczną cielistą przepaskę, przy której jakiekolwiek domysły były w zasadzie zbędne. Oboje prezentowali wzorcową opaleniznę i napompowani sterydami do granic możliwości, przypominali ciężarowców. Obładowani paczkami zdążali w stronę wyjścia.

Idioci! Zamarzną!

Rzeczywiście wieczorna bryza niosła ze sobą chłód.

Christina przyglądała im się z uwagą, a było na co popatrzeć, bo oboje poruszali się niemal w zwolnionym tempie, prezentując jak przed publicznością każde wybrzuszenie, każde rozciągnięcie mięśnia czy ścięgna.

Wreszcie oderwała od nich wzrok i po raz drugi zajrzała do wnętrza sklepu. Tym razem dostrzegła Petera. Stał tam – wysoki, przystojny, mocno zbudowany. Silny. Przysięgłaby, że serce zabiło jej szybciej. Stał między półkami... z muszlami? Trudno powiedzieć, z daleka nie widziała dokładnie. Wzięła głęboki wdech i pchnęła drzwi. Peter się nie odwrócił, za to sprzedawczyni podniosła na nią zbolałe spojrzenie.

– W czym mogę pomóc? – spytała tonem stojącego na ostatnich nogach zombi.

Wyglądała, jakby podanie czegokolwiek było stanowczo ponad jej siły. Tkwiła oparta o ladę, z łokciami na kontuarze i brodą opartą na dłoni. Nawijała na palec jedno z jasnych pasemek przecinających jej kruczoczarne włosy. W nosie, ustach i brwiach miała okrągłe kolczyki, na chudych rękach roiło się od tatuaży.

– Dziękuję, rozejrzę się – powiedziała Christina. Jakoś udało jej się nie wzdrygnąć z obrzydzenia.

Podeszła do Petera, który nadal jej nie zauważał.

– Cześć – powitała go wesoło.

– O! Sie masz!

– Coś taki zajęty? – spytała.

– Oglądam pocztówki.

Dopiero teraz zauważyła, że trzymał w ręku kartki przedstawiające różne ujęcia wielkich rekinów, rozciągniętych na nadbrzeżu, skąpanych we krwi.

– Śliczności – wyrwało jej się zjadliwie.

Bez słowa odłożył kartki na stojak. Wziął w rękę konika morskiego w pudełku z muszelek.

– Dziwaczny, nie?

Popatrzyła na niego z uwagą, po czym skinęła głową.

– Tak. Ale i piękny.

– I taki kruchy. Można mu kark złamać dwoma palcami. – Uśmiechnął się ponuro.

Christina przyglądała mu się w zamyśleniu, nie mając pewności, jak powinna rozumieć komentarz. Czy to była subtelna groźba? Ale dlaczego miałby jej grozić? Tego nie wiedziała, miała natomiast pewność, że Peter jest... niebezpiecznym człowiekiem. I właśnie to ją kręciło.

– Chodźmy stąd – zarządził. Wziął ją pod ramię i wyprowadził na deptak. – Zarezerwowałem pokój w motelu. Niedaleko. – Objął ją mocno.

On nigdy nie pyta. Po prostu wydaje polecenie.

Lubiła takich mężczyzn. Bez dwóch zdań. Na wysokich obcasach z trudem dotrzymywała Peterowi kroku, ale i to jej nie przeszkadzało. Cudowna była taka sekretna schadzka.

Przecięli ulicę i po kilku krokach stanęli przed nędznym motelikiem o łososiowych ścianach, z jaskrawym neonem głoszącym na czerwono: „Morska Bryza". Żarówki w literze „y" były przepalone. Doszedłszy do pokoju z numerem dziewięć, Peter wyjął z kieszeni spodni klucz i otworzył drzwi. Przytrzymał je kurtuazyjnie przed Christiną.

Weszła i rozejrzała się po ascetycznym wnętrzu.

Przynajmniej czysto, pomyślała. Dzięki Bogu.

Peter pchnął drzwi, odwrócił się do Christiny i zamknął ją w potężnych ramionach. Zmiażdżył jej usta gwałtownym pocałunkiem i przycisnął ją do ściany.

Przeszedł ją dreszcz. Peter wepchnął jej wielkie łapska pod spódnicę, ścisnął uda, potem przesunął ręce wyżej, chwycił ją za pośladki i przyciągnął do siebie. Poczuła jego twardy członek i o mało nie spaliła się z pożądania.

– No jak, laluniu, cieszysz się, że mnie widzisz? – wychrypiał Peter.

– Jeszcze jak! – Nogi miała jak z galarety.

I na tym skończyły się czułe słówka. Peter błyskawicznie ściągnął z niej ubranie, potem w równie ekspresowym tempie pozbył się swojego i pociągnął ją do łóżka. Wdarł się w nią bezlitośnie, uderzał gwałtownie i ważna była dla niego tylko własna satysfakcja.

Christina uwielbiała takie brutalne natarcie, jej ciało zareagowało prawie natychmiast i po chwili połączył ich wspólny orgazm.

Szybko się skończyło to zbliżenie. Oboje dyszeli głośno, wyczerpani jak po forsującym biegu, błyszczący od potu. Powoli oddech im się uspokajał. Żadne nie powiedziało słowa, patrzyli sobie w oczy, aż po jakimś czasie ich dłonie ożyły, budząc na nowo namiętność.

Gdy znów odzyskali oddech, Peter zapalił dwa papierosy i jednego podał Christinie.

– Cieszę się, że przyszłaś – powiedział.

Christina zaciągnęła się głęboko.

– Ja też nie żałuję. – Doceniała komplement zawarty w słowach Petera, bo wiedziała, że Rossi nieczęsto deklaruje, iż cieszy go czyjeś towarzystwo.

– Twoja siostra i szwagier nie wiedzą, że tu jesteś? – spytał.

Christina ze śmiechu omal nie zakrztusiła się dymem.

– Jasne, że nie! – Uśmiechnęła się chytrze. – Jeśli ktoś zobaczy mojego rollsa albo mnie gdzieś tutaj, powiem Joannie, że wybrałam się w odwiedziny do przyjaciół w San Francisco. I przejeżdżałam przez Santa Cruz.

– Sprytna jesteś.

– Dlaczego? Bo sypiam z wrogiem?

– Właśnie, właśnie. I nie tylko sypiasz, ale też trochę mu pomagasz w tym i owym.

Oboje roześmiali się głośno.

– Odrobina cierpliwości – podjął Peter – i zrobię tę twoją siostrzyczkę na perłowo. Przyjdzie czas, a będzie mnie błagała, żebym kupił od niej firmę. – W jego głosie brzmiało rozbawienie.

Christina aprobowała jego plany. A konieczność zachowania ich związku w tajemnicy fascynowała ją do takiego stopnia, że aż się temu dziwiła, bo przecież z niejednego pieca chleb jadła.

– Z tego co słyszałam, wzmocnili ochronę. – Wydmuchnęła nosem smugę dymu. – Chyba kupili psa. Więc na razie może być trudniej.

– Poczekamy, zobaczymy. Liczę na twoją pomoc, na informacje.

– Wyciągnę od Joanny, co się da. Ale muszę być ostrożna, bo uzna, że jestem za bardzo zainteresowana sprawami firmy, i zacznie coś podejrzewać. Podejmuję dla ciebie niemałe ryzyko. – Obrzuciła Petera badawczym spojrzeniem. Spodziewała się podziwu i wsparcia.

Spojrzenie mężczyzny stwardniało, zabłysła w nim zimna stal, zdolna zadać śmiertelny cios.

– Dasz sobie radę, laluniu. – Nie odrywając wzroku od Christiny, zgasił papierosa, po czym przycisnął ją do siebie tak mocno, że zabrakło jej tchu. – Zrobisz to dla nas.

– Oczywiście – przytaknęła natychmiast. Potem się uśmiechnęła i odłożyła papierosa. – Możesz na mnie liczyć.

– Tak, wiem. – Pochylił się i pocałował ją, tym razem w usta. Językiem rozsunął jej wargi, powoli, niemal czule. Potem cofnął się niechętnie, jakby z ociąganiem. – A wiesz, co będzie dalej?

Christina pokręciła głową bez słowa.

Nakrył jej pierś dłonią, czubkiem języka połaskotał w ucho i zaczął coś szeptać. Kiedy skończył, połączyły ich kolejne pocałunki, bardziej namiętne i pełne pożądania. Peter przesunął dłoń po brzuchu Christiny, między jej uda.

– Peter... – jęknęła. – Boże...!

Zaczęła poruszać biodrami, jak zwykle natychmiast reagując gotowością na jego szorstkie pieszczoty.

Nagle Peter wstał i Christina została niespodziewanie pozbawiona dotyku jego ust, dłoni, całego ciała.

– Co się stało? – wykrztusiła.

– Będziesz mnie lepiej pamiętała, laluniu. I bardziej za mną tęskniła – wyszczerzył zęby w rekinim uśmiechu. – Aż do następnego razu.

Była potwornie rozczarowana, ale na samą myśl o następnym spotkaniu, kiedy dokończą to, co dzisiaj zaczęli, poczuła gorącą falę podniecenia.

– Nie da się zaprzeczyć – odparła ze zrezygnowanym westchnieniem.

– Czas na mnie – uznał Peter. – Pora wracać do domu.

Christina obserwowała, jak się ubierał. Z jednej strony targała nią wściekłość na faceta, który rozpalił ją do białości i właśnie zamierzał wyjść, z drugiej – nie mógł jej nie cieszyć widok tego przystojnego mężczyzny wkładającego ubranie warte fortunę.

W końcu nachylił się nad nią i pocałował ją długo, głęboko, namiętnie.

– Będziemy w kontakcie – powiedział, prostując się.

– Już zaczynam tęsknić – odrzekła i tak było naprawdę.

Peter rzucił klucz od pokoju na komódkę przy drzwiach, jeszcze w progu odwrócił się i posłał Christinie całusa. Potem zniknął.

Ubierała się powoli, czując rozkoszne zmęczenie całego ciała. Już nie mogła się doczekać następnej randki.

Nienawidziła, a jednocześnie uwielbiała te potajemne schadzki. Nie mogli się pokazywać razem. Po pierwsze, Peter był w trakcie rozwodu i aż do zakończenia sprawy musiał udawać świętego. Po drugie, Christina zdawała sobie sprawę ze swojej zdrady.

Tak, jest zdrajczynią. Sypia z wrogiem. Szkodzi Joannie i Joshowi. Pomaga Peterowi zniszczyć ich firmę. Przekazuje mu poufne informacje. A niedługo jej siostrzyczkę i szwagra spotka kolejna przykra niespodzianka. I bardzo dobrze. Oni zawsze mieli wszystko, czego dusza zapragnie. A zdrada jest niewysoką ceną za Petera. Za jego władzę i pieniądze, za ten podniecający brak skrupułów, który ją tak niesamowicie kręcił.

O tak, pomyślała Christina. Jestem podła. Ale słuszny cel uświęca środki. A tym celem jest moje dobro.

Rozdział trzynasty

Joshua podniósł słuchawkę telefonu w biurze przy szklarniach.

– Słucham?

– Czy mówię z panem Lawrence'em? – odezwał się głęboki męski głos.

Joshowi przeszły ciarki po plecach. Znał ten głos i zaczynał się go bać. Jednak już w następnej chwili gniew okazał się silniejszy.

– Tak, to ja – odparł rzeczowym tonem. – Poznaję pana, panie Rossi.

– Dzwonię, by spytać – podjął Peter Rossi – czy może zmienił pan zdanie na temat sprzedaży firmy. – Z uprzejmych słów wyraźnie przebijało rozbawienie.

Ów kpiący ton doprowadził Joshuę do furii. Nie zdołał opanować emocji.

– Nie! – wykrzyknął. – Nie sprzedam panu firmy! Ani panu, ani nikomu innemu!

Rzucił słuchawkę na widełki, a potem ukrył twarz w dłoniach.

Co za drań, pomyślał. Cholerny skurczysyn.

Wyprostował się, kilka razy odetchnął głęboko, ale tak czy inaczej nie zdołał powstrzymać natłoku myśli.

Czy wzywać policję? Tylko właściwie – do czego? Co im powie? Że za każdym razem, kiedy pojawiają się jakieś kłopoty, dzwoni Peter Rossi z propozycją kupna firmy?

Wstał i wyszedł do sekretariatu, zatrzaskując za sobą drzwi biura.

– Luno – odezwał się, nie patrząc na nią. – Idę do domu. Nie przekazuj żadnych wiadomości.

– Jasne, szefie – odpowiedziała z oczami wielkimi jak spodki.
Wyjściowymi drzwiami także trzasnął.

* * *

Trzasnął również drzwiami od holu i ciężko opadł na drewnianą ławę. Wolno rozwiązał sznurowadła.
– Joanna! – zawołał z ponurą miną. – Joanna!
Nikt się nie odezwał. Gniewnym gestem rzucił buty w kąt i wstał.
– Joanno! – krzyknął znowu. – Gdzie jesteś?!
Najpierw ruszył do kuchni.
Ciekawe, gdzie ją dzisiaj poniosło?
Zaczynał mieć serdecznie dosyć tych ciągłych eskapad żony. Całe popołudnie nikt nie odbierał telefonu, a komórki Joanna nie była uprzejma zaakceptować. Z początku trochę go to śmieszyło, teraz doprowadzało do białej gorączki. Miał nieodparte wrażenie, że zaciska się wokół niego pętla jakiegoś złowrogiego spisku.
W kuchni także nie było Joanny. Ani jej, ani Connie, ani żadnej wiadomości.
Zajrzał po kolei do wszystkich pokojów na parterze. Ani śladu żony. Wbiegł na piętro, wołając ją głośno. Odpowiedziała mu cisza.
Gdzie ona jest, kiedy jej naprawdę potrzebuje?
Zbiegł na dół, wrócił do holu. Wsunął stopy w miękkie mokasyny. Wyszedł na taras i rozejrzał się dookoła.
Nikogo.
Przeszedł po mostku i spojrzał w dół, między jabłonie.
Ani żywego ducha, cholera jasna!
Wpadł do sadu, ruszył w stronę groty i o mało nie wpadł na April.
– O, cześć! – przywitała go z uśmiechem. – Skąd ten pośpiech? – Dopiero teraz dostrzegła wyraz twarzy Josha. – Co się stało?
– Sam chciałbym wiedzieć – wycedził przez zęby. – Joanna ostatnio robi dziwne numery i zaczyna mi się to nie podobać.
– Ooo... Rzeczywiście chyba masz dosyć.
– Wybacz, po prostu...
– Po prostu szlag cię trafia – dokończyła za niego. – Każdemu się czasem zdarza. Chcesz się wygadać?
– Nie – odparł krótko. – Chociaż właściwie... – zreflektował się z mniejszą pewnością siebie. – Może jednak.

April wzięła go pod łokieć i poprowadziła do jednego ze stolików przy basenie.

– Siadaj – zarządziła. – Upuść trochę pary.

Było gorąco i parno, a sam widok powierzchni wody, którą marszczył wiatr, przynosił ochłodę.

Joshua miał minę nietęgą, był wyraźnie zmartwiony i przybity.

A taki zawsze jest wesoły, taki szczęśliwy, pomyślała April. Cóż, w końcu los nikomu nie szczędzi przykrych doświadczeń.

Postanowiła dać mu się wygadać, jeśli będzie chciał, ale nie udzielać żadnych rad.

– Joanna była na lunchu? – spytał Joshua.

– Nie, w ogóle jej dzisiaj nie widziałam. Wyszła, zanim przyjechałam.

– Dziwne. – Wydawał się coraz bardziej zasępiony.

– Pewnie wybrała się na zakupy – powiedziała April z uśmiechem na ustach, ale Bogiem a prawdą, nie wierzyła we własne słowa. Bo i kto się wybiera na zakupy o ósmej rano, jeżeli nie musi? A lunch – to druga sprawa. Joanna przecież zawsze wracała do domu na wspólny posiłek.

– Może i tak – mruknął Joshua. – Ale jakoś nie chce mi się w to wierzyć.

– Zazwyczaj zostawia w kuchni wiadomość... – podsunęła April.

– Dziś nie zostawiła. I właśnie dlatego zaczynam się martwić.

– Dajże spokój. Przecież i tak stale masz ją na wyciągnięcie ręki, niezależnie od pory i okoliczności.

– To prawda – przyznał Joshua. – Ale ostatnio jakoś tak... Sam nie wiem... Mam wrażenie, że dzieje się coś złego.

– Chyba po prostu miałeś ciężki dzień. I trochę cię poniosło.

– No tak... – Josh w zamyśleniu pokiwał głową. – Trudno zaprzeczyć. Ciężki dzień... delikatnie mówiąc!

– A co się stało? Czyżby pan Hara nie zostawił u was okrągłych stu patyków? – spytała April, próbując rozładować atmosferę. Jednak bez skutku.

– Nie, nie... To by jeszcze było pół biedy. – Zgarbił się na krześle. – Mamy naprawdę poważne kłopoty. Ktoś robi nam szkody w szklarniach.

– Jak to?!

– Ano, tak to.

– Mówisz poważnie? Skąd takie podejrzenia?

Joshua podniósł się gwałtownie.

– Napijesz się ze mną? Strasznie mi jest potrzebny kieliszek wina.
– Nie bardzo mam czas... powinnam się już zbierać.
– Tylko jeden kieliszek.
April wiedziała, że Joshua naciska, ponieważ bardzo chciałby zwierzyć się komuś z kłopotów.
– Dobrze, zgoda. Ale tylko jeden.
– Zaraz wrócę. – Szybkim krokiem ruszył do kuchni.
Patrzyła za nim, zastanawiając się, co takiego wydarzyło się w szklarniach, co do tego stopnia wytrąciło Josha z równowagi.
Może diabeł okaże się nie taki straszny... a rzeczywistość nie taka znowu ponura. Skoro nałożyły się na siebie kłopoty z orchideami i niepokój o Joannę...
Znienacka wyrósł przy niej Woody.
– O rany! – Aż krzyknęła. – Ale mnie wystraszyłeś!
– Ty chyba oszalałaś! – szepnął, obrzucając ją płonącym spojrzeniem.
– Co?
– Uważaj, igrasz z ogniem – dodał tak samo cicho, obrócił się na pięcie i zniknął.
Jezus Maria! O co mu chodzi? Trzeba z nim poważnie porozmawiać.
Czy aby na pewno nie popełniła błędu, proponując Woody'emu prace pomocnicze? Nie podejrzewała, że w ogóle stać go na podobne zachowanie. Do tej pory zawsze wzorowo wypełniał powierzone obowiązki. Ale też należało przyznać, iż nigdy wcześniej nie była w tak zażyłych układach ze zleceniodawcami.
– Już nalewam. – Joshua wrócił z dwoma kieliszkami oraz butelką schłodzonego białego wina. – Proszę bardzo. – Podał gościowi jeden i usiadł.
April z przyjemnością wypiła łyk aksamitnego płynu.
– Powiedz mi teraz – poprosiła – co się dokładnie stało w szklarniach. Czy jesteś pewien, że to sabotaż?
– Całkowicie. – Joshua zamilkł na chwilę. – Żebyś dobrze mnie zrozumiała, muszę się cofnąć w czasie o kilka tygodni. Wtedy zawiódł komputerowy system zraszania. Gdyby nie czujność Carla, straty byłyby ogromne. Kwiatom groziło albo przesuszenie, albo zbyt intensywne nawilżanie.
– A, tak, Joanna mi o tym wspominała. Odniosłam wrażenie, że to była kwestia czysto techniczna, po prostu jakaś usterka.
– Pracownicy firmy, która nam ten system instalowała, byli od-

miennego zdania – odparł Joshua. – Uważali, że ktoś majstrował przy programie.

– A może nie chcieli się przyznać do błędu? – zasugerowała April. – Po prostu zrzucili z siebie odpowiedzialność?

– Raczej wątpię. Ta firma cieszy się nieskazitelną reputacją.

– No dobrze. Jeśli jednak istotnie doszło do czegoś takiego, kto mógł zmienić program? I po co?

Joshua spojrzał jej prosto w oczy.

– Nietrudno się domyślić. Bracia Rossi od dłuższego czasu starają się kupić naszą firmę. Ich ziemie otaczają nas ze wszystkich stron, jesteśmy im solą w oku.

– A nie chcecie im sprzedać.

– Nie chcemy. – Joshua pociągnął łyk wina i odstawił kieliszek. – Moglibyśmy uzyskać sumę wystarczającą na spokojną emeryturę albo zainwestować pieniądze w inny interes, ale jest dla nas istotne, że ojciec Joanny kochał tę ziemię. I włożył w firmę wiele serca. Budował ją niemal przez całe życie. A Joanna jest bardzo do niego podobna.

– Ty też od nich nie odstajesz – zauważyła April. – Kochasz orchidee, jesteś oddany swojej pracy.

– To prawda – zgodził się z uśmiechem. – Masz całkowitą rację. – Umilkł i na chwilę zatonął w myślach.

– Twoim zdaniem – podjęła April – za tymi próbami stoją bracia Rossi.

– Jak najbardziej. Tuż po wypadku z systemem zraszania zadzwonił do mnie nie kto inny, tylko właśnie Peter Rossi i kolejny raz złożył mi ofertę.

– Coś podobnego! Nie do wiary!

– Właśnie. Bawi się ze mną w kotka i myszkę.

– Powiedziałeś o tym policji?

– Tak, oczywiście. Ale niewiele to dało. Bo i co można by zrobić?

– Rzeczywiście... A dzisiaj co się stało?

Joshua westchnął ciężko.

– W szklarni wybuchła epidemia jakiegoś grzyba. Chyba to *Phytophthora.* Zaatakował dużą część okazów *Phalaenopsis.*

– O Boże! Czy sytuacja jest poważna?

– Trudno powiedzieć. Na razie chyba choroba objęła tylko jedną szklarnię. Wszystkie *Phalaenopsis.* Trzeba zrobić analizę bakterii, sprawdzić, z czym dokładnie mamy do czynienia, ale w zasadzie to i tak już nie ma większego znaczenia. Musimy pożegnać się z niektórymi okazami, a inne będą wymagały długotrwałej odbudowy. Wiele spośród tych roślin czekało na wysyłkę, teraz będziemy musieli kupić te orchidee u kogoś innego, bo w przeciwnym razie stracimy klientów.

– Straszne!

– Najdziwniejsze w tym wszystkim, że kwiaty miały idealne warunki. Wszystko dokładnie tak jak trzeba. Ruch powietrza, temperatura, wilgotność, nasłonecznienie, odstępy między poszczególnymi sadzonkami... Wszystko wręcz podręcznikowo. W ogóle nie miał prawa się tam pojawić żaden grzyb!

– Wezwałeś policję?

– O, tak, oczywiście. I tak samo jak poprzednio nie znaleźli żadnych śladów włamania. Nic. A Miguel, nocny stróż, tak samo jak ubiegłym razem nie widział ani nie słyszał niczego podejrzanego. Pies też nie podniósł alarmu. – Josh zamilkł na kilka chwil. – Oczywiście sprawcą mógł być któryś z klientów. Ale to czysta teoria, bo niewielu kupującym pozwalamy wchodzić do szklarni, a jeśli już, to zawsze w towarzystwie kogoś z obsługi.

– Mój Boże... Czy tym razem także zadzwonił któryś z braci Rossi?

– A, owszem, jak najbardziej. – Josh z rezygnacją pokręcił głową. – Mówiłem ci, bawią się ze mną w kotka i myszkę.

– Okropność. I dziś też zadzwonił... Peter?

– Tak, właśnie on. Zaczynam się obawiać... Ci ludzie mają opinię bezlitosnych i pozbawionych zasad, ale nie mieści mi się w głowie, jak on śmie dzwonić do mnie... Wygląda na to, że nie ma żadnych skrupułów!

– Co w związku z tym zamierzasz?

– Sęk w tym, że nie wiem. Nie mam bladego pojęcia. Dlatego tak mnie poniosło... Miałem nadzieję, że naradzę się z Joanną...

April przyglądała się Joshowi ze współczuciem. Był wyraźnie zasępiony, wręcz przybity. Najchętniej pogłaskałaby go i przytuliła, niestety, nie mogła tego zrobić.

– Joanna niedługo wróci – odezwała się wreszcie. – Pewnie rzuciła się w wir zakupów i zapomniała o bożym świecie. Sam wiesz, jak łatwo w takiej sytuacji stracić poczucie czasu.

– Dzięki za pocieszenie. Jesteś... fantastyczna.

Znów ogarnęło ją tamto kłopotliwe uczucie, całkowicie nie na miejscu. Zaczerwieniła się lekko.

– Nie ma za co. Jesteście wspaniałą parą... – Dopiła wino, odstawiła kieliszek. – Czas na mnie. Mam mnóstwo pracy w domu.

– Przepraszam, że cię zatrzymałem. Nie dość, że harujesz tutaj cały dzień, to jeszcze pocieszasz mnie po godzinach. – Joshua uśmiechnął się rozbrajająco.

– Nie ma sprawy, naprawdę. – Wstała i zarzuciła torbę na ramię. – Od czego są przyjaciele?

Joshua także się podniósł, zabrał kieliszki i butelkę z winem.

– Tak czy inaczej, wielkie dzięki. I cieszę się, że możemy być przyjaciółmi.

– Ja także.

* * *

Przed nią ciągnęła się plaża. Pozornie nieskończone pasmo wszelkich odcieni szarości tam, gdzie brzeg zalewały fale, poprzez beże mokrego piasku, aż po suchą biel na wydmach. Tu i ówdzie wypełzły na ląd nagie pnie drzew, niczym prehistoryczne stwory, gdzieniegdzie widniały zielonkawe plamy wodorostów. W oddali na tle nieba rysowała się samotna postać wędkarza, a jeszcze dalej sterczały smukłe sylwetki kominów elektrowni w Moss Landing.

Odwróciła się w przeciwną stronę, odgarnęła włosy z twarzy i obiema rękami przytrzymała je z tyłu. Już prawie nie było widać zabudowań Santa Cruz, a perłowa mgła, podnosząca się z oceanu, wkrótce miała je zasłonić całkowicie. Bliżej rozciągał się Joe Camel. Był to wielki pień, wyrzucony przez fale. Nadała mu takie imię, ponieważ przywodził jej na myśl odpoczywającego na pustyni wielbłąda. Znajdował się na drodze do domku plażowego.

Szła bardzo długo i całkowicie straciła poczucie czasu, choć coraz chłodniejsze słońce, opadające nad horyzont, wyraźnie mówiło, iż nadciąga wieczór. Powinna już dawno być w domu.

Dziś jednak nie umiała się zachować właściwie i odpowiedzialnie. Wyjechała natychmiast po wyjściu Josha i nie zostawiła żadnej wiadomości, nie powiedziała nikomu, dokąd się wybiera. Tym razem pozwoliła sobie na taki właśnie luksus. Na ucieczkę, rozmyślne zostawienie wszystkiego za sobą. I nie miała zamiaru nikogo za to przepraszać. Chciała pobyć sama w starym domku na plaży, który kochała całym sercem. Nie było dla niej na całym świecie ważniejszego miejsca niż ten zwyczajny domek bez żadnych luksusów, gdzie spędzała szczęśliwe weekendy oraz wakacje z ojcem i z siostrą, a także gdzie przeżyła pierwsze, rajskie miesiące małżeństwa.

Gdy doszła do pnia w kształcie wielbłąda, nagle całe ciało dziwnie jej zaciążyło. Ręce zmieniły się w ołowiane sztaby, nogi odmówiły posłuszeństwa. Opadła na piasek, z jej dłoni wysunęły się uchwyty dwóch toreb z muszlami. Niektóre okazy były wyjątkowe, ale większość nieszczególna, wiele połamanych. Mimo wszystko miała nadzieję, że i te dadzą się wykorzystać. Co do jednej. Tak postanowiła. Całe czy popękane, pięknie ubarwione czy szare i byle jakie – każda znajdzie swoje miejsce.

Jej wzrok powędrował ku horyzontowi, który powoli zasłaniała mgła. Słońce dotykało już krawędzi wody.

Kończy się jeszcze jeden dzień, pomyślała. Przeminął.

Łzy napłynęły jej do oczu. Pozwoliła im stoczyć się po policzkach. Normalnie próbowałaby je ukryć, ale teraz popłynęły swobodnym strumieniem po twarzy, kapały z brody na sweter, na spodnie, na piasek. Gdzieś z głębi piersi wyrwał się pierwszy szloch. Joanna objęła się ramionami i rozpłakała głośno. Zawodziła wiatrowi do wtóru i krzyczała z żalu, z bezsilności, z bólu. Odpowiadały jej tylko głębokie pomruki oceanu i ptasie krzyki.

Gdy wreszcie atak rozpaczy minął, z wyczerpania bolało ją całe ciało. Zwinęła się w kłębek i oddychała z trudem. Kłujące słone ziarenka przylgnęły jej do twarzy. Długo leżała skulona, bardzo wolno odzyskując świadomość, gdzie jest i co się z nią dzieje.

W końcu usiadła. Zapadał już zmrok.

Z niemałym wysiłkiem wstała, niezdarnie otarła twarz dłońmi i otrzepała ubranie. Czuła się bardzo zmęczona. Podniosła z trudem obie torby z muszlami i zapadając się w miałkim piasku, ruszyła do domku plażowego.

Przy schodach powinna była opłukać nogi pod prysznicem, ale tego nie zrobiła. Owszem, zostawi w całym domu piaszczyste ślady i co z tego? Otworzyła zewnętrzne drzwi z siatki, potem te właściwe. Postawiła torby na krześle i zapaliła światło. Poszła prosto do łazienki. Jej stopy stukały głucho o drewnianą podłogę. Spojrzała w lustro.

– Kochana, jak ty wyglądasz – mruknęła do swojego odbicia.

Zaczął w niej wzbierać śmiech, który łatwo mógł się przerodzić w następny wybuch rozpaczy. Na szczęście zdołała się opanować. Nie chciała już płakać. Obmyła twarz chłodną wodą, przeczesała włosy długimi, pewnymi ruchami. Wyszła z łazienki i ruszyła w stronę sypialni.

Trzeba pościelić łóżko, pomyślała. Sprzątnąć kieliszek, wino i...

– Bez sensu – powiedziała na głos.

Nikt poza mną tu nie przychodzi, więc co za różnica...?

Zabrała muszle, zamknęła dom i poszła do samochodu. Gdy wsiadła, jakiś czas siedziała, oddychając głęboko, by odzyskać spokój i opanowanie. Wreszcie uruchomiła silnik. Mogła już wrócić do domu, żeby na nowo odgrywać rolę szczęśliwej żony.

* * *

Joshua zakręcił prysznic i podśpiewując półgłosem, wyszedł na chłodną, marmurową posadzkę. Akurat zaczął się wycierać ogromnym śnieżnobiałym ręcznikiem, gdy usłyszał warkot silnika. Z mosiężnego wieszaka na drzwiach ściągnął szlafrok i włożył go, przechodząc przez sypialnię.

Nareszcie!, pomyślał, zbiegając po schodach. Ciekawe, gdzie to Joanna podziewała się przez cały dzień. Zaraz się dowie. A w każdym razie przynajmniej usłyszy, co miała mu do powiedzenia.

Dotarł na dół akurat w tej samej chwili, gdy otworzyły się frontowe drzwi i stanęła w nich Joanna z dwiema ogromnymi torbami.

– Cześć, kochanie! – zawołała od progu, rozpromieniona i szczęśliwa.

Joshua odetchnął z ulgą. Opanował go nastrój radosnego podniecenia, jak zawsze w obecności żony.

– Czekaj, czekaj, pomogę ci!

Przytrzymał drzwi, a jednocześnie usiłował wyjąć Joannie torby z rąk.

– Ostrożnie... zacisnęły mi się na palcach!

– Postaw na ziemi.

– Są strasznie brudne! Całe w piachu...

– Trudno, stawiaj.

Joanna uwolniła się od ciężaru, brudząc marmurową posadzkę, i pocałowała męża w usta.

– Witaj, przystojniaku. Dziękuję za pomoc.

Od razu poczuł od niej alkohol. Dziwne. Joanna zawsze pachniała egzotycznymi cytrusami oraz wetiwerią, a tym razem cuchnęło od niej jak z gorzelni. I włosy miała potargane... a ubranie dziwnie wymięte...

– Gdzieś ty się podziewała? Pachniesz jak targ rybny.

– Och, kochany, zachciało mi się zbierać muszle, znalazłam mnóstwo...! Najróżniejszych!

Joshua uśmiechnął się, ujęty niewinnym podnieceniem żony.
– Zaraz ci pokażę! – ciągnęła Joanna, szperając w jednej z toreb. – Zobacz! Prawdziwa macica perłowa! Doskonała na tło do groty.
– Wygląda na to, że udał ci się dzień. Włożę te torby do worków na śmieci.
– Kochany jesteś. – Poszła za nim do kuchni. – Tylko kieliszeczek białego wina może postawić człowieka na nogi po takiej eskapadzie.
– Jakiś czas temu wstawiłem do lodówki dwie butelki, powinny już się schłodzić. – Joshua wyjął z pudełka worki na śmiecie.
– Napijesz się ze mną?
– Chętnie. Zaraz wrócę. – Wychodząc z kuchni, jeszcze się odwrócił. – Może od razu zaniosę te twoje skarby do pralni i namoczę?
– O, tak, dzięki.
Gdy wyszedł do holu, Joanna otworzyła butelkę wina, naszykowała dwa kryształowe kieliszki, ustawiła wszystko na tacy i wyniosła na taras. Usiadła pod wielkim parasolem. Góry powoli ginęły w sinawej zasłonie. Nad basenem także już unosiły się obłoczki mgły. Z jakąż przyjemnością weźmie teraz relaksujący prysznic... Ominęło ją pływanie tego wieczoru, ale była już zbyt zmęczona, żeby się zdecydować na taki wysiłek.
Pojawił się Joshua. Stanął za nią, położył mocne ręce na jej ramionach i pomasował kark.
– Ooo, jak dobrze – westchnęła Joanna z rozmarzonym uśmiechem. Zamknęła oczy i poddała się ciepłym dłoniom ukochanego mężczyzny.
– Jesteś głodna? – spytał Joshua. – Dawno minął czas kolacji, ale Connie zostawiła nam w lodówce zapasy na rok.
– Kolacja...? To już tak późno?
– A i owszem.
– Ojej, nie miałam pojęcia...
– Piłaś coś może? – spytał lekkim tonem. – Nigdy nie zapominasz o kolacji.
– Tak! – przyznała podekscytowana. – To było niesamowite. Zatrzymałam się w „U Umberto" na wino i podziwiałam z tarasu zachód słońca. Niesamowity!
– Przecież nie znosisz tej knajpki.
– A dzisiaj czułam się tam doskonale. To chyba przez ten zachód słońca. W ogóle nie zauważyłam tam tych obrzydliwych sztucznych kwiatów i plastikowych mebli.

– Z czego wynika, że jesteś w wyjątkowo dobrym humorze – uznał Joshua. Jeszcze raz przesunął dłońmi po ramionach żony i usiadł przy stole. – Popijałaś to wino w pojedynkę? – spytał pół żartem, pół serio.

– Byłyśmy we dwie – odparła Joanna, uśmiechając się sennie. – Ja i moja samotność.

Po takiej odpowiedzi nie poczuł się ani odrobinę mądrzejszy, nie wiedział, jak ma to rozumieć i czy wierzyć w słowa żony. Instynkt podpowiadał mu, że Joanna mija się z prawdą. Na pewno zbierała muszle i z pewnością piła, ale czy naprawdę akurat tam? W towarzystwie tych wszystkich surferów i turystów?

Bardzo chciał wiedzieć, co robiła przez cały dzień, ale spojrzawszy jej w oczy, które same się zamykały, postanowił nie naciskać.

Powinienem z nią porozmawiać, uświadomił sobie. Powiedzieć jej o nowych kłopotach w szklarni. Ale nie teraz. Nie w chwili, kiedy, jak widział, ledwo się trzymała na nogach.

– Po powrocie ze szklarni spotkałem tu April – powiedział.

– Jak sobie radzi? Często o niej dzisiaj myślałam.

– Radzi sobie świetnie, ale chyba ma do ciebie kilka pytań. Zdaje się, że w paru kwestiach potrzebuje twojej opinii.

– Załatwimy to jutro – mruknęła sennie Joanna. – Zresztą, ufam jej bez zastrzeżeń. – Odchyliła się na oparcie, zamykając oczy.

– Aha, jeszcze jedno – odezwał się Joshua. – Byłbym zapomniał. Dzwoniła Christina. Może pół godziny temu.

Joanna usiadła prosto i otworzyła oczy.

– Czego chciała moja najdroższa siostra?

– Prosiła, żebyś dała jej znać, czy zajrzysz do niej, tak jak się umawiałyście.

– O Boże! Na śmierć zapomniałam! Przez tę grotę i w ogóle...

– Powiedziałem jej, że nic nie wiem – ciągnął Joshua. – Nie wiedziałem nawet, że się z nią umawiałaś.

Joanna zapatrzyła się w dal.

– Cóż, uznałam, że przyda jej się towarzystwo – powiedziała cicho. – Trudno jej dojść do siebie po rozwodzie. – Spojrzała na męża. – Aż wstyd, że ją tak zaniedbałam. Ona cierpi, a ja...

Joshua zamknął jej dłoń w swojej.

– Nie myśl o tym teraz. – Podniósł się, nadal trzymając ją za rękę. – Chodź, zjesz coś, nie sposób tak o pustym żołądku...

Pozwoliła się podnieść, przygarnąć i czule pocałować. Joshua był prawie nagi, czuła jego ciepło, zapach jego skóry. Zorientowała się, że jest podniecony.

Och, nie... tylko nie to... Nie dam rady, jestem taka zmęczona... Podniosła na niego spojrzenie.

– Josh – szepnęła – jestem wykończona. Powinnam wziąć szybki prysznic i od razu przytulić się do poduszki.

– Naprawdę jestem bez szans? – Nie chciał pogodzić się z odmową.

– Przykro mi, ale lecę z nóg.

– No dobrze... – Blask w jego oczach przygasł. – Ja też niedługo przyjdę na górę. – Wypuścił ją z objęć.

– Dobranoc. – Joanna lekko musnęła wargami usta męża i skierowała się ku drzwiom prowadzącym do kuchni.

Joshua pomyślał, że powinien być zły na żonę, ale jakoś nie potrafił wzbudzić w sobie gniewu. Przyjechała taka szczęśliwa, rozradowana, promieniejąca, a teraz była taka... krucha. Obserwował ją przez chwilę, po czym usiadł i w samotności dokończył wino. Był zbity z tropu. Zagubiony. Przestał cokolwiek rozumieć.

Joanna zniknęła na cały dzień, wróciła do domu na rauszu i twierdzi, że popijała wino w knajpce, której nie znosiła z całego serca. Zapomniała, że umówiła się z siostrą. Nie zjadła kolacji. Ale najgorsze z tego wszystkiego, że nie chciała się z nim kochać.

Nie potrafił sobie przypomnieć, kiedy ostatnio odprawiła go z kwitkiem. Przez wszystkie lata małżeństwa zdarzyło się to zaledwie kilka razy. I zawsze z konkretnego powodu: była chora albo bardzo zła na niego... A teraz? Całkiem nowa sytuacja. Nigdy dotąd nie zdarzyło się, by go odtrąciła z powodu zmęczenia.

Czyżby go już nie kochała?

Nie, nie, to śmieszne. Czysta paranoja. Przecież kochali się, wcale nie tak dawno. I było równie bosko jak zawsze.

Co się wobec tego dzieje, do diabła?!

Rozdział czternasty

Joshua siedział na stołku w marmurowej łazience i osłupiałym wzrokiem wpatrywał się w niewielkie kartonowe pudełko. W oczach miał łzy, czuł się oszukany i zawiedziony.

Powinienem był z nią porozmawiać!, wyrzucał sobie ciągle na nowo.

Oczywiście, doskonale wiedział, dlaczego dotąd tego nie zrobił. Przez ostatnie dni miał tyle do zrobienia w szklarniach, że nie bardzo wiedział, w co najpierw ręce włożyć. Wszyscy pracowali po godzinach, dwojąc się i trojąc, by sprostać zamówieniom, ściągnąć więcej kwiatów, a jednocześnie odizolować i leczyć rośliny zainfekowane grzybem.

A teraz jeszcze to.

Gapił się na pudełko pustym wzrokiem, z przedziwnym uczuciem, że Joanna stała mu się zupełnie obca. Zmieniła się w jakąś zimną, bezduszną istotę, całkowicie pozbawioną serca.

Albo zawsze była taka, pomyślał Joshua, tylko ja tego nie dostrzegałem.

Właśnie zamierzał się położyć spać. Czuł się ledwo żywy, choć przecież było jeszcze stosunkowo wcześnie. Szukał Joanny, by jej życzyć dobrej nocy. Najpierw poszedł do jej gabinetu, bo wcześniej widział, że siedziała przy komputerze. Nie zastał jej tam jednak. Zajrzał do sąsiadującej z gabinetem łazienki i tam, na marmurowym blacie, znalazł to fatalne pudełko. Nawet nie było schowane. Ot, po prostu leżało na widoku.

W pierwszej chwili osłupiał. Następnie ogarnął go ból tak wielki, że stłumił nawet gniew, który musiał zaczekać na swoją kolej. Joshua usiadł zrezygnowany i próbował zmusić otępiały umysł do podjęcia decyzji, co dalej.

Zapytam ją wprost, postanowił. I to już, od razu. Koniec odkładania, ciągłego czekania, braku czasu. Koniec z wymówkami. Dosyć tego.

Chwycił pudełko i zbiegł na dół, do kuchni. Skoro nie znalazł Joanny w sypialni ani w gabinecie, była w kuchni lub na przeszklonej werandzie.

Znalazł ją w kuchni. Akurat nalewała sobie wina do kieliszka. Dostrzegła go kątem oka.

– Napijesz się ze mną? – spytała.

Joshua stanął przed nią i podsunął jej pod oczy fatalne pudełko.

– Dlaczego?! – z trudem wykrztusił to dramatyczne pytanie.

Joanna zbladła jak płótno. Kieliszek wyślizgnął jej się spomiędzy bezwładnych palców i rozprysnął w drobny mak na meksykańskiej terakocie.

– Powiedz mi, dlaczego?! – powtórzył Josh. Chociaż kochał żonę całym sercem i choć nigdy nie podniósł na nią ręki, w tej chwili miał nieprzepartą chęć ją uderzyć. Do tej pory nawet sobie nie wyobrażał, że mógłby chcieć zrobić coś takiego.

– Ja... – zaczęła Joanna niepewnie. – Ja... – Jęknęła rozdzierająco, przycisnęła dłonie do oczu, by powstrzymać łzy, i wybiegła z kuchni, depcząc okruchy szkła.

Joshua został w kuchni sam. Jakiś czas po prostu wpatrywał się w podłogę. Wreszcie odzyskał zdolność myślenia. Otworzył szafkę z koszem na śmieci i wyrzucił kartonik pigułek antykoncepcyjnych. Trzasnął drzwiczkami z całej siły i zdecydowanym krokiem ruszył do sypialni. Musi wreszcie porozmawiać z żoną. Teraz. Natychmiast.

Nacisnął klamkę, ale drzwi nie ustąpiły.

– Joanno! – zawołał. – Otwórz, proszę.

Odpowiedziała mu cisza.

Huknął pięścią w grube deski.

– Otwieraj! – wrzasnął. – Musimy porozmawiać. Natychmiast! – Przyłożył ucho do drewna, lecz nie usłyszał nic. Wściekle załomotał w drzwi, ale zaraz opuścił ręce. Poczuł się śmieszny.

Już i tak postawiłem ją w przykrej sytuacji, pomyślał. Nie ma sensu pogarszać sprawy.

Zszedł na dół, do pokoju gościnnego. Już miał się położyć, gdy jego wzrok padł na zaimprowizowany barek przyszykowany dla odwiedzających – kilka butelek alkoholu i kieliszki na dużej srebrnej tacy. Kubełek na lód był pusty, trudno się dziwić. Mimo wszystko Joshua nalał sobie solidną porcję szkockiej. Zrzucił szlafrok, rozciągnął się na łóżku i patrząc w sufit, sączył whisky. W życiu nie spędził nocy w tym pokoju. Zresztą nie pamiętał nawet, kiedy spał bez Joanny. Wcale nie miał pewności, czy w ogóle uda mu się zasnąć. Myśli kłębiły mu się w głowie, a sprzeczne emocje szarpały nim do tego stopnia, że ogarnęło go niezłomne przekonanie, iż do bladego świtu nie zmruży oka. Objął tęsknym spojrzeniem butelkę szkockiej, ale po chwili namysłu doszedł do wniosku, że kac jest najmniej pożądanym stanem następnego dnia z rana. Zwłaszcza przy tych wszystkich kłopotach.

Muszę przeprowadzić z Joanną poważną rozmowę, postanowił w myślach. I to jutro. Tak dalej być nie może.

Zasnął, nawet nie wiedząc kiedy, głębokim snem sprawiedliwego.

* * *

Obudził się nagle i to od razu ze świadomością, że nie śpi we własnym łóżku. Natychmiast otworzył oczy i obrzucił pokój szybkim spojrzeniem. Wszystko jasne. Przypomniały mu się zdarzenia poprzedniego wieczoru.

Usiadł wolno, spojrzał na zegarek na nocnym stoliku. Dochodziła siódma. Przez szczeliny między zasłonami przesiąkał szarawy świt. Mgła jeszcze się nie podniosła, słońce będzie musiało ją ogrzewać kilka godzin.

Zsunął nogi na podłogę, włożył szlafrok, wstał, przeciągnął się, aż zatrzeszczały kości, i ziewnął szeroko.

– Joanno – zwrócił się do czterech ścian – idę do ciebie.

Trzeba działać szybko, zanim żona wymknie się z domu, uciekając przed konfrontacją. Musiał wykorzystać szansę.

Poszedł na piętro. Drzwi sypialni były otwarte. Czyżby jednak się spóźnił? Cisza. Nikogo. Akurat wtedy dobiegły go jakieś odgłosy z łazienki.

Stłumiony płacz.

W dwóch susach przemknął przez pokój i jednym szarpnięciem otworzył drzwi na oścież. Joanna siedziała przy toaletce, łokcie wsparła na blacie, twarz ukryła w dłoniach.

– Joanno! – Objął ją delikatnie i przytulił. – Co się stało?! Co się z tobą dzieje?

Długo trwało, nim się uspokoiła na tyle, by podnieść na niego wzrok. W oczach miała ból, twarz mokrą od łez i zaczerwienioną, powieki spuchnięte. Oparła mu głowę na ramieniu.

– Kochanie, powiedz mi – poprosił Joshua. – Zrzuć to z siebie.

Ona jednak milczała. Wreszcie wstała, podeszła do umywalki i opłukała twarz chłodną wodą, osuszyła krople ręcznikiem. I dopiero wtedy odwróciła się, zatapiając spojrzenie w niebieskich oczach Josha. Tak długo odsuwała od siebie nieuniknione... Teraz jednak należało wyjawić mu prawdę. Z jednej strony, znalazł pigułki antykoncepcyjne, z drugiej, choroba postępowała na tyle szybko, że nie można było dłużej zwlekać.

– Rzeczywiście, musimy porozmawiać – odezwała się wreszcie. Objęła się rękami i znieruchomiała przygarbiona.

– Joanno, co się dzieje? – Joshua przygarnął ją do siebie.

Dostrzegła strach w jego oczach. Wiedziała, że nie zdoła tego odwlec. Że słowami, które trzeba wypowiedzieć, zada mu głębokie rany. Wzięła go za rękę.

– Chodź, zaparzymy sobie kawę i usiądziemy na tarasie. Dobrze?

– Oczywiście, jak chcesz.

Zeszli razem do kuchni i we dwoje odprawili poranny rytuał parzenia kawy, jakby ten dzień niczym się nie wyróżniał. Wyszli na taras, zanurzony w porannej mgle, jakby odcięty od rzeczywistości. Usiedli pod ogromnym parasolem i otuleni szlafrokami popijali kawę.

W końcu Joshua ujął żonę za rękę. Był napięty i przestraszony.

– Już od jakiegoś czasu uświadamiałem sobie, że coś się między nami zmieniło na gorsze, ale wczoraj zareagowałem zbyt gwałtownie. Znalazłem te pigułki, byłem wstrząśnięty...

– Kochanie, nie ma tu twojej winy. – Joanna utkwiła wzrok w filiżance, jakby na jej dnie szukała właściwych słów. Nie da się tego złagodzić. Musiała zwyczajnie powiedzieć prawdę. Podniosła wzrok na męża. Widziała w jego oczach obawę i najbardziej na świecie pragnęłaby ją stamtąd wypłoszyć. – Niedługo umrę – powiedziała spokojnie.

Joshua drgnął jak ukąszony przez węża. Joanna mocniej ścisnęła jego dłoń. Oczy mu się rozszerzyły, otworzył usta, chcąc coś powiedzieć.

– Zamierzałam jeszcze jakiś czas nie mówić ci o tym, ale już nie mam wyjścia.

– Jak to, nic nie rozumiem... – wyszeptał.
– Jestem śmiertelnie chora...
– Na co?! – wykrzyknął Joshua nieomal z wściekłością. – Co się z tobą dzieje?!
– Mam raka mózgu.
Przyglądał się jej z niedowierzaniem, przekonany, że zwariowała. Nie mieściło mu się w głowie, iż usłyszał prawdę. Wstał, ukląkł przed Joanną, objął ją w pasie i przytulił głowę do jej kolan.
– Co ty mówisz...? – szepnął. – Jesteś pewna?
– Tak. – Czule pogładziła go po włosach. – Jestem całkowicie pewna.
– Ale... Przecież... Na pewno można ci jakoś pomóc! Lekarze... Pójdziemy do najlepszych specjalistów i...
– Josh! – Ucięła jego przemowę tonem nieznoszącym sprzeciwu. – Posłuchaj mnie, proszę. – Przez chwilę szukała najwłaściwszych słów. – Lekarze mogą przedłużyć mi życie najwyżej o kilka miesięcy. Zaaplikują mi naświetlania i chemioterapię.
– A potem...
– Posłuchaj! – Joanna przerwała mu stanowczo. – Joshua, wysłuchaj mnie, bardzo cię proszę. – W milczeniu zebrała myśli. – Nie zamierzam zyskiwać na siłę kilku miesięcy marnej wegetacji. Byłabym tylko ciężarem dla otoczenia i znienawidziłabym za to samą siebie. Nie chcę umierać jak mój ojciec, w udręce i cierpieniu. Chcę umrzeć jak człowiek. Z godnością.
– Ale... Joanno...
– Żadnych „ale" – odrzekła miękko. – Kochanie, objawy choroby dają mi się we znaki coraz częściej. I są coraz groźniejsze. Mam bóle głowy i nudności, a ostatnio doszły jeszcze zaburzenia wzroku...
– Jak... jak się dowiedziałaś? Kiedy poszłaś z tym do lekarza?
– W styczniu wybrałam się do San Francisco na większe zakupy i wówczas byłam u lekarza w Stanford. Już wtedy męczyły mnie częste bóle głowy.
– Nic mi nie powiedziałaś – stwierdził Josh oskarżycielskim tonem. – Słowem nawet nie wspomniałaś, że coś jest nie w porządku.
– To prawda. Postanowiłam żyć normalnie. Tak długo, jak zdołam. I nadal tego pragnę. Lekarz zaproponował środki uśmierzające ból, to mi na razie wystarcza. Chciałabym, żebyś zdawał sobie sprawę ze skutków, jakie może za sobą pociągać mój stan. I żebyś pamiętał, jaką podjęłam decyzję.

– O czym ty mówisz?

– O tym, że chcę umrzeć godnie – odparła. – Tutaj, w domu. Nie zamierzam spędzać ostatnich dni w szpitalu, nie życzę sobie leczenia, które jedynie przedłuży moje męczarnie...

– Ale...

– Joshua, już ci powiedziałam: żadnych „ale". Nie zmienię zdania, nie próbuj mnie przekonywać. Klamka zapadła. – Zamilkła i uścisnęła go mocno. – Mieliśmy dużo szczęścia, kochanie. Dobrze nam się żyło razem. Zostaliśmy obdarzeni najcenniejszym darem na świecie: wzajemnym uczuciem. Z tą świadomością naprawdę mogę odejść w spokoju. Rozumiesz mnie chyba?

Joshua pokiwał głową, choć nie był do końca pewien, czy rzeczywiście rozumiał. Oczy napełniły mu się łzami, które trudno było powstrzymać. Jeszcze nie do końca pojął słowa Joanny. Wydawały mu się nieprawdziwe, jakby dotyczyły cudzego życia albo może zostały wypowiedziane w jakimś filmie.

– Josh? – odezwała się, ujmując w dłonie obie jego ręce.

– Tak?

– Chcę cię prosić o pomoc w bardzo ważnej sprawie.

– Zrobię dla ciebie wszystko – zapewnił, a łzy popłynęły mu z oczu.

– Naprawdę bardzo chcę żyć normalnie, zwyczajnie, tak jak do tej pory – powiedziała Joanna z naciskiem. – Jak gdyby nic się nie stało. Wiem, to nie będzie łatwe, ale tak właśnie zdecydowałam. I proszę cię, żeby o mojej chorobie nie wiedział nikt, kto tego wiedzieć nie musi. Tylko w ten sposób możesz mi osłodzić czas przed odejściem. Jestem najszczęśliwsza wówczas, kiedy nasze życie toczy się utartym szlakiem.

Tylko pokiwał głową, gdyż nie mógł zawierzyć własnemu głosowi. Łzy ciekły mu po policzkach strumieniami.

– Chcę, żebyś pracował jak zwykle. Sama też będę robiła wszystko, jak do tej pory. Wiem, to niełatwe. Ale takie właśnie mam ostatnie życzenie.

– Kto... Kto cię leczy? – wychrypiał Joshua.

– Z myślą o tobie wypisałam wszystkie niezbędne informacje – odparła Joanna. – Kartka jest w górnej prawej szufladzie mojego biurka w gabinecie. Są tam również nazwiska lekarzy, masz do nich wszystkie numery telefonów. Dołączyłam także kilka artykułów prasowych dotyczących tego konkretnego rodzaju nowotworu. Pomogą ci lepiej zrozumieć sytuację.

Joshua oparł głowę na kolanach żony, a ona delikatnie przeczesała mu włosy palcami.

Dziwne, pomyślała. Wydawało mi się, że nie zdołam powstrzymać łez. Że trudno mi będzie wziąć się w garść. Tymczasem... kiedy siedzimy tak blisko, objęci, połączeni naszą miłością... nie jest to takie trudne, jak się spodziewałam.

Joshua nagle podniósł głowę.

– Teraz rozumiem, dlaczego brałaś te pigułki.

– Dowiedziałam się o mojej chorobie zaraz po tym, jak zaplanowaliśmy dziecko, i zdecydowałam, że nie zajdę w ciążę. Nie wiadomo, czy dożyłabym porodu. A gdyby nawet – nikt nie mógł mi zagwarantować, że obejdzie się bez komplikacji. – Nie dodała, że chciała, by miał dziecko z inną kobietą, że postanowiła, iż jego syn czy córka będzie mieć oboje rodziców. Jeszcze przyjdzie czas na te sprawy. I na wiele innych.

– Joanno... jesteś taka dzielna... Sama borykałaś się z tym przez tyle czasu... Żałuję, że nie powiedziałaś mi wcześniej, nie czułabyś się taka osamotniona. W jakimś sensie... jestem na ciebie urażony, że mi nie zaufałaś.

– To nie była kwestia zaufania. Musiałam najpierw dojść do ładu z własnymi emocjami. Nie chciałam cię odsuwać, ale po prostu nie umiałam z tobą o tym rozmawiać.

– Cieszę się, że wreszcie się na to zdobyłaś.

– Ja też. – Umilkła i potargała mu włosy. – A teraz – poleciła – wstaniesz i przygotujesz się do wyjścia. Jak co dzień. Niedługo przyjedzie April, zjawi się Connie... Mamy mnóstwo pracy.

– Nie potrafię się zachowywać jak gdyby nigdy nic! To czyste szaleństwo!

– Nieprawda. Nie ma w tym ani odrobiny szaleństwa. I pamiętaj, że właśnie o takie zachowanie cię proszę. Normalne, zwykłe, jakby nic szczególnego się nie działo.

– Nie do wiary.

– A jednak. Tylko na tym mi zależy. Kocham życie, jest mi z tobą dobrze, chcę wykorzystać każdą chwilę, jaka została nam dana. Pomóż mi spełnić to życzenie. Wiem, że proszę o bardzo wiele, ale pragnę tego ponad wszystko. W ten sposób łatwiej będzie mi odejść.

Joshua wstał i spojrzał na żonę. W oczach miał ból i rozpacz.

Dobry Boże, pomyślała, oby tylko zdołał wziąć się w garść!

W głębi serca miała przekonanie, że mu się to uda.

– Musisz się zbierać – powiedziała. – Przed wyjściem zajrzyj i pocałuj mnie na do widzenia. A jeśli będziesz mógł, przyjdź na lunch jak zwykle.

Joshua stał bez ruchu. Nie chciał odejść.

– Josh, pora na ciebie – ponagliła go miękko.

Wreszcie przestąpił z nogi na nogę i wolno wszedł do domu. Joanna powiodła za nim wzrokiem, chcąc utrwalić sobie w pamięci każdy ruch jego barków, kołysanie ramion, sposób stawiania kroków. Ogarnęła ją fala miłości. Poczuła pod powiekami łzy. Udało jej się jednak zachować spokój. Powstrzymać płacz.

Tylko otarła jedną słoną kropelkę z kącika oka.

Och, Joshua, westchnęła w duchu. Żałuję, że muszę odejść.

Po chwili wyprostowała się i upiła łyk kawy.

Umieram, pomyślała, ale zanim odejdę, muszę jeszcze wiele zrobić.

Księga druga

APRIL I JOSH

Jesień i zima 2000 roku

Rozdział piętnasty

April siedziała przy stole w kuchni, popijając kawę i skubiąc grzanki. Jedna była z dżemem z czarnej porzeczki, druga z marmoladą pomarańczową. Koło talerza leżały poranne gazety. Gdy zadzwonił telefon, sięgnęła po słuchawkę, nie odrywając oczu od artykułu.

– Halo?

– April?

Joshua?, zdumiała się w myślach. Natychmiast odsunęła gazetę.

– Cześć, Josh. Co u ciebie?

– Poświęć mi kilka chwil – poprosił niepewnie. – Muszę z tobą porozmawiać o pewnej ważnej sprawie.

Ciekawe, co to za ważna sprawa, zastanowiła się April. W głosie Josha nie usłyszała zwykłej wesołości. A właściwie to był wyraźnie smutny.

– Oczywiście – powiedziała. – Zamieniam się w słuch. O co chodzi?

Jednak Joshua jakoś nie potrafił zebrać się w sobie.

– Masz dziwny głos – dorzuciła.

– Widzisz... Ja raczej... – westchnął zrezygnowany. – April, nie chcę ci przeszkadzać, ale naprawdę muszę z tobą porozmawiać. I to nie przez telefon. Sprawa jest wyjątkowo ważna.

– Rozumiem. Przyjechać do ciebie?

– Nie, nie. Lepiej nie. – Zamilkł, wyraźnie się zastanawiając. – Czy moglibyśmy się spotkać gdzieś przy kawie? W jakimś spokojnym miejscu?

Mój Boże, pomyślała April. Zdaje się, że jest czymś bardzo zmartwiony.

– Jeśli nie masz nic przeciwko temu, zapraszam cię do siebie – zaproponowała. – Kawę już wstawiam. Odpowiada ci to?
– Bardzo – odrzekł z wyraźną ulgą. – Już jadę.
– Czekam. Wiesz, jak do mnie trafić?
– Tak. Joanna tyle razy opowiadała mi o jeździe do ciebie, że znam drogę na pamięć. – W jego głosie zabrzmiała znajoma nutka humoru.
April uśmiechnęła się w duchu. Może nie jest tak źle, jak sądziła?
– Będę za jakieś pół godziny – powiedział Joshua.
– Świetnie.
– No to, na razie.
– Do zobaczenia.
April odłożyła słuchawkę i dłuższy czas wpatrywała się w przestrzeń. Potem próbowała czytać artykuł, ale nie mogła się skupić, ledwie dostrzegała litery. Wreszcie zrezygnowała, zamknęła gazetę, odłożyła ją na bok i wstała, by zaparzyć kawę.
Co tam się mogło stać? Przecież Joshua nie dzwoniłby do niej z byle błahostką. I z pewnością nie prosiłby o spotkanie w cztery oczy, gdyby nie miał jakiegoś wyjątkowo ważnego powodu. Pytanie tylko, o co może mu chodzić... Czyżby Lawrence'owie nagle doszli do wniosku, że nie podoba im się jej praca? Postanowili zrezygnować z groty?
Miała zamiar wyrzucić fusy z kubka do kosza, ale chybiła.
– A niech to!
Urwała kilka kawałków papierowego ręcznika i kiedy zaczęła sprzątać bałagan, uświadomiła sobie, że drżą jej ręce.
Dlaczego jestem taka zdenerwowana?, zdziwiła się.
W głębi serca znała odpowiedź. Choć starała się stłumić w sobie uczucie do Joshuy Lawrence'a, jej wysiłki nie przynosiły oczekiwanych rezultatów, a nawet chyba dawały wręcz przeciwny skutek. A nie było to uczucie, jakie mogła żywić siostra wobec brata... O, nie.
A teraz jeszcze i to. Rozmowa w cztery oczy.
Wycierając podłogę, April przysięgła sobie po raz kolejny, że niezależnie od tematu wynurzeń Josha, ona opanuje natłok gwałtownych emocji. Ze względu na jego żonę. Ponieważ Joanna stała jej się bliska jak siostra. I dlatego April gotowa była uczynić wszystko, by oszczędzić bólu przyjaciółce. I nic, a już zwłaszcza zakazana miłość do Joshuy, nie może zakłócić szczęścia tamtych dwojga.

* * *

Joanna prowadziła mercedesa krętą górską drogą, od czasu do czasu zerkając na niewielkie pudełko w kolorze przygaszonej pomarańczy, ozdobione brązową kokardą. Leżało na siedzeniu pasażera, tuż obok i za każdym razem, gdy rzuciła na nie okiem, uśmiechała się z dumą. Któregoś dnia, robiąc zakupy, wstąpiła do Hermèsa. Tam zobaczyła apaszkę ozdobioną wzorem w muszle. Natychmiast pomyślała, iż to drobiazg wprost stworzony dla April, toteż kupiła chustkę bez chwili wahania, kazała ją elegancko zapakować i postanowiła dać przyjaciółce przy najbliższej sposobności.

Instynkt podszepnął jej, że można by to zrobić już dziś, więc w drodze powrotnej z salonu piękności, świeżo uczesana, wypoczęta i w doskonałym nastroju, postanowiła wstąpić do April.

Zatrzymała się przed znakiem stopu. Lepiej było go nie lekceważyć, droga naprawdę należała do niebezpiecznych. Przepuściła samochód z przeciwka, potem wolno pokonała zwężony odcinek szosy, wreszcie znów ruszyła nieco szybciej. Z ciekawością przyglądała się letnim domkom zawieszonym na skałach po drugiej stronie wąwozu. Niektóre zostały tak zręcznie ukryte między gęstymi drzewami, że trudno je było dostrzec. I na tym, między innymi, polegał ich urok.

Za następnym zakrętem stał domek April. Joanna zwolniła. Miała zamiar, jak poprzednio, zaparkować tuż za autem gospodyni, ale gdy wyjechała zza zakrętu, okazało się, iż na wąskim podjeździe nie ma wolnego miejsca.

Tuż za starym dżipem stał land cruiser Josha.

Joanna zatrzymała samochód. Myśli kłębiły jej się w głowie, serce waliło jak młotem. Szybko podjęła decyzję, wcisnęła gaz i odjechała. Miała nadzieję, że nie zauważyli jej mercedesa.

Na najbliższym skrzyżowaniu skręciła w lewo, w jakąś podporządkowaną drogę. Akurat trafiła na zatoczkę, więc zatrzymała się tam i długi czas siedziała bez ruchu, niewidzącym wzrokiem patrząc w okno. Serce nadal biło jak na alarm.

Boże jedyny, pomyślała, aż mi się ręce trzęsą!

Kilkakroć odetchnęła głęboko, by uspokoić nerwy i oczyścić umysł. Kolejny raz spojrzała na wytworną paczuszkę z kokardą. Prezent dla April.

Zaczęła się śmiać.

Najpierw bezgłośnie, jakby dyskretnie, potem coraz gwałtowniej, aż w końcu pochyliła się i mało nie popłakała ze śmiechu.

Udało się! Tak! Tylko... nie przewidziała, że będzie zazdrosna. Mało tego: czuła się osamotniona i zdradzona i... Ach, Boże!

Wtedy popłynęły łzy. Płakała spokojnie, cicho, nienawidząc siebie samej za to uczucie zazdrości, której nie chciała. Za złość do Josha i April, za pretensję, że między nimi zrodziło się coś niepowtarzalnego. Wyraźna więź, którą sama zadzierzgnęła, umacniała i na której tak bardzo jej zależało.

Oczywiście, że przyjechał tutaj, pomyślała. A dokąd miał pójść? Cudownie! Fantastycznie, że akurat z April chciał porozmawiać w tak trudnej chwili.

Gdy łzy w końcu obeschły, zdjęła okulary przeciwsłoneczne i wytarła oczy chusteczką. Nagle znowu zaczęła się śmiać – ale tym razem w jej śmiechu brzmiał bezsilny, pełen bezradności ton.

Co za ironia! Osiągnęła cel. Powinna być szczęśliwa. A wcale się nie cieszyła.

Nadszedł czas, by się z tym oswoić. Należało przewidzieć, że ciepłe uczucia Josha dla innej kobiety będą ją bolały. Nawet jeśli to kobieta przez nią wybrana.

W końcu Joanna uspokoiła się i wyjechała na szosę. Postanowiła wrócić do domu inną drogą, nie przejeżdżając już obok domu April.

Prowadziła wolno, by mieć czas na rozmyślania. We wspomnieniach wróciła do początków swojej choroby.

Gdy tylko się dowiedziała, że nie zostało jej wiele czasu, postanowiła, że na jej miejscu w życiu Joshuy pojawi się inna kobieta. Ponieważ jej dzielny mąż, wbrew pozorom, potrzebował wsparcia mądrej partnerki. Fizycznego, emocjonalnego i duchowego. Jak każdy człowiek zresztą.

Kochała go tak bardzo, iż postanowiła znaleźć mu kogoś, kto ją zastąpi.

Pierwszą kandydatką była robiąca karierę dekoratorka wnętrz, Julie Gillette. Joanna zatrudniła ją do pomocy przy zamawianiu tapet i farb i szybko uznała za fascynującą kobietę. Z początku nowa znajoma wydawała się doskonałą kandydatką na drugą żonę Joshuy. Niestety, zaledwie po kilku dniach Joanna odkryła z przykrością, iż Julie, przy wszystkich swoich zaletach – a było ich niemało – miała także jedną cechę stanowczo niepożądaną: kochała pieniądze i eksponowaną pozycję towarzyską. Nie było w tym w zasadzie nic złego, ale taka postawa nie współgrała z podejściem do życia re-prezentowanym przez Joshuę. Innymi słowy, jako para nie zaszliby daleko.

Następnie trafiła się Rachel Lewis, z zawodu fotografik. Joanna poznała ją, pracując nad albumem z orchideami. Na tamtym etapie była jeszcze przekonana, że tekst powinien zostać urozmaicony zdjęciami, a nie rysunkami - na które zdecydowała się później - i dlatego umówiła się z kilkoma fotografami, by zobaczyć z bliska ich osiągnięcia. Przy tej okazji spotkała Rachel, która okazała się zarówno doskonałym fachowcem, jak i piękną kobietą. Uroda Rachel nie podlegała dyskusji, natomiast w czasie kolejnych rozmów wyszedł na jaw poważny mankament: okazała się osobą emocjonalnie słabą, brakowało jej wewnętrznej siły, na której mógłby polegać Josh. Najwyraźniej z trudnością radziła sobie z własnymi problemami, wobec czego, oczywiście, nie mogła wspierać kogoś innego.

Przewinęło się jeszcze kilka innych kandydatek, które wzbudziły nadzieję w Joannie. Ot, choćby Frieda. Piękna, rozwiedziona właścicielka księgarni. Idealna kandydatka, gdyby nie była lesbijką. Albo Laura, młoda bogata miłośniczka jazdy konnej – o zrównoważonym charakterze, przypominająca araba czystej krwi. Niestety, okazała się mało inteligentna i niewykształcona, chociaż uczyła się w najlepszych szkołach.

Wreszcie Joanna trafiła na April. Kobietę idealną dla Josha. Poszukiwania zakończyły się szczęśliwie i to akurat wtedy, kiedy właściwie już się poddała i pogodziła z myślą, że Joshua będzie dalej szedł przez życie sam. Właśnie wtedy pojawiła się April, partnerka doskonała, o ogromnej sile charakteru, z pewnością zdolna w razie potrzeby wesprzeć ukochanego mężczyznę. April, która będzie szczęśliwa, zarówno dając, jak biorąc.

Joanna uśmiechnęła się z triumfem. Pokonała strach i żal, burza uczuć wreszcie ucichła, przynajmniej na jakiś czas. Nie mogła się doczekać poniedziałku, gdy podaruje April tę uroczą apaszkę, zdobioną wzorem z tęczowych muszli. Cudnie będzie zobaczyć na twarzy przyjaciółki zachwyt.

Spodoba jej się na pewno, pomyślała zadowolona. Obojgu im się spodoba.

* * *

– Joanna umiera... – powtórzyła zszokowana April.

Joshua pochylił głowę.

– Nie chciała mi o tym powiedzieć. Nie dowiedziałbym się i dzisiaj, gdybym przypadkiem nie znalazł tych pigułek... – Podniósł wzrok i napotkał pełne współczucia spojrzenie April. – Widzisz, bardzo długo odkładaliśmy decyzję o powiększeniu rodziny. Kiedy w końcu uznaliśmy, że nadszedł na to czas, zrezygnowaliśmy ze środków antykoncepcyjnych... A później Joanna dowiedziała się o swojej chorobie... – Umilkł i pokręcił głową. – Wtedy na nowo zaczęła brać pigułki. Nie wiedziała, czy dożyje do końca ciąży, obawiała się komplikacji, nie chciała skrzywdzić nienarodzonego dziecka...

April patrzyła na niego w milczeniu, targana sprzecznymi uczuciami. Nie bardzo mogła uwierzyć w to, co usłyszała.

– Josh... Dobry Boże... – Z trudem powstrzymywała łzy. – Nie wiem, co ci powiedzieć... Ale zapewniam, że zrobię wszystko, co w ludzkiej mocy, by wam pomóc. Powiedz tylko słowo. Naprawdę, zrobię wszystko. – Oczy miała pełne smutku, ale nie uroniła ani jednej łzy. Na płacz przyjdzie czas później.

Joshua wbił wzrok w kubek z kawą, stojący przed nim na kuchennym stole.

– Dziękuję ci, April. – Spojrzał na nią z wdzięcznością. – Wiem, że bardzo polubiłaś Joannę, inaczej niczego bym ci nie zdradził. Powiedziałem ci nie tylko dlatego, że musiałem zrzucić z siebie ten ciężar, ale też po to, żebyś pierwsza o wszystkim się dowiedziała. Moim zdaniem masz do tego prawo.

April położyła dłoń na ręku Josha.

– Dobrze zrobiłeś – zapewniła go. – Miło mi, że obdarzyłeś mnie zaufaniem. Oczywiście masz rację, kocham Joannę całym sercem, jest wspaniała... brak mi słów. Zawsze chciałam mieć siostrę – i znalazłam ją w Joannie. – Głos uwiązł jej w gardle. – Kocham was oboje – dodała po chwili. Poczerwieniała, mówiąc te słowa. – I zawsze jestem gotowa pomagać wam ze wszystkich sił. Zrobię dla was wszystko.

Joshua zamknął jej rękę w dłoniach.

Boże jedyny, pomyślał. Chciałbym móc teraz jej powiedzieć, że także ją kochamy. I że ja ją kocham.

Byłaby to jednak zdrada wobec Joanny. Nawet taka myśl wydawała się niestosowna.

– Zdaję sobie sprawę z tego, że możemy na tobie polegać – odrzekł ciepło. – Jesteś dla nas jak członek rodziny. Na pewno o tym wiesz.

April pokiwała głową.

– Tak – szepnęła po prostu. Jej spojrzenie zbłądziło za okno, zatonęło w gęstych liściach. – Josh – spojrzała mu prosto w oczy – mam do ciebie jedną prośbę.

– Jaką?

– Lepiej nie przyznawaj się Joannie, że mi opowiedziałeś o jej chorobie. Zaczekajmy, aż sama się na to zdecyduje.

Joshua w milczeniu pokiwał głową.

April wysunęła rękę z jego dłoni i nerwowym gestem przeczesała włosy.

– Na pewno niedługo to zrobi.

– Prawdopodobnie – zgodził się Joshua. – Ma coraz więcej objawów. Częstsze bóle głowy, zaburzenia widzenia, nudności... Lekarstwa trochę pomagają, ale i tak niedługo będzie ci się musiała wytłumaczyć...

– Zostanę przy was – obiecała April spokojnie.

– Dziękuję. W imieniu nas obojga. – Joshua poruszył się niespokojnie. – Będę się zbierał. Nie wiem, kiedy Joanna wróci do domu, a wolę być pierwszy. Boję się o nią, nie chcę jej zostawiać samej. Najchętniej zamknąłbym ją na cztery spusty... ale ona nie znosi żadnych ograniczeń...

– I trudno ci się z tym pogodzić?

– Właśnie.

Joshua wstał, April także.

– Umówiłyśmy się, że przyjadę do was dopiero w poniedziałek rano. Jeśli byłabym potrzebna wcześniej, daj mi znać, proszę. Możesz dzwonić o każdej porze dnia i nocy. Nigdzie się nie wybieram na weekend.

– Dobrze. – Joshua uśmiechnął się smutno. – Będziemy improwizowali na bieżąco...

– Tak, raczej tak. – Odprowadziła go aż do mostka. – Pamiętaj, w razie potrzeby dzwoń bez wahania. Jestem do waszej dyspozycji.

– Będę pamiętał. Wiem, że mogę na ciebie liczyć. – Tak bardzo chciał ją objąć i przytulić, podziękować tym gestem za zrozumienie, za dobroć.

April jakby wyczuła jego pragnienie, objęła go i przycisnęła do siebie.

– Musimy być silni – wyszeptała.

– To prawda.

Wszedł na mostek i ruszył ku drodze.

April patrzyła za nim długo, aż wsiadł do samochodu i odjechał, machając na pożegnanie. Dopiero wtedy wróciła do domu. Zamknęła za sobą drzwi, oparła się o nie i przymknęła oczy. Z ust wyrwało jej się głośne westchnienie. I wtedy łzy, tak długo powstrzymywane, spłynęły po policzkach. Szlochała, jakby nie miała nigdy przestać. Opłakiwała Joannę, Josha i siebie.

* * *

Joshua wjechał na podwórze i natychmiast zauważył mercedesa Joanny. Odetchnął z ulgą. Zaparkował wóz i szybkim krokiem poszedł do domu. Uświadomił sobie, że po rozmowie z April czuje się silniejszy. Nie wiedział dokładnie dlaczego, ale miał wrażenie, iż pomogła mu sama świadomość, że może liczyć na wsparcie przyjaciółki.

Zdawał sobie także sprawę z nowej, mocniejszej więzi, jaką połączyła ich wspólna tajemnica. Z jednej strony cieszyła go ta sytuacja, z drugiej – budziła w nim poczucie winy. Może za bardzo polubił towarzystwo April?

Podobał mu się jej skromny domek, miły i przytulny, pełen bajkowego uroku.

Podobnie jak wszystko, do czego przyłoży rękę Joanna, uświadomił sobie.

W sieni się zorientował, że buty ma zupełnie czyste, więc nie musi ich zmieniać, wobec tego od razu poszedł do kuchni. Tam jednak nie było Joanny. Nie dostrzegł jej także na tarasie. Stanął w holu i zawołał ją po imieniu, lecz odpowiedziała mu cisza. Kierowany impulsem wyszedł na taras, minął mostek, basen i sad, aż znalazł się przy grocie.

Tam ją zobaczył. Zatrzymał się przed drzwiami i patrzył, jak wędrowała wzdłuż ściany, muskając palcami muszle. Od czasu do czasu odsuwała się o krok czy dwa i spoglądała krytycznym wzrokiem na to, co zostało zrobione.

Wszedł do środka.

– Joanno! – zawołał miękko.

Odwróciła się do niego, wcale nie zaskoczona. Na twarzy miała promienny uśmiech. Robiła wrażenie całkowicie spokojnej, nawet szczęśliwej.

– Piękniejе z dnia na dzień, prawda? – odezwała się jasnym głosem.

– Istotnie.

– Ma w sobie coś ze mnie, nie uważasz?

– Cała moja Joanna! – odparł Joshua. – Twój pomysł, twoja wyobraźnia... – Nagłe łzy nie pozwoliły mu skończyć.

Joanna otarła je delikatnie.

– Nie płacz – powiedziała. – Damy sobie radę. Nie wolno się załamywać. – Pocałowała go czule w usta. – Nie jesteś sam.

* * *

Następnego ranka Joanna przebudziła się wyjątkowo wcześnie, jakaś nieswoja. Coś ją zaniepokoiło. Wyciągnęła rękę do Josha, lecz go nie znalazła.

Ach, to dlatego, pomyślała. Niesamowite, jak można się przyzwyczaić... Wystarczy, że go przy mnie zabrakło, a już jestem niespokojna.

Wstała z łóżka, zarzuciła szlafrok i na bosaka poszła do łazienki. Połknęła pierwszą tego dnia pigułkę, zapobiegawczy środek przeciwbólowy. Ochlapała twarz, wymyła zęby, przeczesała włosy. Przyjrzała się swojemu odbiciu w lustrze.

Dziwne, wcale nie sprawiam wrażenia chorej. W zasadzie wyglądam całkiem dobrze.

Uśmiechnęła się i zgasiła światło.

Czas poszukać Josha.

Ruszyła w stronę schodów, ale zatrzymała się przy gabinecie męża. Drzwi były otwarte na oścież, światło zapalone. Joshua siedział przy biurku, monitor komputera rzucał na jego twarz migotliwe blaski. Na blacie piętrzyły się jakieś papiery; zapewne były między nimi artykuły i notatki, o których mu wspomniała. Zastukała lekko w drzwi i weszła do środka.

– Josh?

Drgnął i obrócił się gwałtownie. Oczy miał czerwone i zapuchnięte, włosy potargane, ubranie wygniecione. W pokoju panował zaduch.

– Wyglądasz na zmęczonego – odezwała się zaniepokojona.

– Nic dziwnego. – Uśmiechnął się ponuro. – Jestem zmęczony.

Podeszła i objęła go od tyłu, a potem pogładziła po włosach. Wiedziała, czym się zajmował, bo nietrudno się było domyślić, ale i tak spytała:

– Co robisz?

– Myszkowałem po sieci – rzekł ochryple. – Chciałem się dowiedzieć jak najwięcej o... na temat... – Podniósł na nią smutne spojrzenie.

– Śmiało, Josh. Odwagi. Powiedz to wyraźnie. Choroba nowotworowa. Rak. Widzisz? To tylko słowo.

– Wybacz mi... po prostu nadal nie mogę uwierzyć... – Wyraźnie walczył ze łzami.

Przytuliła go czule i ucałowała w czoło.

Musi się wziąć w garść!

Sama też z trudem powstrzymywała łzy. Kochała go ponad wszystko na świecie i nie mogła okazać słabości, bo złamałaby mu serce.

– Dojdziesz z tym jakoś do ładu, kochanie – oznajmiła, siląc się na pogodny ton. Zmierzwiła mu włosy. – Powiedz mi, co znalazłeś.

– Szukałem organizacji skupiających ludzi, którzy mają do czynienia z tą chorobą. Wpadło mi w oko Amerykańskie Stowarzyszenie Osób Chorych na Raka Mózgu, Towarzystwo Walki z Rakiem, Narodowy Instytut Onkologiczny, Krajowa Fundacja do Walki z Nowotworami Mózgu... Sporo tego. Całą noc przeglądałem witryny w Internecie. Wczoraj zadzwoniłem do doktora Saltzmana z Palo Alto i dostałem od niego sporo informacji, odpowiedział na wszystkie moje pytania. Chciałem jednak bliżej zapoznać się z tematem, dlatego przesiedziałem całą noc przy komputerze.

– Nic dziwnego, że jesteś wykończony. Chodź, napijemy się kawy. A może wolisz wziąć prysznic i położyć się spać?

– Nie, nie. Teraz nie potrafiłbym zasnąć. Niech będzie kawa.

Trzymając się za ręce, zeszli do kuchni. Joanna wrzuciła do młynka ciemnobrązowe ziarna i włączyła ekspres, Joshua przyszykował tosty oraz świeżo wyciśnięty sok z pomarańczy, a potem nakrył stół na tarasie. Gdy w końcu usiedli do śniadania, poranne słońce już rozprawiało się z mgłą.

– Twój lekarz jest wymieniany w witrynie „Najlepsi lekarze" – odezwał się Josh.

– Wiem. Ale nie stamtąd się o nim dowiedziałam, chociaż zajrzałam chyba na każdą stronę w sieci, gdzie znajdowała się choćby wzmianka o tej chorobie.

– Joanno – Joshua utkwił w żonie spojrzenie – zdajesz sobie sprawę, że pojawiają się coraz to nowe techniki leczenia i są coraz skuteczniejsze. Jest też wiele...

– Josh – przerwała mu. – Wiem o tym, możesz mi wierzyć. Czytałam wszystko, co znalazłam na ten temat, rozmawiałam z całymi zastępami lekarzy. Wszyscy mówią mi właściwie to samo: można jedynie zyskać na czasie. Ale nie tak znowu wiele.

– Są też pewne badania eksperymentalne... – Nie dawał za wygraną.

Joanna uderzyła otwartą dłonią w blat stołu.

– Dość! W tej chwili przestań! Nie chcę tego dłużej słuchać! – Głos jej się załamał, w oczach zabłysły łzy.

Joshua zerwał się na równe nogi, opadł na klęczki i objął żonę.

– Wybacz mi – jęknął. – Kochanie, ja tylko chciałem... Po prostu nie umiem się z tym pogodzić... Szukałem czegoś... Chciałem cudu. Nie możesz tak odejść!

– Spójrz na mnie.

Podniósł na nią wzrok i dojrzał niezłomną siłę. Oraz całkowity brak jakichkolwiek wątpliwości.

– Powiedziałam ci, że nie chcę umierać jak tata, w bólu i cierpieniu. Nie będę odwlekać momentu odejścia. Nie zamierzam też zostać królikiem doświadczalnym. Joshua, spójrz prawdzie w oczy. Można mnie utrzymać przy życiu, ale tak naprawdę nie byłabym żywa. Podjęłam taką, a nie inną decyzję i mam nadzieję, że ją uszanujesz.

Po dłuższej chwili ciszy Josh wolno skinął głową. Nie widział sposobu, by przekonać żonę do zmiany zdania, choć nie umiał sobie wytłumaczyć, jakim cudem tak spokojnie podchodziła do straszliwego wyroku śmierci.

– Joanno, jak ty sobie dajesz z tym radę? Nie czujesz nienawiści do losu?

– Był taki czas – przyznała z błyskiem w oku – że przeklinałam Boga i ludzi... Cały świat. Ale to już minęło. Teraz pogodziłam się z nieuniknionym. I z własną bezsilnością wobec losu. – Uśmiechnęła się smutno. – Odzyskałam spokój – dodała cicho. – Mam nadzieję, że i tobie się to uda. – Pochyliła się, ucałowała go i uścisnęła. – Jedzmy – powiedziała. – Czeka mnie dziś wyjątkowo pracowity dzień.

– A co planujesz?

– Muszę się spakować. Wybieram się na kilka dni do Christiny. Najwyższy czas jej powiedzieć, jak wyglądają sprawy. Muszę to zrobić osobiście, nie przez telefon. Nawet nie zauważysz mojej nieobecności, bo przecież masz pełne ręce roboty.

Joshua był pod wrażeniem jej opanowania.

– Czy aby na pewno powinnaś jechać sama?

– Powiedziałam ci już, że chcę żyć zupełnie normalnie. Aż do końca. – Nagle się roześmiała. – Wizyta u Christiny nie jest może szczytem moich pragnień, ale postaram się zachowywać przyzwoicie.

Joshua zgodnie pokiwał głową, lecz w głębi serca nadal burzył się przeciwko decyzjom żony.

– Zajrzysz dzisiaj do szklarni? – spytała Joanna.

– Nie. W tym tygodniu nie mam żadnych spotkań, więc Carl się wszystkim zajmie. Planowałem popracować w cieplarni, w jaskini rozpusty.

– A może najpierw byś się przespał? Wyglądasz jak zombi.

– Dobrze, może rzeczywiście się położę.

– Obiecujesz?

Joshua pokiwał głową.

– Obiecuję – odrzekł ze słabym uśmiechem.

Wiedział jednak, że tego nie zrobi. Nie zdołałby zasnąć.

Rozdział szesnasty

April leżała na rusztowaniu, rozciągnięta na plecach. Do sufitu miała mniej niż pół metra. Z ogromnym skupieniem układała w szybkoschnącym cemencie okrągłe muszle w odcieniach od różu do pomarańczowego. Uważnie obserwowała nakreślone wcześniej linie, bo każda pomyłka wymagałaby trudnych i czasochłonnych poprawek.

Argopecten circularis, pomyślała z kwaśnym uśmiechem. W życiu nie przypuszczałam, że tyle się dowiem o tym małżu. Chcąc nie chcąc, musiałam.

Pracowała caluteńki dzień, z krótką przerwą na obiad. Woody już poszedł, a ona została najdłużej, jak mogła. Po pamiętnej rozmowie z Joshem poświęcała pracom w grocie każdą chwilę. Poza tym chciała, żeby Joanna po powrocie z Montecito mogła się ucieszyć niespodziewanie żwawym postępem prac.

Oczami wyobraźni widziała już gotowy sufit. Choć wiedziała, że nie uda jej się skończyć go w ciągu tych kilku dni, zamierzała przynajmniej zrobić jak najwięcej. Zdobienie sufitu stanowiło najtrudniejszą część zadania, chociażby z tego prostego powodu, że trzeba było pracować na leżąco, z podniesionymi rękami. Jakby tego było mało, bardzo dawały jej się we znaki upał i duchota, wyjątkowo dokuczliwe w górze, mimo stale włączonych wiatraków.

Umieściła ostatnią muszlę na końcu wyrysowanej linii i odetchnęła z ulgą.

Dosyć na dzisiaj, uznała. Tym razem już na serio.

Podejmowała tę decyzję już kilka razy, ale pracowała dalej, starając się zbliżyć do zamknięcia przynajmniej jednego fragmentu zdobienia.

– Heeej, tam na górze! – zawołał Joshua od wejścia.
– Cześć! – odkrzyknęła April.
– Późno się robi. Nie wystarczy ci na dzisiaj?
– Właśnie skończyłam.
Joshua przyjrzał się sufitowi. Już było widać, że wnętrze będzie jedyne w swoim rodzaju, fascynujące, egzotyczne. Szkice nawet nie umywały się do rzeczywistości. I nic dziwnego, w końcu przecież stworzenie takiego cudu wymagało nieskończonej cierpliwości i wielkiego nakładu pracy.
April przesunęła się do brzegu rusztowania i opuściła nogi na niższy poziom. Gdy dotarła na sam dół, ściągnęła gumowe rękawice. Rozprostowała ramiona, zatoczyła kółko głową, najpierw w jedną, potem w drugą stronę.
– Najgorsze, co może być. – Westchnęła. – Pojęcia nie mam, jak dawał sobie z tym radę Michał Anioł. Zresztą nie on jeden. Pewnie wszyscy artyści miewają potworne skurcze.
– Ale chyba gra jest warta świeczki? – zaśmiał się Joshua.
Jak dobrze słyszeć jego śmiech, pomyślała April. Od wyjazdu Joanny nawet się nie uśmiechnął.
Przyjrzała się uważnie sufitowi.
– Masz rację – przyznała. – Będzie rewelacyjny.
– April, może zostaniesz na kolacji? Connie jak zwykle coś upichciła, a ja strasznie nie lubię jeść sam. No i po takim dniu pracy naprawdę należy ci się przyzwoity posiłek. A także chwila odpoczynku.
Nie bardzo wiedziała, co odpowiedzieć. Szybko jednak uświadomiła sobie, że zachowuje się jak dziecko. Przecież chciała zjeść z nim tę kolację, więc niby dlaczego miałaby sobie odmówić tej przyjemności? A Josh też poczuje się lepiej, jeśli nie będzie musiał siedzieć w domu sam.
– Chętnie zostanę, dziękuję. – Otrzepała ręce. – O Boże! Zobacz, jak ja wyglądam! Cała w cemencie, kurzu...
– Nie przejmuj się. Wykąp się albo weź prysznic, jak wolisz.
– Zaraz będę gotowa – obiecała April, rozwiązując wielki fartuch. – Chociaż i tak będę wyglądała trochę niestosownie...
– Jak artystka po pracy – uśmiechnął się Joshua. – Nie ma w tym nic niestosownego.
– Jeszcze tylko pozbieram rzeczy i zaraz przyjdę.
– Możesz skorzystać z łazienki dla gości w domu albo z tej w domku nad basenem.

– Tę nad basenem już znam, więc tam się ogarnę – zdecydowała April.

– Niech ci będzie – zgodził się Joshua. – Wobec tego do zobaczenia na tarasie.

Po jego wyjściu szybko uporządkowała grotę, przygotowała wszystko na następny ranek i zebrała narzędzia, które trzeba było umyć. Jak co dzień włożyła je do wiadra, wzięła też swoją przepastną torbę, zgasiła światło i wyszła, dokładnie zamykając za sobą ogromne przeszklone drzwi.

Znalazłszy się w jednej z dwóch łazienek w domku nad basenem, najpierw starannie umyła i osuszyła narzędzia, dopiero potem spojrzała w lustro.

– Kompletna beznadzieja – zawyrokowała. Wyszorowała ręce, zeskrobując nawet z ramion ledwo zastygły cement, a następnie obmyła twarz i szyję. Wycierając się, zerknęła ponownie w lustro. – O Boże! Włosy! – jęknęła. Rzeczywiście, włosy miała równo pokryte białą warstwą cementowego pyłu. – Wyglądam jak kiepsko ucharakteryzowana aktorka. Jakbym usiłowała dodać sobie lat wyłącznie siwizną... – Chwyciła szczotkę i energicznie wyszczotkowała włosy. – No i nic z tego – oceniła po jakimś czasie, całkowicie zgodnie z prawdą. Westchnęła i odłożyła szczotkę. – Ech, trudno. Mniejsza o fryzurę! Będę po prostu sobą. Josh musi się pogodzić ze stanem faktycznym.

Strząsnęła pył z ubrania, chwyciła torbę i poszła na taras.

W czasie gdy usiłowała doprowadzić się do porządku, wiele się tutaj zmieniło. W każdym kąciku paliła się latarenka, stół został pięknie nakryty, jak zwykle lnianym obrusem i wykrochmalonymi serwetkami. Znalazły się na nim talerze z Prowansji, kryształowe kieliszki do wina i błyszczące srebrne sztućce. Na samym środku pyszniła się orchidea w doniczce, pokryta maleńkimi, delikatnymi kwiatkami, które kaskadą rozsypały się po blacie. Niemal chciało się je pogłaskać.

– Prawdziwa piękność, prawda? – Joshua wychodził właśnie z kuchni, w dłoniach trzymał butelkę wina.

– Rzeczywiście, prześliczna. Taka delikatna.

– *Barkeria specabilis* – powiedział. – Z rodziny *Cattleya*. – Podsunął April krzesło. – Siadaj, proszę. Connie zaraz przyniesie jedzenie.

– Dziękuję. – Usiadła z prawdziwą przyjemnością.

Joshua zajął miejsce naprzeciwko i napełnił kieliszki winem.

– Twoje zdrowie, Michale Aniele – wygłosił toast, unosząc swój. – Chociaż pewnie powinienem powiedzieć: Michalino Anielska. Wznoszę toast za ten niesamowity, przepiękny strop w grocie.

April z uśmiechem wzięła kieliszek.

– A ja za ciebie – powiedziała – i za twoje przepiękne orchidee.

Gdy sączyli wino, pojawiła się Connie z kolacją. Postawiła tacę na stole.

– Nałożycie sobie sami, dobrze? Ja muszę się już zbierać.

– Jakoś pewnie damy sobie radę – uśmiechnął się Joshua. – Dziękuję ci, Connie.

– Nie ma za co. Cała przyjemność po mojej stronie. – Ledwo dostrzegalnie uniosła głowę i spojrzała na gościa czarnymi jak noc oczyma, lekko zamglonymi, jakby ukrywały jakąś mroczną tajemnicę. – Smacznego.

– Dziękujemy – powiedziała April.

Gosposia szybko wróciła do domu.

– Czasami nie mogę się oprzeć wrażeniu, że ona za mną nie przepada – przyznała się April przyciszonym głosem.

– Dlaczego? – Joshua był wyraźnie zdziwiony. Zaczął im nakładać na talerze zieloną sałatę, potem kurczaka, następnie pieczone młode ziemniaki, wreszcie zieloną fasolkę.

– Jak to pięknie wygląda! – odezwała się w niej artystka.

– A smakuje pewnie jeszcze lepiej. Connie przyprawia potrawy w niezrównany sposób... nikt jej nie dorówna. Ale, ale: powiedz, dlaczego sądzisz, że ona nie darzy cię sympatią?

– Trudno to sprecyzować. Natomiast daje się odczuć w tysiącu najróżniejszych drobiazgów. W zasadzie odnosi się do mnie uprzejmie, jednak z lekką rezerwą. Mam wrażenie, że po prostu nie chce zaakceptować naszej przyjaźni.

– Między tobą a mną?

– Nie, nie to miałam na myśli – zaprzeczyła April. – Chociaż... to chyba także nie bez znaczenia. – Uśmiechnęła się z zakłopotaniem. – Niekiedy odnoszę wrażenie, że jest o mnie zazdrosna. Może sądzi, że wchodzę jej w paradę... sama nie wiem. Przecież Joanna i Connie są ze sobą dość mocno zżyte...

– To prawda – przyznał Joshua – nie sposób zaprzeczyć. Z drugiej strony, Joanna ma wiele przyjaciółek, więc nie bardzo rozumiem, dlaczego Connie miałaby akurat ciebie nie lubić.

– Dajmy temu spokój. – April wzruszyła lekko ramionami. – Pewnie to tylko moja wyobraźnia. Stale jestem w pobliżu, budowa groty zajmuje Joannie sporo czasu, a normalnie pewnie spędzałaby go właśnie z Connie.

Joshua podniósł na nią wzrok.

– Nie pomyślałem o tym – przyznał. – Może to i racja. Joanna zawsze miała do Connie całkowite zaufanie. Ta dziewczyna jest niemalże członkiem naszej rodziny.

– Tak, wiem. I właśnie dlatego nie chcę... jak by to powiedzieć... stawać między nimi. Zwłaszcza teraz. – Włożyła do ust kawałek ziemniaka. – Mmm... Przepyszne.

– Widzisz? Mówiłem ci: smakuje jeszcze lepiej, niż wygląda. April, posłuchaj mnie – podjął poważnym tonem. – Zapewniam cię, że nikomu w niczym nie przeszkadzasz. Nic dziwnego, że Joanna obdarzyła cię pełnym zaufaniem. Znalazła w tobie prawdziwą przyjaciółkę. I vice versa, jak sądzę.

– O tak – przytaknęła April.

– I to najważniejsze – oświadczył Joshua stanowczo. – Nie masz się czym przejmować. Connie z pewnością da sobie radę. Jest drobna i wydaje się krucha, ale twarda z niej kobieta. A jeśli Joanna znalazła w tobie bratnią duszę, możemy się tylko cieszyć.

– Muszę ci powiedzieć, że i ja zyskałam w niej przyjaciółkę, o jakiej nawet nie marzyłam. Nigdy wcześniej nie miałam bratniej duszy. Jakoś tak się złożyło. – Umilkła i odetchnęła głęboko. Łzy napływały jej do oczu, a przecież nie mogła płakać przy Joshu. Szybko podniosła kieliszek do ust.

* * *

Joanna uznała, że najwyższy czas poprawić makijaż przed wieczornym przyjęciem. Włączyła światło w luksusowej, wyłożonej marmurami łazience z ogromnymi lustrami. Zdumiała ją liczba własnych odbić. Powietrze przesycone było słodkim zapachem gardenii – trzy ich doniczki zdobiły ogromnych rozmiarów gładki blat, na którym znajdowały się wszelkie akcesoria toaletowe, o jakich można by zamarzyć – wszystkie w najlepszym gatunku. Podeszła do lustra wiszącego nad jedną z dwóch złotych umywalek i przyjrzała się sobie z uwagą.

Całkiem nieźle. A nawet zupełnie dobrze. Biją ode mnie zdrowie i radość życia!

Uśmiechnęła się ponuro i zbliżyła twarz do gładkiej tafli.

Może odrobina różu... Tak. Zdecydowanie.

Sięgnęła po niewielki kompaktowy zestaw i lekko musnęła policzki różem „Sunset" Givenchy'ego. Odsunęła się o krok.

Teraz jest dobrze, uznała. Wszyscy dzisiejsi goście będą opaleni na brąz, więc w ten sposób lepiej się do nich dopasuję.

Większość przyjaciół Christiny przez okrągły rok przemieszczała się po świecie w pogoni za słońcem, tak więc zawsze byli opaleni. Bez sensu. Płacili potem lekarzom grube pieniądze za usuwanie skutków nadmiernego nasłonecznienia, po czym od nowa wystawiali się na działanie promieni słońca.

Joanna zatrzasnęła wieczko zestawu i cofnęła się, by sprawdzić efekt. Zawirowała przed ogromnymi lustrami. Świetnie. Była doskonale ubrana. Miała na sobie luźną bluzkę z długimi rękawami i dość głębokim dekoltem, do niej długi szal z tego samego co bluzka jedwabnego muślinu oraz szerokie spodnie z cieniutkiej dzianiny w tym samym kolorze. Komplet od Chanel. I uszyty jakby specjalnie dla niej. Wyglądała elegancko, ale też swobodnie, jakby osiągnięcie owego efektu nie wymagało żadnego wysiłku. Mało kto wiedział, ile pracy trzeba włożyć w takie dopasowanie wszystkich elementów, by sprawiać wrażenie, że się w tym celu nic nie zrobiło.

Trąciła palcem jeden z kolczyków w kształcie łezki. Odpowiedział jej błyskiem w gładkiej tafli lustra. Uwielbiała te kolczyki, ponieważ dostała je w prezencie ślubnym od Josha, który w tamtych czasach właściwie nie mógł sobie na nie pozwolić. Kropelki złota, ozdobione brylantami i maleńkimi rubinami. Na pierwszą rocznicę ofiarował jej naszyjnik do kompletu. Nieczęsto nosiła kosztowną biżuterię, ale tego wieczoru zrobiła wyjątek, ponieważ Christina, bywając na przyjęciach u nich w domu, zawsze wkładała mnóstwo drogich świecidełek, wobec czego Joanna postanowiła dostosować się do jej stylu. No i był jeszcze jeden powód: chciała wyglądać możliwie najlepiej, przekazując siostrze niewesołą wiadomość.

Wróciła do sypialni i głęboko odetchnęła cudną wonią świeżych kwiatów.

Pochyliła się nad ogromną różą.

– Mmmm! Sama słodycz.

Christina zawsze dąży do doskonałości, pomyślała.

Pościel była z najdelikatniejszego płótna, na nocnym stoliku leżały równo ułożone najnowsze książki i czasopisma, w niewielkiej lodówce czekały alkohole, soki, woda oraz świeże owoce.

O tak, Christina umiała rozpieszczać gości.

Joanna usiadła na łóżku i zsunęła z nóg sandałki na wysokich obcasach. Od Manolo Blahnika. Objęła je zachwyconym spojrzeniem. Prawdziwe dzieło sztuki zdobione kryształowymi kwiatuszkami.

Jesteś niemądra, skarciła się w myślach. Jak można się zajmować takimi błahostkami w sytuacji gdy... Cóż, z drugiej strony, pozwalają oderwać myśli od...

Niespecjalnie miała ochotę brać udział w uroczystej kolacji, zwłaszcza dzisiaj, ale postanowiła dostosować się do zwyczajów Christiny. Przyjechała do Montecito, by osobiście przekazać jej niewesołą wiadomość, ponieważ uważała, że tak właśnie wypada postąpić. Poza tym, uznała, iż po kolejnym rozwodzie siostrze przyda się towarzystwo. No i może smutne wiadomości oderwą ją od własnych smutków.

Tymczasem Christina, ku zaskoczeniu Joanny, była w pogodnym, a nawet radosnym nastroju. Ani jednym słowem nie wspomniała o eksmężu, nie zająknęła się też na temat samotności, która nieodmiennie gnębiła ją w okresach pomiędzy kolejnymi małżeństwami.

Ciekawe dlaczego?

Z pewnością myśli ma zaprzątnięte czymś niezmiernie dla niej ważnym. Cóż takiego mogło ją napełnić niespodziewaną radością życia?

Joanna podniosła torebkę leżącą obok łóżka, poszperała w niej chwilę i wyjęła płaską buteleczkę z pigułkami. Wieczko odskoczyło z cichym pyknięciem. Włożyła do ust od razu dwie. Sięgnęła po wodę stojącą na nocnym stoliku, popiła lekarstwo.

Lepiej dmuchać na zimne, pomyślała. I od razu połknąć tabletki, na wypadek gdyby miał nadejść ten potworny ból głowy.

Czuję się bardzo dobrze, zapewniła sama siebie z przekonaniem. Naprawdę. Ale koniecznie muszę dzisiaj porozmawiać z Christiną.

Odkładała tę rozmowę od przyjazdu, powtarzając sobie stale, że nie ma powodu się śpieszyć. Czas jednak uciekał i zbliżał się dzień powrotu do domu. A ona nie znalazła sposobności, by poruszyć smutny temat. Stale były zajęte, a na dodatek Christina wydawała się taka szczęśliwa i pełna energii, że Joanna nie miała serca psuć jej nastroju.

Rozległo się lekkie pukanie, więc otworzyła drzwi.

– Gotowa, siostrzyczko? – spytała Christina.

– Jak najbardziej.

– Wyglądasz pięknie! Jak ty to robisz? I to jakby zupełnie od niechcenia! Ja całe godziny siedzę przed lustrem, żeby przypominać człowieka, a tu – proszę!

Joanna przewróciła oczami.

– Christino, przestań! Oczu od ciebie oderwać nie można, a ty się krygujesz. Z drugiej strony, jeśli chcesz posłuchać komplementów, to dobrze trafiłaś. Jesteś prześliczna, a ta suknia wygląda, jakby była na ciebie szyta!

– W rzeczy samej! – zaśmiała się Christina. – Uszył ją dla mnie Josephus Thimister z Paryża. I żądał czterech przymiarek! Jednej więcej niż zwykle. – Obróciła się dookoła, demonstrując piękną suknię sięgającą podłogi. – Boska, co?

– Nieziemska – przyznała Joanna.

Kreacja została uszyta z artystycznie dopasowanych skrawków tiulu oraz jedwabiu w kolorze tak delikatnego różu, iż przywodził na myśl nagie ciało. Christina sprawiała wrażenie ubranej wyłącznie w brylantowe kolczyki, naszyjnik, bransoletki oraz pierścionki.

– To co, idziemy? – rzuciła, poprawiając włosy w tysiącu odcieni blond. – Wypijemy coś, zanim nadciągną tłumy.

Wyszła z sypialni pierwsza, a za nią podążyła Joanna, by w przestronnym marmurowym salonie przy drinku oczekiwać przybycia zaproszonych.

* * *

Przyjęcie się skończyło, goście wyszli. Siostry usiadły w oranżerii, urządzonej w stylu neoklasycznym. Przez szklane ściany zaglądał do wnętrza wymyślnie oświetlony ogród z basenem oraz fantazyjną kaskadą spływającą ze wzgórza.

Joanna nie czuła się tu najlepiej. Dostawała gęsiej skórki na widok ustawionych rzędem na cokołach marmurowych popiersi oraz antycznych rzeźb, przedstawiających różne części ciała.

Christina wyraźnie była w nastroju do pogaduszek.

– Dobrze się bawiłaś? – spytała, wypuszczając nosem siną chmurę dymu.

– Tak. Zwykle bywam na zupełnie innych przyjęciach. Poważnych, nawet dostojnych... A u ciebie było zabawnie.

Christina zmierzyła siostrę nieufnym spojrzeniem.

– Co ty wygadujesz? Przecież widziałam, wynudziłaś się za wszystkie czasy!

– Ależ skąd! – wykrzyknęła Joanna. – Może wydawałam się trochę... nieobecna myślami, roztargniona, ale przyjęcie było świetne.

– No dobrze, żarty na bok. – Christina spoważniała. – Masz jakieś kłopoty z Joshem?

– Nie, skądże! – odparła Joanna ze śmiechem.

– Siostrze możesz powiedzieć. Ja znam mężczyzn. Wszyscy oni to świnie! – Zawahała się. – No, może prawie wszyscy.

Joanna znów się roześmiała.

– Nie, nie, daj spokój! To nie tak. Między mną a Joshem wszystko jest w jak najlepszym porządku.

– Wobec tego, o co chodzi? – spytała Christina, zaciągając się papierosem.

Joanna rozejrzała się dookoła.

– Wyjdźmy na taras – poprosiła. – Nie chciałabym, żeby nas usłyszał ktoś ze służby.

– Daj spokój! Robią taki raban w kuchni, że nie usłyszeliby armatnich wystrzałów.

– Będę się lepiej czuła na zewnątrz... Muszę ci powiedzieć coś naprawdę ważnego. Ale zachowaj tę sprawę w sekrecie...

Christina zerwała się na równe nogi i wyciągnęła rękę do siostry.

– Dla ważnej i dyskretnej sprawy gotowa jestem wybrać się nawet do Santa Barbara.

Wyszły na taras i usiadły na leżakach. Wiał lekki, przyjemnie chłodny wiatr.

– No dobrze. – Christina, walcząc z bryzą, usiłowała zapalić kolejnego papierosa. – Możesz mówić.

Joanna najpierw dłuższą chwilę patrzyła jej w oczy.

– Zanim ci powiem – odezwała się w końcu – musisz mi obiecać, że nikomu nie zdradzisz mojej tajemnicy.

– Przecież wiesz, że możesz mi ufać.

– Naprawdę nikomu – podkreśliła Joanna. – Tak jak w czasach, kiedy we dwie spiskowałyśmy przeciwko tacie. Tylko że teraz sprawa jest znacznie poważniejsza.

Christina miała oczy okrągłe ze zdumienia i ciekawości, ale nie odezwała się słowem.

– Obiecujesz? – naciskała Joanna.

– Tak – odrzekła Christina i wolno skinęła głową. Dziwnie się czuła. Ogarnął ją trudny do wytłumaczenia lęk. Joanna nigdy nie zachowywała się w ten sposób.

Młodsza siostra zatopiła spojrzenie w źrenicach starszej.
– Niedługo umrę – powiedziała zwyczajnie.
– Nnn... nie rozumiem – wykrztusiła Christina.
– Mam raka mózgu. Zostało mi najwyżej kilka miesięcy.
Christina zaniemówiła na chwilę. Nie dowierzała, bała się, była wręcz zszokowana.
– Jak to? Ale... przecież... – jąkała się z oczami pełnymi łez. – Joanno! To niemożliwe! – wykrzyknęła ochryple.
– A jednak to prawda. Mówię ci, bo jesteś moją siostrą i masz prawo wiedzieć, co się dzieje.
Christina zerwała się z leżaka i chwyciła siostrę za ramiona.
– Kłamiesz! – syknęła. – Albo sobie ze mnie żartujesz!
Joanna łagodnie ujęła w dłonie jej ręce.
– Nie kłamię, kochanie. I nigdy w życiu nie mówiłam równie poważnie. Przykro mi, ale taka właśnie jest prawda.
Christina z płaczem rzuciła jej się w ramiona.
– A Josh? – wyszlochała przez łzy. – Już wie?
– Tak. I powiem ci to, co powiedziałam jemu: chcę żyć normalnie, jak dotąd. Nie życzę sobie żadnych zmian w związku z moją chorobą. Rozumiesz mnie?
– Normalnie?!? – wybuchnęła Christina.
– Ależ tak. Tak samo jak zawsze. Dla mojego dobra.
Christina jakiś czas patrzyła na nią bez słowa.
– Chyba rozumiem – odezwała się wreszcie.
– Musimy wszyscy być silni – powiedziała Joanna – choć to nie będzie łatwe.
Christina wyprostowała się. Oczy miała błyszczące od łez.
– Potrafię znieść niejedno – oznajmiła z mocą. – I obojętne, co się stanie, zawsze możesz na mnie liczyć.
Joanna wstała, objęła ją ramieniem i serdecznie ucałowała w policzek.
– Wiem o tym, siostrzyczko. I za to cię kocham.
– Jeśli tylko zdołam ci w czymś pomóc, daj mi znać – szepnęła Christina.
Nie miała pewności, czy mówi szczerze. Jej słowa porwał wiatr, łatwo było o nich zapomnieć. Przytulona do Joanny, zacisnęła mocno powieki i usiłowała zaprowadzić jakiś porządek w chaosie własnych uczuć.
Już sama nie wiem, co myśleć. Muszę pamiętać, co dla mnie dobre... Mieć na względzie plany Petera...

* * *

Joshua upił łyk wina i podniósł wzrok na April.

– Ja też nigdy nie miałem bratniej duszy, do czasu gdy poznałem Joannę.

Usłyszała w jego głosie tęskną nutę. Pozostało jej mieć nadzieję, że nie skierowała rozmowy na bolesny temat.

– Joanna mogła wybrać, kogo chciała – ciągnął Josh – ale...

– Ty byłeś jej przeznaczony.

– Najwyraźniej. – Uśmiechnął się smutno. – Byliśmy dla siebie stworzeni. – Patrzył gdzieś w dal. – Zdarzył się prawdziwy cud. Gdy się poznaliśmy, nie miałem prawie nic. Pracowałem u jej ojca. Odkładałem zaledwie kilka dolarów tygodniowo. Ale dla niej to nie miało najmniejszego znaczenia. Była piękna, miała poczucie humoru i bujną wyobraźnię. Pewnie dzięki temu we mnie uwierzyła. – Uśmiechnął się do wspomnień. – Byliśmy najszczęśliwszą parą na świecie. – Twarz mu się skurczyła z bólu. Umilkł.

– Takie właśnie zrobiliście na mnie wrażenie – odezwała się April, by przerwać dręczącą ciszę.

– Naprawdę? – Oczy miał błyszczące od łez.

– Jak najbardziej. Od razu rzuciło mi się w oczy, że osiągnęliście harmonię, o której zawsze marzyłam. O której marzy większość ludzi.

Joshua zrozumiał cały sens jej słów. Pojął, że April jest samotna, a w każdym razie nie spotkała jeszcze swojej drugiej połowy. Sięgnął przez stół i wziął ją za rękę.

– Znajdziesz go – powiedział z mocą. – Kiedyś poznasz najwspanialszego mężczyznę na świecie.

Niewiele brakowało, a wyrwałaby rękę, zreflektowała się w ostatniej chwili. W końcu, są przecież zaprzyjaźnieni. Nawet więcej: łączy ich wielka tajemnica. A ten uścisk dłoni, tak niewinny, tak przyjacielski, stanowił jedynie wyraz wsparcia. Czemu wobec tego poczuła znajome ukłucie winy? Czemu upajała się tym dotknięciem?

– Taka kobieta jak ty – ciągnął Joshua – z pewnością znajdzie tego, kogo szuka. Za pierwszym razem źle trafiłaś, to prawda, ale życie toczy się dalej. – Ciągle trzymał ją za rękę, aż w pewnej chwili zdał sobie sprawę, iż być może pozwala sobie na zbyt wiele. Ale przecież był to tylko przyjacielski gest. Zresztą, April najwyraźniej nie zwróciła na niego większej uwagi.

Gdyby nie Joanna... pomyślał. Gwałtownie cofnął dłoń i zaczerwienił się aż po uszy. Nie powinien nawet tak myśleć! Zwłaszcza w tej sytuacji.

– Dziękuję za podniesienie na duchu – powiedziała April z wymuszonym uśmiechem. – Każdemu się przyda kilka słów otuchy. Chyba czasami siebie nie doceniam.

– A powiedz mi, jaki był w życiu codziennym Roger Woodward? Oczywiście nie chcę być wścibski...

– Nie jesteś. Nie mam nic przeciwko twojemu pytaniu. – Umilkła, zbierając myśli. – Roger jako partner życiowy był... uroczym zerem – stwierdziła w końcu rozbawionym tonem. – Byliśmy małżeństwem przez cztery lata, lecz niekiedy mam wrażenie, że nasz związek nie trwał dłużej niż dwa tygodnie. Stale w pośpiechu.

– Nie brakuje ci Hollywoodu i życia w blasku sławy? Przecież związek z gwiazdą ekranu na pewno miał swoje plusy.

– Wcale mi tego nie brakuje. Kiedy poznałam Rogera, był jeszcze nikomu nieznanym, początkującym aktorem, a ja studiowałam architekturę. – Lekko wzruszyła ramionami. – Historia, jakich wiele. Rzuciłam uczelnię, żeby mu pomagać, a on chodził na kolejne castingi, obiecując, że kiedy zostanie sławny, wrócę na studia. Tyle tylko, że kiedy dostał swoją wielką szansę, nie miał ochoty dać mi wolnej ręki. Jak wielu aktorów był egocentrykiem. Wymagał ode mnie poświęcenia dla siebie – i dla swojej kariery. A ja doszłam do wniosku, że taka rola mi nie odpowiada. Chciałam także coś osiągnąć.

– I to się stało przyczyną rozstania.

– W jakimś stopniu – przytaknęła. – Najpierw projektowałam ogrody dla przyjaciół, potem zaczęłam eksperymentować z płytkami i kamieniami. Oraz muszlami – dokończyła z uśmiechem.

– I całe szczęście – roześmiał się Joshua.

– Tak czy inaczej, w końcu postanowiliśmy się rozwieść – zakończyła. – I za te marne grosze, które od niego dostałam, kupiłam sobie domek w górach.

– Dlaczego dostałaś marne grosze?

– Nie chciałam nikomu niczego zawdzięczać – wyjaśniła. – A już zwłaszcza jemu. Chciałam żyć wreszcie na własny rachunek. Poza tym, akurat wtedy trafiło mi się właśnie tutaj całkiem przyzwoite zlecenie, które bardzo mi odpowiadało. No i tak to się jakoś ułożyło.

– Widać, że lubisz swoją pracę.

– Można by nawet powiedzieć, że ją kocham. Nie mam nic przeciwko roli pani domu, ale chciałabym robić coś więcej. Innymi słowy: usmażyć omlet, nie rozbijając jajek. – Uśmiechnęła się rozbrajająco. – Marzy mi się, że któregoś dnia będę miała rodzinę. Dom z prawdziwego zdarzenia, dzieci...

– Tak... rozumiem cię. Ja też miałem takie plany. – Joshua zwiesił głowę i umilkł na dłuższy czas. W końcu poniósł wzrok. – Miałaś szczęśliwe dzieciństwo?

– Cóż... – April szukała najwłaściwszych słów. – Było w nim wiele jasnych chwil. Ale często czułam się samotna. Moi rodzice się rozwiedli, mama codziennie wychodziła do pracy... Tata wyprowadził się na Wschodnie Wybrzeże i prawie go nie widywałam.

– Jakoś mi to znajomo brzmi – stwierdził Joshua. – Moi rodzice także byli rozwiedzeni, ojca prawie nie znałem. Mama pracowała, więc w zasadzie byłem zdany na siebie samego.

– Założę się, że pomysłów ci nie brakowało.

– Co racja, to racja – uśmiechnął się Joshua. – Zawsze mnie gdzieś nosiło... Można by powiedzieć, że szybko nauczyłem się życia. – Podniósł na nią oczy. – Ty też?

– I tak, i nie. Z jednej strony, miałam dużo swobody, z drugiej, stale chciałam udowadniać... nie wiem, jak to powiedzieć... Usiłowałam tworzyć pozory, lepsze niż rzeczywistość. Przedstawiać się w lepszym świetle. Przekonywać otoczenie, że jest mi lepiej, niż było naprawdę.

Joshua usłyszał w jej głosie echo bolesnych wspomnień.

– Jednym słowem, w domu nie było najlepiej i chciałaś z niego jak najszybciej odejść? Zacząć lepsze życie na własną rękę?

April pokiwała głową.

– Tak. Szczerze mówiąc... – zaśmiała się głośno. – Co za okropny zwrot! Nie znoszę go. Zawsze kiedy ktoś tak zaczyna zdanie, zamierza mnie okłamać.

Joshua także się uśmiechnął.

– To samo jest z: „prawda jest taka". Wtedy też człowiek od razu wie, że zaraz zostanie poczęstowany stekiem kłamstw. – Upił łyk wina i odstawił kieliszek. – No ale dokończ to, co mówiłaś.

Widać było, że naprawdę chce tego słuchać, że jest ciekawy jej przeszłości, pragnie się o niej jak najwięcej dowiedzieć. Poznać ją. April spuściła wzrok i przyjrzała się swoim dłoniom.

– Chciałam powiedzieć, że... wstydziłam się biedy – wyjaśniła. – Mieszkałyśmy blisko Beverly Hills, większość moich kolegów i koleżanek miała ogromne domy, jeździła drogimi samochodami, nosiła modne ciuchy. Niektórzy mieli rodzeństwo, inni nawet oboje rodziców... Właściwie każde z nich było ode mnie lepsze.

Joshua popatrzył na nią w milczeniu, twarz mu nagle poczerwieniała. Zęby miał zaciśnięte, pobielały mu kłykcie dłoni, w której trzymał kieliszek.

April poczuła się zakłopotana. Najwyraźniej sprawiła mu przykrość, zbytnio się zagłębiła w swoje osobiste sprawy. Czuła, jak fala gorąca ogarnia jej szyję i twarz. Szybko podniosła kieliszek do ust.

Boże jedyny, pomyślała. Wszystko popsułam. Ten wspaniały człowiek był mną rzeczywiście zainteresowany, a ja go zanudzam jakimiś bzdurnymi nieszczęściami z dzieciństwa. Przecież nikt nie chce słuchać o smutnej przeszłości.

Ledwo do niej dotarł głos Josha.

– April, mam wrażenie, jakbyśmy razem dorastali!

Zwróciła na niego zdumione spojrzenie. Zniknęło wszelkie napięcie. Wpatrywały się w nią hipnotyzujące niebieskie oczy, rozjaśnione uśmiechem, który podnosił zaledwie kąciki ust.

– Co...? Jak to? Nie rozu... – Zamilkła. – Co powiedziałeś?

– Powiedziałem, że dorastaliśmy w takich samych warunkach. – Ujął znowu jej dłoń. – Oboje poznaliśmy wstyd i upokorzenie. Byliśmy biedakami, żyliśmy wśród bogaczy, a w każdym razie – wśród ludzi, których uważaliśmy za lepszych. – Lekko zacisnął palce.

W oczach April pojawiły się nieproszone łzy. Słowa więzły jej w gardle.

– Polubiłem cię od razu, od pierwszego spotkania poczułem do ciebie instynktowną sympatię. Teraz już wiem dlaczego. Nie dość, że jesteście z Joanną takie podobne do siebie, to jeszcze masz za sobą prawie taką samą przeszłość, jak moja. I chyba dlatego, że ta przeszłość jest dla mnie tak ważna, wyczułem w tobie bratnią duszę.

– To... niesamowite – wykrztusiła April w końcu. Bezlitosne łzy spłynęły jej po twarzy.

– Racja! – Joshua delikatnie otarł jej policzki lnianą serwetką. – Teraz lepiej, prawda?

– Tak. O, tak. – Chętnie by się do niego przytuliła... – O wiele lepiej. Tyle tylko, że mi się zrobiło jakoś nijako. Czuję się głupio. Urządziłam scenę jak z opery mydlanej. Przepraszam...

– Ciii... Nie było żadnej sceny. Po prostu, powiedziałaś mi coś o sobie i wzruszyłaś się trochę. Tak się szczęśliwie złożyło, że wybrałaś sobie na powiernika najwłaściwszą osobę pod słońcem.

– Gdy się uśmiechnął, w ciepłym blasku świecy błysnęły śnieżnobiałe zęby. – Głowa do góry! Dobraliśmy się w korcu maku!

– Dziękuję. Już się przeraziłam, że popełniłam straszny błąd, za dużo powiedziałam, zbyt mocno skupiłam się na własnych sprawach. Wszystko przez to, że jesteście tacy fantastyczni. Ciepli, mili, serdeczni. Nie macie przede mną tajemnic, traktujecie mnie jak członka rodziny. Dlatego pozwoliłam sobie na zbyt wiele wynurzeń.

– Przy nas możesz być sobą – zapewnił ją Joshua. – Możesz się z nami czuć bezpiecznie.

– Miło mi to słyszeć – podziękowała mu. – Och, czuję się jak idiotka! – zaśmiała się lekko.

– To dlatego, że pozwoliłaś sobie na szczerość. Teraz dopiero potrafisz ocenić, ile mnie kosztowała rozmowa z tobą na temat choroby Joanny.

Oboje się roześmieli, zachwyceni porozumieniem, które wzmocniło łączącą ich więź.

– Myślę, że do Joanny i jej ojca przyciągnął mnie blask ich świata – podjął Joshua poważnym tonem. – Zupełnie innego niż mój, uporządkowanego i spokojnego. Ach, i oczywiście orchidee. Wyjątkowo pomocny element zmieniania świata na lepszy. Miałem nadzieję, iż coś zyskają dzięki moim staraniom.

– Doskonale cię rozumiem. Mnie z tego samego powodu ciągnęło zawsze do architektury i niecodziennych projektów... Właśnie dlatego rysuję rośliny i planuję ogrody. I dlatego podjęłam się wykonania tej groty. Ciągle staram się porządkować chaos, upiększać świat i przez to, niestety, często... – umilkła znowu.

– Czujesz się wyobcowana? – podsunął Joshua.

– Właśnie. Nigdzie nie czuję się naprawdę dobrze. Mam wrażenie, jakby cały świat był zrzeszony w jakimś klubie, do którego ja nie należę. Ale, przyznaję, niekiedy udaje mi się przerzucić most nad tą przepaścią. Tak się na przykład czułam, kiedy was poznałam.

– Ze mną jest identycznie. – Joshua się uśmiechnął. – Zapewne dlatego, że w dzieciństwie także często czułem się gorszy... i tak dalej.

– Na pewno. Z całą pewnością – przytaknęła April żarliwie. – Najwyższy czas skończyć z przeszłością i zacząć cieszyć się życiem.

Joshua stuknął się w czoło.

– O Boże! Deser! Kompletnie zapomniałem. Mam nadzieję, że zdołasz jeszcze coś zjeść.

– Oj, nie wiem.

– Musisz koniecznie. Connie upiekła tartę owocową. Lepszej nigdzie nie dostaniesz. Zaczekaj chwilę, zaraz przyniosę.

April odprowadziła go wzrokiem. I dokładnie w chwili, gdy Josh wchodził do kuchni, uświadomiła sobie, że go kocha. Nie mogła się dłużej oszukiwać, choć czuła się z tą miłością paskudnie.

Jestem beznadziejnie zakochana w Joshu Lawrensie, pomyślała. W mężczyźnie żonatym. I, co gorsza, mężu mojej najlepszej przyjaciółki. Mojej śmiertelnie chorej...

Zalało ją poczucie winy.

Nie mogę tego zrobić Joannie. Ani Joshowi. Ani sobie. Muszę ukrócić wszelkie spotkania i rozmowy poza pracą. Zwłaszcza pod nieobecność Joanny.

Choć z jednej strony dobrze jej było z Joshem sam na sam, z drugiej – żałowała, iż Joanna wyjechała do Montecito.

Szybkim ruchem nalała wina do kieliszka i wypiła spory łyk. Niestety, utraciło swój poprzedni smak. Już nie pieściło łagodnie podniebienia, nie zachwycało aromatycznym bukietem. Miało posmak grzechu i wyrzutów sumienia oraz przykrą woń zdrady.

Zanim Joshua wrócił z deserem, udało jej się wziąć w garść i powitała go uśmiechem. A on się zawahał, jakby niepewny własnych reakcji, nim odpowiedział jej tym samym. Ponieważ w kuchni uświadomił sobie rzecz straszną: pokochał April Woodward. I musiał stawiać czoło sile popychającej go ku tej kobiecie pomimo świadomości, że to owoc zakazany.

Boże jedyny! Skąd w ogóle takie myśli?! Zwłaszcza teraz, gdy Joanna... umiera.

No cóż – serce nie sługa. Nieważne, co postanowisz, jeśli los tak zechce, chcąc nie chcąc, wpadniesz w sidła miłości.

Rozdział siedemnasty

April napełniła maszynkę do prażenia kukurydzy i ustawiła pod wylotem duży metalowy garnek. Do niego będą spadały wielkie, puszyste ziarna. Woody w tym czasie rozpuszczał w rondlu masło. Maszynka była wyposażona w pojemnik do topienia masła, ale wielkość naczynia stanowczo nie spełniała wymagań obojga.

Słysząc pierwsze wystrzały, April roześmiała się wesoło.

– Co cię tak cieszy? – spytał Woody.

– Zobacz, używamy wyrafinowanej maszynki do dietetycznego prażenia kukurydzy gorącym powietrzem, zamiast przygotować popcorn w rondlu, a potem zalewamy tę niskokaloryczną kukurydzę kostką stopionego masła. Czysty absurd!

– Fakt. Kretyństwo. Tyle tylko, że maszynka jest super.

– To prawda – zgodziła się April.

Częstotliwość kukurydzianych wystrzałów zaczęła przypominać serię z broni maszynowej. April nie mogła się powstrzymać i wrzuciła do ust kilka białych, ciepłych ziaren.

Do niczego. Bez masła i soli – mdłe i byle jakie.

Po powrocie do domu zastała nagraną na sekretarce wiadomość od Woody'ego. Prosił o telefon. Ciągle była na niego zła z powodu niedorzecznych uwag, na jakie sobie pozwolił, gdy zobaczył ją rozmawiającą z Joshem, ale w końcu postanowiła mu wybaczyć. Naprawdę dobrze się z nim pracowało, choć od czasu owego pamiętnego komentarza przepadły gdzieś ich swobodne pogaduszki. Może czas już oczyścić atmosferę. A poza wszystkim innym, przyjaciel miał głos wyraźnie skruszony. Przy okazji obiecała sobie porozmawiać z Woodym o jego przykrym zachowaniu.

Zadzwoniła do niego, wysłuchała przeprosin i błagań, by dała się wyciągnąć na kolację. Odmówiła, ponieważ zamierzała skubnąć coś w domu, wziąć kąpiel, a potem iść do łóżka i pogapić się w telewizor. Wtedy Woody zaproponował zorganizowanie nocy wideo-popcornowej. Wiedział, że temu April się nie oprze.

– Wygrałeś – przyznała. – Możesz być za jakąś godzinę. Tylko mi nie przynoś żadnych superprodukcji, na których krew się leje strumieniami. Nie mam dzisiaj najmniejszej ochoty oglądać scen przemocy. Mówię zupełnie poważnie. Nawet śmiesznych.

Teraz była zadowolona, że przyszedł. I że był sobą. Ciepłym, sympatycznym przyjacielem, a nie szyderczym macho, w jakiego zmienił się u Lawrence'ów. Na dodatek przyniósł francuski film kostiumowy „Śmieszność". Jeszcze go nie oglądała, ale słyszała o nim wiele dobrego. Co oznaczało, iż Woody jest naprawdę skruszony. W przeciwnym razie nie pokazałby się z takim dziełem.

Maszynka wyrzuciła ostatnie gorące ziarenka.

April obrzuciła krytycznym spojrzeniem wielki garnek.

– Twoim zdaniem tyle nam wystarczy?

Woody też zajrzał do garnka.

– Mowy nie ma. – Potrząsnął czarnymi lokami. – Na dwie osoby? Do dobrego filmu?

– Tak właśnie podejrzewałam. – Podstawiła pod wylot drugi garnek i ponownie napełniła maszynkę. – Doprawisz tę uprażoną, póki ciepła?

– Sie robi. Masła też na pewno zabraknie. – Wylał wszystko z rondla do garnka, solidnie posolił, a potem zamknął wieko i zaczął potrząsać całością jak Carmen Miranda kastanietami.

– Nieźle! – zaśmiała się April.

Woody spokojnie dokończył występ i odstawił garnek.

– Nie przeczę.

– Chciałabym cię spytać o jeden drobiazg. – Cóż, chwila dobra jak każda inna. – Co cię napadło wtedy u Lawrence'ów? Po jakie licho wygadujesz takie bzdury?

– Jak by ci to powiedzieć... – Wrzucił następną porcję masła do rondla. – Tacy ludzie to szczwane lisy, w życiu nie wyczaisz, co im raptem do łbów strzeli.

– Daj spokój, jesteś śmieszny. – Rozpoczęły się regularne strzały pękającej kukurydzy. – Oni są bardzo mili.

– Wolno ci tak uważać. – Woody wzruszył ramionami. – A ja im nie ufam. Bogata rozpuszczona suka rozbija się tym swoim mercem, jakby świat do niej należał... A on też nie lepszy. Zarozumiały dureń. Pręży muskuły, podrywa naiwniaczki i rżnie na prawo i lewo.

April patrzyła na niego osłupiała. Miała wrażenie, że mówią o zupełnie różnych osobach.

– Ty chyba zwariowałeś – wykrztusiła w końcu. – To bzdury wyssane z palca! Nie wiem, czy są bardzo bogaci, ale przyjmuję, że przynajmniej dobrze sytuowani. Na pewno jednak nie zachowują się w ten sposób i nie są zarozumiali. A Joshua Lawrence nikogo nie podrywa! Są wzorowym małżeństwem.

Woody zerknął na nią z ukosa.

– Już mówiłem, że wolno ci tak uważać. – Wyłączył maszynkę i wlał stopione masło do garnka. Dopiero wtedy podniósł wzrok na April. – Mogę ci opowiedzieć o jej siostrze takie ciekawostki, że włosy ci staną dęba – oznajmił.

Jakiś czas przyglądała mu się bez słowa.

– O niej rzeczywiście wiem niewiele – odrzekła w końcu. – Ale ich znam, widuję oboje codziennie. Naprawdę nie są tacy, jak mówisz. – Stanęła jej przed oczami Joanna, jej serdeczna hojność, przyjaźń – i choroba. Nie mogła dłużej słuchać takich kalumnii. – Woody – podjęła z ogniem w oczach. – Nie chcę słyszeć złego słowa na tych ludzi. Rozumiesz? Nigdy więcej.

– Skoro opowiadam bzdury – zirytował się – to dlaczego pan Joshua Lawrence pożerał cię wzrokiem?

– Ty chyba jesteś nienormalny. Opowiadał mi o kłopotach w pracy. I nic więcej się nie działo.

– Nooo... Proszę, proszę... A wyglądało całkiem inaczej. Tobie się wydaje, że ślepy jestem czy co? Ten facet się do ciebie klei jak sto pięćdziesiąt!

– Czy ty mnie słyszałeś? Powiedziałam, że nie chcę więcej rozmawiać na ten temat, więc daj już sobie spokój. Brakuje ci obiektywnego spojrzenia.

– Może i tak. Ale chciałaś poznać moje zdanie. No to usłyszałaś.

Maszynka do prażenia kukurydzy wypluła kilka ostatnich ziaren popcornu.

– Proszę bardzo. – April podała Woody'emu garnek. – Jeszcze sól.

W końcu przeszli do sypialni i umościli się na wielkim łóżku pośród mnóstwa poduszek, ustawiając między sobą dwie miski z popcornem. April obserwowała leniwie, jak Woody włącza telewizor, a potem magnetowid, ale myślami błądziła zupełnie gdzie indziej. Musiała przyznać, że choć często zachowywał się niepoważnie jak dziecko, nie był ani ślepy, ani głupi.

Wręcz przeciwnie: można go było z czystym sumieniem nazwać bystrym i wnikliwym obserwatorem. Wobec czego należało uważać, bo coś zobaczył. Ponieważ odkrył zażyłość łączącą ją z Joshem. Wystarczyło, aby popatrzył na nich, gdy rozmawiali na tarasie. Skoro on się domyślił, to może i Connie? Albo nawet... sama Joanna?

Żołądek podszedł jej do gardła. Sięgnęła po miskę z popcornem, nabrała pełną garść ciepłych ziaren, wsadziła je do ust i zaczęła gryźć, ale właściwie nie czuła smaku. Owszem, wiedziała, co czuje do Joshuy Lawrence'a, nie sposób zaprzeczyć, że go kochała, ale miała nadzieję, iż zdoła ukryć tę miłość. A co z Joshem? Czyżby Woody miał rację? Czy Joshua odwzajemnia jej uczucie?

Od dawna zgadywała, że więź łącząca ją z mężem Joanny wykracza poza granice przyjaźni. Mało tego: domyślała się, że Joshua nie ma nic przeciwko temu. Nie miała jednak żadnej pewności, a także najmniejszej ochoty roztrząsać tego teraz. Gdzieś w głębi mózgu zaczynał się odzywać dzwonek alarmowy. Bała się, że skoro Woody się czegoś dopatrzył, może się też znaleźć inny spostrzegawczy obserwator w ich otoczeniu – i ktoś w końcu złamie Joannie serce. A tego by nie zniosła.

– Gotowa? – spytał Woody, wyrywając ją z zamyślenia. – Możemy zaczynać?

– Gotowa – przytaknęła April. – Kukurydzy już spróbowałam, jak widać.

* * *

Minął jakiś czas. Woody tylko udawał, że patrzy w telewizor, w rzeczywistości bowiem przyglądał się April. Ona utkwiła spojrzenie w ekranie jak zahipnotyzowana. Chłonęła film równie zachłannie jak kukurydzę. Woody był zadowolony, choć francuski dramat kostiumowy wcale go nie interesował. Lubił dogadzać April. W zasadzie, w ogóle lubił dogadzać kobietom. W każdym razie tym, na których mu zależało. Których pragnął. April była jedną z najbardziej godnych pożądania kobiet, jakie spotkał na swojej drodze. I stanowiła nie lada wyzwanie. A on nie przepadał za łatwymi zdobyczami. Przesunął wzrokiem po jej piersiach, wyraźnie zarysowanych pod cienkim t-shirtem.

Jeszcze będzie moja, pomyślał. Bez dyskusji. Będzie mi jadła z ręki. Jak wszystkie.

Rozdział osiemnasty

Joshua wolno szedł przez szklarnię, Carl posuwał się tuż za nim. Rozglądali się uważnie na boki, wypatrując miejsc, gdzie należało odtworzyć sadzonki zainfekowane przez *Phalaenopsis*. Za ogromną cenę udało się odkupić kwiaty zniszczone przez grzyb i były rzeczywiście piękne. Koszty wzrosły jednak niepomiernie, gdyż choroba zaatakowała wiele roślin, wobec czego nie wystarczyło własnych orchidei na zrealizowanie zamówień i trzeba było, nie licząc się z wielkością strat, dokupić odpowiednie okazy u innych hurtowników, by nie stracić klientów.

– Ja tam swoje wiem – oświadczył Carl po raz kolejny. – Przydałaby się lepsza ochrona. Na przykład kamery.

Joshua pokręcił głową.

– Przesadzasz. W nocy czuwa tu Miguel, i to z psem. A w dzień klient może wejść do szklarni wyłącznie w towarzystwie pracownika. Czyli z eskortą.

– Niby to wszystko prawda – uznał Carl – ale pamiętaj, że ten, kto przyniósł te cholerne grzyby, też wszedł z eskortą. A na dodatek Miguel nie lubi psów... Dlaczego się upierasz?

– Nic podobnego! – żachnął się Joshua. – Doskonale zdajesz sobie sprawę, że mogliśmy sami wprowadzić do szklarni zakażone kwiaty, co oczywiście wyszło na jaw dopiero po pewnym czasie. Istnieje taka możliwość. Po drugie, do tej pory nie każdy wchodził do szklarni z naszym pracownikiem. Nie każdy miał eskortę.

– To prawda – zgodził się Carl. – Nie każdy. Ale jest o wiele bardziej prawdopodobne, że szklarnie zostały zainfekowane nocą. Chcesz wiedzieć, co ja o tym myślę?

– Mów.
– Mnie się wydaje, że ty nie chcesz uwierzyć, że ktoś to robi specjalnie – oznajmił Carl stanowczo. – Oszukujesz się i nie chcesz sam przed sobą przyznać, że tak jest naprawdę.
Joshua nie miał siły tłumaczyć, iż od czasu, gdy dowiedział się o chorobie Joanny, trudno mu się skupić na sprawach dotyczących pracy.
– Josh! – rozległ się za nimi kobiecy głos. – Szefie!
Luna biegła najszybciej, jak mogła na niebotycznych obcasach, grzęznąc w żwirze. Pokaźny biust dziewczyny, obciągnięty dopasowaną bluzką, falował efektownie. Było na co popatrzeć. Carl roześmiał się głośno, Joshua tylko się uśmiechnął.
– Co się stało? – spytał.
– Ten, jak mu tam – wykrztusiła bez tchu – czeka w biurze.
– Aha. A kto? – Joshua nie dawał za wygraną.
Sposób przekazywania informacji przez Lunę pozostawia nieco do życzenia, pomyślał z rozbawieniem.
– Ten... Japończyk!
– Który? – Teraz Joshua był rzeczywiście zaciekawiony.
– No wiesz, ten z czarnymi włosami i... No, ten taki potwornie bogaty!
– Mogłaś mnie wezwać pagerem. Albo przez interkom...
– Ja bym tam nie wysiedziała! A poza tym powiedział, że chce się widzieć z szefem natychmiast, więc chciałam mu pokazać, że robię, co mogę.
– Dziękuję ci, Luno.
W takim razie będzie to pan Hara. On zwykle tak się śpieszy. Prawdopodobnie spodobały mu się nasze orchidee i wrócił po więcej. A może to nawet pan Nakamura?
Szybkim krokiem ruszył do biura.

* * *

Joshua rozparł się w fotelu, założył ręce za głowę, spojrzał w sufit i zadowolony odetchnął pełną piersią.
Jest jednak sprawiedliwość na tym świecie!, pomyślał.
Pan Nakamura zostawił okrągłą sumkę, która z okładem wystarczy na pokrycie strat poniesionych z winy *Phalaenopsis*. Podobne wizyty zdarzały się coraz częściej, w miarę jak firma zyskiwała międzynarodową renomę, ale Joshua nadal do nich nie przywykł i za

każdym razem miał wrażenie, iż zespołowi pracującemu przy kwiatach udało się odnieść ogromny, lecz jednorazowy sukces. Nie umiał spocząć na laurach, nie czuł się rozpieszczanym przez los bogaczem.

Muszę przekazać Joannie dobre wieści, pomyślał. I to natychmiast.

Sięgnął po słuchawkę, wystukał numer. Po trzech sygnałach odebrała Connie.

– Witaj, chciałbym rozmawiać z Joanną.

– Nie ma.

– A gdzie jest? Chciałbym ją złapać jak najszybciej.

– Nie wiem.

– Jak to: nie wiesz? – zdumiał się Joshua.

Jasna cholera! Joanna nie powinna wychodzić sama, nie powinna tak znikać. Co będzie, jeśli...

– Wiem tylko – pojęła Connie zirytowana – że ona się bardzo dziwnie zachowuje.

– Co przez to rozumiesz? – Joshowi zrobiło się zimno ze strachu.

– Bo ja wiem... Trudno powiedzieć.

– Connie, zlituj się nade mną... O co chodzi?

– Sprzątałam niedawno domek na plaży – oznajmiła Connie.

– I co?

– Nie wierzyłam własnym oczom.

– Dlaczego? Co tam znalazłaś?

– Domek wyglądał, jakby przez niego przeszła trąba powietrzna.

– A dokładnie? – Joshua był coraz bardziej zdenerwowany i zmartwiony.

– Dosłownie. Wszędzie pełno pustych butelek po winie. A inne, jeszcze z winem, niezakorkowane. Na podłodze – jak w chlewie: piasek, brud, wodorosty... Łóżko nawet niezarzucone... Naprawdę, jak w chlewie. – Umilkła, wyraźnie szukając słów. Gdy znowu się odezwała, w jej głosie brzmiała złość. – Roboty było na caluteńki dzień.

Joshua miał ściśnięty żołądek, na czole pojawiły się kropelki potu. Doskonale zdawał sobie sprawę, że Joanna gdzieś musiała się podziewać, kiedy znikała z domu przez ostatnich kilka tygodni. Zaszywała się gdzieś, aby dojść ze sobą do ładu. Zupełnie sama. Teraz już wiedział gdzie.

– Bardzo mi przykro, Connie – odezwał się, gdy wreszcie mógł zaufać własnemu głosowi. – Powinnaś była mi powiedzieć wcześniej.

– Nie chciałam cię martwić.

– Tak czy inaczej, jadę do domu – zdecydował. – Zaraz będę. – Uznał, że najwyższy czas zawiadomić Connie, co się dzieje, by zrozumiała niezwykłe zachowanie Joanny.

– Jasne – rzuciła słuchawkę.

Joshua jakiś czas siedział przy biurku i niewidzącym wzrokiem wpatrywał się w przestrzeń. Jak to w kilka minut może się zmienić nastrój. W jednej chwili uniesienie i radość z pomyślnie przeprowadzonej transakcji, w następnej ponura świadomość nieuchronnego złego losu, która wszystko pogrąża w cieniu.

Teraz już nic nie ma znaczenia, pomyślał. Liczy się tylko Joanna.

Powoli wstał i zajrzał do holu.

– Luna, skończyłem na dzisiaj. Gdyby wyskoczyło coś bardzo ważnego, będę w domu.

Sekretarka, jak zwykle ze słuchawką przyklejoną do ucha, zasłoniła dłonią mikrofon.

– Tak jest, szefie – odrzekła z uśmiechem. – Niczym się nie przejmuj, wszystko będzie w porządku. – Odsłoniła mikrofon i natychmiast z jej ust popłynął wartki potok hiszpańskich słów.

Joshua wyszedł na parking i wskoczył do land cruisera. Skręciwszy w drogę szybkiego ruchu na północ, do domu, mijał po prawej stronie tereny należące do braci Rossi.

– Jasna cholera! – zaklął głośno. Ostro wcisnął hamulec i mało brakowało, a byłby skręcił na ich parking. Rozmyślił się w ostatniej chwili. Pojechał dalej, z nowym ciężarem i nowym zmartwieniem, jakby miał ich jeszcze za mało.

Na parkingu przed biurem Rossich stał samochód Carla. Jego, bez najmniejszych wątpliwości.

Co Carl robi u konkurencji?, zapytał Joshua sam siebie. Przecież nie pojechał tam w interesach, trudno sobie wyobrazić, co miałby tam załatwiać. A gdyby nawet, to dlaczego słowem mi o tym nie wspomniał? Szlag!

Ze złością uderzył otwartą dłonią w kierownicę. Ale jedynym skutkiem był ostry ból ręki.

Czy już naprawdę cały świat obrócił się przeciwko niemu?!

* * *

Zatrzymał wóz na podwórzu. Samochodu Joanny nie było, stał za to dżip należący do April oraz van Connie. Jak zwykle zmienił w przedpokoju ubłocone w szklarni buty na mokasyny.

Connie zastał w kuchni, tak jak się spodziewał.

– Cześć. – Ledwo uniosła powieki. Takie spojrzenie oznaczało, że nie miała najmniejszej ochoty z nim rozmawiać.

– Witaj, Connie. Domyślam się, że nadal nie wiesz, gdzie zniknęła Joanna?

– Nie wiem. W domu jej nie ma. Tylko April siedzi w stajni, razem z tym swoim pomocnikiem.

W głosie gosposi wyraźnie dało się słyszeć dezaprobatę. Dlaczego Connie nie lubiła April? Czyżby była zazdrosna? Trudno zgadnąć. Tak czy inaczej, Josh teraz nie miał zamiaru łamać sobie nad tym głowy.

Wyszedł na taras, minął basen i jabłonie, aż dotarł do stajni, która powoli stawała się grotą. Wsunął głowę przez drzwi i rozejrzał się po wnętrzu. April tkwiła wysoko na rusztowaniu, jej towarzysz pracował przy jednej ze ścian.

– Cześć! – zawołał Joshua. – Jak wam idzie?

– O, Josh! – ucieszyła się April. Ściągnęła z twarzy papierową maseczkę. – Robota pali nam się w rękach. – Zeszła z rusztowania i ściągnęła gumowe rękawice.

Woody porzucił na chwilę układanie drobnych kawałków macicy perłowej wykorzystywanych jako tło i zmierzył ich dwoje długim spojrzeniem, po czym w milczeniu wrócił do pracy.

– Sam zobacz. – April wskazała strop szerokim gestem. – Sufit już prawie gotowy.

Joshua po raz pierwszy miał okazję podziwiać jej dzieło nieomal w całości. Z wrażenia przez chwilę nie mógł wydobyć głosu. Sufit przedstawiał wieczorne niebo, roziskrzone dziesiątkami gwiezdnych konstelacji, a wszystko to zostało stworzone z kamyków i muszli.

– Boże! – wyrwało mu się. – Ale piękne! Nie wiedziałem, że to będzie takie... skomplikowane, takie precyzyjne... jakie żywe kolory!

– Prawda? – ucieszyła się April. – Rewelacyjny efekt.

– Aż trudno uwierzyć. – Joshua z podziwem pokręcił głową. – Joanna już widziała?

– Nie. Zajrzała tu zaraz po powrocie z Montecito, ale wtedy sufit jeszcze nie robił takiego wrażenia. Mam nadzieję, że spodoba jej się końcowy efekt.

– Na pewno! W życiu nie widziałem czegoś podobnego. Wszystko tu jest. Słuchotki kalifornijskie, przegrzebki, macica perłowa, porcelanka monetka, stożek, jeżokraby, sercówki, turban zielony, nawet zawiaśnik kolczasty! Coś podobnego!

– Znasz się na muszlach – zdziwiła się April.

– Interesowały go od zawsze – rozległ się głos Joanny. – Prawdę mówiąc, to właśnie on mnie zaraził tą pasją.

Oboje odwrócili się w jej stronę. Stała w progu, uśmiechnięta i szczęśliwa. Torby z zakupami oparła o framugę.

– Witaj, kochanie. – Podeszła do Josha i ucałowała go czule w policzek.

– Dzień dobry, moja piękna.

Joanna uścisnęła serdecznie April i ją także pocałowała. Wreszcie spojrzała w górę. Dłuższy czas przyglądała się sufitowi z niekłamanym zachwytem.

– April – odezwała się wreszcie – jesteś cudotwórczynią. Aż trudno uwierzyć... Piękne! To prawdziwe czary... Bosko! Jak w niebie!

– Cóż, sufit powinien mieć jak najwięcej wspólnego z niebem – roześmiała się April.

– Przecież wiesz, o co mi chodzi. Fantastyczny. Idealny. Och, już się nie mogę doczekać, kiedy będzie gotowa reszta.

– Pracujemy najszybciej, jak możemy – zapewniła ją April. – Ach, no właśnie. Akurat przyszły gipsowe popiersia do nisz, chcesz obejrzeć?

Twarz Joanny wykrzywił ból.

– Nie... może później... Teraz się położę...

Wyszła, zostawiając torby z zakupami.

Woody obserwował jej zniknięcie z krzywym uśmiechem.

Taaa, jasne, pomyślał. Nic dziwnego, że musi się położyć. Jak ich zobaczyła razem, to od razu się pochorowała. I bardzo dobrze.

April spojrzała na Josha. Oboje mieli w oczach ten sam smutek.

– Zajrzę do Joanny – powiedział cicho.

– Ucałuj ją ode mnie – poprosiła, mocno zaniepokojona.

Joanna nigdy się tak nie zachowywała. Taka nieuprzejma reakcja była całkiem do niej niepodobna.

* * *

W sypialni panowały ciemności. Kotary starannie zaciągnięto, nie paliło się żadne światło. Joshua ledwie dostrzegł żonę leżącą na łóżku. Ubrana była w krótki jedwabny szlafroczek. Podszedł i cicho przysiadł na brzegu materaca.

– Jak się czujesz? – zapytał z niepokojem.

– Jako tako. Muszę trochę odpocząć.

– Przynieść ci coś?

– Nie, niczego mi nie trzeba. Naprawdę. Nie przejmuj się, po prostu potrzebuję trochę odpoczynku i spokoju.

– Dobrze. – Joshua wstał. – Gdybyś jednak czegoś chciała, zawołaj mnie.

– Zawołam – szepnęła. – Dziękuję.

Joshua wyszedł z pokoju i dokładnie zamknął za sobą drzwi. Zrobił dwa kroki i zachwiawszy się, oparł czoło o ścianę. Serce nieznośnie ciążyło mu w piersi.

Boże jedyny! Spraw, żeby nie cierpiała.

Strach, namacalny i rzeczywisty, obezwładnił go i pozbawił możliwości jakiegokolwiek działania. Trwało to całą wieczność. W końcu przerażający uścisk nieco się rozluźnił i dopiero wtedy Joshua zdołał się poruszyć. Poszedł do swojego gabinetu, nalał sobie porcję szkockiej i wyciągnął się na fotelu. Nie potrafił się na niczym skupić, całkowicie opanowany przez straszne uczucie, które po raz pierwszy z bliska pokazało mu swoją przerażającą twarz.

Była to samotność.

Rozdział dziewiętnasty

Joanna stanęła w progu stajni, gdzie April i Woody starannie wykładali ściany muszlami. Nie zamierzała im przeszkadzać, ale bardzo chciała popatrzeć, jak pracują. Ostatnio coraz częściej musiała odpoczywać, mówiła sobie, że po prostu chce trochę poczytać, ale tak czy inaczej, potrzebowała coraz więcej pauz, przerw w aktywnym życiu, by odzyskać utraconą energię i zebrać siły. Dlatego przez kilka dni nie mogła tu zajrzeć i bardzo była ciekawa postępów prac.

– April – odezwała się półgłosem.

– Och, Joanna! – ucieszyła się projektantka. – Chodź, chodź. Nie zauważyłam, kiedy się zjawiłaś. – Siedziała dość wysoko na rusztowaniu, układając muszle w samym kącie.

– Nie przeszkadzałoby wam, gdybym chwilę popatrzyła? Będę cicho jak myszka, obiecuję.

– Zostań. Usiądź sobie, zobacz, tam są krzesła. Tylko trzymaj się w przyzwoitej odległości, bo inaczej za chwilę cała będziesz obsypana cementem.

– Dobrze. Będę udawała, że mnie tu w ogóle nie ma.

Woody zerknął na nią spod oka, ale się nie odezwał. Sprawiał wrażenie całkowicie pochłoniętego swoim zadaniem.

Joanna rozstawiła sobie krzesło i usiadła. Rozejrzała się dookoła. Prace postępowały nieco szybciej, niż przewidywał grafik. Zdarzały się dni, gdy gołym okiem dawało się zauważyć ogromne postępy. Bywały jednak też i takie, gdy pozornie nie zmieniało się nic, gdyż April mozoliła się akurat nad jakimś skomplikowanym detalem, wymagającym czasu i cierpliwości.

Mijający dzień szczęśliwie należał do tych, co z dumą ukazywały niebagatelne postępy. Joanna, rozglądając się po wnętrzu, które wyraźnie nabierało charakteru, odkrywała z radością, jak niewiele brakuje do ukończenia dzieła. Sufit, rozjarzony perłowymi gwiazdozbiorami, okazał się imponujący; nisze, gdzie miały stanąć rzeźby obłożone muszlami, były całkowicie gotowe. Ozdobiono je, podobnie jak okna i drzwi, wymyślnymi gzymsami, oczywiście z kamieni oraz muszli. Ściany wydawały się błyszczeć, jak gdyby ozdobiono je drogimi kamieniami. Zostało jeszcze kilka pustych miejsc na orchidee z muszli.

Joanna musiała zaciskać usta, by nie rozpraszać pracujących pochwałami. Dała sobie słowo, że zaczeka z wyrazami uznania do obiadu, jako że przyjaciółka obiecała dotrzymać im dzisiaj towarzystwa.

April pracowała w skupieniu, lecz stale czuła obecność Joanny, która ostatnio zaglądała do groty znacznie rzadziej. Zwłaszcza w ciągu minionych dwóch, może trzech tygodni. Znając przyczynę takiego stanu rzeczy, April tym bardziej starała się zachowywać jak gdyby nigdy nic. Pracowała najszybciej, jak mogła, wbrew rozsądkowi mając nadzieję, iż zdąży przed... przed śmiercią Joanny.

Przysunęła sobie muszle bliżej, usiadła na piętach i uważnie przyjrzała się linii. Doskonale. Idealnie prosto.

– Woody, bądź aniołem – poprosiła – i podaj mi *Cardita crassicosta*, dobrze?

– Jedną sekundę. – Starannie osadził w cemencie kolejny fragment macicy perłowej.

Siedział po turecku, twarzą do ściany, całkowicie pochłonięty pracą – i od stóp do głów obsypany białym cementem. Oboje woleli codziennie zeskrobywać pod prysznicem wszechobecny pył, niż nosić foliowe czepki.

– Hej, Woody, posiwiałeś ostatnio!

– Przyganiał kocioł garnkowi! Gdzie twój uroczy blond? – Wstał, znalazł pudło z odpowiednimi muszlami i podał je April.

– Serdeczne dzięki. – Ustawiła karton na rusztowaniu.

– Nie ma sprawy. – Znowu usiadł po turecku i wrócił do pracy.

Joanna długi czas przyglądała im się ze swojego kąta. Stanowili zgrany tandem, rozumieli się bez słów. Byli idealnie zestrojeni. Jak starzy przyjaciele.

Albo kochankowie.

Musiała obiektywnie przyznać, że Woody jest atrakcyjnym mężczyzną. Z pewnością nie mógł narzekać na brak zainteresowania kobiet. Zwłaszcza takich, które miały ochotę na przelotny romans bez zobowiązań.

Obserwowała tych dwoje uważnie od kilku tygodni. Zauważyła, że Woody otaczał April troskliwą opieką, wyczuwała w nim zazdrość o jej zażyłość z innymi ludźmi. Ponieważ miała prawo zakładać, iż nie jest w niej naprawdę zakochany, musiała przyjąć, że chce ją dopisać do listy swoich zdobyczy. Najwyraźniej zamierzał odgrywać rolę kochającego starszego brata aż do skutku.

April najwyraźniej niczego nie podejrzewała i rzeczywiście traktowała go jak dobrego przyjaciela. Śmiała się swobodnie z jego przygód miłosnych, ufając mu całkowicie, choć zdaniem Joanny powinna być ostrożniejsza z tym podstępnym draniem. Nie bardzo wiedziała, jak powinna zareagować. Przecież nie życzyła sobie stanowczo, by ktokolwiek stanął na drodze zażyłości między April a nią oraz... Joshem, oczywiście.

Z zamyślenia wyrwał ją głos przyjaciółki, która właśnie zeszła z rusztowania.

– Prawie cię nie widać, wcale nie słychać...

– Obiecałam, że będę się zachowywać cichutko jak myszka. Grota z godziny na godzinę pięknieje, nie chcę wam przeszkadzać.

April potoczyła dookoła krytycznym spojrzeniem.

– Rzeczywiście, nie jest źle. – W jej głosie brzmiała nieskrywana duma.

– Pamiętasz, że jemy razem lunch?

– Tak, tak. Tylko zajrzę do łazienki w domku przy basenie i trochę się ogarnę.

– Dobrze. Wobec tego spotkamy się na tarasie. Posiedzę tu sobie jeszcze kilka chwil, pooddycham atmosferą.

– Niemożliwa jesteś – odrzekła April z rozbawieniem. – Co to za atmosfera? Chyba robocza, przesycona cementem. Ale rób, jak chcesz. – Jeszcze odwróciła się do pomocnika. – Wrócę za jakąś godzinę.

– Będę na czas. – Woody starannie wytarł ręce w szmatkę.

Joanna przyglądała mu się bez słowa.

– Wracasz na lunch do domu? – spytała wreszcie. Oboje nadal odgrywali tę farsę: udawali, że dopiero co się poznali.

Nawet nie podniósł wzroku.

– Czasami. Ale zwykle wpadam do jakiejś knajpki.

– Musisz któregoś dnia zjeść z nami – powiedziała, bardziej z uprzejmości niż ze szczerego serca.

– Zwykle jadam w towarzystwie – odparł Woody. – Ale dzięki. – Rzucił szmatkę na ziemię. – No to spadam. – Minął próg i dumnym krokiem ruszył pod górę, w stronę jabłoni.

I bardzo dobrze, pomyślała Joanna. Spadaj.

Rozdział dwudziesty

Christina dotarła na miejsce pierwsza. W gęstej mgle z trudnością odnalazła parking na końcu osiedla. Stały tam zaledwie dwa samochody.

Uważnie rozejrzała się dookoła i skierowała ku drewnianemu pomostowi wiodącemu przez wydmy do domków krytych cedrowymi gontami. Całe szczęście, że do Petera należał ostatni w rzędzie, ponieważ inaczej bardzo trudno byłoby trafić. Pytanie tylko, w którym rzędzie.

Rany, dlaczego to zawsze wygląda tak samo, pomyślała rozeźlona. Czy my naprawdę musimy się spotykać w takich nędznych dziurach?

Doskonale znała odpowiedź na to pytanie. Tak właśnie musiało być, gdyż nie wolno im było pokazywać się razem. I dlatego właśnie akurat dzisiaj spotykali się w domku plażowym, który stał na uboczu.

Porywisty wiatr od oceanu szarpał ogromne eukaliptusy i udręczone sosny. Drobne, ostre ziarenka piasku wbijały się w skórę.

Boże jedyny!

Wyjęła z torebki jedwabną apaszkę i osłoniła nią twarz.

Co za pogoda!

Dziś jednak mógł nastąpić nawet koniec świata, było jej wszystko jedno. Ponieważ dzisiaj miała się spotkać z Peterem.

Ruszyła w górę po stromych schodach, mocno trzymając się poręczy. Cienkie wysokie szpilki stanowczo nie ułatwiały marszu.

Powinnam była włożyć pantofle na płaskim obcasie, pomyślała.

Zaraz jednak porzuciła tę myśl. Peter lubił, gdy była odstawiona od stóp do głów. Zachwycał się wtedy, że Christina wygląda tak dystyngowanie. Roześmiała się głośno. To, co będą robili za kilka chwil, można by określić na wiele różnych sposobów, ale z pewnością nie tym słowem.

Na szczycie schodów mgła okazała się jeszcze gęściejsza. Christina stanęła niezdecydowana, rozglądając się za jakimś znakiem, który by ją skierował do właściwego rzędu domków.

W życiu tam nie trafi!

Akurat wtedy dostrzegła, prawie na wprost, drewnianą tabliczkę z mosiężnymi numerami zmatowiałymi od wiatru. Numer osiemset trzy znajdował się na prawo. Poszła w kierunku wskazanym przez strzałkę i wkrótce zobaczyła, że ma do pokonania jeszcze jeden długi ciąg drewnianych schodów.

Westchnęła głęboko, podniosła wzrok na niebieskie stopnie i przeklęła wszystkie wypalone papierosy oraz swoje trzydzieści sześć lat.

Wreszcie stanęła u celu. Wspinając się na palce, sięgnęła do gzymsu i znalazła klucz.

Jest!, ucieszyła się w myślach. Przepustka do krainy rozkoszy.

Weszła do domku, zsunęła wreszcie apaszkę z twarzy i stanowczym gestem zamknęła za sobą drzwi. Zrzuciła z udręczonych nóg pantofle i rozejrzała się dookoła z nieskrywanym zaciekawieniem. Na wprost widziała jadalnię, za nią kuchnię i salonik o wielkich oknach, a właściwie przeszklonej ścianie, która sięgała od podłogi do sufitu, otwierając się na morze. Tego dnia nie dało się podziwiać krajobrazu, ponieważ za szybą kłębiła się szarobura zasłona.

Christina podniosła szpilki i przeszła do saloniku. Cały domek urządzony był w różnych odcieniach bieli, umeblowanie składało się z rozłożystych kanap i foteli oraz niedrogich drewnianych stolików.

Nudne, ale praktyczne, uznała.

Zostawiła pantofle obok kanapy w salonie, apaszkę przerzuciła przez ramię. Podeszła bliżej okna, ciekawa, czy uda jej się dostrzec choć skrawek oceanu.

Mgła jest fascynująca, pomyślała. Można się w nią wpatrywać godzinami. Człowiek ma wrażenie zawieszenia w nicości, nie znajduje oparcia...

Przypomniało jej się, że ich dawny domek plażowy, tak starannie urządzony przez Joannę i Josha, znajduje się na tej samej plaży. Stary, wyjątkowy, jedyny w swoim rodzaju. Kiedyś wiele takich staroci z charakterem stało wzdłuż wybrzeża, teraz natomiast, gdy rozprzestrzenił się agrobiznes, kierowany przez rzutkich ludzi interesu, jak Peter, oraz profesjonalnych deweloperów, budowano osiedla składające się z jednakowych pudełek. Warto przy tym pamiętać, iż do firmy Rossi Brothers należały już prawie wszystkie wartościowe grunty w okolicy.

Stary domek nad morzem jest w tej sytuacji wart fortunę, uprzytomniła sobie.

Nagle ktoś ją złapał od tyłu. Zesztywniała w potężnych ramionach, czując na karku gorący oddech.

Krzyknęła, serce zamarło jej w piersi – i w tej samej chwili uświadomiła sobie, że to on.

– Rany boskie...! – jęknęła. Kolana się pod nią ugięły. – Ty... Ty...!

– Przestraszyłem cię, laluniu? – Językiem wyrysował mokrą słoną ścieżkę na jej szyi.

– Mało nie umarłam ze strachu! Przecież to mógł być... nie wiem, choćby jakiś morderca albo gwałciciel... Na takim pustkowiu!

Peter zaśmiał się głośno, odwrócił Christinę do siebie i wbił w nią spojrzenie smoliście czarnych oczu.

– A to nie gwałciciel, tylko ja...

– Myślałam... Przeraziłam się... – Ciągle jeszcze drżała.

Pocałował ją w usta, zachłannie, gwałtownie. Potem odsunął Christinę od siebie, ale nadal trzymał w mocnym uścisku jak w imadle.

– Lubisz to, maleńka, co?

Znów poczuła dreszcze, ale tym razem nie ze strachu. Miała wrażenie, jakby gdzieś w głębi jej ciała zadrgała struna, dostrajająca się do oczekiwań Petera. Nie potrafiła nad tym zapanować. Serce waliło jej jak młotem, zmieniła się w czyste pożądanie, zniknęły wszelkie inne myśli, jakby je zagarnęła mgła kłębiąca się za oknem.

– Tak, tak... Uwielbiam. Tak.

– Wiedziałem.

Ściągnął jej apaszkę z ramienia i skręcił w gruby sznur. Zafascynowana Christina przyglądała się jego zręcznym, zdecydowanym ruchom. I zanim uświadomiła sobie, do czego Peter zmierza, już miała zawiązane oczy.

– Ej! Nic nie widzę!

– Ciii... – Wziął ją za ręce i poprowadził.

– Dokąd idziemy? – szepnęła. – Co robisz?

– Ciii... – powtórzył. – Nie pożałujesz.

Rozebrał ją szybko i bezceremonialnie, głodny jej nagiego ciała, potem sam ściągnął ubranie. Christina go nie widziała i nie potrafiłaby wyrazić słowami, jak bardzo pragnie widoku tego muskularnego ciała, jak bardzo chce czuć je tuż obok, na sobie i w sobie.

Czyżby myśl stała się rozkazem? Gorąca dłoń musnęła piersi Christiny, opadła między jej uda, przesunęła się po pośladkach i powędrowała w górę przez środek pleców.

Christina mało nie oszalała z podniecenia, ale nie chciała psuć scenariusza, stała więc bez ruchu, bez słowa i omal bez tchu, stłumiwszy w sobie nawet westchnienie zadowolenia.

Teraz poczuła dwie dłonie na piersiach, naciskające najpierw lekko, jakby niezdecydowanie, potem coraz bardziej stanowczo. Palce muskały jej różowe sutki, z początku delikatnie, później coraz mocniej, aż chwilami rozkosz zmieniała się w ból. Nagle wszystko ustało.

Prawy sutek objęły gorące, wilgotne usta. Język poruszał się coraz szybciej, a jednocześnie któraś dłoń odnalazła drogę między udami i pieściła wilgotne zakamarki.

– Peter... jeszcze...!

– Nieźle, laluniu, co? Zadowolona?

– Tak – wychrypiała z oczami pełnymi łez, zafascynowana siłą ciała mężczyzny, który nią rządził. – Tak.

Pociągnął ją w stronę łóżka, chwycił na ręce i rzucił w pościel.

– Och! – Christinie zabrakło tchu.

Zanim jednak zdążyła zaprotestować, zanim się zorientowała, co się dzieje, Peter już był nad nią. Kolanami rozepchnął jej nogi na boki i wtargnął w nią, wcisnął się aż do końca, wypełniając ją po granice możliwości.

Przez chwilę miała wrażenie, że ją rozedrze, choć przecież była od dawna gotowa, ale gdy bezlitośnie w nią uderzał, jej ciało szybko zaczęło odpowiadać tym samym, otwierając się na jego przyjęcie. Gdy wycofywał się prawie całkowicie, miała ochotę szlochać z rozpaczy, ale zaraz wracał, jeszcze mocniej i gwałtowniej, przyciskając ją do materaca.

Nagle zabłysły jej przed oczami gwiazdy, zalała ją gorąca fala i wstrząsnęły nią drgania. Peter uderzył po raz ostatni, krzyknął i eksplodował, a potem opadł bez sił. Christina jęknęła, po jej ciele przebiegł ostatni dreszcz. Osłabła, niezdolna do najmniejszego ruchu.

Leżeli, powleczeni słonym woalem potu, z wysiłkiem łapiąc powietrze. Obejmowali się mocno. Dużo czasu upłynęło, nim odzyskali oddech i głos.

– Peter... – Odchrząknęła. Udało jej się w pewnym stopniu pozbyć chrapliwego tonu. – Możesz mnie... straszyć, kiedy tylko zechcesz.

Zachichotali oboje. Rossi stoczył się na materac.

– Podobało ci się, mała, nie? – stwierdził z dumą w głosie.

– Tak, podobało mi się – przyznała szczerze. Sięgnęła do apaszki, ale Peter odepchnął jej dłonie. Sam rozwiązał chustkę i okręcił ją wokół dłoni jak bokser, chroniący rękę bandażem. Przycisnął pięścią brzuch Christiny.

– Musimy to kiedyś powtórzyć – powiedział. – Zagramy mocniejszą scenkę. Dorzucimy jakieś gadżety.

Nie żartował. Naprawdę chciał podkręcić sprężynę. Z jednej strony Christina miała wrażenie, że ta propozycja jest dziwaczna, wynaturzona, wręcz odrażająca, z drugiej – było jej wszystko jedno. Chciała mieć tego mężczyznę, ze wszystkich sił pragnęła go zatrzymać. Dopiero przy nim poznała naprawdę świetny seks. Więc – dlaczego by nie?

Wobec tego zgodnie pokiwała głową.

Peter pochylił się nad nią i pocałował w usta. Potem podniósł się i sięgnął po papierosy. Christina usiadła przy nim, oparła mu głowę na piersiach. Objął ją za ramiona.

– No to teraz mów, co takiego ważnego się zdarzyło u tej twojej siostrzyczki. – Wydmuchnął w górę smugę szaroniebieskiego dymu. – Państwo Lawrence są źli z powodu najnowszych kłopotów?

– Słuchaj, stało się coś takiego, że nie uwierzysz.

– Może jednak?

– Chodzi o coś znacznie poważniejszego niż kłopoty w szklarniach. – Christina zrobiła efektowną pauzę. – Joanna jest śmiertelnie chora. Niedługo umrze. – Podała tę sensacyjną wiadomość głosem pozbawionym emocji, ale żołądek miała dziwnie ściśnięty.

Peter przyjrzał jej się z wyraźnym zainteresowaniem. Usta rozciągnęły mu się w szerokim uśmiechu.

– Jaja sobie robisz.

– Nie, poważnie. Zostało jej najwyżej kilka miesięcy. Ma raka. – Zgasiła papierosa w popielniczce na nocnym stoliku i natychmiast odwróciła się z powrotem do Petera. Leciutko powiodła palcem wokół jego ust. – Teraz wystarczy, że cierpliwie zaczekasz, a ziemia będzie twoja. I szklarnie, i domy, wszystko. Joshua nie ma głowy do interesów, chętnie się pozbędzie tego całego kramu.

Peter, nie odrywając od niej wzroku, wyjął z ust papierosa, a drugą ręką wsunął sobie jej palec do ust. Dłoń natomiast powędrowała dalej, wzdłuż ramienia, aż do piersi, do różowego sutka.

Christina wstrzymała oddech i osunęła się na łóżko. W następnej chwili Peter znów przebijał ją, zdawałoby się, na wylot, jak nikt nigdy wcześniej. Pomyślna wiadomość błyskawicznie rozpaliła w nim ogień.

Warto było mu powiedzieć, myślała Christina. Zapłacę za jego podniecenie każdą cenę.

Rozdział dwudziesty pierwszy

Ogromny jasnobeżowy rolls-royce corniche wjechał majestatycznie na podjazd. Dach miał opuszczony. Christina siedziała rozparta na mięciutkiej skórzanej tapicerce jaśniejszej o ton od karoserii. Pasy bezpieczeństwa miały dokładnie ten sam odcień. Między dwoma upierścienionymi palcami trzymała nieodłącznego papierosa, jak modny dodatek.

Connie, zaciekawiona pomrukiem silnika, wyjrzała przez okno.

– Szlag by to! – wyrwało jej się szczerze. – Silikonowa wiedźma!

Nienawidziła Christiny z całego serca. Tak głęboko, iż nie sposób było tego nie zauważyć. Zresztą, nie zawsze miała ochotę kryć się ze swoją antypatią.

Akurat przygotowywała, razem z April, niewyszukany lunch, który miały zanieść nad basen.

– Co się stało? – April natychmiast zauważyła zmianę nastroju Connie.

– Przyjechała siostra Joanny – prychnęła gosposia.

– Jak to? – zdziwiła się April. – Tak bez uprzedzenia?

– U niej to normalne. Właśnie wylądowała na podwórzu. Razem z tą swoją miotłą wartą fortunę.

April nie mogła powstrzymać serdecznego śmiechu. Domyślała się, jakimi uczuciami gosposia darzy Christinę oraz wszystkie podobne jej kobiety, wiedziała także, co o tym myślą Joanna i Josh. Nie przejmowali się szczególnie złością Connie, czasem nawet żartowali na ten temat.

Żadne z nich trojga nie uświadamiało sobie, jak głębokie było owo uczucie nienawiści. Żadne z nich nie wiedziało także, iż wypływało z trudnej wprost do wyobrażenia, najpodlejszej, najbardziej prymitywnej zawiści. Connie gotowa była oddać wszystko, by żyć tak jak Christina, mieć wszystko to, co miała siostra Joanny, i móc się zachowywać tak jak tamta.

– Pójdę ją wprowadzić – zaoferowała się April. – Możesz się nie pokazywać. I nie trzeba tu ściągać Joanny, zabiorę Christinę do groty, a potem nad basen.

Odstawiła tacę z talerzami i sztućcami i poszła do frontowych drzwi.

Gdy je otworzyła, uderzył ją niezwykły widok.

Christina była wystrojona jak na wieczorny spacer po słynnej Via Condotti. Właśnie stała przy otwartym bagażniku ogromnego auta, więc można ją było podziwiać w pełnej krasie. Włosy miała osłonięte zawiązaną z tyłu barwną apaszką paryskiej firmy Hermès, do tego czarny kapelusz gauczo na głowie. Wielkie okulary przeciwsłoneczne w stylu Jackie Onasis zakrywały jej prawie całą twarz. Biała jedwabna koszula była jedynie zawiązana w talii, guziki okazały się całkowicie zbędne, więc dekolt sięgał pępka. Stroju dopełniały obcisłe jedwabne spodnie do pół łydki oraz krwistoczerwone sandałki na wysokich szpilkach i cukierkowa torebka w tym samym odcieniu, z pewnością od Louisa Vuittona.

– Christina? – odezwała się April po dłuższej chwili.

Przybyła zsunęła okulary na czubek nosa i zmierzyła ją uważnym spojrzeniem.

– Owszem... – wycedziła. – A kto pyta?

– Przepraszam. – April zeszła ze schodów. – Nazywam się April Woodward. – Wyciągnęła dłoń na powitanie. – Pracuję u Joanny.

– Taaak, widzę. – Christina zignorowała jej rękę. – Jakaś brudna robota.

April przed obiadem usiłowała doprowadzić swoje ubranie do jakiego takiego stanu, niestety, jej wysiłki nie odniosły pożądanego skutku.

– Nie da się ukryć – przyznała.

– Aha.

– Joanna chyba nie spodziewa się gościa?

– Ależ skąd! – obruszyła się Christina. – Zamierzam jej zrobić niespodziankę, a gdybym ją uprzedziła, z niespodzianki byłyby nici, prawda?

Nie sposób zaprzeczyć tej logice.

Na schodach pojawiła się Connie. Zmierzyła gościa podejrzliwym spojrzeniem.

– Dobrze, że jesteś – powitała ją Christina. – Bądź tak miła i zajmij się bagażami.

– Chętnie pomogę – zaproponowała April.

– Nie trzeba. Connie da sobie radę.

– Dobrze. Wobec tego zapraszam do groty, Joanna z pewnością się ucieszy.

– Do jakiej groty? Pierwsze słyszę. Co tu się znowu dzieje?

– To najnowszy pomysł Joanny – odrzekła April tajemniczo i ruszyła przodem.

Connie zajrzała do bagażnika. Twarz jej zapłonęła.

Walizki od Louisa Vuittona! Pewnie! I to ile! Ale szczęściara!

* * *

– Świetnie wyglądasz! – Christina wyciągnęła do siostry szczupłe, opalone ramiona.

Joanna podniosła się z leżaka. Uścisnęła gościa i obie ceremonialnie ucałowały powietrze w pobliżu swoich policzków.

– To ty robisz piorunujące wrażenie! – odparła.

– Phi! Jestem kobietą po przejściach, odsysaniu tłuszczu i dwóch liftingach twarzy. – Christina uśmiechnęła się jednak, ukazując olśniewająco białe zęby, których pielęgnacja także kosztowała fortunę. – Ale efekty są niezłe, co?

Joanna roześmiała się serdecznie.

– Rzeczywiście, niezłe.

– Powiedz no mi, co to za historia z tą całą... grotą? – Christina podparła się pod boki i pierwszy raz spojrzała na budowlę. – O rany... Aaale! – Aż się zachłysnęła i z ciekawością zajrzała do środka.

– Wyrazy uznania należą się tej osobie – rzekła Joanna, wskazując April. – Rozumiem, że już się poznałyście, ale pozwólcie, że was sobie przedstawię. April, to moja siostra, Christina. Christino, poznaj April Woodward, prawdziwą cudotwórczynię, która wyczarowała wszystkie te skarby.

– Miło cię poznać.

– Mnie także – zrewanżowała się Christina uprzejmie, obrzucając April uważniejszym spojrzeniem.

– Och, a to jest pomocnik April – powiedziała Joanna, wskazując Woody'ego. – Woody, to moja siostra, Christina.

Młody mężczyzna ledwo podniósł wzrok znad muszli. Z marsem na czole mruknął coś, kiwnął głową i przestał się interesować towarzyskimi ceregielami.

– Ja też się cieszę, że cię poznałam – wycedziła Christina z nieskrywaną ironią. Przeniosła spojrzenie na Joannę. – Ogromne przedsięwzięcie! – zauważyła z niejakim podziwem.

– To prawda. Tysiące muszli i kamieni oraz mnóstwo pracy.

– To fantastyczne, chociaż chyba trochę przesadne... A w ogóle, skąd ci to przyszło do głowy? Zwłaszcza teraz... – Uświadomiła sobie, że powiedziała za dużo. – Rozumiesz, o co mi chodzi. Na pewno masz z tym urwanie głowy!

April dzielnie trzymała język za zębami, ale Christina miała sokoli wzrok. Od razu spostrzegła, że miejscowa cudotwórczyni zżyma się w duchu.

Ona wie o chorobie Joanny, pomyślała.

Zainteresowało ją ogromnie, dlaczego jakaś obca kobieta została dopuszczona do tak poufnych spraw. Postanowiła zapytać o to siostrę przy najbliższej okazji.

– Robię to, ponieważ tego chcę – odparła Joanna, wiedząc, iż z taką odpowiedzią trudno dyskutować. – Christino, właśnie mieliśmy siadać do stołu. Zjesz z nami?

– Z rozkoszą. Tylko najpierw muszę się odświeżyć. No i zobaczę, co ta mała zrobiła z moimi bagażami.

– Wobec tego pójdziemy razem – zaproponowała Joanna. Odwróciła się do April. – Zjemy troszkę później, dobrze? – Mrugnęła do niej porozumiewawczo. – Za jakieś pół godzinki. Czekamy przy basenie.

April z uśmiechem skinęła głową.

Siostry poszły w stronę domu. Christina jak czapla pięła się pod górę na wysokich obcasach.

– Co to za jedna? – spytała, gdy tylko oddaliły się od groty.

– April? – upewniła się Joanna. – Prawdziwy geniusz. Specjalizuje się w pracach z muszli i kamieni. Kiedyś zobaczyliśmy jej dzieło w ogrodzie u Ingrid Wilson. Obojgu nam się bardzo spodobało, toteż postanowiliśmy urządzić grotę w starej stajni. April to wyjątkowa osoba. Znalazłam w niej prawdziwą przyjaciółkę.

Christinie, zawsze irracjonalnie zazdrosnej o sympatie młodszej siostry, nie spodobały się te słowa.

– A ten jej facet? – spytała. – Co to za jeden?

– Nazywa się Woody Pearlman. Zawodowo oprawia obrazy, ma

pracownię w Capitoli, ale od czasu do czasu pomaga April przy większych zleceniach.

– Ładniutki. – Christina zachichotała jak nastolatka. – Ale niewychowany.

– Cały Woody, cały on – odparła Joanna.

– Hmmm... – Christina nie zamierzała rezygnować z tematu. – Szkoda, że taki nastroszony. Zdaje się, że pod tymi paskudnymi roboczymi ciuchami kryje się całkiem apetyczne ciałko. Chętnie bym sprawdziła, na co go stać.

– Christino! – Joanna roześmiała się głośno. – Czasami własnym uszom nie wierzę!

– Dobrze, już, dobrze, żartowałam... Ale... ślinka cieknie na jego widok.

– Bezwstydna!

Weszły do kuchni. Connie akurat wybierała się z tacą nad basen.

– Bagaże zaniosłam do tego pokoju gościnnego, co zawsze.

– Rozpakowałaś?

Connie podniosła na Christinę leniwe spojrzenie.

– Nieee – powiedziała wolno. – Chyba nie powinnam ruszać takich drogich rzeczy.

Christina popatrzyła na Joannę z rozbawieniem i złością.

Młodsza siostra tylko bezradnie rozłożyła ręce.

– Pomogę ci się rozgościć – zaproponowała.

– Nie, daj spokój. Poradzę sobie sama. Na pewno chcesz odpocząć przed obiadem albo coś takiego...

– To nie jest konieczne – ucięła Joanna chłodno. – Ale jak wolisz. Wobec tego spotkamy się przy basenie.

– Dobrze. – Christina wymaszerowała z kuchni i podążyła ku schodom wiodącym na piętro.

Joanna odwróciła się do Connie.

– Wiem, że nie lubisz Christiny – powiedziała – i wiem, że bywa naprawdę przykra, ale czy mogłabyś się postarać zachowywać trochę bardziej uprzejmie?

Gosposia obrzuciła ją mrocznym spojrzeniem spod ciężkich powiek.

– Myślisz, że jej nie lubię?

– Ja to wiem z całą pewnością – odparła Joanna. – I ty wiesz, że ja wiem.

– W ogóle nie myślę o tej silikonowej lalce – prychnęła Connie.

Joanna westchnęła ciężko i wyszła. Po ostatnim zdaniu dziewczyny ledwo powstrzymała uśmiech. Nie mogła jednak pozwolić sobie na taką reakcję, bo nie chciała, by gosposia uznała, iż w stosunku do Christiny wszystko jej wolno. Wiedziała, że i bez kąśliwych uwag Peruwianki czeka ją dość kłopotów z siostrą. Usiadła przy stole ustawionym nad brzegiem basenu, pod wielkim parasolem.

Kusiło ją, by zadzwonić do Josha i powiedzieć mu o niespodziewanej wizycie, ale w końcu postanowiła nie przeszkadzać mu w pracy.

Biedny Josh, pomyślała. I tak ostatnio ma mnóstwo kłopotów, jeszcze mu do szczęścia potrzebna moja siostra.

Przymknęła oczy, napawając się ciszą i ciepłem.

Nie powinnam była mówić Christinie o chorobie, uznała. Ona nawet mimo najlepszych chęci bywa trudna do zniesienia. Potrafi w ciągu kilku godzin, najdalej paru dni, doprowadzić Josha do białej gorączki. No i, co gorsza, zapewne nie będzie umiała zachowywać się, jak gdyby nic się nie stało. Ech... I co teraz?

Wiedziała doskonale, że siostra będzie usiłowała jej pomagać na wszelkie możliwe sposoby – a jej starania w większości okażą się mocno chybione. A ponieważ Christina była manipulatorką z zapędami do przejmowania kontroli nad wszystkim i wszystkimi, w krótkim czasie odsunie od Joanny Connie, Josha, a także April, czyli wszystkich najbliższych.

Nie można dopuścić do takiej sytuacji. Koniecznie trzeba coś z tym zrobić. I to najlepiej już, od razu.

Wstała i poszła do groty. Na początek zamierzała zaprosić April także na kolację. Zyska na tym podwójnie. Po pierwsze – miłe towarzystwo, po drugie – zamknie Christinie usta. Siostra nie będzie rozprawiała o chorobie w obecności osoby, którą uważała za obcą.

* * *

Lunch przeszedł gładko. Oczywiście rozmowę zdominowała Christina, zasypując Joannę i Josha najnowszymi ploteczkami z życia sławnych i bogatych od San Francisco po Montecito. Po jedzeniu siostry zajęły się zbieraniem naczyń. Normalnie byłoby to zajęcie Connie, zwłaszcza przy gościach, ale tym razem gosposia uznała, że musi koniecznie załatwić jakąś niecierpiącą zwłoki sprawę daleko od domu Lawrence'ów. Joanna doskonale wiedziała, czym podyktowana była taka decyzja, lecz nie protestowała.

Popołudnie minęło nie wiadomo kiedy i nastała pora kolacji. Tym razem jedli na tarasie, a posiłek upłynął w identycznej atmosferze jak poprzednio. I znów Christina z Joanną składały talerze.

– Chętnie wam pomogę – zaproponowała April już po raz drugi. – Pozwólcie mi się do czegoś przydać.

– Nie ma mowy – odparła Joanna. – Jesteś gościem. We dwie doskonale damy sobie radę.

– A poza tym – przyłączyła się Christina – chcemy poplotkować w cztery oczy, jak siostra z siostrą.

– Oczywiście – poparła ją gładko Joanna.

Z pełnymi tacami poszły do kuchni. Na tarasie zostali tylko April z Joshem.

Joshua upił łyk kawy i spojrzał na swą towarzyszkę ze znaczącym uśmiechem.

– I co myślisz o starszej siostrze? – spytał.

– Cóż... Z pewnością to osoba, która przyciąga uwagę... Jest piękna, inteligentna, ma cięty język, poczucie humoru, ale... – Spuściła wzrok i lekko wzruszyła ramionami.

– Ale...?

– Wydaje się apodyktyczna, dumna i ma pogardliwy stosunek do reszty świata... – podniosła na Josha niepewne spojrzenie.

– Mów, mów! – zaśmiał się w głos. – Teraz nie wolno ci zamilknąć. Właśnie mnie zaciekawiłaś.

– I tak już powiedziałam za dużo – wycofała się April. – Stanowczo przekroczyłam wszelkie granice przyzwoitości.

– Daj spokój, przecież wiesz, że jesteś tu na prawach członka rodziny! – Roześmiał się znowu. – Chociaż z rodziną, jak wiadomo, człowiek najlepiej wychodzi na zdjęciu.

– Nie chcę być niegrzeczna. Nie zamierzam jej krytykować. Przecież ja tej kobiety właściwie nie znam.

– Coś mi się zdaje, że i tak trafiłaś w dziesiątkę – stwierdził Joshua z rozbawieniem. – Szczerze mówiąc, wolałbym, żeby starsza siostrzyczka tu nie zawitała. Joanna z pewnością także. Jakoś nie podejrzewam, żeby ta wizyta była jej wybitnie na rękę. Szczególnie teraz...

April mimowolnie zadrżała. Straszna była myśl o czyjejś bliskiej śmierci. W dodatku odejść miała istota tak dobra, taka kochana... Joanna w zasadzie wyglądała na całkiem zdrową, jedynym sygnałem złego stanu były coraz częstsze chwile odpoczynku, toteż nic dziwnego, że trudno by u niej dostrzec śmiertelną chorobę. Natomiast kiedy się o ten temat zahaczało w rozmowie, zagrożenie stawało się bardziej realne, nawet zbyt prawdziwe. Jakby słowa podkreślały istnienie zła. April wolała zmienić temat.

– Jak tam w szklarniach? – spytała. – Joanna ostatnio nic o nich nie wspominała.

– Odpukać w niemalowane – Joshua stuknął kłykciami w blat – wszystko w najlepszym porządku. Mam nadzieję, że to koniec nieszczęść na długi czas. – Podniósł na April pogodne spojrzenie. – O postępy w twojej pracy nie muszę pytać. Joanna jest pełna podziwu dla ciebie. Ja także.

April poczerwieniała. Komplementy sprawiły jej ogromną przyjemność, lecz jednocześnie czuła się winna.

Zawsze, kiedy Joshua mówi mi coś miłego, odnoszę wrażenie, jakbym zdradzała Joannę. Wszystko przez to, że tak bardzo go lubię. I najchętniej słuchałabym go dniami i nocami... Boże, co robić?

* * *

Christina rozparła się na skórzanej sofie Chesterfield i wyjrzała przez okno. Wykrzywiła wargi w ironicznym uśmiechu. Długimi paznokciami pomalowanymi krwistoczerwonym lakierem nerwowo przeczesała włosy. Ciężkie złote bransoletki z drogimi kamieniami zadźwięczały na chudych nadgarstkach. Wypiła solidny łyk brandy i zaciągnęła się papierosem.

Więc to tak, pomyślała. Dobra wróżka z groty została na kolacji. A teraz czaruje Josha. Interesujące.

Rysy jej twarzy zastygły w wyrazie złości.

Cały ten Joshua Lawrence gówno mnie obchodzi, ale niech mnie szlag, jeśli jakaś wścibska przybłęda będzie się plątała po moim rodzinnym domu! Genialna projektantka pożal się Boże! Artystka! Już ja szybciutko zakończę te jej gościnne występy!

Wściekłym ruchem zgasiła papierosa, zerwała się na równe nogi i ruszyła na taras. W drzwiach omal nie wpadła na siostrę wracającą z łazienki.

– Dokąd tak pędzisz? – zdziwiła się Joanna.

– Na taras. Widzę, że Joshua wyjątkowo miło spędza czas z tą całą April. – Znacząco uniosła brew.

– Daj im spokój – zaśmiała się Joanna. – Nic złego się nie dzieje. A my wreszcie mamy okazję spokojnie porozmawiać.

Christina z ociąganiem wróciła na wielką skórzaną sofę.

– A co to właściwie za imię, „April"...!

– Nie irytuj się, nie ma powodu. Ona naprawdę jest najmilszą istotą pod słońcem.

– Pewnie! – Christina zapaliła kolejnego papierosa i wypuściła w powietrze długą smugę dymu. – Jak myślisz, rżnie się z tym swoim przystojniakiem?

– Nie mam zielonego pojęcia – odparła Joanna, lekko zirytowana.

Nie podobało jej się zainteresowanie siostry Woodym. Zżymała się w duchu, bo Christina była pod tym względem taka sama jak jej eksmężowie: oni szukali przygód, stale zmieniając partnerki, najczęściej na coraz młodsze, ona chętnie zabawiała się z chłopcami.

Joanna stanowczo nie życzyła sobie komplikacji w postaci romansu siostry z pomocnikiem April. O, nie. Nagle uświadomiła sobie, że jest tylko jedno wyjście z tej sytuacji. Od dawna już miała w głowie pewien plan, dotyczący gburowatego pana Woody'ego Pearlmana. Wystarczy, że wprowadzi go w życie nieco wcześniej, niż zamierzała. I w ten sposób upiecze dwie pieczenie przy jednym ogniu.

Zadowolona z siebie odwróciła się do siostry, gotowa poświęcić jej całą uwagę.

– To jak, kochanie – zapytała – długo planujesz u nas zostać?

Rozdział dwudziesty drugi

Joshua bez tchu wpadł do domu i pognał od razu do sypialni. Zaalarmowany telefonem od April całą drogę ze szklarni gnał, jakby go wszyscy diabli gonili.

Przyjaciółka wyszła naprzeciw i zanim zdążył się odezwać, położyła palec na ustach.

– Zasnęła – powiedziała szeptem.

– Ale... Ale... co się stało? – Z trudem łapał oddech.

Pogładziła go po ramieniu.

– Zejdźmy na dół – zaproponowała. Wzięła go za rękę i poprowadziła do schodów. Gest ten był tak naturalny, że żadne nie zwróciło na niego uwagi.

Razem wyszli na taras i usiedli przy tekowym stole.

– Mów, proszę. Co się stało? – Joshuę dławił strach.

April uścisnęła go za rękę, chcąc dodać mu sił.

– Byłyśmy w grocie – odezwała się cicho – gdy nagle Joannę potwornie rozbolała głowa. Miała też zaburzenia wzroku. Od razu zadzwoniłam po lekarza. Nie było go w gabinecie, więc nalegałam, aby go wezwano przez pager. – Odetchnęła głęboko, by odzyskać równowagę. – Zgodnie z jego zaleceniami dałam jej silne środki przeciwbólowe oraz tabletki nasenne. Powiedział, że będzie dłuższy czas głęboko spała, a po przebudzeniu powinna się czuć dużo lepiej.

Joshua nie odrywał wzroku od jej twarzy. Pogładził April po dłoni.

– Bogu dzięki, że jesteś z nami! Wiem... wiem, że mamy przed sobą bardzo trudny okres, szczególnie pod koniec... Nie musisz nam pomagać. Znajdę pielęgniarkę...

– Daj spokój – obruszyła się April. – Mowy nie ma. Joanna przez większość czasu czuje się zupełnie dobrze. Mnie sprawia przyjemność jej towarzystwo przy pracy, więc tak czy inaczej, mam na nią oko. Niepotrzebna tu żadna dodatkowa osoba.

– Doceniam twoje dobre chęci...

– Obiecuję ci, że będę się opiekowała Joanną. Daję słowo.

Joshua spojrzał na nią z wdzięcznością. Cudowna kobieta. Teraz zauważył, że April ma na sobie roboczy strój, włosy w nieładzie i cała jest obsypana białym cementowym pyłem.

– Oderwałem cię od pracy...

– Och, daj spokój. Przecież to najmniej istotne!

– Niby są rzeczy ważniejsze... – Zmarszczył brwi. – A gdzie się podziały Christina i Connie?

– Nie wiem. Joanna wspomniała tylko, że Christina znowu gdzieś zniknęła. Connie była rano, sprzątała trochę, a potem chyba wybrała się po zakupy.

– I nadal jej nie ma?

– Nie. Joanna mówiła też, że Connie ma sporo zajęcia przy Christinie... To znaczy, nie drążyła tematu, tylko tak sobie rozmawiałyśmy... Akurat ustalałyśmy, które muszle będą pasować do orchidei... i tak się jakoś zgadało. – Odwróciła wzrok, bo łzy napłynęły jej do oczu. – Tak było miło i nagle... – Głos jej się załamał. – Zupełnie bez powodu...

Joshua znów ujął ją za rękę.

– April, jesteś wyjątkowo dzielna.

– Dzielna to jest Joanna.

Siedzieli w milczeniu, zatopieni w myślach. Wreszcie April spojrzała na zegarek.

– Wracam do pracy – oznajmiła stanowczo. – Miałam zamiar zajrzeć do szklarni, żeby ostatecznie zdecydować, które orchidee ozdobią grotę, ale Woody się dzisiaj nie pojawił, więc spadło na mnie sporo innych prac.

– Dlaczego nie przyszedł?

– Nie mam pojęcia. Liczyłam na niego. Pierwszy raz mu się coś takiego zdarzyło, więc zupełnie nie wiem, co o tym myśleć. Może musiał nadgonić własną robotę. – Spojrzała na Josha z uśmiechem. – Najwyraźniej taki dzisiaj pechowy dzień.

– Na to wygląda.

– Możesz spokojnie wrócić do szklarni. Zajrzę do Joanny od czasu do czasu. Lekarz powiedział, że będzie długo spała, więc i tak w niczym jej teraz nie pomożesz, a ja jestem pod ręką, tak czy inaczej.

– Kochana jesteś, ale nie pojadę już dzisiaj do firmy. Zadzwonię do Carla, niech się zajmie interesami, a ja może spróbuję coś osiągnąć w jaskini rozpusty.

– Ale nie masz nic przeciwko temu, żebym raz czy drugi sprawdziła, jak się czuje Joanna?

– Nie, oczywiście, że nie. We dwójkę będzie nam łatwiej... – Zamyślił się. – Ciekaw jestem, czy Christina po powrocie będzie chciała zjeść obiad.

– Jeśli nawet, to przecież jest dorosła i wie, gdzie stoi lodówka, prawda?

– Słuszna uwaga! – uznał Joshua z rozpromienioną twarzą.

* * *

Christina leżała na wielkim łożu małżeńskim, rozpięta jak motyl w gablocie. Ręce i nogi miała przywiązane do rogów stelaża, na oczach tę samą barwną apaszkę od Hermèsa co poprzednio. Nie widziała nic.

Drżała ze strachu i zniecierpliwienia. Choć trzykrotnie wychodziła za mąż i miała wielu kochanków, nigdy w życiu nie była tak podniecona. Każdym nerwem dostroiła się do Petera, z napięciem usiłując odgadnąć, w jaki sposób teraz będzie sobie radził z jej nienasyconym apetytem.

Teraz wyczuła jakiś ruch w pokoju, a w pewnej chwili schłodził ją niespodziewany powiew, jakby mgła skłębiona za oknami dostała się do wnętrza i musnęła ją sinymi wstęgami.

Co on robi?

Wyczuwała jego obecność, ciepło bijące od rozgrzanego ciała, gotowego bezlitośnie ją wykorzystać. Uda jej drżały z pożądania. Nagle wślizgnął się w nią jego palec. Krzyknęła – zaskoczona, a jednocześnie zadowolona i natychmiast straciła resztki panowania nad sobą. Bez wahania poddała się jego woli, wiła się, dyszała, błagała o więcej.

Dłoń zniknęła, zostawiając po sobie straszną pustkę. Materac ugiął się po obu stronach Christiny. Od razu wiedziała, że Peter przygotowuje się do ataku. Miała rację. Wsunął dłonie pod jej pośladki i wbił się w nią gwałtownie.

Jej ciało natychmiast odpowiedziało orgazmem. Wyrwał jej się głośny okrzyk, gdy uciekała przed nim, a jednocześnie za nim goniła, ogarnięta pierwotną ekstazą, jakiej istnienia nawet nie podejrzewała. Wreszcie i Peter eksplodował z jękiem, a wtedy Christina wygięła się w łuk, by poczuć jego rozkosz do końca.

Oboje leżeli bez ruchu, zdyszani jak po długim biegu. W powietrzu uniosła się ciężka woń zmęczenia, pożądania i spełnionej namiętności.

Długo trwało, nim Christina wreszcie odzyskała oddech i mogła coś powiedzieć, ale i wtedy zdobyła się tylko na westchnienie.

Peter natomiast w milczeniu zsunął się z niej i wstał z łóżka.

Co on robi? Ciągle jeszcze nie miała dosyć.

Słyszała, że chodzi po pokoju... dobiegły ją szmery, jakby się ubierał!

Co on znowu wykombinował?!

Szarpnęła więzy – bezskutecznie.

– Peter – wyszeptała w końcu. – Co robisz?

Odpowiedziała jej cisza. Potem usłyszała lekki zgrzyt zapinanego suwaka, szczęk klamerki paska od spodni. I szelest tkaniny, gdy kochanek wkładał marynarkę.

– Peter! – Tym razem w jej głosie pobrzmiewała irytacja. – Co jest, do cholery?!

Nadal nie odpowiadał. Spróbowała się oswobodzić – na próżno.

– Peter! – krzyknęła. – Rozwiąż mnie!

I wtedy usłyszała czyjś szept.

Szept?!

Wyobraźnia podsunęła jej setki możliwości. Christina nie mogła myśleć logicznie, strach sparaliżował ją, pozbawił zdrowego rozsądku. Oblała się zimnym potem.

– Peter!!! – zawołała, wyrywając się z całej siły. – Rozwiąż mnie! Teraz! Natychmiast! – Zaczęła szlochać jak dziecko. – Proszę cię!

I wtedy... usłyszała śmiech.

Nie był to jednak śmiech mężczyzny.

Nie, to śmiała się kobieta. Okrutnie i szyderczo.

Przez chwilę Christina myślała, że zemdleje. Zebrała się jednak w sobie i szarpnęła więzy z całej siły. Nic to nie dało. Zaczęła się miotać jak szalona, krzyczała i płakała, błagała, by ktoś ją uwolnił.

Nagle czyjaś dłoń zakryła jej usta i ledwo mogła oddychać.

– Spokojnie, laluniu – odezwał się Peter. – Nie denerwuj się. Jestem tutaj.

Christina pisnęła przerażona.

– Teraz odsunę rękę – oznajmił – żebyś mogła swobodnie oddychać, ale jeśli chociaż miaukniesz, zatkam cię na dobre. Dotarło?

Gorliwie pokiwała głową.

Tak, tak, myślała rozpaczliwie. Zrobię wszystko, co zechcesz. Tylko już przestań.

Materac się poruszył, usłyszała Petera:

– Idź i zaczekaj w samochodzie.

Znów usłyszała śmieszek – wyraźnie kobiecy. Potem dobiegł ją odgłos szybkich drobnych kroków, gdy ktoś wyszedł z pokoju. Wreszcie trzasnęły drzwi domku.

Christina dygotała na całym ciele, ale nie z podniecenia, tylko z wyczerpania i strachu.

Peter wstał z łóżka.

– Teraz cię rozwiążę, laluniu – powiedział. – A potem wychodzę. Łapiesz?

Bez słowa pokiwała głową.

Zręcznie uwolnił jej nogi. Radził sobie z tym równie dobrze jak z zawiązywaniem. Przesunął się po łóżku i oswobodził lewą rękę Christiny. Wreszcie mogła poruszyć stopami, aby przywrócić krążenie w zdrętwiałych kończynach.

– No to znikam – oznajmił. – Zatrzaśnij za sobą drzwi.

– Ale co... Kto to...

– Rób, co ci mówię. – W głosie mężczyzny zabrzmiał groźny ton. – I żadnych pytań.

– Peter... – zakwiliła żałośnie. – Kto to był? I... co z nami?

– Z jakimi „nami"? – roześmiał się szyderczo. – Nie jesteś mi już potrzebna. Zapomnij o mnie. A jak będziesz się naprzykrzać, gorzko pożałujesz, jasne?

Nie wierzyła własnym uszom. Z wściekłości aż jej pociemniało w oczach. Chętnie by się na niego rzuciła, gryzła i drapała, rozdarła go na strzępy! Strach jest jednak potężną siłą, więc nie pisnęła słowa ani nie drgnęła.

– Ciao – rzucił Peter.

Usłyszała, jak wychodzi z pokoju, a następnie zamyka frontowe drzwi.

Lewą ręką ściągnęła apaszkę z oczu. Nie było to łatwe, bo Peter zawiązał ją naprawdę mocno. Zamrugała kilka razy, nim wzrok na nowo przyzwyczaił się do światła. Rozejrzała się dookoła. Oczywiście nikogo nie zobaczyła.

Najszybciej jak mogła oswobodziła prawą rękę. Potrząsając nią i rozcierając nadgarstki, zerwała się na równe nogi i pognała do drzwi wejściowych. Otworzyła je, wyjrzała ostrożnie zza framugi. Niestety, parking przesłaniała mgła. Nie było widać niczego i nikogo. Tylko ptasie krzyki przeszywały niebo, śląc w powietrze przenikliwą skargę.

Wróciła do sypialni. Ubrała się, usiadła na łóżku i skryła twarz w dłoniach. Po policzkach spłynęły jej zdradliwe ciche łzy, potem dołączył się do nich szloch, jeden i drugi, aż wreszcie wrzasnęła ze złości i miotała się, waląc pięściami w materac.

W końcu gniew się wypalił. Wyczerpana, obolała, długi czas leżała bez ruchu.

Wreszcie wstała i ruszyła chwiejnym krokiem do łazienki. Włączyła światło, spojrzała w lustro.

Piękny widok!

Wyszarpnęła kilka chusteczek z kartonika ustawionego na blacie, by zetrzeć rozmazany tusz. Wróciła do sypialni po torbę i wyłowiła z niej po kolei wszystkie kosmetyki niezbędne do zrobienia makijażu.

Znów popatrzyła na siebie w lustrze. Najpierw podkład, potem róż, tusz i szminka. Nie było to łatwe, bo ręce wciąż jej drżały, ale w końcu osiągnęła cel. Wrzuciła kosmetyki do torby i już miała zgasić światło, gdy przyszła jej do głowy całkiem nowa myśl. Ponownie wyjęła ołówek do brwi i zastygła przed lustrem z narzędziem zemsty w dłoni.

Nie, to na nic, pomyślała. Za łatwo wyczyścić.

Wróciła do sypialni i weszła na łóżko. Zdjęła ze ściany krajobraz morski, prawdziwy landszaft i z całej siły cisnęła nim w lustro na drzwiach szafy. Srebrna tafla pokryła się gęstą pajęczyną, okruchy szkła poleciały na podłogę.

Dobrze. Bardzo dobrze, pomyślała z zadowoleniem, choć w tej satysfakcji nie było ani odrobiny radości.

Kawałkiem szkła pracowicie wydrapała w tynku duże litery, pogrubiając je kilkakrotnie. Wreszcie usiadła na łóżku, wsunęła stopy w pantofle, podniosła z podłogi torbę i poszła do drzwi. W progu odwróciła się jeszcze i obrzuciła taksującym spojrzeniem swoje dzieło. Nad wezgłowiem widniały trzy słowa: WAL SIĘ SAM. Niżej, pośrodku – tylko jedno: ZŁAMASIE. Od niego prowadziła w dół strzałka, wskazująca łóżko.

Zadowolona z efektu, zarówno literackiego, jak i artystycznego, Christina odwróciła się, wyszła z domku i spokojnie zamknęła za sobą drzwi.

Rozdział dwudziesty trzeci

Promienie słońca przedarły się przez mgłę i rozsiały w jadalni złoty blask. Joshua wyszedł już do pracy, Connie sprzątała na piętrze. April zajrzała tylko na chwilę, przywitała się w biegu i pomknęła do groty. Od kilku dni pracowała sama, bo Woody nie wiedział, w co najpierw ręce włożyć u siebie w zakładzie. Miał się pojawić dopiero w przyszłym tygodniu.

Dlatego też siostry tylko we dwie popijały poranną kawę.

– Cudownie się dzisiaj czuję – powiedziała Joanna. Minął tydzień od pamiętnego bólu głowy i kłopotów z widzeniem, więc epizod, choć przerażający, zaczynał nabierać kształtów odległego wspomnienia. – Dzwoniłaś do Vincenta?

– A, owszem. Wczoraj wieczorem, kiedy mi wspomniałaś, że jesteś poumawiana i cały dzień masz zajęty, już nie miałam siły go ścigać, ale dzisiaj wstałam o bladym świcie i od razu go złapałam. – Christina zabębniła nerwowo paznokciami o blat.

– Już nie spał?

– Dziwne, ale nie spał. Coś tam napomknął, że kto rano wstaje... Ale raczej o inne dawanie mu chodziło. Podejrzewam aluzję do napiwków.

Młodsza siostra uśmiechnęła się ze zrozumieniem.

– Dziwisz mnie trochę – wyznała – bo włosy masz idealne. – Nie umknął jej uwagi także nienaganny makijaż. – Nawet jeśli Vincent jest taki dobry, jak mówią, nie bardzo widzę, co właściwie miałby poprawiać.

Christina pogładziła dłonią nienaganną fryzurę.

– Kochana, włosy nigdy nie są idealne. A Vincent, chociaż mieszka w dziurze zabitej dechami, jest jednym z najlepszych fryzjerów na świecie. Dzięki niemu wyglądam, jakbym nie robiła nic szczególnego z włosami, a efekt jest. Znać rękę mistrza.

– Aha, rozumiem – bąknęła Joanna, niespecjalnie zainteresowana tematem. Nie pojmowała, jak można tyle pieniędzy i czasu poświęcać na poprawianie urody. Przecież to strasznie nudne. Chyba że... to właśnie nuda prowadzi do obsesji na temat wyglądu.

– Szkoda, że nie możesz ze mną jechać – powiedziała Christina, nawet nie pytając, czy siostra chciałaby się z nią wybrać. – Vincent na pewno zrobiłby coś z twoimi włosami.

– Będę dziś bardzo zajęta, nie mam ani jednej wolnej chwili. Poza tym lubię się strzyc u Jonathana.

– Ależ on cię obcina zawsze tak samo! – wykrzyknęła Christina z oburzeniem.

– I bardzo dobrze.

– Koszmar!

– Jeśli chcesz, podrzucę cię do fryzjera – zaproponowała Joanna. – Chyba że wolisz jechać własnym wozem.

– Czy ja wiem... – zastanowiła się Christina. – Może zajrzę jeszcze do jakiegoś sklepu... Lepiej jedźmy osobno. – Zniżyła głos. – Czy jesteś pewna, że poradzisz sobie sama? Jeśli wolisz, zostanę w domu albo pojadę z tobą.

– Nie, nie trzeba – odparła Joanna. – Dzięki za troskę, ale na pewno wszystko będzie w porządku. Jedź śmiało.

– Jak uważasz. – Christina wstała i przeciągnęła się. – Wezmę żakiet i jadę. Vincent nie lubi czekać. – Pochyliła się i cmoknęła powietrze obok policzka siostry. – Trzymaj się.

– Cześć. Baw się dobrze.

– Jasne! – zaświergotała i wyszła.

Joanna czas jakiś jeszcze siedziała zapatrzona w okno i pogrążona w rozmyślaniach. Christina ostatnio zachowywała się dziwnie. Ze dwa razy wyglądała na zapłakaną, ale kiedy Joanna ją o to spytała, smutek skończył się natychmiast i starsza siostra zaczęła dla odmiany demonstrować nieoczekiwaną wesołość. Co dziwne, wiecznie była czymś zajęta, właściwie ciągle gdzieś znikała. A to robiła wypady do pobliskich sklepów, a to umawiała się z przyjaciółmi, o których Joanna pierwszy raz słyszała, co chwilę biegała do fryzjera... Zdumiewała siostrę i szwagra co krok.

Cóż, dopóki jest zadowolona z życia, wszystko w porządku, pomyślała Joanna. Muszę się zająć własnymi sprawami. Czas ucieka, a ja nie mam chwili do stracenia.

* * *

Joanna szybko pokonała zdradliwą górską drogę. Po dziesięciu minutach znalazła się w banku. Pewnych transakcji nie sposób załatwić przez telefon ani za pośrednictwem Internetu.

Wróciła do samochodu z dużą, wypchaną kopertą w torbie.

Ruszyła do Capitoli, gdzie cieszyły oko wiktoriańskie domy w pastelowych kolorach, a w licznych butikach oferowano po zawyżonych cenach rękodzieła okolicznych mieszkańców.

Ponieważ był środek tygodnia, bez trudu zaparkowała dosłownie przed wejściem do pracowni Woody'ego.

Wyprostowała się dumnie i gotowa na wszystko weszła do środka.

Za kontuarem siedziała jakaś nastolatka. Jej długie tlenione włosy kontrastowały z piękną opalenizną.

– Dzień dobry – odezwała się grzecznie. – W czym mogę pomóc?

– Chciałabym porozmawiać z panem Pearlmanem.

– Nie ma go.

– Jest w domu?

– Nie wiem... – Nastolatka była wyraźnie zbita z tropu. – Chętnie przekażę mu wiadomość...

Joanna zmierzyła ją uważnym spojrzeniem. Dziewczyna kłamała, to więcej niż pewne.

– Nie, dziękuję, zajrzę później.

Po wyjściu ze sklepu od razu skręciła za róg budynku. Woody miał mieszkanie nad zakładem. Wiedziała, bo któregoś dnia zgadały się z April na ten temat.

Drewniane, poszarzałe od słońca zewnętrzne schody okazały się bardzo strome. Wzięła głęboki oddech.

Nie ma rady, naprzód.

Udało jej się dotrzeć na górę bez niemiłych przygód. Otworzyła zardzewiałe drzwi z siatki i zastukała w drewnianą ramę, z której odłaziła farba. Cisza. Zapukała głośniej. I tym razem nikt się nie pojawił.

Wtedy zauważyła niegdyś biały, umocowany na framudze przycisk dzwonka. Wcisnęła go, choć nie miała szczególnej nadziei, że to cokolwiek da. Ku jej zdumieniu gdzieś w mieszkaniu zabrzmiał głośny brzęczyk.

Po chwili drzwi się uchyliły, a Woody wytknął głowę przez szparę. Czarne wielkie oczy rozszerzyły mu się ze zdumienia, ale szybko wziął się w garść i zrobił swoją zwykłą, zblazowaną minę.

– Sie masz – wycedził, ledwo otwierając usta. – Co jest?

– Chciałabym z tobą porozmawiać.

– Trochę jakby zajęty jestem.

– Mam do ciebie pewną sprawę – oświadczyła Joanna. – Powiedzmy, że jeśli nie znajdziesz dla mnie kilku minut, przejdzie ci koło nosa niebagatelna suma.

– Chwilunia. Coś na siebie wrzucę.

– Dobrze, zaczekam. – Dopiero teraz Joanna spostrzegła, że młody mężczyzna przytrzymuje ręcznik na biodrach.

Zniknął, ale nie zamknął drzwi. Mimo to czekała cierpliwie na zewnątrz. Czuła obrzydzenie na samą myśl o tym, co zamierzała zrobić, ale niekiedy człowiek musi działać wbrew swoim najświętszym zasadom.

Woody wrócił i otworzył szerzej drzwi.

– No, już – rzucił, wskazując kciukiem za siebie. Najwyraźniej było to zaproszenie.

Weszła więc i rozejrzała się ciekawie. Została mile zaskoczona widokiem pięknych, starannie oprawionych rysunków oraz przyciągających wzrok reprodukcji, zajmujących właściwie całe ściany. Większość stanowiły dzieła miejscowych artystów. Umeblowanie było dość kosztowne, zarazem nowoczesne i funkcjonalne. Gdzieś z głębi mieszkania dobiegał jazz, wygłuszony przez zamknięte drzwi.

– Tylko nie za długo, bo muszę zaraz iść do pracowni – odezwał się Woody.

– Dobrze.

Nie bardzo wiedziała, jak zacząć.

– No, o co chodzi? – Obrzucił ją uważnym spojrzeniem. Ubrany tylko w workowate szorty, wydawał się wyższy i bardziej muskularny niż w grocie. Czarne włosy kłębiły się gęstą masą, ciemne oczy rzucały niepokojące błyski.

– Nie chcę wtykać nosa w nie swoje sprawy – odezwała się Joanna niepewnie – ale muszę ci zadać osobiste pytanie.

– No? – Zmierzył ją hardym spojrzeniem. Ręce założył na piersiach i zakołysał się na piętach. Najwyraźniej bawił go jej brak pewności siebie, ale sam też był podenerwowany. – Ja tam nie mam żadnych tajemnic – oświadczył. – Strzelaj.

– Czy kochasz April? – spytała Joanna prosto z mostu.

Zamarł na chwilę w bezruchu. Potarł policzek i odwrócił wzrok. Wreszcie spojrzał na nią butnie.

– Nie twój interes.

– Podobno nie masz żadnych tajemnic – przypomniała.

– Bo nie mam.

– Wobec tego...

– To jest pytanie zbyt osobiste. Ale skoro tak bardzo chcesz wiedzieć, to... Owszem, może być, że kocham April.

– Może być? – powtórzyła Joanna jak echo. – Czyli nie jesteś pewien? – W napięciu czekała na odpowiedź. Przyszła tutaj święcie przekonana, że Woody jest egoistycznym łobuzem, zimnym uwodzicielem, słucha jedynie testosteronu i żyje w przekonaniu, że żadna kobieta mu się nie oprze.

– W sumie... – podrapał się po głowie... – Znam April nie od dzisiaj, byłem kumplem jej eks i w ogóle. Mądra z niej kobieta, prawdziwa artystka i niczego sobie... – Wzruszył ramionami.

Kawał lodu w żołądku Joanny natychmiast stopniał. Już wiedziała, że wygra.

– A co ona czuje do ciebie?

– Traktuje mnie jak przyjaciela – odparł bez wahania. – Albo jak starszego brata. – Wyszczerzył zęby w uśmiechu. – Tyle tylko że starszy brat zwykle nie rżnie siostrzyczki.

Joanna skrzywiła się lekko.

– O ile mi wiadomo, nigdy do tego nie doszło.

Woody spochmurniał.

– Skoro tak cholernie dużo wiesz, to po co pytasz? – Znów zaczął się kołysać na piętach. – A poza tym, kto wie, może jej się to spodobać, nie? Wszystkim innym się podoba.

Te przechwałki nie zrobiły na niej wrażenia. Ani jej nie wystraszyły.

– Chcę, żebyś zostawił April – powiedziała. – Żebyś od niej odszedł. Żebyś wymyślił jakąś zgrabną historyjkę i zniknął z jej życia. Raz na zawsze.

– Palma ci odbiła?

– Mówię zupełnie poważnie. Jestem gotowa ci zapłacić. Znikniesz z jej życia?

– Chcesz mi zapłacić?

– Jeśli znikniesz z życia April na zawsze.

– Wariatka.

– Nie odpowiedziałeś na moje pytanie. Sformułuję je inaczej. Czy jesteś gotów w zamian za pięćdziesiąt tysięcy dolarów raz na zawsze usunąć się z życia April?

– Pięćdziesiąt patyków? – powtórzył Woody osłupiały.

Joanna w milczeniu skinęła głową.

– Poważnie?

Skinęła głową po raz drugi.

Wbił wzrok w podłogę. Fala kręconych włosów opadła mu na czoło. W końcu podniósł spojrzenie na Joannę.

– Niech będzie. Pięćdziesiąt kawałków i już mnie nie ma.

– Zadzwonisz do niej z jakąś wiarygodną wymówką i nigdy więcej się nie spotkacie.

– Dobra. Zadzwonię. Dzisiaj wieczorem. Powiem jej, że spotkałem swój ideał. I że musi się trzymać ode mnie z daleka, bo w przeciwnym razie moja lalunia będzie zazdrosna i mnie rzuci. Zniknę z życia April Woodward raz na zawsze.

Joanna uznała, iż może mu wierzyć, chociaż był bezdyskusyjnym łajdakiem. Wyjęła z torby grubą brązową kopertę.

– Proszę.

Nie chciał sprawić jej satysfakcji, ale ciekawość zwyciężyła. Oddarł brzeg opakowania. Rzeczywiście, pięćdziesiąt tysięcy dolarów.

– I nikomu ani słowa – dodała. – Jeśli zdradzisz się przed April, i tak nie będziesz miał u niej szans, bo natychmiast dowie się ode mnie, że wziąłeś pieniądze.

Woody niedbale rzucił kopertę na kanapę. Joanna powiodła za nią wzrokiem i osłupiała. Na podłodze ujrzała parę czarnych sandałków na wysokim obcasie, od Gucciego, takich samych jak Christiny. Na siedzisku leżał niedbale rzucony skórzany żakiet, biały, w czarne łaty, również od Gucciego i także identyczny z tym, jaki Joanna widziała u siostry. A na żakiecie – czarna skórzana torebka. Rzecz jasna, od Gucciego. I oczywiście identyczną miała Christina.

Woody dostrzegł jej spojrzenie, zrozumiał wyraz twarzy.

– Tak to właśnie jest. – Bezczelnie wzruszył ramionami. – Lecą na mnie. Wszystkie.

– Oprócz April – odparowała Joanna z krzywym uśmiechem. Odwróciła się i wyszła.

Woody stanął na progu.

– A gdybym się nie zgodził?

– Nie było takiej możliwości.

Śpiesznie pokonała strome schody, wsiadła do auta, uruchomiła silnik i niecierpliwie wcisnęła gaz. Chciała się jak najszybciej oddalić od Woody'ego i zapomnieć o scenie, w której właśnie brała udział. Choć sama ją wyreżyserowała, czuła do siebie wstręt, była zawstydzona. A jeszcze przy okazji zyskała niechciany dowód wątpliwej konduity swojej siostry.

Boże jedyny, chyba jesteśmy bardziej podobne do siebie, niż byłabym skłonna przyznać. Jedna daje łapówki, druga ma niecięzkie obyczaje...

Światło na skrzyżowaniu zmieniło się na zielone. Joanna wcisnęła pedał gazu do oporu. Byle szybciej wrócić do domu, wziąć gorący prysznic, spłukać z siebie wstrętne wspomnienia.

Z pewnością nie mam prawa odsądzać Christiny od czci i wiary. Nie jestem od niej lepsza. Nigdy dotąd nie upadłam tak nisko. Dałam łapówkę! Przekupiłam człowieka, któremu April ufała, mimo wszelkich jego wad.

Tak czy inaczej, nie żałowała tego kroku. Dzięki niemu skutecznie usunęła z życia przyjaciółki konkurencję, ułatwiając drogę Joshowi.

Natomiast zaskoczyła ją Christina.

Co ona wyprawia...?

W końcu doszła do wniosku, że nie powinno jej to obchodzić. Woody zniknie z życia April i tylko to się liczy. A przy okazji poznała prawdziwy charakter tego człowieka.

Chociaż zachowała się podle, nie żałowała swojego uczynku, ponieważ przyświecał jej szczytny cel. Dobrze zrobiła. To oczywiste.

Rozdział dwudziesty czwarty

Minąwszy mostek przy basenie, Joanna dostrzegła Christinę rozciągniętą na leżaku. Ogromny słomiany kapelusz zasłaniał jej głowę, wielkie okulary przeciwsłoneczne zakrywały prawie całą twarz. Czytała jakiś kolorowy magazyn. Miała na sobie pomarańczowe bikini i smażyła się na słońcu, nie myśląc o skutkach starzenia się skóry.

– O, już wstałaś – odezwała się na widok Joanny. – Jak się dzisiaj czujesz, kochanie?

– Dobrze.

– Na pewno?

– Tak.

– Masz ochotę przejrzeć włoskie wydanie „Vogue"? Prezentują kolekcję zimową.

– Nie, dziękuję. Idę do groty, porozmawiać z April.

– Aha. Nie pobrudź się cementem. Lepiej byłoby, gdybyś została na słońcu. Zobacz, jak tu przyjemnie.

– Nie przyzwyczajaj się zanadto – odrzekła Joanna, obrzucając ją chłodnym spojrzeniem. – Wyjeżdżasz stąd najdalej jutro z samego rana.

Christina opuściła czasopismo na kolana i zsunęła okulary.

– Nie rozumiem...

– Wyraziłam się zupełnie jasno. Powiedziałabym ci wczoraj, ale wróciłaś tak późno, że już się nie widziałyśmy.

– Bo widzisz... Ja...

– Nie musisz się tłumaczyć. Po prostu pakuj manatki. Jutro po śniadaniu się pożegnamy. I bez ciebie nie wiem, w co najpierw ręce włożyć.

– Ale...

– Nie ma o czym dyskutować – ucięła Joanna.

Minęła ją i poszła do groty. Nie zamierzała rozmawiać z siostrą o wczorajszych wypadkach. Nie miała pojęcia, co jej powiedział Woody, i wcale jej to nie obchodziło. Chciała tylko pozbyć się Christiny z domu.

April stała na drabinie. Pracowała dziś sama. Powitała Joannę z uśmiechem.

– Cześć, miło mi cię widzieć. Chcesz zobaczyć szkice orchidei?

– Ale tu pięknie! – Joanna ogarnęła gestem całe wnętrze. – Wiem, że mówiłam to już sto razy, ale powtórzę sto pierwszy: grota jest znacznie ładniejsza, niż przypuszczałam.

– Jak już mówiłam sto razy i powtórzę sto pierwszy, masz w tym niemały udział – odparła April.

Joanna przetarła krzesło papierowym ręcznikiem i usiadła.

– Gdzie Woody? – spytała niby to mimochodem. – Nie pomaga ci dzisiaj?

April zeszła z drabiny.

– Zaraz ci wszystko opowiem, zaczekaj chwilę. Przyda mi się parę minut odpoczynku. – Zdjęła kitel, ściągnęła rękawice i przetarła twarz wilgotnym ręcznikiem. Wreszcie nalała wody do szklanki. – Napijesz się?

– Nie, dziękuję.

April z przyjemnością wypiła kilka solidnych łyków, po czym przysunęła sobie plastikowe krzesło i usiadła.

– Najwyższy czas na przerwę – uznała.

– Nie chcę ci przeszkadzać – zaczęła się tłumaczyć Joanna – tylko po prostu uwielbiam patrzeć, jak pracujesz.

– Nie przeszkadzasz mi – zapewniła ją April. – Jeśli już, to Woody miewał jakieś anse.

– No tak. Chyba za mną nie przepada.

– Możesz się tym już nie przejmować. Sprawa umarła śmiercią naturalną – oznajmiła April.

– Jak to?

– Woody był uprzejmy zadzwonić do mnie z informacją, że się wypisuje z układu. Nie nadąża z własną robotą, więc musi sobie odpuścić moją. Ale to nie wszystko! – Uniosła w górę palec wskazujący. – Wyznał mi też, że poznał jakąś wyjątkową kobietę, fantastyczną, idealną, jedyną. Wobec czego nie będzie się ze mną więcej widywał – zakończyła ze wzruszeniem ramion.

– Widzę, że nie spędza ci to snu z powiek. Chociaż pewnie będzie ci go brakowało. W końcu byliście przyjaciółmi.

– Szczerze mówiąc, mam mieszane odczucia – przyznała April. – Z jednej strony, przyzwyczaiłam się do naszego układu. Woody pocieszał mnie, kiedy miałam chandrę, zapraszał do kina czy na kolację, dzięki niemu nie byłam samotna.

– Tak, wspominałaś.

– Rzecz w tym, że od jakiegoś czasu zaczął mnie irytować. Zrobiło się go koło mnie jakoś za dużo, za bardzo się kleił. Nie chciałam go odpychać ani specjalnie trzymać na dystans, bo bałam się go urazić. Muskulaturę ma imponującą, ale nie grzeszy nadmiarem pewności siebie.

– Na pewno jakoś dałby sobie radę.

April pokiwała głową.

– I to chyba dość szybko. – Uśmiechnęła się szeroko. – Opowiadał mi o swoich niezliczonych podbojach... Zresztą, kobiety zawsze leciały do niego jak pszczoły do miodu. Widziałam na własne oczy.

– Nic dziwnego.

– Od jakiegoś czasu nasza sielanka straciła trochę uroku, bo Woody za mocno się ode mnie uzależnił. A jednocześnie za bardzo chciał mnie chronić. W każdym razie – jak na przyjaciela. Ja też chyba za mocno do niego przylgnęłam. Czasami lepiej samemu radzić sobie z samotnością.

– To prawda. Człowiek musi się nauczyć polegać na sobie, czerpać energię z własnych rezerw.

– W przeciwnym razie nigdy nie pozna swoich możliwości, prawda? I nie nauczy się być sobą. – April zamyśliła się, patrząc w dal. – Jednym słowem – wróciła do rzeczywistości – w zasadzie kamień spadł mi z serca. Zwłaszcza że ostatnio Woody zaczął robić pewne aluzje na temat seksu... Nie był agresywny, właściwie nawet nie naciskał, ale ciągle wisiało nad nami coś dwuznacznego. A to mi nie odpowiadało.

– Skoro nie czujesz się porzucona, to wszystko w porządku. Na pewno znajdziesz swoją bratnią duszę.

– Tym się nie przejmuję. Gorzej z pracą. Kto mi teraz będzie pomagał? Oto pytanie za milion dolarów. Muszę się rozejrzeć za jakąś parą chętnych rąk.

– Ja ci chętnie pomogę.

– Ty? – zdumiała się April. – Ale ty... To znaczy...

– Boisz się, bo jestem chora. Bo umieram na raka.

April oblała się rumieńcem, nie mogąc wykrztusić słowa. Zresztą, i tak nie wiedziałaby, co powiedzieć.

– Tak, tak, wiem, że wiesz – odezwała się Joanna miękko. – I wcale mi to nie przeszkadza.

– Jak się dowiedziałaś?

– Hm... Może jestem wyjątkowo spostrzegawcza? Widzę ukradkowe spojrzenia, zatroskane miny... Och, niekoniecznie zawsze z mojego powodu, ale czasem... Dostrzegam gniewną reakcję na głupie wpadki Christiny... – Nagle roześmiała się głośno. – Oczywiście nie bez znaczenia był fakt, że w dniu, kiedy powiedziałam o chorobie Joshowi, zobaczyłam jego samochód przed twoim domem – oznajmiła z psotną miną. – Akurat miałam do ciebie zajrzeć, ale w tej sytuacji musiałam zmienić plany, nie chciałam wam przeszkadzać.

April przyglądała się jej bez słowa, kompletnie osłupiała. Wreszcie jednak i ona się roześmiała.

– Jesteś niemożliwa!

– Bardzo mi na rękę – ciągnęła Joanna poważniejszym tonem – że Joshua zwierzył się właśnie tobie.

– Czułam się... wyróżniona – przyznała April nieśmiało.

– Głowa do góry. Cieszą mnie wasze wspólne tajemnice. Nie masz pojęcia, jak bardzo. Dobrze, że wiesz o wszystkim. I że nie oczekujesz, iż przestanę żyć jeszcze przed śmiercią. Nie przekonujesz mnie do przerwania prac nad grotą, rozumiesz, że to pamiątka, którą chcę po sobie zostawić. Dla Josha. I dla ciebie.

– Tak, rozumiem – szepnęła April.

– Robię to, co wydaje mi się naturalne i właściwe – tłumaczyła dalej Joanna. – Jesteście oboje z Joshem wyjątkowo dzielni. Niełatwo żyć jak gdyby nigdy nic, wiedząc to, co wiecie. Dobrze, że możecie się wspierać nawzajem, a zwłaszcza że Joshua znalazł w tobie przyjaciółkę.

– Musiał się z kimś podzielić bólem...

– Na szczęście wybrał ciebie. Bardzo potrzebuje oparcia.

– Wiem.

– Zawsze stanowiliśmy doskonale zgraną parę. Od samego początku. I teraz smuci mnie tylko jedno: świadomość, że kiedy umrę, nasz duet przestanie istnieć. Zależy mi ogromnie, najbardziej na świecie, by Joshua znów miał kogoś bliskiego. – Podniosła wzrok na April. – On kocha życie. I to nie tylko ze względu na mnie. Uwielbia orchidee, sprawia mu przyjemność prowadzenie firmy... Mam nadzieję, że nie porzuci tego zajęcia. Chciałabym, żeby nadal walczył z braćmi Rossi. Znam go jednak i wiem: lepiej będzie mu szło przy wsparciu mądrej partnerki. Dlatego właśnie mam ogromną nadzieję, że ożeni się po raz drugi. Im szybciej po mojej śmierci, tym lepiej. – Zatopiła uważne spojrzenie w źrenicach April. – To dla mnie rzecz największej wagi. Najważniejsza na świecie. Joshua musi mieć kogoś, z kim będzie budował wspólne życie.

April gubiła się w natłoku sprzecznych emocji. Nie umiała nic powiedzieć, choć doskonale rozumiała, co słyszy. Chciała być silna. Spełnić oczekiwania serdecznej przyjaciółki.

– A teraz – zaproponowała Joanna pogodnie – pokaż mi, co mam robić. – Podniosła się i ujęła April za ramię. – Naucz mnie pracy, którą wykonywał Woody.

* * *

Dzień okazał się znacznie bardziej wyczerpujący od innych, nic dziwnego zatem, że April szła do swojego ukochanego starego dżipa kompletnie wykończona. Sama praca wymagała ogromnego skupienia i bardzo przyzwoitej kondycji, a na dodatek dziś jeszcze trzeba było uczyć wszystkiego Joannę. Szczęściem okazała się równie pojętną co chętną uczennicą, więc pod wieczór wykonywała pracę Woody'ego tak samo dobrze jak on, tylko wolniej.

Najbardziej wyczerpująca okazała się jednak rozmowa z Joanną. April była poruszona do głębi. Chciało jej się płakać, a przecież musiała trzymać się w ryzach.

Była ledwo żywa.

Już miała zamknąć drzwiczki, gdy ktoś ją zawołał. Szła ku niej Christina, jak zwykle nienagannie uczesana i ubrana z najwyższą starannością. Miała na sobie drukowaną jedwabną koszulę oraz jedwabne spodnie. Luksusowa biżuteria rzucała w gasnącym świetle dnia ostre błyski.

– Nie masz pojęcia, jak się cieszę, że cię jeszcze złapałam! Muszę z tobą zamienić słówko.

– Słucham. O co chodzi?

– Jesteś bardzo miłą dziewczyną – Christina dokładała starań, by zabrzmiało to szczerze, ale efekt osiągnęła mizerny – dlatego na pewno zrozumiesz, co mam ci do powiedzenia.

– To znaczy?

– Chodzi mi o Woody'ego Pearlmana – wyjaśniła Christina – tego młodego człowieka, który ci pomagał.

– Tak, znam Woody'ego. I co z nim?
– Wiem, że byliście przyjaciółmi, i to nawet bliskimi... Znacie się dość długo. No, ale czasy się zmieniają i teraz my ze sobą chodzimy. Na poważnie.
April musiała zdobyć się na niemały wysiłek, by nie okazać zdumienia.
– Rozumiem.
– Co za tym idzie, oczekuję, że okażesz się kobietą cywilizowaną, za którą ma cię moja siostra, i zachowasz w stosunku do niego odpowiedni dystans.
April zmierzyła Christinę długim spojrzeniem.
– Nie obawiaj się żadnych kłopotów z mojej strony – oświadczyła wreszcie. – Woody już nie zamierza się ze mną widywać.
– No cóż, tak to w życiu bywa. Nawet Woody ma prawo zmienić zdanie. – Chwyciła April mocno za ramię. – Więc trzymaj się od niego z daleka – dokończyła ciszej, tonem groźby. – Zrozumiano?
– Oczywiście. Rozumiem cię doskonale – odparła April, bynajmniej nie zbita z tropu. – Nie mam zamiaru ingerować w... wasze stosunki. W najmniejszym stopniu. Uważam iż doskonale do siebie pasujecie.
– Naprawdę? – rozpromieniła się tamta.
– Ależ tak. On przeleciał prawie wszystkie chętne w okolicy, a ty, z tego, co słyszałam, zaliczyłaś większość facetów, więc dobraliście się jak w korcu maku. – Spokojnie zdjęła z ramienia rękę Christiny, uruchomiła silnik i wcisnęła gaz. Ruszyła z miejsca, jakby opuszczała miejsce ohydnej zbrodni.
Christina cofnęła się, jej twarz wykrzywiła furia. Poczerwieniała jak burak.
– Ty suko! – wycedziła przez zęby. – Ja ci jeszcze pokażę!

Rozdział dwudziesty piąty

Po wyjeździe Christiny atmosfera wyraźnie się oczyściła.

April i Joanna wykańczały grotę we dwie. Usta im się nie zamykały, a wspólnych tematów miały wiele: od zwykłych ploteczek po roztrząsanie sensu życia.

Z początku April się niepokoiła, że wspólna praca niekorzystnie wpłynie na układ ze zleceniodawczynią, jednak bardzo szybko jej obawy okazały się płonne. Po dwóch tygodniach więź między nimi wyraźnie się zacieśniła, ponieważ Joanna traktowała serio swoje zajęcie.

Jedno tylko nie dawało April spokoju: owa przykra scena z Christiną w ostatni wieczór jej wizyty u Lawrence'ów. Wiele razy się zastanawiała, czy powinna o tym opowiedzieć przyjaciółce, aż w końcu Joanna sama rozwiązała ten problem, zupełnie jakby znała jej myśli.

– Wiesz, April, od kilku dni chcę ci coś powiedzieć, ale jakoś nie mogę się zebrać i znaleźć odpowiednich słów.

– Nie żartuj! Najlepiej mów prosto z mostu.

Joanna odłożyła kielnię.

– Dobrze. Wobec tego, powiem bez ogródek: choć trudno w to uwierzyć, wymarzoną kobietą Woody'ego okazała się Christina. Są razem.

April zamknęła oczy, westchnęła, otworzyła oczy i wybuchnęła śmiechem.

Joanna patrzyła na nią zdumiona.

– Co cię tak rozbawiło?

– Bo wiesz – April złapała się za brzuch – miałam ci to powiedzieć, tylko nie wiedziałam jak!

– Żartujesz?! – Teraz i Joanna zaczęła się śmiać. – A skąd wiesz?

– Dzień przed wyjazdem Christina w niewybredny sposób kazała mi się trzymać z daleka od Woody'ego.

– Coś podobnego! Nie wiedziałam, że ją stać na coś takiego.

W końcu April powtórzyła przyjaciółce dokładnie, jak przebiegła rozmowa z Christiną, i obie uśmiały się serdecznie. I ta beztroska wesołość sprawiła, że wreszcie pozbyły się na dobre niemiłego wspomnienia starszej siostry.

– Przez cały czas bardzo dziwnie się zachowywała – zauważyła Joanna. – Znikała na całe dnie... Podobno robiła zakupy i spotykała się z przyjaciółmi, o których w życiu nie słyszałam, ponoć nawet zajrzała do szklarni! – Spoważniała. – Chyba nie znałam Christiny. W każdym razie, nie tak dobrze, jak mi się zdawało. Jest dla mnie zagadką i pewnie tak już zostanie. Tyle tylko – wyraźnie poweselała – że teraz to wcale nie jest ważne. Ważna jesteś ty i Joshua.

April pogładziła ją po policzku, Joanna uścisnęła jej dłoń. Jakiś czas siedziały melancholijnie zamyślone.

Nagle Joanna zesztywniała.

– Muszę... się położyć. – W jej oczach błysnął strach. Podniosła się z trudem i zachwiała.

April natychmiast ją podtrzymała.

– Odprowadzę cię.

Joanna tylko kiwnęła głową.

* * *

Josh i April siedzieli na tarasie, a Joanna spała, oszołomiona lekami. We dwójkę łatwiej było znosić ogromny smutek. Joshua zrobił się nagle dużo starszy. Zniknął gdzieś beztroski chłopiec.

– Dobrze, że byłaś z Joanną – uśmiechnął się niewesoło. – W przeciwnym razie... – Ścisnął ją za rękę.

– Przestań się zamartwiać – powiedziała April stanowczo. – Byłam i już. Takie gdybanie nie ma sensu. Damy sobie radę. Joanna zostanie w domu, tak jak postanowiła. Jeśli będzie trzeba, to się do was wprowadzę.

Joshua miał ochotę uścisnąć ją i pocałować.

– Masz rację – przyznał. – We dwoje damy sobie radę.

April zrobiło się ciepło na sercu, choć jednocześnie ukłuło ją poczucie winy. Oto Joshua powiedział „my". Podświadomie połączył ich oboje.

– Zajrzę do niej – zaproponowała, niechętnie wysuwając dłoń z jego ręki. – Nigdy nie wiadomo... – Wstała.

– Ja też pójdę.

Joanna leżała w półmroku, twarz miała pogodną. Oddychała spokojnie. Tylko maleńkie kropelki potu na czole przypominały o niedawnych przejściach.

Joshua delikatnie ujął żonę za rękę i pogładził czule.

– Wszystko będzie dobrze – odezwał się cicho.

I choć nie doczekał się odpowiedzi, długo jeszcze szeptał Joannie słowa otuchy.

April ze łzami w oczach patrzyła na tę wzruszającą scenę szczerego oddania.

Wreszcie pochylił się, musnął ustami czoło śpiącej i wstał.

Na schodach April spojrzała na zegarek.

– Powinna spać jeszcze przynajmniej godzinę. Chcesz coś zjeść w tym czasie? – spytała. – Connie wzięła dzisiaj wolne, ale zostawiła spore zapasy, więc wystarczy coś podgrzać.

– Chętnie zjem – przyznał się Joshua. – Zaraz ci pomogę, ale najpierw zadzwonię do szklarni. Carl niedługo wychodzi, muszę z nim zamienić kilka słów. Spróbuję też przekręcić do Connie. Trzeba jej powiedzieć, może się okazać potrzebna po godzinach...

– Poza tym powinna znać prawdę.

– Tak.

Stanęli w holu.

– Rozejrzę się w kuchni – powiedziała April.

– Zaraz wracam. – Joshua poszedł do biblioteki.

W lodówce rzeczywiście znalazła zapasy dla pułku wojska na miesiąc, między innymi słynną zupę z krewetek, pieczonego kurczaka oraz potrawkę z drobiu z awokado i ziemniakami.

Kochana dziewczyna, pomyślała. Ma dużo roboty, ale zawsze jest co zjeść. I to wcale nie najgorzej!

Wyjęła pojemnik z zupą, wstawiła do kuchenki mikrofalowej. Właśnie zaczęła się zastanawiać, że więcej chyba i tak nie zjedzą, gdy pojawił się Joshua.

– W szklarniach wszystko w porządku – powiedział.

– To dobrze. A złapałeś Connie?

– Nie. Pewnie wyszła. Zadzwonię później. Albo porozmawiam z nią rano.

– Zobacz, lodówka pełna, ale czy zjemy coś oprócz zupy?

– Na pewno nam wystarczy.

* * *

Skończyli jeść, zajrzeli do Joanny, która nadal spokojnie spała, i postanowili odpocząć na tarasie, choć noc przyniosła ze sobą chłód.

– Miałam dzisiaj pojechać do szklarni – powiedziała April. – Joanna dała mi kod do bramy.

– Czy to oznacza – zapytał z uśmiechem Joshua – że w końcu jednak dokonałyście wyboru?

– Owszem. – April pokiwała głową. – Zresztą, o co chodzi? Przecież zajęło nam to zaledwie kilka miesięcy. – Zastanowiła się chwilę. – Wiesz, jednak wybiorę się tam dziś, jeśli nie masz nic przeciwko temu. Chyba że chcesz, żebym została na noc.

– Nie, nie trzeba. – Joshua pokręcił głową. – Na pewno dam sobie radę, zresztą nic się nie będzie działo. Nie wiem tylko, czy warto jechać tam dzisiaj, w końcu do szklarni jest kawałek drogi...

– Chciałabym zabrać te orchidee jak najszybciej. Muszę się z nimi oswoić. Jeśli mam je narysować, powinnam je obejrzeć. Widzisz, Josh – zagryzła wargi – zdaję sobie sprawę, że czas ucieka... Nie mogę o tym zapomnieć.

Joshua skinął głową i w milczeniu spuścił wzrok.

– Przepraszam, nie chciałam ci sprawić przykrości.

– April, nie wiem, co bym bez ciebie zrobił. – Zamilkł na dłuższą chwilę, po czym dodał żartobliwym tonem: – Uciekaj, bo mi zaśniesz w jakiejś szklarni.

* * *

April cały czas pilnowała prędkościomierza, bo na tym odcinku drogi wyjątkowo często trafiały się patrole policji. Nie miała najmniejszej ochoty na mandat. Przez otwarte okna wpadało rześkie wieczorne powietrze, wiatr gładził ją po twarzy, rozwiewał włosy, łagodził napięcia wyczerpującego dnia. Taka jazda to prawdziwy odpoczynek, a połączona z wizytą w szklarni pełnej orchidei – wręcz zbawcza terapia.

Wybrane okazy nie należały do szczególnie kosztownych, dlatego postanowiła zabrać je do domu. Chciała je oglądać przez kilka dni, rano i wieczorem, w zmieniającym się świetle. Pragnęła jak najefektowniej odwzorować je za pomocą muszli, a najlepsze pomysły przychodziły jej do głowy, gdy dobrze poznała kwiat, mogła się mu przyjrzeć pod różnymi kątami, bez pośpiechu.

Zjechała na drogę prowadzącą bezpośrednio do szklarni i wkrótce zatrzymała wóz na parkingu. Pierwszy raz była tutaj nocą, pierwszy raz wstąpiła w niesamowitą ciszę, którą mącił jedynie koncert nocnych owadów. Gdy wystukała kod na pilocie, rozległ się metaliczny szczęk i oba skrzydła bramy płynnie rozsunęły się na boki. Ruszyła ścieżką prowadzącą do szklarni z *Phalaenopsis*.

Ciekawe, gdzie też się podział słynny Miguel ze swoim groźnym psem obronnym, pomyślała. Pewnie obaj się zdrzemnęli. Najwyraźniej pies nie jest taki dobry, jak miał być.

W pewnej chwili ciarki jej przeszły po plecach.

Ktoś tu jest, pomyślała. I to nie pies!

Zastygła bez ruchu, nadstawiając uszu. Z pewnością coś się tam działo. Nadal jednak nie słyszała psa, a przecież powinien już ujadać jak oszalały!

Znowu!

Po drugiej stronie żywopłotu. Jakby dyszenie? I jęki?

O Boże! Czyżby ktoś potrzebował pomocy? Może jakiś włamywacz skrzywdził Miguela?!

Nie śmiała nawet drgnąć, stała jak zaklęta w kamień, cała zmieniona w słuch.

Oho! Tym razem... jakby dwa jękliwe głosy... męski i kobiecy...

Skradając się z największą ostrożnością, zrobiła trzy kroki, jakie dzieliły ją od końca żywopłotu. Wytężyła słuch, wstrzymując oddech. Teraz słyszała wyraźniej: z pewnością były tam dwie osoby – mężczyzna i kobieta.

Bezszelestnie wyjrzała zza żywopłotu.

O mało nie padła trupem z wrażenia.

Cofnęła się gwałtownie, ale po cichu, i na powrót ukryła za krzewami.

Zadrżała, chłodny pot wystąpił jej na czoło. Jednocześnie z trudnością powstrzymywała śmiech.

Kilka razy odetchnęła głęboko, a potem najszybciej, jak się dało, wróciła do samochodu. Nie zapalając świateł, wycofała się z parkingu.

Na autostradzie zaczęła oddychać swobodniej. I dopiero wówczas zdała sobie sprawę, że zachowała się absurdalnie. Wreszcie pozwoliła sobie na wybuch śmiechu.

Pięknie, pomyślała. Pięknie! Niech no tylko Joanna i Josh się dowiedzą. Tego się nie spodziewali.

I nagle śmiech zamarł jej w gardle.

Boże! Ale ze mnie idiotka! Przecież to oznacza... właśnie się dowiedziałam, kto jest sprawcą niedawnych kłopotów! Joanna będzie zdruzgotana. Joshua też.

Łudziła się, że się myli, ale była to płonna nadzieja.

Czas jakiś zastanawiała się, czy w ogóle mówić Joannie o swoim odkryciu. A może powinna iść z tym od razu do Josha? Niech on zdecyduje, czy ją zawiadomić...

Tak czy inaczej, zaczekam do jutra, postanowiła. Dziś już nie będę go niepokoiła. Nie jest to dobry czas na takie wieści. Po wszystkim, co się dzisiaj zdarzyło... Jutro z samego rana porozmawiamy w cztery oczy.

Wcisnęła mocniej gaz.

Nie chcę być posłańcem przynoszącym złe wieści..., pomyślała bezradnie. Ale, zdaje się, nie mam wyboru. Muszę mu powiedzieć, co widziałam. Wtedy wreszcie prawda wyjdzie na jaw. Niestety, przykra.

Rozdział dwudziesty szósty

April przyjechała do Lawrence'ów wcześniej niż zwykle, chcąc złapać Josha samego. Plymouth już stał na podwórzu, czyli Connie, jak co dzień, stawiła się w pracy. Co zresztą potwierdzała niebiańska woń świeżo parzonej, mocnej kawy.

Gdy weszła do kuchni, gosposia podniosła wzrok znad deski, na której siekała warzywa.

– Wcześnie dziś jesteś – zauważyła.

– Muszę pogadać z Joshem – wyjaśniła April. – Jest gdzieś tutaj?

– Dokładnie przed tobą! – zaśmiała się Connie. – Na tarasie.

– Och! No tak. Chyba się jeszcze nie obudziłam.

– Idź, przyniosę ci kawę.

– Dziękuję, chętnie się napiję. – Wyszła na taras, gdzie Lawrence'owie siedzieli przy dużym, okrągłym stole. – Witajcie! – Pochyliła się i ucałowała Joannę w oba policzki, z Joshem wymieniła serdeczny uścisk ręki.

– Wcześnie się dzisiaj zjawiłaś – zauważyła Joanna.

W ciągu nocy wszystkie jej dolegliwości jak gdyby ustąpiły.

– Jak się czujesz? – spytała April, siadając.

– Przy tobie fantastycznie! Jak nowo narodzona.

– Szczerze? – upewniła się April.

– Możesz wierzyć albo nie, ale naprawdę czuję się wyśmienicie.

– To cudnie.

Rzeczywiście Joanna wyglądała dobrze i choć może nie tryskała energią jak zwykle, sprawiała wrażenie wyjątkowo ożywionej.

– Kochani – odezwała się, przechylając głowę – wiem, że sprawiam wam kłopoty. Nie powinnam być w domu, tylko w hospicjum...

– Przestań – przerwała jej April. – Nie mów tak i nawet tak nie myśl.

– Ale to prawda. Dlatego tak bardzo chcę ci podziękować za wszystko, co dla mnie robisz. Bardzo mi zależy, żeby zostać w domu.

Joshua objął żonę i pogładził czule.

– Kocham cię, nie pamiętasz?

Joanna przytuliła się do niego.

– Pamiętam. I dziękuję wam obojgu za spełnianie moich wariackich kaprysów.

– Daj spokój. – Joshua zaśmiał się głośno. – No, chociaż jeśli chodzi o te wariackie kaprysy, to może masz trochę racji.

Roześmiali się wszyscy troje.

– Josh – rozległ się głos Connie. Gosposia stała w drzwiach na taras. – Telefon do ciebie. Carl dzwoni.

Joshua natychmiast spoważniał, na jego twarzy odmalowała się troska.

– Zaraz wrócę – powiedział. – Mam nadzieję, że nie stało się nic złego. – Wyszedł za Connie do kuchni.

April opanowały złe przeczucia. Lawrence'owie nadal o niczym nie wiedzieli...

– Mam trochę papierkowej roboty – odezwała się Joanna – siądę do niej teraz, od razu z samego rana, a potem przyjdę ci pomóc, dobrze?

– Dobry Boże, Joanno! Przecież wcale nie musisz mi pomagać! Powinnaś bardziej dbać o siebie. Nie wolałabyś dzisiaj odpocząć?

– Nie, nie... *Carpe diem* i tak dalej – odparła z uśmiechem. – Ale jeszcze skorzystam z okazji, skoro zostałyśmy same i coś ci powiem. Może to zabrzmi głupio, ale...

– Mów śmiało. Nie zawsze twoje wypowiedzi muszą mieć ciężar gatunkowy rozpraw intelektualnych.

Zaśmiały się obie, ale Joanna szybko spoważniała.

– Mam nadzieję, że moja śmierć i wspomnienie naszej przyjaźni nie przeszkodzą ci żyć dalej całą pełnią.

– Nie bardzo rozumiem...

– Powinnaś wyjść za mąż, urodzić dzieci. Powiedziałaś, że pragniesz kiedyś założyć rodzinę, doskonale pamiętam. Chciałabym, żeby twoje marzenia się spełniły. Chciałabym, żebyście oboje z Joshem byli szczęśliwi.

– Ale...

Joanna położyła jej palec na ustach.

– Ciii... Kocham was. Oboje. I jego, i ciebie.

* * *

April już od dobrych dwudziestu minut pracowała w grocie, gdy niespodzianie pojawił się Josh. Od razu poznała, że coś jest nie tak.

– Co się stało?

Joshua stanął w wejściu, przygarbiony i smutny.

– Zniszczono rośliny w laboratorium. – Wolno pokręcił głową. – Młodziutkie siewki.

– Josh...

– Co oznacza – ciągnął – że tym razem ponieśliśmy ogromne straty. Przynajmniej jeśli chodzi o czas. Sam stworzyłem każdą z tych roślinek. To były wyłącznie moje krzyżówki. – Westchnął ciężko. – Czy to się nigdy nie skończy? Już nie mam siły.

– Posłuchaj. Przyjechałam dzisiaj wcześniej, bo chciałam ci w cztery oczy powiedzieć coś ważnego.

– Dlaczego akurat w cztery oczy?

– Bo to dotyczy szklarni, a nie chciałam martwić Joanny.

– Mów jaśniej.

– Wczoraj wieczorem, idąc do szklarni, usłyszałam jakieś dziwne dźwięki. – April szybko wyrzucała z siebie słowa. – Okazało się, że to Miguel i Connie uprawiali seks...

Joshua miał oczy jak spodki.

– Co takiego?! Chyba ci się coś pomyliło!

Niecierpliwie potrząsnęła głową.

– Byli tuż przy ścieżce, za żywopłotem. A dokładnie, za laboratorium. Pies siedział przy nich, w kagańcu, łańcuch był przypięty do słupka.

– Rany boskie!

– A Connie i Miguel robili swoje, jakby... jakby zapomnieli o bożym świecie.

Joshua objął ją i przytulił.

– April, jest mi bardzo przykro, że byłaś świadkiem takiej sceny. – Pokręcił głową. – Nie do wiary! – Puścił ją i ruszył długim krokiem w głąb groty. Zawrócił i stanął przed April. – Joanna traktuje Connie jak siostrę. A Miguel jest dla nas prawie członkiem rodziny... Nie potrafię uwierzyć, że któreś z nich maczało palce w tym wszystkim...

– Nie chcę cię przekonywać na siłę – odrzekła – ale moim zdaniem powinieneś się nad tym poważnie zastanowić. Joanna mówiła mi, że Connie chce się wyrwać z własnego środowiska, że jest ambitna, dumna i postanowiła piąć się w górę. Ty sam powiedziałeś, że umawia się na randki jedynie z mężczyznami, którzy mają przed sobą przyszłość. Koniecznie z białymi. – Spojrzała mu prosto w oczy. – Zastanów się, po co, dlaczego kochała się z Miguelem? Mówicie o nim „prosty człowiek". I słusznie. W dodatku nie jest biały. Przecież Connie nie powinna go w ogóle zauważać.

Joshua zwiesił głowę.

– Byłem głupi – przyznał. – Ślepy i głuchy. Nie wiem, jak ja to powiem Joannie.

– A może... może by jej nie mówić? – zaproponowała April niepewnie.

– Zastanowię się. – Zamilkł na chwilę. – Najpierw jednak porozmawiam z Miguelem. Spróbuję czegoś się od niego dowiedzieć. Potem dopiero zdecyduję, co dalej.

– Sensowny plan – pochwaliła April.

– Powinienem od razu jechać do szklarni.

– Jedź. Jeśli Joanna będzie czegoś potrzebowała, ja tu jestem.

– Będę ci wdzięczny. Na razie jest w gabinecie, siedzi nad jakimiś papierami. Naturalnie o niczym jeszcze nie wie. Później zamierza ci pomagać.

– Wobec czego siłą rzeczy będziemy razem. Możesz spokojnie jechać do szklarni.

– Jadę. Naprawdę jest mi przykro, że natknęłaś się na taką paskudną scenę.

– Jakoś to przeżyję. – Uśmiechnęła się niewesoło.

Joshua uścisnął ją krótko.

– Czas na mnie.

Odwrócił się i wyszedł, a jej serce o mało nie wyskoczyło z piersi. Boże jedyny, pomyślała. Nic na to nie poradzę. Ja go po prostu kocham. I coś mi się wydaje, że on kocha mnie.

* * *

Miguel niespokojnie poprawił się na fotelu przed biurkiem Joshuy. Nieczęsto bywał w biurze pracodawcy i nie czuł się tutaj dobrze. Po pierwsze, Luna zwykle się z niego naśmiewała, a po drugie, jeśli szef chciał się z nim widzieć, na pewno chodziło o jakąś poważną, pewnie niemiłą sprawę.

Joshua natomiast patrzył na Miguela i myślał, że nie ma najmniejszej ochoty robić tego, co zrobić musiał.

– Miguelu – odchrząknął. – Czy zdarza się, że ktoś cię w czasie pracy odwiedza?

Meksykanin zacisnął powieki i gwałtownie potrząsnął głową.

– Nigdy. Nikt – odpowiedział szybko. – Ja zawsze jestem sam.

– Na pewno? – spytał Joshua spokojnym tonem.

Stróż tylko mocniej zacisnął powieki.

– Nikt – wykrztusił po dłuższej chwili. – Nigdy nikt nie przychodzi. Nigdy.

Joshua znał wszystkich swoich pracowników, Miguela także. I wiedział, bez cienia wątpliwości, że Meksykanin kłamie. Zasmuciło go to, ale też trudno było biedaka obciążać jakąkolwiek odpowiedzialnością. Był to mężczyzna o umyśle dziecka.

– Miguelu – odezwał się łagodnie – a może o czymś zapomniałeś?

– Nieee, proszę pana. O niczym nie zapomniałem – odparł stróż, kręcąc głową.

– Chyba jednak tak. Bo przecież odwiedza cię Connie, prawda?

– Connie? – powtórzył Miguel, szeroko otwierając oczy.

– No tak, Connie. Widziano was razem. Podobno miło spędzacie czas. – Joshua porozumiewawczo zmrużył oko.

Miguel uśmiechnął się od ucha do ucha. I w tym samym momencie zorientował się, że wpadł w pułapkę. Zapiszczał jak skarcony szczeniak i zaczął płakać.

– Ja przepraszam, proszę pana – wybełkotał. – Ja bardzo przepraszam.

Joshua nienawidził samego siebie za to, że doprowadził do łez tego biedaka, ale musiał zakończyć sprawę. Wstał, obszedł biurko i pochylił się nad Miguelem. Położył mu dłonie na ramionach.

– Nic nie szkodzi – zapewnił go solennie. – Nie gniewam się.

Meksykanin w dalszym ciągu szlochał.

– Posłuchaj mnie, Miguelu – ciągnął Joshua. – Potrzebuję twojej pomocy. Bo tylko ty potrafisz mi pomóc. Rozumiesz? Nikt inny. Jak sądzisz, dasz radę? Pomożesz mi ocalić szklarnie?

Stróż podniósł na niego wzrok.

– Ja? – zapytał niebotycznie zdumiony.

– Tak, właśnie ty. I tylko ty. – Zrobił przerwę dla efektu. – Powiedz mi, czy Connie myszkowała po szklarniach?

– Myszkowała? – Miguel był wyraźnie zdumiony. – Ona jest mała, ale...

– Czy zaglądała do szklarni, a może coś ruszała? – naciskał Joshua. – Czy wczoraj weszła do laboratorium?

Tamten patrzył na niego bez słowa.

– Zastanów się, proszę. To bardzo ważna sprawa. Pamiętaj, tylko ty możesz uratować szklarnie. Powiedz mi, co robiliście, kiedy przychodziła Connie.

– M... miło spędzaliśmy czas.

– A gdzie? W szklarniach? Czy na zewnątrz?

– Różnie – przyznał się Miguel. – Czasami w szklarniach. Czasami gdzie indziej. Kazała mi otwierać.

– A ostatnim razem byliście w laboratorium?

– To tam, gdzie te szklane półki? No tak.

Joshua poklepał go po ramieniu i wstał. Z trudem wierzył własnym uszom, ale nie sposób zaprzeczać prawdzie! Connie pracowała dla braci Rossi. Kochana, wierna Connie. Zdradziła ich bez żadnych skrupułów. Zrobiło mu się niedobrze. A jednocześnie ogarnął go wielki smutek. Jakby najlepszy przyjaciel odwrócił się od nich bez żadnego powodu.

– No dobrze, Miguelu. Chodźmy, odwiozę cię do domu.

Meksykanin podniósł się z fotela, a Joshua otworzył mu drzwi. Gdy znaleźli się w holu, Luna szybko odłożyła słuchawkę i uśmiechnęła się, pokazując bielusieńkie zęby, dziś efektownie kontrastujące z czekoladowobrązową szminką.

– Miguel! – zaćwierkała. – Jakiś ty dzisiaj elegancki! Te podarte dżinsy...! Aaale seksowne!

Meksykanin dał susa w stronę wyjścia, a Joshua obrzucił sekretarkę piorunującym spojrzeniem.

– Odpuść mu.

Uśmiech natychmiast zniknął z warg Luny, wydęła usta.

– Jadę do domu – oznajmił Joshua. – Bronisz twierdzy razem z Carlem.

– Dopiero co przyjechałeś! – zdziwiła się Luna. – To znaczy, chciałam powiedzieć: jasne, szefie. Tak jest.

Gdy Joshua wychodził z budynku, śpiesząc za Miguelem, już trzymała w ręku słuchawkę.

* * *

Zaparkował obok auta Connie. Od razu ruszył w stronę domu, ale zmienił zdanie i postanowił najpierw zajrzeć do Joanny, do groty.

Był prawie na miejscu, gdy usłyszał głośny śmiech. Ze zdumienia aż przystanął. To ona tak się śmiała, z całą pewnością, na końcu świata poznałby ten melodyjny głos. Uśmiechnął się także.

Siedziała po turecku na podłodze, tuż za przeszklonymi drzwiami, od stóp do głów pokryta białym pyłem. Podobnie jak April oraz jakiś nieznajomy młody człowiek. Wszyscy troje pili mrożoną herbatę. Najwyraźniej akurat zrobili sobie przerwę. Gdy ucichł śmiech, rozległy się wesołe głosy. Gadali jak najęci, jakby nic innego na świecie się nie liczyło.

Przyglądał im się przez chwilę i w końcu postanowił nie przeszkadzać, nie psuć pogodnego nastroju. Zawrócił do domu.

Connie obierała ziemniaki, podśpiewując pod nosem.

– O, Josh! Szybko wróciłeś.

– Owszem. I to z twojego powodu. Muszę z tobą poważnie porozmawiać.

– Nie ma sprawy. – Wzruszyła ramionami. – Ale już i tak wiem, co do mnie masz.

– Wiesz? – Joshua był mocno zaskoczony.

– Joanna mi wszystko powiedziała. O tym, że ma raka i niedługo umrze... – Znowu wzruszyła ramionami. – Postanowiła mnie zawiadomić, bo i tak nie może już ukryć objawów choroby.

Joshua milczał.

– Bardzo mi przykro. – Connie zerknęła na niego spod oka. – Pamiętam, jak mój wujek umierał na raka. To było okropne. No, ale zdarza się. I nigdy nie wiadomo, na kogo trafi.

Głos miała tak pozbawiony emocji, że Joshua osłupiał. Przecież nieomal należała do rodziny! Czy cały czas udawała? Nie było odpowiedzi na to pytanie. Tak czy inaczej, musiał załatwić sprawę, z którą tutaj przyszedł. Zaczynał też rozumieć, że ich gosposia jest zupełnie inną kobietą, niż sądzili.

– Nie zamierzałem z tobą rozmawiać o chorobie Joanny – powiedział.

– Nie? A o czym?

– O tym, że chodzisz na randki z Miguelem.

Dziewczyna wybuchnęła głośnym śmiechem.

– Ja! – Poczerwieniała, mało się nie rozpłakała ze śmiechu. – Z Miguelem! – Plasnęła dłońmi o uda.

Ta żywiołowa reakcja wydała się Joshowi przesadna, jakby Connie usiłowała w ten sposób lepiej zamaskować kłamstwo.

– Dobre sobie! – powiedziała już nieco spokojniej. – On ci to wyznał?

– Tak. Właśnie on.

– Przecież to kompletny głupek. *Mongolito*, nie? – wypluła szydercze słowo. – Jemu nie można wierzyć. – Wróciła do obierania ziemniaków.

– Widziano cię z nim nocą na terenie szklarni.

Wyraz rozbawienia zniknął, na twarzy dziewczyny pojawiła się złość.

– A niby kto mnie widział? – zapytała, celując w Josha obieraczką.

Joshua milczał. Patrzył na nią smutnym wzrokiem.

– No? Kto ci nakłamał?

– April.

– No nie! Jeszcze tego brakowało. Przecież to wariatka!

– Nie, Connie. April nie jest wariatką i ty o tym doskonale wiesz. Po co niby miałaby zmyślać takie rzeczy? W jakim celu miałaby opowiadać, że widziała, jak się gzisz z Miguelem przy laboratorium?

Connie powoli odłożyła obieraczkę na blat. Jej twarz przybrała wyzywający wyraz. Wiedziała, że dalsze zaprzeczenia nie mają sensu. Wydało się.

– Powiedz mi, dlaczego nam to zrobiłaś? – odezwał się Joshua. – Kochaliśmy cię i sądziliśmy, że możemy ci zaufać. Czy bracia Rossi tak dobrze płacą?

– Nie wiem, o czym mówisz – odparła.

– Wiesz, wiesz. – Westchnął znużony. – Nie chciałem... i nie mogłem uwierzyć... Traktowaliśmy cię jak członka rodziny. Pomagaliśmy ci. Connie... przecież nawet w tej chwili wynajęty przez nas prawnik głowi się, co zrobić, żebyś dostała zieloną kartę!

Jednym ruchem ściągnęła fartuch i rzuciła na granitowy blat.

– Nie będę tego słuchała – oświadczyła butnie. – Wsadźcie sobie gdzieś tę waszą łaskawą pomoc. Już jej nie potrzebuję. Ani was. Ani żadnego cholernego prawnika! – Oczy jej błyszczały. – Wychodzę za mąż za Petera Rossiego! Wyobraź sobie, że woli mnie od tej wielkiej pani, siostrzyczki twojej Joanny!

– Co? Nic nie rozumiem! – Joshua nie posiadał się ze zdumienia.

– A tak! Ja odwalałam brudną robotę, a Christina się z nim bzykała. Ale to ja go dostałam, nie ona! I teraz będę bogatsza od was wszystkich razem wziętych!

Obróciła się na pięcie i jak burza wypadła z kuchni.

Joshua czas jakiś stał bez ruchu, wreszcie pokręcił głową i po raz kolejny westchnął.

Skończył się szczęśliwy czas, pomyślał. A przyszłe lata niosą ze sobą tylko samotność.

Chciał iść do groty, ale się zreflektował. Nie warto psuć humoru szczęśliwej, ciężko pracującej trójce. Poza tym czekało go jeszcze jedno niewdzięczne zadanie. Musiał porozmawiać z Carlem. Powiedzieć mu, że to jego siostra pomagała braciom Rossi zniszczyć firmę.

Wówczas przypomniał sobie, że jakiś czas temu widział na podjeździe braci Rossi samochód Carla.

On także jest przeciwko mnie? O Boże! Nie do wiary!

Pewności jednak nie miał, więc postanowił wreszcie się dowiedzieć.

Wybiegł z kuchni, wskoczył do samochodu i raz jeszcze pojechał do szklarni.

* * *

Wokół basenu migotały dziesiątki płomyczków. Świeczki stały na ogrodowym murze, zwieszały się w latarenkach z gałęzi drzew, użyczały ciepłego blasku sprzętom i pływały po spokojnej powierzchni turkusowej wody. Środek stołu, przy którym mieli jeść kolację, zdobiła duża orchidea, *Miltonia spectabilis* z gatunku *moreliana*. Egzotyczne kwiaty, pyszniące się całą gamą barw od ciemnego fioletu po najdelikatniejszy róż, spływały na blat wonną kaskadą.

Joshua przygotował na grillu soczyste *filet mignon*, do nich pieczone ziemniaki i sałatkę z różnych rodzajów zielonej sałaty, a wszystko to zostało podlane wyśmienitym *Chateau Katour*, przechowywanym na specjalne okazje.

– Fantastyczna kolacja! – pochwaliła Joanna, odstawiając kieliszek.

– Wypada mi jedynie przyklasnąć – zawtórowała jej April.

– Uprzejmie paniom dziękuję. – Joshua się skłonił. – Cała przyjemność po mojej stronie.

– A czemuż to zawdzięczamy te rozkosze podniebienia? – spytała Joanna.

– E, nie, niczemu szczególnemu. Po prostu byłem w odpowiednim nastroju – odrzekł wesoło.

– Rozumiem. – Joanna uznała, że nic z niego nie wyciągnie. – A gdzie się podziała Connie? Chyba dzisiaj miała być do wieczora?

Joshua wymienił porozumiewawcze spojrzenie z April. Zawiadomił ją o rozwoju wypadków, gdy Joanna przebierała się do kolacji. Choć zdawał sobie sprawę, że i tak będzie musiał przekazać żonie przykre wieści, starał się odwlekać tę chwilę jak najdłużej. Miał nadzieję na przyjemną kolację we troje, bez dyskutowania o niemiłych wydarzeniach. Najwyraźniej jednak los chciał inaczej i trzeba było poruszyć temat gosposi jeszcze przy stole.

– No już, mów – poprosiła Joanna. – Przecież widzę, że coś się stało. Chciałabym wiedzieć co.

– Cóż... Jak by to... – Joshua jeszcze szukał bezbolesnego wyjścia. – Jednym słowem, Connie zniknęła.

– Jak to: zniknęła? – zaniepokoiła się Joanna. – Nie rozumiem.

– No tak. – Joshua brnął w zaparte. – Dziś po południu nie zastałem ani jej, ani jej rzeczy.

Joanna dłuższą chwilę przyglądała mu się uważnie. Wreszcie pokiwała głową i ciężko westchnęła.

– Odeszła od nas.

Joshua tylko spuścił głowę.

Na twarzy Joanny rozlał się głęboki smutek.

– To ona chciała nas zrujnować, prawda? – spytała.

Joshua skinął głową w milczeniu. I on był pogrążony w żalu.

April natomiast miała wyraz twarzy nieprzenikniony jak maska.

Nagle Joanna zaczęła się śmiać. Szczerze, wesoło, z głębi serca. Tamci dwoje spojrzeli po sobie zdumieni. Normalnie śmiech Joanny był zaraźliwy, tym razem jednak nie mogli się do niej przyłączyć.

W końcu się uspokoiła.

– Szkoda, że siebie nie widzicie! – wykrzyknęła. – Dajcie spokój! Po czymś takim naprawdę nie wiadomo, czy się śmiać, czy płakać, więc lepiej to pierwsze, chyba się ze mną zgodzicie? – Mimo wszystko miała łzy w oczach. Otarła je szybko. – Tyle lat... Uważałam ją za kogoś bliskiego... Mam nadzieję, że przynajmniej dobrze jej zapłacili.

– Ale znaleźliśmy wreszcie źródło kłopotów – zauważyła April. – Choć to mizerne pocieszenie.

– Cała April! – zawołała Joanna. – Wieczna optymistka!

April nie była pewna, czy przyjaciółka traktuje tę cechę jak zaletę czy raczej wadę.

– To dobrze czy źle? – spytała.

– Bardzo dobrze! I tak trzymaj! – Przeniosła spojrzenie na Josha. – Czy któryś z Rossich zadzwonił?

– Tak, owszem. Jak zwykle, Peter.

– Cóż, odejście Connie nie oznacza, że tamci nie będą już próbowali nas wykupić, ale przynajmniej teraz już nie mają wśród nas swojego człowieka... – Przygwoździła męża spojrzeniem. – A może się mylę?

– Sądziłem, że jest jeszcze jedna osoba...

– Kto?!

– Carl. Ale to na szczęście nieprawda. Któregoś dnia zobaczyłem jego samochód na parkingu u Rossich, więc miałem powody do obaw. Zwłaszcza odkąd się dowiedziałem, co robiła nasza kochana Connie. Okazało się jednak, że pojechał do nich, bo zaproponowali mu pracę. Zajęcie miało być nieproporcjonalnie dobrze płatne, więc bez wątpienia chcieli go po prostu przekupić. Nie przyjął posady.

– Bóg łaskaw! – ucieszyła się Joanna. – Odzyskuję wiarę w ludzi.

– Nie śpiesz się zanadto. – Josh postanowił, że najlepiej załatwić już wszystko za jednym zamachem.

– To jeszcze nie koniec?!

– Jeszcze nie. Dowiedziałem się też, że Christina miała romans z Peterem.

– Co takiego?! – Joanna nie wierzyła własnym uszom.

– Skąd wiesz? – zapytała April, równie zaskoczona.

– Od Connie. Nie jestem pewien, czy można jej wierzyć, ale jeśli tak rzeczywiście było, to prawdopodobnie wyciągał informacje od twojej siostry. A teraz podobno rzucił Christinę i będzie się żenił z naszą gosposią.

Joanna milczała przez chwilę. Wreszcie pokręciła głową, jakby czegoś nie rozumiała.

– Chyba powinnam być wstrząśnięta – odezwała się w końcu – ale jakoś nie jestem. Może raczej nieco zaskoczona. – Spojrzała na April. – Pewnie zajęła się Woodym, kiedy straciła Petera.

– Biedny Woody – westchnęła April. – Cóż, jedno warte drugiego.

Zaśmiały się obie, Josh także im zawtórował.

– I tak to już jest – odezwała się Joanna, kiedy umilkli. – Zdradziła nas Christina, porzuciła Connie... Sytuacja wyglądałaby niewesoło, gdyby nie fakt... – wyciągnęła jedną rękę do Josha, drugą do April – że mamy siebie nawzajem.

– Jasne – powiedział Joshua.

– Jasne – powtórzyła April jak echo, ściskając lekko dłoń przyjaciółki. Potem spoważniała. Spojrzała na Josha. – Co zrobiła tym razem? Czy jest bardzo źle?

Joshua aż jęknął.

– Nawet nie mam siły o tym myśleć.

– Musisz – oświadczyła Joanna. – A im szybciej damy sobie z tym radę, tym lepiej.

– Niektóre nowe okazy zostały całkowicie zniszczone. Jeszcze nawet nie do końca wiem ile.

Teraz to ona jęknęła.

– Te nowe okazy – Josh zwrócił się do April – to hybrydy, moje dzieło. Były jeszcze młodziutkie, dopiero zaczynały rosnąć.

– Co zamierzasz?

– Będę musiał zacząć od początku. Gorzej być nie mogło. No, chyba żeby podpalili szklarnie. Najpierw będę musiał dojść, które krzyżówki straciliśmy. Były dokładnie oznaczone, więc nie jest to trudne zadanie, ale żmudne i pracochłonne. A potem spróbuję je odtworzyć. Zajmie mi to dużo czasu.

– Chętnie ci pomogę – zaoferowała się April. – Oczywiście musiałabym się dużo nauczyć, ale zrobię to z przyjemnością.

– Dziękuję za propozycję, coś mi się jednak zdaje, że na razie masz pełne ręce roboty. A tak przy okazji, cóż to za piękny młodzian wam dzisiaj pomagał?

– Randy Jarvis – odpowiedziała April. – Pracował ze mną parę razy, więc zadzwoniłam spytać, czy nie zastąpiłby Woody'ego. Okazało się, że akurat ma trochę czasu, więc od razu wziął się do roboty.

– Świetnie. Bo chyba macie sporo zajęcia.

– A i owszem. – April przeniosła wzrok na Joannę. – Zamierzamy stworzyć piękną grotę, prawda?

– I to szybko! – Joanna uśmiechnęła się trochę nieśmiało. – A potem będziesz mogła pomagać w szklarni.

Rozdział dwudziesty siódmy

Dni uciekały w zastraszającym tempie. April i Randy prawie nie wychodzili z groty, Joanna najpierw im pomagała, potem coraz częściej kładła się na leżaku i tylko patrzyła, ciesząc się z szybkiego postępu prac. W końcu nadszedł czas, gdy raczej zostawała w domu i prawie nie wychodziła z sypialni.

April nigdy nie kwestionowała żadnych jej decyzji, niczego nie sugerowała, nie proponowała pomocy. Wiedziała, że Joanna sama powie, czego potrzebuje, więc tym bardziej nie chciała podważać jej wiary w siebie czy, co gorsza, naruszać prywatności. Głęboko ukrywała swój ogromny smutek. Niekiedy było to bardzo trudne. W takich razach jeszcze bardziej poświęcała się pracy. Szukała w niej zapomnienia. Ucieczki przed świadomością zbliżającej się śmierci przyjaciółki.

Nie mogła jej zatrzymać. Bywało, że Joanna uciekała wzrokiem gdzieś w dal, jakby już spoglądała na inny, lepszy świat, cierpliwie czekając, kiedy nadejdzie jej pora, by przejść na drugą stronę.

April widziała też rozpacz Josha i pomagała mu, by zgodnie z pragnieniem żony zachowywał się zwyczajnie. Starał się spełniać życzenia Joanny: codziennie wychodził do pracy w szklarniach, załatwiał tysiące drobnych spraw nawarstwiających się każdego dnia – i ukrywał w sercu ból, nieutulony żal.

Joannie jest o wiele trudniej, myślał w takich chwilach.

Praca okazała się, na szczęście, doskonałą terapią. Poświęcał mnóstwo czasu odtwarzaniu zniszczonych krzyżówek, miał też nadzieję z nadejściem zimy wyhodować wyjątkową orchideę, specjalnie dla Joanny.

Któregoś dnia, jakiś miesiąc po ostatnich kłopotach w szklarni, April jadła obiad z Lawrence'ami. Joanna czuła się wyjątkowo dobrze, oczy miała błyszczące, śmiała się i mówiła przez cały czas.

Następczyni Connie, Peruwianka Elizabeth, podała na deser wspaniały krem. Obie przyjaciółki wyjadły go do ostatniej łyżeczki.

– Boże, ale pychota! – westchnęła April, kładąc rękę na brzuchu.

– Mmmmniam! – zgodziła się z nią Joanna. – Cieszę się, że zatrudniliśmy Elizabeth. Nie stała się członkiem rodziny jak Connie, ale ma to pewnie także swoje dobre strony: przynajmniej nie będzie mogła nas tak perfidnie zdradzić! Natomiast gotuje... bosko! – Zaśmiała się zadowolona, a April jej zawtórowała. – Aha, chciałam ci coś pokazać. – Wzięła do ręki lokalny dziennik. – Podejrzewam, że cię to zainteresuje. – Podała gazetę przyjaciółce.

April zerknęła na zdjęcia ze ślubu i od razu rozpoznała państwa młodych.

– Boże słodki! – wyrwało jej się. – Mówić sobie mogła, co chciała, jednak... No proszę! – Szybko przebiegła wzrokiem treść notki.

CESPEDES I ROSSI SĄ MAŁŻEŃSTWEM!

W minioną sobotę, w obecności sędziego Thomasa Quinna, w Watsonville odbyła się ceremonia zaślubin Connie Louise Cespedes oraz Petera Anthony'ego Rossiego. Pan młody jest prezesem Rossi Brothers Inc., firmy dominującej w agrobiznesie, zajmującej się zwłaszcza kupnem i sprzedażą upraw orchidei, panna młoda otrzymała stanowisko wiceprezesa.

April oddała dziennik Joannie.

– Wygląda na to, że każde ma, co chciało.

– Aha – przytaknęła Joanna. – Moim zdaniem pasują do siebie. Oboje są ambitni i pozbawieni skrupułów. Dobrali się w korcu maku. Podobnie jak Christina i Woody.

– Masz o nich jakieś wieści?

Joanna uśmiechnęła się figlarnie.

– Moja starsza siostra dzwoniła, nie dalej jak dziś rano. Nie powinnam sobie z niej żartować, bo wiem, że jest w rozpaczy, ale nic na to nie poradzę. – Zamilkła tajemniczo.

– No mów! Bo się spalę z ciekawości!

– Moja ukochana siostrzyczka oraz Woody stanęli na ślubnym kobiercu.

– Żartujesz!

– Jestem śmiertelnie poważna. Ale to nie wszystko.

– Co jeszcze?

– On ją już zdradza! Dobre sobie, co? Jak ci się podoba taki dowód sprawiedliwości dziejowej?

– Bardzo współczuję Christinie. Ale nie mogę powiedzieć, żeby mi to specjalnie popsuło humor.

– Mnie także nie – przyznała Joanna. – Powiedziałam jej, co myślę o namiętnych randkach z Peterem Rossim, przy okazji także nakładłam mnóstwo na temat Woody'ego, a potem wszystko hurtem wybaczyłam. – Podniosła wzrok na April. – Przebaczenie jest, moim zdaniem, szalenie istotne. Trudno żyć z bagażem pretensji. Taki ciężar tylko zgina człowiekowi kark. Teraz widzę to tak: Christina zawsze pozostanie moją siostrą, a rodziny się nie wybiera. Tymi, których wybrałam, jesteście wy dwoje – Joshua i ty. – Wzięła przyjaciółkę za rękę. – Posłuchaj mnie uważnie.

April tylko skinęła głową.

– Długo szukałam idealnej partnerki dla Josha. Najwyraźniej chciałam zabawić się w Boga, wyręczyć los. – Jej fiołkowe oczy lśniły. – I nagle ty spadłaś jak z nieba. Uszczęśliwiłaś i mnie, i jego... Pozostaje mi mieć nadzieję, że oboje spełnicie moje marzenie: będziecie żyli pełnią życia, będziecie się nim cieszyli. – Urwała, a jej twarz rozjaśnił łagodny uśmiech. – Nie powiem już nic więcej. Myślę, że wiesz... że rozumiesz, o co mi chodzi.

April zakręciło się w głowie. Nie pojmowała, jakim cudem Joanna powiedziała to wszystko tak spokojnie. Nie wiedziała, co odpowiedzieć, więc tylko ze łzami w oczach ucałowała przyjaciółkę i uścisnęła ją czule.

– Pójdę się zdrzemnąć – powiedziała Joanna. – Później wpadnę sprawdzić, czy pilnie przykładasz się do roboty.

Wstała i odeszła.

April odprowadziła ją wzrokiem.

* * *

Godzinę później, gdy Joanna już spała, April pożyczyła od Randy'ego telefon komórkowy i wyszła przed grotę. Numer, który był jej potrzebny, znalazła bez najmniejszego trudu w książce telefonicznej. Wystukała rząd cyfr. Po trzecim sygnale odezwał się żeński głos.

– Rossi Brothers, słucham?

– Chciałabym mówić z Connie Rossi.

– Kto dzwoni?

– April Woodward. – Pozostało jej mieć nadzieję, że na sam dźwięk nazwiska sekretarka nie przerwie połączenia.

– Proszę zaczekać.

Wobec czego April czekała cierpliwie – dłuższy czas. Nagle usłyszała w słuchawce Connie.

– Czego chcesz? – W głosie dawnej gosposi Lawrence'ów brzmiało samozadowolenie, przebijała z niego próżność.

– Mam do ciebie pewną sprawę. Chcę ci powiedzieć, że jeśli zdarzy się jeszcze jeden, choćby najdrobniejszy, wypadek w szklarniach, pójdę prosto na policję. Z największą przyjemnością, wręcz z dziką rozkoszą opowiem, co widziałam tej nocy, kiedy zostały zniszczone orchidee w laboratorium. O tym, jak się zabawiałaś z nocnym stróżem, żeby zyskać dostęp do szklarni. Miguel potwierdzi moje słowa. I nie tylko on, bo Joshua także powtórzy, co mu powiedziałaś w kuchni, zanim uprzejmie zniknęłaś. – Zacisnęła kciuki i dodała z wielkim przekonaniem, choć całkowicie niezgodnie z prawdą. – A jeszcze do kompletu Christina zezna, że Peter Rossi wyciągał od niej poufne informacje.

Jakiś czas w słuchawce panowała cisza.

– To tylko twoje słowa przeciwko moim – odezwała się wreszcie Connie.

– Nooo, niezupełnie. Moje słowo, plus zeznanie Miguela, oświadczenie Joshuy i wyjaśnienia Christiny. – April ponownie zacisnęła kciuki. – Powinnaś też wiedzieć, że już wynajęliśmy prawnika, który ma ci wytoczyć sprawę, gdyby cokolwiek się stało. – Zaczerpnęła głęboko powietrza. – No i na koniec rzecz ostatnia, choć równie ważna. Mam paru przyjaciół w wydawnictwach prasowych, więc mogę ci zaręczyć, że w razie czego żądni sensacji czytelnicy będą mogli przeczytać sążniste artykuły na temat twoich wyczynów. Postaram się, żeby zamieszczono w nich twoje śliczne zdjęcie ślubne. – Usłyszała ciężkie westchnienie byłej gosposi. – Dlatego najlepiej zrobisz, jeśli przekonasz męża, żeby sobie odpuścił firmę Lawrence'ów. Niech lepiej zacznie ostrzyć zęby na kogoś innego. Rozumiemy się?

– Taaak... – wycedziła Connie. – Rozumiemy. Niepotrzebnie się denerwujesz. Komu potrzebna jakaś farma orchidei? – Przerwała połączenie.

April wyłączyła telefon i odetchnęła z ulgą. Teraz pozostało jej tylko wierzyć, że ta rozmowa odniesie pożądany skutek. Nie miała na to żadnej gwarancji, ale znając Connie, dla której pozory były szalenie istotne (zwłaszcza od czasu, gdy została żoną pana Petera Rossiego - bogatego, pnącego się w górę białego biznesmena), pozwoliła sobie na luksus wiary w powodzenie swojego planu. Ta dziewczyna powinna zrobić wszystko, co w jej mocy, by zająć męża czymś innym.

Wróciła do groty, oddała Randy'emu telefon i energicznie zabrała się do pracy. Chciała ją skończyć jak najszybciej. Ze względu na Joannę, na Josha i siebie samą.

* * *

Joanna patrzyła z okna sypialni w stronę, gdzie znajdowała się grota. Nie widziała jej, oczywiście, ale potrafiła sobie wyobrazić, co się tam dzieje. Uśmiechnęła się do siebie, zadowolona i szczęśliwa. Wkrótce dzieło zostanie ukończone, a efekt z pewnością przejdzie najśmielsze oczekiwania. Spełni się jej marzenie. Powstanie zakątek szczęścia. Dla April i Josha.

Odwróciła się od okna, wzięła torebkę i zeszła do holu. Objęła spojrzeniem błyszczące drewno, marmurowe podłogi... całe to piękno, które zapoczątkował jej ojciec, a oni we dwoje rozwinęli. Lekkim krokiem wyszła przez frontowe drzwi, wsiadła do ulubionego mercedesa, włożyła okulary przeciwsłoneczne, wyjechała z garażu i robiąc rundę po podwórzu, przyjrzała się uroczemu domowi obrośniętemu winoroślą. Minęła dwa kamienne słupy stojące na straży bramy i pojechała, nie oglądając się za siebie.

* * *

April zerknęła na zegarek.

Czas kończyć na dzisiaj, pomyślała. A Joanny jak nie było, tak nie ma. Może przespała całe popołudnie? Taka była ożywiona przy stole, pewnie musi teraz odzyskać siły.

– Randy, gotów do odwrotu? – spytała pomocnika.

– Już sprzątam – odrzekł zmęczonym głosem. – Tak się zamyśliłaś, że ogłuchłaś i oślepłaś. Mam dosyć na dzisiaj. Jestem wykończony.

– No to się porządnie wyśpij, bo jutro będzie to samo. – Uśmiechnęła się serdecznie. – Jestem ci naprawdę wdzięczna.

– No wiesz, darmo nie haruję! – zaśmiał się Randy. Skończył składać narzędzia i wziął kurtkę. – Trzymaj się, do jutra – rzucił i już go nie było.

April zdjęła fartuch, otrzepała ubranie, zebrała narzędzia i poszła je wyczyścić w domku nad basenem. Umyła wszystkie i wytarła, wyszczotkowała włosy, wyszorowała, na ile dała radę, twarz i ręce. Zdecydowała, że przed powrotem do domu zajrzy jeszcze do Joanny.

W kuchni zastała Elizabeth.

– Gdzie Joanna? – spytała.

– Nie wiem – odpowiedziała nowa gosposia. – Nie widziałam jej od obiadu.

– Dziękuję. Poszukam.

Weszła na piętro i na palcach zbliżyła się do sypialni. Drzwi pozostały uchylone, więc pchnęła je lekko i zajrzała do środka.

Łóżko było puste. I nawet zasłane.

Pewnie jest w łazience, pomyślała April.

– Joanno! – zawołała.

Odpowiedziała jej cisza.

– Joanno! – krzyknęła głośniej.

Drzwi od łazienki także pozostały uchylone, ale i tutaj nie znalazła przyjaciółki. Wobec tego zeszła na dół i przeszukała wszystkie pokoje na parterze. Na próżno.

Co się dzieje? Gdzie ona zniknęła?

Wróciła do kuchni.

– Na pewno nie widziałaś jej od obiadu? – spytała gosposię.

– Na pewno. Czy coś się stało?

– Nigdzie jej nie ma – powiedziała April. – A w każdym razie, nie mogę jej znaleźć.

Akurat wtedy usłyszała samochód wjeżdżający na podjazd. Wybiegła do holu. Może to ona? Jednym szarpnięciem otworzyła frontowe drzwi i wypadła na schody.

Z land cruisera wysiadł Joshua.

– Cześć. Gdzie Joanna? – spytał.

– Nie wiem. Właśnie jej szukam.

– Jak to? Nic ci nie powiedziała? Nie ma jej samochodu!

– Nie ma?! Josh... Nic nie rozumiem. Po obiedzie poszła odpocząć. Potem miała przyjść do groty i nie przyszła. Dlatego chciałam do niej zajrzeć, ale nigdzie jej nie ma... Nie przyszło mi do głowy sprawdzać, czy jest samochód.

– Pytałaś Elizabeth? Czy Joanna zostawiła jakąś wiadomość?

– Nie, nie zostawiła. Gosposia nie widziała jej od obiadu. – April podniosła na niego spojrzenie pełne obawy. – Gdzie ona się podziała? Co się z nią dzieje?

Razem poszli do kuchni, Joshua raz jeszcze wypytał Elizabeth, ale nie dowiedział się niczego nowego.

– Chodź, usiądziemy w bibliotece i spokojnie się zastanowimy – zaproponował.

Usiedli na wielkiej skórzanej kanapie i Joshua zaczął głośno myśleć.

– Przy obiedzie była wesoła i ożywiona. Zachowywała się, jakby nic złego się nie działo...

– Śmiałyśmy się i plotkowałyśmy... – Głos uwiązł jej w gardle, do oczu napłynęły łzy.

Joshua objął ją i pogładził. Wargami musnął jej czoło.

– Nie płacz, proszę. Nie zniosę widoku twoich łez.

Przytuliła się do niego, odsuwając na bok poczucie winy. Tylko na chwilę.

Zdawałoby się, że trwali tak zaledwie przez moment, lecz w rzeczywistości upłynęło sporo czasu. Wreszcie odsunęli się niechętnie.

– Przepraszam cię, nie chciałem...

– Nie przepraszaj. Jestem tak samo winna jak ty. Ja... Och, zostawmy to teraz. Zastanówmy się, gdzie szukać Joanny.

Joshua pokiwał głową, zatopiony w myślach. Patrzył w podłogę, jego umysł pracował gorączkowo.

– Wiem, dokąd pojechała – oznajmił, podnosząc głowę. – Jestem pewien.

– Dokąd? – zapytała April, wstając.

– Chcesz jechać ze mną?

– Oczywiście.

Joshua skoczył na równe nogi.

– Chodźmy. – Ruszył do holu.

Nie minęła minuta, a już byli w drodze.

* * *

Zanim zjechali z autostrady na drogę prowadzącą do odludnego kawałka plaży Pajaro Dunes, słońce już skryło się za horyzontem. Na niebo wypłynął księżyc w pełni, jego blask skąpał ziemię w złowrogiej, zimnej poświacie. Na nieboskłonie zbierały się czarne chmury.

Jadąc nad brzeg oceanu, mijali ogromne pola truskawkowe, uprawy brukselki, brokułów i karczochów. Nie napotkali żadnego innego samochodu; Joshua, sztywny i spięty, ze wzrokiem utkwionym w pustej drodze, mocno dociskał pedał gazu. April także milczała. Nigdy tu nie była, lecz domyślała się, dokąd jadą.

Stary domek na plaży. Jakże by inaczej.

Zarówno ten domek, jak i ocean zawsze były dla Joanny bardzo ważne. Tutaj cierpiała w samotności, tu pogodziła się ze śmiertelną chorobą.

I widać w tym miejscu chciała spędzić ostatnie chwile.

Z jednej strony April doskonale rozumiała przyjaciółkę, z drugiej dostawała gęsiej skórki na myśl, że Joanna jest całkiem sama na tym odludziu. A może przyjechała tutaj na spotkanie... ze śmiercią?

Skręcili z asfaltu w piaszczystą drogę porośniętą tak gęsto trawą, jakby zieleń postanowiła odzyskać władanie także nad tym wąskim pasmem piasku. Noc zabierała ostatnie szarości dziennego światła. Wkrótce pojawiła się przed nimi ledwie widoczna, zardzewiała brama. Otwarta. Pomiędzy prętami kołysał się błyszczący łańcuch o ciężkich ogniwach.

Joshua zwolnił.

– Jest – powiedział z ulgą.

Minęli bramę i łagodny zakręt. Reflektory toyoty wyłuskały ze smolistej czerni chromowany zderzak mercedesa.

– Zaczekasz? – spytał głosem bez wyrazu.

– Nie. – April potrząsnęła głową. – Idę z tobą.

Na chwilę zapadła cisza.

– Dziękuję.

Wysiedli i razem podeszli do domku. Gdzieś w środku widać było przyćmione światło.

Gdy weszli na ganek, nagle ciemność rozdarł oślepiający błysk. Zaraz potem w górze przetoczył się ogłuszający ryk gromu i z nieba lunęły potoki wody.

Joshua wyjął z kieszeni klucz, ale drzwi okazały się otwarte. Na wprost wejścia wielkie okno na całą ścianę ukazywało Pacyfik, teraz ukryty w ciemności.

– Tu jest Joanna – powiedział Josh. – Zapaliła światło.

– Chodźmy – rzekła April. – Jestem z tobą.

Joanna miała pogodną twarz i wydawać by się mogło, że spokojnie śpi. Pół leżała, pół siedziała, oparta na poduszkach, by widzieć nieskończony bezmiar wody. Ciepłe światło spływało z lampki, która żółtym kręgiem otaczała torby pełne muszli. Plon ostatniego spaceru po plaży.

Stanęli nad nią we dwoje i patrzyli bez słowa. Nie dopatrzyli się żadnego ruchu, nie usłyszeli oddechu.

Joshua przyklęknął, ujął żonę za ręce, przyłożył ucho do jej piersi, szukając bicia serca, którego znaleźć nie mógł.

Usiadł obok bezwładnego ciała i wziął Joannę w ramiona. Kołysał ją delikatnie, a bezgłośne łzy płynęły mu po policzkach.

April także płakała. Nigdy dotąd nie poniosła większej straty, nie czuła większego bólu.

Nad plażą srożył się sztorm. Świat żegnał Joannę Lawrence.

Po długim czasie Joshua wypuścił żonę z objęć. Pochylił się nad nią i pocałował czule.

Wstał, spojrzał na April. Nie pierwszy raz widział na jej twarzy smutek, ale nigdy dotąd tak ogromny. Wyciągnęła do niego dłoń. Podał jej rękę i razem pożegnali najukochańszą istotę.

Koniec jest początkiem

Zima 2000 roku

Mimo żałoby dni chłostane zimowymi deszczami minęły szybko i w powietrzu czuło się już zapowiedź wiosny.

April stała na środku groty, przyglądając się efektom wielomiesięcznej wytężonej pracy. Pamiętała, że jej wkład w powstanie tego cudu, choć ważny, nie był jedyny. Gdyby nie pomysł Joanny, gdyby nie jej upór, siła oraz energia, na wzgórzu w dalszym ciągu stałaby dawna stajnia.

Od śmierci żony Joshua nie zajrzał tu ani razu, nawet gdy grota została ukończona. Nie mógł. April natomiast walczyła ze smutkiem, zmuszając się do zakończenia pracy. A było to niełatwe zadanie.

Starała się także pomagać w szklarniach, by Josh mógł więcej czasu poświęcać krzyżowaniu orchidei, tworzeniu nowych hybryd, od których w tak znacznym stopniu zależało powodzenie firmy.

Tak minęło kilka miesięcy. Ból nieco zelżał, rozpacz otuliła mgiełka czasu. Oboje dojrzeli do tego, by uroczyście otworzyć grotę. Przejąć spadek po Joannie. I miało to nastąpić dziś wieczór.

April przesunęła dookoła wzrokiem, wciąż zadziwiona, choć od kilku miesięcy spędzała tutaj większość czasu. Całe wnętrze, co do centymetra, zostało pokryte muszlami i kamieniami. Na suficie pyszniło się lśniące niebo, roziskrzone gwiazdami, na ścianach widniały fantastyczne „rysunki" egzotycznych orchidei, wykonane z barwnych muszli.

W niszach ustawiono na cokołach popiersia. Jeszcze niedawno przedstawiały one sławnych ludzi, dziś przemieniły się w niesamowite istoty nie z tego świata, całkowicie pokryte muszlami. Okna i drzwi ozdabiały barwne girlandy, naśladujące skomplikowane płaskorzeźby Grinlinga Gibbonsa.

Na samym środku tryskała niewielka fontanna, kształtem przywodząca na myśl basen dla ptaków. Woda opadała do okrągłej sadzawki, na której dnie April stworzyła mozaikę z kamyków, jakby splecionych wodorostów, przypominających wiązankę orchidei. Po obu stronach fontanny zwieszały się z sufitu dwa żyrandole, także ozdobione muszlami. Pod nimi stanęły srebrzyste weneckie stoliki i krzesła, rzecz jasna z motywem z muszli. Na każdym stoliku migotała latarenka z kryształowymi szybkami. April zapaliła świece.

Przyniosła srebrne wiaderko z lodem, w którym chłodziła się butelka szampana Louis Roderer Cristal. Dwa smukłe kryształowe kieliszki, rosyjskie antyki, czekały na napełnienie szlachetnym trunkiem.

Wreszcie przeniosła spojrzenie na centralną część dłuższej ściany, która aż do dziś pozostawała zasłonięta dużym płótnem. Uśmiechnęła się do siebie. Nikomu nie zdradziła, co się tam kryje. Pracowała nad tą niespodzianką w tajemnicy przez kilka długich tygodni. Teraz przyglądała jej się z dumą i satysfakcją. Oto pyszniła się przed nią perłowobiała orchidea, ułożona prawie wyłącznie z muszli słuchotki kalifornijskiej. Pod spodem litery z wygładzonych przez fale otoczaków układały się w nazwę rośliny. *Phalaenopsis Joanna*. Na jednym z weneckich stolików stał żywy kwiat. Hybryda, którą Joshua wyhodował dla swojej żony i nazwał jej imieniem. Śnieżnobiała, lśniąca, jedyna w swoim rodzaju.

April nie mogła się doczekać, co powie twórca orchidei na widok jej wizerunku na ścianie.

Cofnęła się i raz jeszcze zlustrowała wnętrze uważnym spojrzeniem.

– Tak – powiedziała głośno. – Dziś możemy wznieść toast.

Nadszedł czas zamknięcia tego rozdziału. Zakończyła się ogromna praca, bardziej artystyczna niż rzemieślnicza. April, dumna ze swego dzieła, spoglądała na poszczególne muszle. Tu *Laliotis ruber* i *Lischcea imperialis*, tam *Spondylas princeps* i *Wrightianus*, jeszcze *Babelomurex spinosus* oraz *Ocinebra erinaceus*, a także prowokacyjna *Purpura patual*.

Boże jedyny, pomyślała. Ileż ja się przy tej pracy nauczyłam! I to nie tylko o muszlach, ale o projektowaniu i przemienianiu marzeń w rzeczywistość... O wykorzystaniu możliwości... O, tak, możliwości zawsze są najważniejsze.

Joanna nauczyła ją widzieć nieskończone piękno tworzenia dzięki tym wyjątkowym, a tak skromnym materiałom.

Wyłączyła żyrandole i ruszyła po Josha. W progu odwróciła się po raz ostatni.

Zyskałam coś jeszcze, uświadomiła sobie. Poznałam przyjaźń i miłość.

* * *

April weszła do groty pierwsza, sprawdziła, czy świece nadal się palą, i przytłumiła światło żyrandoli, by stworzyć romantyczny nastrój. Potem włączyła fontannę, która od razu zanuciła swoją dźwięczną pieśń. Całość zapierała dech w piersiach, a autorka tego cudu, nieco spokojniejsza, stanęła w drzwiach, i powiedziała Joshowi, że już może wejść.

– Na pewno wszystko skończone? – zapytał półżartem.

– Finito – potwierdziła April z uśmiechem.

– Wobec tego, najwyższy czas na uroczysty toast! – orzekł, wchodząc do środka.

Powoli ogarnął wnętrze uważnym spojrzeniem. Nie umknął mu żaden szczegół, żaden efekt. Uśmiech na jego twarzy zastąpił podziw.

Obserwowała tę przemianę z rosnącą dumą, ale wreszcie zaczęło ją niepokoić milczenie Josha. Czekała na pochwałę, na słowa uznania i na pewno doczekałaby się ich od Joanny.

Wreszcie Joshua popatrzył na nią. Jego wzrok przyciągnęła najpierw znajoma apaszka od Hermèsa. Ta ze wzorem w muszle, prezent od Joanny. Dopiero potem przeniósł spojrzenie na twarz April.

– Spełniłaś jej marzenie – powiedział cicho. – A nawet zrobiłaś jeszcze więcej. – Umilkł. – Nie ma drugiej równie pięknej groty.

April odetchnęła z ulgą, a Joshua przytulił ją mocno.

– Bałaś się, że mi się nie spodoba?

– Tak.

Roześmiał się głośno, wziął ją pod brodę i pocałował w usta.

– Napijmy się szampana. – Odkorkował butelkę, nalał trunek do obu kieliszków i podał jeden April. – Chciałbym wznieść toast. Za życie. I za naszą wspólną przyszłość.

– Za naszą przyszłość. – Zadźwięczał kryształ.

Serce zatrzepotało jej w piersi. Choć ostatnie miesiące minęły w smutku i żałobie, nie mogła zapomnieć o swoim uczuciu, potrzebie wzajemności i namiętności.

Joshua odstawił kieliszek, April powtórzyła jego gest. Położył ręce na jej ramionach, zajrzał w oczy. Zatopiła spojrzenie w jego źrenicach. Widziała w nich cień rozpaczy. Na szczęście zniknęło niedawne przygnębienie. Czas leczy rany. Stopniowo w obojgu budziły się chęci do życia, tęsknota za bratnią duszą, pragnienie miłości.

Joshua pogładził April po twarzy. Ujął ją za rękę.

– Tak miała wyglądać ta grota – powiedział. – Dokładnie tak, jak wygląda. Oto spadek, jaki zostawiła nam Joanna. Ta grota i nasza miłość.

Odgarnął z czoła niesforne włosy i ciepło ucałował April w policzek. Zaczynali nowy etap życia. Pod znakiem wspólnej przyszłości.